SPIDER-GWEN

GWEN STACY

WRITER
JASON LATOUR

ARTISTS
ROBBI RODRIGUEZ
WITH CHRIS VISIONS (#5B)

COLOR ARTIST
RICO RENZI

LETTERER
VC's CLAYTON COWLES

COVER ART
ROBBI RODRIGUEZ

ASSISTANT EDITOR
DEVIN LEWIS

ASSOCIATE EDITOR
ELLIE PYLE

SENIOR EDITOR
NICK LOWE

Gwen Stacy created by STAN LEE & STEVE DITKO

collection editor JENNIFER GRÜNWALD
assistant editor CAITLIN O'CONNELL • associate managing editor KATERI WOODY
editor, special projects MARK D. BEAZLEY • vp production & special projects JEFF YOUNGQUIST

director, licensed publishing SVEN LARSEN • svp print, sales & marketing DAVID GABRIEL
editor in chief C.B. CEBULSKI • chief creative officer JOE QUESADA
president DAN BUCKLEY • executive producer ALAN FINE

SPIDER-GWEN: GWEN STACY. Contains material originally published in magazine form as EDGE OF SPIDER-VERSE #2, SPIDER-GWEN (2015A) #1-5 and SPIDER-GWEN (2015B) #1-6. First printing 2019. ISBN 978-1-302-91986-3. Published by MARVEL WORLDWIDE, INC., a subsidiary of MARVEL ENTERTAINMENT, LLC. OFFICE OF PUBLICATION: 135 West 50th Street, New York, NY 10020. © 2019 MARVEL No similarity between any of the names, characters, persons, and/or institutions in this magazine with those of any living or dead person or institution is intended, and any such similarity which may exist is purely coincidental. Printed in Canada. DAN BUCKLEY, President, Marvel Entertainment; JOHN NEE, Publisher; JOE QUESADA, Chief Creative Officer; TOM BREVOORT, SVP of Publishing; DAVID BOGART, Associate Publisher & SVP of Talent Affairs; DAVID GABRIEL, SVP of Sales & Marketing, Publishing; JEFF YOUNGQUIST, VP of Production & Special Projects; DAN CARR, Executive Director of Publishing Technology; ALEX MORALES, Director of Publishing Operations; DAN EDINGTON, Managing Editor; SUSAN CRESPI, Production Manager; STAN LEE, Chairman Emeritus. For information regarding advertising in Marvel Comics or on Marvel.com, please contact Vit DeBellis, Custom Solutions & Integrated Advertising Manager, at vdebellis@marvel.com. For Marvel subscription inquiries, please call 888-511-5480. Manufactured between 9/6/2019 and 10/8/2019 by SOLISCO PRINTERS, SCOTT, QC, CANADA.

10 9 8 7 6 5 4 3 2 1

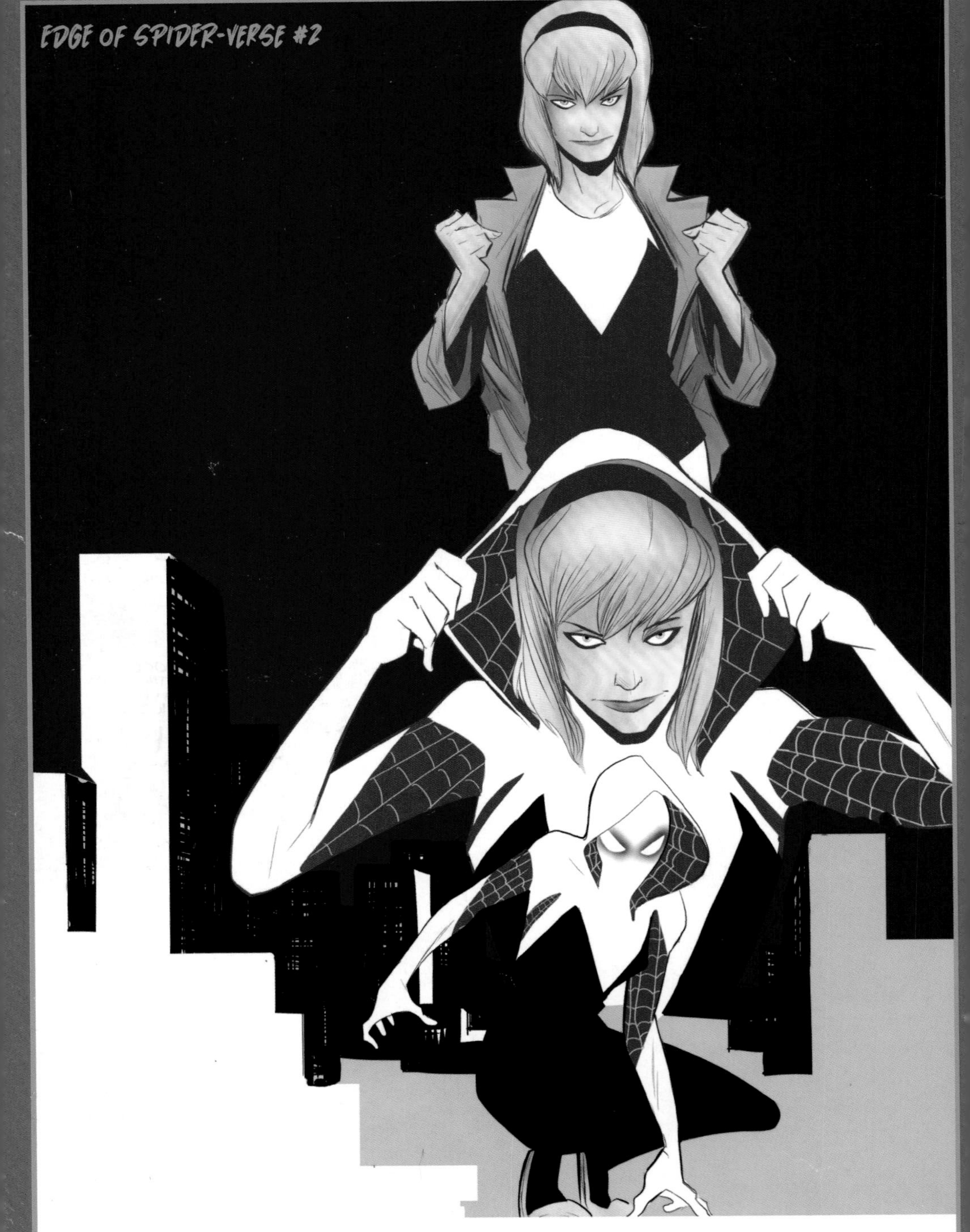
EDGE OF SPIDER-VERSE #2

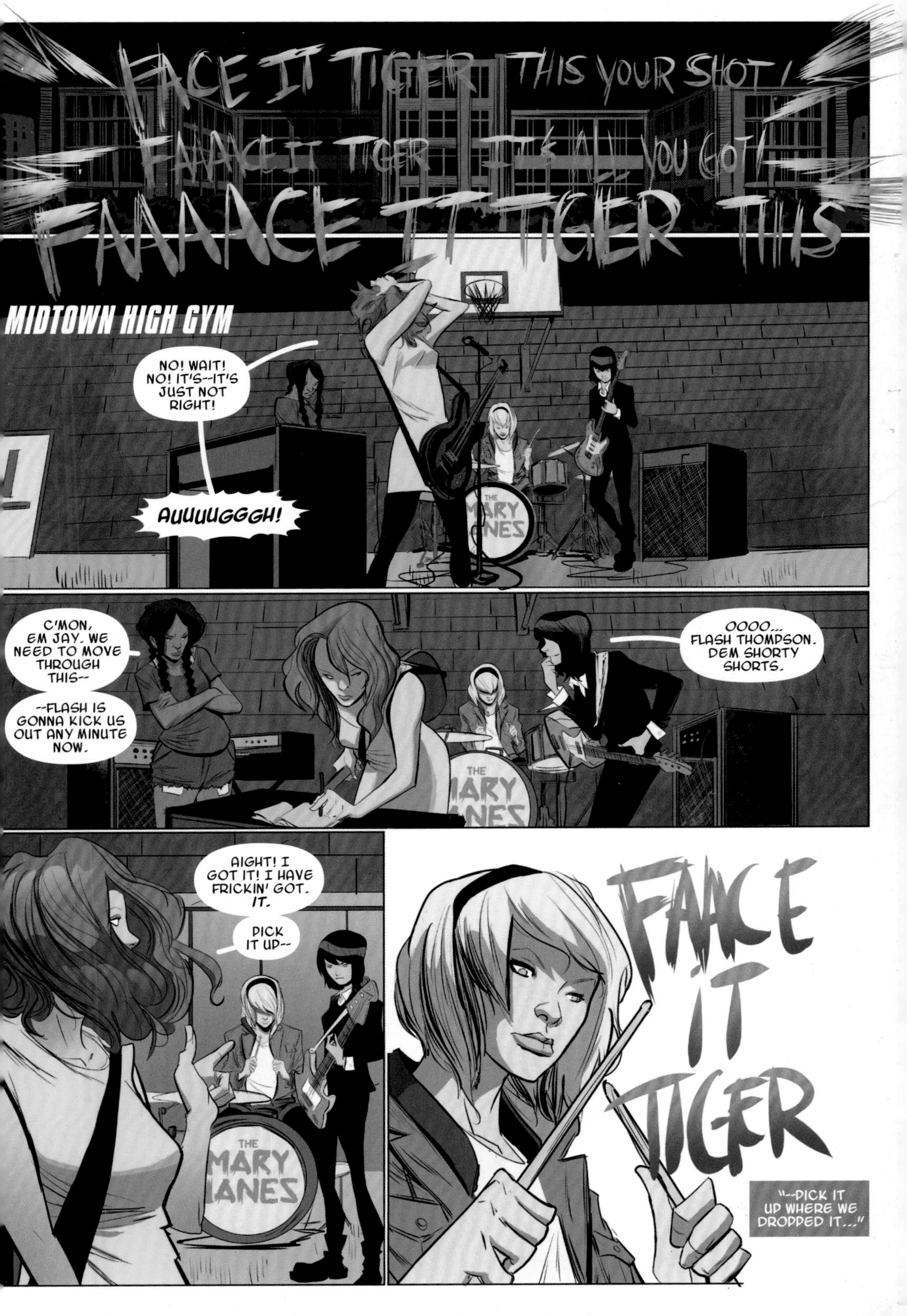

FACE IT TIGER THIS YOUR SHOT!
FAAACE IT TIGER IT'S ALL YOU GOT!
FAAACE IT TIGER THIS
MIDTOWN HIGH GYM
NO! WAIT! NO! IT'S--IT'S JUST NOT RIGHT!
AUUUUGGGH!
C'MON, EM JAY. WE NEED TO MOVE THROUGH THIS--
--FLASH IS GONNA KICK US OUT ANY MINUTE NOW.
OOOO... FLASH THOMPSON. DEM SHORTY SHORTS.
AIGHT! I GOT IT! I HAVE FRICKIN' GOT. IT.
PICK IT UP--
FAAACE IT TIGER
"--PICK IT UP WHERE WE DROPPED IT..."

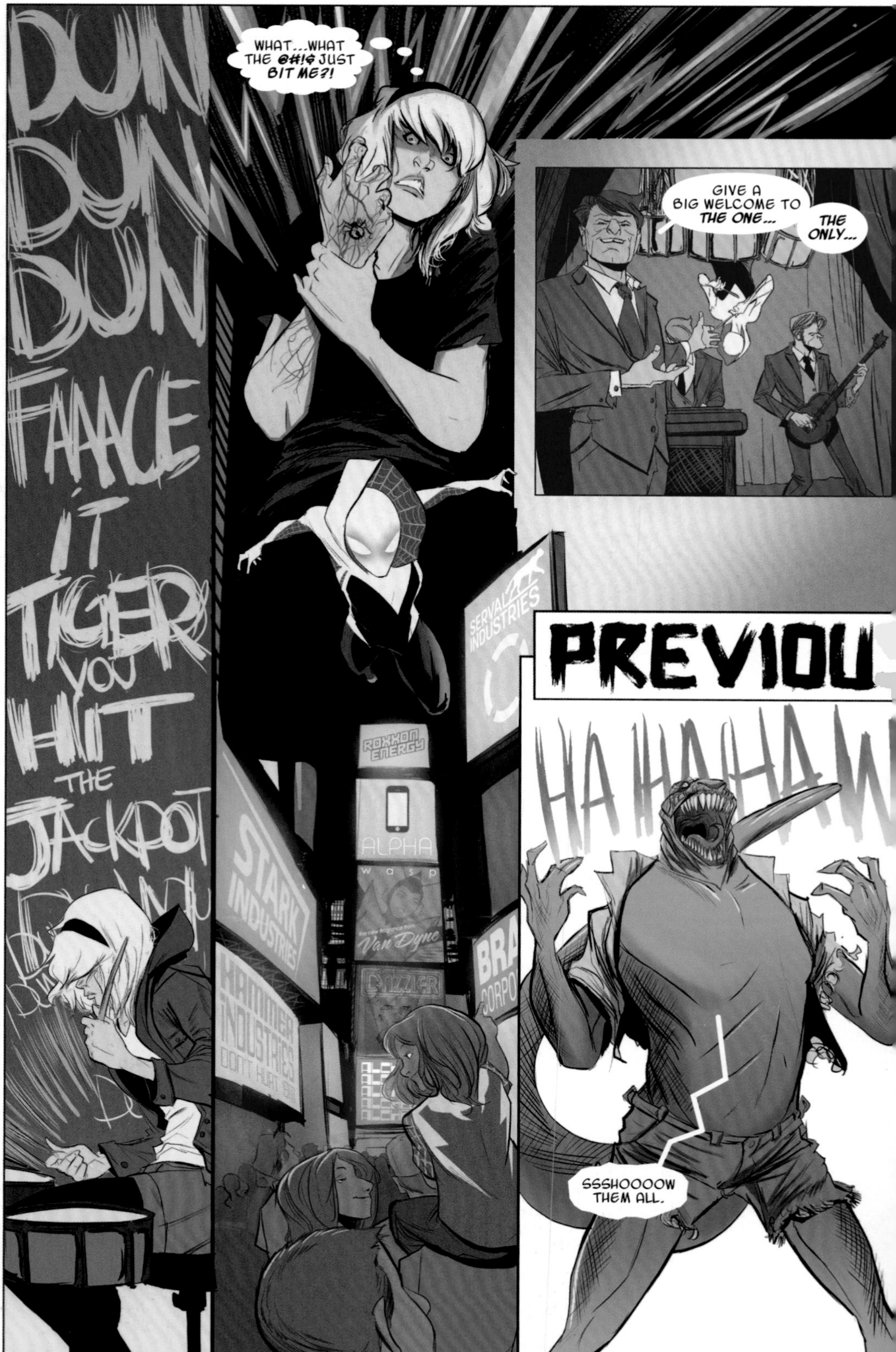
DUN DUN DUN DUN
FAAACE IT TIGER YOU HIT THE JACKPOT
WHAT...WHAT THE @#!$ JUST BIT ME?!
GIVE A BIG WELCOME TO THE ONE...
THE ONLY...
SERVAL INDUSTRIES
ROXXON ENERGY
ALPHA
wasp
Van Dyne
STARK INDUSTRIES
HAMMER INDUSTRIES DON'T HURT 'EM
DAZZLER
PREVIOU
HAHAHAHA
SSSHOOOOW THEM ALL.

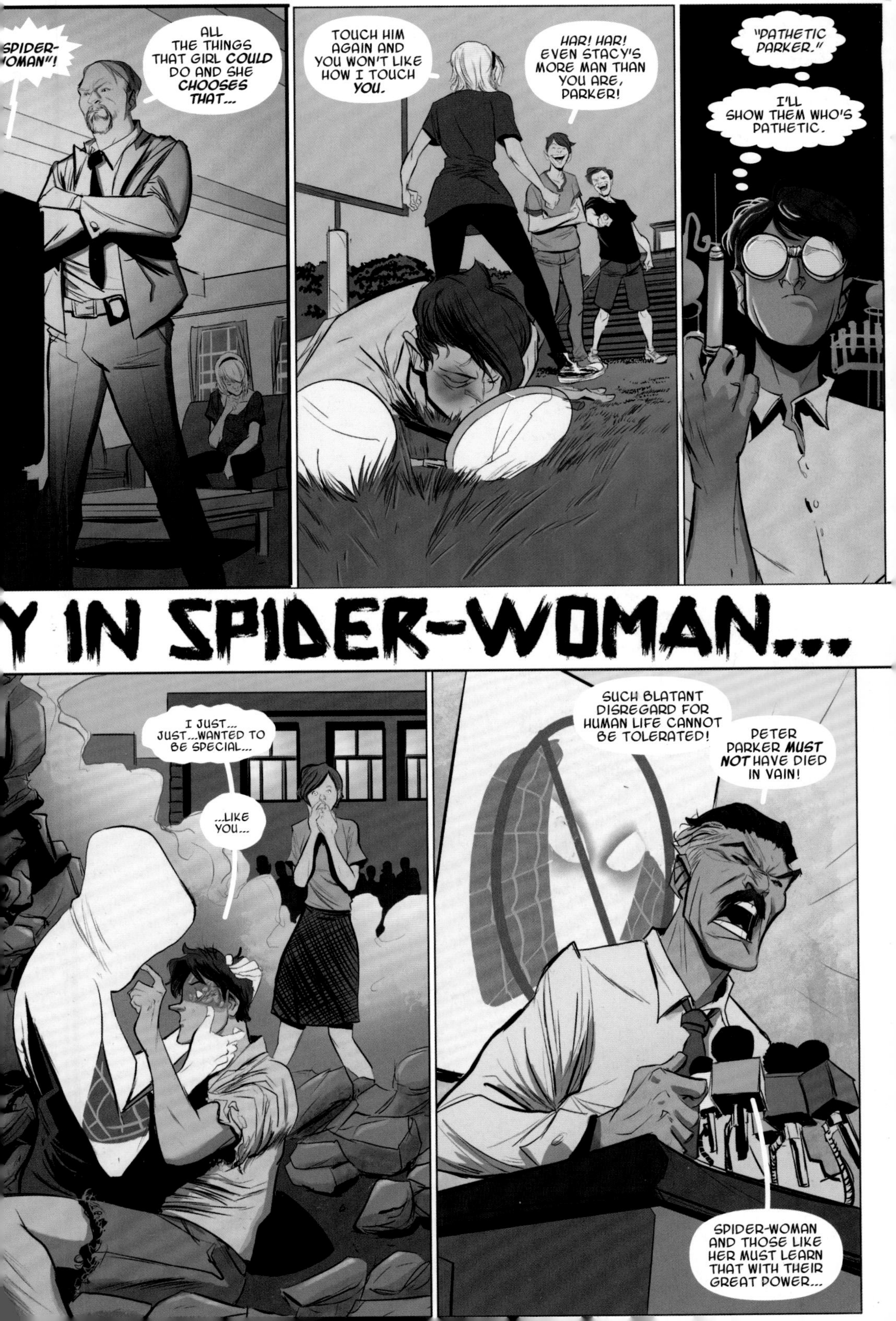
SPIDER-WOMAN"!
ALL THE THINGS THAT GIRL COULD DO AND SHE CHOOSES THAT...
TOUCH HIM AGAIN AND YOU WON'T LIKE HOW I TOUCH YOU.
HAR! HAR! EVEN STACY'S MORE MAN THAN YOU ARE, PARKER!
"PATHETIC PARKER."
I'LL SHOW THEM WHO'S PATHETIC.
Y IN SPIDER-WOMAN...
I JUST... JUST...WANTED TO BE SPECIAL...
...LIKE YOU...
SUCH BLATANT DISREGARD FOR HUMAN LIFE CANNOT BE TOLERATED!
PETER PARKER MUST NOT HAVE DIED IN VAIN!
SPIDER-WOMAN AND THOSE LIKE HER MUST LEARN THAT WITH THEIR GREAT POWER...

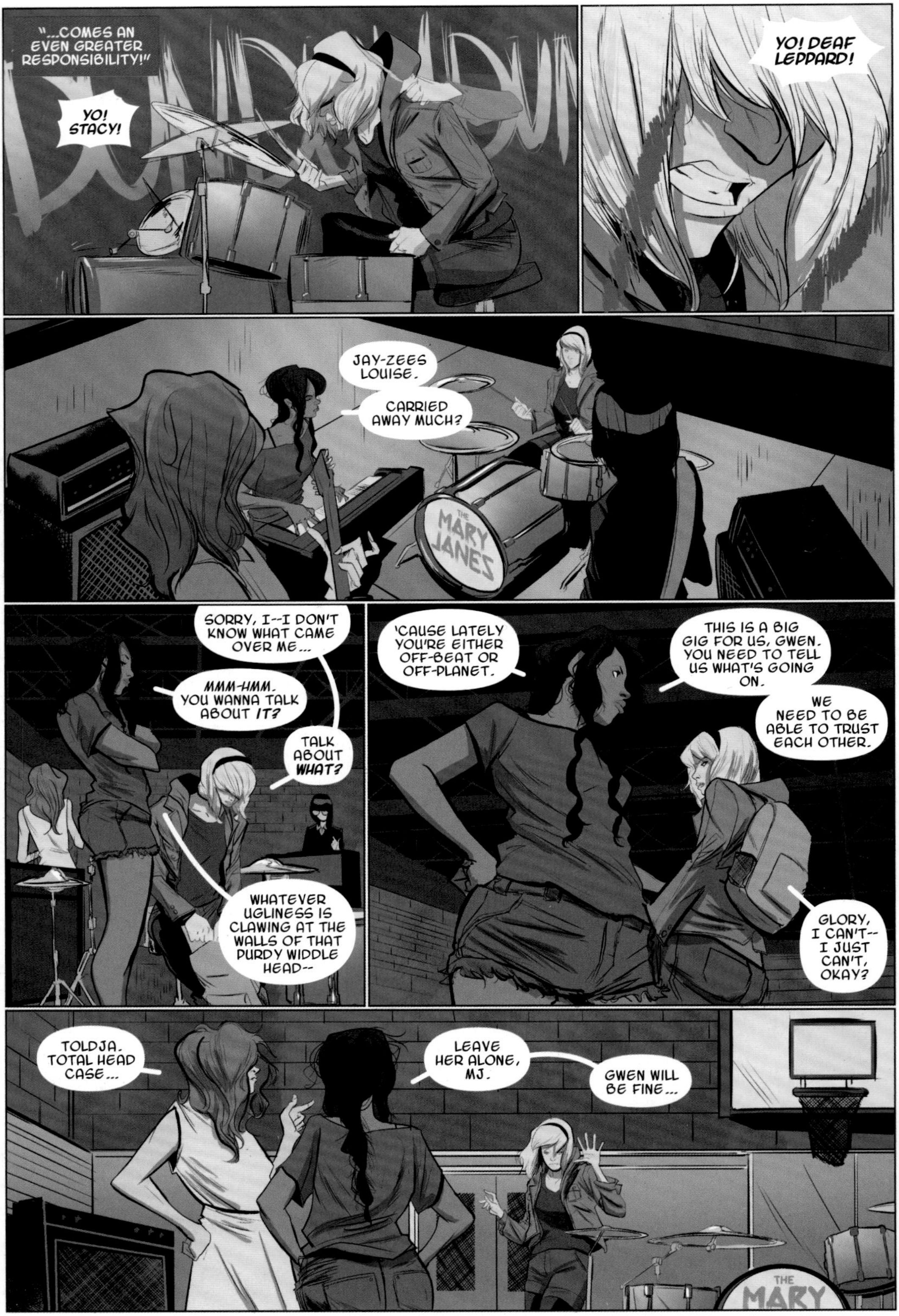
"...COMES AN EVEN GREATER RESPONSIBILITY!"
YO! STACY!
YO! DEAF LEPPARD!
JAY-ZEES LOUISE.
CARRIED AWAY MUCH?
THE MARY JANES
SORRY, I--I DON'T KNOW WHAT CAME OVER ME...
MMM-HMM. YOU WANNA TALK ABOUT IT?
TALK ABOUT WHAT?
WHATEVER UGLINESS IS CLAWING AT THE WALLS OF THAT PURDY WIDDLE HEAD--
'CAUSE LATELY YOU'RE EITHER OFF-BEAT OR OFF-PLANET.
THIS IS A BIG GIG FOR US, GWEN. YOU NEED TO TELL US WHAT'S GOING ON.
WE NEED TO BE ABLE TO TRUST EACH OTHER.
GLORY, I CAN'T-- I JUST CAN'T, OKAY?
TOLDJA. TOTAL HEAD CASE...
LEAVE HER ALONE, MJ.
GWEN WILL BE FINE...
THE MARY

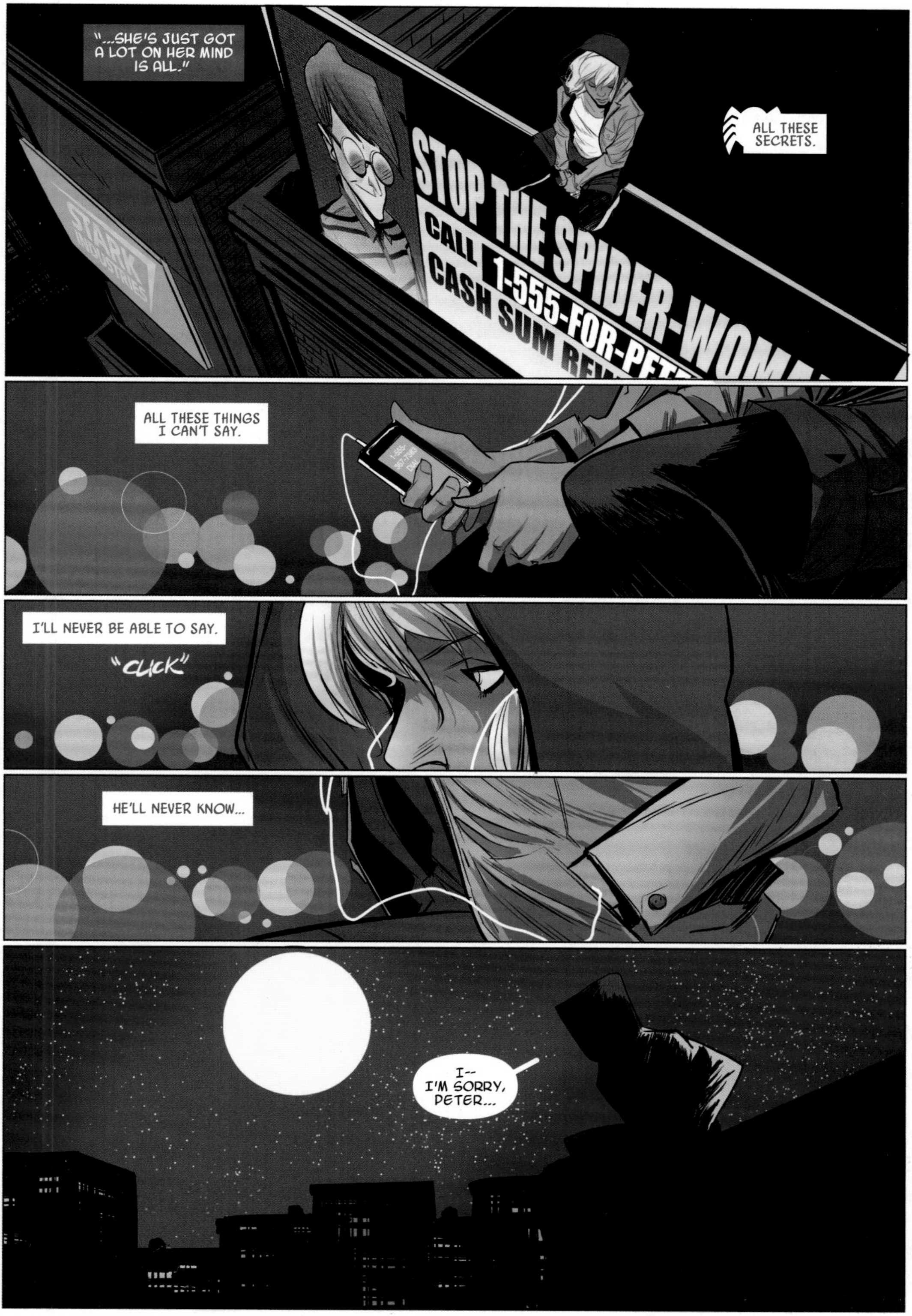
"...SHE'S JUST GOT A LOT ON HER MIND IS ALL."
STARK INDUSTRIES
STOP THE SPIDER-WOM
CALL 1-555-FOR-PET
CASH SUM REV
ALL THESE SECRETS.
ALL THESE THINGS I CAN'T SAY.
I'LL NEVER BE ABLE TO SAY.
"CLICK"
HE'LL NEVER KNOW...
I-- I'M SORRY, PETER...

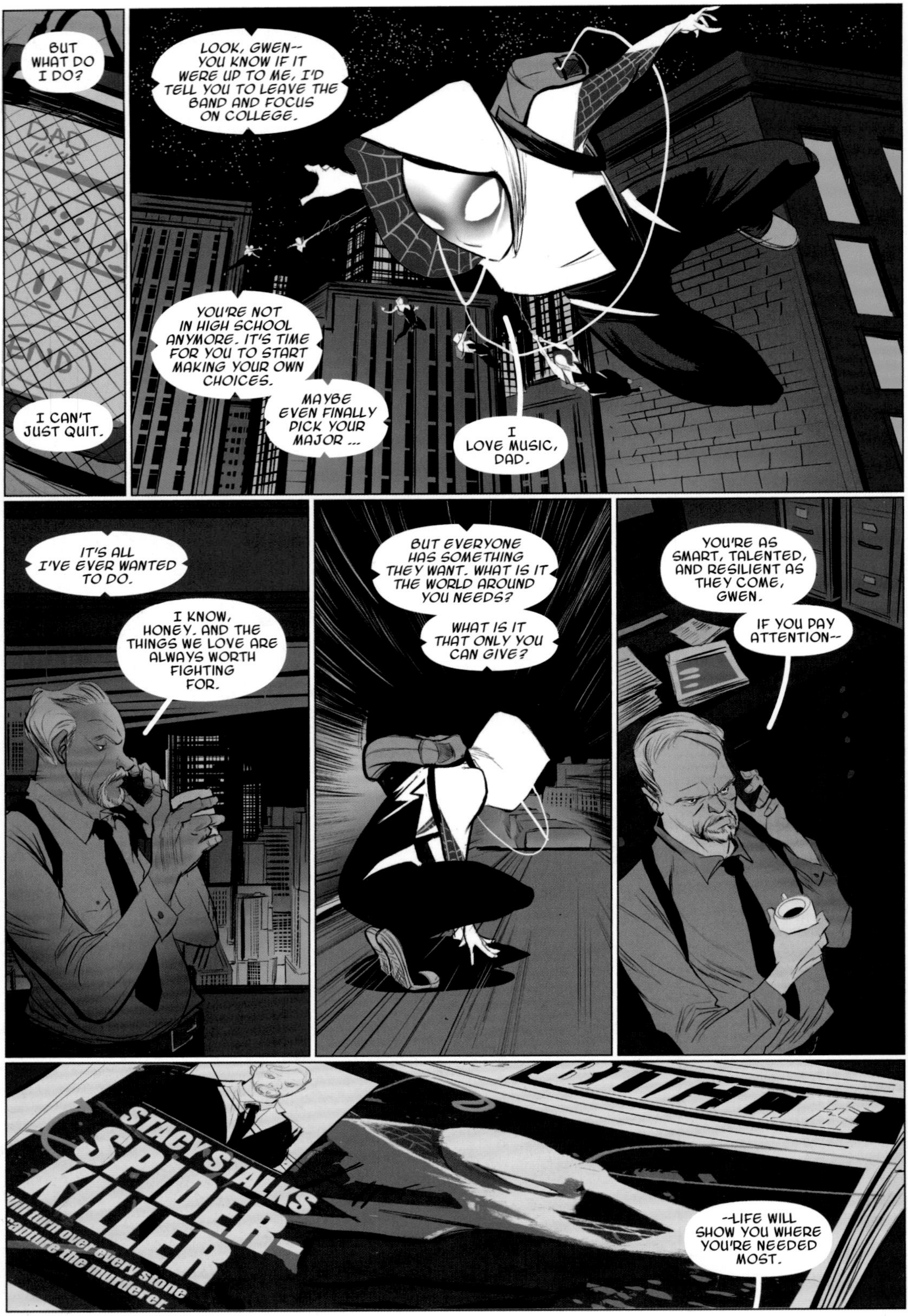
BUT WHAT DO I DO?
LOOK, GWEN-- YOU KNOW IF IT WERE UP TO ME, I'D TELL YOU TO LEAVE THE BAND AND FOCUS ON COLLEGE.
YOU'RE NOT IN HIGH SCHOOL ANYMORE. IT'S TIME FOR YOU TO START MAKING YOUR OWN CHOICES.
MAYBE EVEN FINALLY PICK YOUR MAJOR ...
I CAN'T JUST QUIT.
I LOVE MUSIC, DAD.
IT'S ALL I'VE EVER WANTED TO DO.
I KNOW, HONEY. AND THE THINGS WE LOVE ARE ALWAYS WORTH FIGHTING FOR.
BUT EVERYONE HAS SOMETHING THEY WANT. WHAT IS IT THE WORLD AROUND YOU NEEDS?
WHAT IS IT THAT ONLY YOU CAN GIVE?
YOU'RE AS SMART, TALENTED, AND RESILIENT AS THEY COME, GWEN.
IF YOU PAY ATTENTION--
STACY STALKS SPIDER-KILLER
will turn over every stone
capture the murderer.
--LIFE WILL SHOW YOU WHERE YOU'RE NEEDED MOST.

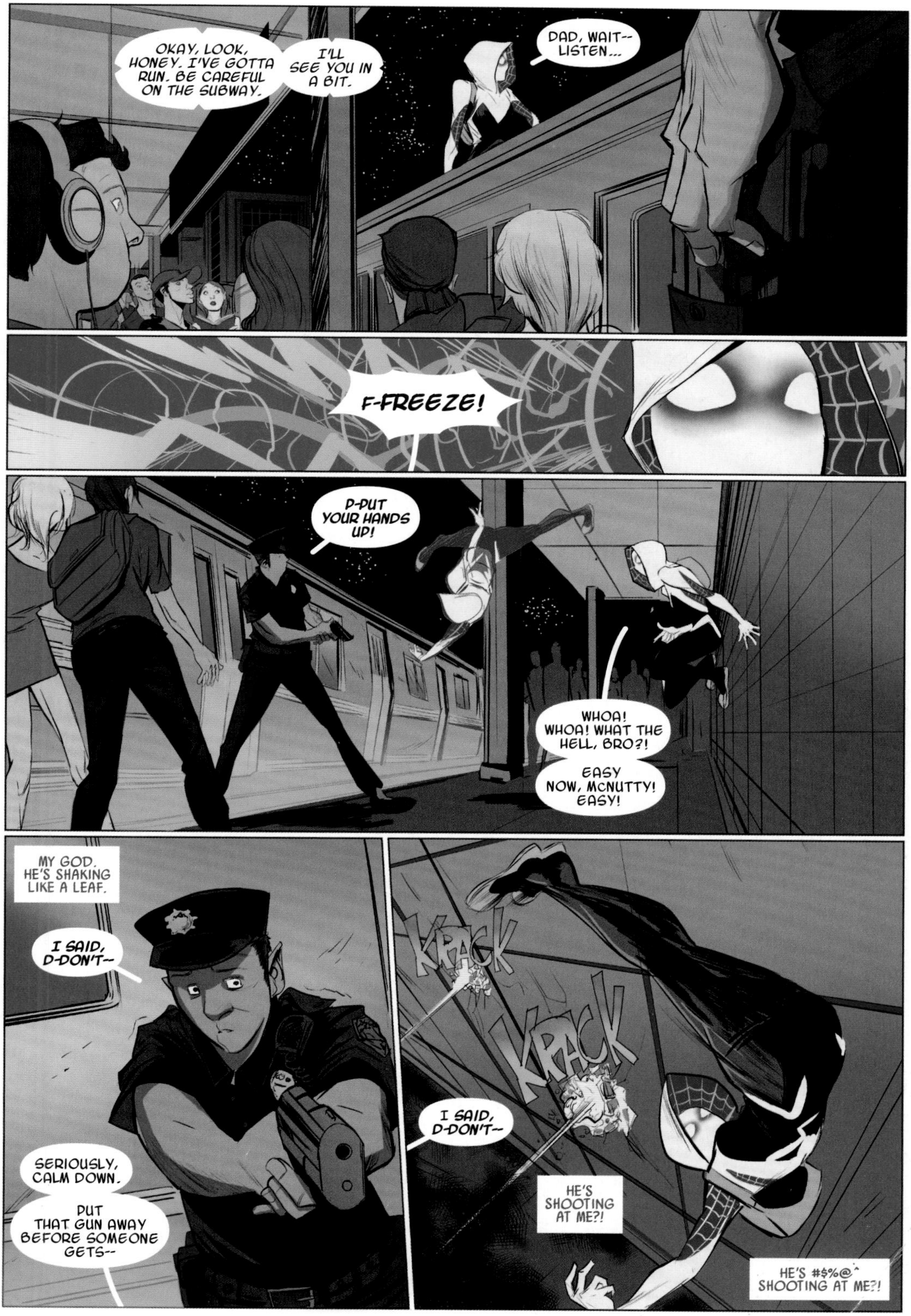

OKAY, LOOK, HONEY. I'VE GOTTA RUN. BE CAREFUL ON THE SUBWAY.
I'LL SEE YOU IN A BIT.
DAD, WAIT-- LISTEN...
F-FREEZE!
D-PUT YOUR HANDS UP!
WHOA! WHOA! WHAT THE HELL, BRO?!
EASY NOW, McNUTTY! EASY!
MY GOD. HE'S SHAKING LIKE A LEAF.
I SAID, D-DON'T--
SERIOUSLY, CALM DOWN.
PUT THAT GUN AWAY BEFORE SOMEONE GETS--
KRACK
KRACK
I SAID, D-DON'T--
HE'S SHOOTING AT ME?!
HE'S #$%@^ SHOOTING AT ME?!

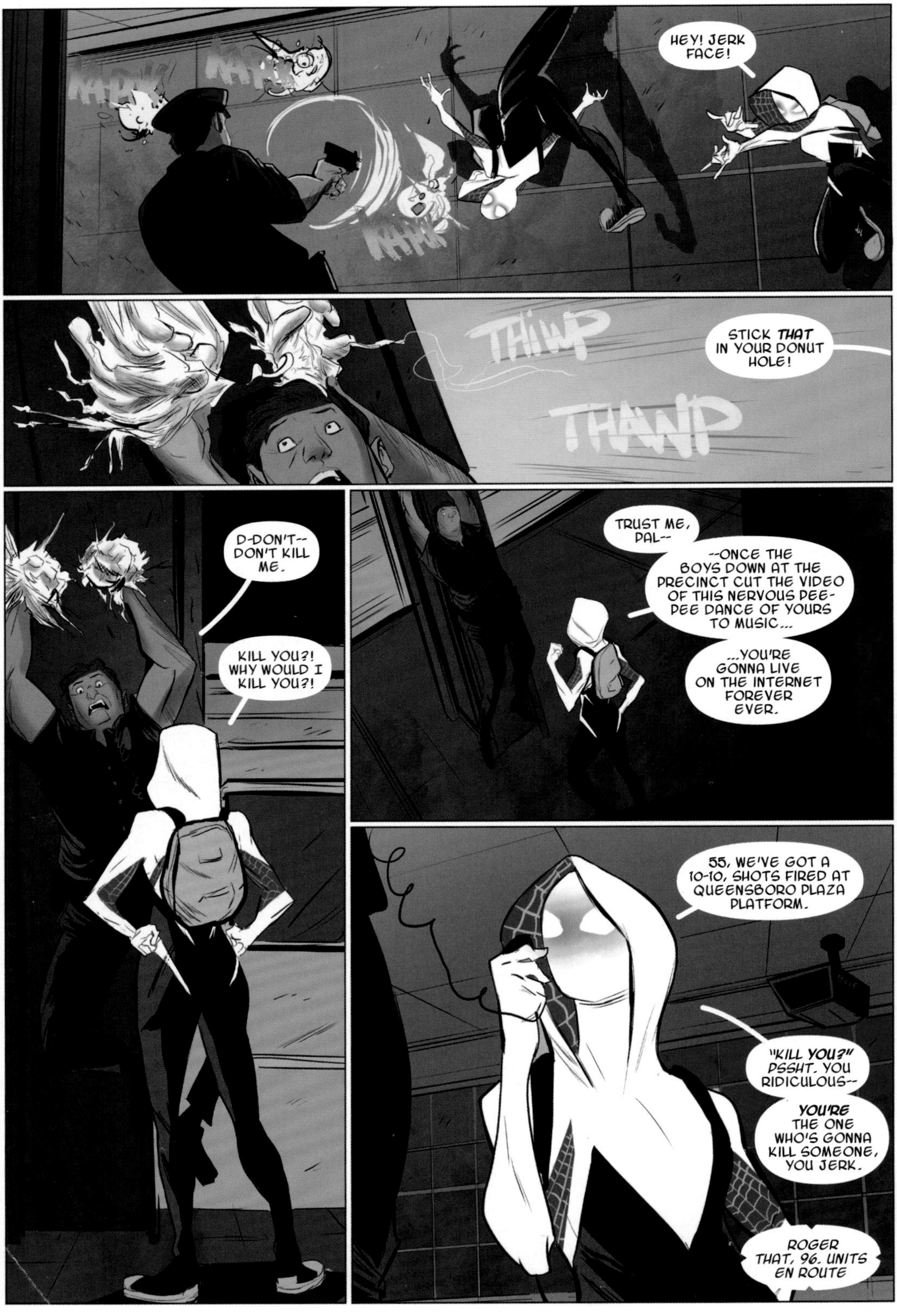
KAPOW
KAPOW
KAPOW
HEY! JERK FACE!
THWP
THAWP
STICK THAT IN YOUR DONUT HOLE!
D-DON'T-- DON'T KILL ME.
KILL YOU?! WHY WOULD I KILL YOU?!
TRUST ME, PAL--
--ONCE THE BOYS DOWN AT THE PRECINCT CUT THE VIDEO OF THIS NERVOUS PEE-PEE DANCE OF YOURS TO MUSIC...
...YOU'RE GONNA LIVE ON THE INTERNET FOREVER EVER.
55, WE'VE GOT A 10-10, SHOTS FIRED AT QUEENSBORO PLAZA PLATFORM.
"KILL YOU?" PSSHT. YOU RIDICULOUS--
YOU'RE THE ONE WHO'S GONNA KILL SOMEONE, YOU JERK.
ROGER THAT, 96. UNITS EN ROUTE

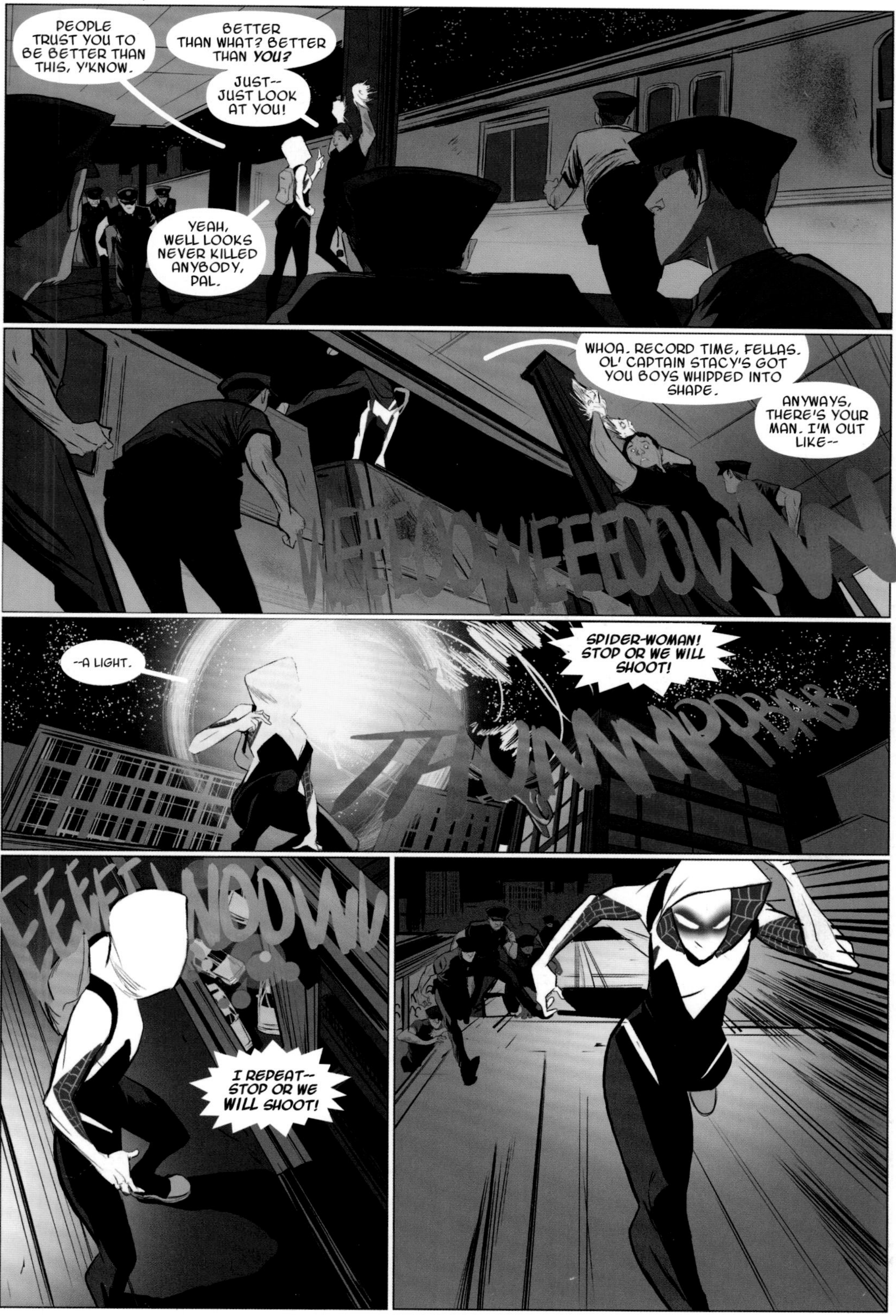
PEOPLE TRUST YOU TO BE BETTER THAN THIS, Y'KNOW.
BETTER THAN WHAT? BETTER THAN *YOU?*
JUST-- JUST LOOK AT YOU!
YEAH, WELL LOOKS NEVER KILLED ANYBODY, PAL.
WHOA. RECORD TIME, FELLAS. OL' CAPTAIN STACY'S GOT YOU BOYS WHIPPED INTO SHAPE.
ANYWAYS, THERE'S YOUR MAN. I'M OUT LIKE--
--A LIGHT.
SPIDER-WOMAN! STOP OR WE WILL SHOOT!
I REPEAT-- STOP OR WE **WILL** SHOOT!

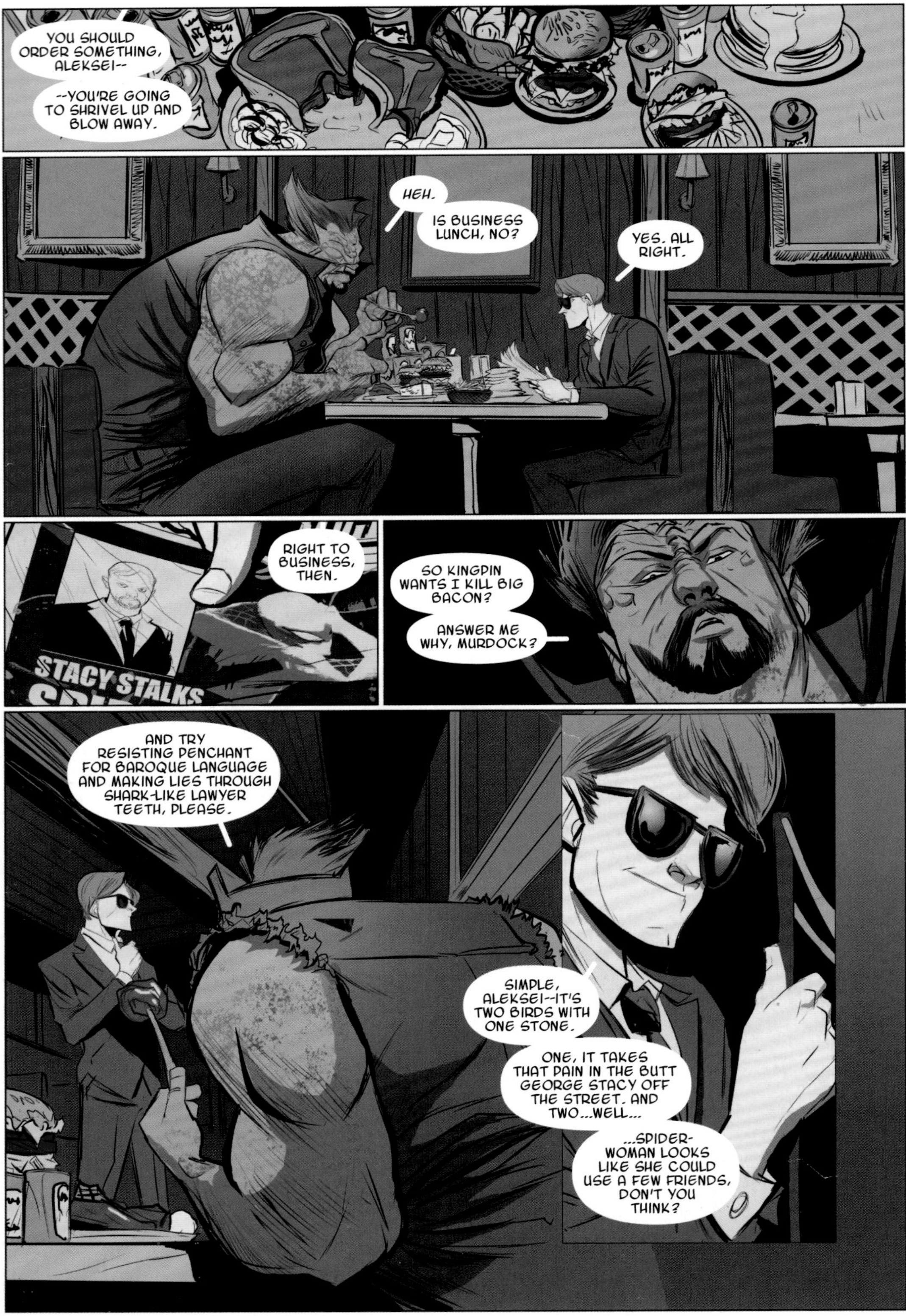
YOU SHOULD ORDER SOMETHING, ALEKSEI--
--YOU'RE GOING TO SHRIVEL UP AND BLOW AWAY.
HEH.
IS BUSINESS LUNCH, NO?
YES. ALL RIGHT.
STACY STALKS
RIGHT TO BUSINESS, THEN.
SO KINGPIN WANTS I KILL BIG BACON?
ANSWER ME WHY, MURDOCK?
AND TRY RESISTING PENCHANT FOR BAROQUE LANGUAGE AND MAKING LIES THROUGH SHARK-LIKE LAWYER TEETH, PLEASE.
SIMPLE, ALEKSEI--IT'S TWO BIRDS WITH ONE STONE.
ONE, IT TAKES THAT PAIN IN THE BUTT GEORGE STACY OFF THE STREET. AND TWO...WELL...
...SPIDER-WOMAN LOOKS LIKE SHE COULD USE A FEW FRIENDS, DON'T YOU THINK?

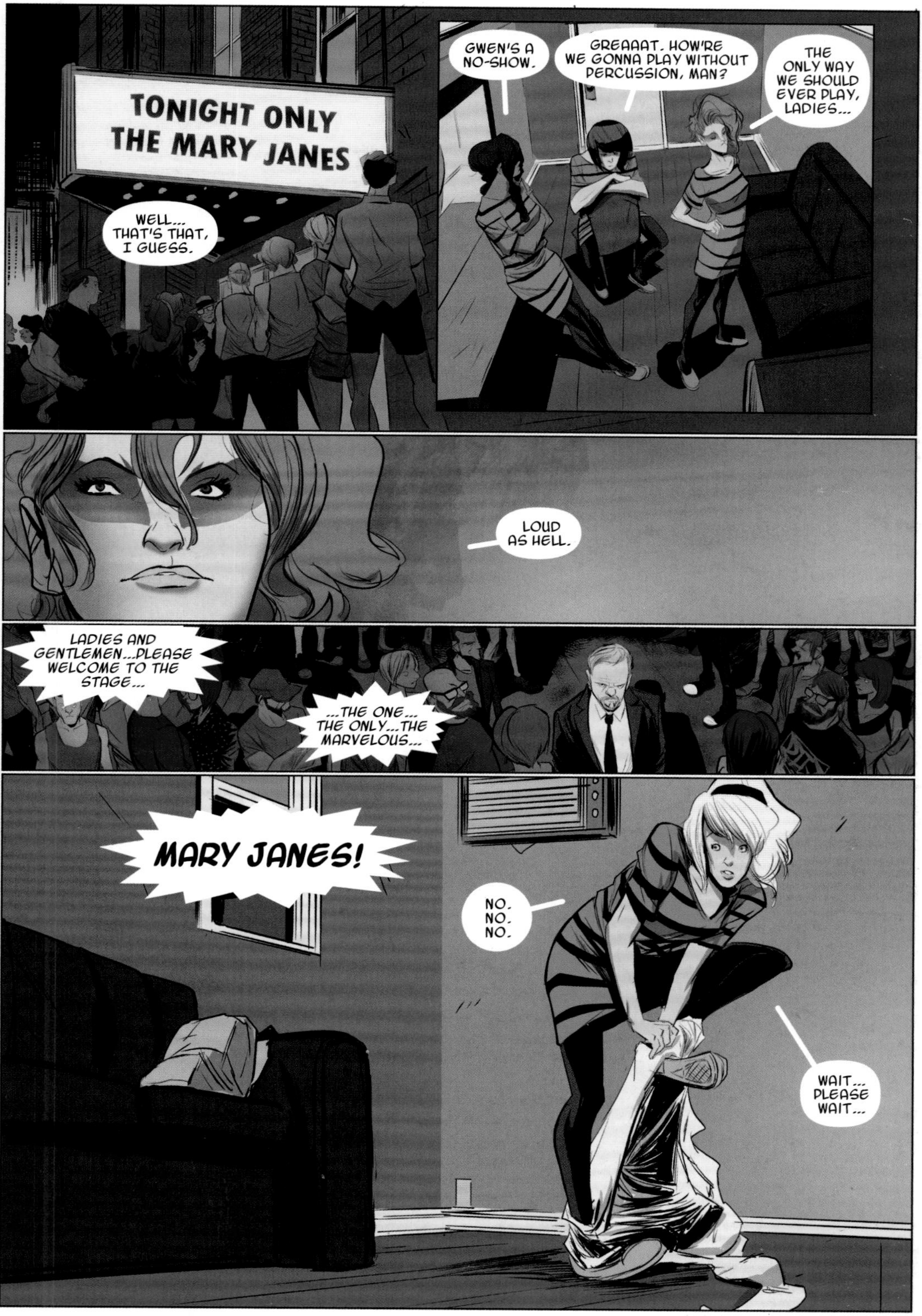
TONIGHT ONLY
THE MARY JANES
WELL... THAT'S THAT, I GUESS.
GWEN'S A NO-SHOW.
GREAAAT. HOW'RE WE GONNA PLAY WITHOUT PERCUSSION, MAN?
THE ONLY WAY WE SHOULD EVER PLAY, LADIES...
LOUD AS HELL.
LADIES AND GENTLEMEN...PLEASE WELCOME TO THE STAGE...
...THE ONE... THE ONLY...THE MARVELOUS...
MARY JANES!
NO. NO. NO.
WAIT... PLEASE WAIT...

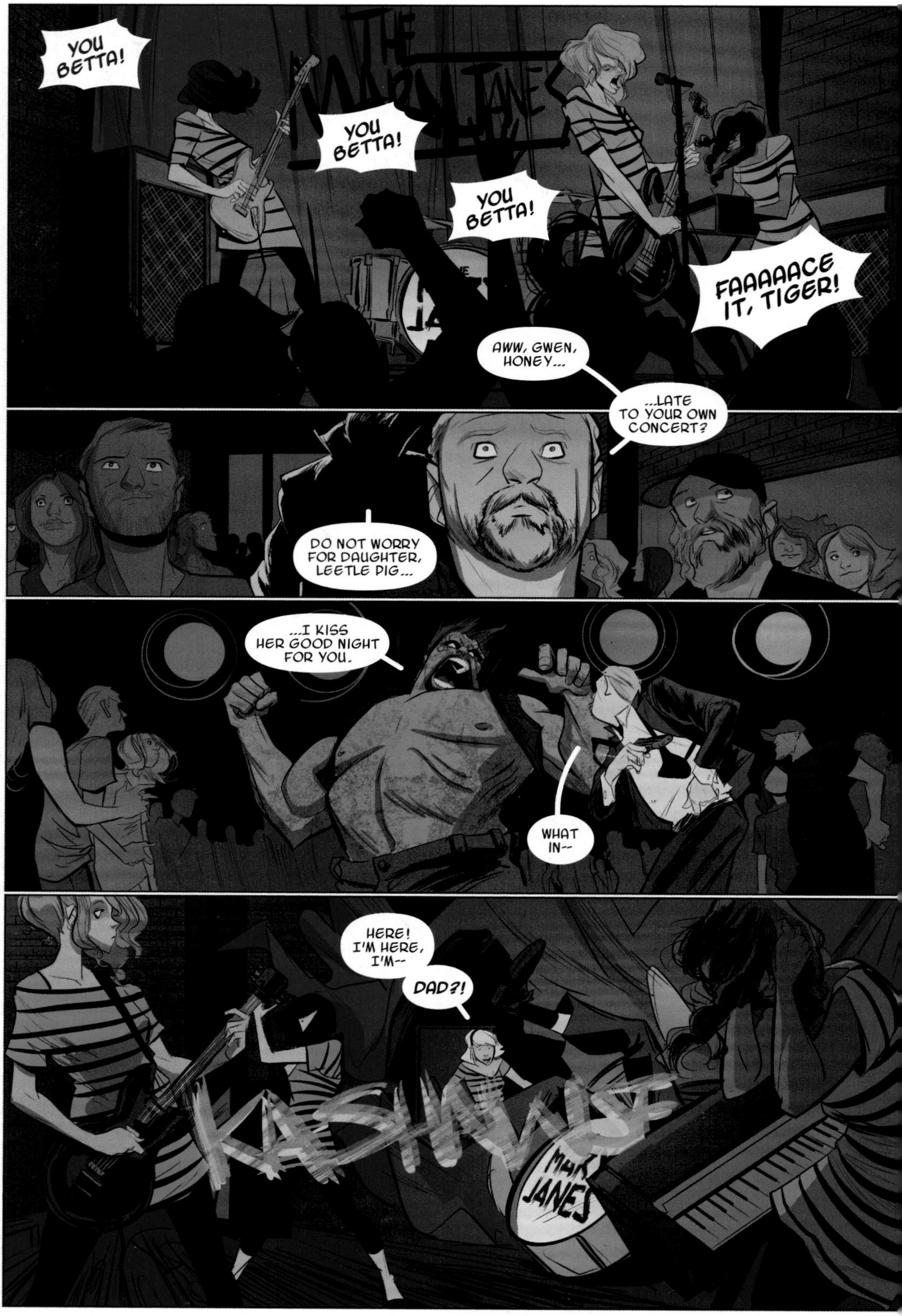
YOU BETTA!
YOU BETTA!
YOU BETTA!
FAAAAACE IT, TIGER!
AWW, GWEN, HONEY...
...LATE TO YOUR OWN CONCERT?
DO NOT WORRY FOR DAUGHTER, LEETLE PIG...
...I KISS HER GOOD NIGHT FOR YOU.
WHAT IN--
HERE! I'M HERE, I'M--
DAD?!
KASHWISF
JANES

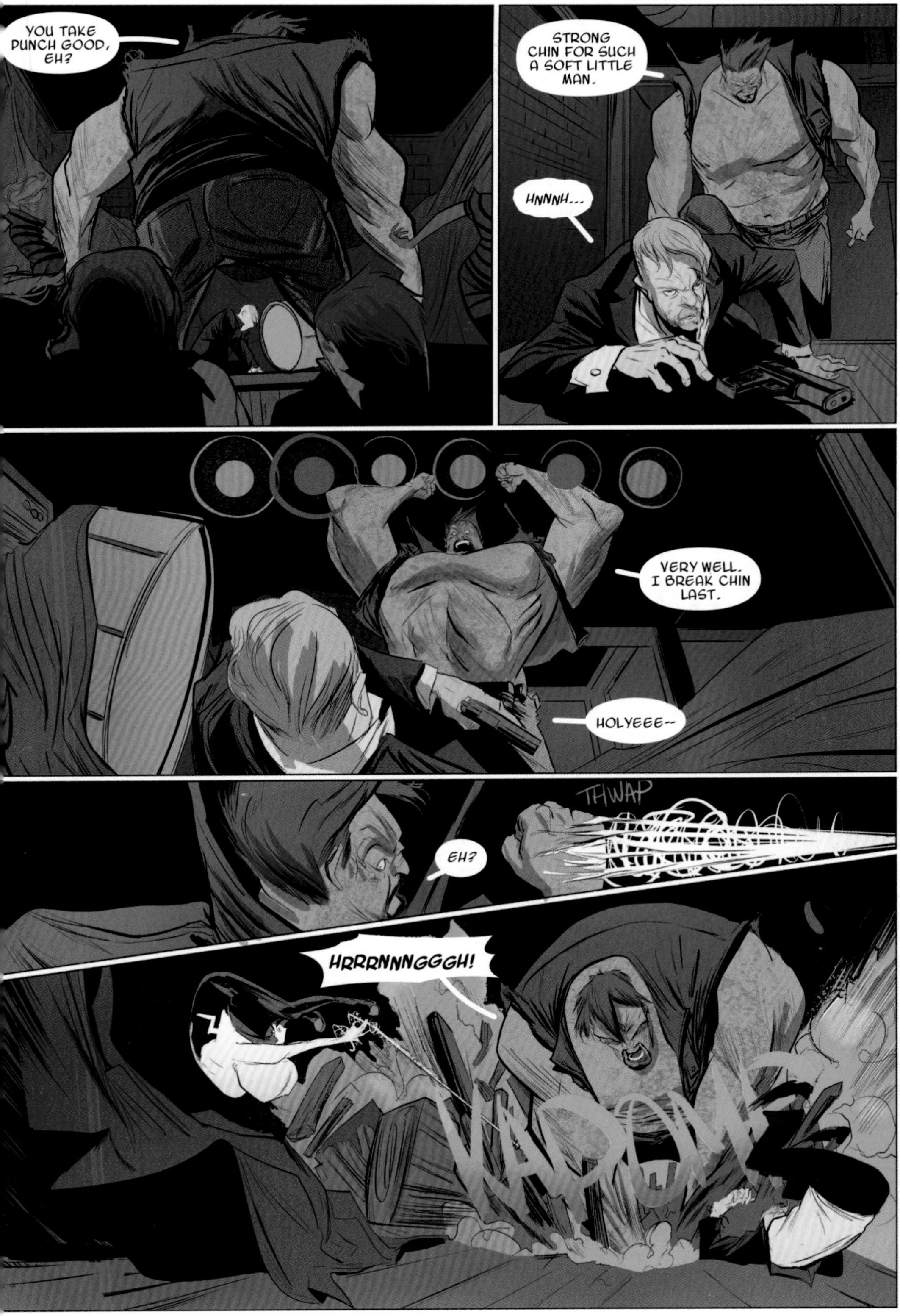
YOU TAKE PUNCH GOOD, EH?
STRONG CHIN FOR SUCH A SOFT LITTLE MAN.
HNNNH...
VERY WELL. I BREAK CHIN LAST.
HOLYEEE--
THWAP
EH?
HRRRNNNGGGH!
VADOOM

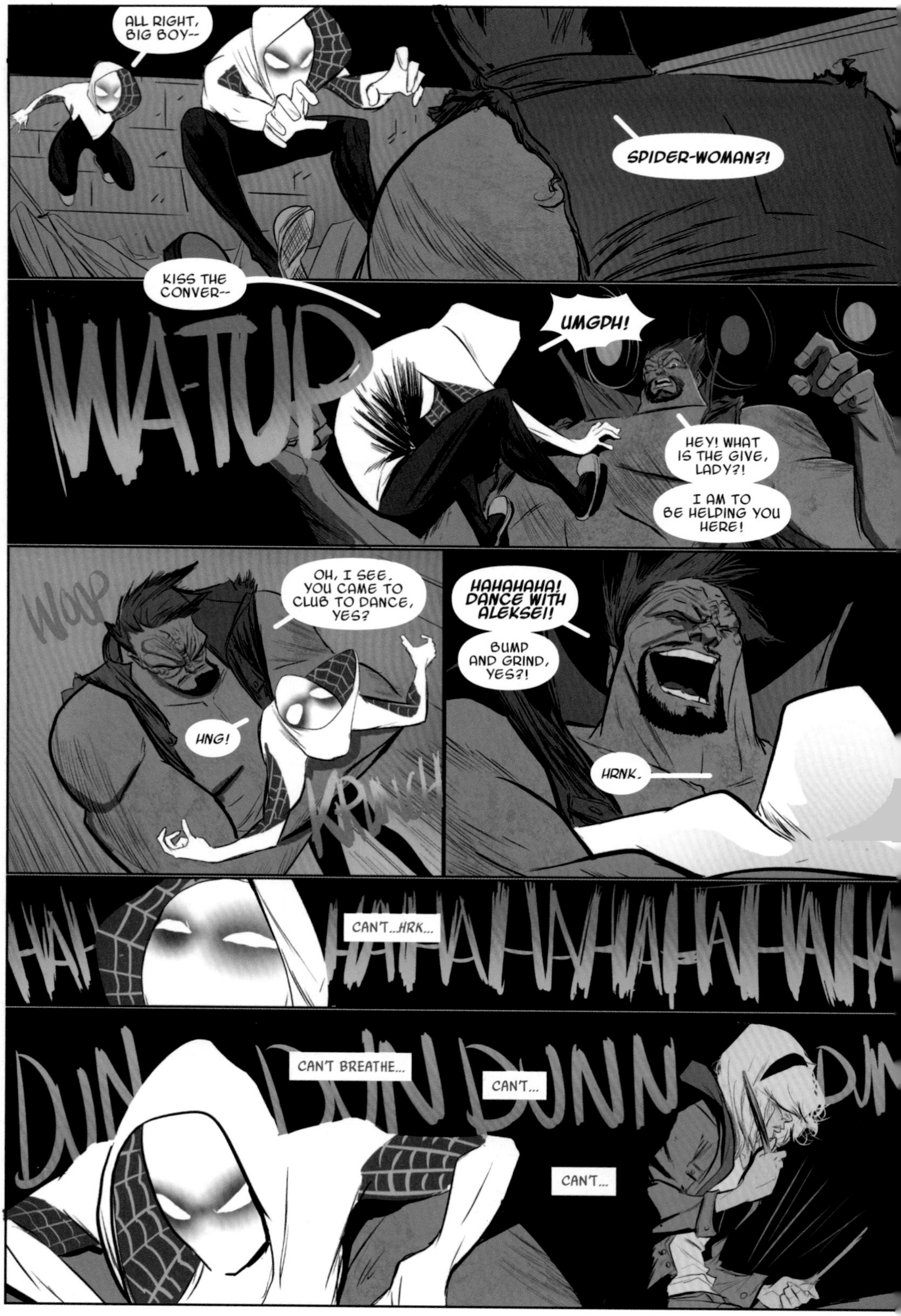

ALL RIGHT, BIG BOY--
SPIDER-WOMAN?!
KISS THE CONVER--
WATUP
UMGPH!
HEY! WHAT IS THE GIVE, LADY?!
I AM TO BE HELPING YOU HERE!
WOOP
OH, I SEE. YOU CAME TO CLUB TO DANCE, YES?
HNG!
KRUNCH
HAHAHAHA! DANCE WITH ALEKSEI!
BUMP AND GRIND, YES?!
HRNK.
CAN'T...HRK...
CAN'T BREATHE...
CAN'T...
CAN'T...
DUNN DUNN DUNN

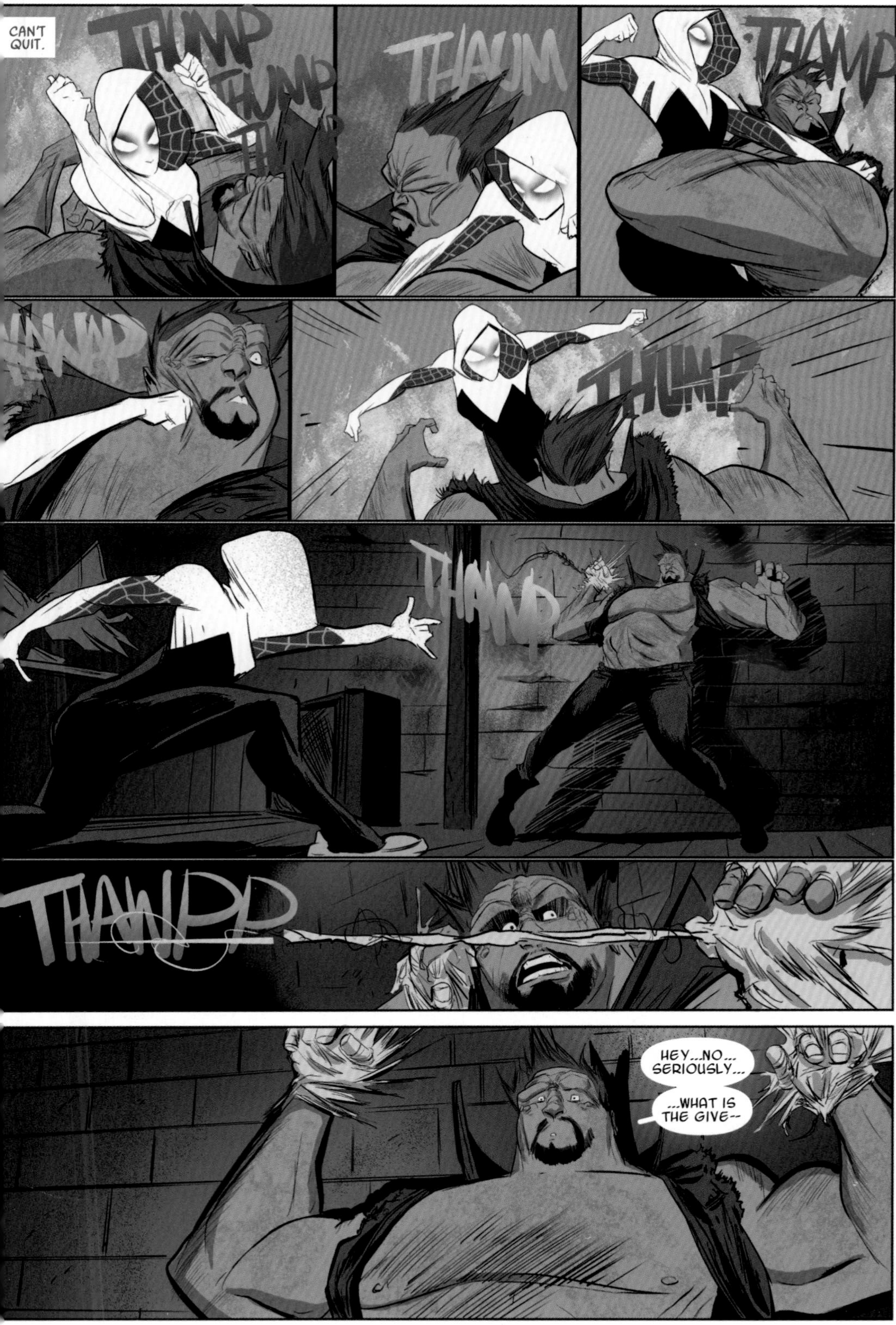
CAN'T QUIT.
THUMP
THUMP
THUMP
THAUM
THAMP
WAMP
THUMP
THAMP
THAWPP
HEY...NO... SERIOUSLY...
...WHAT IS THE GIVE--

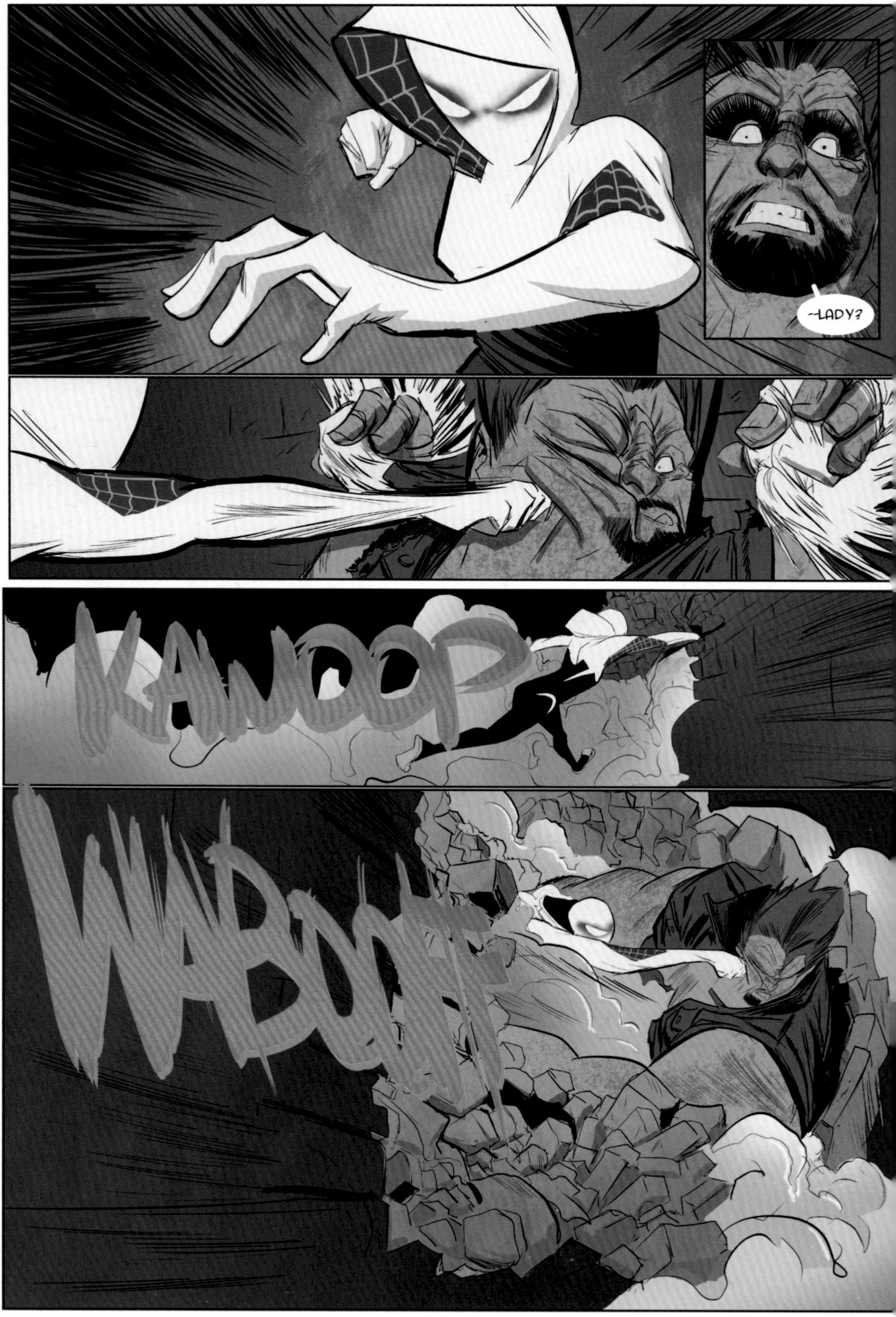
--LADY?
KANOOP
WABOOF

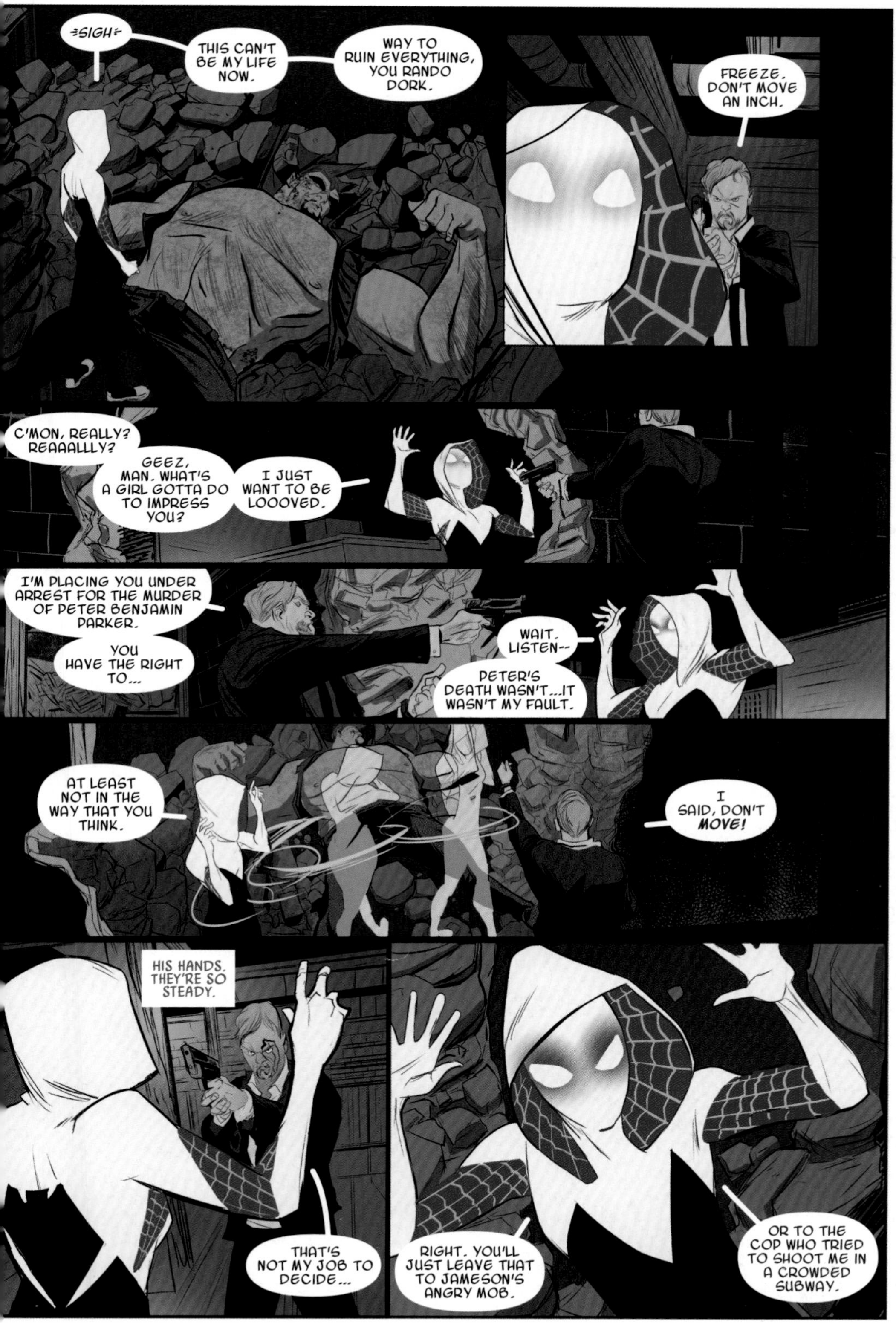
≠SIGH≠
THIS CAN'T BE MY LIFE NOW.
WAY TO RUIN EVERYTHING, YOU RANDO DORK.
FREEZE. DON'T MOVE AN INCH.
C'MON, REALLY? REAAALLLY?
GEEZ, MAN. WHAT'S A GIRL GOTTA DO TO IMPRESS YOU?
I JUST WANT TO BE LOOOVED.
I'M PLACING YOU UNDER ARREST FOR THE MURDER OF PETER BENJAMIN PARKER.
YOU HAVE THE RIGHT TO...
WAIT. LISTEN--
PETER'S DEATH WASN'T...IT WASN'T MY FAULT.
AT LEAST NOT IN THE WAY THAT YOU THINK.
I SAID, DON'T *MOVE!*
HIS HANDS. THEY'RE SO STEADY.
THAT'S NOT MY JOB TO DECIDE...
RIGHT. YOU'LL JUST LEAVE THAT TO JAMESON'S ANGRY MOB.
OR TO THE COP WHO TRIED TO SHOOT ME IN A CROWDED SUBWAY.

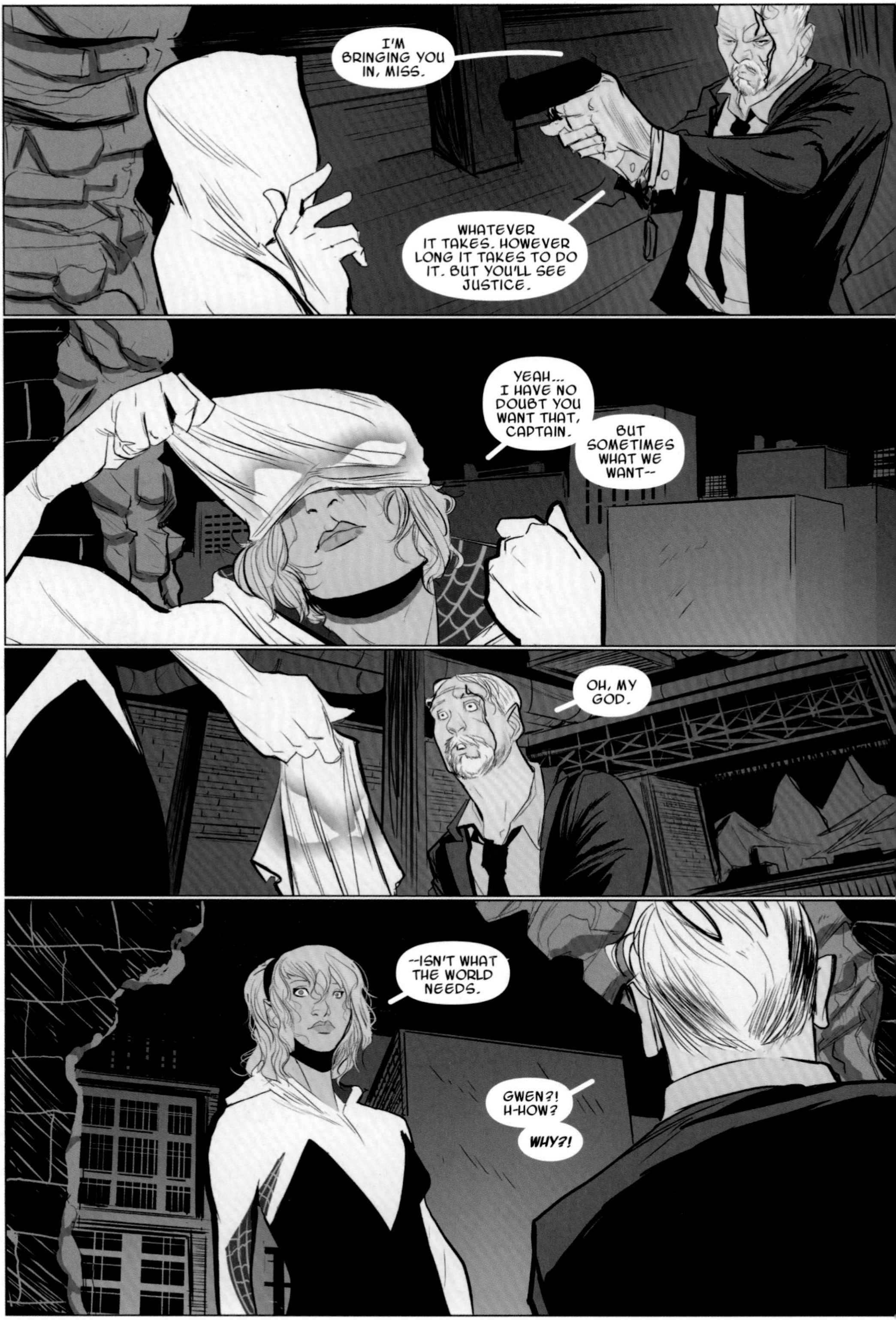
I'M BRINGING YOU IN, MISS.
WHATEVER IT TAKES. HOWEVER LONG IT TAKES TO DO IT. BUT YOU'LL SEE JUSTICE.
YEAH... I HAVE NO DOUBT YOU WANT THAT, CAPTAIN.
BUT SOMETIMES WHAT WE WANT--
OH, MY GOD.
--ISN'T WHAT THE WORLD NEEDS.
GWEN?! H-HOW?
WHY?!

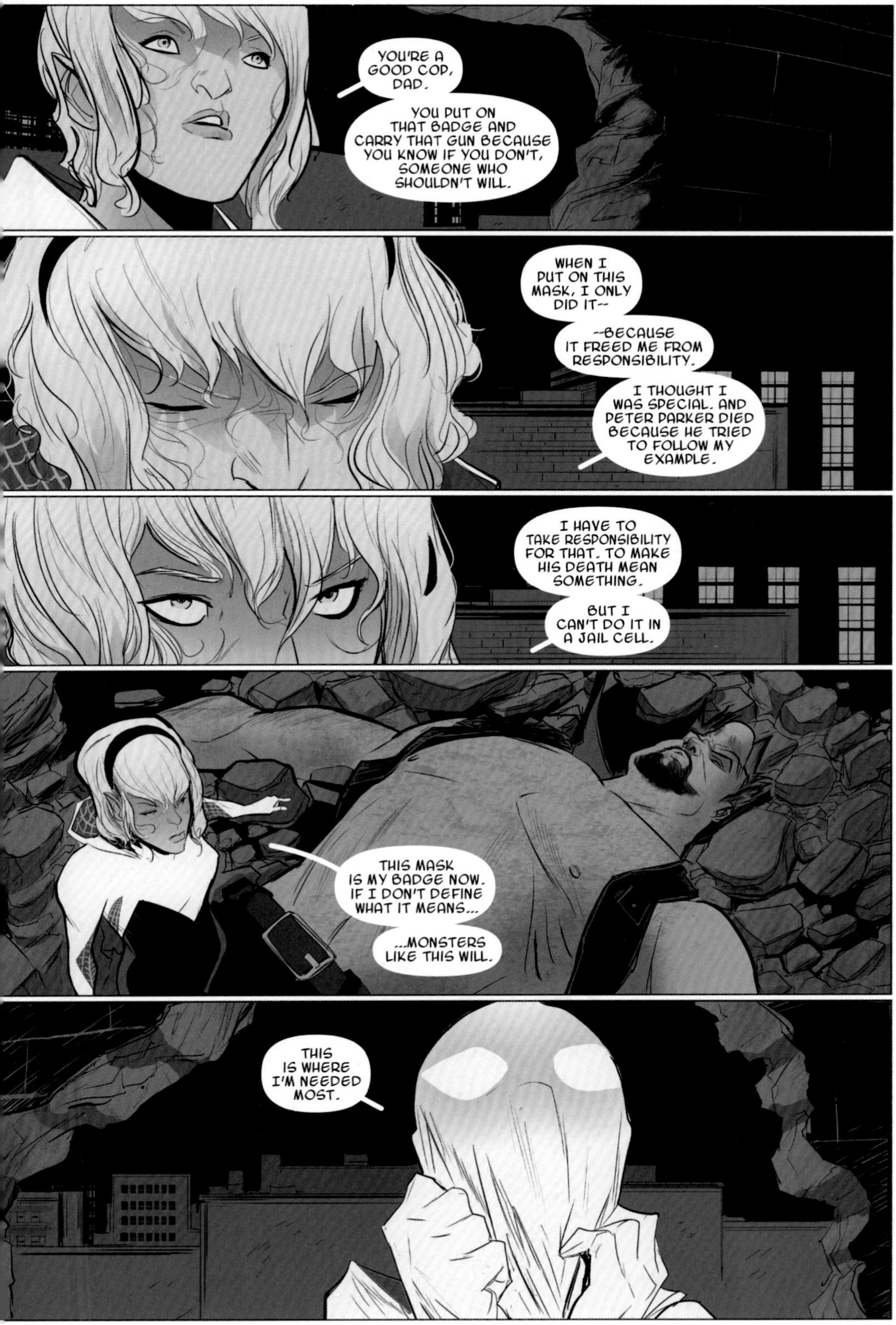
YOU'RE A GOOD COP, DAD.
YOU PUT ON THAT BADGE AND CARRY THAT GUN BECAUSE YOU KNOW IF YOU DON'T, SOMEONE WHO SHOULDN'T WILL.
WHEN I PUT ON THIS MASK, I ONLY DID IT--
--BECAUSE IT FREED ME FROM RESPONSIBILITY.
I THOUGHT I WAS SPECIAL. AND PETER PARKER DIED BECAUSE HE TRIED TO FOLLOW MY EXAMPLE.
I HAVE TO TAKE RESPONSIBILITY FOR THAT. TO MAKE HIS DEATH MEAN SOMETHING.
BUT I CAN'T DO IT IN A JAIL CELL.
THIS MASK IS MY BADGE NOW. IF I DON'T DEFINE WHAT IT MEANS...
...MONSTERS LIKE THIS WILL.
THIS IS WHERE I'M NEEDED MOST.

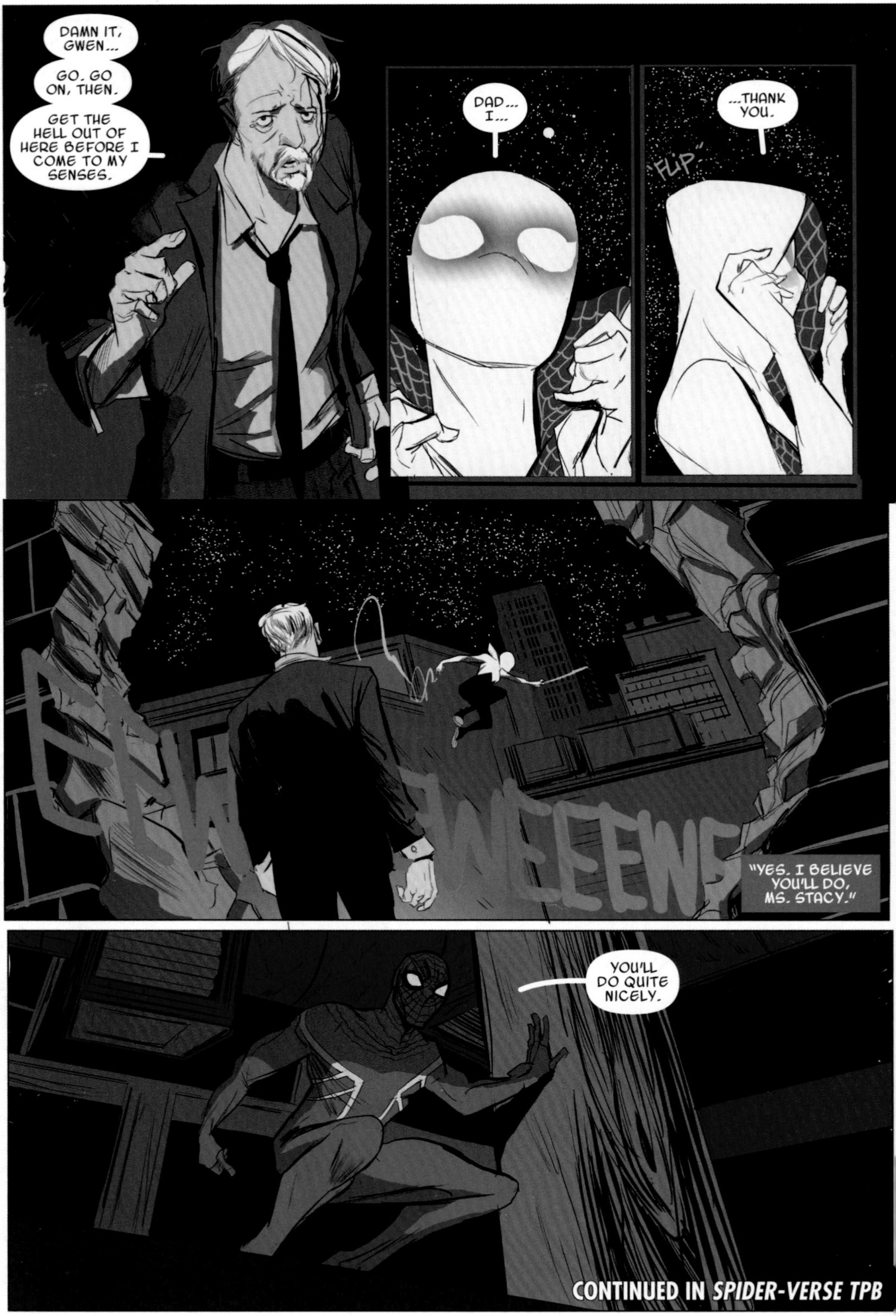

DAMN IT, GWEN...
GO. GO ON, THEN.
GET THE HELL OUT OF HERE BEFORE I COME TO MY SENSES.
DAD... I...
...THANK YOU.
FLIP
"YES. I BELIEVE YOU'LL DO, MS. STACY."
YOU'LL DO QUITE NICELY.
CONTINUED IN *SPIDER-VERSE TPB*

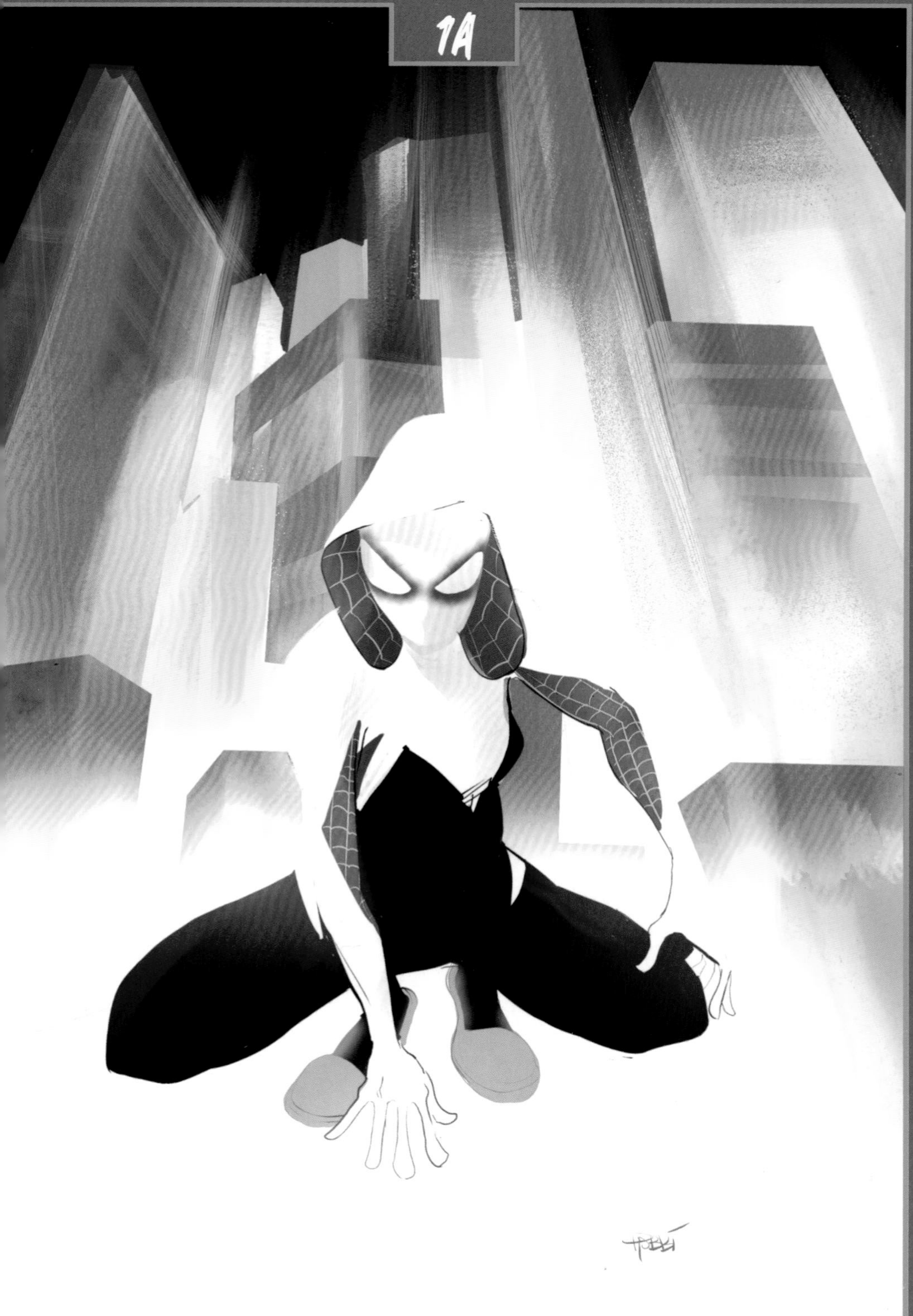
1A

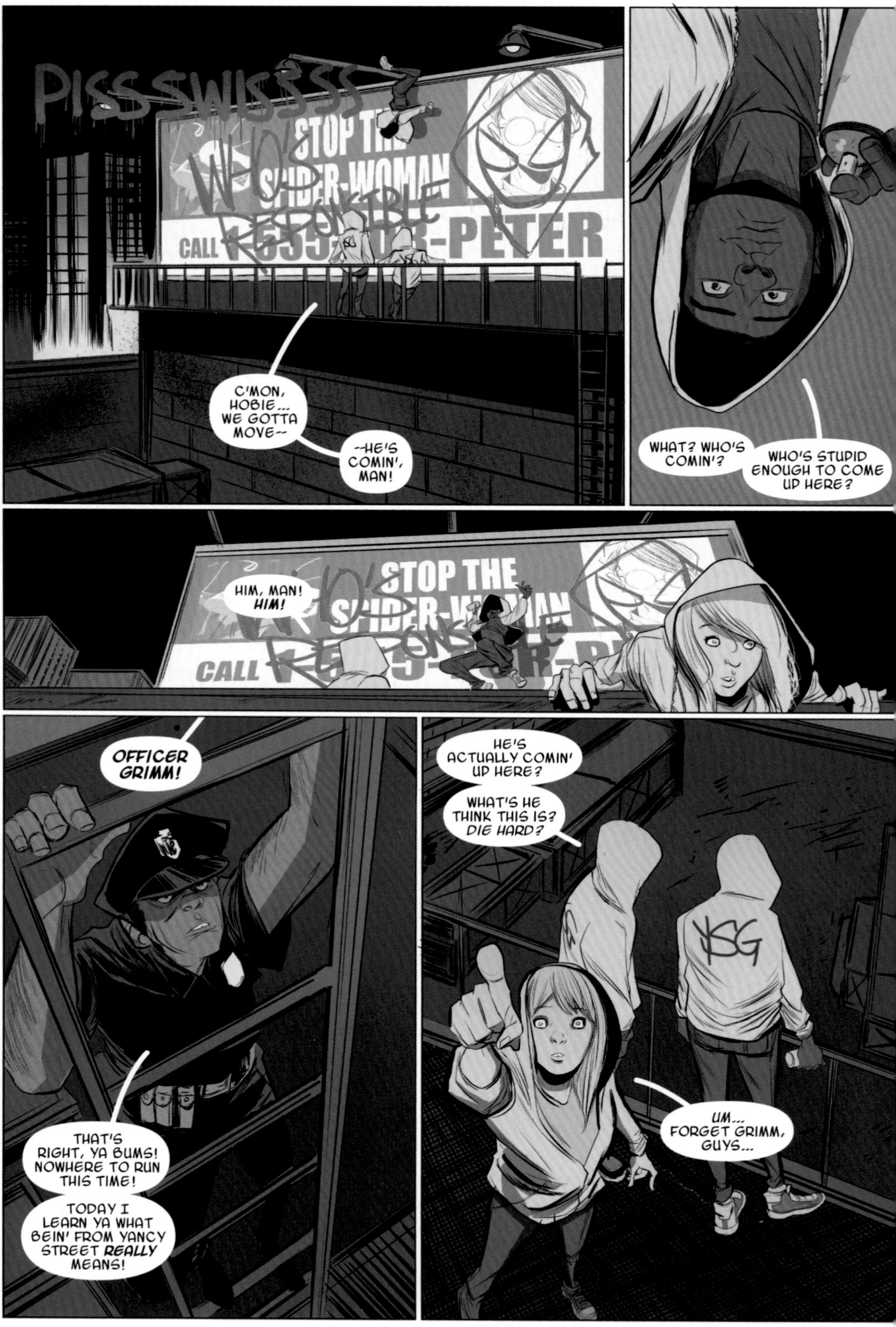
PISSSWISSSS
STOP THE SPIDER-WOMAN
CALL 1-555-FOR-PETER
WHO'S RESPONSIBLE
C'MON, HOBIE... WE GOTTA MOVE--
--HE'S COMIN', MAN!
WHAT? WHO'S COMIN'?
WHO'S STUPID ENOUGH TO COME UP HERE?
HIM, MAN! *HIM!*
STOP THE SPIDER-WOMAN
CALL
OFFICER GRIMM!
THAT'S RIGHT, YA BUMS! NOWHERE TO RUN THIS TIME!
TODAY I LEARN YA WHAT BEIN' FROM YANCY STREET *REALLY* MEANS!
HE'S ACTUALLY COMIN' UP HERE?
WHAT'S HE THINK THIS IS? *DIE HARD?*
YSG
UM... FORGET GRIMM, GUYS...

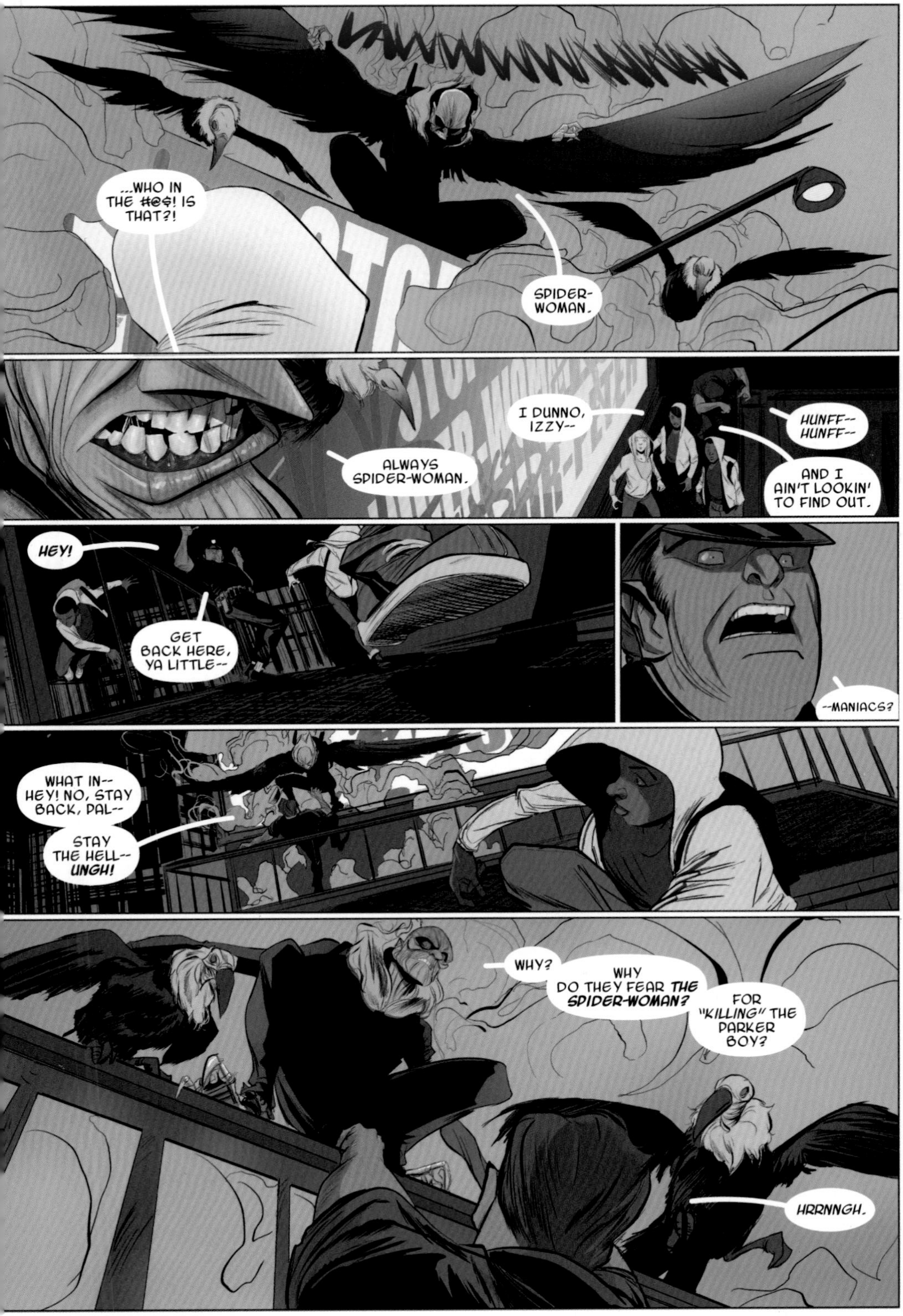

VAWWWWWWWRAW
...WHO IN THE #@$! IS THAT?!
SPIDER-WOMAN.
ALWAYS SPIDER-WOMAN.
I DUNNO, IZZY--
HUNFF-- HUNFF--
AND I AIN'T LOOKIN' TO FIND OUT.
HEY!
GET BACK HERE, YA LITTLE--
--MANIACS?
WHAT IN-- HEY! NO, STAY BACK, PAL--
STAY THE HELL-- UNGH!
WHY?
WHY DO THEY FEAR THE SPIDER-WOMAN?
FOR "KILLING" THE PARKER BOY?
HRRNNGH.

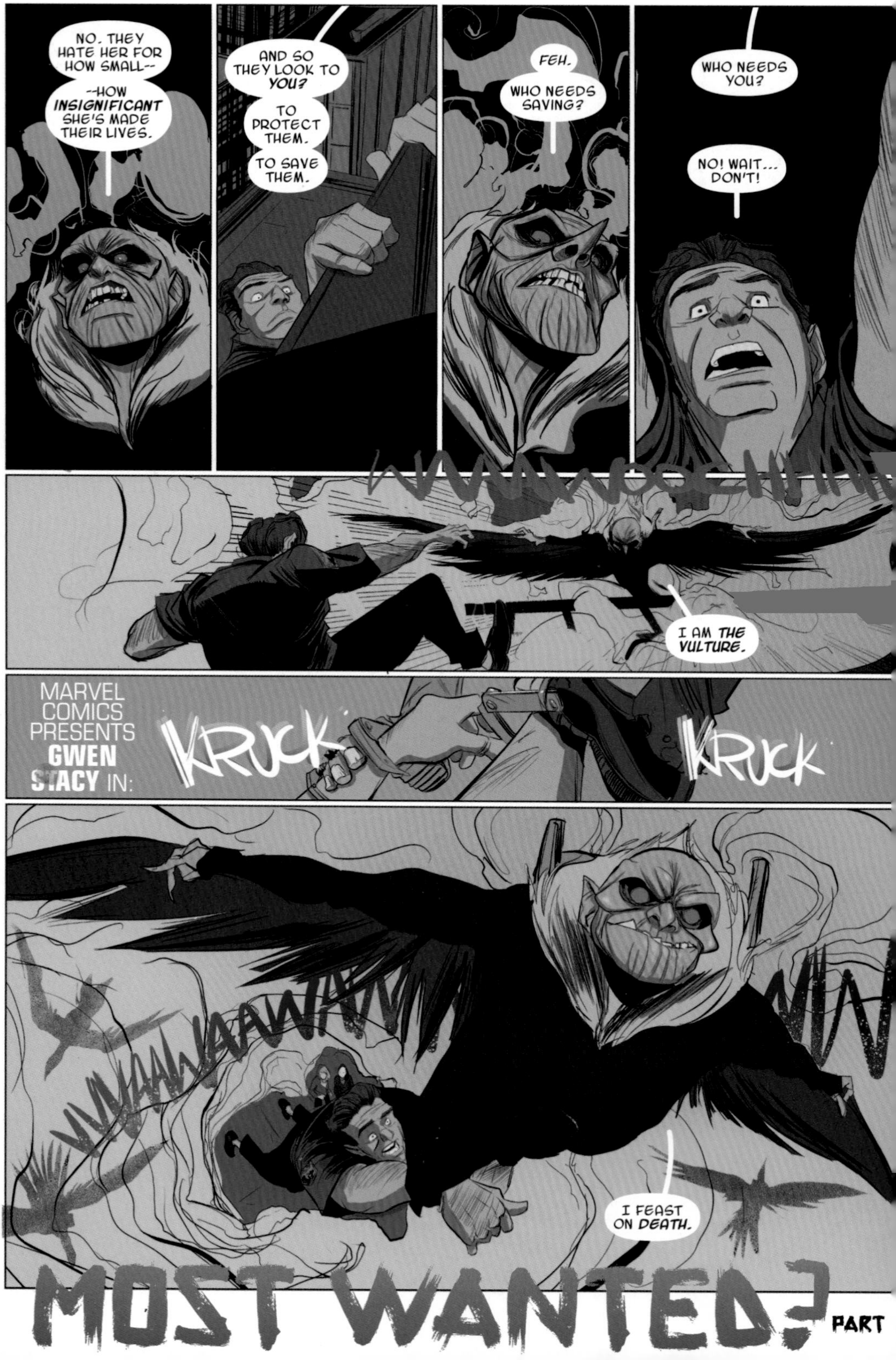

NO. THEY HATE HER FOR HOW SMALL--
--HOW *INSIGNIFICANT* SHE'S MADE THEIR LIVES.
AND SO THEY LOOK TO *YOU?*
TO PROTECT THEM.
TO SAVE THEM.
FEH.
WHO NEEDS SAVING?
WHO NEEDS YOU?
NO! WAIT... DON'T!
I AM *THE VULTURE.*
MARVEL COMICS PRESENTS GWEN STACY IN:
KRUCK
KRUCK
I FEAST ON *DEATH.*
MOST WANTED? PART

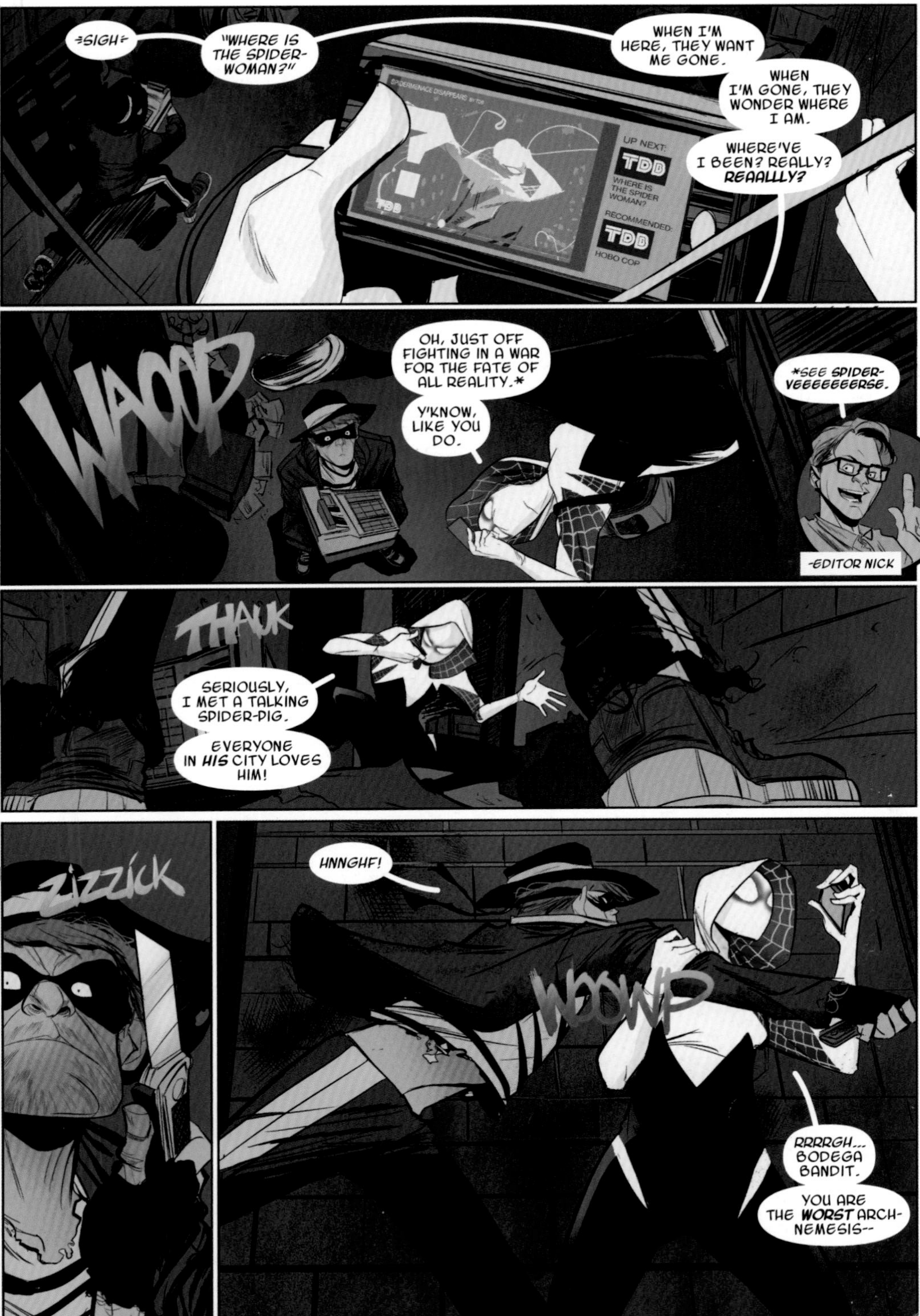

=SIGH=
"WHERE IS THE SPIDER-WOMAN?"
SPIDERMENACE DISAPPEARS
UP NEXT:
TDB
WHERE IS THE SPIDER WOMAN?
RECOMMENDED:
TDB
HOBO COP
WHEN I'M HERE, THEY WANT ME GONE.
WHEN I'M GONE, THEY WONDER WHERE I AM.
WHERE'VE I BEEN? REALLY? **REAALLLY?**
WAOOP
OH, JUST OFF FIGHTING IN A WAR FOR THE FATE OF ALL REALITY.*
Y'KNOW, LIKE YOU DO.
*SEE **SPIDER-VEEEEEEEERSE.**
-EDITOR NICK
THAUK
SERIOUSLY, I MET A TALKING SPIDER-PIG.
EVERYONE IN **HIS** CITY LOVES HIM!
ZIZZICK
HNNGHF!
WOOWP
RRRRGH... BODEGA BANDIT.
YOU ARE THE **WORST** ARCH-NEMESIS--

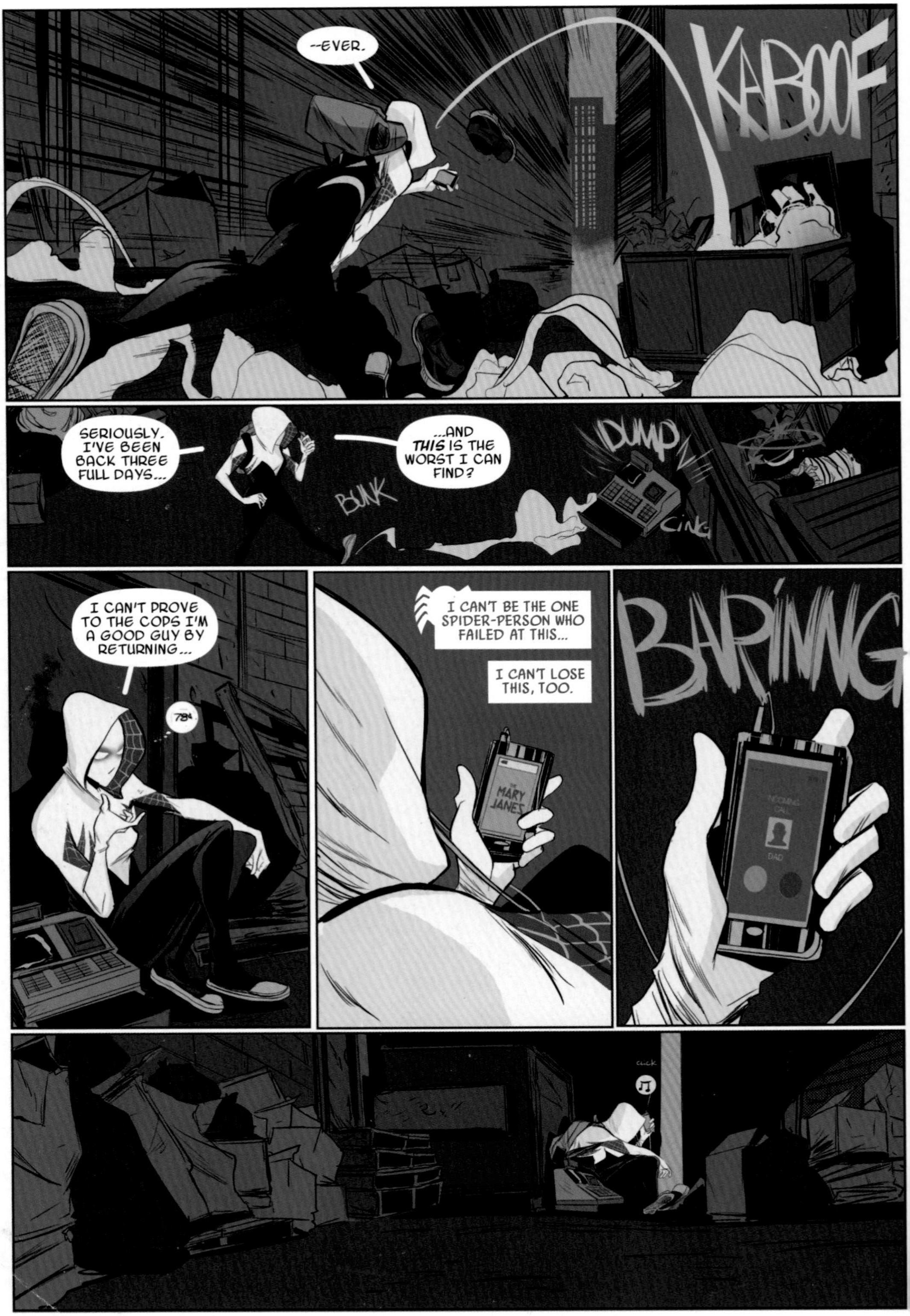
--EVER.
KABOOF
SERIOUSLY. I'VE BEEN BACK THREE FULL DAYS...
...AND THIS IS THE WORST I CAN FIND?
BUNK
DUMP
CING
I CAN'T PROVE TO THE COPS I'M A GOOD GUY BY RETURNING...
I CAN'T BE THE ONE SPIDER-PERSON WHO FAILED AT THIS...
I CAN'T LOSE THIS, TOO.
THE MARY JANES
BARINNG
DAD
click

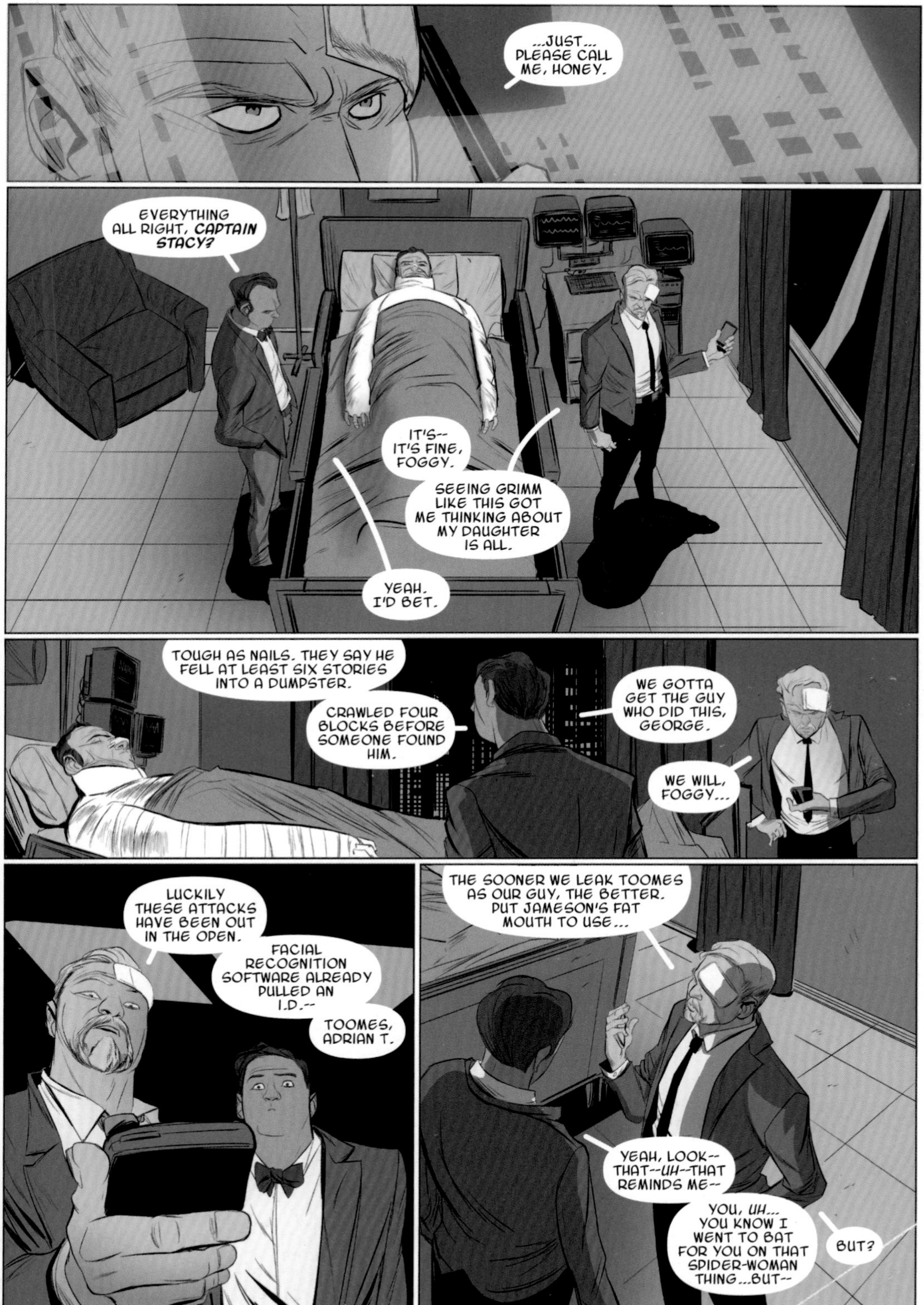
...JUST... PLEASE CALL ME, HONEY.
EVERYTHING ALL RIGHT, CAPTAIN STACY?
IT'S-- IT'S FINE, FOGGY.
SEEING GRIMM LIKE THIS GOT ME THINKING ABOUT MY DAUGHTER IS ALL.
YEAH. I'D BET.
TOUGH AS NAILS. THEY SAY HE FELL AT LEAST SIX STORIES INTO A DUMPSTER.
CRAWLED FOUR BLOCKS BEFORE SOMEONE FOUND HIM.
WE GOTTA GET THE GUY WHO DID THIS, GEORGE.
WE WILL, FOGGY...
LUCKILY THESE ATTACKS HAVE BEEN OUT IN THE OPEN.
FACIAL RECOGNITION SOFTWARE ALREADY PULLED AN I.D.--
TOOMES, ADRIAN T.
THE SOONER WE LEAK TOOMES AS OUR GUY, THE BETTER. PUT JAMESON'S FAT MOUTH TO USE...
YEAH, LOOK-- THAT--UH--THAT REMINDS ME--
YOU, UH... YOU KNOW I WENT TO BAT FOR YOU ON THAT SPIDER-WOMAN THING...BUT--
BUT?

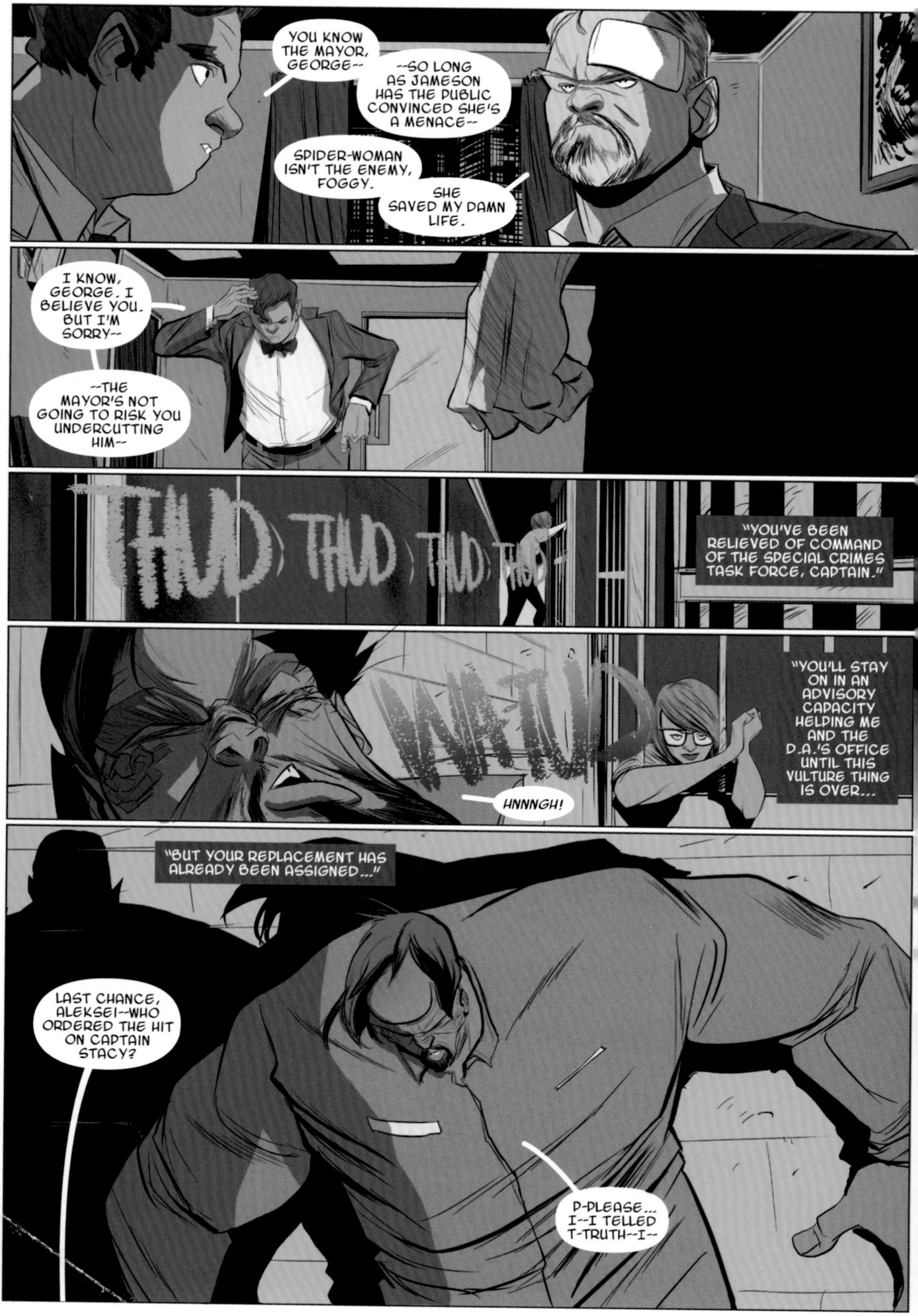
YOU KNOW THE MAYOR, GEORGE--
--SO LONG AS JAMESON HAS THE PUBLIC CONVINCED SHE'S A MENACE--
SPIDER-WOMAN ISN'T THE ENEMY, FOGGY.
SHE SAVED MY DAMN LIFE.
I KNOW, GEORGE. I BELIEVE YOU. BUT I'M SORRY--
--THE MAYOR'S NOT GOING TO RISK YOU UNDERCUTTING HIM--
THUD THUD THUD THUD
"YOU'VE BEEN RELIEVED OF COMMAND OF THE SPECIAL CRIMES TASK FORCE, CAPTAIN."
WHUD
"YOU'LL STAY ON IN AN ADVISORY CAPACITY HELPING ME AND THE D.A.'S OFFICE UNTIL THIS VULTURE THING IS OVER...
HNNNGH!
"BUT YOUR REPLACEMENT HAS ALREADY BEEN ASSIGNED..."
LAST CHANCE, ALEKSEI--WHO ORDERED THE HIT ON CAPTAIN STACY?
P-PLEASE... I--I TELLED T-TRUTH--I--

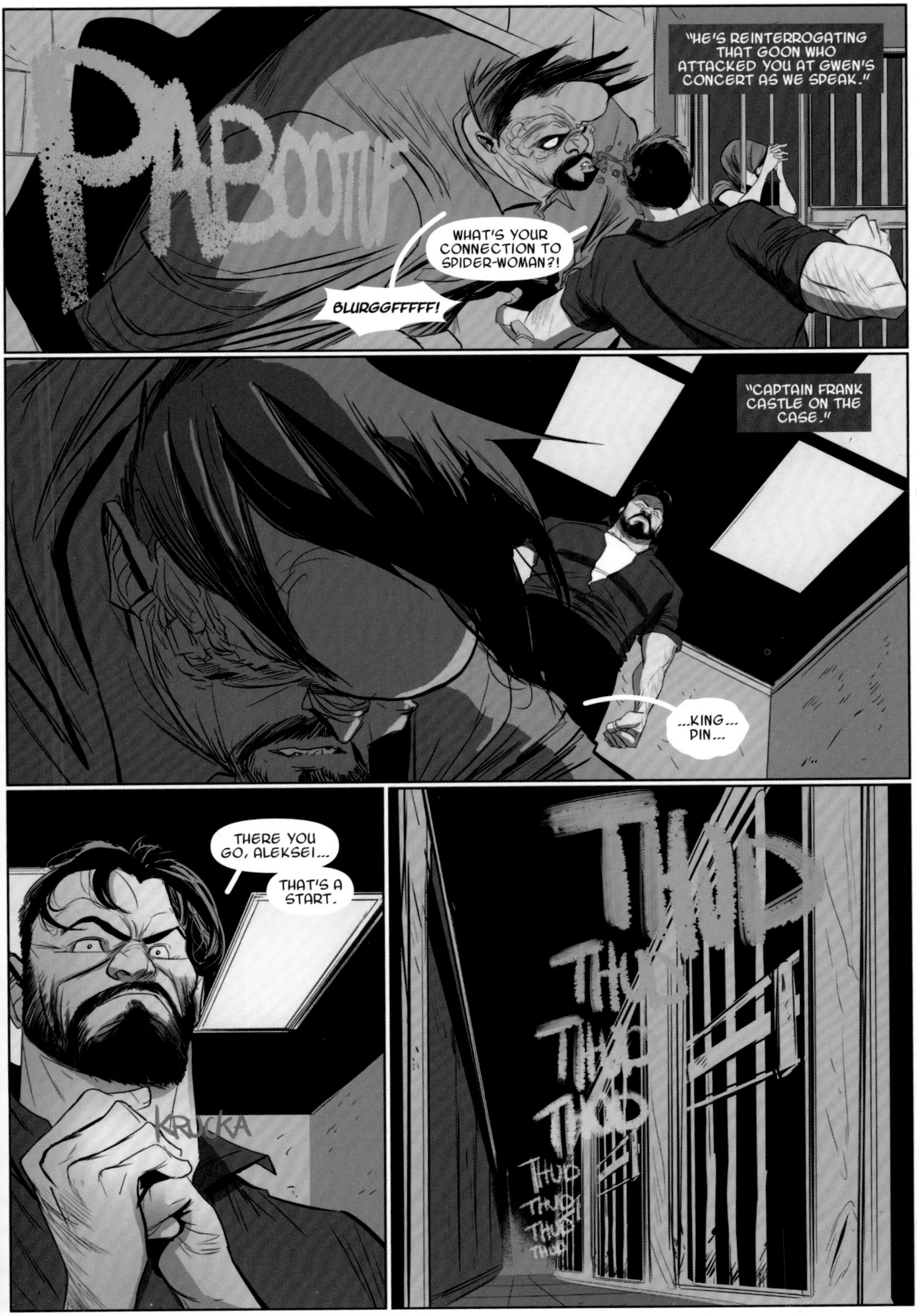
PABOOTUF
"HE'S REINTERROGATING THAT GOON WHO ATTACKED YOU AT GWEN'S CONCERT AS WE SPEAK."
WHAT'S YOUR CONNECTION TO SPIDER-WOMAN?!
BLURGGFFFFF!
"CAPTAIN FRANK CASTLE ON THE CASE."
...KING... PIN...
THERE YOU GO, ALEKSEI...
THAT'S A START.
KRUCKA
THUD
THUD
THUD
THUD
THUD
THUD
THUD
THUD

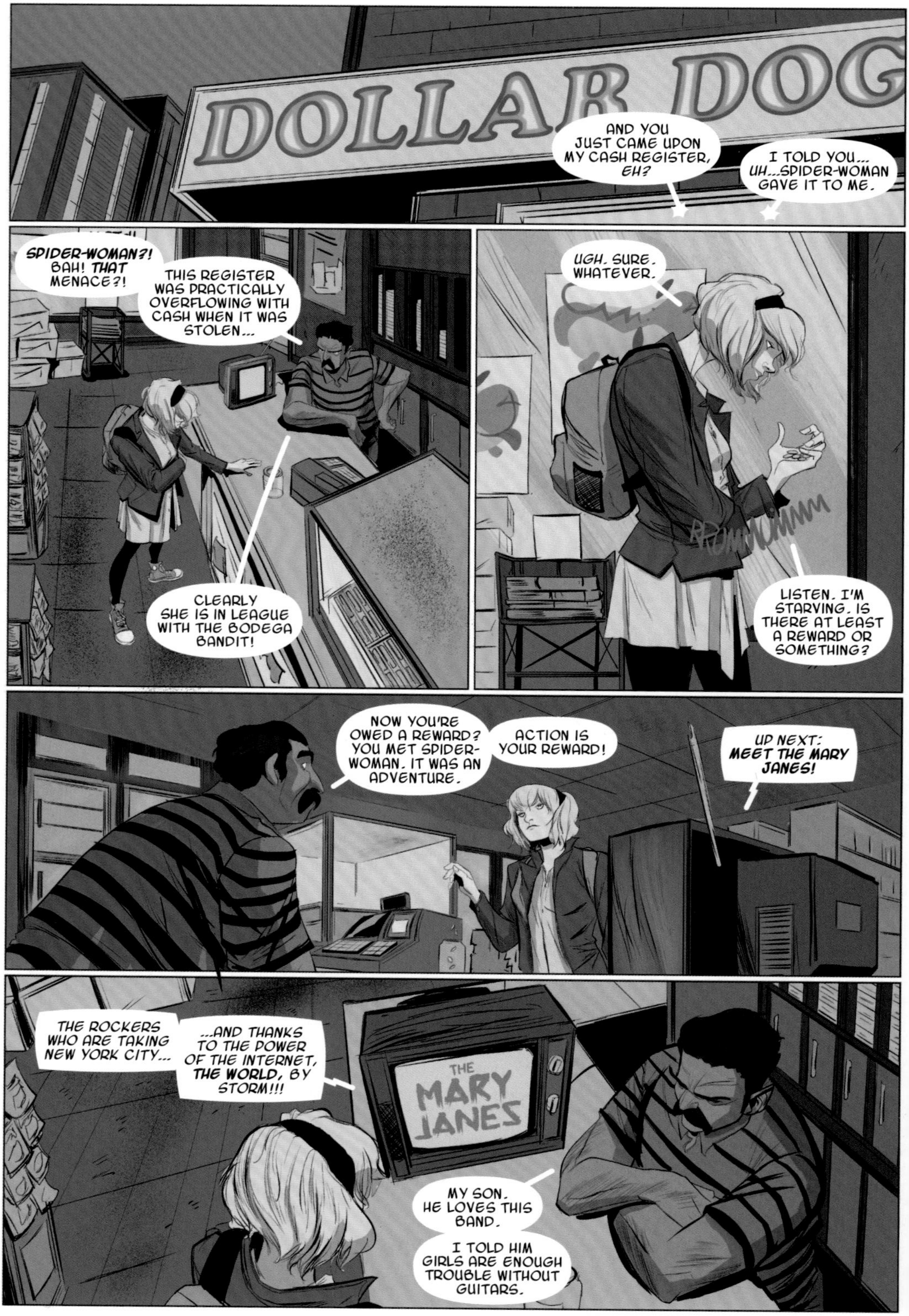
DOLLAR DOG
AND YOU JUST CAME UPON MY CASH REGISTER, EH?
I TOLD YOU... UH...SPIDER-WOMAN GAVE IT TO ME.
SPIDER-WOMAN?! BAH! THAT MENACE?!
THIS REGISTER WAS PRACTICALLY OVERFLOWING WITH CASH WHEN IT WAS STOLEN...
CLEARLY SHE IS IN LEAGUE WITH THE BODEGA BANDIT!
UGH. SURE. WHATEVER.
LISTEN. I'M STARVING. IS THERE AT LEAST A REWARD OR SOMETHING?
NOW YOU'RE OWED A REWARD? YOU MET SPIDER-WOMAN. IT WAS AN ADVENTURE.
ACTION IS YOUR REWARD!
UP NEXT: MEET THE MARY JANES!
THE ROCKERS WHO ARE TAKING NEW YORK CITY...
...AND THANKS TO THE POWER OF THE INTERNET, THE WORLD, BY STORM!!!
THE MARY JANES
MY SON. HE LOVES THIS BAND.
I TOLD HIM GIRLS ARE ENOUGH TROUBLE WITHOUT GUITARS.

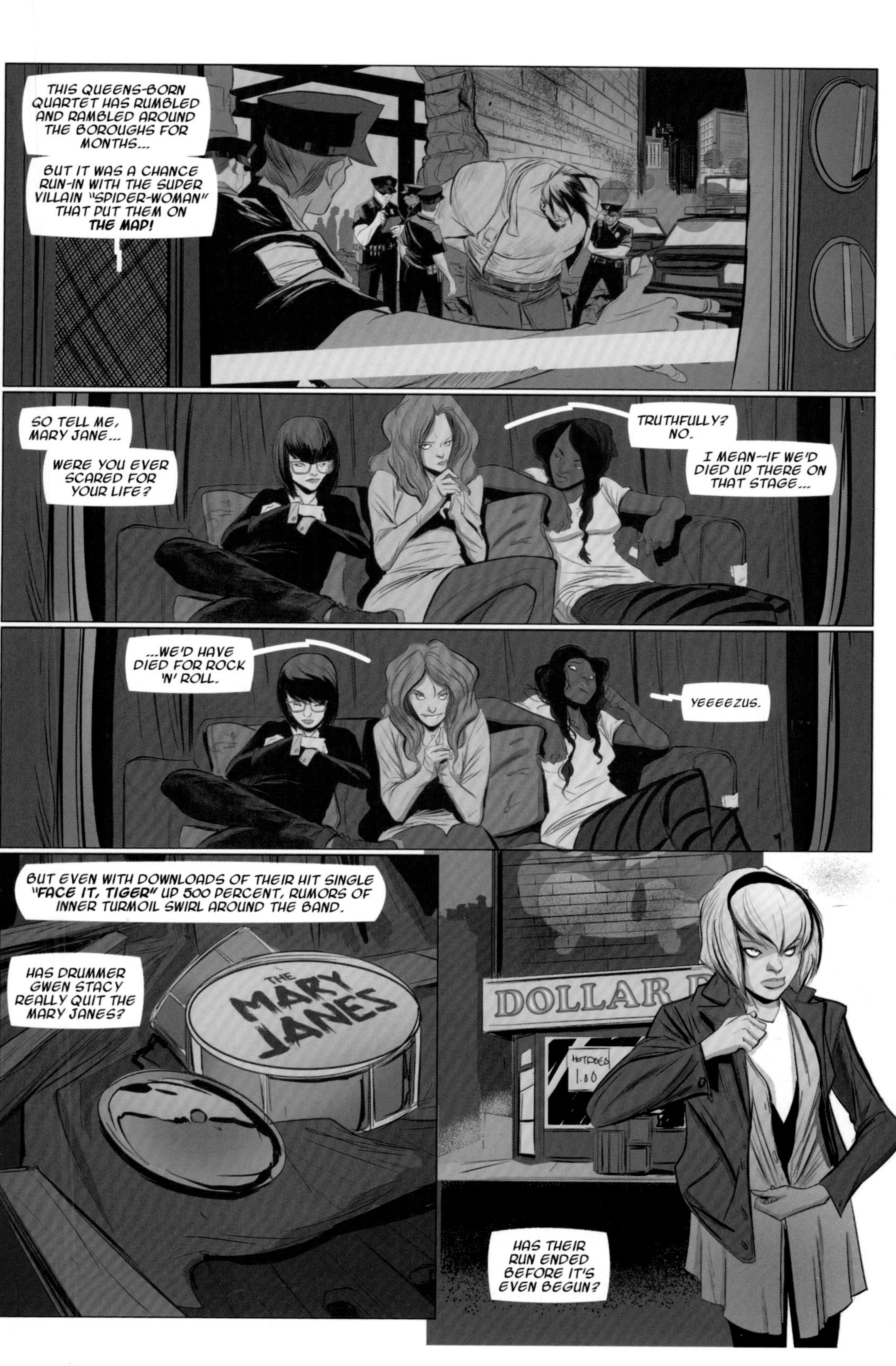
THIS QUEENS-BORN QUARTET HAS RUMBLED AND RAMBLED AROUND THE BOROUGHS FOR MONTHS...
BUT IT WAS A CHANCE RUN-IN WITH THE SUPER VILLAIN "SPIDER-WOMAN" THAT PUT THEM ON THE MAP!
SO TELL ME, MARY JANE...
WERE YOU EVER SCARED FOR YOUR LIFE?
TRUTHFULLY? NO.
I MEAN--IF WE'D DIED UP THERE ON THAT STAGE...
...WE'D HAVE DIED FOR ROCK 'N' ROLL.
YEEEEZUS.
BUT EVEN WITH DOWNLOADS OF THEIR HIT SINGLE "FACE IT, TIGER" UP 500 PERCENT, RUMORS OF INNER TURMOIL SWIRL AROUND THE BAND.
HAS DRUMMER GWEN STACY REALLY QUIT THE MARY JANES?
THE MARY JANES
DOLLAR
HAS THEIR RUN ENDED BEFORE IT'S EVEN BEGUN?

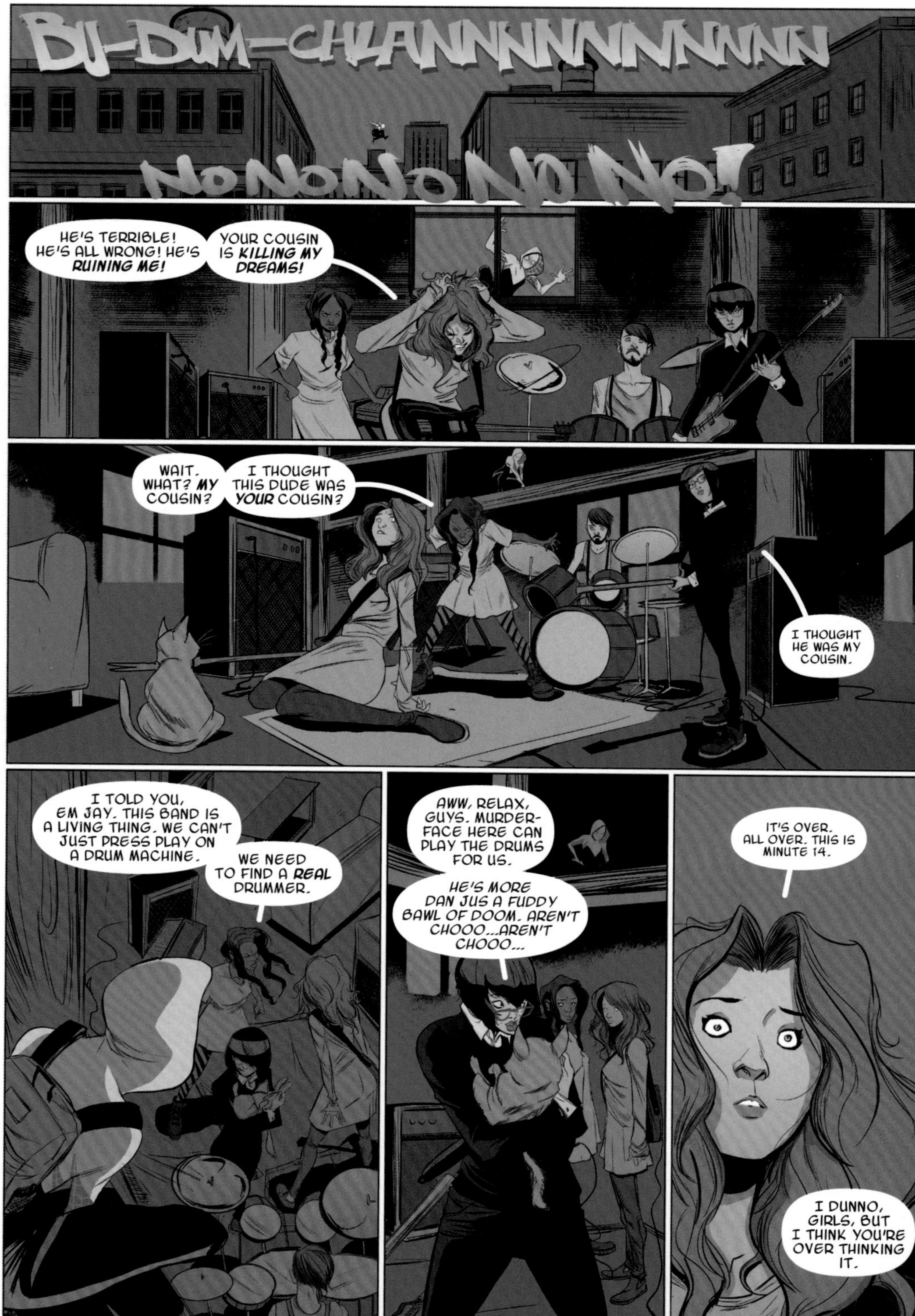
BU-DUM-CHLANNNNNNNNNN
NO NO NO NO NO NO!
HE'S TERRIBLE! HE'S ALL WRONG! HE'S RUINING ME!
YOUR COUSIN IS KILLING MY DREAMS!
WAIT. WHAT? MY COUSIN?
I THOUGHT THIS DUDE WAS YOUR COUSIN?
I THOUGHT HE WAS MY COUSIN.
I TOLD YOU, EM JAY. THIS BAND IS A LIVING THING. WE CAN'T JUST PRESS PLAY ON A DRUM MACHINE.
WE NEED TO FIND A REAL DRUMMER.
AWW, RELAX, GUYS. MURDER-FACE HERE CAN PLAY THE DRUMS FOR US.
HE'S MORE DAN JUS A FUDDY BAWL OF DOOM. AREN'T CHOOO...AREN'T CHOOO...
IT'S OVER. ALL OVER. THIS IS MINUTE 14.
I DUNNO, GIRLS, BUT I THINK YOU'RE OVER THINKING IT.

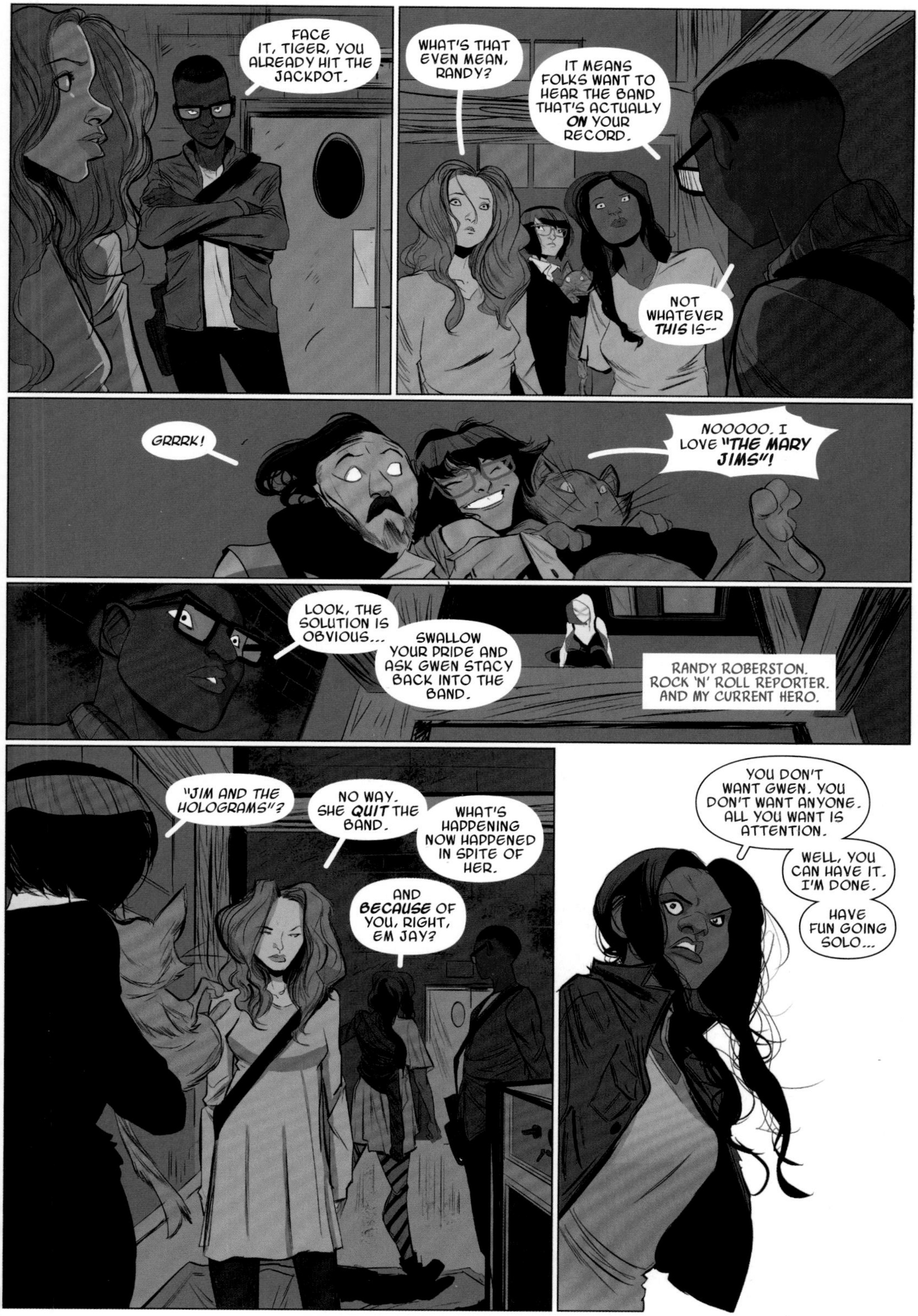

FACE IT, TIGER, YOU ALREADY HIT THE JACKPOT.
WHAT'S THAT EVEN MEAN, RANDY?
IT MEANS FOLKS WANT TO HEAR THE BAND THAT'S ACTUALLY ON YOUR RECORD.
NOT WHATEVER THIS IS--
GRRRK!
NOOOOO. I LOVE "THE MARY JIMS"!
LOOK, THE SOLUTION IS OBVIOUS...
SWALLOW YOUR PRIDE AND ASK GWEN STACY BACK INTO THE BAND.
RANDY ROBERSTON. ROCK 'N' ROLL REPORTER. AND MY CURRENT HERO.
"JIM AND THE HOLOGRAMS"?
NO WAY. SHE QUIT THE BAND.
WHAT'S HAPPENING NOW HAPPENED IN SPITE OF HER.
AND BECAUSE OF YOU, RIGHT, EM JAY?
YOU DON'T WANT GWEN. YOU DON'T WANT ANYONE. ALL YOU WANT IS ATTENTION.
WELL, YOU CAN HAVE IT. I'M DONE.
HAVE FUN GOING SOLO...

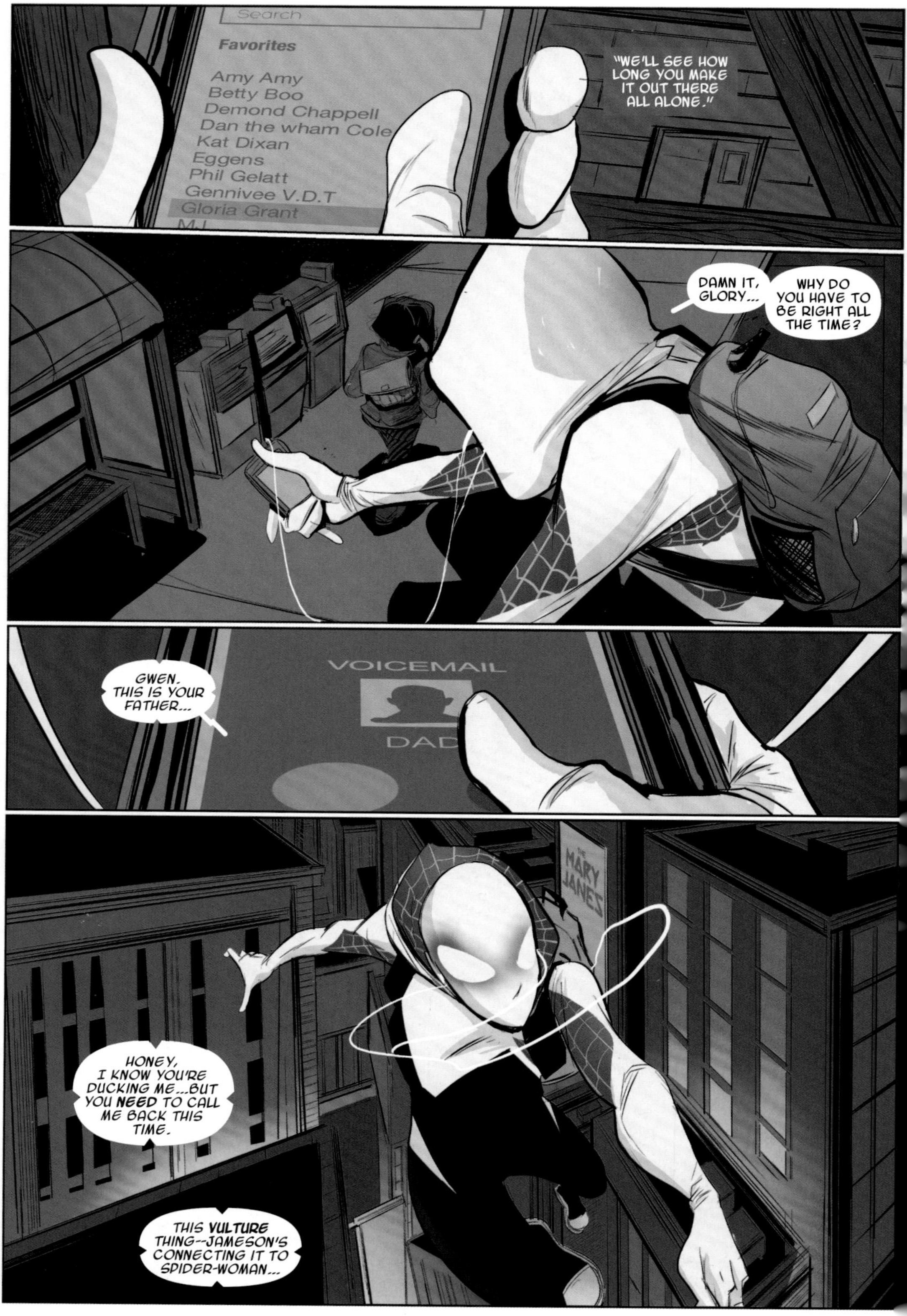
Search
Favorites
Amy Amy
Betty Boo
Demond Chappell
Dan the wham Cole
Kat Dixan
Eggens
Phil Gelatt
Gennivee V.D.T
Gloria Grant
"WE'LL SEE HOW LONG YOU MAKE IT OUT THERE ALL ALONE."
DAMN IT, GLORY...
WHY DO YOU HAVE TO BE RIGHT ALL THE TIME?
VOICEMAIL
DAD
GWEN. THIS IS YOUR FATHER...
THE MARY JANES
HONEY, I KNOW YOU'RE DUCKING ME...BUT YOU NEED TO CALL ME BACK THIS TIME.
THIS VULTURE THING--JAMESON'S CONNECTING IT TO SPIDER-WOMAN...

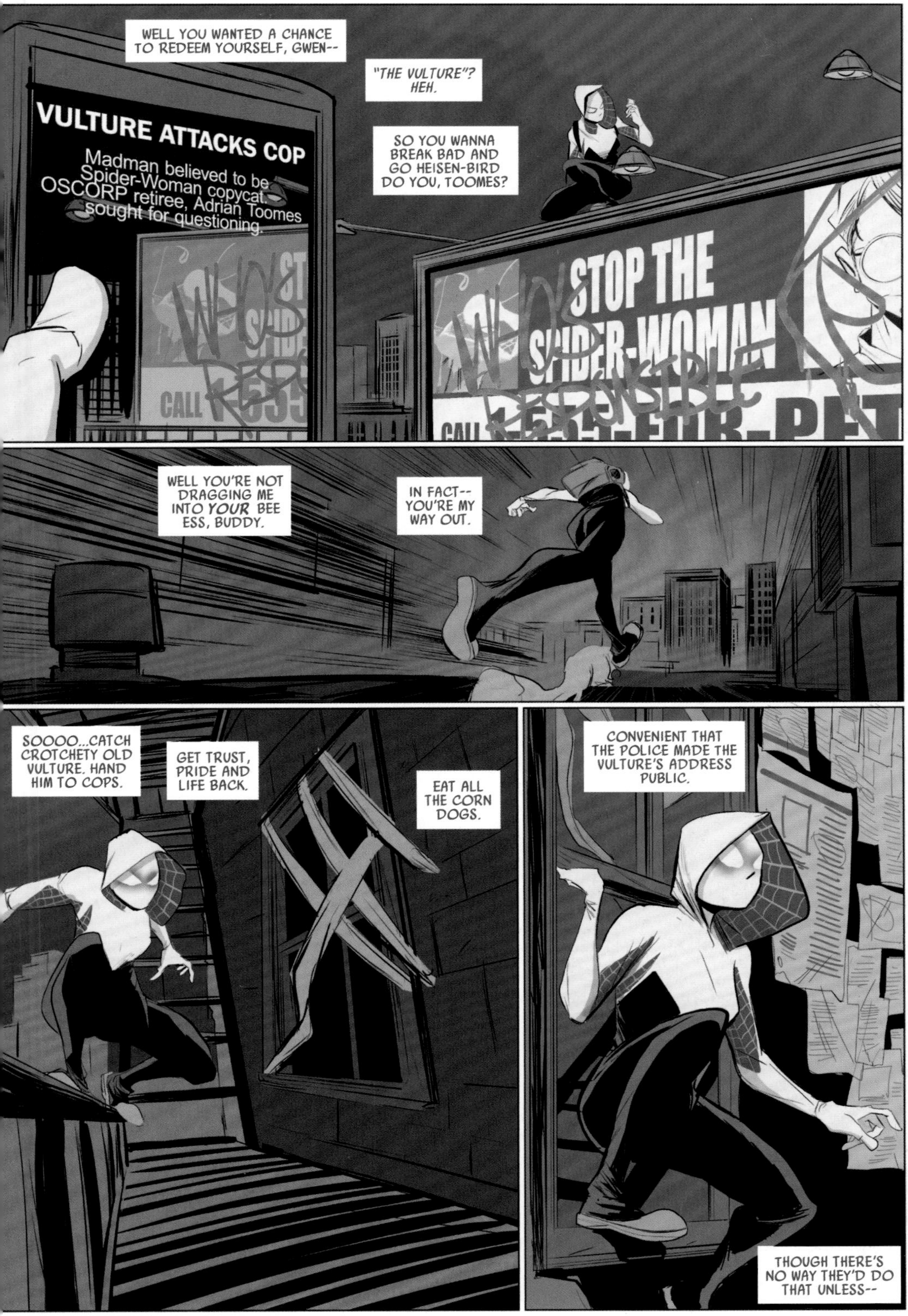
WELL YOU WANTED A CHANCE TO REDEEM YOURSELF, GWEN--
VULTURE ATTACKS COP
Madman believed to be Spider-Woman copycat. OSCORP retiree, Adrian Toomes sought for questioning.
"THE VULTURE"? HEH.
SO YOU WANNA BREAK BAD AND GO HEISEN-BIRD DO YOU, TOOMES?
STOP THE SPIDER-WOMAN
WHO'S RESPONSIBLE
CALL
WELL YOU'RE NOT DRAGGING ME INTO *YOUR* BEE ESS, BUDDY.
IN FACT-- YOU'RE MY WAY OUT.
SOOOO...CATCH CROTCHETY OLD VULTURE. HAND HIM TO COPS.
GET TRUST, PRIDE AND LIFE BACK.
EAT ALL THE CORN DOGS.
CONVENIENT THAT THE POLICE MADE THE VULTURE'S ADDRESS PUBLIC.
THOUGH THERE'S NO WAY THEY'D DO THAT UNLESS--

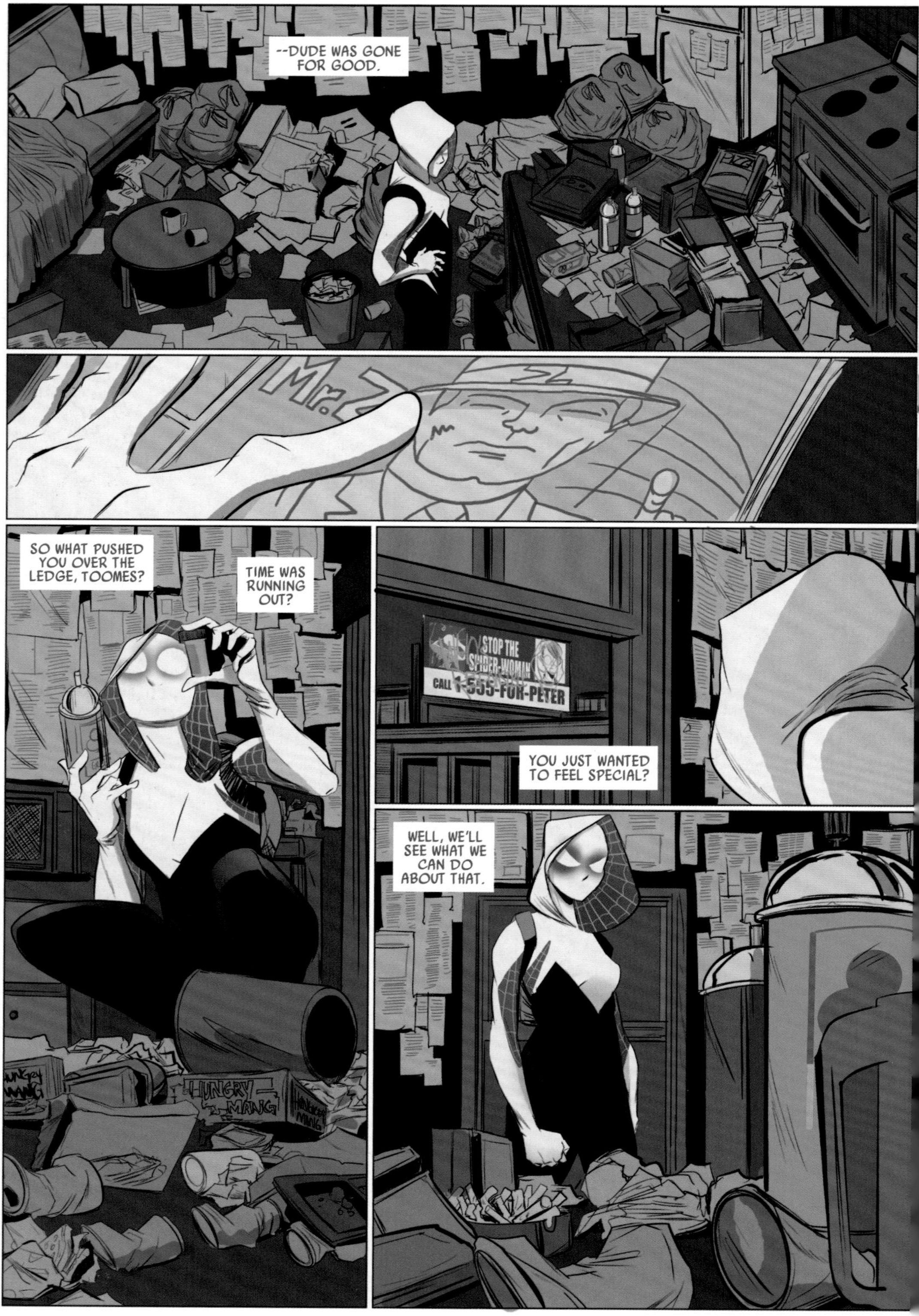
--DUDE WAS GONE FOR GOOD.
Mr. Z
SO WHAT PUSHED YOU OVER THE LEDGE, TOOMES?
TIME WAS RUNNING OUT?
STOP THE SPIDER-WOMAN
CALL 1-555-FOR-PETER
YOU JUST WANTED TO FEEL SPECIAL?
WELL, WE'LL SEE WHAT WE CAN DO ABOUT THAT.
HUNGRY MANIG

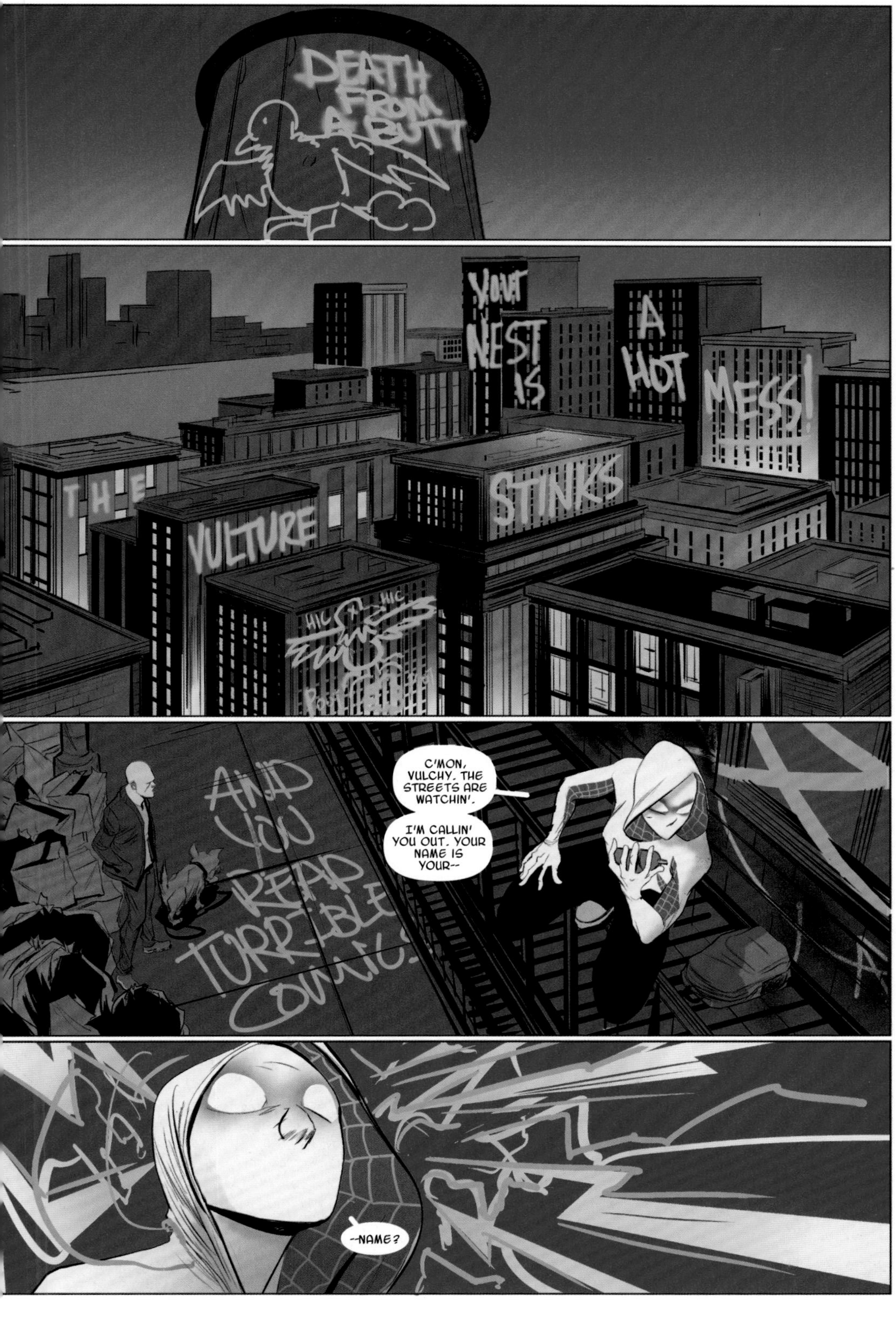
DEATH FROM A BUTT
YOUR NEST IS A HOT MESS!
THE VULTURE STINKS
AND YOU READ TURR-IBLE COMICS!
C'MON, VULCHY. THE STREETS ARE WATCHIN'.
I'M CALLIN' YOU OUT. YOUR NAME IS YOUR--
--NAME?

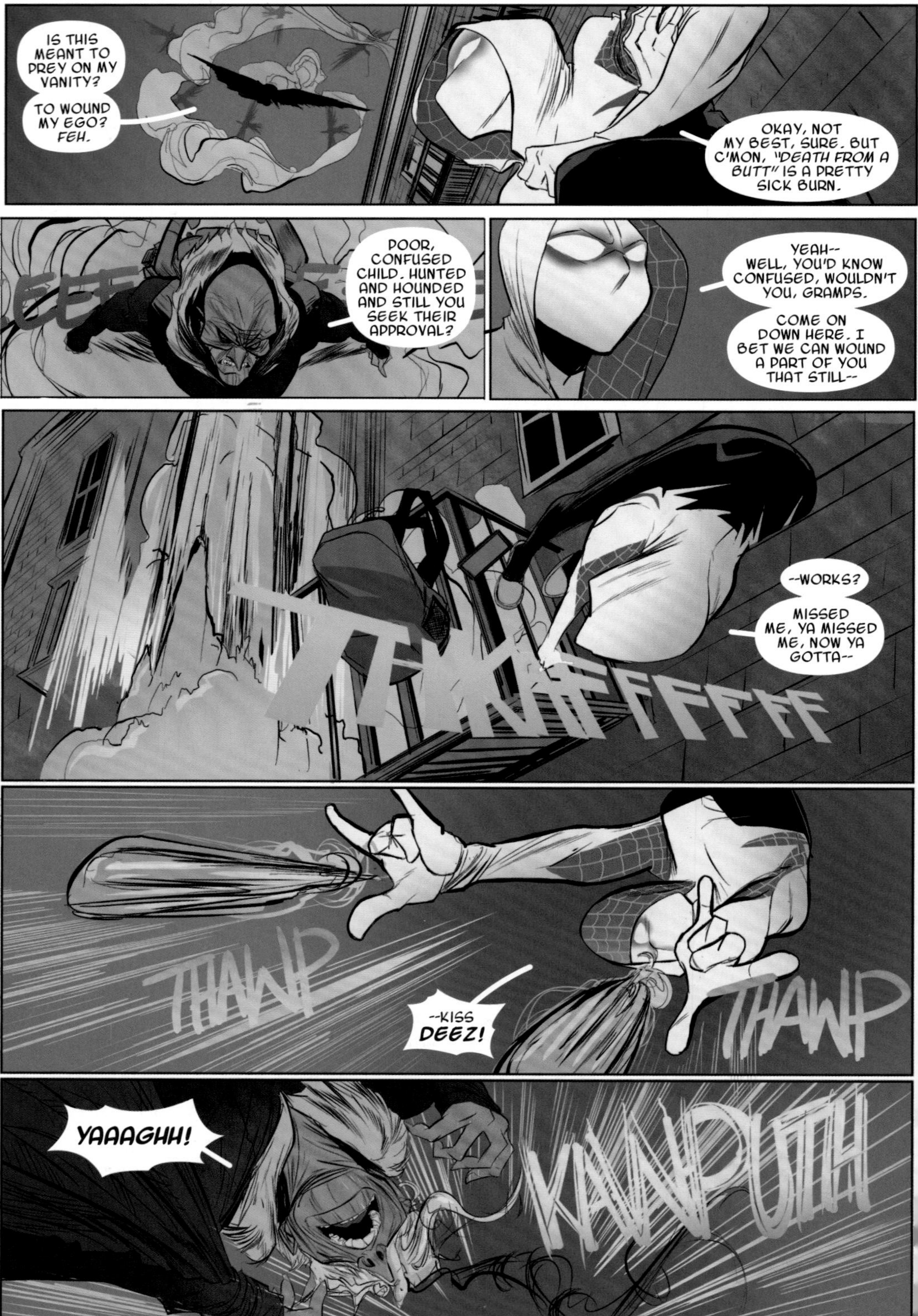

IS THIS MEANT TO PREY ON MY VANITY?
TO WOUND MY EGO? FEH.
OKAY, NOT MY BEST, SURE. BUT C'MON, "DEATH FROM A BUTT" IS A PRETTY SICK BURN.
POOR, CONFUSED CHILD. HUNTED AND HOUNDED AND STILL YOU SEEK THEIR APPROVAL?
YEAH-- WELL, YOU'D KNOW CONFUSED, WOULDN'T YOU, GRAMPS.
COME ON DOWN HERE. I BET WE CAN WOUND A PART OF YOU THAT STILL--
--WORKS?
MISSED ME, YA MISSED ME, NOW YA GOTTA--
THWIFFFFFF
THAWP
--KISS DEEZ!
THAWP
YAAAGHH!
KWAPUTH

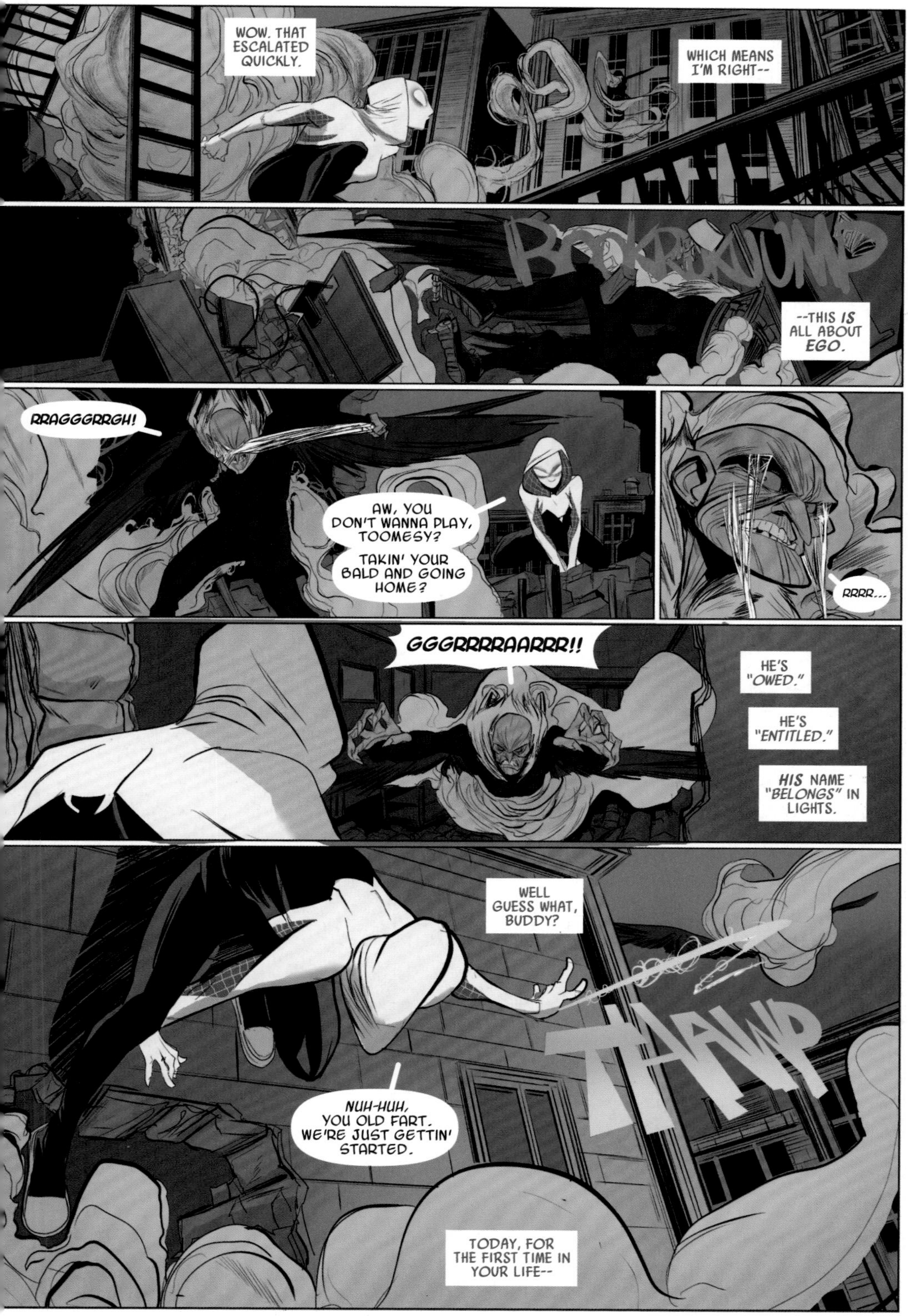
WOW. THAT ESCALATED QUICKLY.
WHICH MEANS I'M RIGHT--
BOOKRUUUMP
--THIS IS ALL ABOUT EGO.
RRAGGGRRGH!
AW, YOU DON'T WANNA PLAY, TOOMESY?
TAKIN' YOUR BALD AND GOING HOME?
RRRR...
GGGRRRRAARRR!!
HE'S "OWED."
HE'S "ENTITLED."
HIS NAME "BELONGS" IN LIGHTS.
WELL GUESS WHAT, BUDDY?
THAWP
NUH-HUH, YOU OLD FART. WE'RE JUST GETTIN' STARTED.
TODAY, FOR THE FIRST TIME IN YOUR LIFE--

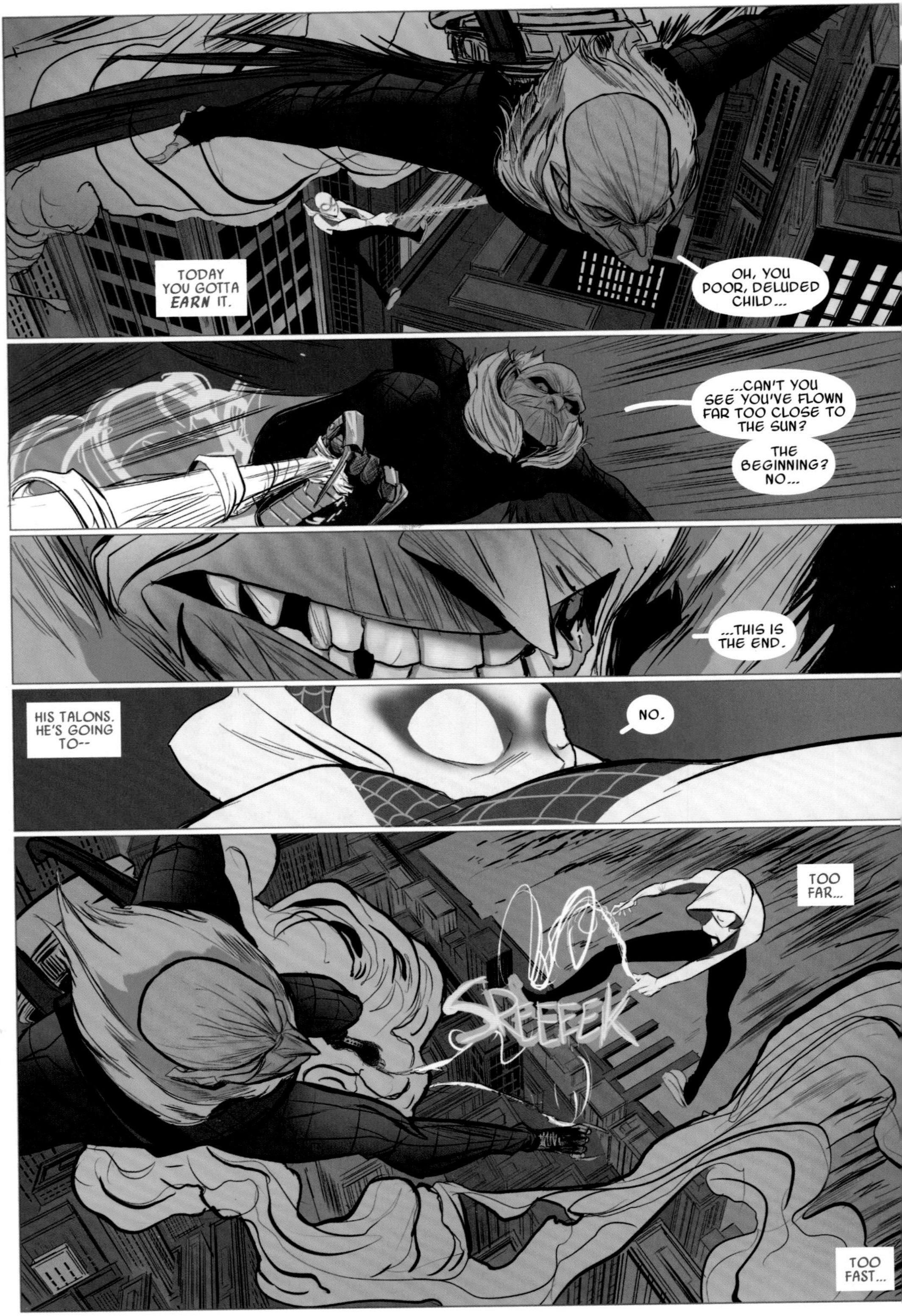
TODAY YOU GOTTA EARN IT.
OH, YOU POOR, DELUDED CHILD...
...CAN'T YOU SEE YOU'VE FLOWN FAR TOO CLOSE TO THE SUN?
THE BEGINNING? NO...
...THIS IS THE END.
HIS TALONS. HE'S GOING TO--
NO.
TOO FAR...
SREEEEK
TOO FAST...

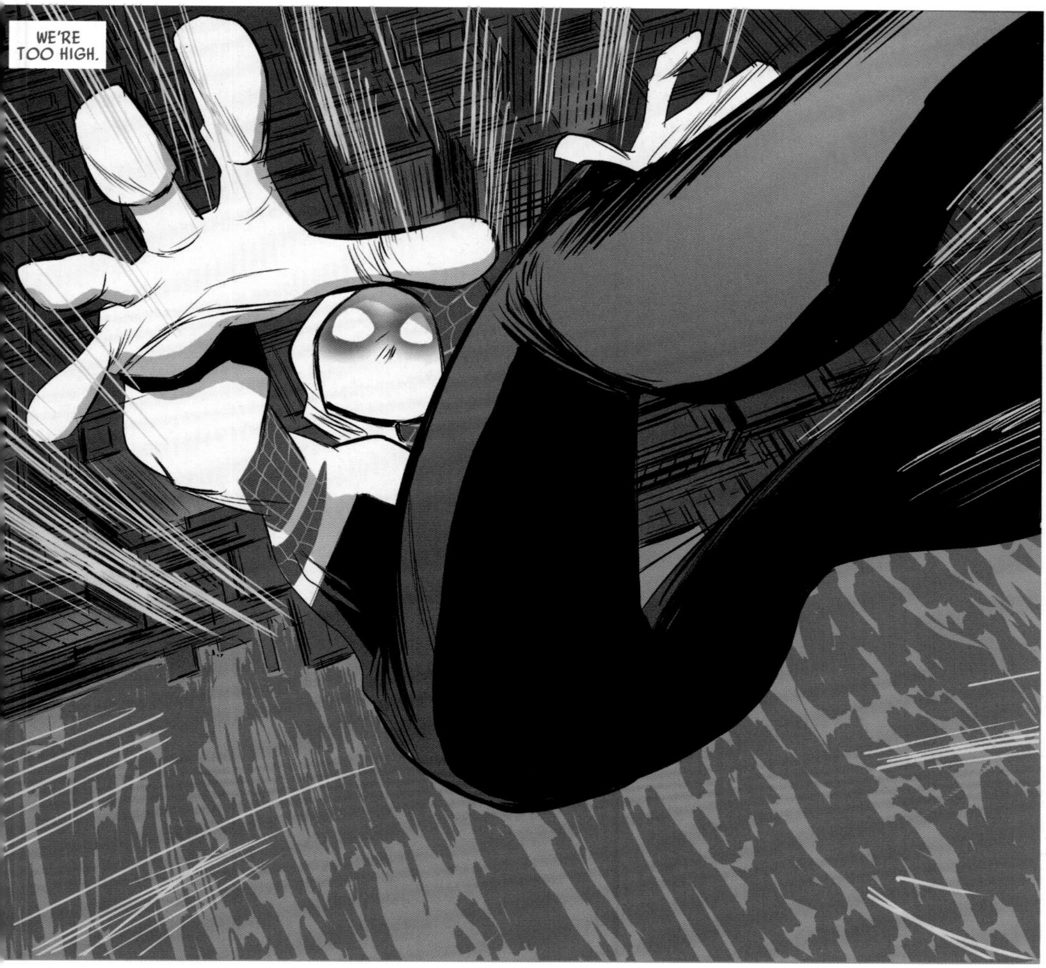
WE'RE TOO HIGH.

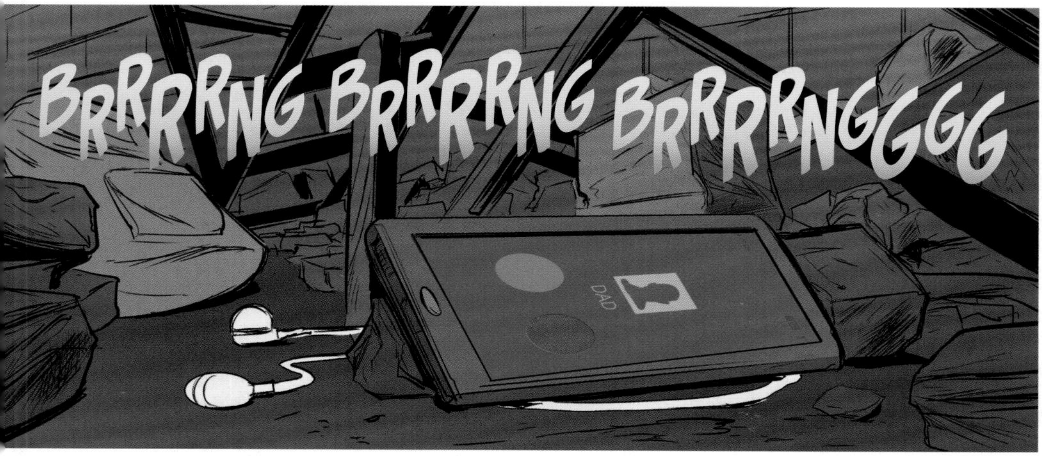
BRRRRNG BRRRRRNG BRRRRRNGGGG
DAD

2A

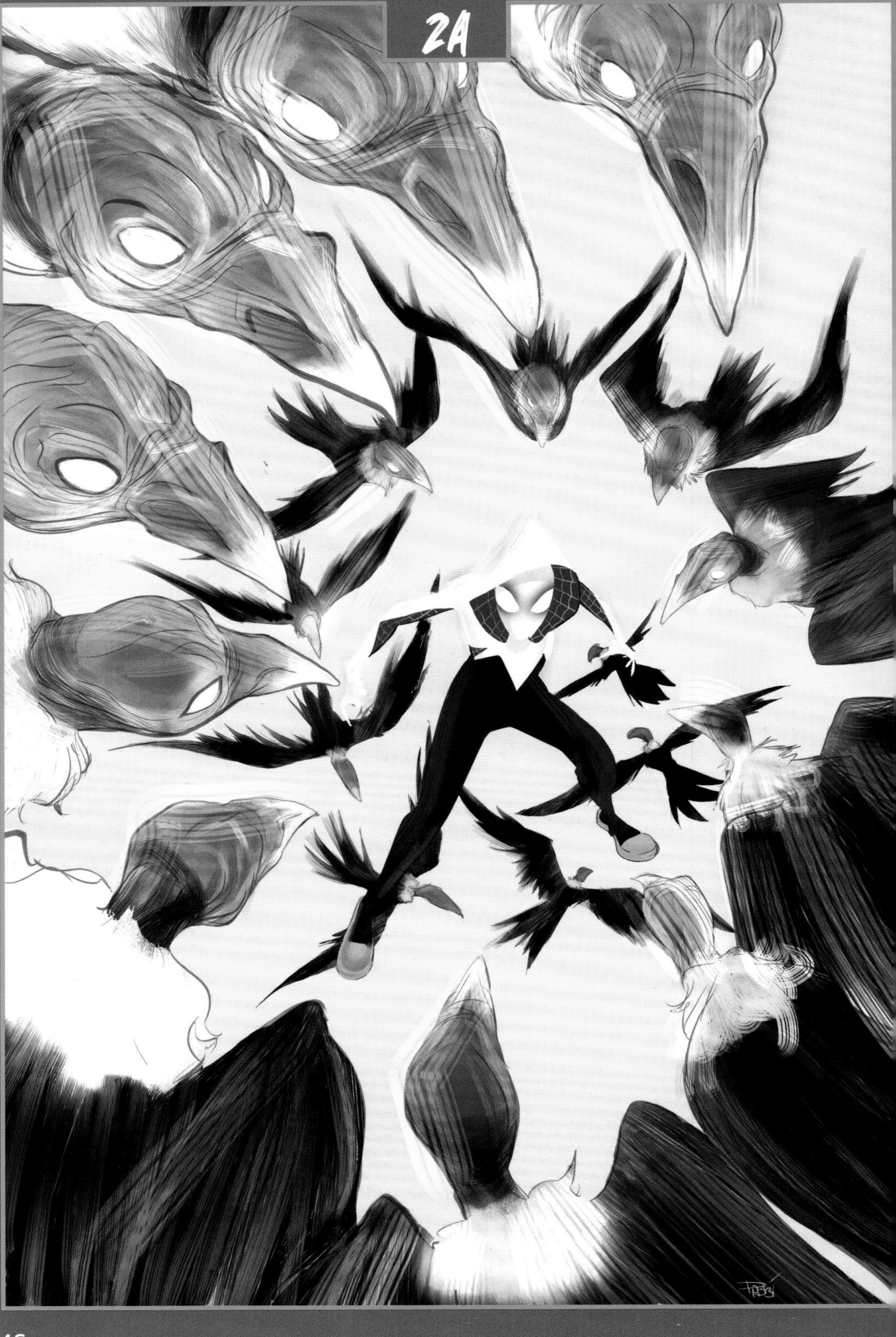

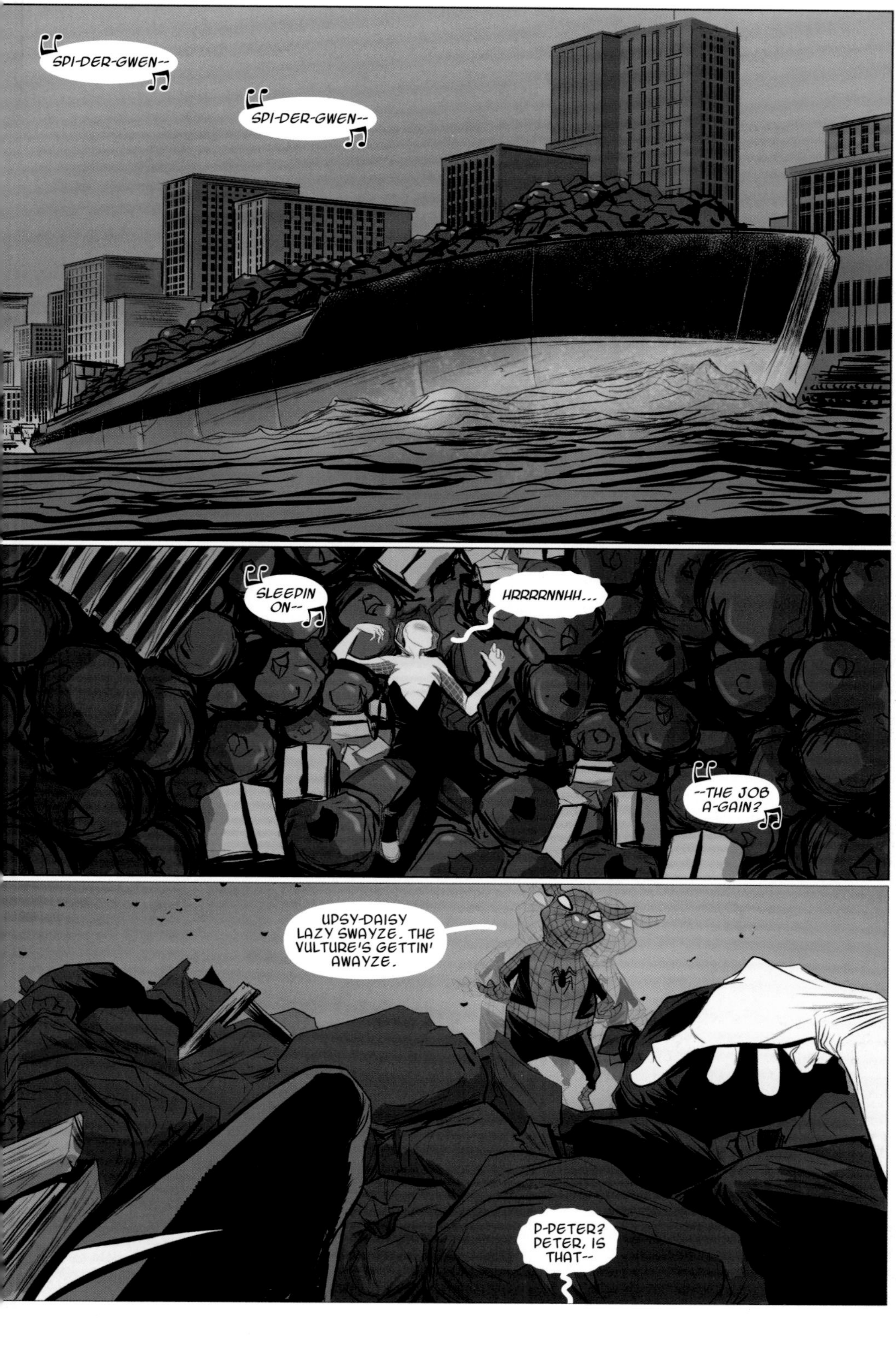
SPI-DER-GWEN--
SPI-DER-GWEN--
SLEEPIN ON--
HRRRRNNHH...
--THE JOB A-GAIN?
UPSY-DAISY LAZY SWAYZE. THE VULTURE'S GETTIN' AWAYZE.
P-PETER? PETER, IS THAT--

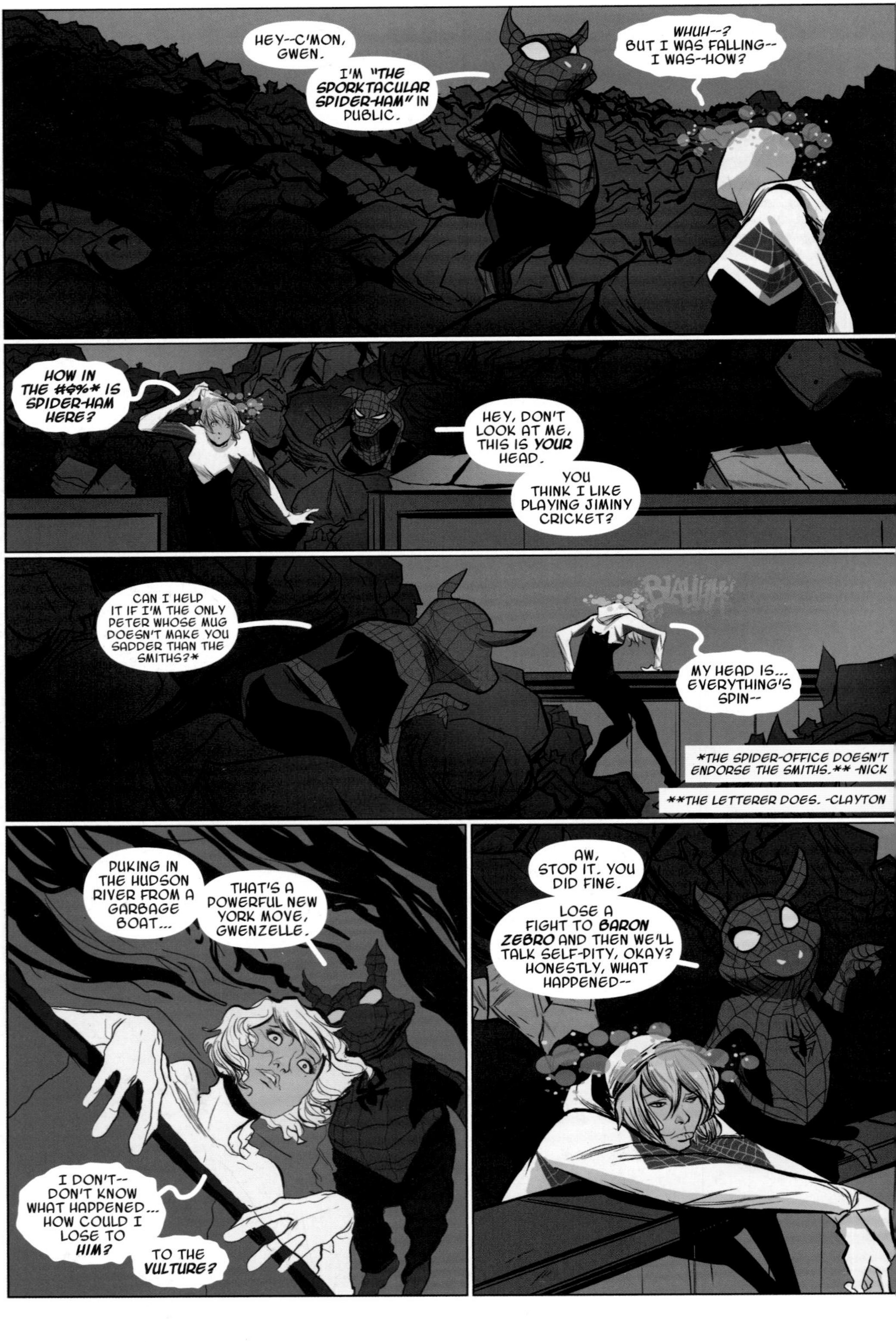
HEY--C'MON, GWEN.
I'M "THE SPORKTACULAR SPIDER-HAM" IN PUBLIC.
WHUH--? BUT I WAS FALLING-- I WAS--HOW?
HOW IN THE #$%* IS SPIDER-HAM HERE?
HEY, DON'T LOOK AT ME, THIS IS YOUR HEAD.
YOU THINK I LIKE PLAYING JIMINY CRICKET?
CAN I HELP IT IF I'M THE ONLY PETER WHOSE MUG DOESN'T MAKE YOU SADDER THAN THE SMITHS?*
MY HEAD IS... EVERYTHING'S SPIN--
*THE SPIDER-OFFICE DOESN'T ENDORSE THE SMITHS.** -NICK
**THE LETTERER DOES. -CLAYTON
PUKING IN THE HUDSON RIVER FROM A GARBAGE BOAT...
THAT'S A POWERFUL NEW YORK MOVE, GWENZELLE.
I DON'T-- DON'T KNOW WHAT HAPPENED... HOW COULD I LOSE TO HIM?
TO THE VULTURE?
AW, STOP IT. YOU DID FINE.
LOSE A FIGHT TO BARON ZEBRO AND THEN WE'LL TALK SELF-PITY, OKAY? HONESTLY, WHAT HAPPENED--

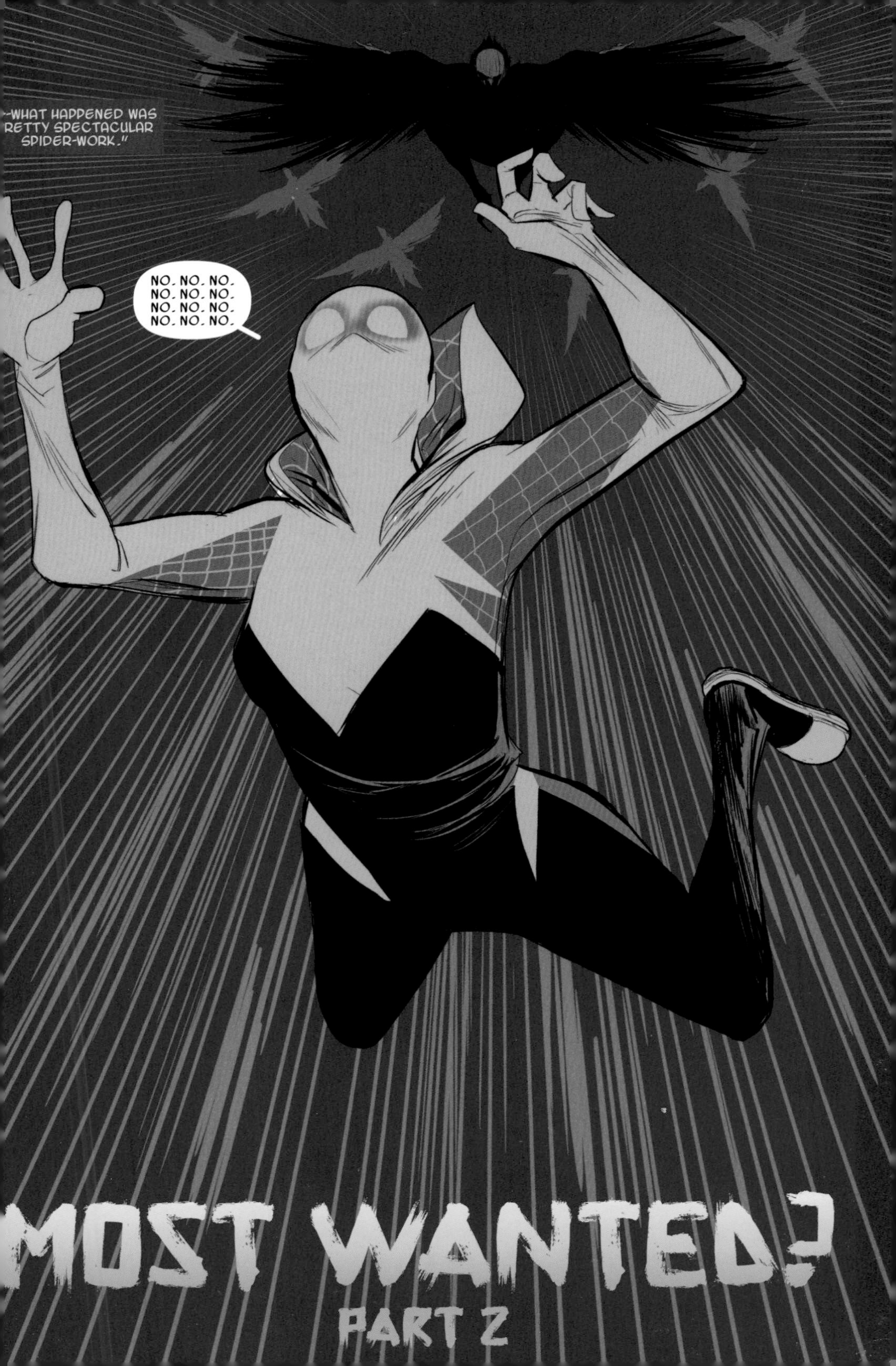

"--WHAT HAPPENED WAS
RETTY SPECTACULAR
SPIDER-WORK."
NO. NO. NO. NO. NO. NO. NO. NO. NO. NO. NO. NO.
MOST WANTED?
PART 2

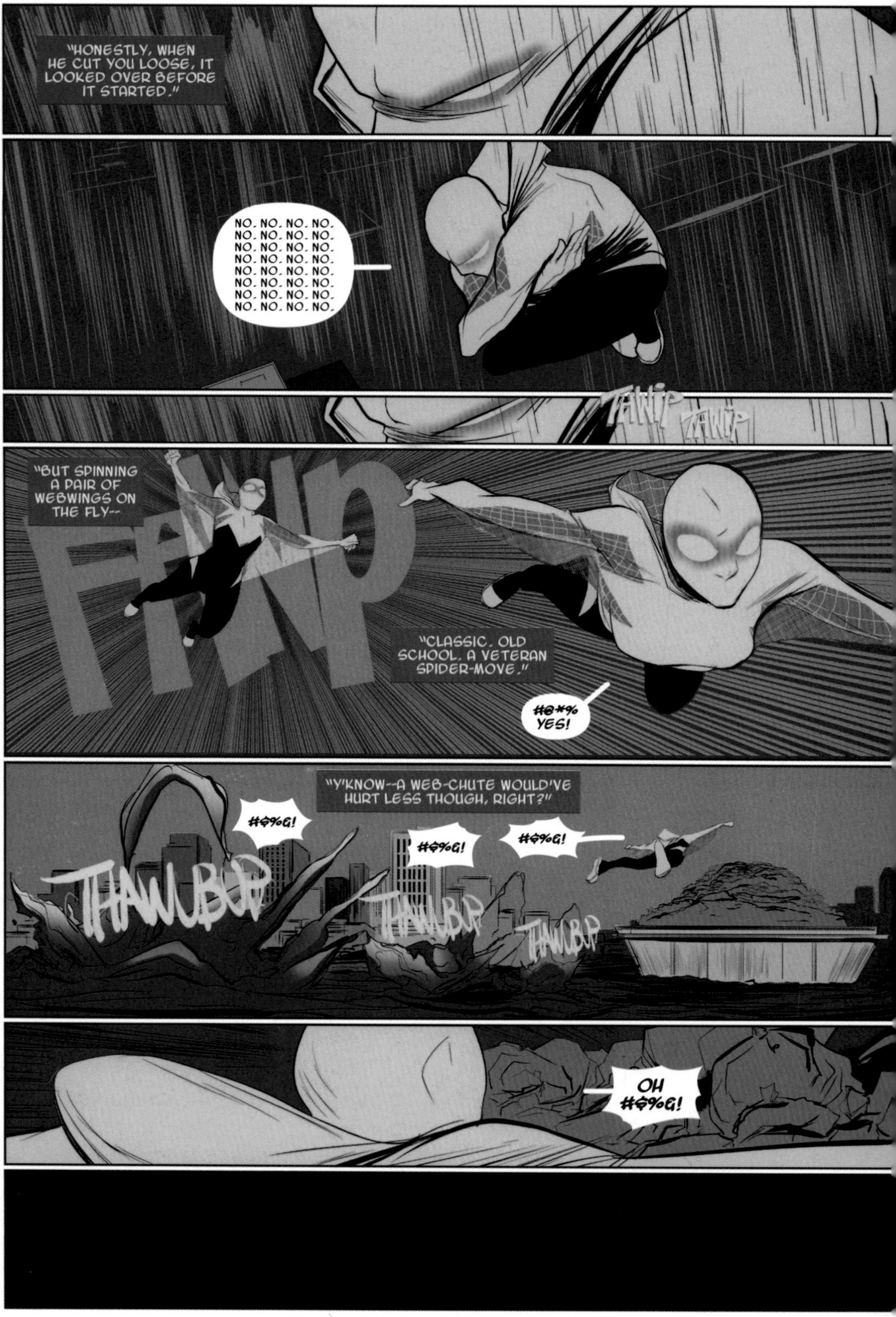
"HONESTLY, WHEN HE CUT YOU LOOSE, IT LOOKED OVER BEFORE IT STARTED."
NO. NO. NO. NO. NO. NO. NO. NO. NO. NO. NO. NO. NO. NO. NO. NO. NO. NO. NO. NO. NO. NO. NO. NO. NO. NO. NO. NO. NO. NO. NO. NO.
TAWIP
TAWIP
"BUT SPINNING A PAIR OF WEBWINGS ON THE FLY--
"CLASSIC. OLD SCHOOL. A VETERAN SPIDER-MOVE."
#@*% YES!
"Y'KNOW--A WEB-CHUTE WOULD'VE HURT LESS THOUGH, RIGHT?"
#$%&!
#$%&!
#$%&!
THAWUBUP
THAWUBUP
THAWUBUP
OH #$%&!

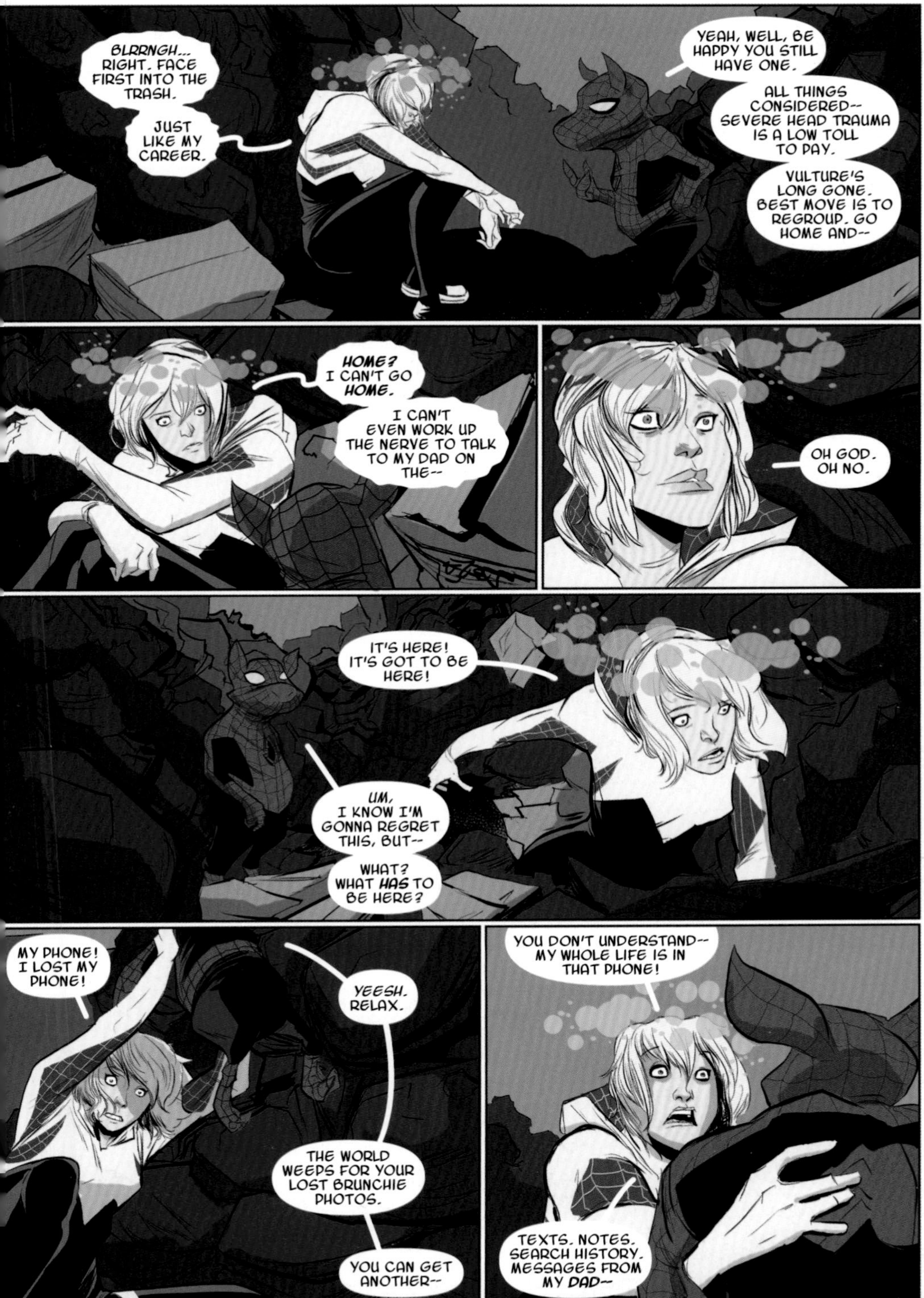
BLRRNGH... RIGHT. FACE FIRST INTO THE TRASH.
JUST LIKE MY CAREER.
YEAH, WELL, BE HAPPY YOU STILL HAVE ONE.
ALL THINGS CONSIDERED-- SEVERE HEAD TRAUMA IS A LOW TOLL TO PAY.
VULTURE'S LONG GONE. BEST MOVE IS TO REGROUP. GO HOME AND--
HOME? I CAN'T GO *HOME*.
I CAN'T EVEN WORK UP THE NERVE TO TALK TO MY DAD ON THE--
OH GOD. OH NO.
IT'S HERE! IT'S GOT TO BE HERE!
UM, I KNOW I'M GONNA REGRET THIS, BUT--
WHAT? WHAT *HAS* TO BE HERE?
MY PHONE! I LOST MY PHONE!
YEESH. RELAX.
THE WORLD WEEPS FOR YOUR LOST BRUNCHIE PHOTOS.
YOU CAN GET ANOTHER--
YOU DON'T UNDERSTAND-- MY WHOLE LIFE IS IN THAT PHONE!
TEXTS. NOTES. SEARCH HISTORY. MESSAGES FROM MY *DAD*--

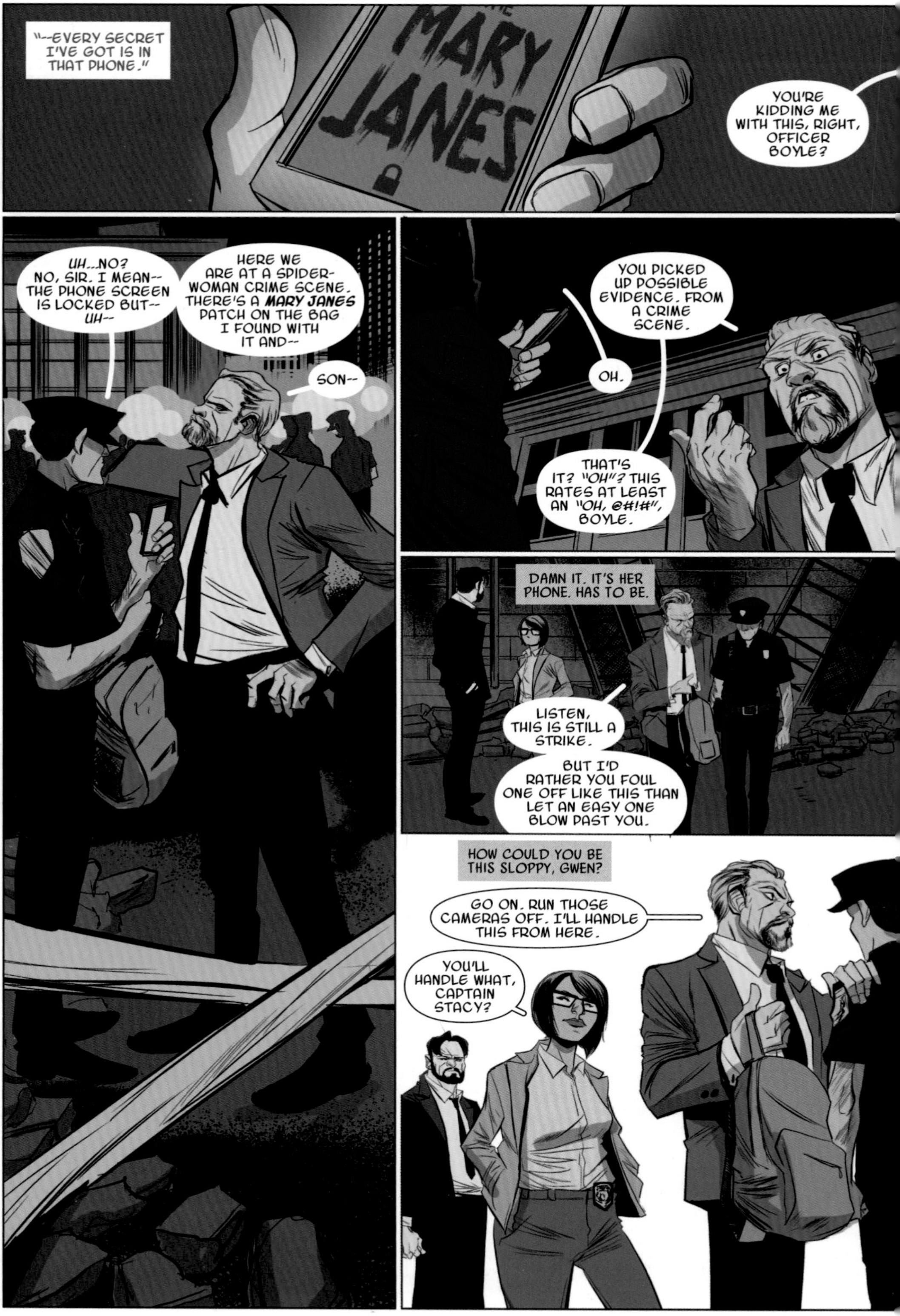
MARY JANES
"--EVERY SECRET I'VE GOT IS IN THAT PHONE."
YOU'RE KIDDING ME WITH THIS, RIGHT, OFFICER BOYLE?
UH...NO? NO, SIR. I MEAN--THE PHONE SCREEN IS LOCKED BUT--UH--
HERE WE ARE AT A SPIDER-WOMAN CRIME SCENE. THERE'S A MARY JANES PATCH ON THE BAG I FOUND WITH IT AND--
SON--
YOU PICKED UP POSSIBLE EVIDENCE. FROM A CRIME SCENE.
OH.
THAT'S IT? "OH"? THIS RATES AT LEAST AN "OH, @#!#", BOYLE.
DAMN IT. IT'S HER PHONE. HAS TO BE.
LISTEN, THIS IS STILL A STRIKE.
BUT I'D RATHER YOU FOUL ONE OFF LIKE THIS THAN LET AN EASY ONE BLOW PAST YOU.
HOW COULD YOU BE THIS SLOPPY, GWEN?
GO ON. RUN THOSE CAMERAS OFF. I'LL HANDLE THIS FROM HERE.
YOU'LL HANDLE WHAT, CAPTAIN STACY?

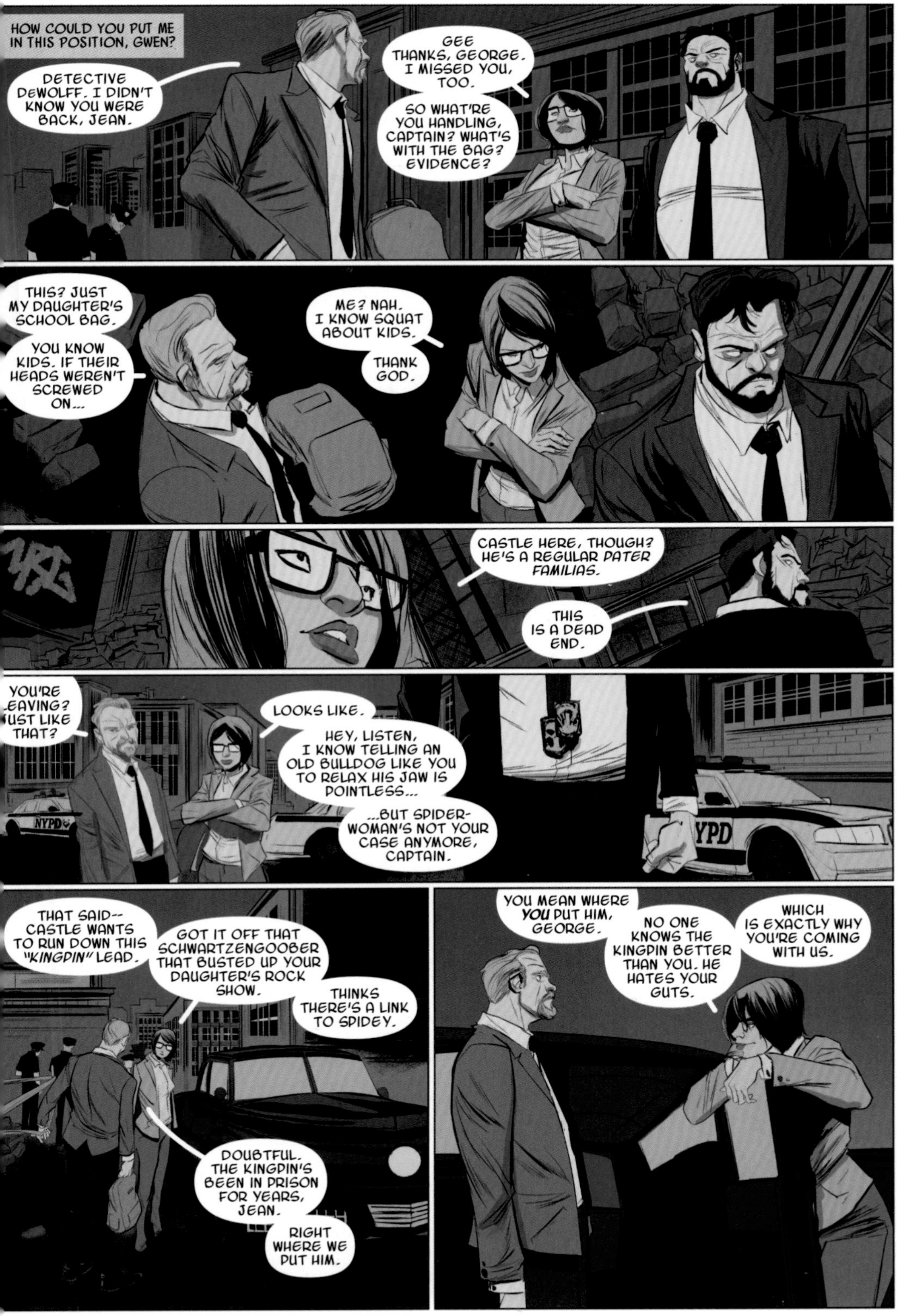
HOW COULD YOU PUT ME IN THIS POSITION, GWEN?
DETECTIVE DeWOLFF. I DIDN'T KNOW YOU WERE BACK, JEAN.
GEE THANKS, GEORGE. I MISSED YOU, TOO.
SO WHAT'RE YOU HANDLING, CAPTAIN? WHAT'S WITH THE BAG? EVIDENCE?
THIS? JUST MY DAUGHTER'S SCHOOL BAG.
YOU KNOW KIDS. IF THEIR HEADS WEREN'T SCREWED ON...
ME? NAH. I KNOW SQUAT ABOUT KIDS.
THANK GOD.
CASTLE HERE, THOUGH? HE'S A REGULAR PATER FAMILIAS.
THIS IS A DEAD END.
YOU'RE LEAVING? JUST LIKE THAT?
LOOKS LIKE.
HEY, LISTEN, I KNOW TELLING AN OLD BULLDOG LIKE YOU TO RELAX HIS JAW IS POINTLESS...
...BUT SPIDER-WOMAN'S NOT YOUR CASE ANYMORE, CAPTAIN.
NYPD
THAT SAID-- CASTLE WANTS TO RUN DOWN THIS "KINGPIN" LEAD.
GOT IT OFF THAT SCHWARTZENGOOBER THAT BUSTED UP YOUR DAUGHTER'S ROCK SHOW.
THINKS THERE'S A LINK TO SPIDEY.
DOUBTFUL. THE KINGPIN'S BEEN IN PRISON FOR YEARS, JEAN.
RIGHT WHERE WE PUT HIM.
YOU MEAN WHERE YOU PUT HIM, GEORGE.
NO ONE KNOWS THE KINGPIN BETTER THAN YOU. HE HATES YOUR GUTS.
WHICH IS EXACTLY WHY YOU'RE COMING WITH US.

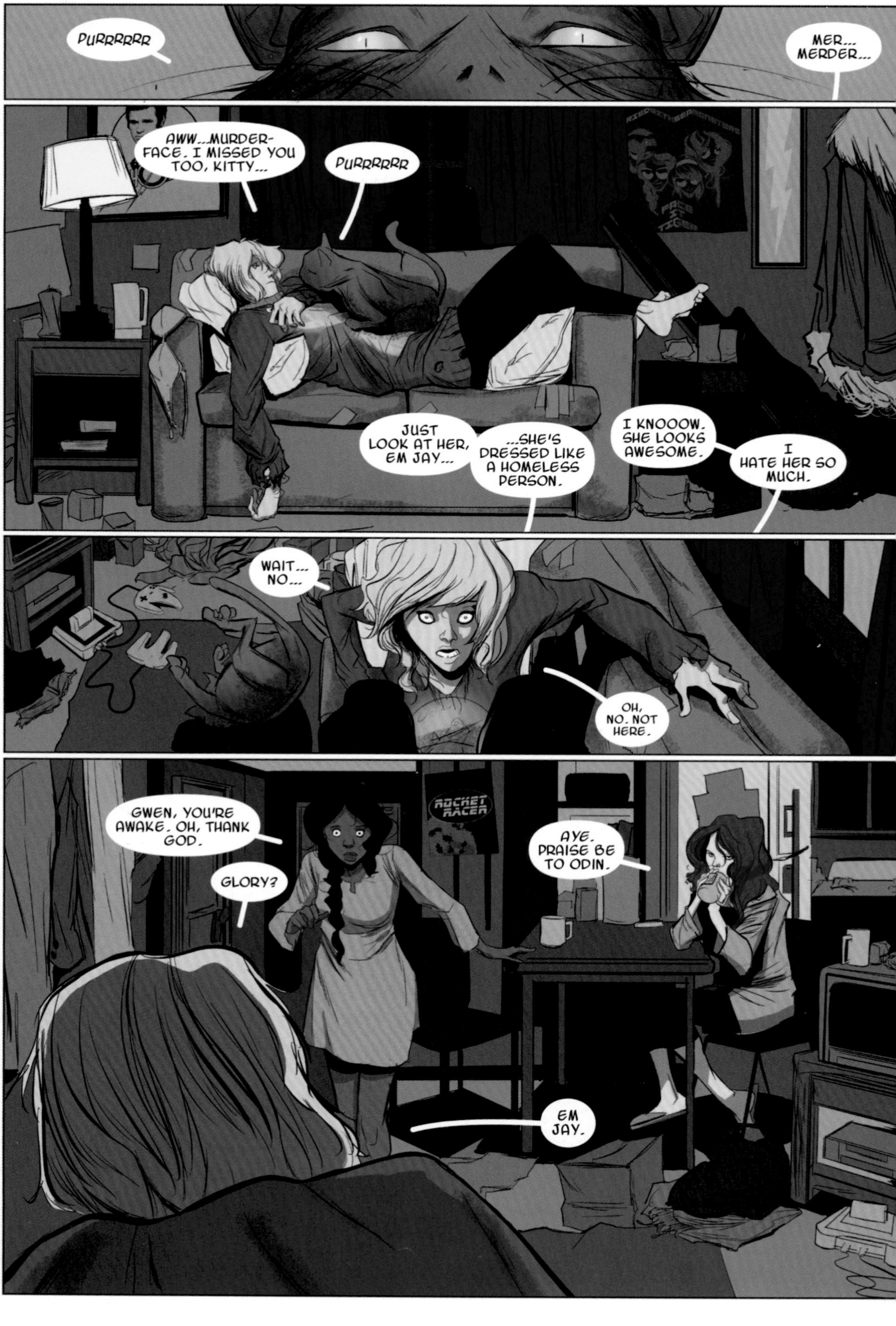
PURRRRRR
MER... MERDER...
AWW...MURDER-FACE. I MISSED YOU TOO, KITTY...
PURRRRRR
JUST LOOK AT HER, EM JAY...
...SHE'S DRESSED LIKE A HOMELESS PERSON.
I KNOOOW. SHE LOOKS AWESOME.
I HATE HER SO MUCH.
WAIT... NO...
OH, NO. NOT HERE.
ROCKET RACER
GWEN, YOU'RE AWAKE. OH, THANK GOD.
GLORY?
AYE. PRAISE BE TO ODIN.
EM JAY.

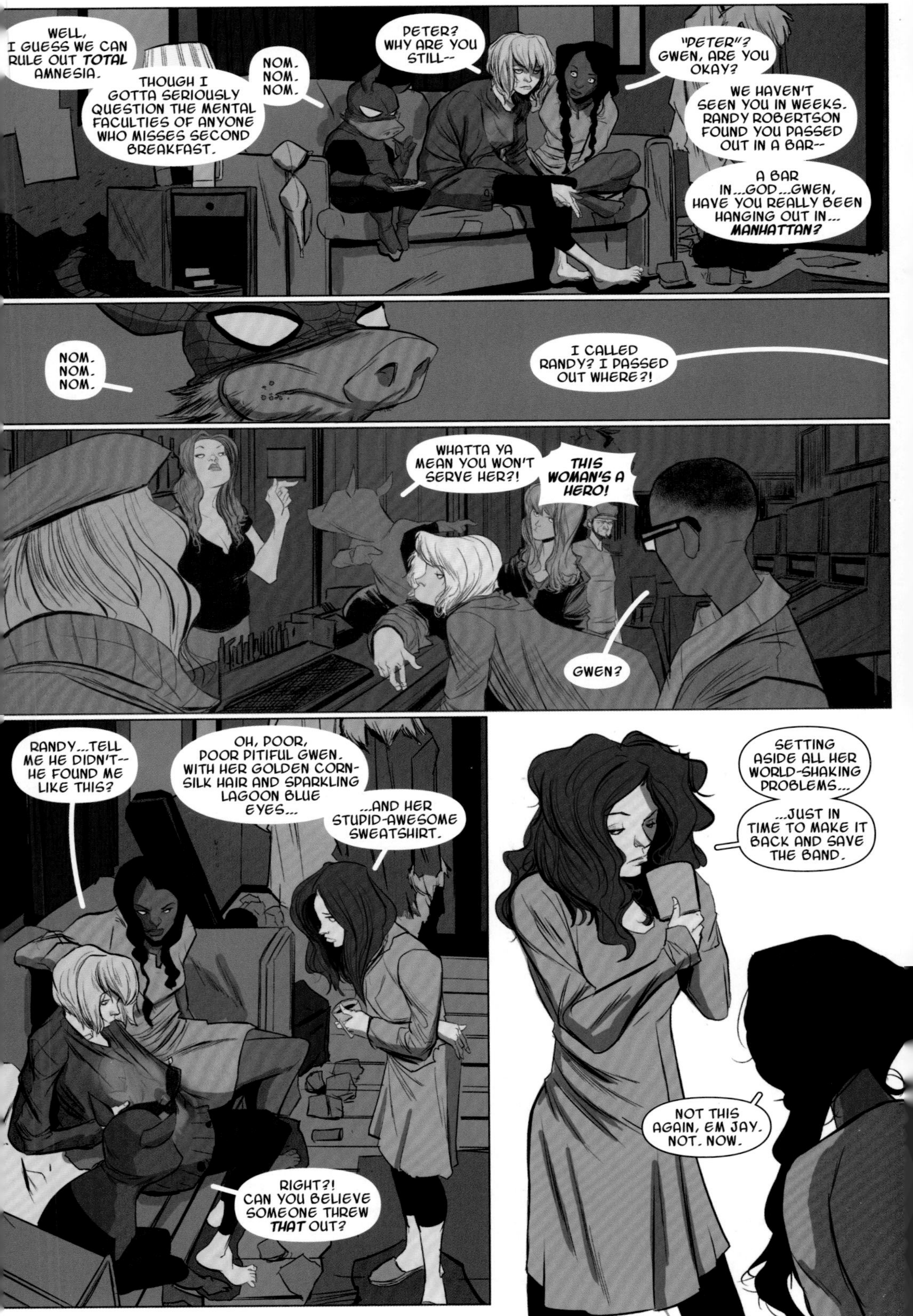
WELL, I GUESS WE CAN RULE OUT *TOTAL* AMNESIA.
THOUGH I GOTTA SERIOUSLY QUESTION THE MENTAL FACULTIES OF ANYONE WHO MISSES SECOND BREAKFAST.
NOM. NOM. NOM.
PETER? WHY ARE YOU STILL--
"PETER"? GWEN, ARE YOU OKAY?
WE HAVEN'T SEEN YOU IN WEEKS. RANDY ROBERTSON FOUND YOU PASSED OUT IN A BAR--
A BAR IN...GOD...GWEN, HAVE YOU REALLY BEEN HANGING OUT IN... ***MANHATTAN?***
NOM. NOM. NOM.
I CALLED RANDY? I PASSED OUT WHERE?!
WHATTA YA MEAN YOU WON'T SERVE HER?!
THIS WOMAN'S A HERO!
GWEN?
RANDY...TELL ME HE DIDN'T-- HE FOUND ME LIKE THIS?
OH, POOR, POOR PITIFUL GWEN. WITH HER GOLDEN CORN-SILK HAIR AND SPARKLING LAGOON BLUE EYES...
...AND HER STUPID-AWESOME SWEATSHIRT.
RIGHT?! CAN YOU BELIEVE SOMEONE THREW *THAT* OUT?
SETTING ASIDE ALL HER WORLD-SHAKING PROBLEMS...
...JUST IN TIME TO MAKE IT BACK AND SAVE THE BAND.
NOT THIS AGAIN, EM JAY. NOT. NOW.

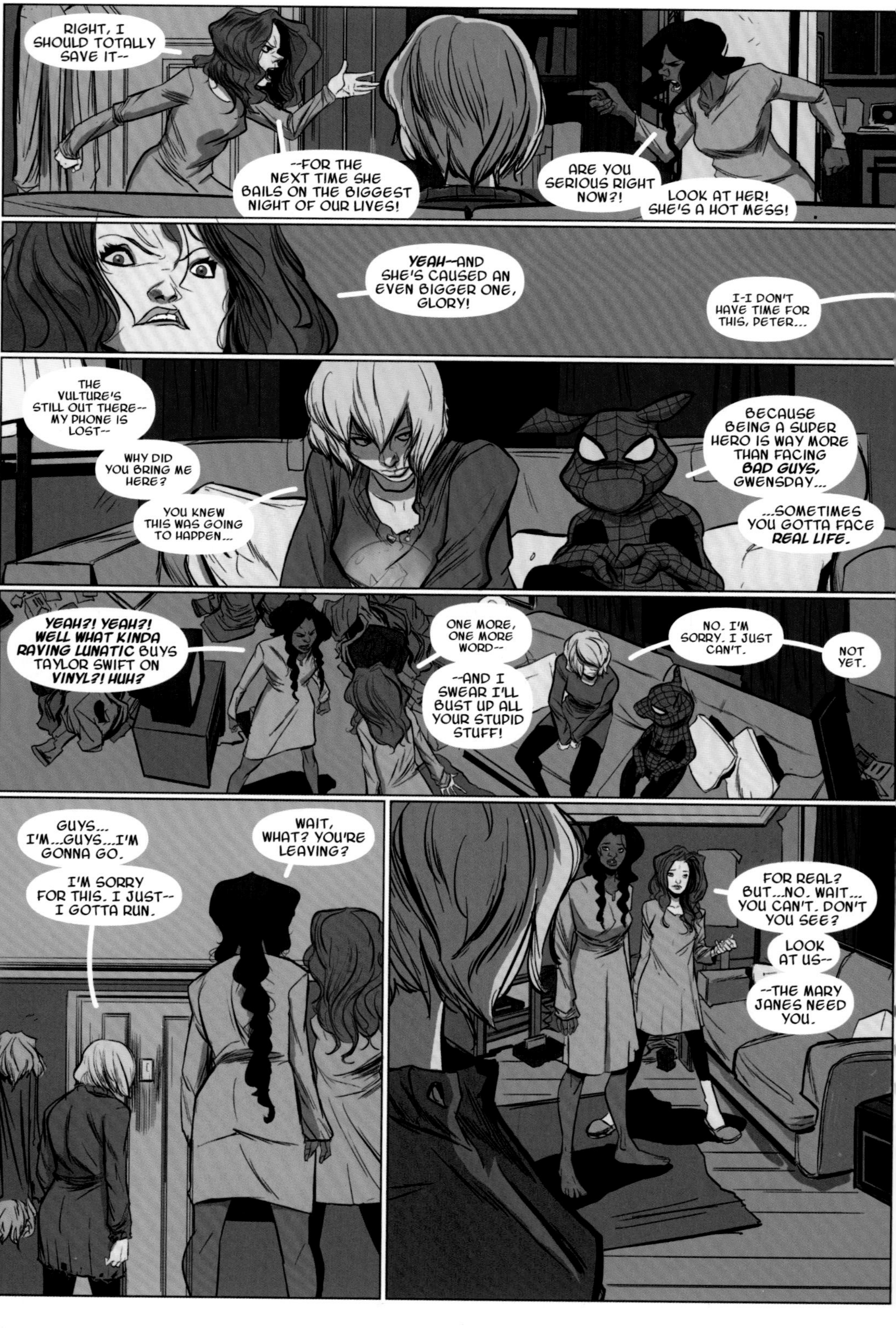
RIGHT, I SHOULD TOTALLY SAVE IT--
--FOR THE NEXT TIME SHE BAILS ON THE BIGGEST NIGHT OF OUR LIVES!
ARE YOU SERIOUS RIGHT NOW?!
LOOK AT HER! SHE'S A HOT MESS!
YEAH--AND SHE'S CAUSED AN EVEN BIGGER ONE, GLORY!
I-I DON'T HAVE TIME FOR THIS, PETER...
THE VULTURE'S STILL OUT THERE-- MY PHONE IS LOST--
WHY DID YOU BRING ME HERE?
YOU KNEW THIS WAS GOING TO HAPPEN...
BECAUSE BEING A SUPER HERO IS WAY MORE THAN FACING BAD GUYS, GWENSDAY...
...SOMETIMES YOU GOTTA FACE REAL LIFE.
YEAH?! YEAH?! WELL WHAT KINDA RAVING LUNATIC BUYS TAYLOR SWIFT ON VINYL?! HUH?
ONE MORE, ONE MORE WORD--
--AND I SWEAR I'LL BUST UP ALL YOUR STUPID STUFF!
NO. I'M SORRY. I JUST CAN'T.
NOT YET.
GUYS... I'M...GUYS...I'M GONNA GO.
I'M SORRY FOR THIS. I JUST-- I GOTTA RUN.
WAIT, WHAT? YOU'RE LEAVING?
FOR REAL? BUT...NO. WAIT... YOU CAN'T. DON'T YOU SEE?
LOOK AT US--
--THE MARY JANES NEED YOU.

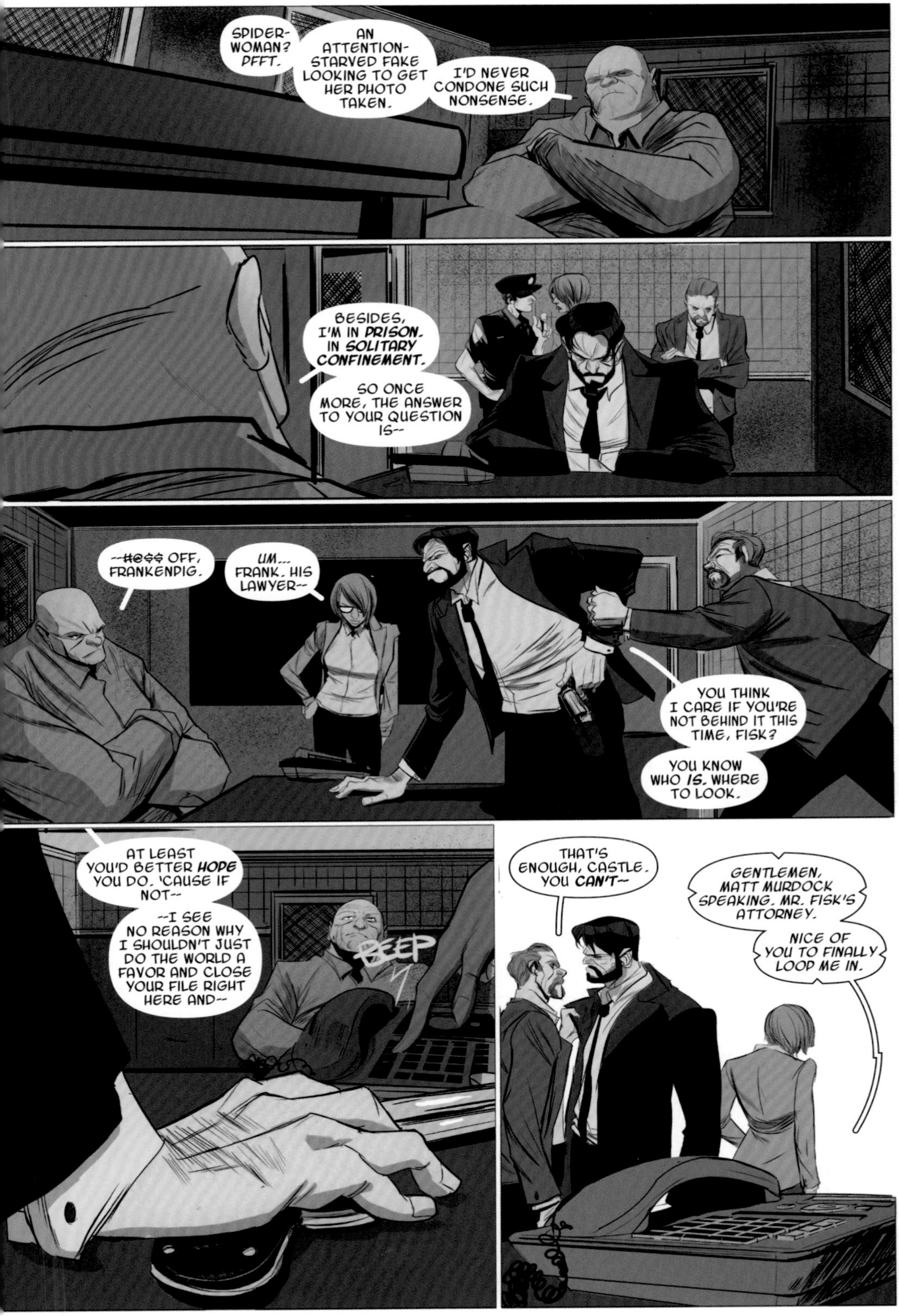
SPIDER-WOMAN? PFFT.
AN ATTENTION-STARVED FAKE LOOKING TO GET HER PHOTO TAKEN.
I'D NEVER CONDONE SUCH NONSENSE.
BESIDES, I'M IN PRISON. IN SOLITARY CONFINEMENT.
SO ONCE MORE, THE ANSWER TO YOUR QUESTION IS--
--#@$$ OFF, FRANKENPIG.
UM... FRANK. HIS LAWYER--
YOU THINK I CARE IF YOU'RE NOT BEHIND IT THIS TIME, FISK?
YOU KNOW WHO IS. WHERE TO LOOK.
AT LEAST YOU'D BETTER HOPE YOU DO. 'CAUSE IF NOT--
--I SEE NO REASON WHY I SHOULDN'T JUST DO THE WORLD A FAVOR AND CLOSE YOUR FILE RIGHT HERE AND--
BEEP
THAT'S ENOUGH, CASTLE. YOU CAN'T--
GENTLEMEN, MATT MURDOCK SPEAKING. MR. FISK'S ATTORNEY.
NICE OF YOU TO FINALLY LOOP ME IN.

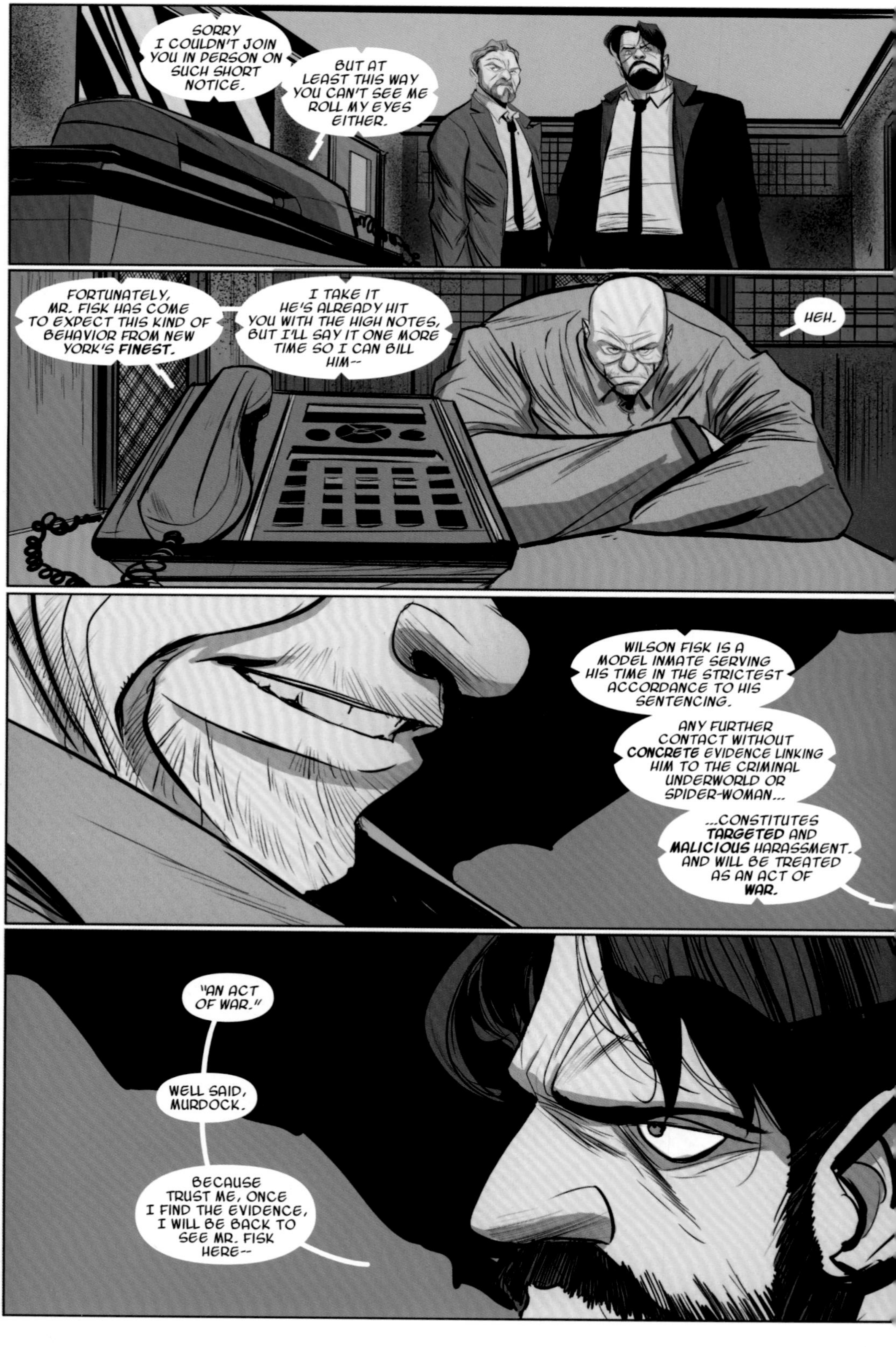
SORRY I COULDN'T JOIN YOU IN PERSON ON SUCH SHORT NOTICE.
BUT AT LEAST THIS WAY YOU CAN'T SEE ME ROLL MY EYES EITHER.
FORTUNATELY, MR. FISK HAS COME TO EXPECT THIS KIND OF BEHAVIOR FROM NEW YORK'S FINEST.
I TAKE IT HE'S ALREADY HIT YOU WITH THE HIGH NOTES, BUT I'LL SAY IT ONE MORE TIME SO I CAN BILL HIM--
HEH.
WILSON FISK IS A MODEL INMATE SERVING HIS TIME IN THE STRICTEST ACCORDANCE TO HIS SENTENCING.
ANY FURTHER CONTACT WITHOUT CONCRETE EVIDENCE LINKING HIM TO THE CRIMINAL UNDERWORLD OR SPIDER-WOMAN...
...CONSTITUTES TARGETED AND MALICIOUS HARASSMENT. AND WILL BE TREATED AS AN ACT OF WAR.
"AN ACT OF WAR."
WELL SAID, MURDOCK.
BECAUSE TRUST ME, ONCE I FIND THE EVIDENCE, I WILL BE BACK TO SEE MR. FISK HERE--

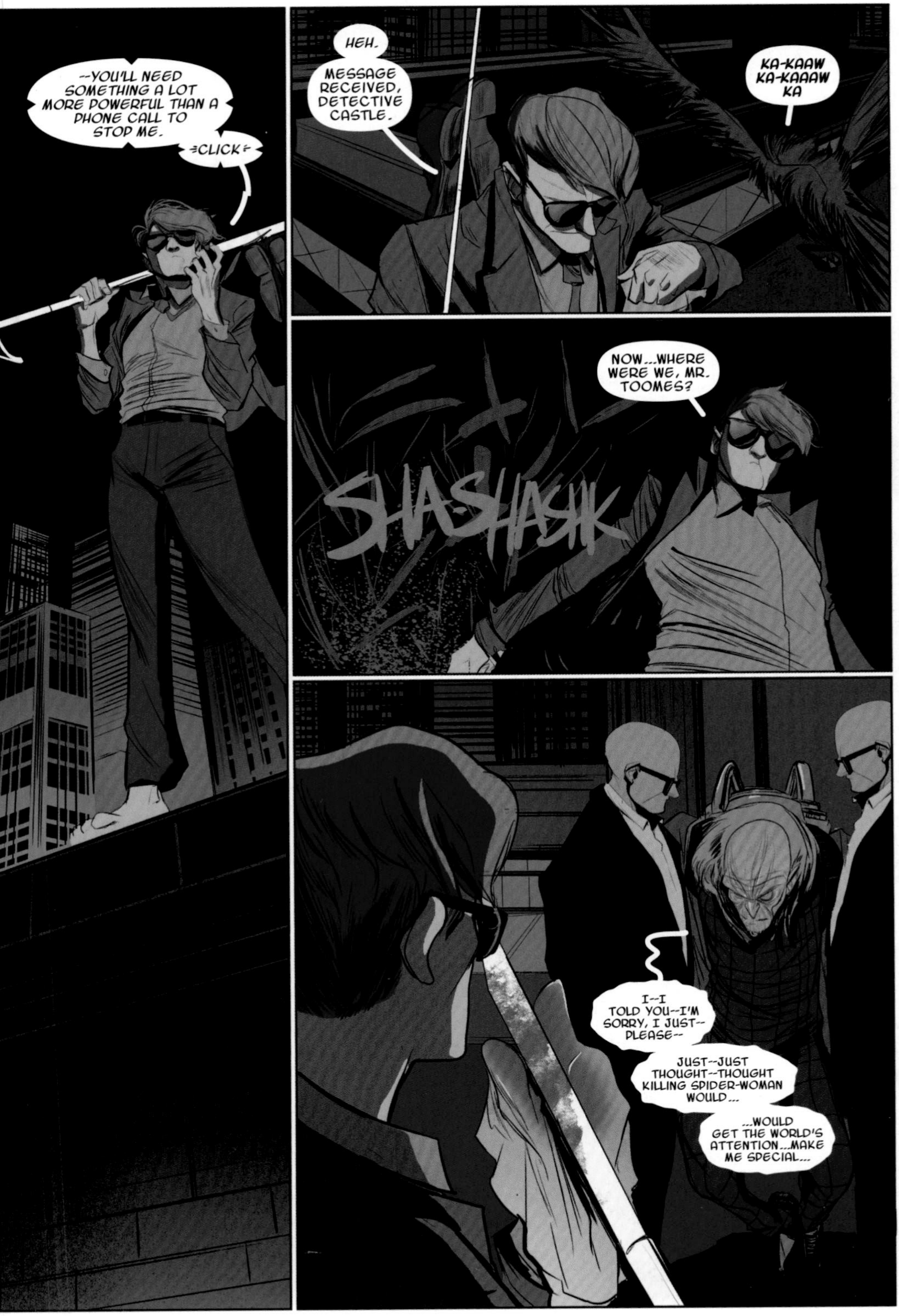
--YOU'LL NEED SOMETHING A LOT MORE POWERFUL THAN A PHONE CALL TO STOP ME.
=CLICK=
HEH.
MESSAGE RECEIVED, DETECTIVE CASTLE.
KA-KAAW KA-KAAAW KA
NOW...WHERE WERE WE, MR. TOOMES?
SHASHASK
I--I TOLD YOU--I'M SORRY, I JUST--PLEASE--
JUST--JUST THOUGHT--THOUGHT KILLING SPIDER-WOMAN WOULD...
...WOULD GET THE WORLD'S ATTENTION...MAKE ME SPECIAL...

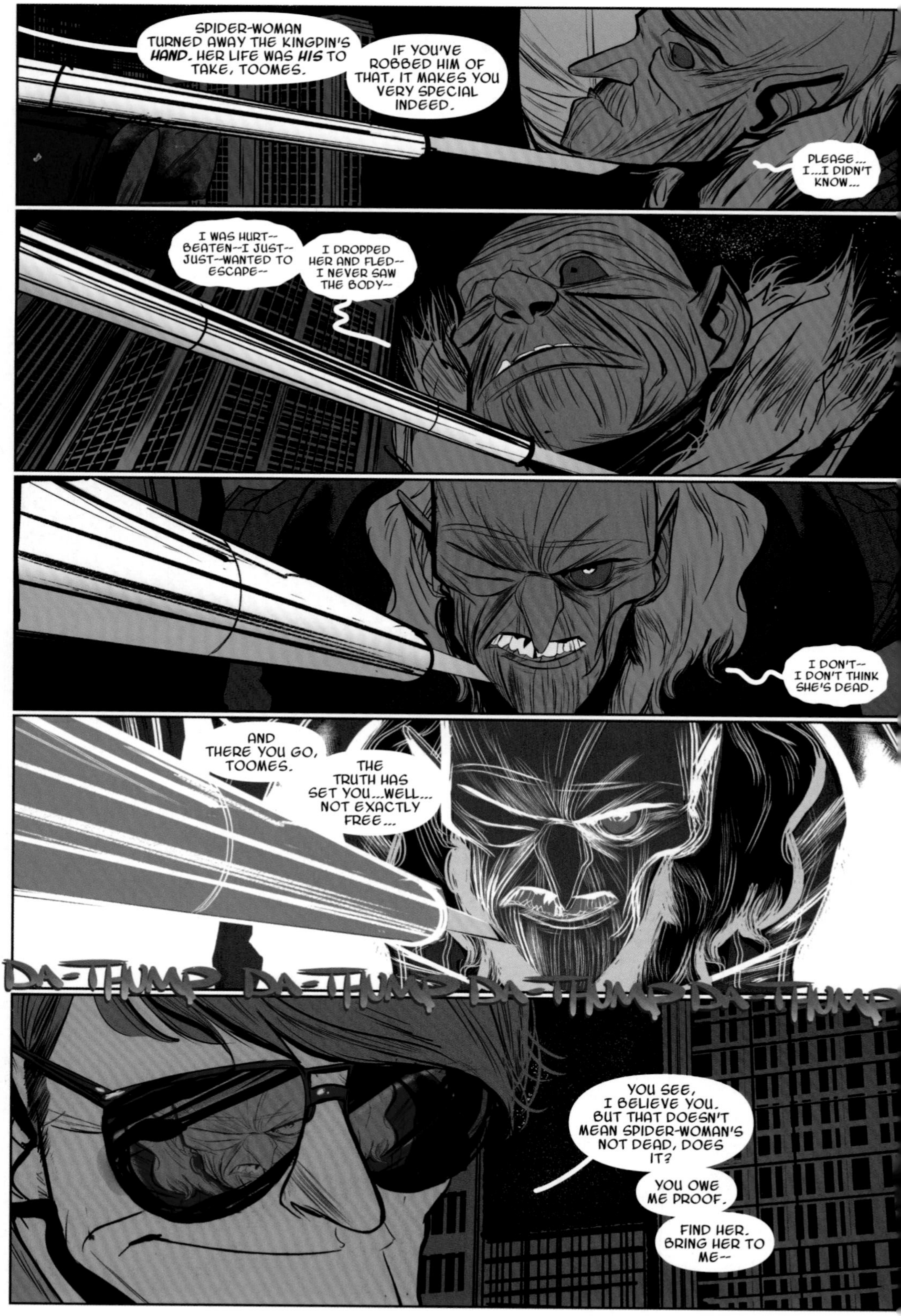
SPIDER-WOMAN TURNED AWAY THE KINGPIN'S HAND. HER LIFE WAS HIS TO TAKE, TOOMES.
IF YOU'VE ROBBED HIM OF THAT, IT MAKES YOU VERY SPECIAL INDEED.
PLEASE... I...I DIDN'T KNOW...
I WAS HURT--BEATEN--I JUST--JUST--WANTED TO ESCAPE--
I DROPPED HER AND FLED--I NEVER SAW THE BODY--
I DON'T--I DON'T THINK SHE'S DEAD.
AND THERE YOU GO, TOOMES.
THE TRUTH HAS SET YOU...WELL... NOT EXACTLY FREE...
DA-THUMP DA-THUMP DA-THUMP DA-THUMP
YOU SEE, I BELIEVE YOU. BUT THAT DOESN'T MEAN SPIDER-WOMAN'S NOT DEAD, DOES IT?
YOU OWE ME PROOF.
FIND HER. BRING HER TO ME--

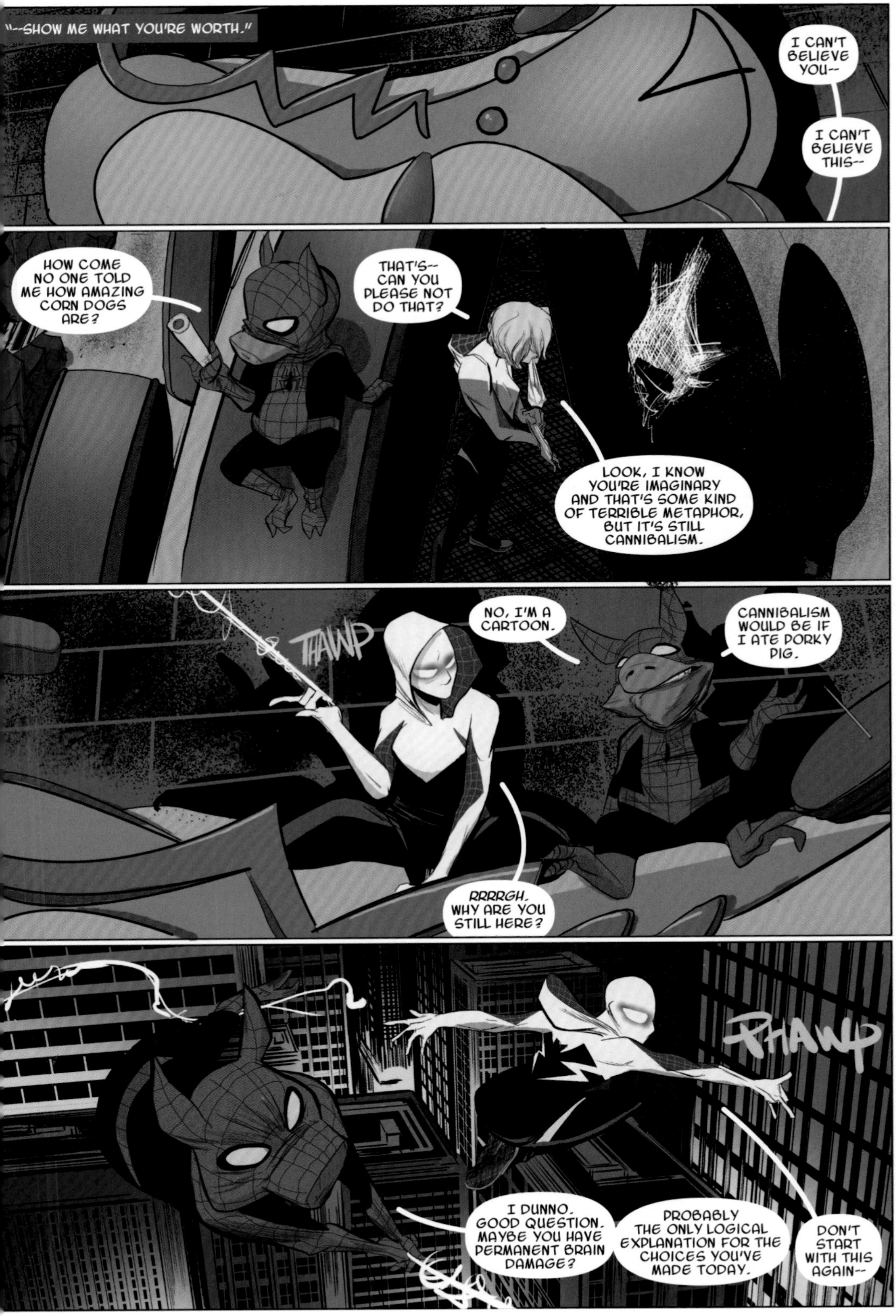
"--SHOW ME WHAT YOU'RE WORTH."
I CAN'T BELIEVE YOU--
I CAN'T BELIEVE THIS--
HOW COME NO ONE TOLD ME HOW AMAZING CORN DOGS ARE?
THAT'S-- CAN YOU PLEASE NOT DO THAT?
LOOK, I KNOW YOU'RE IMAGINARY AND THAT'S SOME KIND OF TERRIBLE METAPHOR, BUT IT'S STILL CANNIBALISM.
THAWP
NO, I'M A CARTOON.
CANNIBALISM WOULD BE IF I ATE PORKY PIG.
RRRRGH. WHY ARE YOU STILL HERE?
PHAWP
I DUNNO. GOOD QUESTION. MAYBE YOU HAVE PERMANENT BRAIN DAMAGE?
PROBABLY THE ONLY LOGICAL EXPLANATION FOR THE CHOICES YOU'VE MADE TODAY.
DON'T START WITH THIS AGAIN--

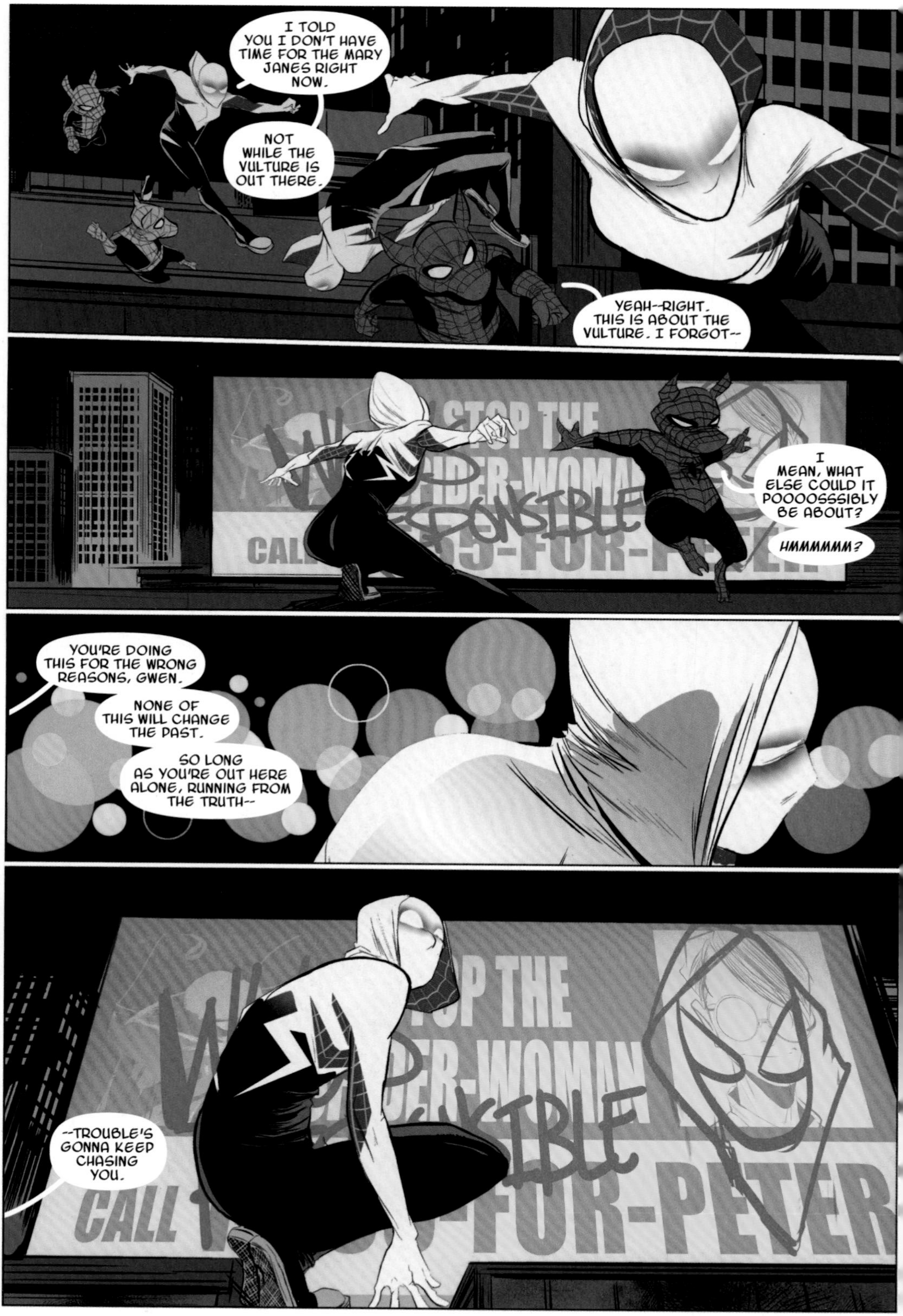
I TOLD YOU I DON'T HAVE TIME FOR THE MARY JANES RIGHT NOW.
NOT WHILE THE VULTURE IS OUT THERE.
YEAH--RIGHT. THIS IS ABOUT THE VULTURE. I FORGOT--
I MEAN, WHAT ELSE COULD IT POOOOSSSIBLY BE ABOUT?
HMMMMMM?
YOU'RE DOING THIS FOR THE WRONG REASONS, GWEN.
NONE OF THIS WILL CHANGE THE PAST.
SO LONG AS YOU'RE OUT HERE ALONE, RUNNING FROM THE TRUTH--
--TROUBLE'S GONNA KEEP CHASING YOU.

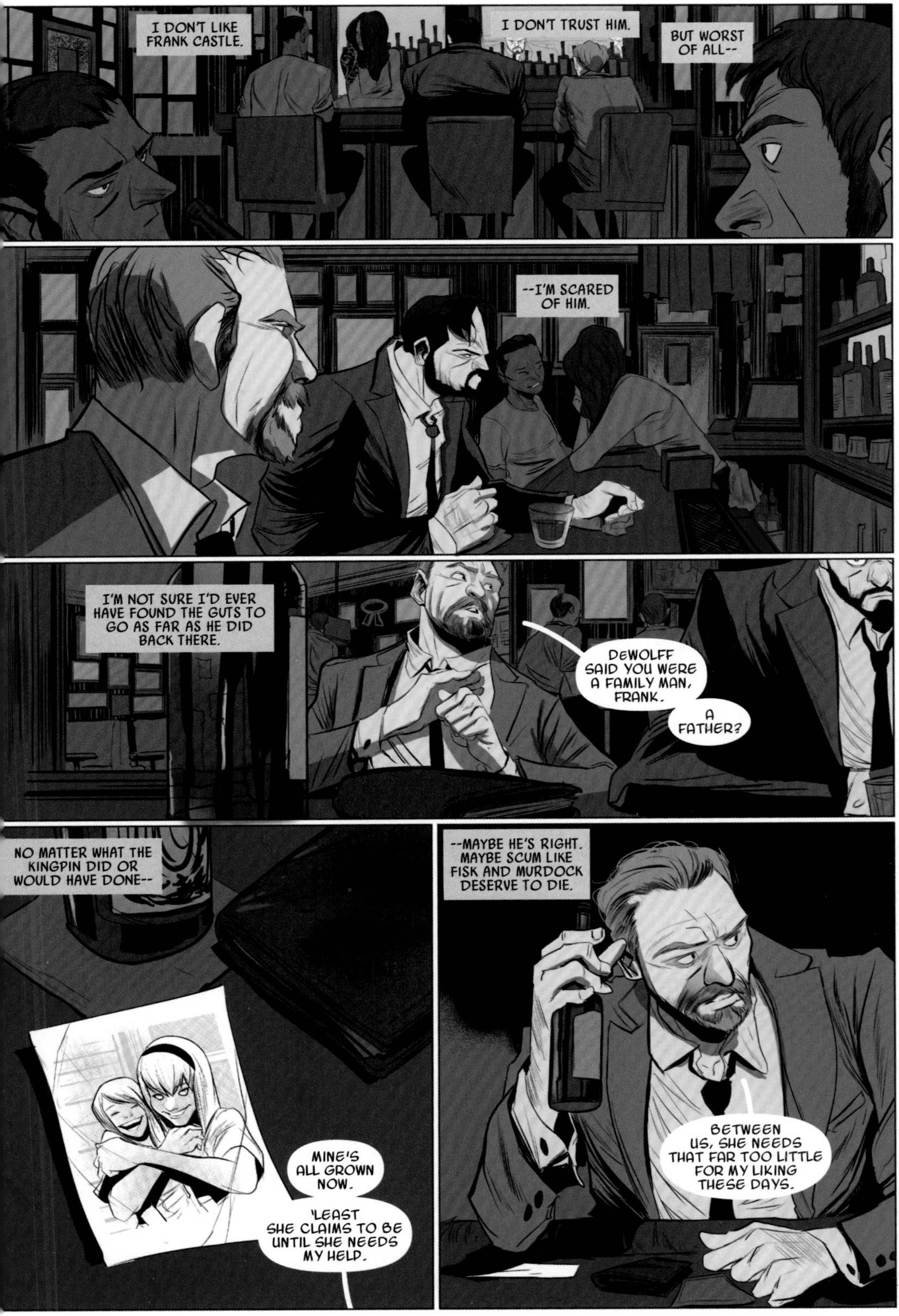
I DON'T LIKE FRANK CASTLE.
I DON'T TRUST HIM.
BUT WORST OF ALL--
--I'M SCARED OF HIM.
I'M NOT SURE I'D EVER HAVE FOUND THE GUTS TO GO AS FAR AS HE DID BACK THERE.
DEWOLFF SAID YOU WERE A FAMILY MAN, FRANK.
A FATHER?
NO MATTER WHAT THE KINGPIN DID OR WOULD HAVE DONE--
MINE'S ALL GROWN NOW.
'LEAST SHE CLAIMS TO BE UNTIL SHE NEEDS MY HELP.
--MAYBE HE'S RIGHT. MAYBE SCUM LIKE FISK AND MURDOCK DESERVE TO DIE.
BETWEEN US, SHE NEEDS THAT FAR TOO LITTLE FOR MY LIKING THESE DAYS.

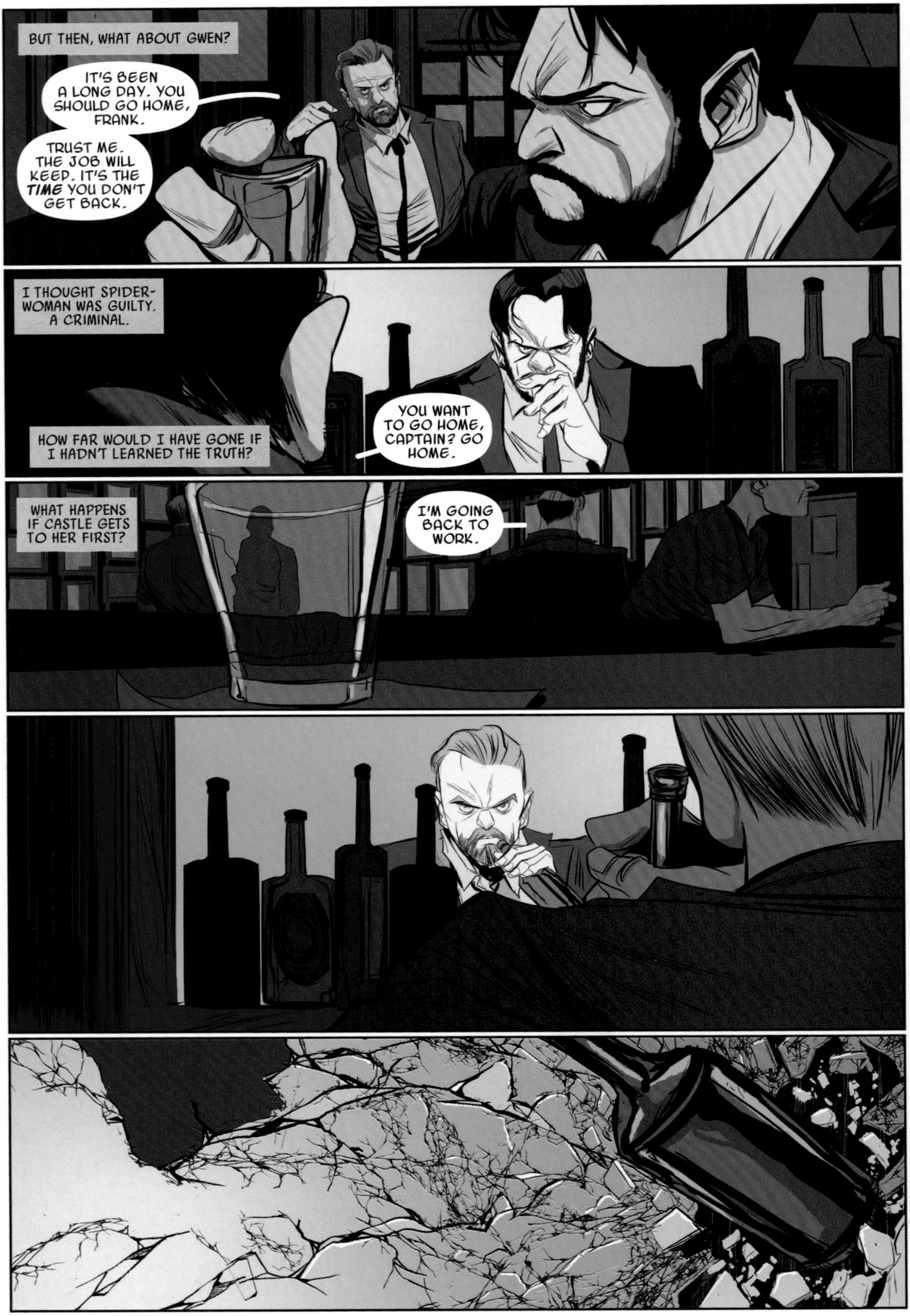
BUT THEN, WHAT ABOUT GWEN?
IT'S BEEN A LONG DAY. YOU SHOULD GO HOME, FRANK.
TRUST ME. THE JOB WILL KEEP. IT'S THE TIME YOU DON'T GET BACK.
I THOUGHT SPIDER-WOMAN WAS GUILTY. A CRIMINAL.
HOW FAR WOULD I HAVE GONE IF I HADN'T LEARNED THE TRUTH?
YOU WANT TO GO HOME, CAPTAIN? GO HOME.
WHAT HAPPENS IF CASTLE GETS TO HER FIRST?
I'M GOING BACK TO WORK.

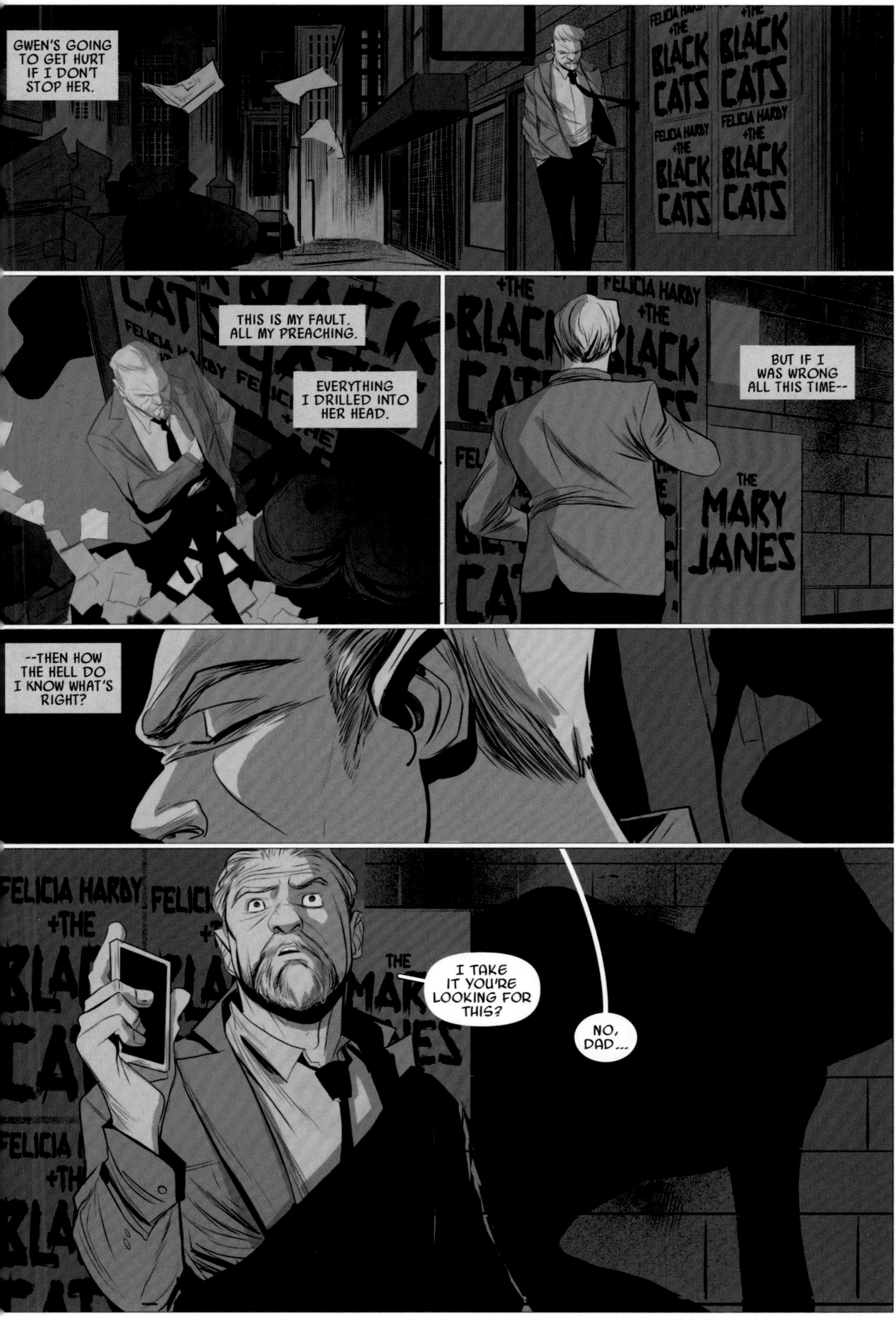
GWEN'S GOING TO GET HURT IF I DON'T STOP HER.
FELICIA HARDY +THE BLACK CATS
THIS IS MY FAULT. ALL MY PREACHING.
EVERYTHING I DRILLED INTO HER HEAD.
BUT IF I WAS WRONG ALL THIS TIME--
THE MARY JANES
--THEN HOW THE HELL DO I KNOW WHAT'S RIGHT?
I TAKE IT YOU'RE LOOKING FOR THIS?
NO, DAD...

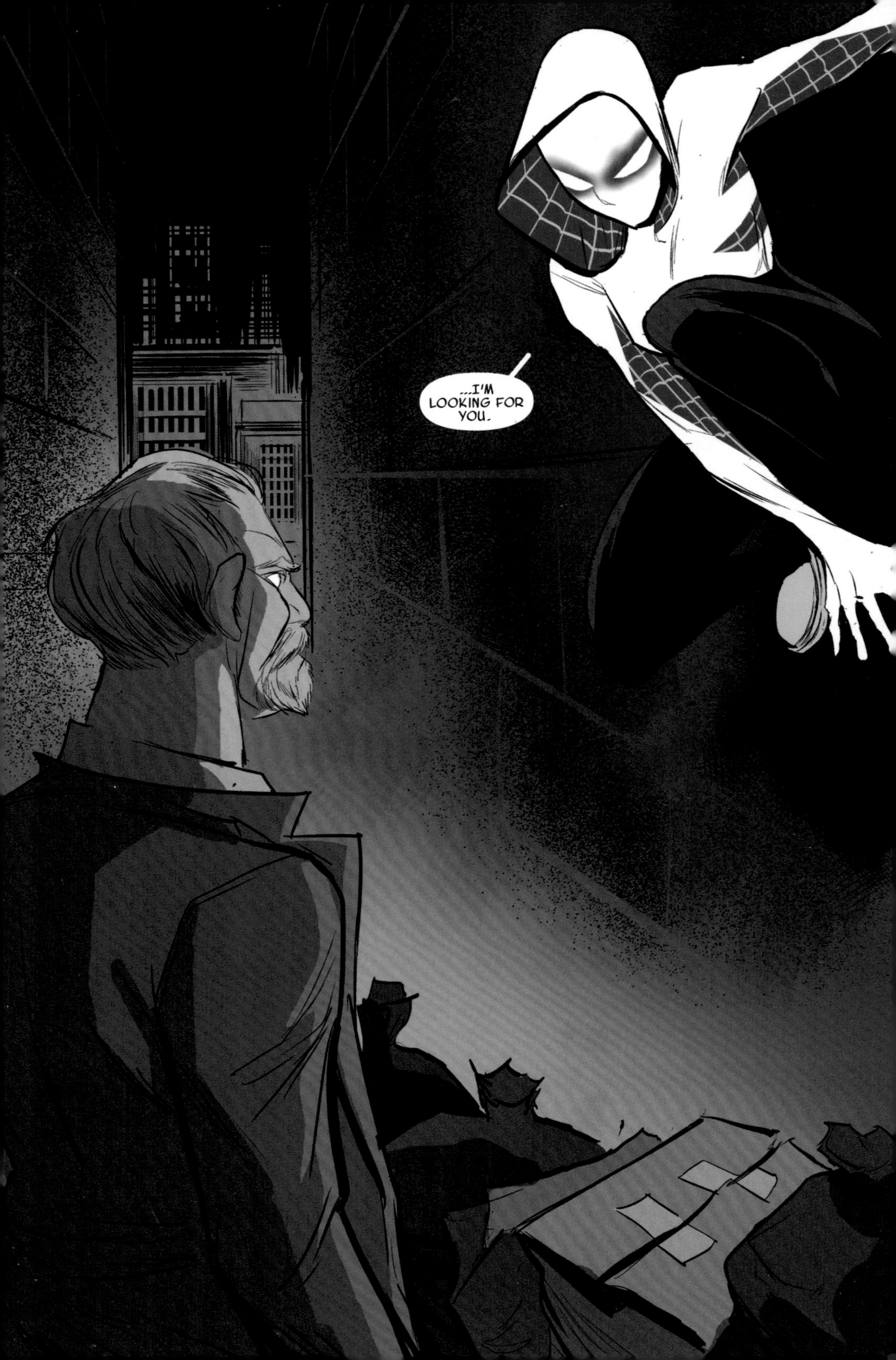
...I'M LOOKING FOR YOU.

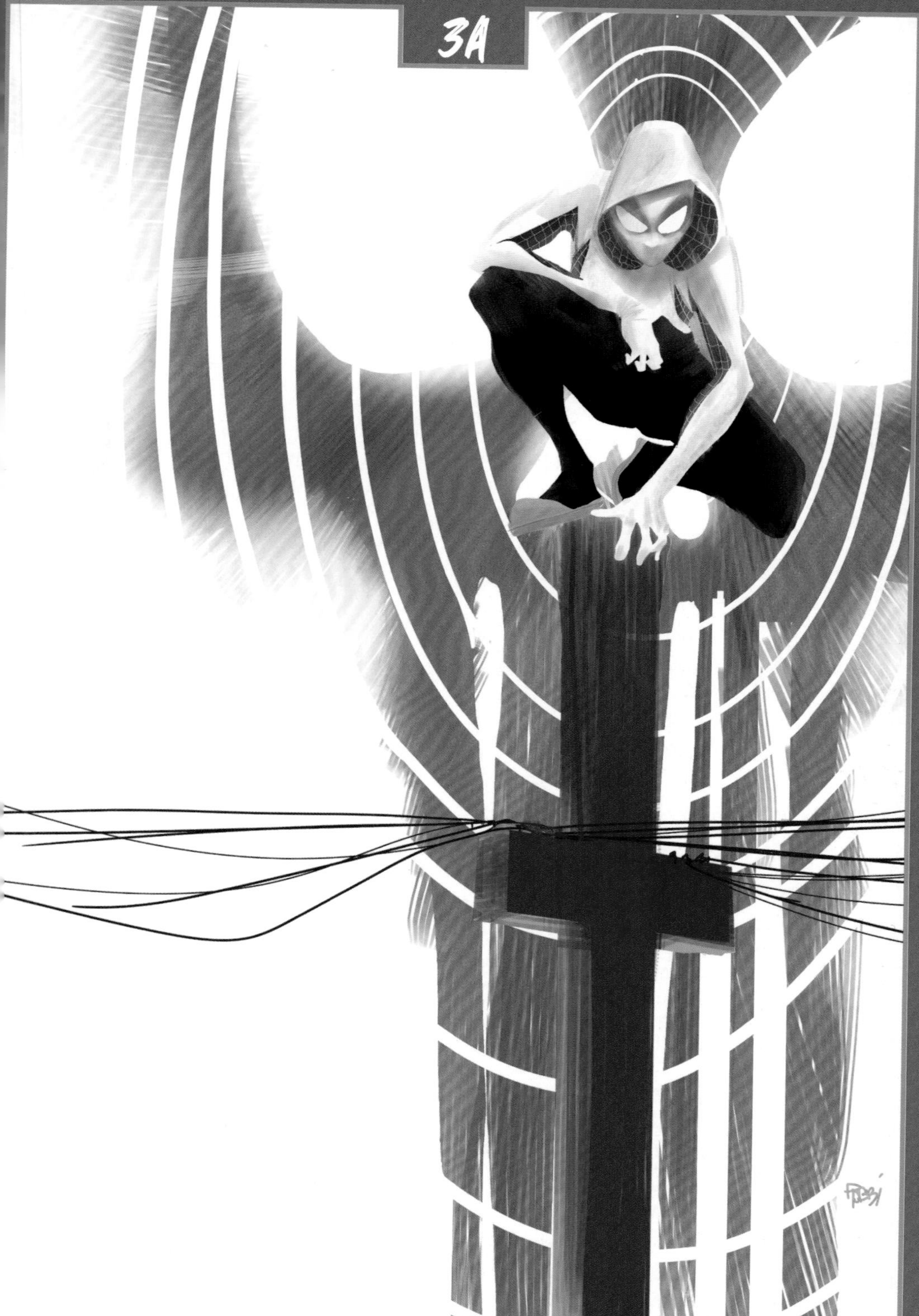
3A

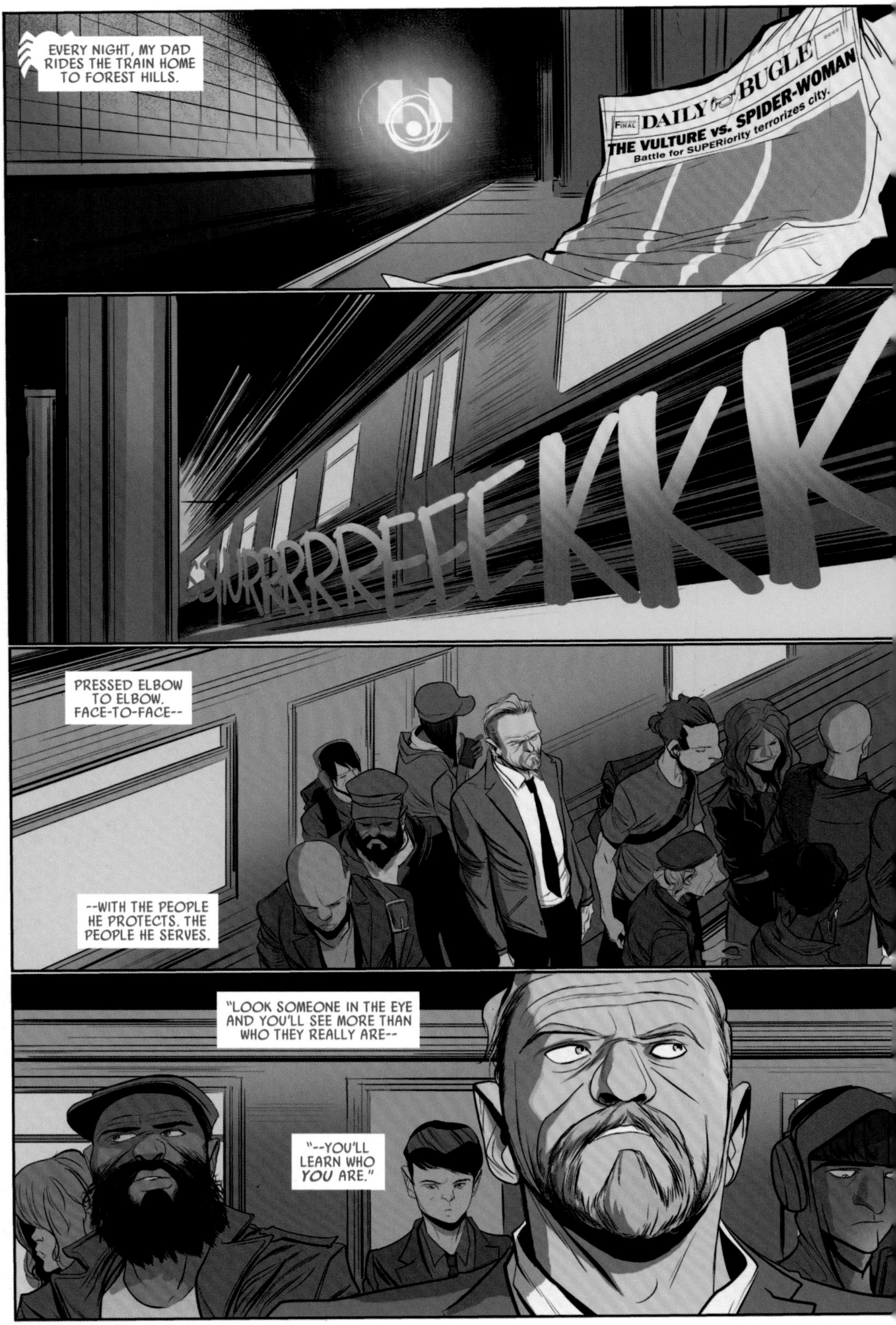
EVERY NIGHT, MY DAD RIDES THE TRAIN HOME TO FOREST HILLS.
DAILY BUGLE
FINAL
THE VULTURE vs. SPIDER-WOMAN
Battle for SUPERiority terrorizes city.
SCHURRRRRREEEKKK
PRESSED ELBOW TO ELBOW. FACE-TO-FACE--
--WITH THE PEOPLE HE PROTECTS. THE PEOPLE HE SERVES.
"LOOK SOMEONE IN THE EYE AND YOU'LL SEE MORE THAN WHO THEY REALLY ARE--
"--YOU'LL LEARN WHO *YOU* ARE."

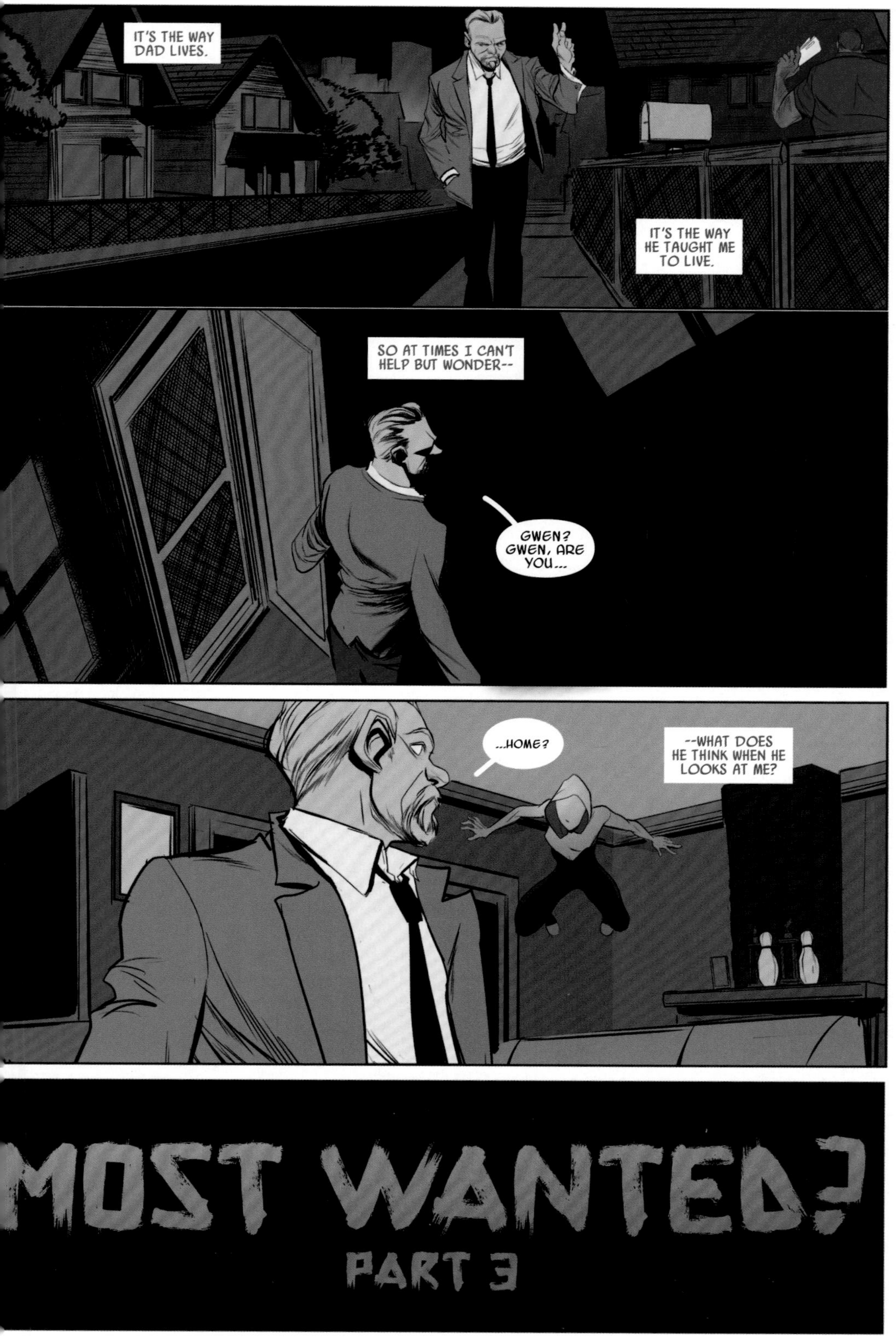
IT'S THE WAY DAD LIVES.
IT'S THE WAY HE TAUGHT ME TO LIVE.
SO AT TIMES I CAN'T HELP BUT WONDER--
GWEN? GWEN, ARE YOU...
...HOME?
--WHAT DOES HE THINK WHEN HE LOOKS AT ME?
MOST WANTED?
PART 3

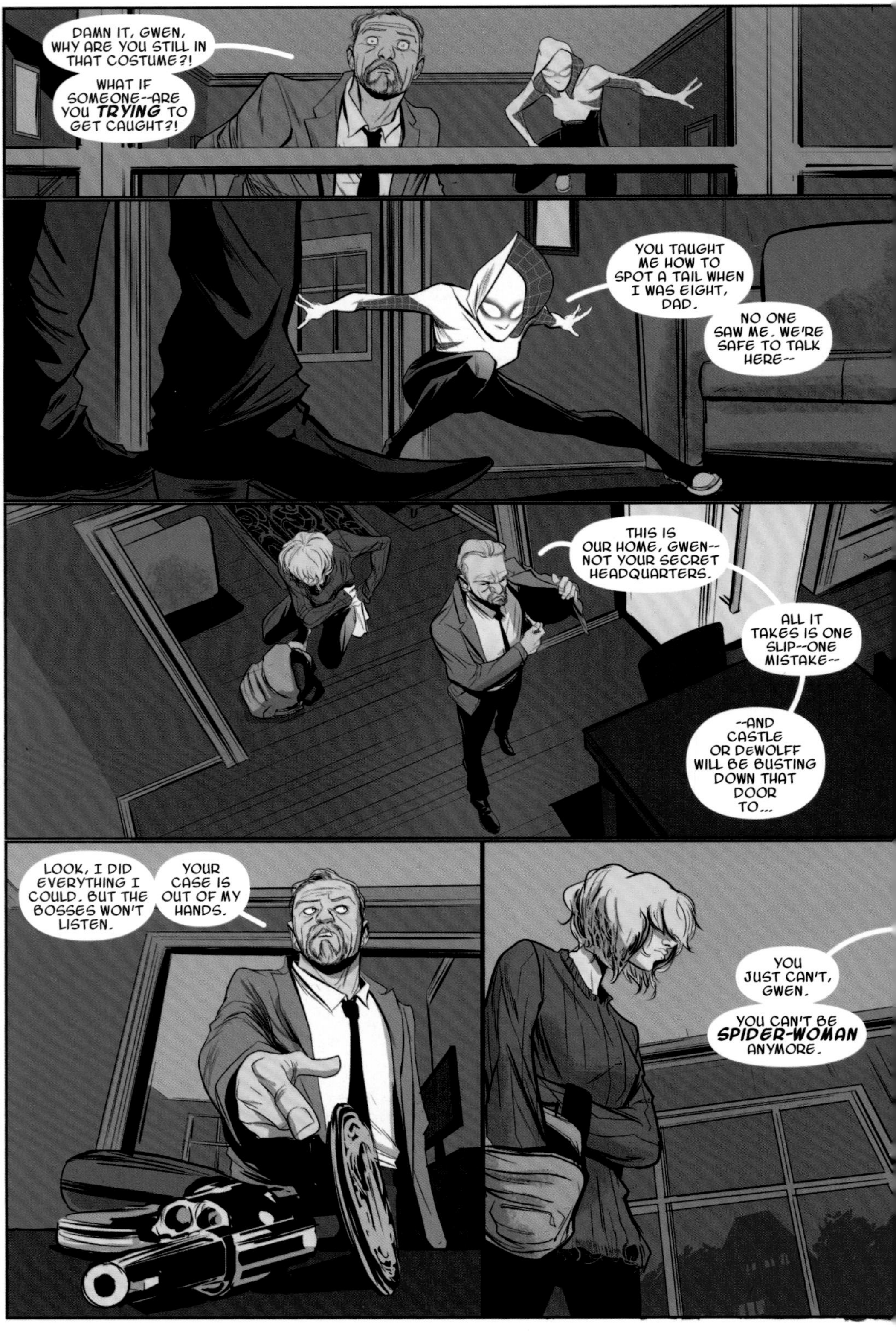
DAMN IT, GWEN, WHY ARE YOU STILL IN THAT COSTUME?!
WHAT IF SOMEONE--ARE YOU TRYING TO GET CAUGHT?!
YOU TAUGHT ME HOW TO SPOT A TAIL WHEN I WAS EIGHT, DAD.
NO ONE SAW ME. WE'RE SAFE TO TALK HERE--
THIS IS OUR HOME, GWEN--NOT YOUR SECRET HEADQUARTERS.
ALL IT TAKES IS ONE SLIP--ONE MISTAKE--
--AND CASTLE OR DEWOLFF WILL BE BUSTING DOWN THAT DOOR TO...
LOOK, I DID EVERYTHING I COULD. BUT THE BOSSES WON'T LISTEN.
YOUR CASE IS OUT OF MY HANDS.
YOU JUST CAN'T, GWEN.
YOU CAN'T BE SPIDER-WOMAN ANYMORE.

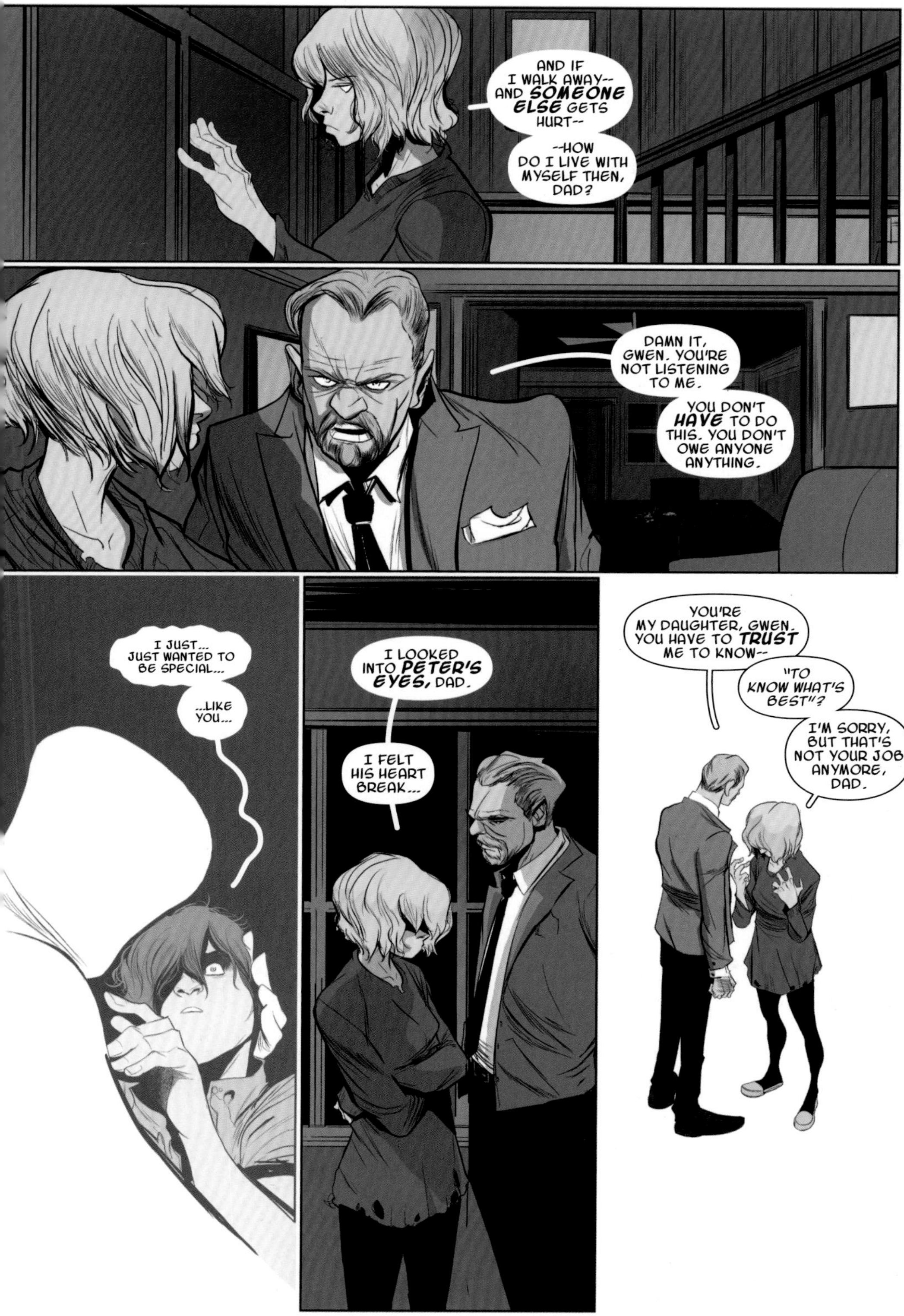
AND IF I WALK AWAY-- AND SOMEONE ELSE GETS HURT--
--HOW DO I LIVE WITH MYSELF THEN, DAD?
DAMN IT, GWEN. YOU'RE NOT LISTENING TO ME.
YOU DON'T HAVE TO DO THIS. YOU DON'T OWE ANYONE ANYTHING.
I JUST... JUST WANTED TO BE SPECIAL...
...LIKE YOU...
I LOOKED INTO PETER'S EYES, DAD.
I FELT HIS HEART BREAK...
YOU'RE MY DAUGHTER, GWEN. YOU HAVE TO TRUST ME TO KNOW--
"TO KNOW WHAT'S BEST"?
I'M SORRY, BUT THAT'S NOT YOUR JOB ANYMORE, DAD.

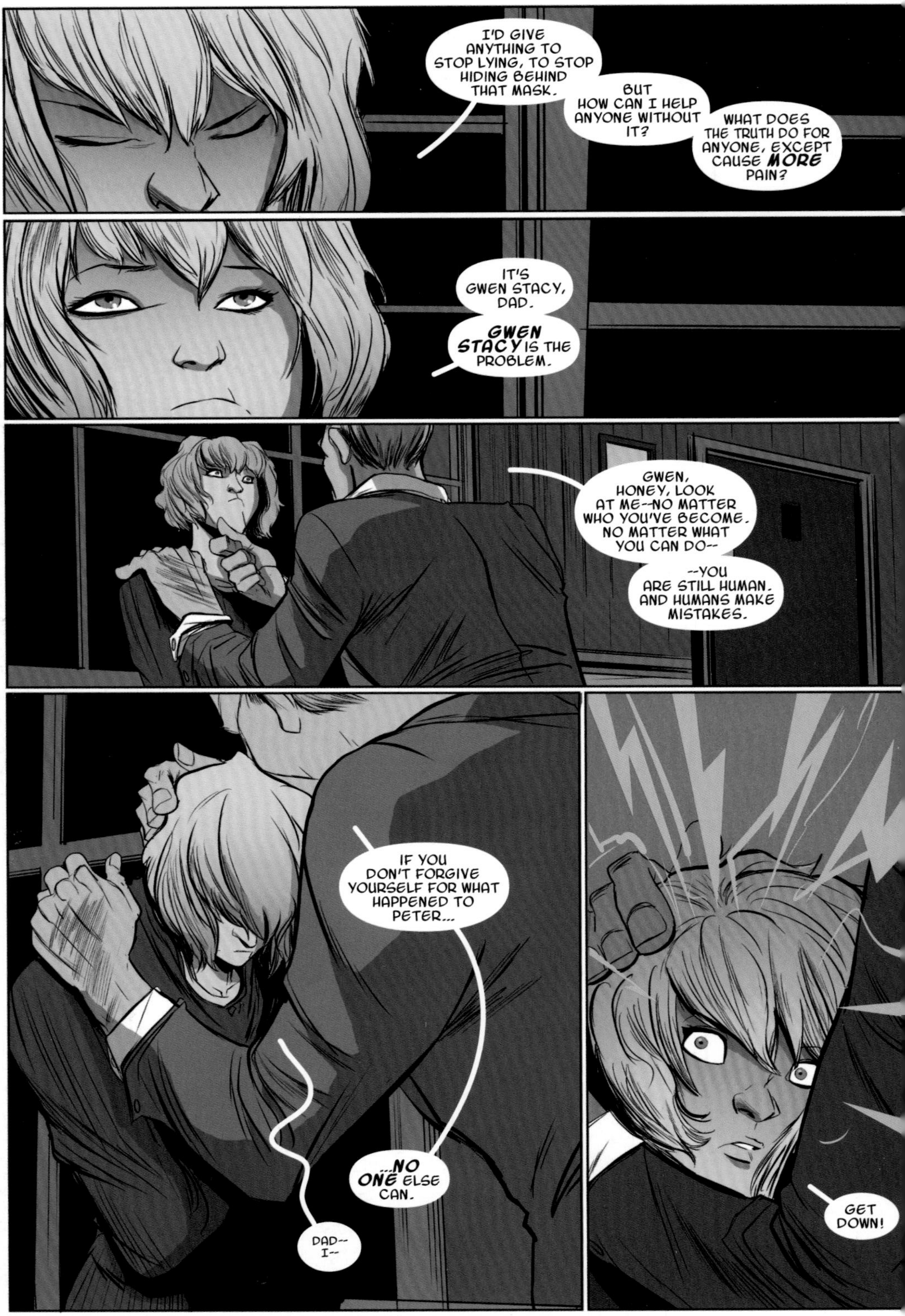
I'D GIVE ANYTHING TO STOP LYING, TO STOP HIDING BEHIND THAT MASK.
BUT HOW CAN I HELP ANYONE WITHOUT IT?
WHAT DOES THE TRUTH DO FOR ANYONE, EXCEPT CAUSE **MORE** PAIN?
IT'S GWEN STACY, DAD.
GWEN STACY IS THE PROBLEM.
GWEN, HONEY, LOOK AT ME--NO MATTER WHO YOU'VE BECOME. NO MATTER WHAT YOU CAN DO--
--YOU ARE STILL HUMAN. AND HUMANS MAKE MISTAKES.
IF YOU DON'T FORGIVE YOURSELF FOR WHAT HAPPENED TO PETER...
...**NO ONE** ELSE CAN.
DAD-- I--
GET DOWN!

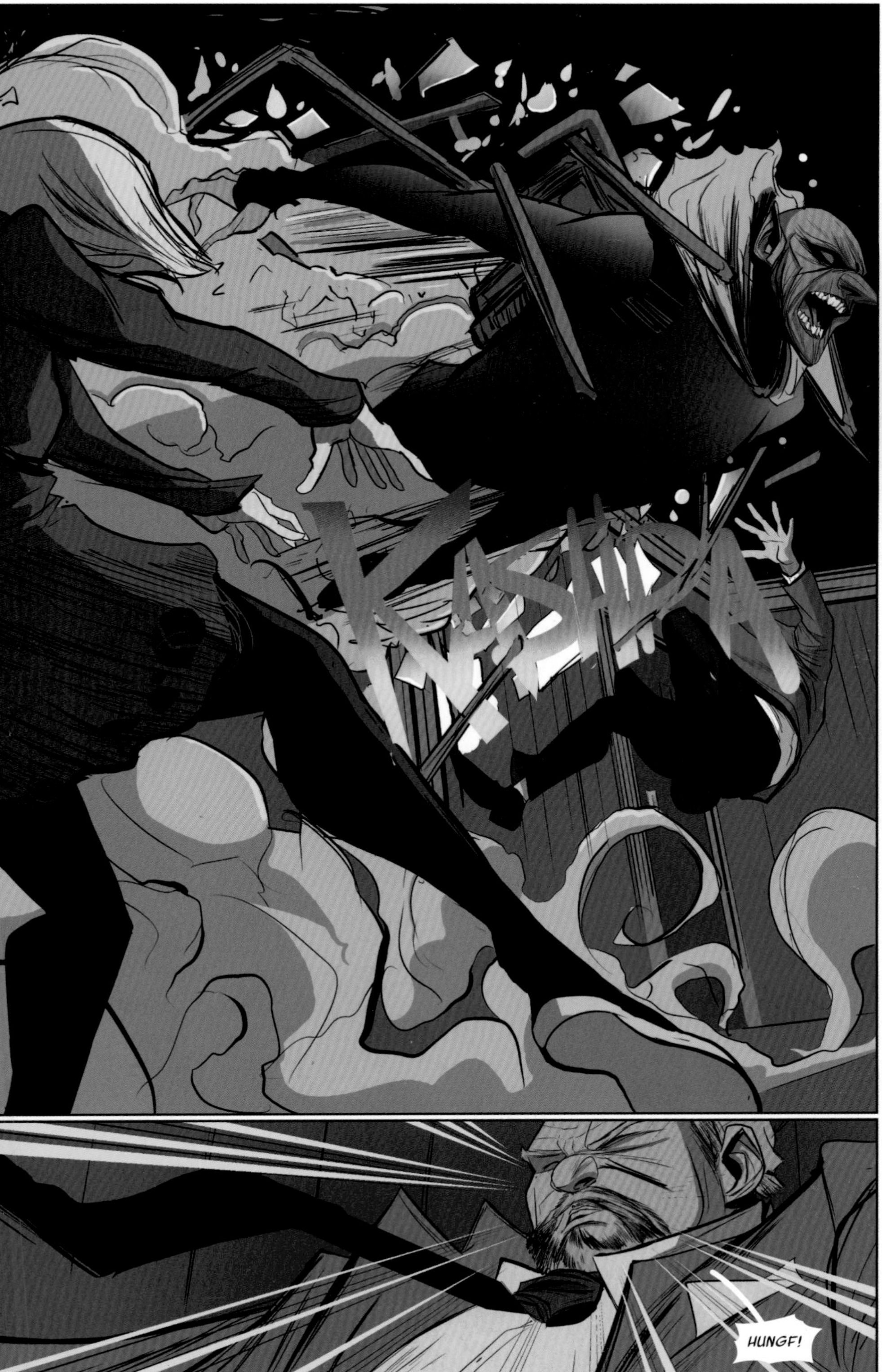
HUNGF!

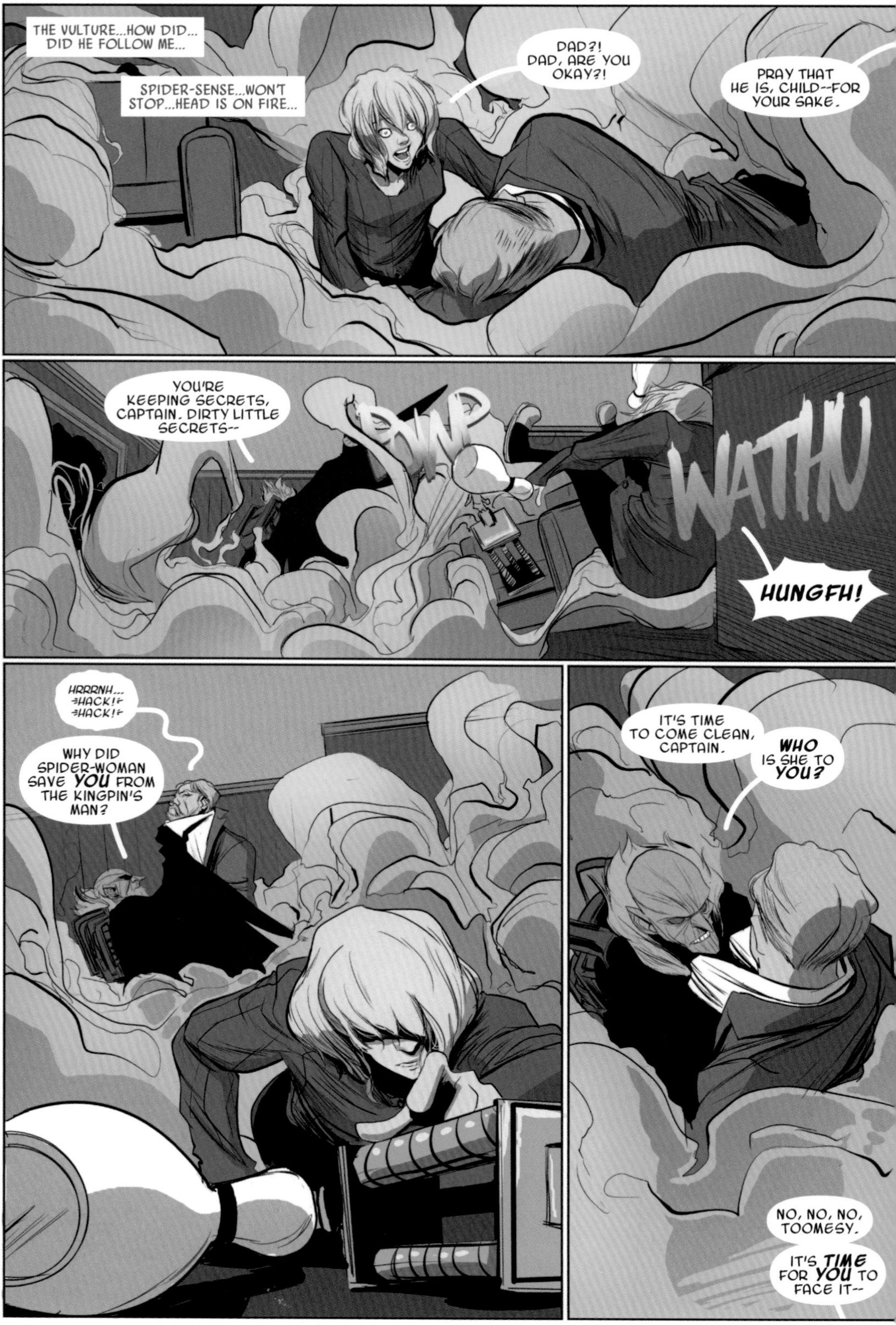
THE VULTURE...HOW DID... DID HE FOLLOW ME...
SPIDER-SENSE...WON'T STOP...HEAD IS ON FIRE...
DAD?! DAD, ARE YOU OKAY?!
PRAY THAT HE IS, CHILD--FOR YOUR SAKE.
YOU'RE KEEPING SECRETS, CAPTAIN. DIRTY LITTLE SECRETS--
WATHU
HUNGFH!
HRRRNH... HACK! HACK!
WHY DID SPIDER-WOMAN SAVE YOU FROM THE KINGPIN'S MAN?
IT'S TIME TO COME CLEAN, CAPTAIN.
WHO IS SHE TO YOU?
NO, NO, NO, TOOMESY.
IT'S TIME FOR YOU TO FACE IT--

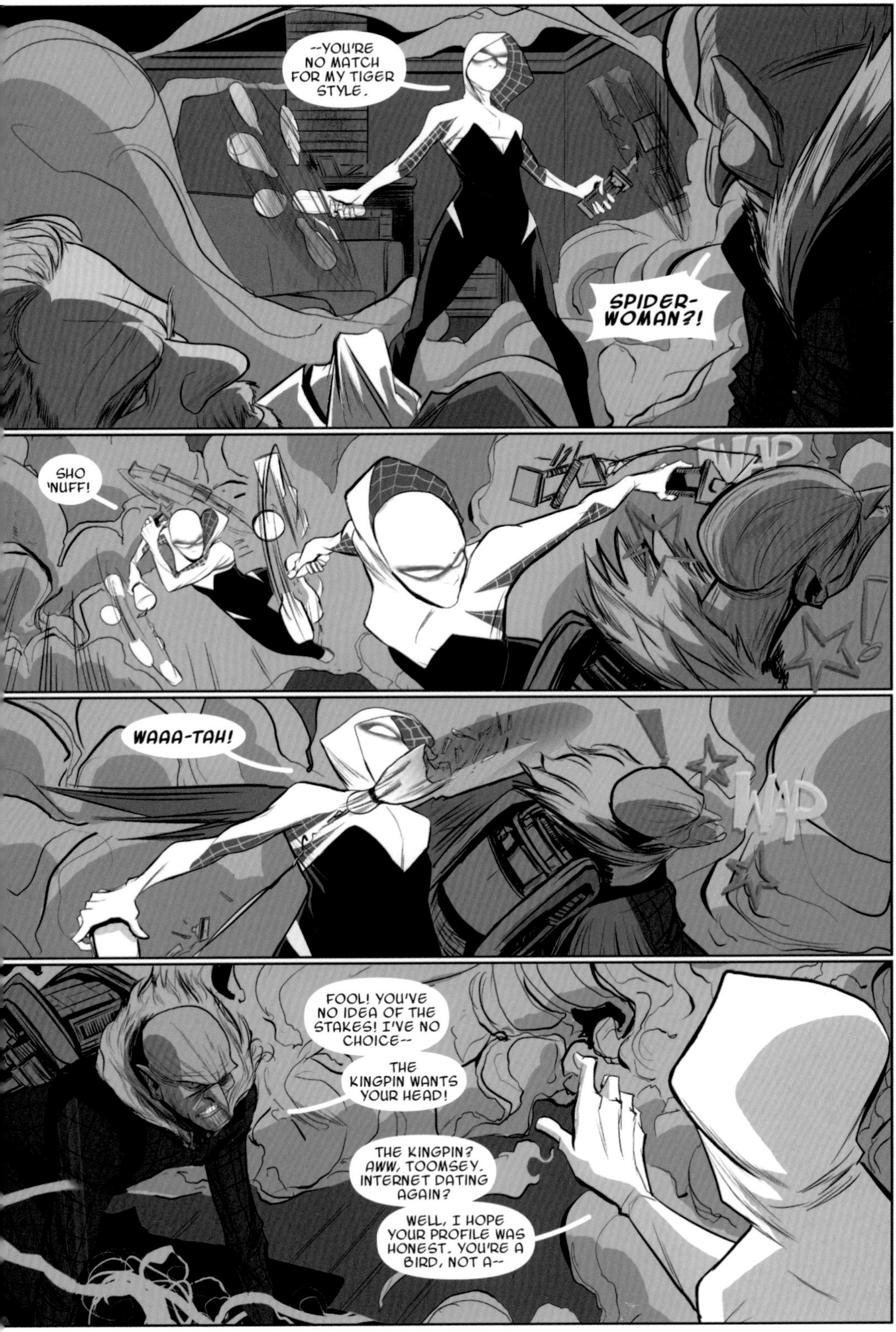
--YOU'RE NO MATCH FOR MY TIGER STYLE.
SPIDER-WOMAN?!
SHO 'NUFF!
WAP
WAAA-TAH!
WAP
FOOL! YOU'VE NO IDEA OF THE STAKES! I'VE NO CHOICE--
THE KINGPIN WANTS YOUR HEAD!
THE KINGPIN? AWW, TOOMSEY. INTERNET DATING AGAIN?
WELL, I HOPE YOUR PROFILE WAS HONEST. YOU'RE A BIRD, NOT A--

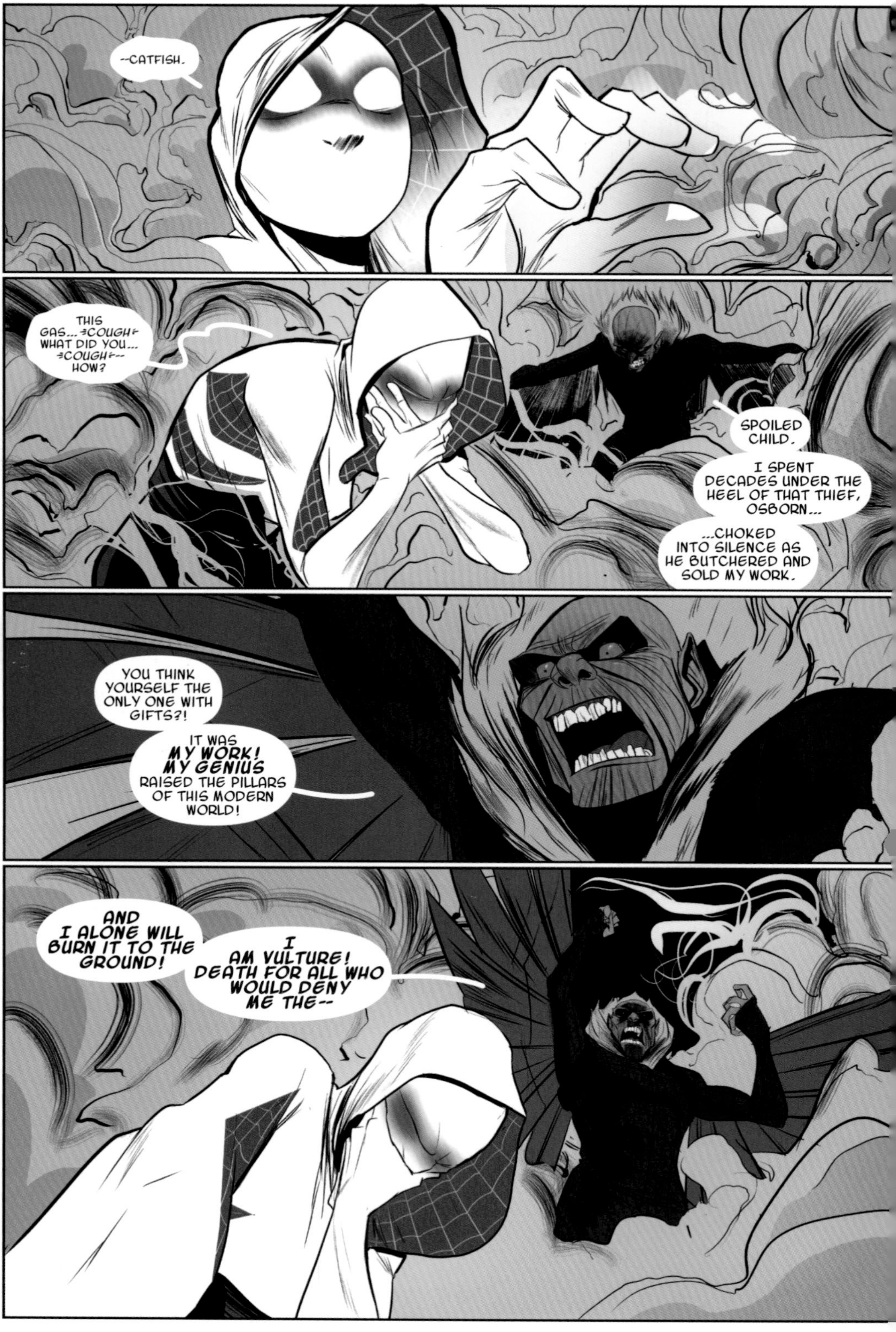
--CATFISH.
THIS GAS... ≠COUGH≠ WHAT DID YOU... ≠COUGH≠-- HOW?
SPOILED CHILD.
I SPENT DECADES UNDER THE HEEL OF THAT THIEF, OSBORN...
...CHOKED INTO SILENCE AS HE BUTCHERED AND SOLD MY WORK.
YOU THINK YOURSELF THE ONLY ONE WITH GIFTS?!
IT WAS MY WORK! MY GENIUS RAISED THE PILLARS OF THIS MODERN WORLD!
AND I ALONE WILL BURN IT TO THE GROUND!
I AM VULTURE! DEATH FOR ALL WHO WOULD DENY ME THE--

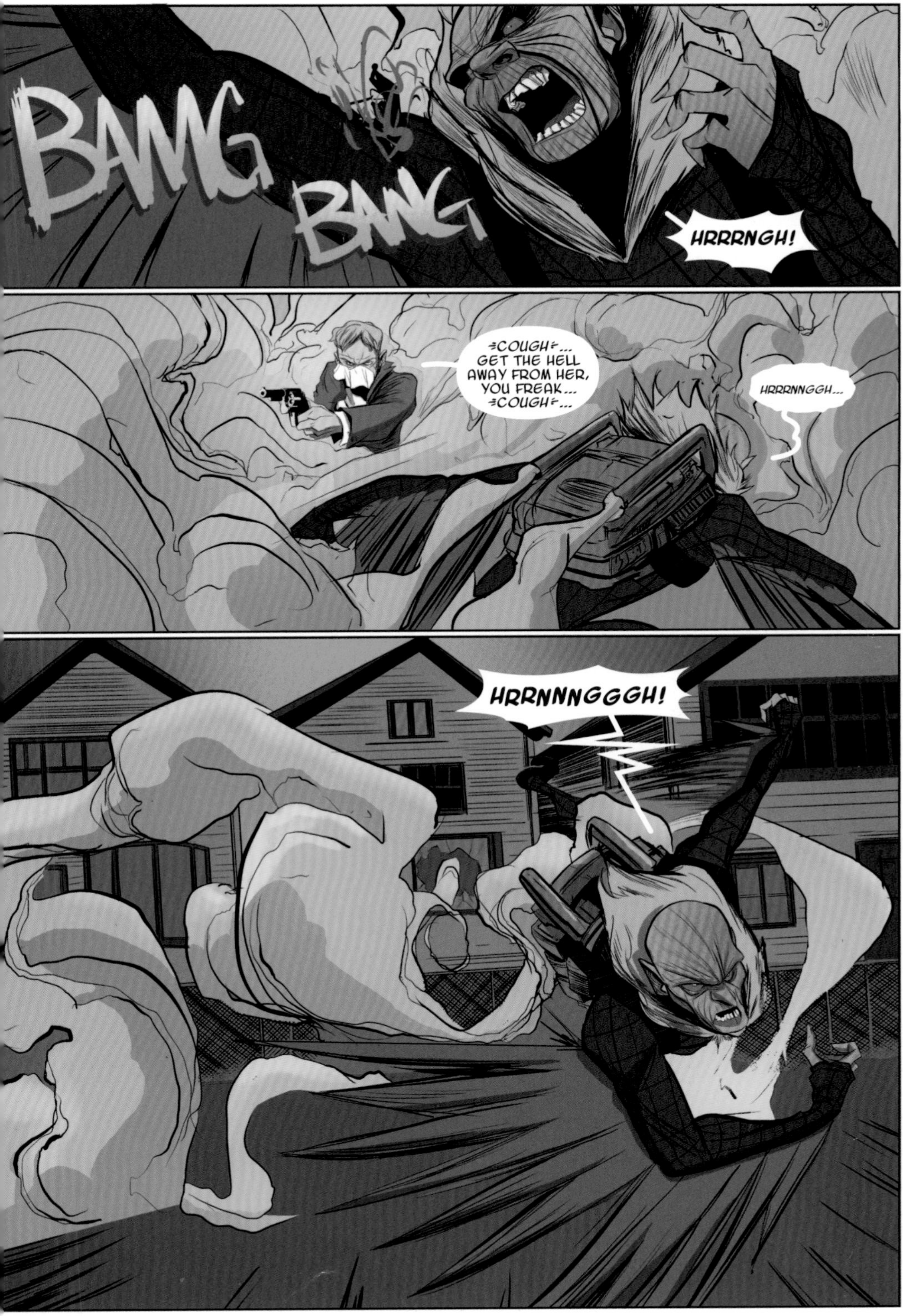
BANG
BANG
HRRRNGH!
=COUGH=... GET THE HELL AWAY FROM HER, YOU FREAK... =COUGH=...
HRRRNNGGH...
HRRNNNGGGH!

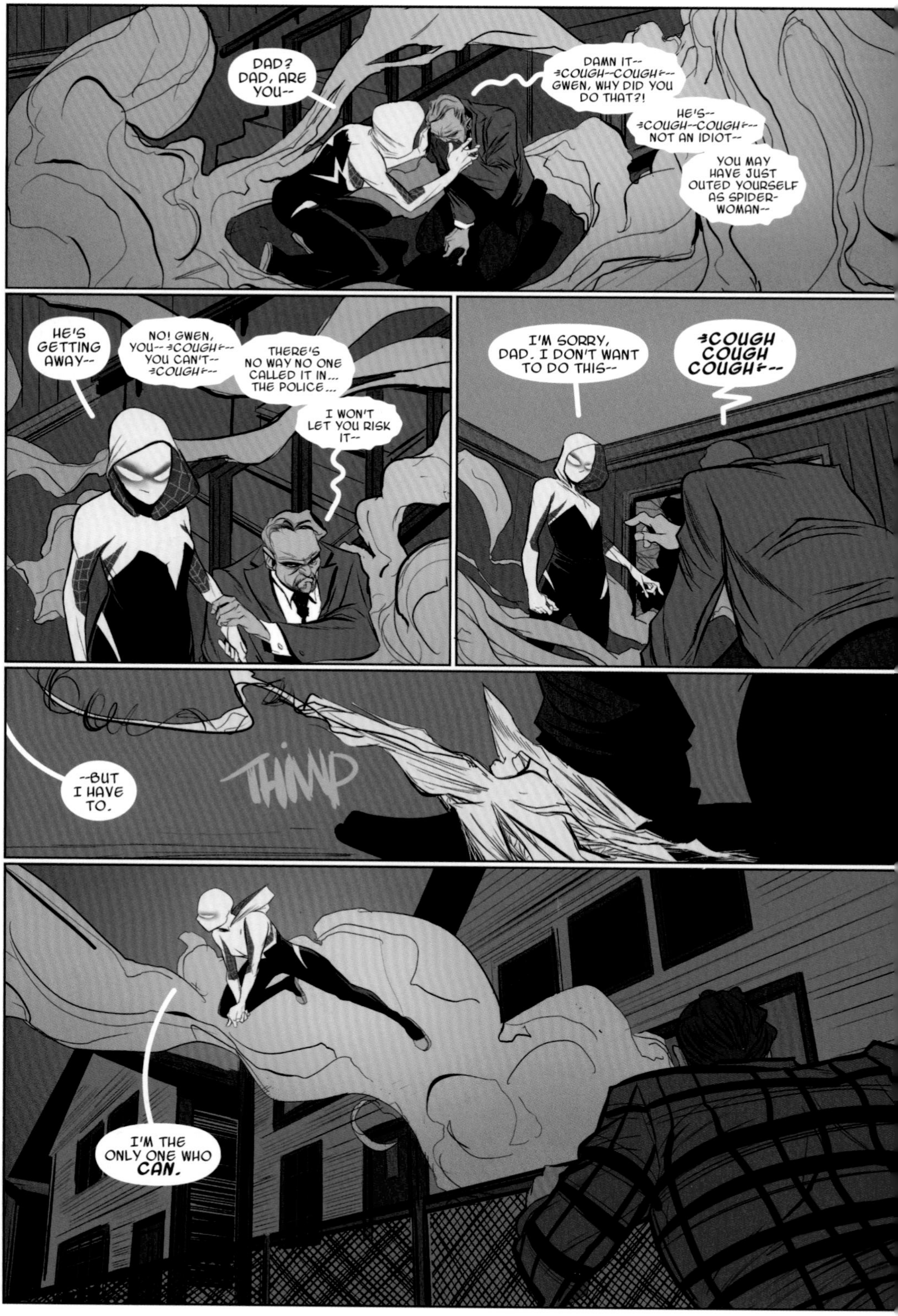

DAD? DAD, ARE YOU--
DAMN IT-- ≥COUGH--COUGH≤-- GWEN, WHY DID YOU DO THAT?!
HE'S-- ≥COUGH--COUGH≤-- NOT AN IDIOT--
YOU MAY HAVE JUST OUTED YOURSELF AS SPIDER-WOMAN--
HE'S GETTING AWAY--
NO! GWEN, YOU-- ≥COUGH≤-- YOU CAN'T-- ≥COUGH≤--
THERE'S NO WAY NO ONE CALLED IT IN... THE POLICE...
I WON'T LET YOU RISK IT--
I'M SORRY, DAD. I DON'T WANT TO DO THIS--
≥COUGH COUGH COUGH≤--
--BUT I HAVE TO.
THWP
I'M THE ONLY ONE WHO CAN.

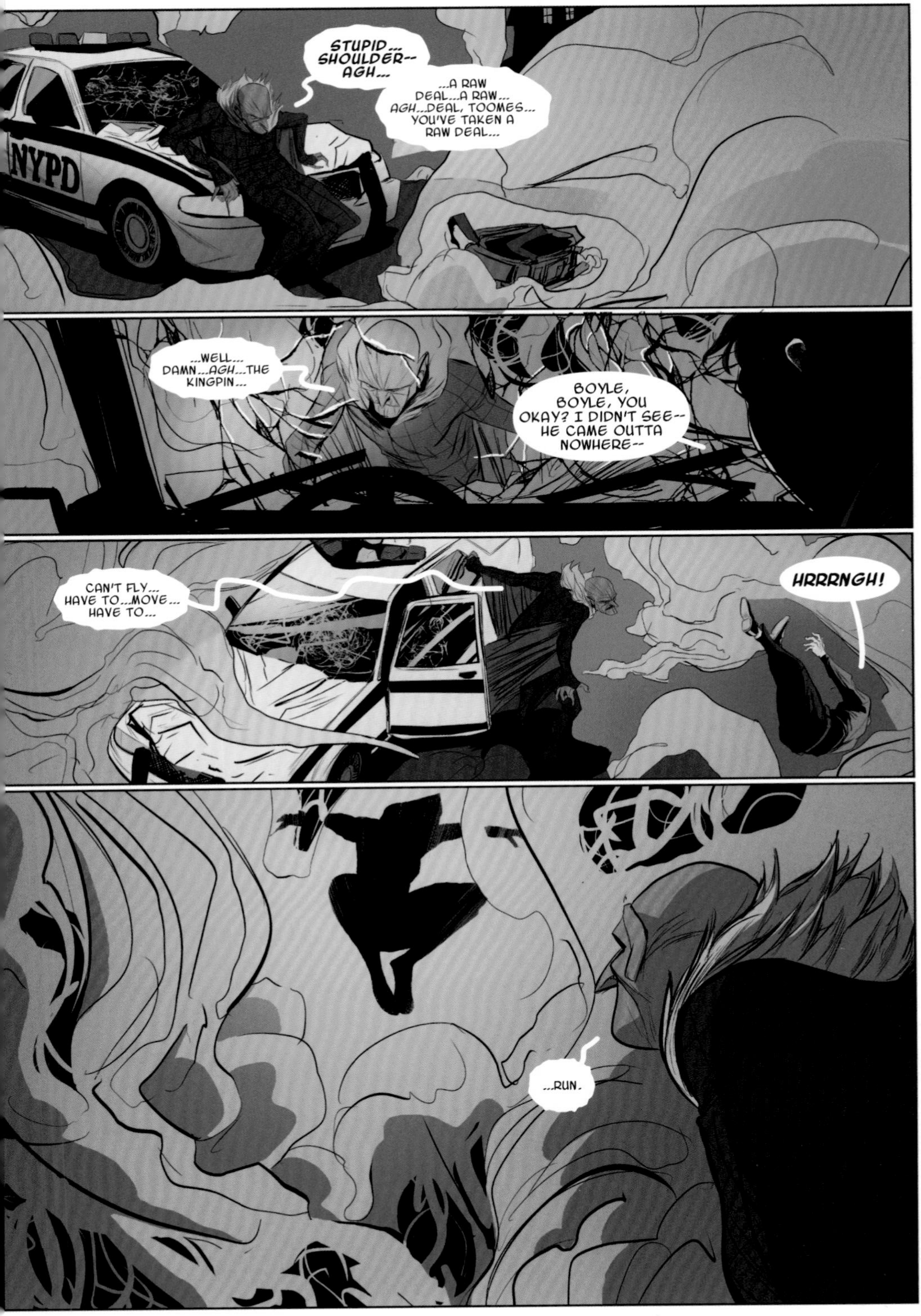
STUPID... SHOULDER-- AGH...
...A RAW DEAL...A RAW... AGH...DEAL, TOOMES... YOU'VE TAKEN A RAW DEAL...
...WELL... DAMN...AGH...THE KINGPIN...
BOYLE, BOYLE, YOU OKAY? I DIDN'T SEE-- HE CAME OUTTA NOWHERE--
CAN'T FLY... HAVE TO...MOVE... HAVE TO...
HRRRNGH!
...RUN.

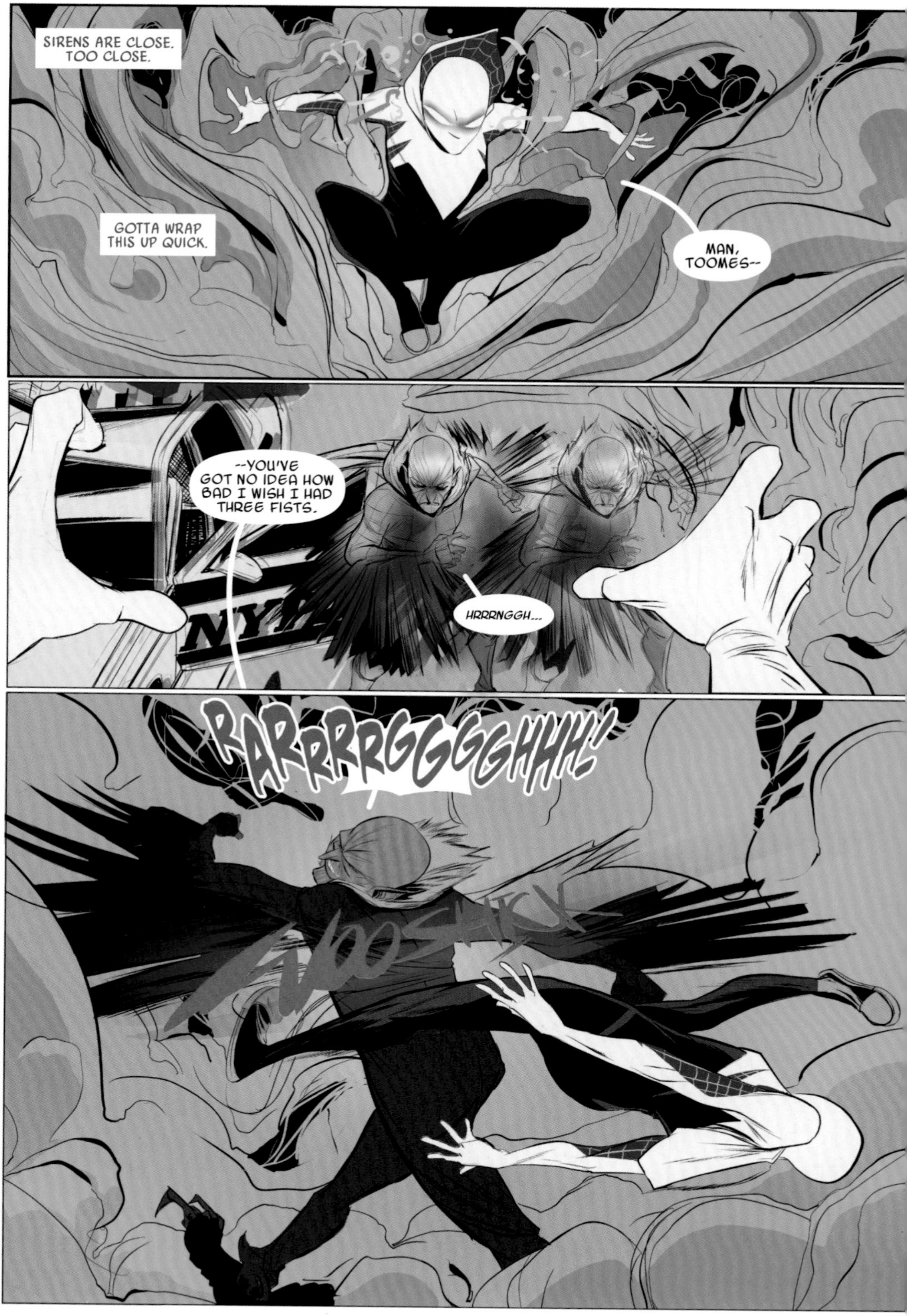

SIRENS ARE CLOSE. TOO CLOSE.
GOTTA WRAP THIS UP QUICK.
MAN, TOOMES--
--YOU'VE GOT NO IDEA HOW BAD I WISH I HAD THREE FISTS.
HRRRNGGH...
RARRRGGGGHHH!

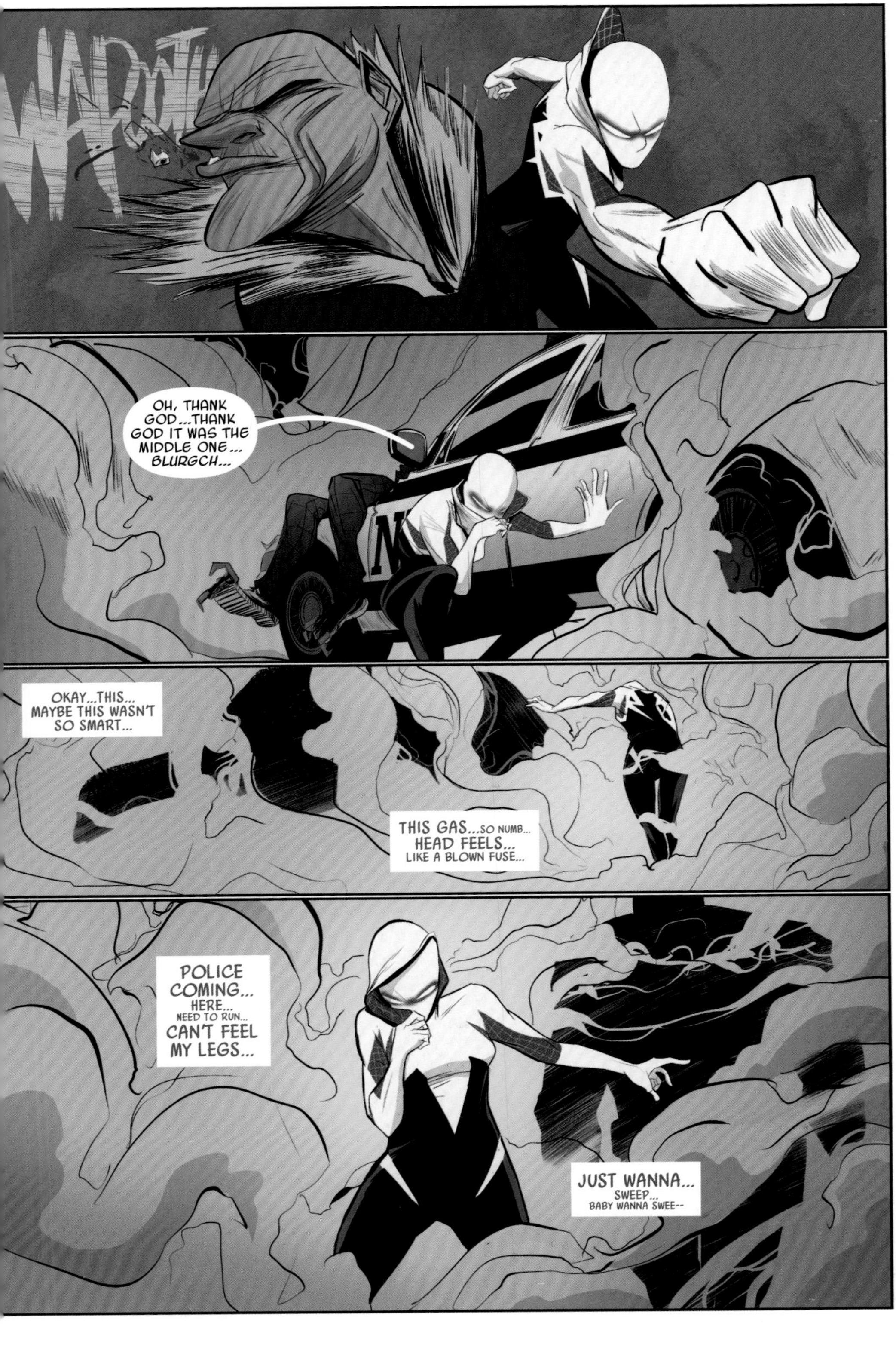
OH, THANK GOD...THANK GOD IT WAS THE MIDDLE ONE... BLURGCH...
OKAY...THIS... MAYBE THIS WASN'T SO SMART...
THIS GAS...SO NUMB... HEAD FEELS... LIKE A BLOWN FUSE...
POLICE COMING... HERE... NEED TO RUN... CAN'T FEEL MY LEGS...
JUST WANNA... SWEEP... BABY WANNA SWEE--

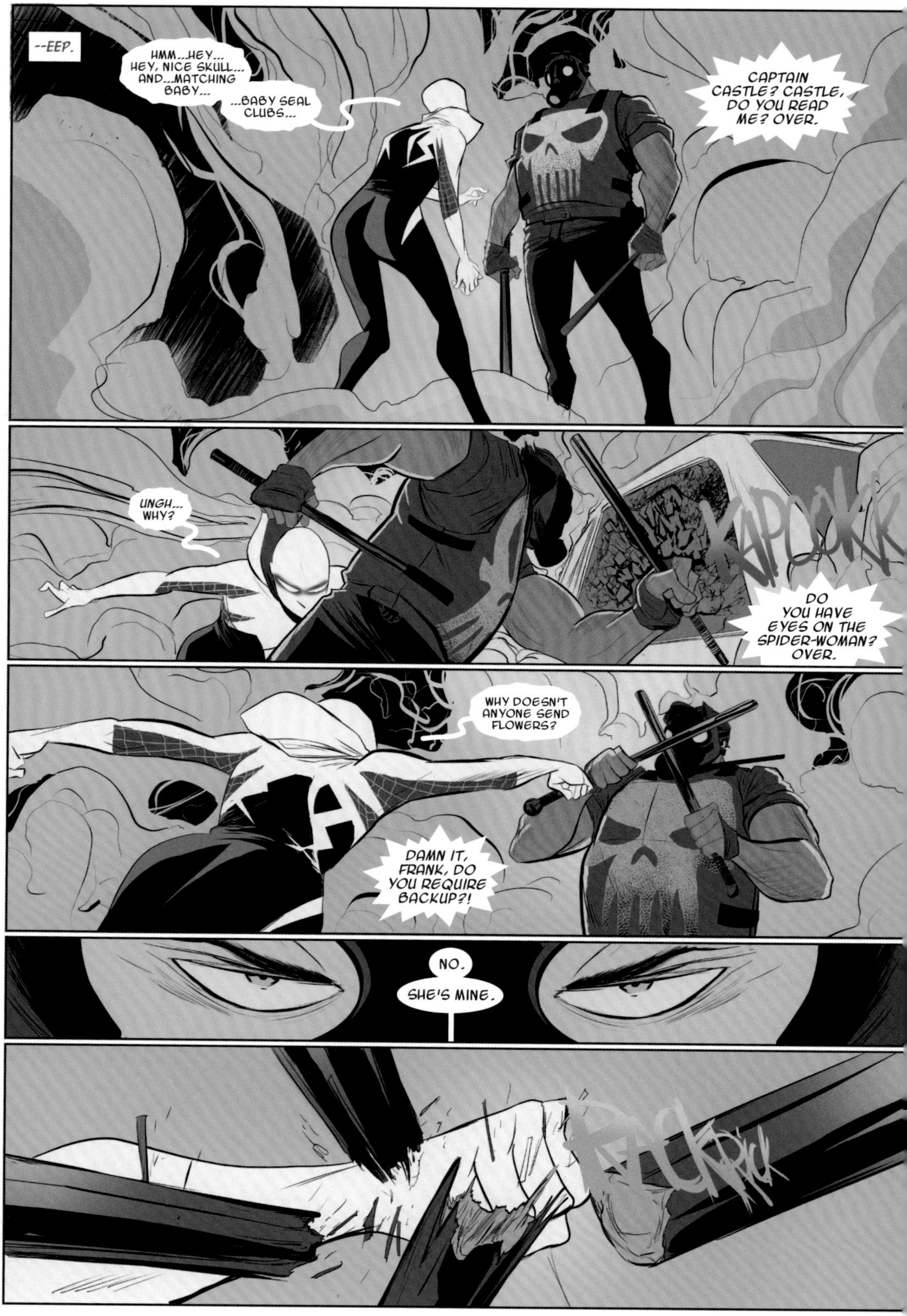
--EEP.
HMM...HEY... HEY, NICE SKULL... AND...MATCHING BABY...
...BABY SEAL CLUBS...
CAPTAIN CASTLE? CASTLE, DO YOU READ ME? OVER.
UNGH... WHY?
KAPOOKK
DO YOU HAVE EYES ON THE SPIDER-WOMAN? OVER.
WHY DOESN'T ANYONE SEND FLOWERS?
DAMN IT, FRANK, DO YOU REQUIRE BACKUP?!
NO.
SHE'S MINE.

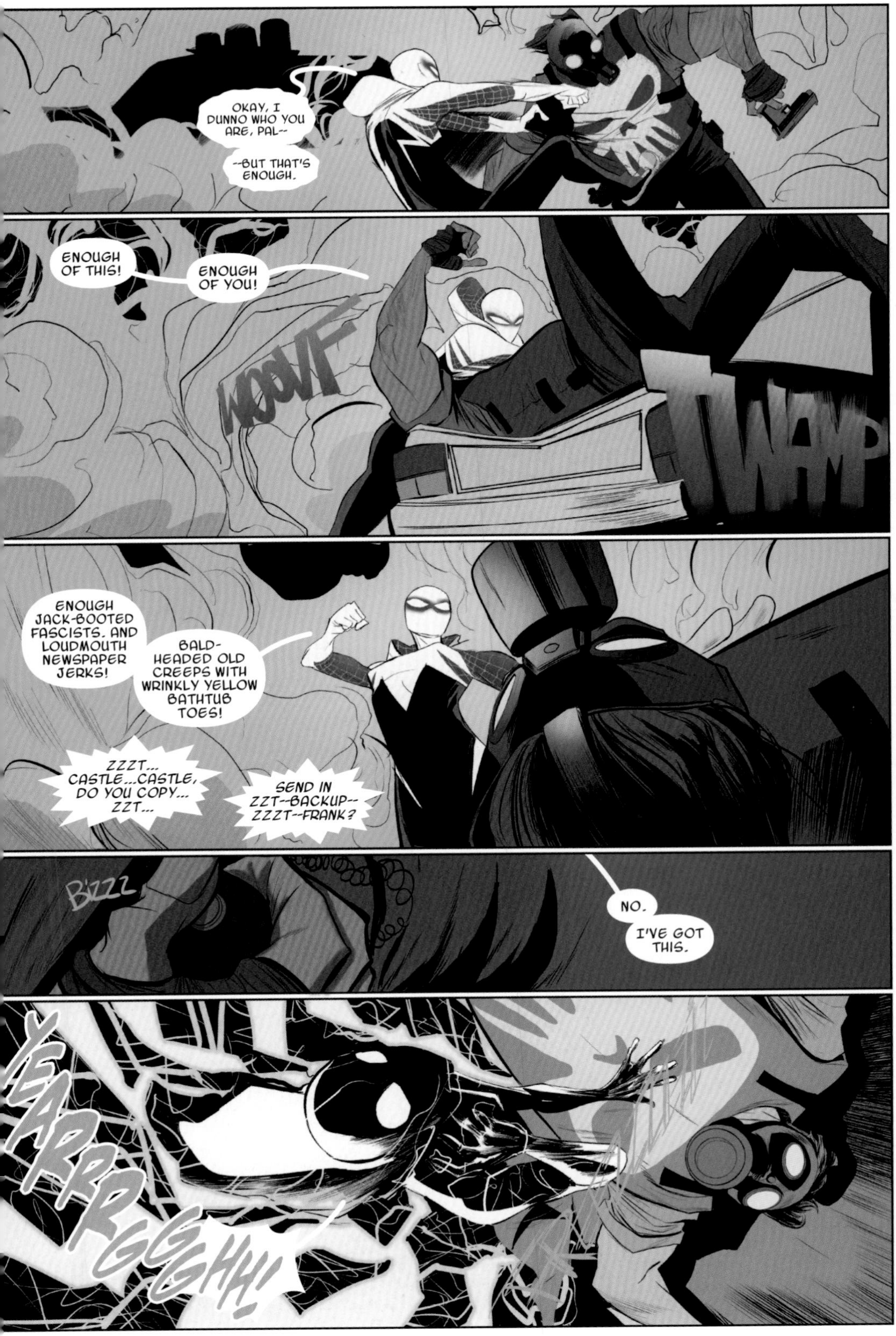
OKAY, I DUNNO WHO YOU ARE, PAL--
--BUT THAT'S ENOUGH.
ENOUGH OF THIS!
ENOUGH OF YOU!
WOOVF
TWAMP
ENOUGH JACK-BOOTED FASCISTS. AND LOUDMOUTH NEWSPAPER JERKS!
BALD-HEADED OLD CREEPS WITH WRINKLY YELLOW BATHTUB TOES!
ZZZT... CASTLE...CASTLE, DO YOU COPY... ZZT...
SEND IN ZZT--BACKUP-- ZZZT--FRANK?
BZZZ
NO.
I'VE GOT THIS.
YEARRRGGGHH!

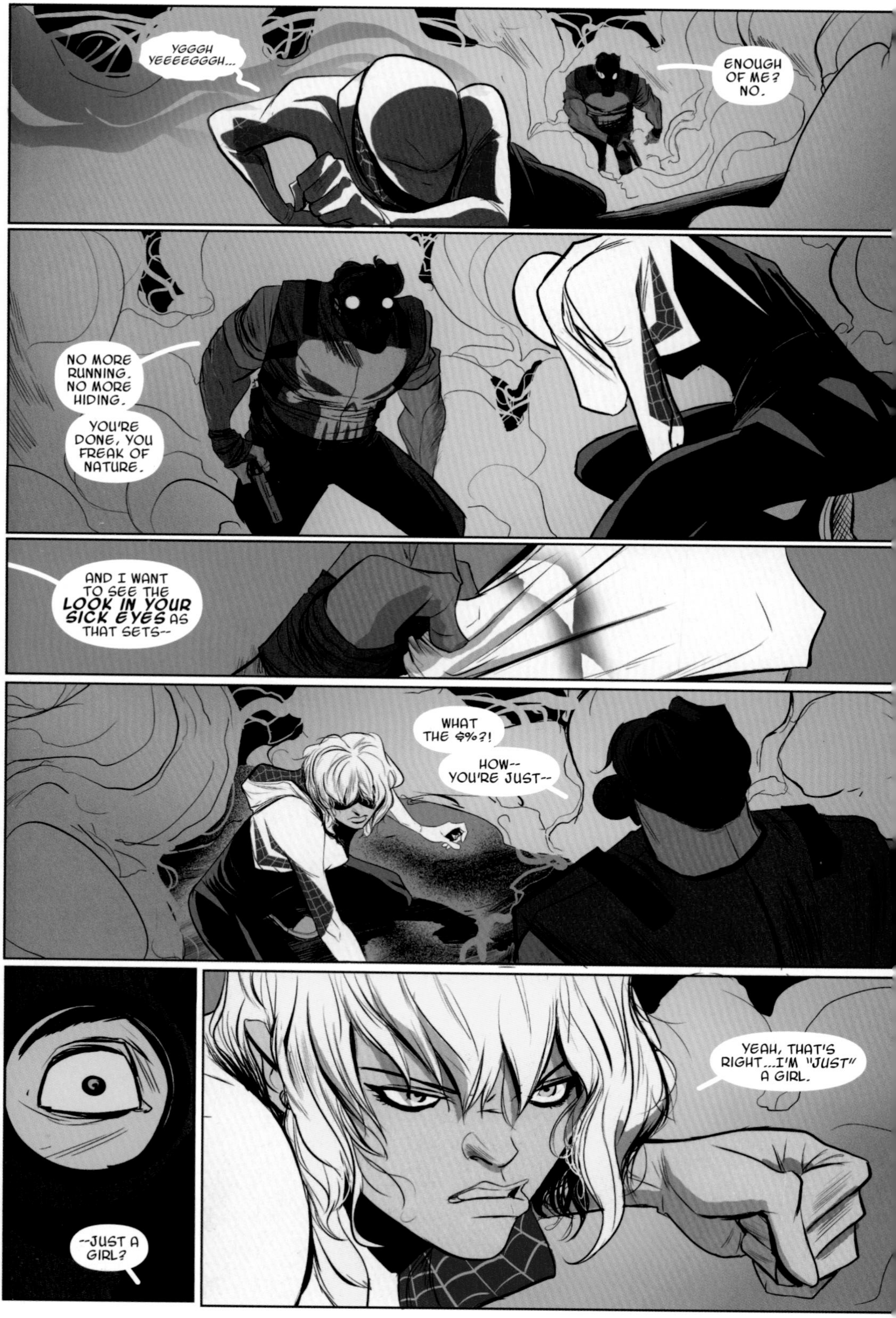
YGGGH YEEEEGGGH...
ENOUGH OF ME? NO.
NO MORE RUNNING. NO MORE HIDING.
YOU'RE DONE, YOU FREAK OF NATURE.
AND I WANT TO SEE THE LOOK IN YOUR SICK EYES AS THAT SETS--
WHAT THE $%?!
HOW-- YOU'RE JUST--
--JUST A GIRL?
YEAH, THAT'S RIGHT...I'M "JUST" A GIRL.

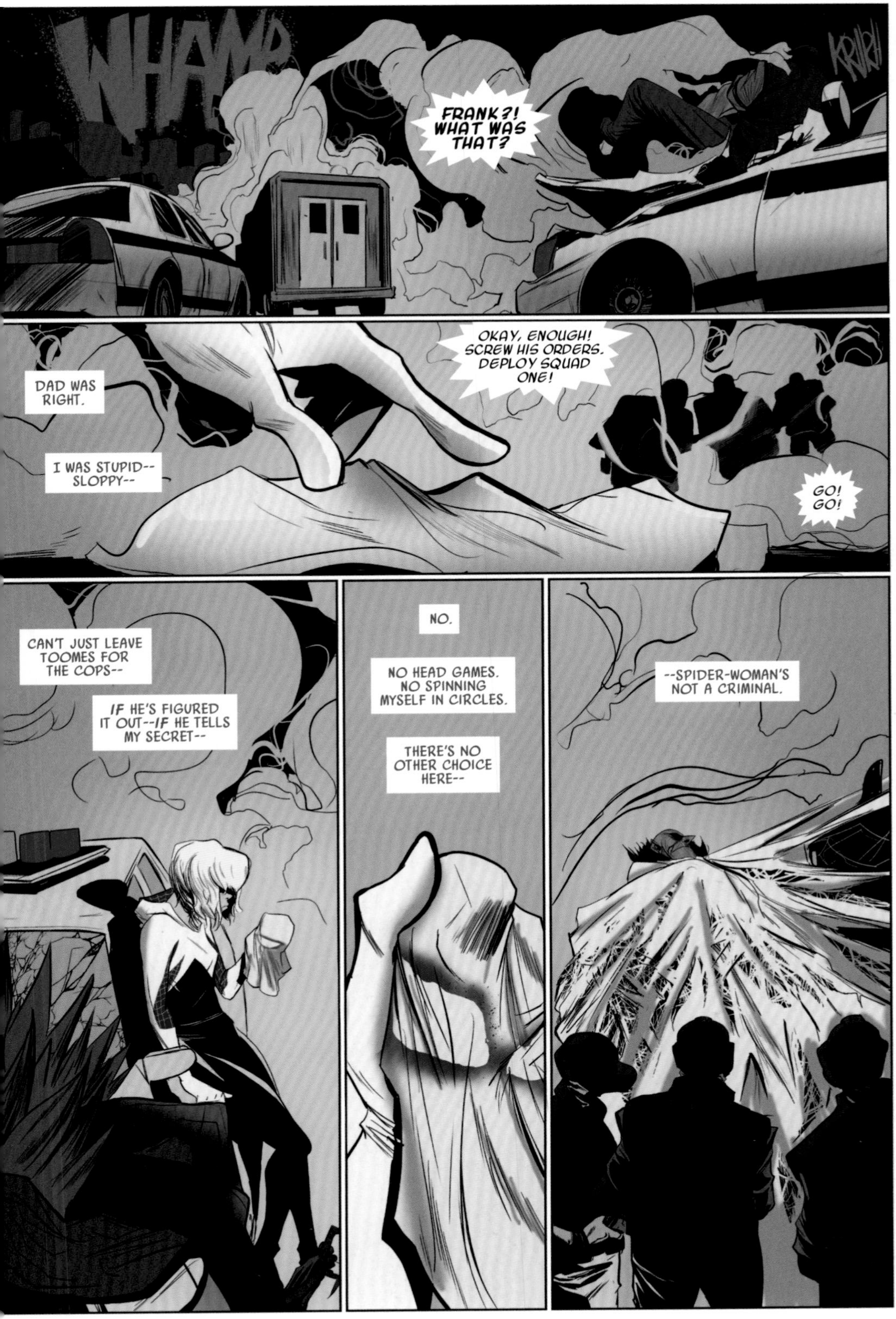
WHAMP
KRUNCH
FRANK?! WHAT WAS THAT?
DAD WAS RIGHT.
OKAY, ENOUGH! SCREW HIS ORDERS. DEPLOY SQUAD ONE!
I WAS STUPID-- SLOPPY--
GO! GO!
CAN'T JUST LEAVE TOOMES FOR THE COPS--
IF HE'S FIGURED IT OUT--IF HE TELLS MY SECRET--
NO.
NO HEAD GAMES. NO SPINNING MYSELF IN CIRCLES.
THERE'S NO OTHER CHOICE HERE--
--SPIDER-WOMAN'S NOT A CRIMINAL.

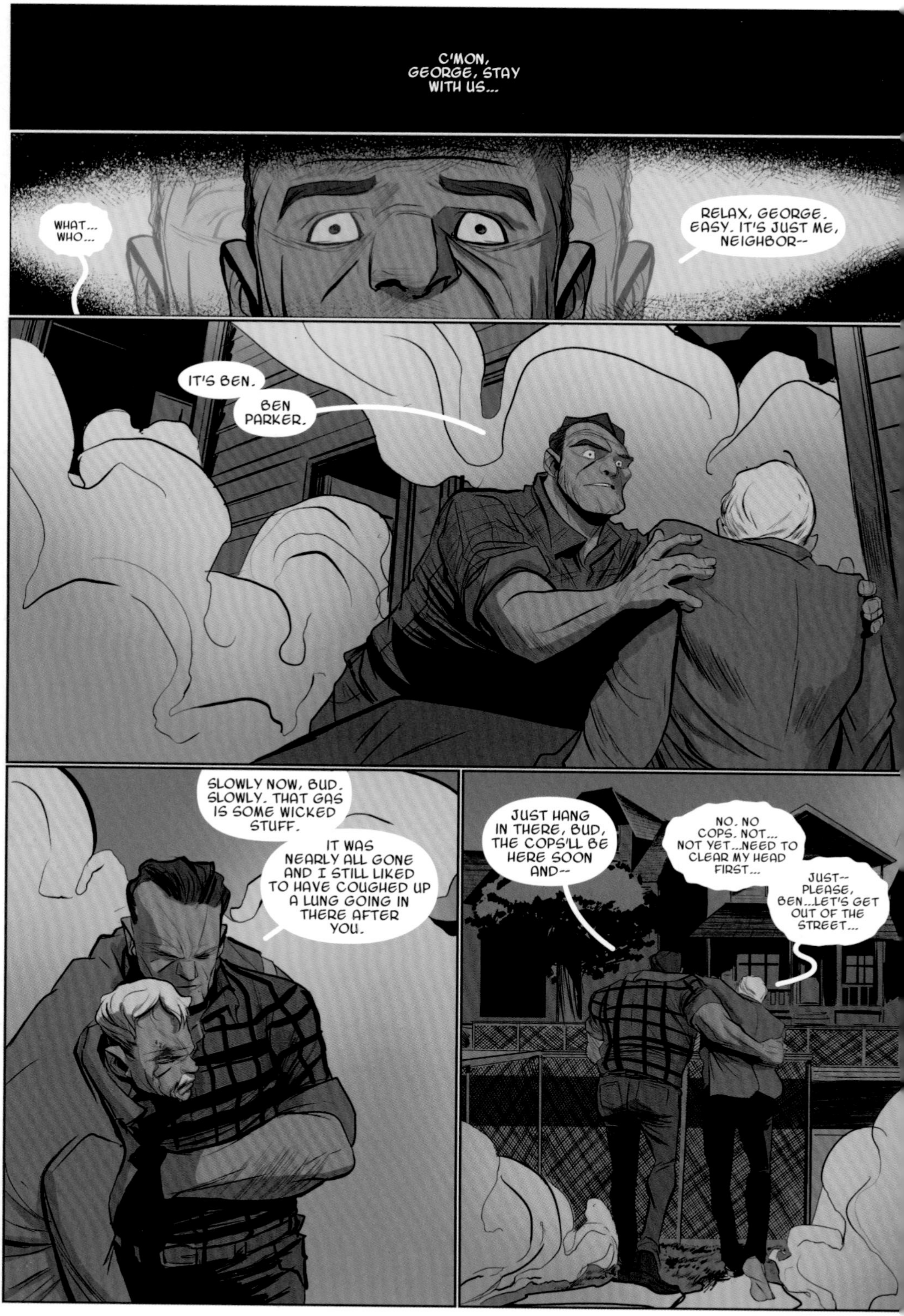
C'MON, GEORGE, STAY WITH US...
WHAT... WHO...
RELAX, GEORGE. EASY. IT'S JUST ME, NEIGHBOR--
IT'S BEN.
BEN PARKER.
SLOWLY NOW, BUD. SLOWLY. THAT GAS IS SOME WICKED STUFF.
IT WAS NEARLY ALL GONE AND I STILL LIKED TO HAVE COUGHED UP A LUNG GOING IN THERE AFTER YOU.
JUST HANG IN THERE, BUD, THE COPS'LL BE HERE SOON AND--
NO. NO COPS. NOT... NOT YET...NEED TO CLEAR MY HEAD FIRST...
JUST-- PLEASE, BEN...LET'S GET OUT OF THE STREET...

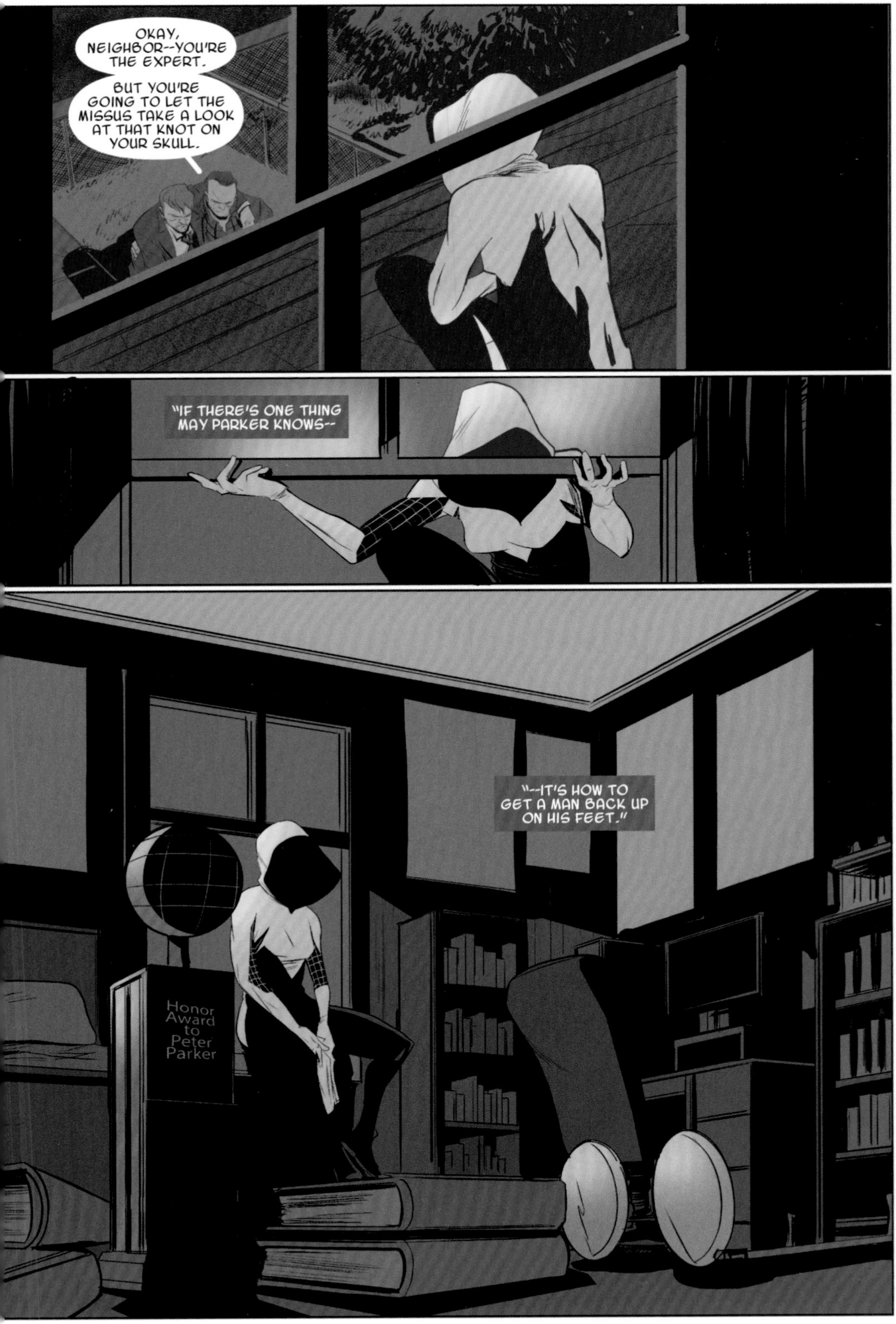
OKAY, NEIGHBOR--YOU'RE THE EXPERT.
BUT YOU'RE GOING TO LET THE MISSUS TAKE A LOOK AT THAT KNOT ON YOUR SKULL.
"IF THERE'S ONE THING MAY PARKER KNOWS--
"--IT'S HOW TO GET A MAN BACK UP ON HIS FEET."
Honor Award to Peter Parker

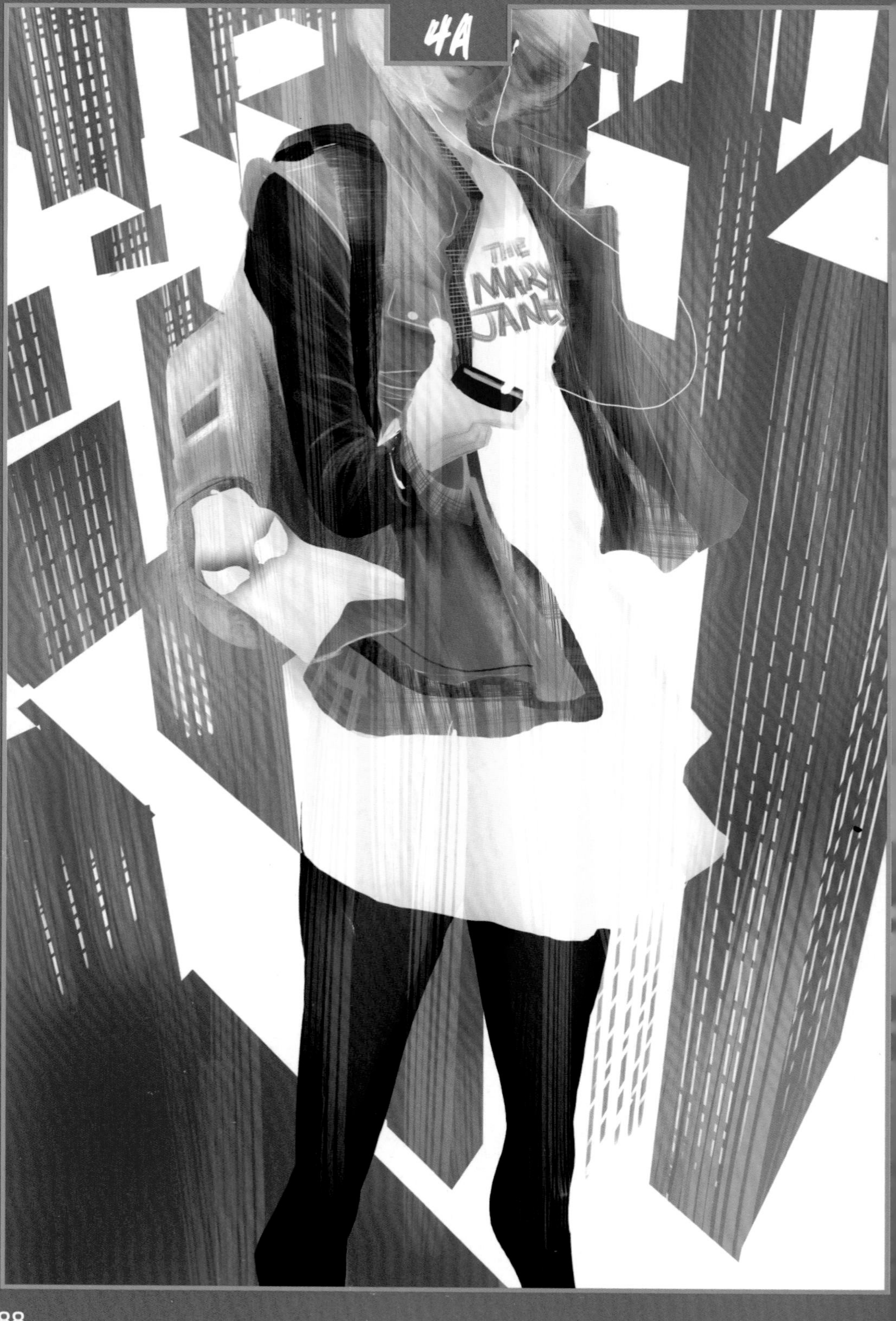
4A
THE
MARY
JANE

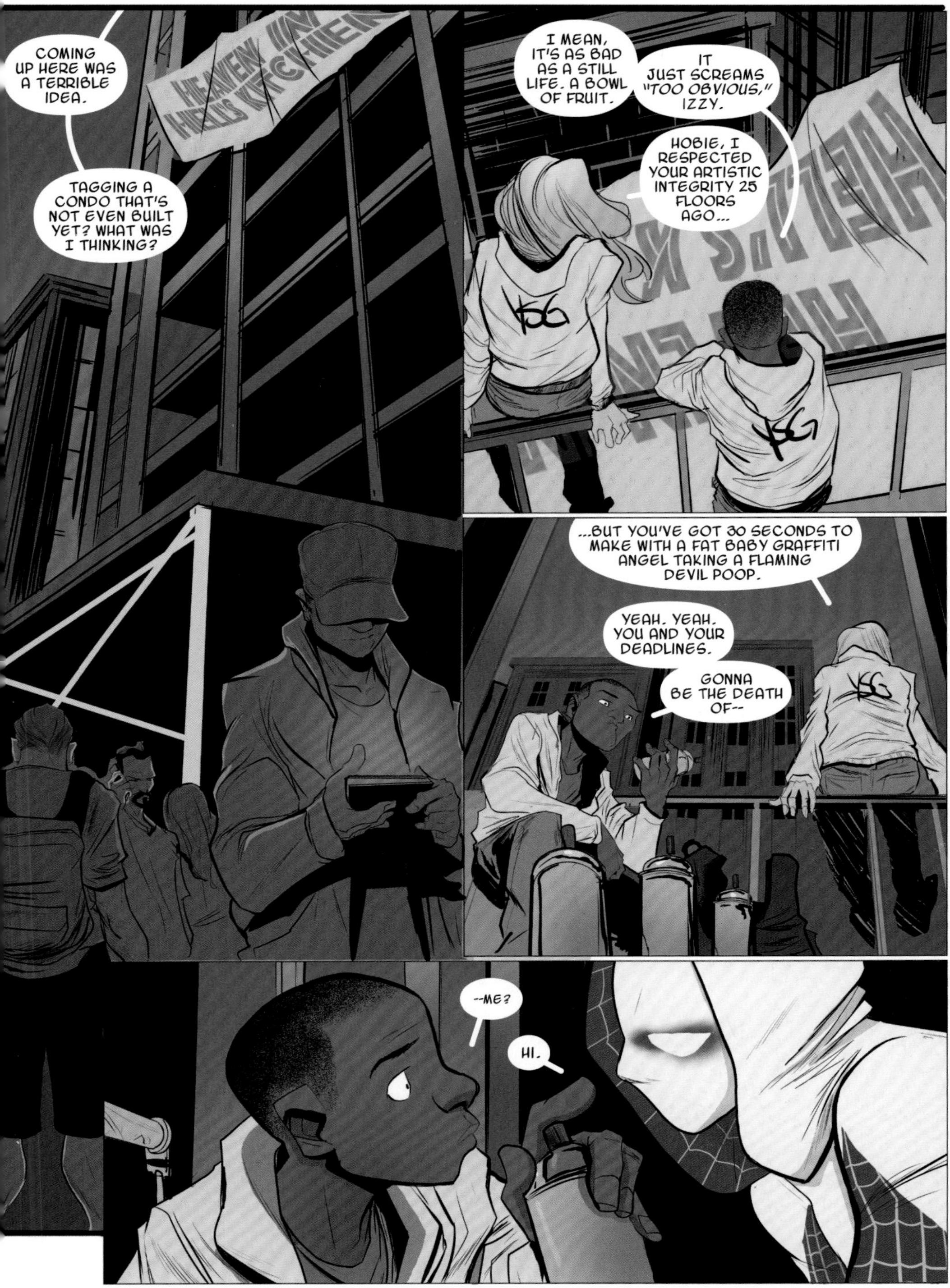
COMING UP HERE WAS A TERRIBLE IDEA.
TAGGING A CONDO THAT'S NOT EVEN BUILT YET? WHAT WAS I THINKING?
HEAVEN IN HELL'S KITCHEN
I MEAN, IT'S AS BAD AS A STILL LIFE. A BOWL OF FRUIT.
IT JUST SCREAMS "TOO OBVIOUS," IZZY.
HOBIE, I RESPECTED YOUR ARTISTIC INTEGRITY 25 FLOORS AGO...
...BUT YOU'VE GOT 30 SECONDS TO MAKE WITH A FAT BABY GRAFFITI ANGEL TAKING A FLAMING DEVIL POOP.
YEAH. YEAH. YOU AND YOUR DEADLINES.
GONNA BE THE DEATH OF--
--ME?
HI.

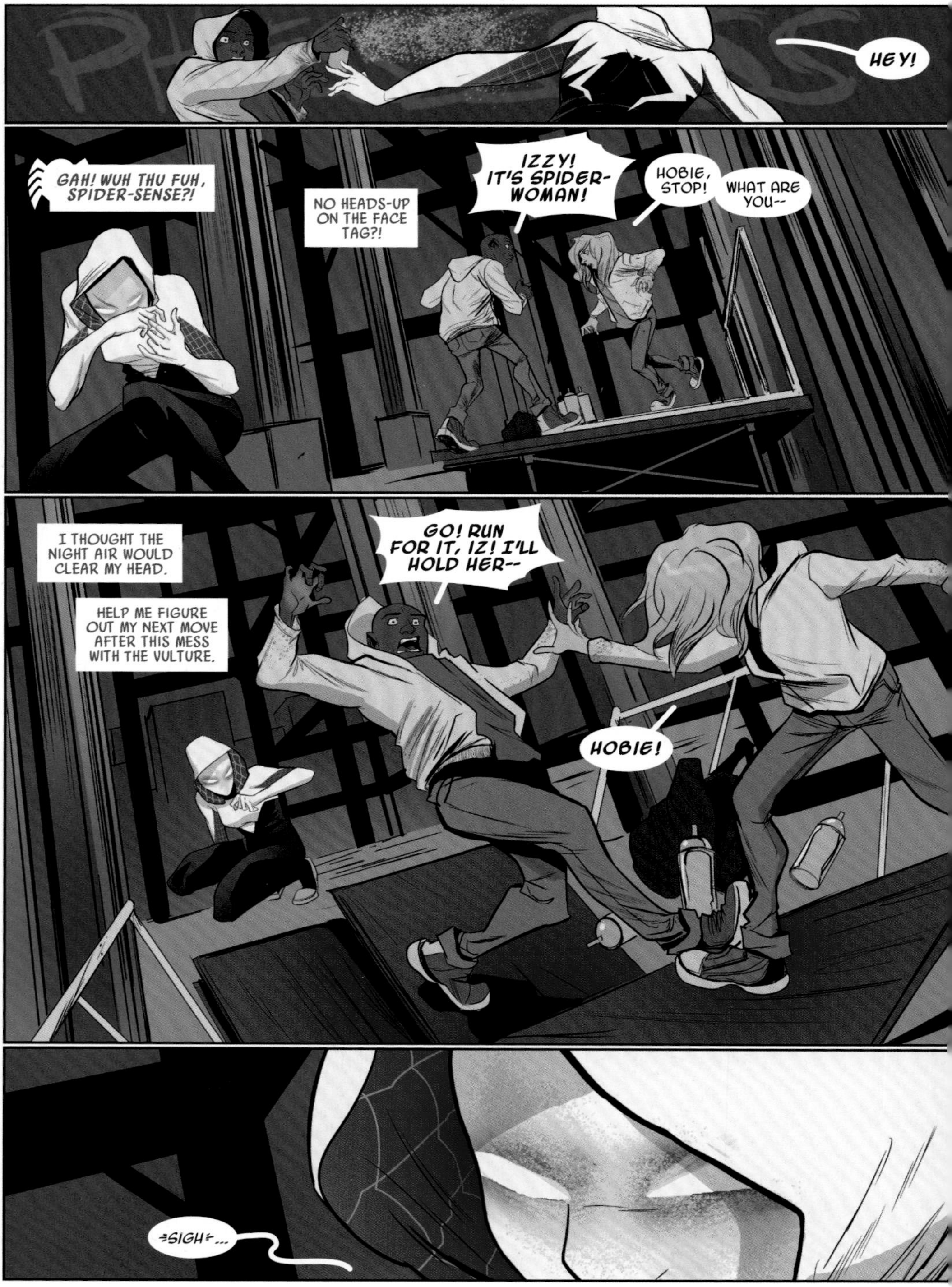
HEY!
GAH! WUH THU FUH, SPIDER-SENSE?!
NO HEADS-UP ON THE FACE TAG?!
IZZY! IT'S SPIDER-WOMAN!
HOBIE, STOP!
WHAT ARE YOU--
I THOUGHT THE NIGHT AIR WOULD CLEAR MY HEAD.
HELP ME FIGURE OUT MY NEXT MOVE AFTER THIS MESS WITH THE VULTURE.
GO! RUN FOR IT, IZ! I'LL HOLD HER--
HOBIE!
=SIGH=...

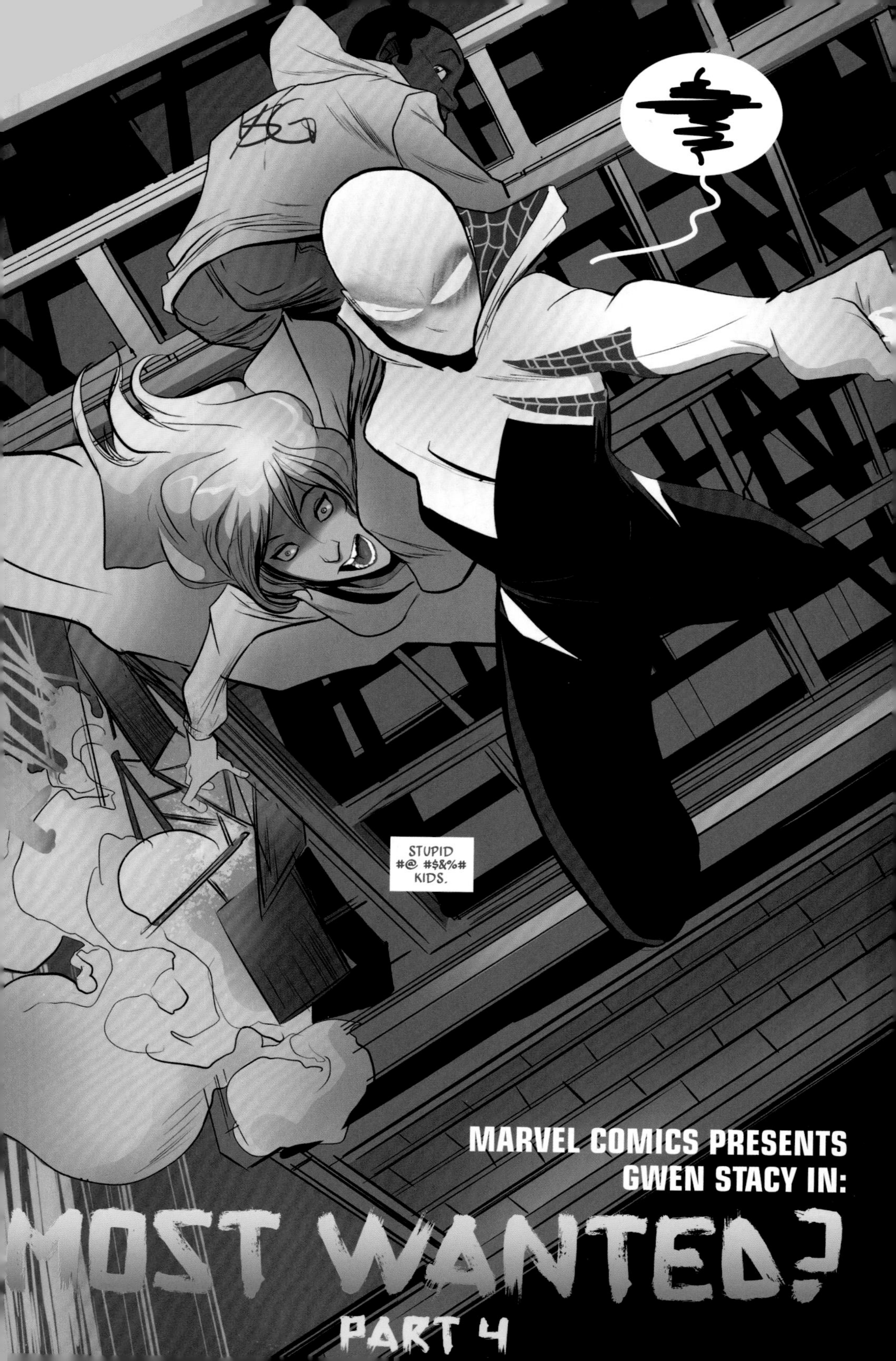
STUPID #@ #$&%# KIDS.
MARVEL COMICS PRESENTS GWEN STACY IN:
MOST WANTED?
PART 4

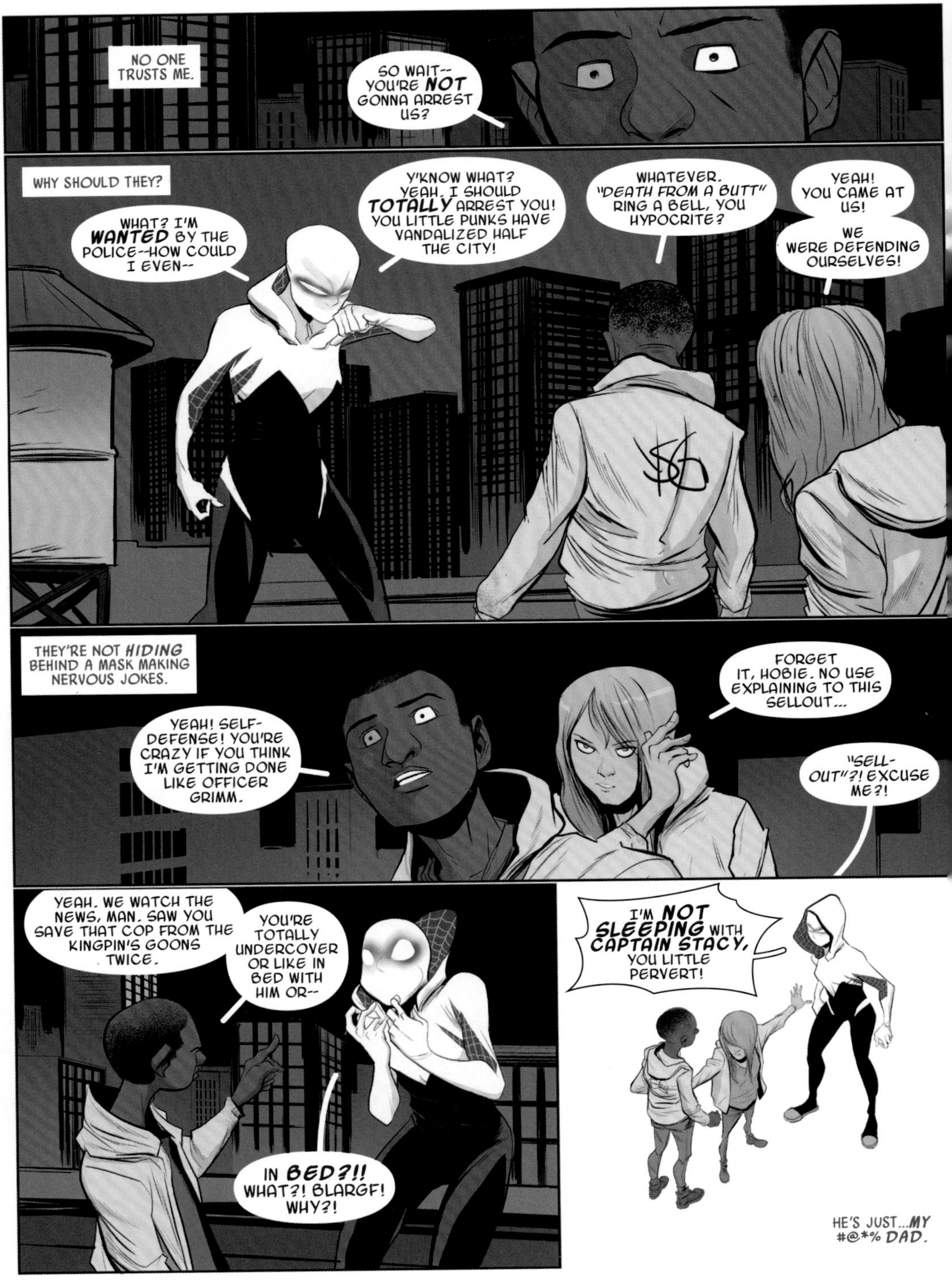
NO ONE TRUSTS ME.
SO WAIT-- YOU'RE NOT GONNA ARREST US?
WHY SHOULD THEY?
WHAT? I'M WANTED BY THE POLICE--HOW COULD I EVEN--
Y'KNOW WHAT? YEAH, I SHOULD TOTALLY ARREST YOU! YOU LITTLE PUNKS HAVE VANDALIZED HALF THE CITY!
WHATEVER. "DEATH FROM A BUTT" RING A BELL, YOU HYPOCRITE?
YEAH! YOU CAME AT US!
WE WERE DEFENDING OURSELVES!
THEY'RE NOT HIDING BEHIND A MASK MAKING NERVOUS JOKES.
YEAH! SELF-DEFENSE! YOU'RE CRAZY IF YOU THINK I'M GETTING DONE LIKE OFFICER GRIMM.
FORGET IT, HOBIE. NO USE EXPLAINING TO THIS SELLOUT...
"SELL-OUT"?! EXCUSE ME?!
YEAH. WE WATCH THE NEWS, MAN. SAW YOU SAVE THAT COP FROM THE KINGPIN'S GOONS TWICE.
YOU'RE TOTALLY UNDERCOVER OR LIKE IN BED WITH HIM OR--
IN BED?!! WHAT?! BLARGF! WHY?!
I'M NOT SLEEPING WITH CAPTAIN STACY, YOU LITTLE PERVERT!
HE'S JUST...MY #@*% DAD.

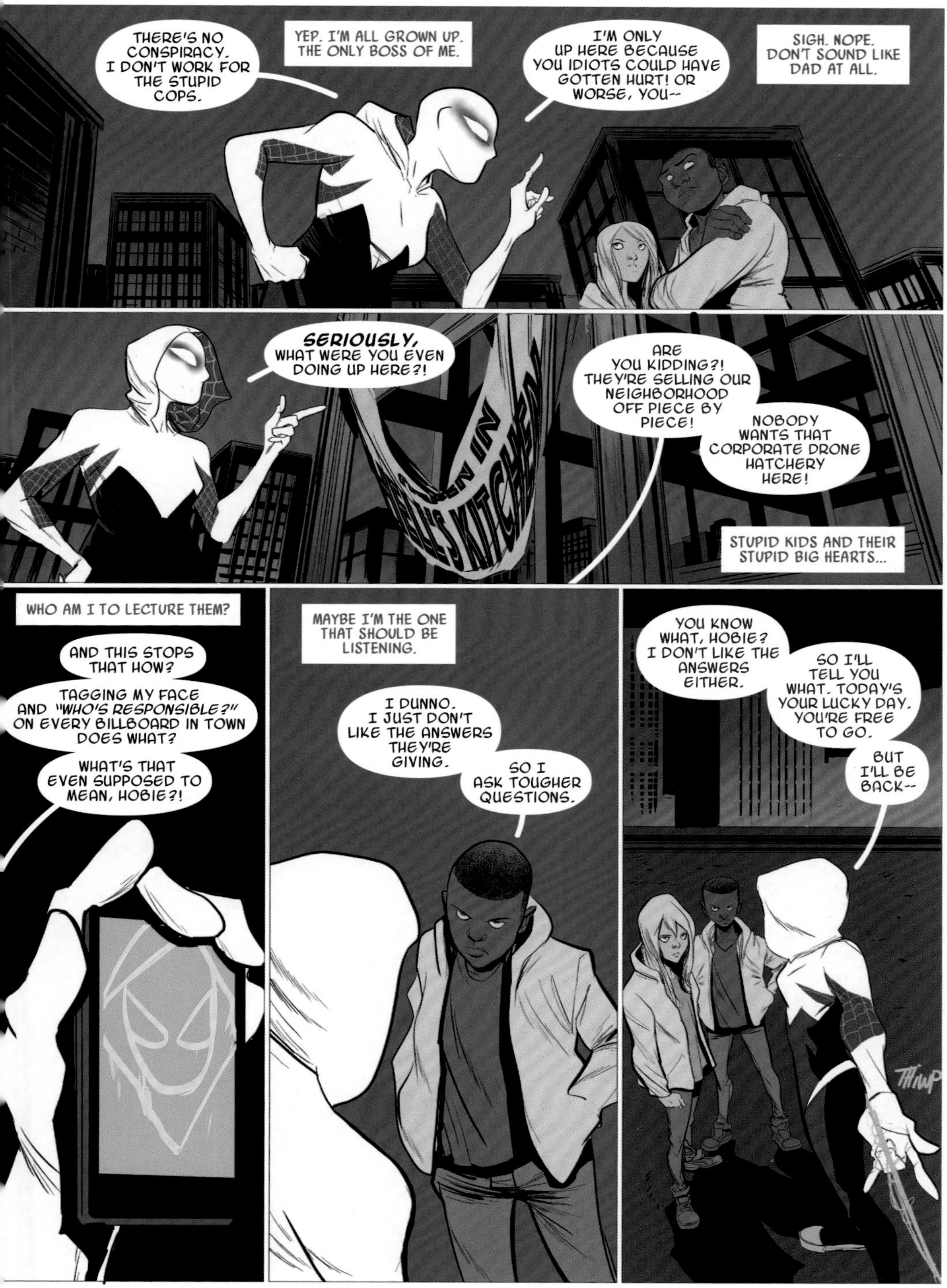
THERE'S NO CONSPIRACY. I DON'T WORK FOR THE STUPID COPS.
YEP. I'M ALL GROWN UP. THE ONLY BOSS OF ME.
I'M ONLY UP HERE BECAUSE YOU IDIOTS COULD HAVE GOTTEN HURT! OR WORSE, YOU--
SIGH. NOPE. DON'T SOUND LIKE DAD AT ALL.
SERIOUSLY, WHAT WERE YOU EVEN DOING UP HERE?!
ARE YOU KIDDING?! THEY'RE SELLING OUR NEIGHBORHOOD OFF PIECE BY PIECE!
NOBODY WANTS THAT CORPORATE DRONE HATCHERY HERE!
STUPID KIDS AND THEIR STUPID BIG HEARTS...
WHO AM I TO LECTURE THEM?
AND THIS STOPS THAT HOW?
TAGGING MY FACE AND "WHO'S RESPONSIBLE?" ON EVERY BILLBOARD IN TOWN DOES WHAT?
WHAT'S THAT EVEN SUPPOSED TO MEAN, HOBIE?!
MAYBE I'M THE ONE THAT SHOULD BE LISTENING.
I DUNNO. I JUST DON'T LIKE THE ANSWERS THEY'RE GIVING.
SO I ASK TOUGHER QUESTIONS.
YOU KNOW WHAT, HOBIE? I DON'T LIKE THE ANSWERS EITHER.
SO I'LL TELL YOU WHAT. TODAY'S YOUR LUCKY DAY. YOU'RE FREE TO GO.
BUT I'LL BE BACK--
THWP

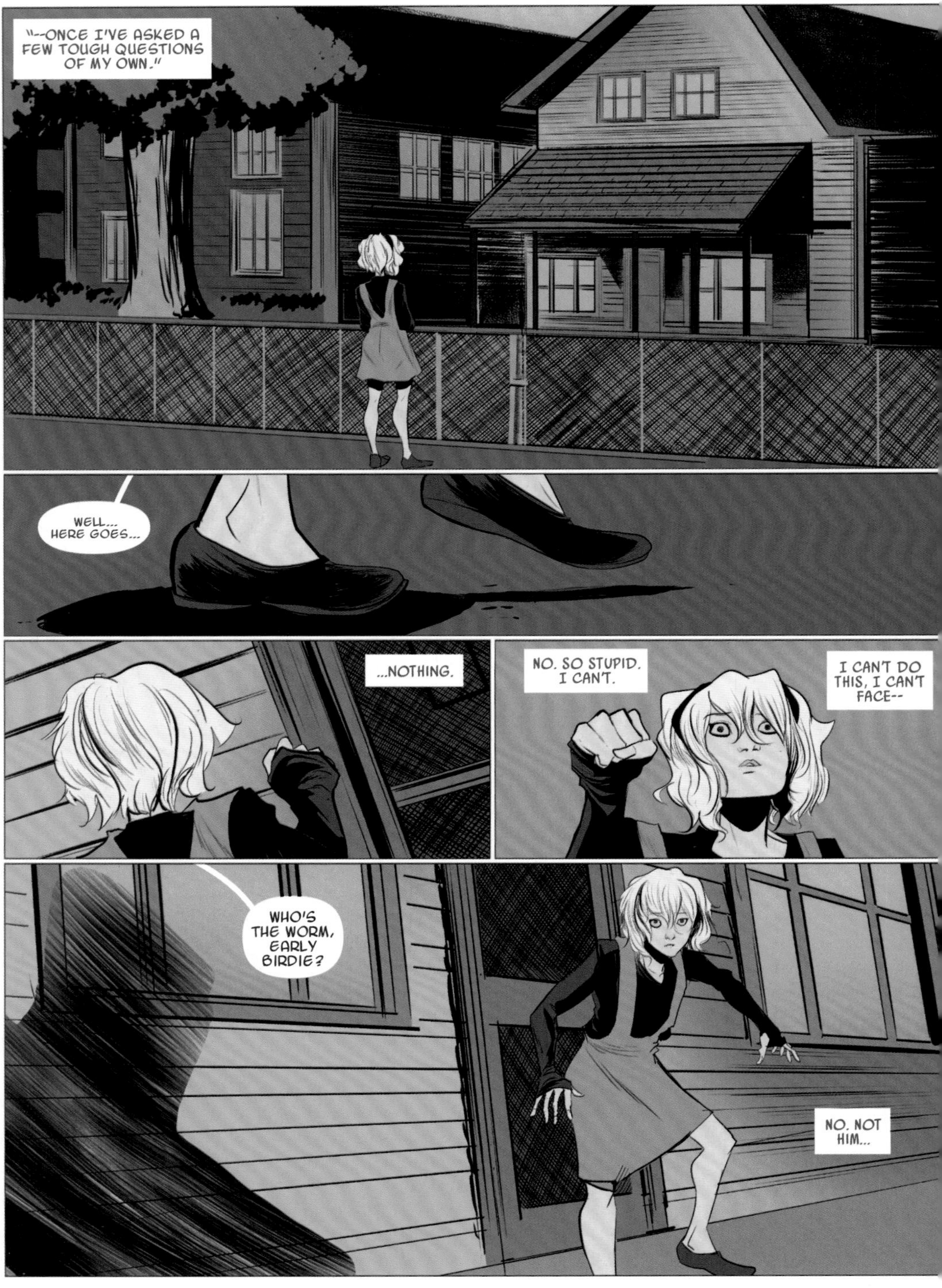
"--ONCE I'VE ASKED A FEW TOUGH QUESTIONS OF MY OWN."
WELL... HERE GOES...
...NOTHING.
NO. SO STUPID. I CAN'T.
I CAN'T DO THIS, I CAN'T FACE--
WHO'S THE WORM, EARLY BIRDIE?
NO. NOT HIM...

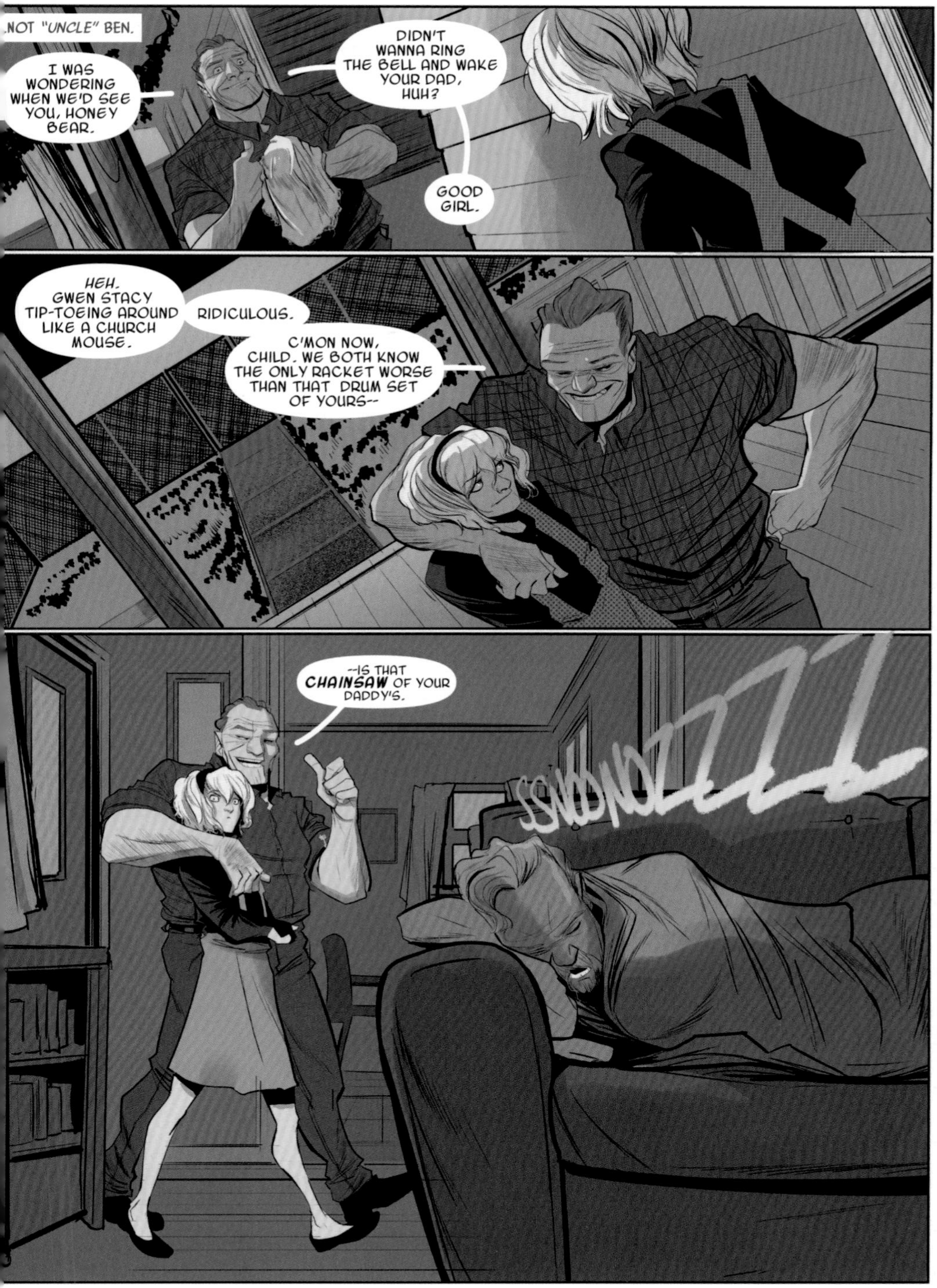
.NOT "UNCLE" BEN.
I WAS WONDERING WHEN WE'D SEE YOU, HONEY BEAR.
DIDN'T WANNA RING THE BELL AND WAKE YOUR DAD, HUH?
GOOD GIRL.
HEH. GWEN STACY TIP-TOEING AROUND LIKE A CHURCH MOUSE.
RIDICULOUS.
C'MON NOW, CHILD. WE BOTH KNOW THE ONLY RACKET WORSE THAN THAT DRUM SET OF YOURS--
--IS THAT CHAINSAW OF YOUR DADDY'S.
SSNOONOZZZZZ

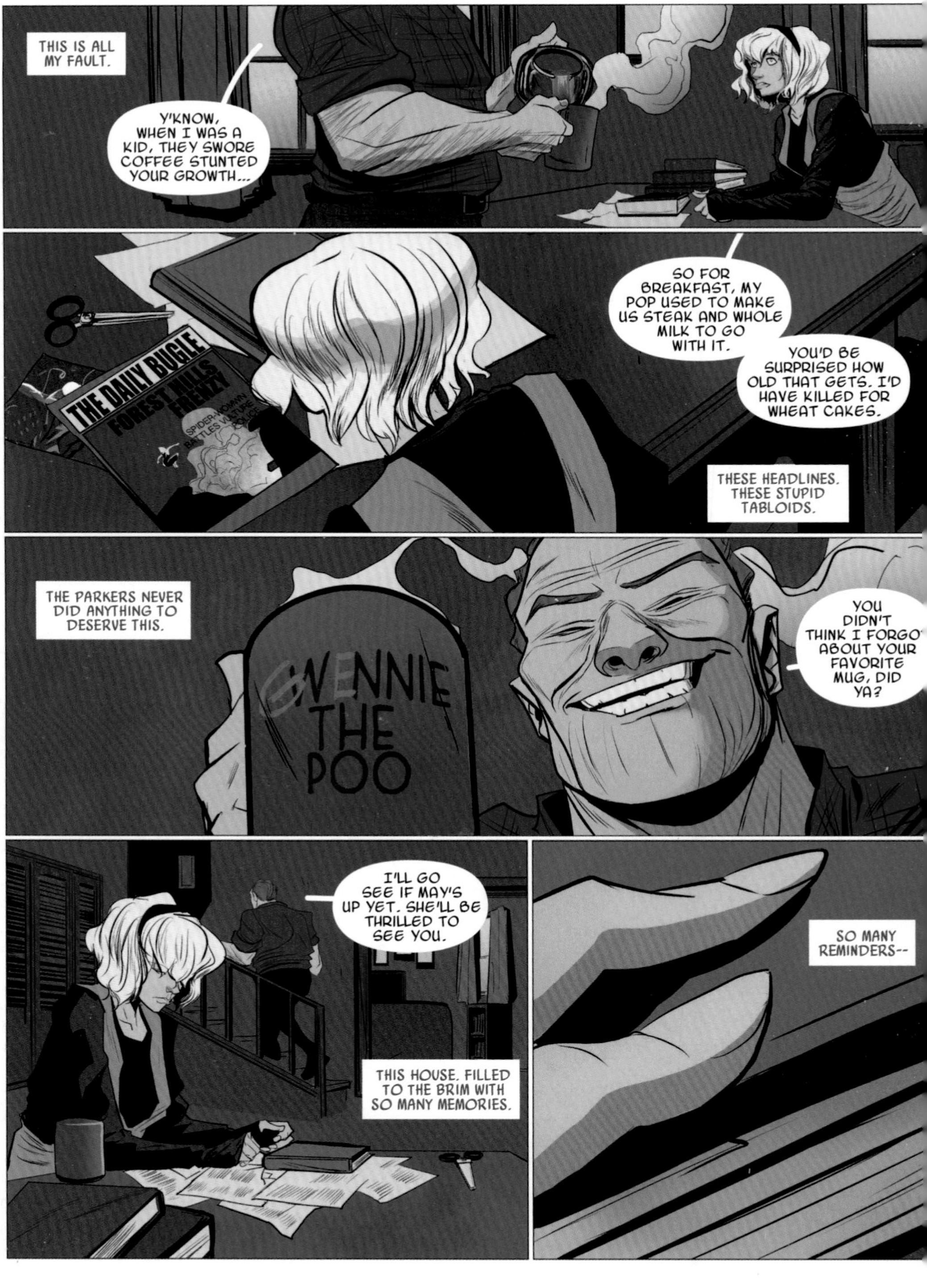
THIS IS ALL MY FAULT.
Y'KNOW, WHEN I WAS A KID, THEY SWORE COFFEE STUNTED YOUR GROWTH...
SO FOR BREAKFAST, MY POP USED TO MAKE US STEAK AND WHOLE MILK TO GO WITH IT.
YOU'D BE SURPRISED HOW OLD THAT GETS. I'D HAVE KILLED FOR WHEAT CAKES.
THE DAILY BUGLE
FOREST HILLS FRENZY
THESE HEADLINES. THESE STUPID TABLOIDS.
THE PARKERS NEVER DID ANYTHING TO DESERVE THIS.
WENNIE THE POO
YOU DIDN'T THINK I FORGO ABOUT YOUR FAVORITE MUG, DID YA?
I'LL GO SEE IF MAY'S UP YET. SHE'LL BE THRILLED TO SEE YOU.
THIS HOUSE. FILLED TO THE BRIM WITH SO MANY MEMORIES.
SO MANY REMINDERS--

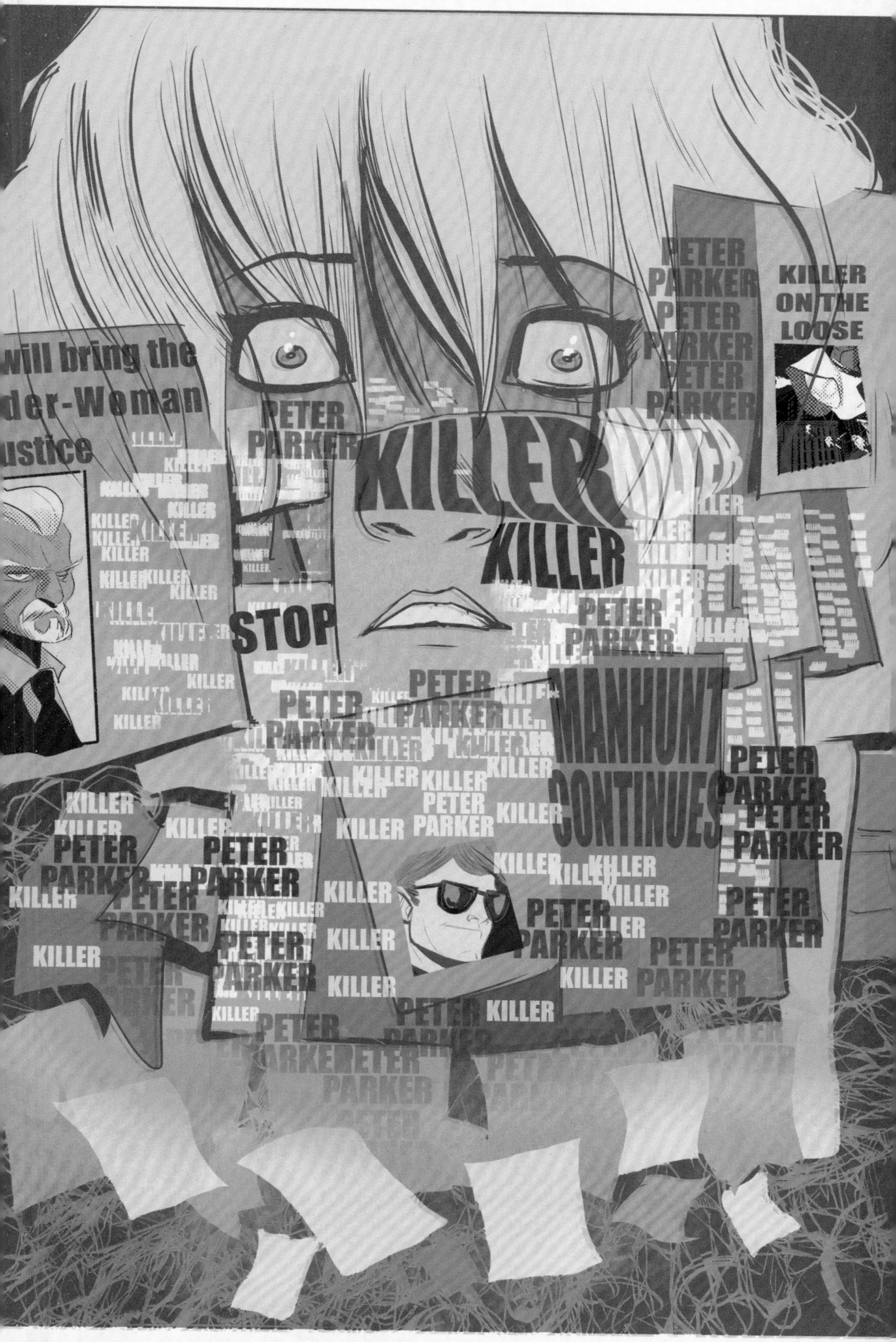
will bring the
der-Woman
ustice
PETER
PARKER
PETER
PARKER
PETER
PARKER
KILLER
ON THE
LOOSE
PETER
PARKER
KILLER
KILLER
STOP
PETER
PARKER
MANHUNT
CONTINUES
PETER
PARKER
KILLER
PETER
PARKER
KILLER
PETER
PARKER
KILLER
PETER
PARKER
PETER
PARKER
KILLER
PETER
PARKER
KILLER

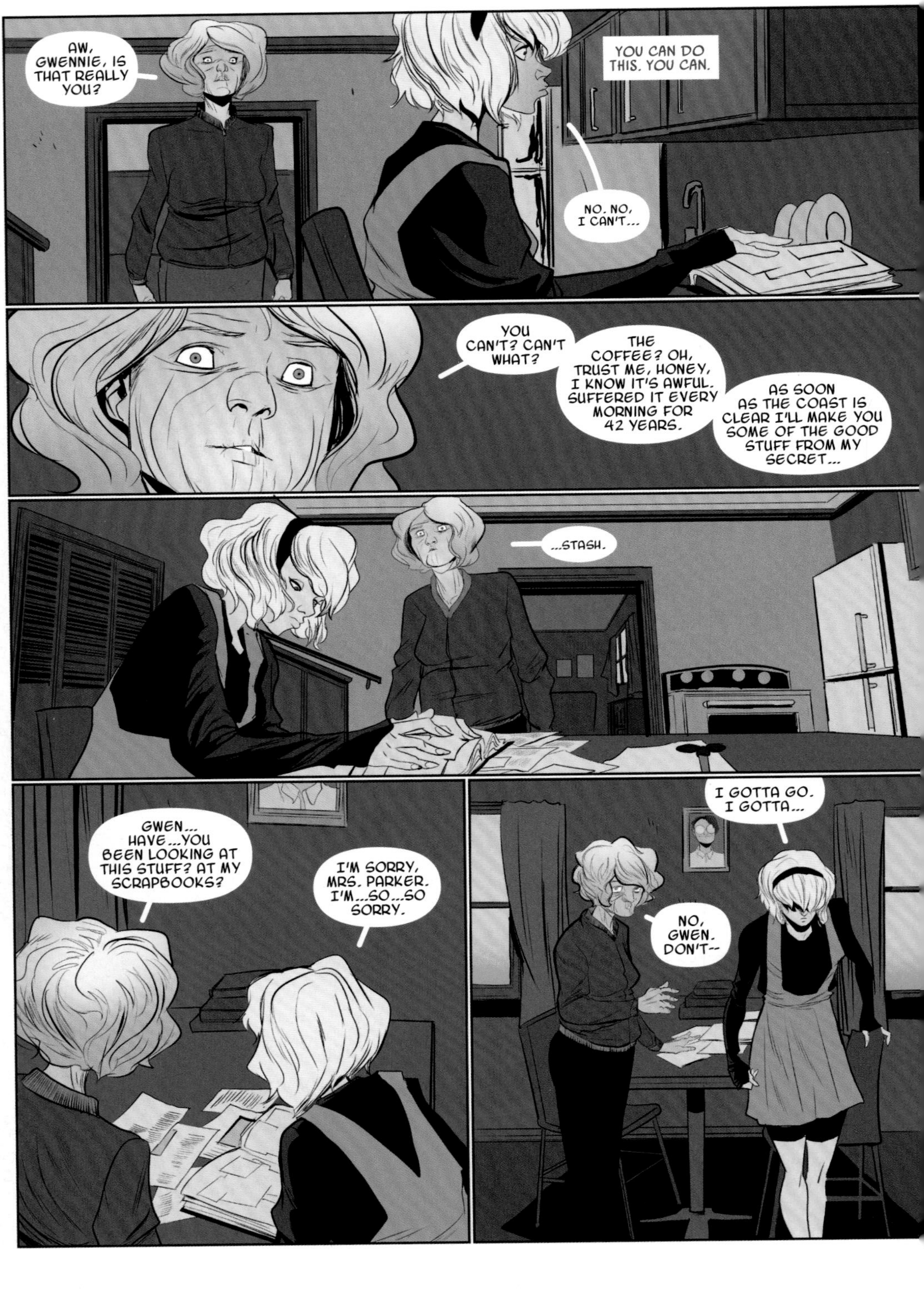
AW, GWENNIE, IS THAT REALLY YOU?
YOU CAN DO THIS. YOU CAN.
NO. NO, I CAN'T...
YOU CAN'T? CAN'T WHAT?
THE COFFEE? OH, TRUST ME, HONEY, I KNOW IT'S AWFUL. SUFFERED IT EVERY MORNING FOR 42 YEARS.
AS SOON AS THE COAST IS CLEAR I'LL MAKE YOU SOME OF THE GOOD STUFF FROM MY SECRET...
...STASH.
GWEN... HAVE...YOU BEEN LOOKING AT THIS STUFF? AT MY SCRAPBOOKS?
I'M SORRY, MRS. PARKER. I'M...SO...SO SORRY.
I GOTTA GO. I GOTTA...
NO, GWEN. DON'T--

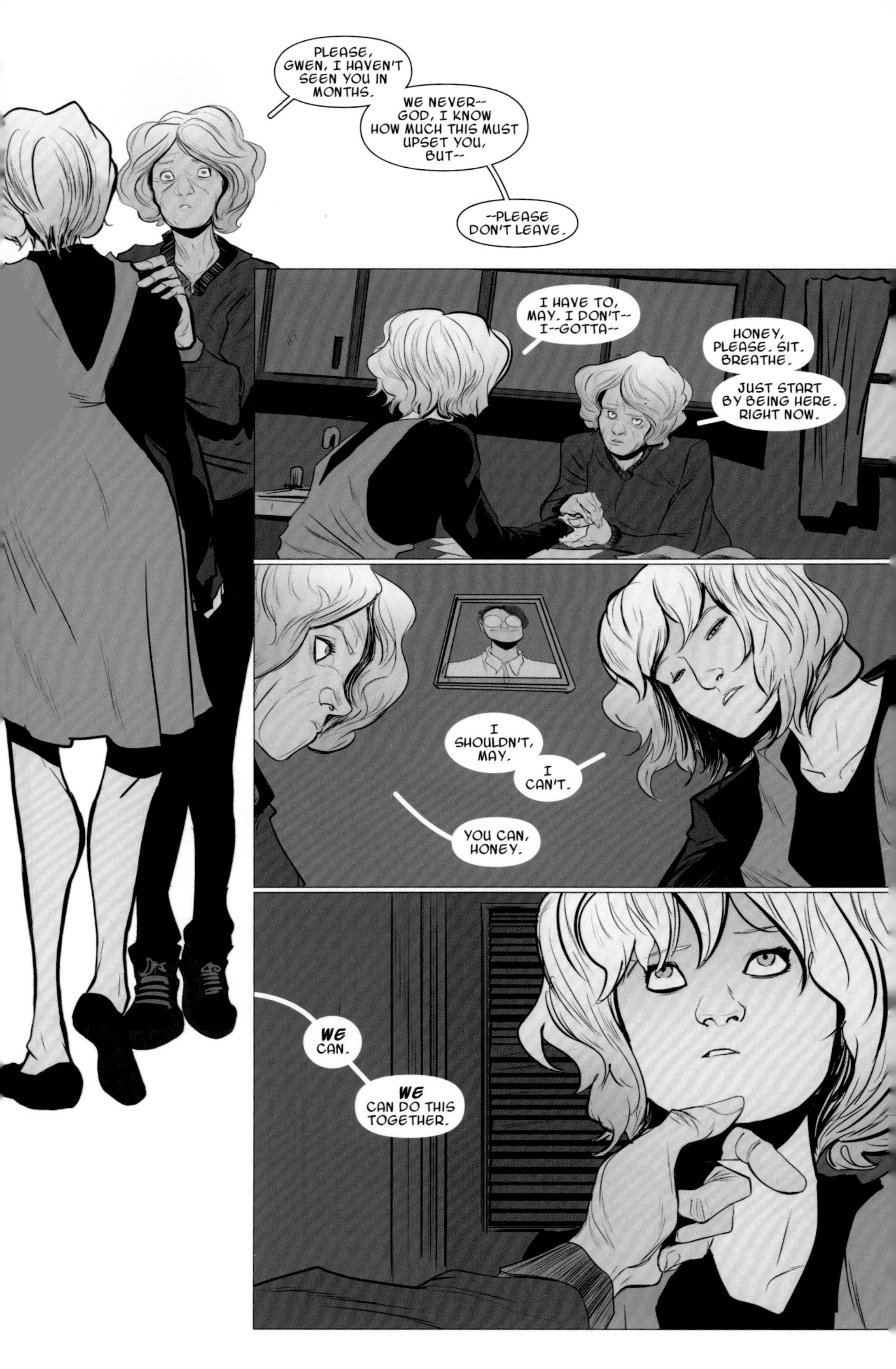
PLEASE, GWEN, I HAVEN'T SEEN YOU IN MONTHS.
WE NEVER-- GOD, I KNOW HOW MUCH THIS MUST UPSET YOU, BUT--
--PLEASE DON'T LEAVE.
I HAVE TO, MAY. I DON'T-- I--GOTTA--
HONEY, PLEASE. SIT. BREATHE.
JUST START BY BEING HERE. RIGHT NOW.
I SHOULDN'T, MAY.
I CAN'T.
YOU CAN, HONEY.
WE CAN.
WE CAN DO THIS TOGETHER.

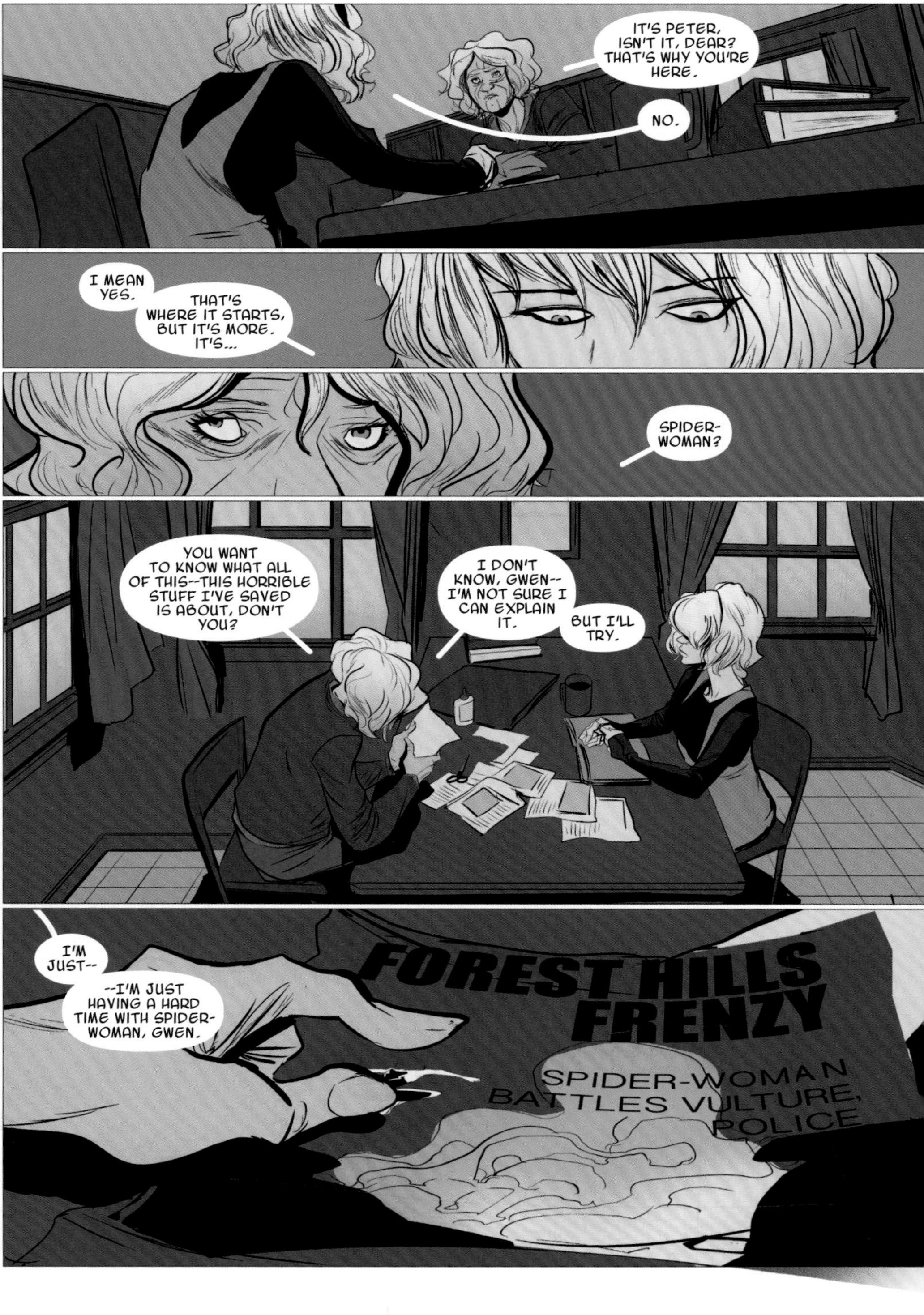
IT'S PETER, ISN'T IT, DEAR? THAT'S WHY YOU'RE HERE.
NO.
I MEAN YES.
THAT'S WHERE IT STARTS, BUT IT'S MORE. IT'S...
SPIDER-WOMAN?
YOU WANT TO KNOW WHAT ALL OF THIS--THIS HORRIBLE STUFF I'VE SAVED IS ABOUT, DON'T YOU?
I DON'T KNOW, GWEN-- I'M NOT SURE I CAN EXPLAIN IT.
BUT I'LL TRY.
I'M JUST--
--I'M JUST HAVING A HARD TIME WITH SPIDER-WOMAN, GWEN.
FOREST HILLS FRENZY
SPIDER-WOMAN BATTLES VULTURE, POLICE

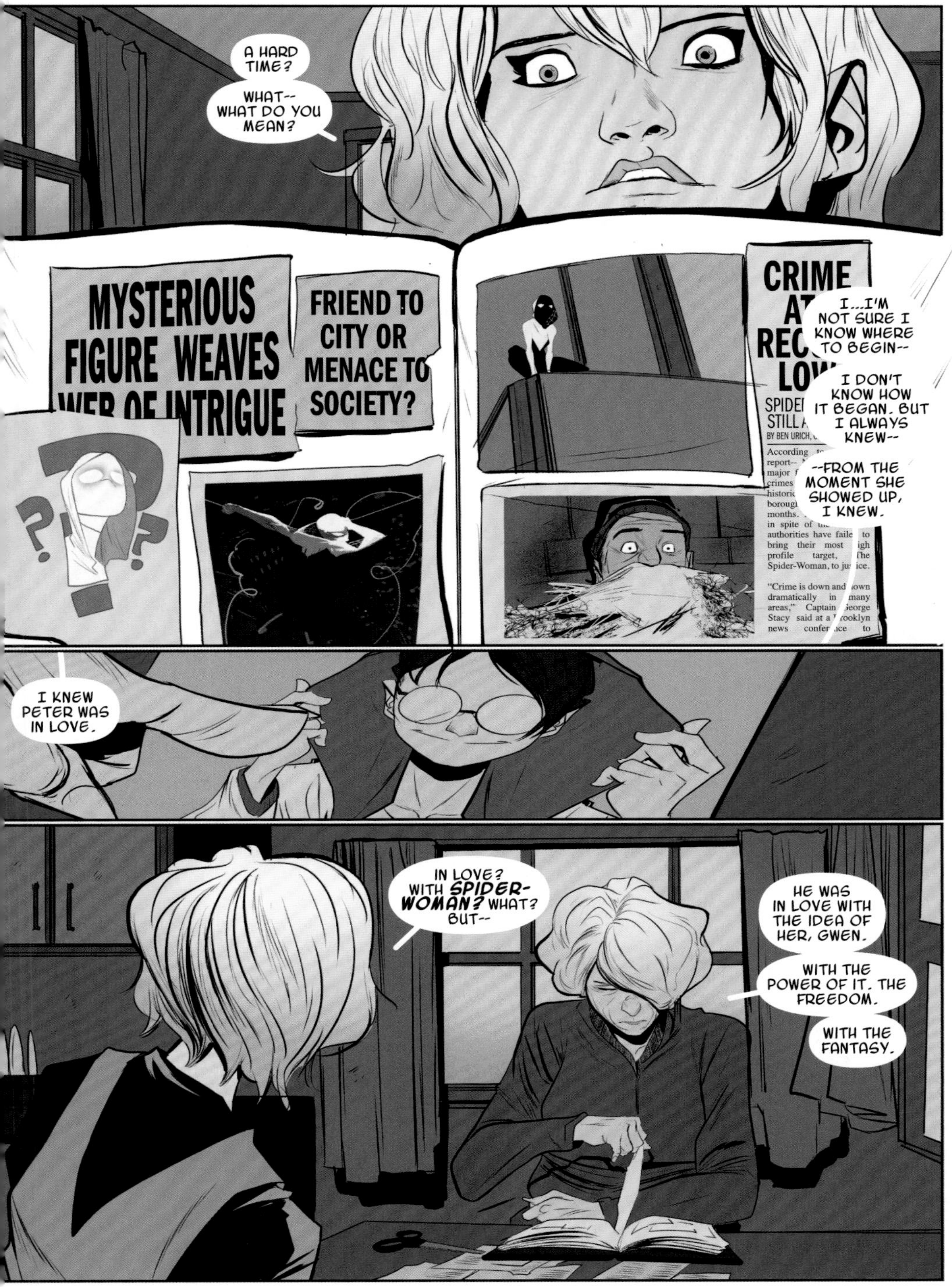
A HARD TIME?
WHAT-- WHAT DO YOU MEAN?
MYSTERIOUS FIGURE WEAVES WEB OF INTRIGUE
FRIEND TO CITY OR MENACE TO SOCIETY?
CRIME
BY BEN URICH
in spite of the
authorities have faile to
bring their most high
profile target, The
Spider-Woman, to justice.
"Crime is down and down
dramatically in many
areas," Captain George
Stacy said at a Brooklyn
news conference to
I...I'M NOT SURE I KNOW WHERE TO BEGIN--
I DON'T KNOW HOW IT BEGAN. BUT I ALWAYS KNEW--
--FROM THE MOMENT SHE SHOWED UP, I KNEW.
I KNEW PETER WAS IN LOVE.
IN LOVE? WITH SPIDER-WOMAN? WHAT? BUT--
HE WAS IN LOVE WITH THE IDEA OF HER, GWEN.
WITH THE POWER OF IT. THE FREEDOM.
WITH THE FANTASY.

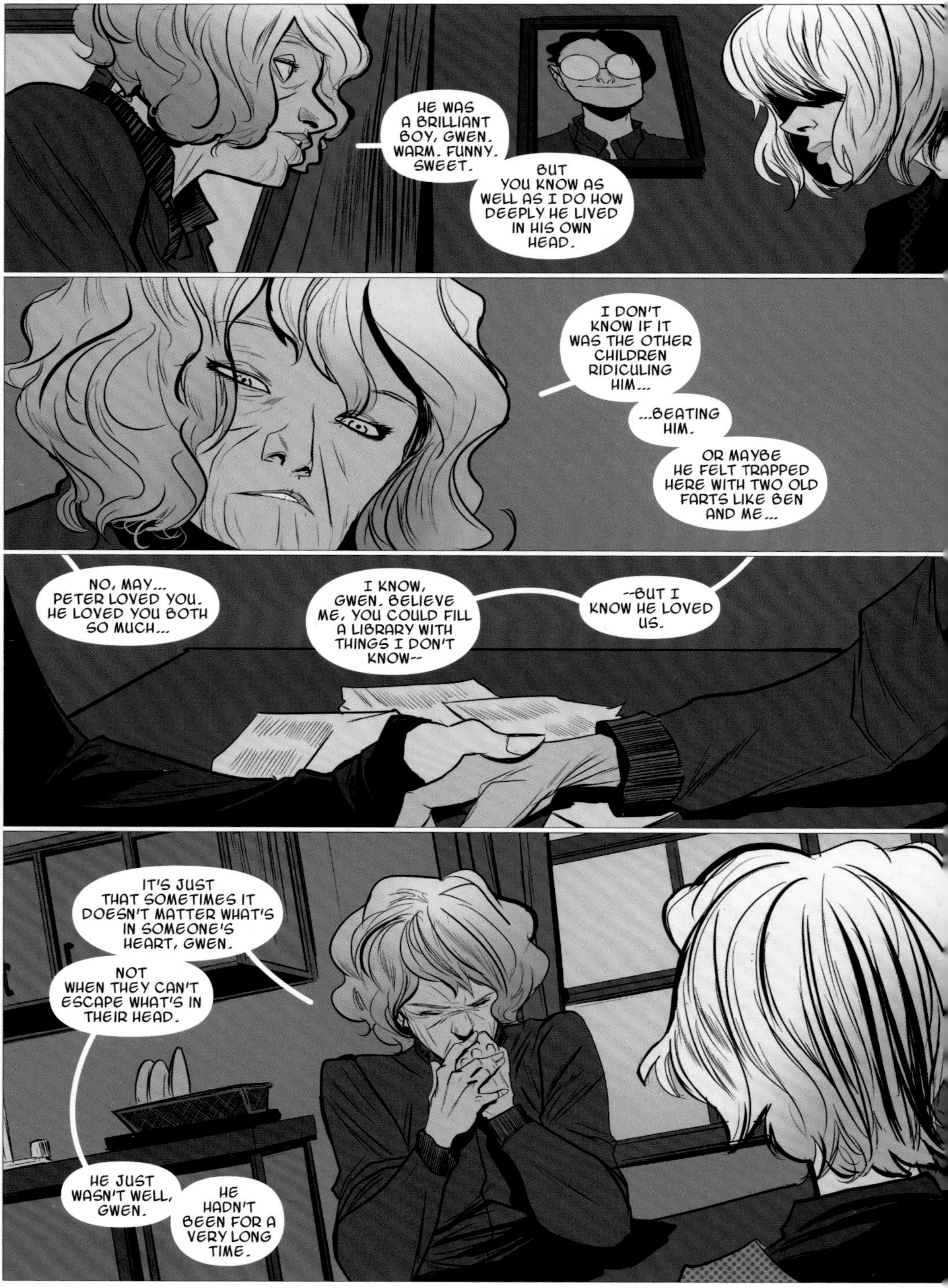
HE WAS A BRILLIANT BOY, GWEN. WARM. FUNNY. SWEET.
BUT YOU KNOW AS WELL AS I DO HOW DEEPLY HE LIVED IN HIS OWN HEAD.
I DON'T KNOW IF IT WAS THE OTHER CHILDREN RIDICULING HIM...
...BEATING HIM.
OR MAYBE HE FELT TRAPPED HERE WITH TWO OLD FARTS LIKE BEN AND ME...
NO, MAY... PETER LOVED YOU. HE LOVED YOU BOTH SO MUCH...
I KNOW, GWEN. BELIEVE ME, YOU COULD FILL A LIBRARY WITH THINGS I DON'T KNOW--
--BUT I KNOW HE LOVED US.
IT'S JUST THAT SOMETIMES IT DOESN'T MATTER WHAT'S IN SOMEONE'S HEART, GWEN.
NOT WHEN THEY CAN'T ESCAPE WHAT'S IN THEIR HEAD.
HE JUST WASN'T WELL, GWEN.
HE HADN'T BEEN FOR A VERY LONG TIME.

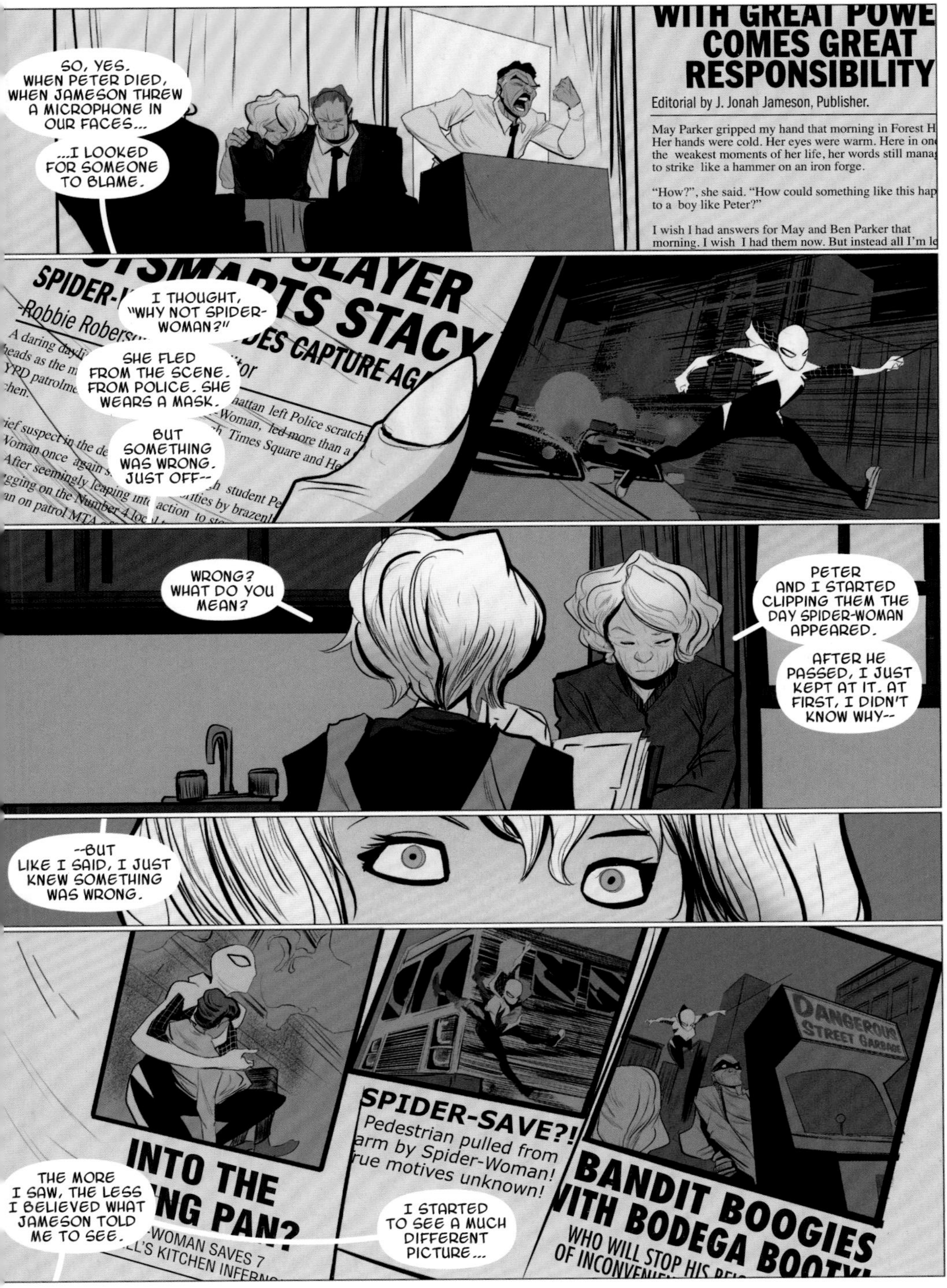
SO, YES. WHEN PETER DIED, WHEN JAMESON THREW A MICROPHONE IN OUR FACES...
...I LOOKED FOR SOMEONE TO BLAME.
WITH GREAT POWE
COMES GREAT
RESPONSIBILITY
Editorial by J. Jonah Jameson, Publisher.
May Parker gripped my hand that morning in Forest H
Her hands were cold. Her eyes were warm. Here in one
the weakest moments of her life, her words still manag
to strike like a hammer on an iron forge.
"How?", she said. "How could something like this hap
to a boy like Peter?"
I wish I had answers for May and Ben Parker that
morning. I wish I had them now. But instead all I'm le
SLAYER
TS STACY
DES CAPTURE AG
-Robbie Roberson
I THOUGHT, "WHY NOT SPIDER-WOMAN?"
SHE FLED FROM THE SCENE. FROM POLICE. SHE WEARS A MASK.
BUT SOMETHING WAS WRONG. JUST OFF--
WRONG? WHAT DO YOU MEAN?
PETER AND I STARTED CLIPPING THEM THE DAY SPIDER-WOMAN APPEARED.
AFTER HE PASSED, I JUST KEPT AT IT. AT FIRST, I DIDN'T KNOW WHY--
--BUT LIKE I SAID, I JUST KNEW SOMETHING WAS WRONG.
INTO THE
NG PAN?
-WOMAN SAVES 7
LL'S KITCHEN INFERN
SPIDER-SAVE?!
Pedestrian pulled from
arm by Spider-Woman!
rue motives unknown!
DANGEROUS
STREET GARBAGE
BANDIT BOOGIES
WITH BODEGA BOOTY!
WHO WILL STOP HIS REI
OF INCONVENIEN
THE MORE I SAW, THE LESS I BELIEVED WHAT JAMESON TOLD ME TO SEE.
I STARTED TO SEE A MUCH DIFFERENT PICTURE...

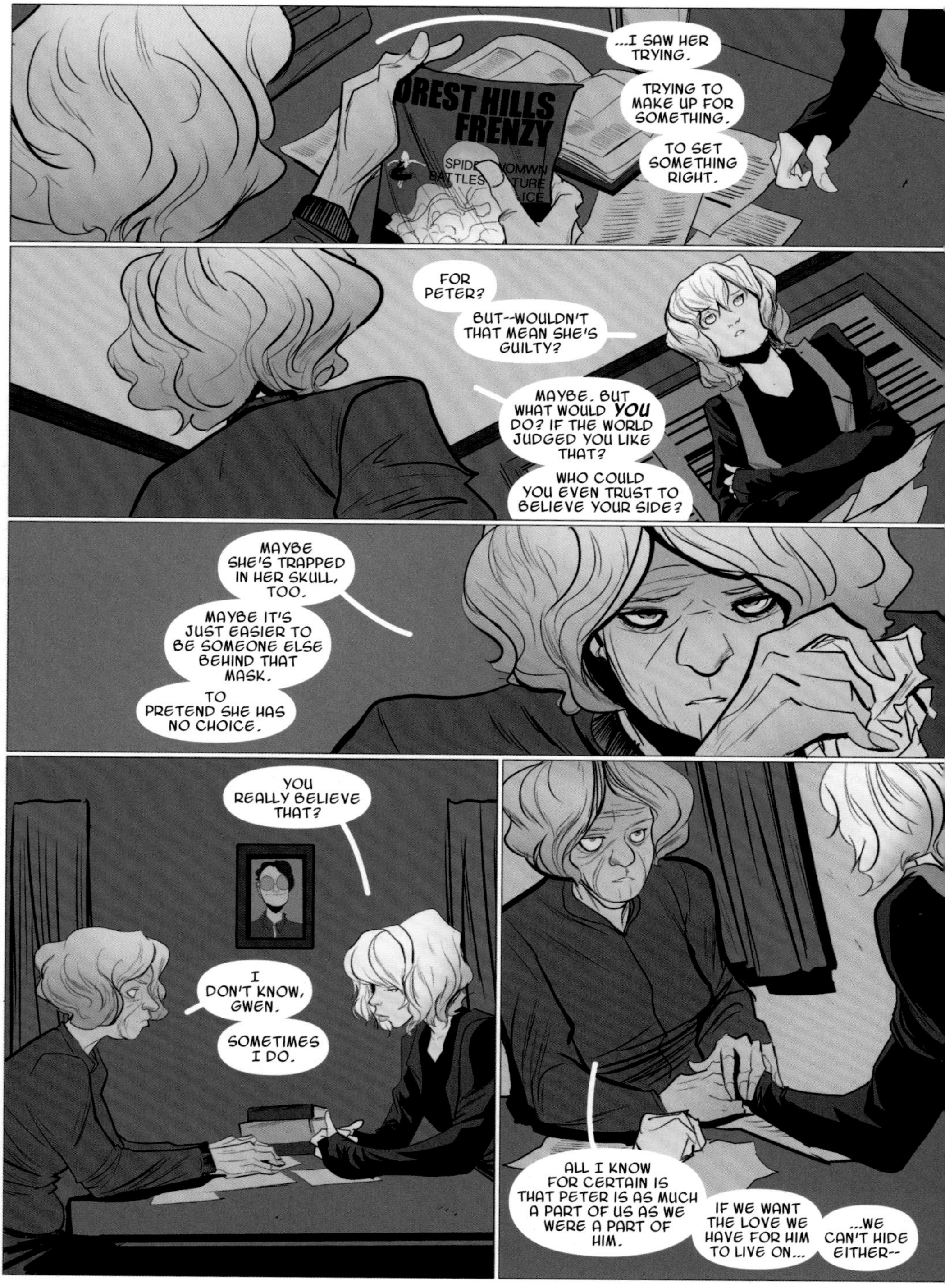

OREST HILLS
FRENZY
...I SAW HER TRYING.
TRYING TO MAKE UP FOR SOMETHING.
TO SET SOMETHING RIGHT.
FOR PETER?
BUT--WOULDN'T THAT MEAN SHE'S GUILTY?
MAYBE. BUT WHAT WOULD YOU DO? IF THE WORLD JUDGED YOU LIKE THAT?
WHO COULD YOU EVEN TRUST TO BELIEVE YOUR SIDE?
MAYBE SHE'S TRAPPED IN HER SKULL, TOO.
MAYBE IT'S JUST EASIER TO BE SOMEONE ELSE BEHIND THAT MASK.
TO PRETEND SHE HAS NO CHOICE.
YOU REALLY BELIEVE THAT?
I DON'T KNOW, GWEN.
SOMETIMES I DO.
ALL I KNOW FOR CERTAIN IS THAT PETER IS AS MUCH A PART OF US AS WE WERE A PART OF HIM.
IF WE WANT THE LOVE WE HAVE FOR HIM TO LIVE ON...
...WE CAN'T HIDE EITHER--

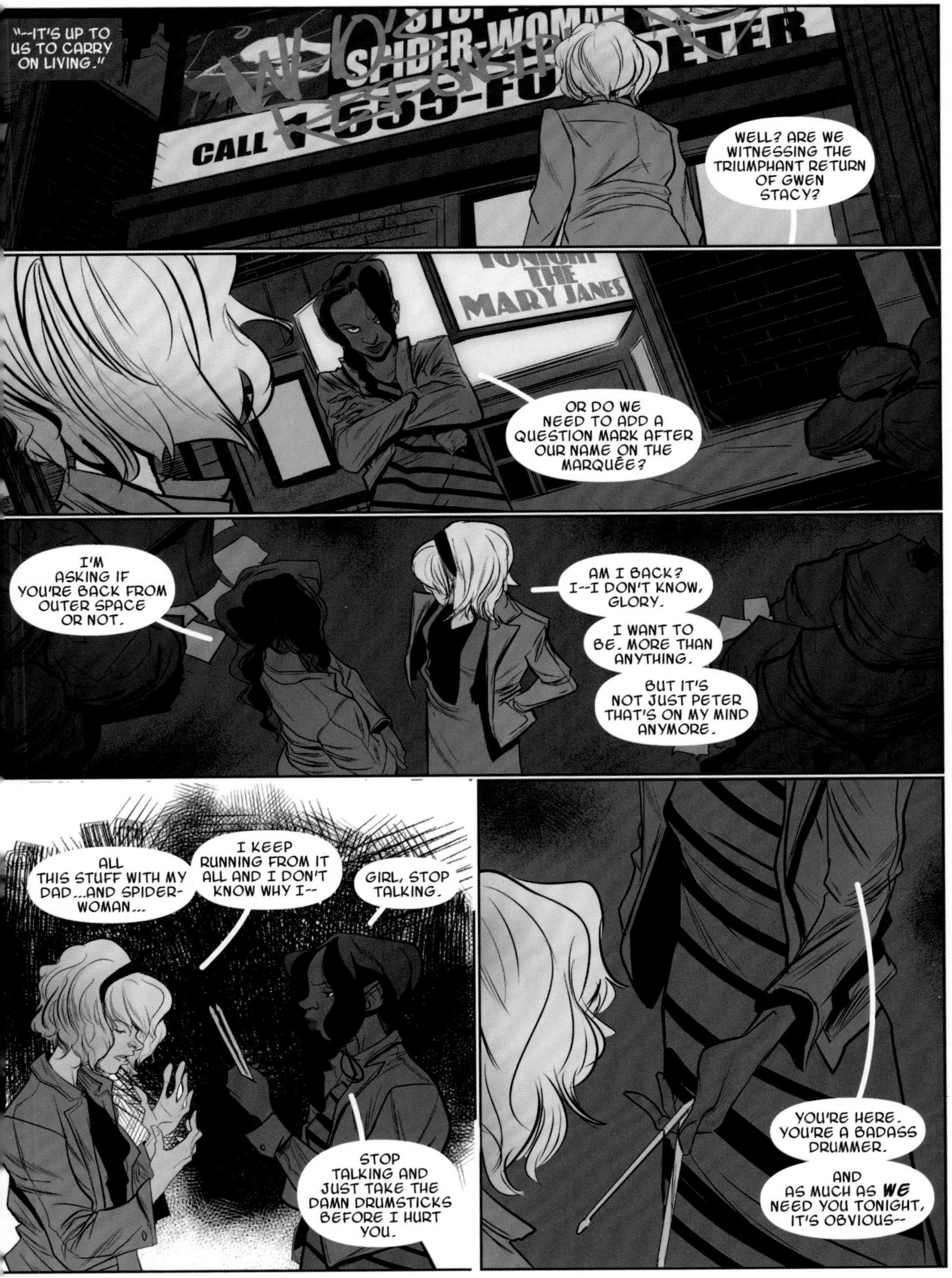
"--IT'S UP TO US TO CARRY ON LIVING."
CALL
WELL? ARE WE WITNESSING THE TRIUMPHANT RETURN OF GWEN STACY?
THE MARY JANES
OR DO WE NEED TO ADD A QUESTION MARK AFTER OUR NAME ON THE MARQUEE?
I'M ASKING IF YOU'RE BACK FROM OUTER SPACE OR NOT.
AM I BACK? I--I DON'T KNOW, GLORY.
I WANT TO BE. MORE THAN ANYTHING.
BUT IT'S NOT JUST PETER THAT'S ON MY MIND ANYMORE.
ALL THIS STUFF WITH MY DAD...AND SPIDER-WOMAN...
I KEEP RUNNING FROM IT ALL AND I DON'T KNOW WHY I--
GIRL, STOP TALKING.
STOP TALKING AND JUST TAKE THE DAMN DRUMSTICKS BEFORE I HURT YOU.
YOU'RE HERE. YOU'RE A BADASS DRUMMER.
AND AS MUCH AS WE NEED YOU TONIGHT, IT'S OBVIOUS--

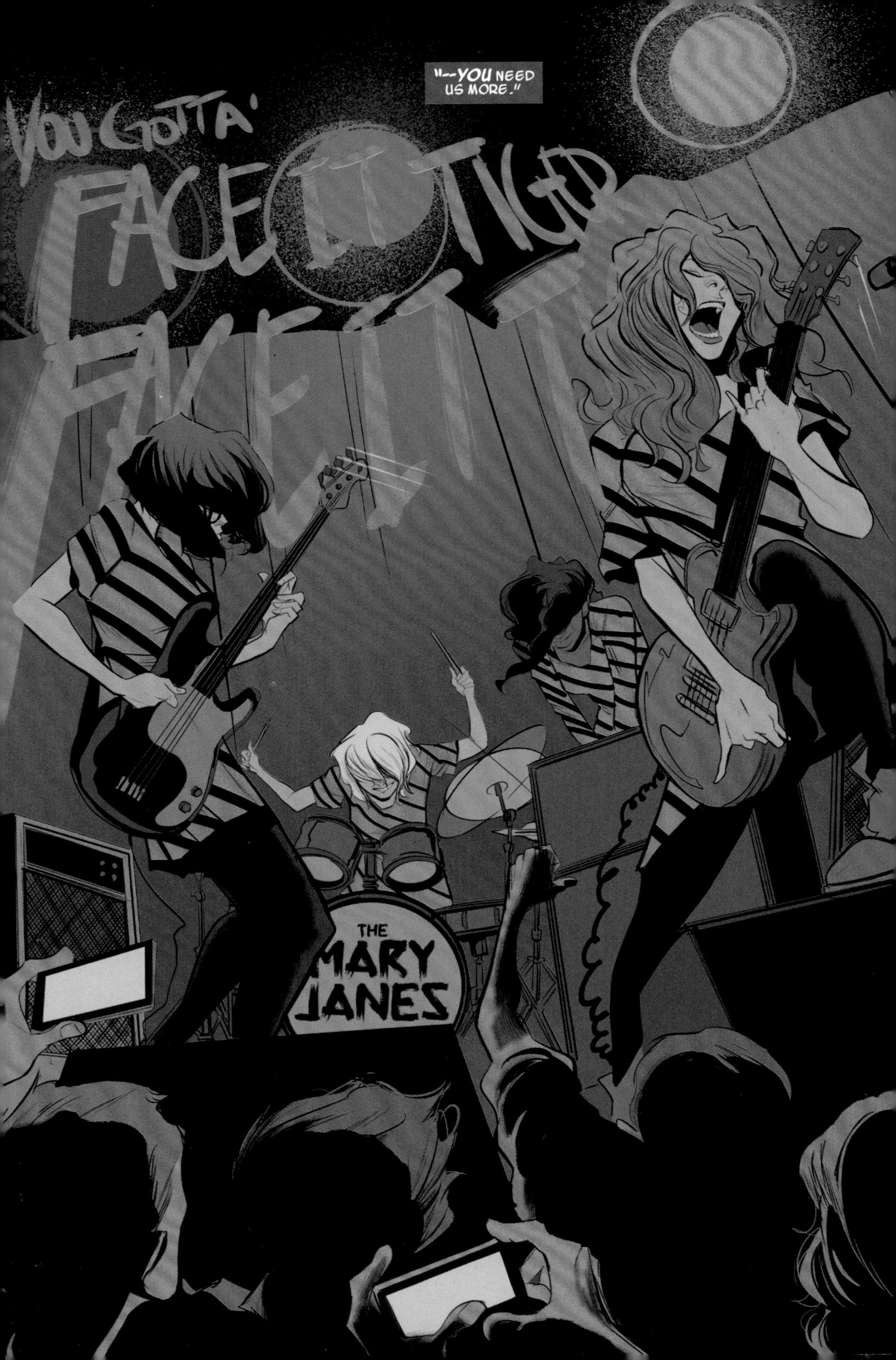
"--YOU NEED US MORE."
YOU GOTTA'
FACE IT TIGER
THE MARY JANES

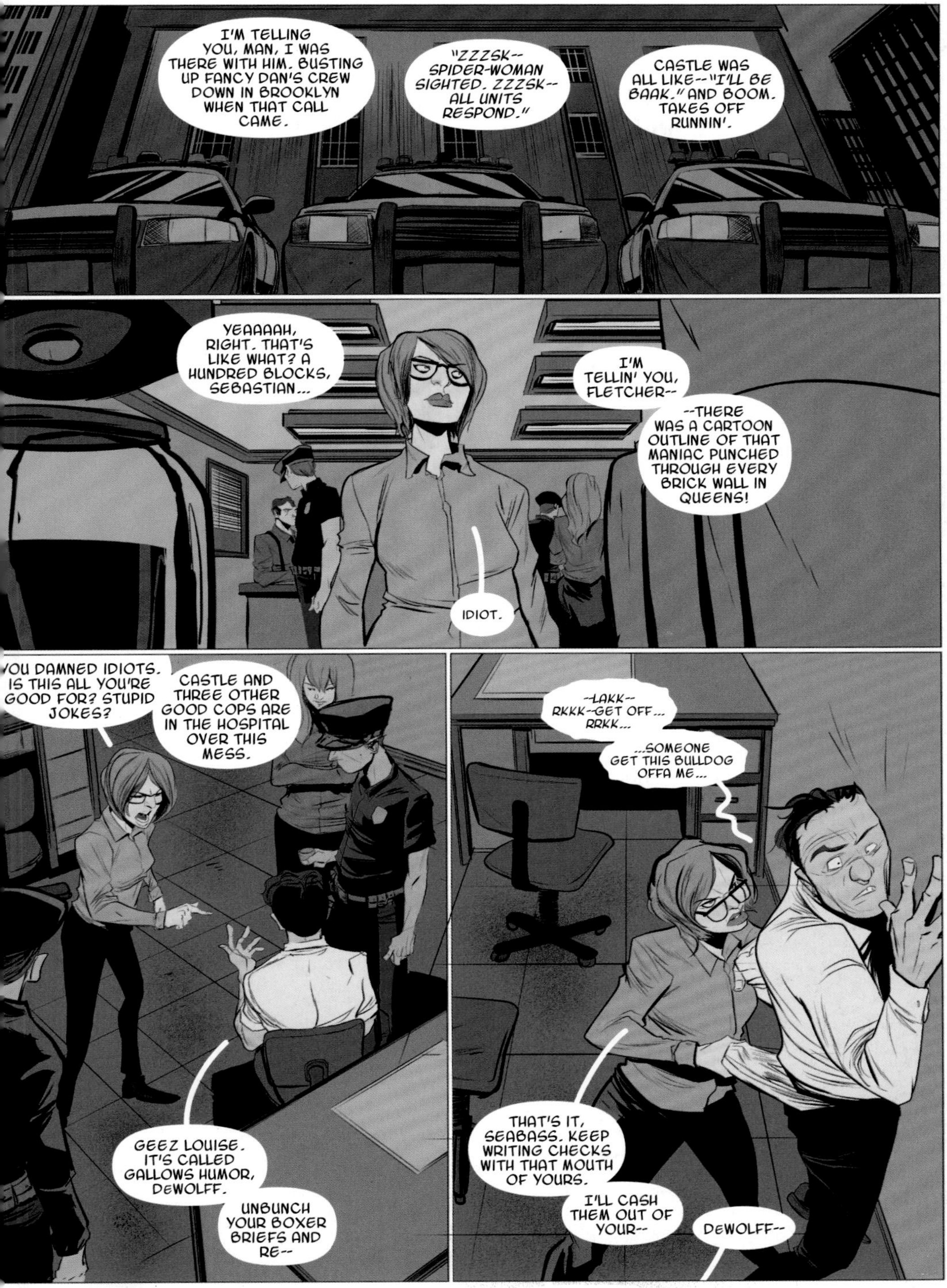
I'M TELLING YOU, MAN, I WAS THERE WITH HIM. BUSTING UP FANCY DAN'S CREW DOWN IN BROOKLYN WHEN THAT CALL CAME.
"ZZZSK-- SPIDER-WOMAN SIGHTED. ZZZSK-- ALL UNITS RESPOND."
CASTLE WAS ALL LIKE--"I'LL BE BAAK." AND BOOM. TAKES OFF RUNNIN'.
YEAAAAH, RIGHT. THAT'S LIKE WHAT? A HUNDRED BLOCKS, SEBASTIAN...
I'M TELLIN' YOU, FLETCHER--
--THERE WAS A CARTOON OUTLINE OF THAT MANIAC PUNCHED THROUGH EVERY BRICK WALL IN QUEENS!
IDIOT.
YOU DAMNED IDIOTS. IS THIS ALL YOU'RE GOOD FOR? STUPID JOKES?
CASTLE AND THREE OTHER GOOD COPS ARE IN THE HOSPITAL OVER THIS MESS.
GEEZ LOUISE. IT'S CALLED GALLOWS HUMOR, DEWOLFF.
UNBUNCH YOUR BOXER BRIEFS AND RE--
--LAKK-- RKKK--GET OFF... RRKK...
...SOMEONE GET THIS BULLDOG OFFA ME...
THAT'S IT, SEABASS. KEEP WRITING CHECKS WITH THAT MOUTH OF YOURS.
I'LL CASH THEM OUT OF YOUR--
DEWOLFF--

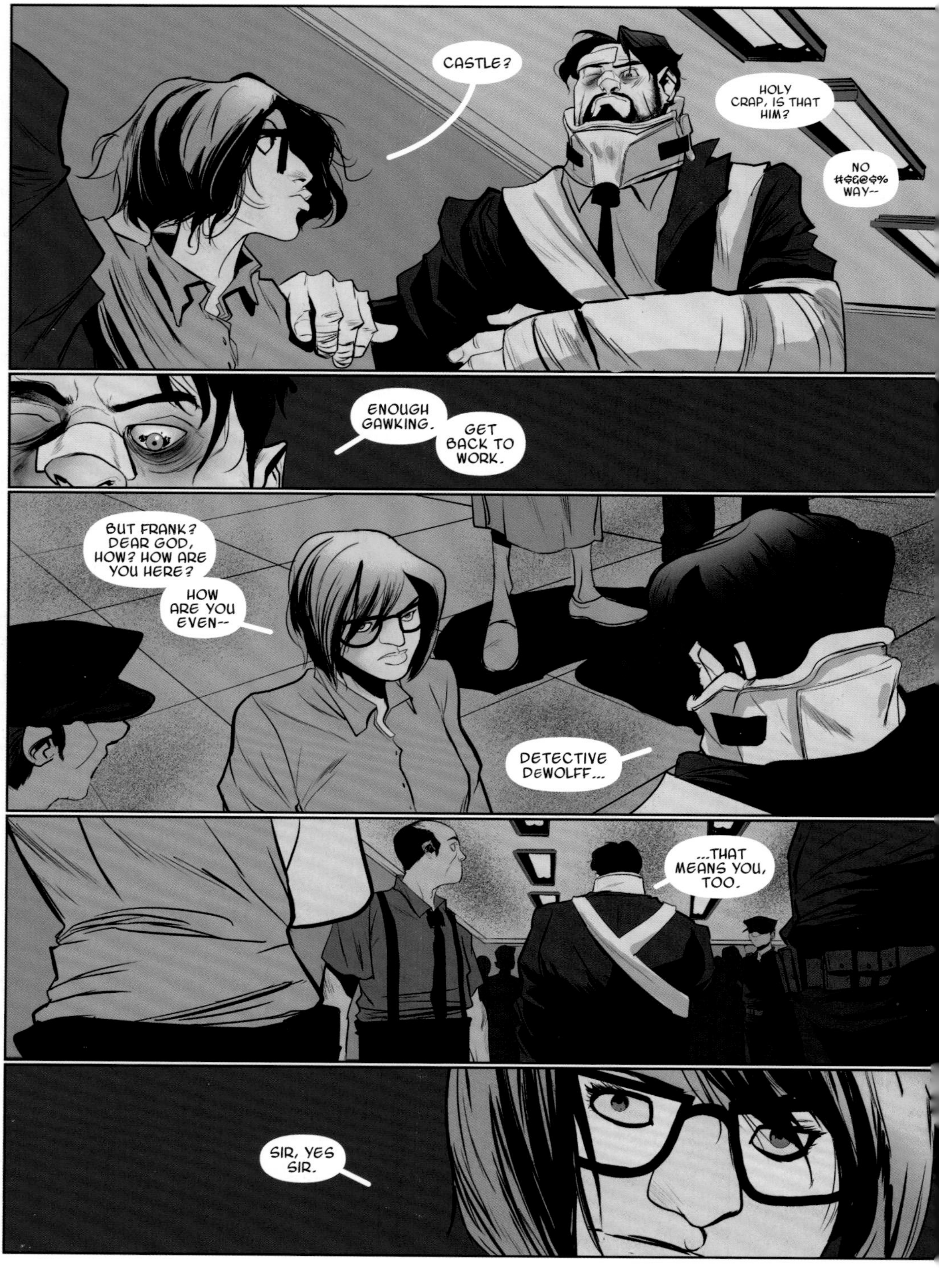
CASTLE?
HOLY CRAP, IS THAT HIM?
NO #$&@$% WAY--
ENOUGH GAWKING.
GET BACK TO WORK.
BUT FRANK? DEAR GOD, HOW? HOW ARE YOU HERE?
HOW ARE YOU EVEN--
DETECTIVE DeWOLFF...
...THAT MEANS YOU, TOO.
SIR, YES SIR.

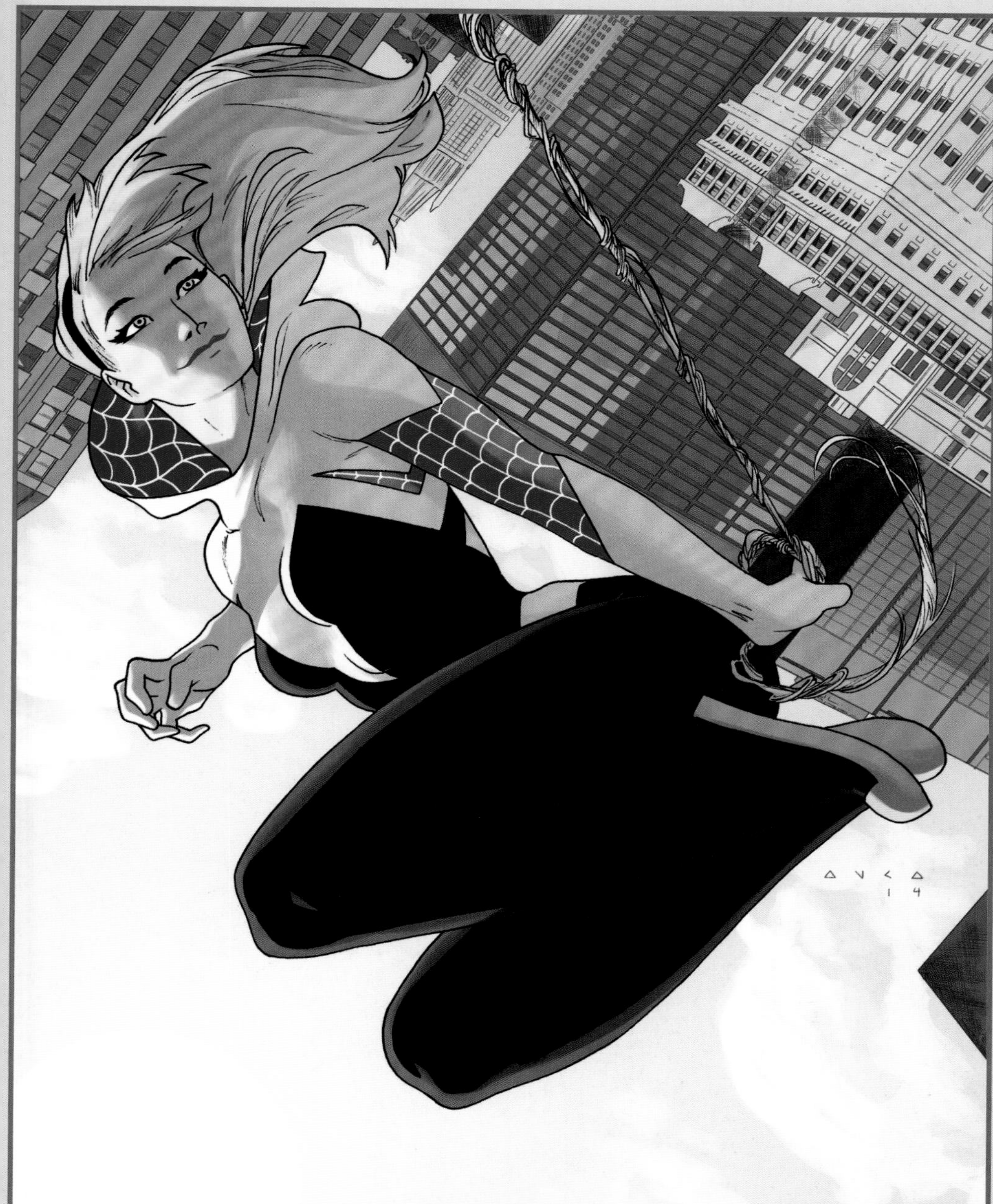

SPIDER-GWEN #1A VARIANT
BY KRIS ANKA

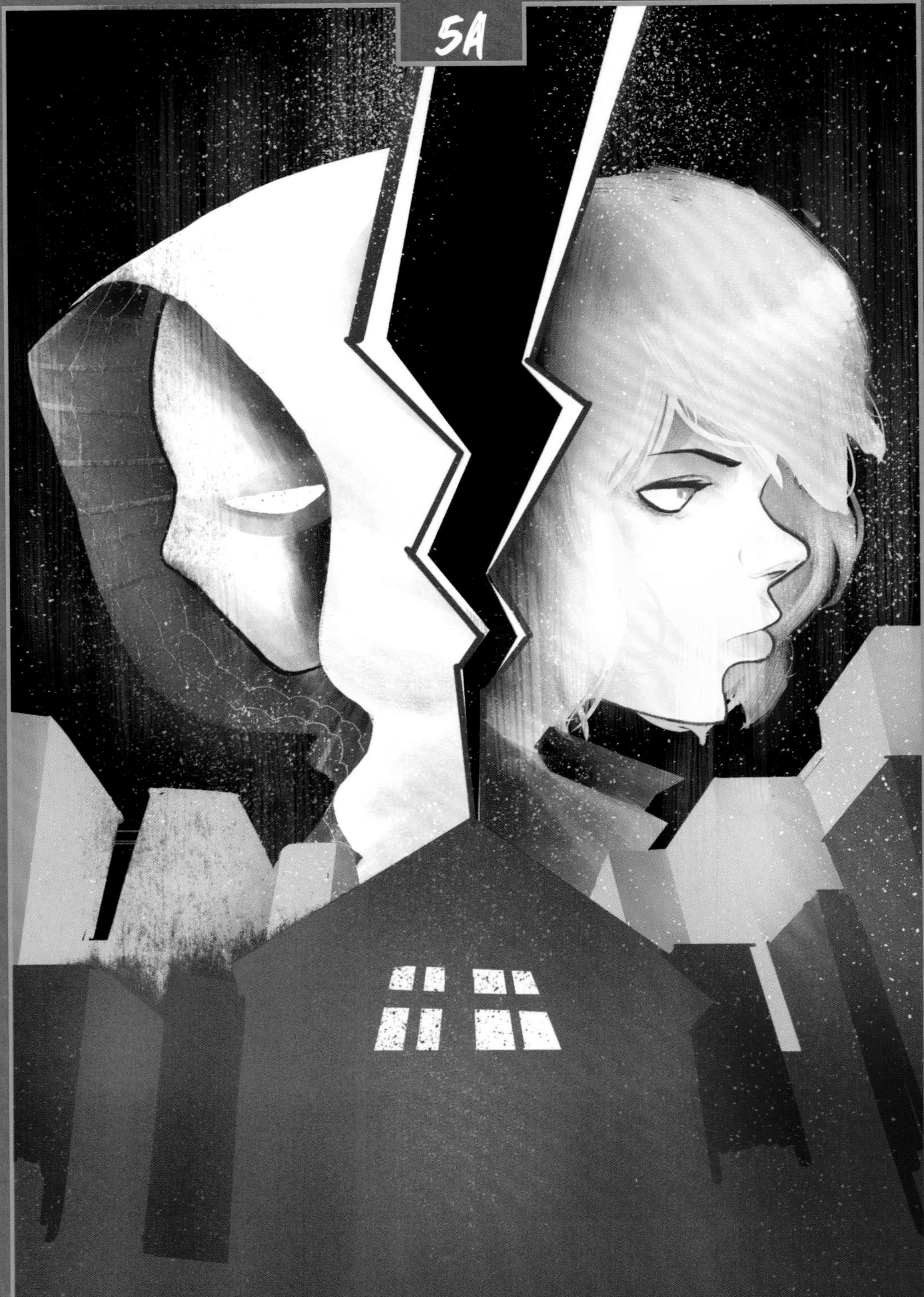
5A

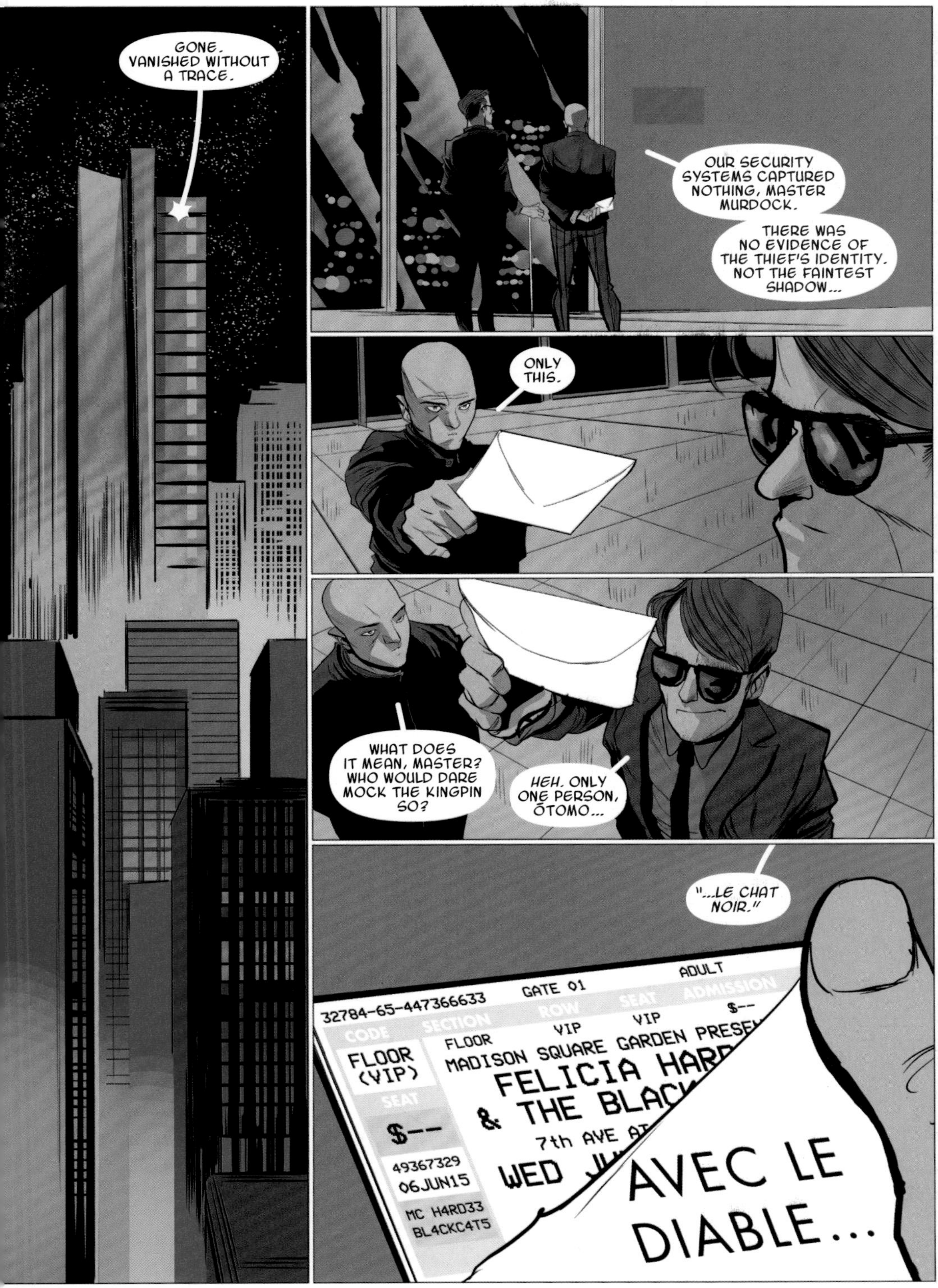
GONE. VANISHED WITHOUT A TRACE.
OUR SECURITY SYSTEMS CAPTURED NOTHING, MASTER MURDOCK.
THERE WAS NO EVIDENCE OF THE THIEF'S IDENTITY. NOT THE FAINTEST SHADOW...
ONLY THIS.
WHAT DOES IT MEAN, MASTER? WHO WOULD DARE MOCK THE KINGPIN SO?
HEH. ONLY ONE PERSON, ŌTOMO...
"...LE CHAT NOIR."
32784-65-447366633
GATE 01
ADULT
CODE SECTION ROW SEAT ADMISSION
FLOOR VIP VIP $--
FLOOR (VIP)
SEAT
$--
49367329
06JUN15
MC H4RD33
BL4CKC4T5
MADISON SQUARE GARDEN PRESE
FELICIA HARD
& THE BLAC
7th AVE AT
WED JU
AVEC LE DIABLE...

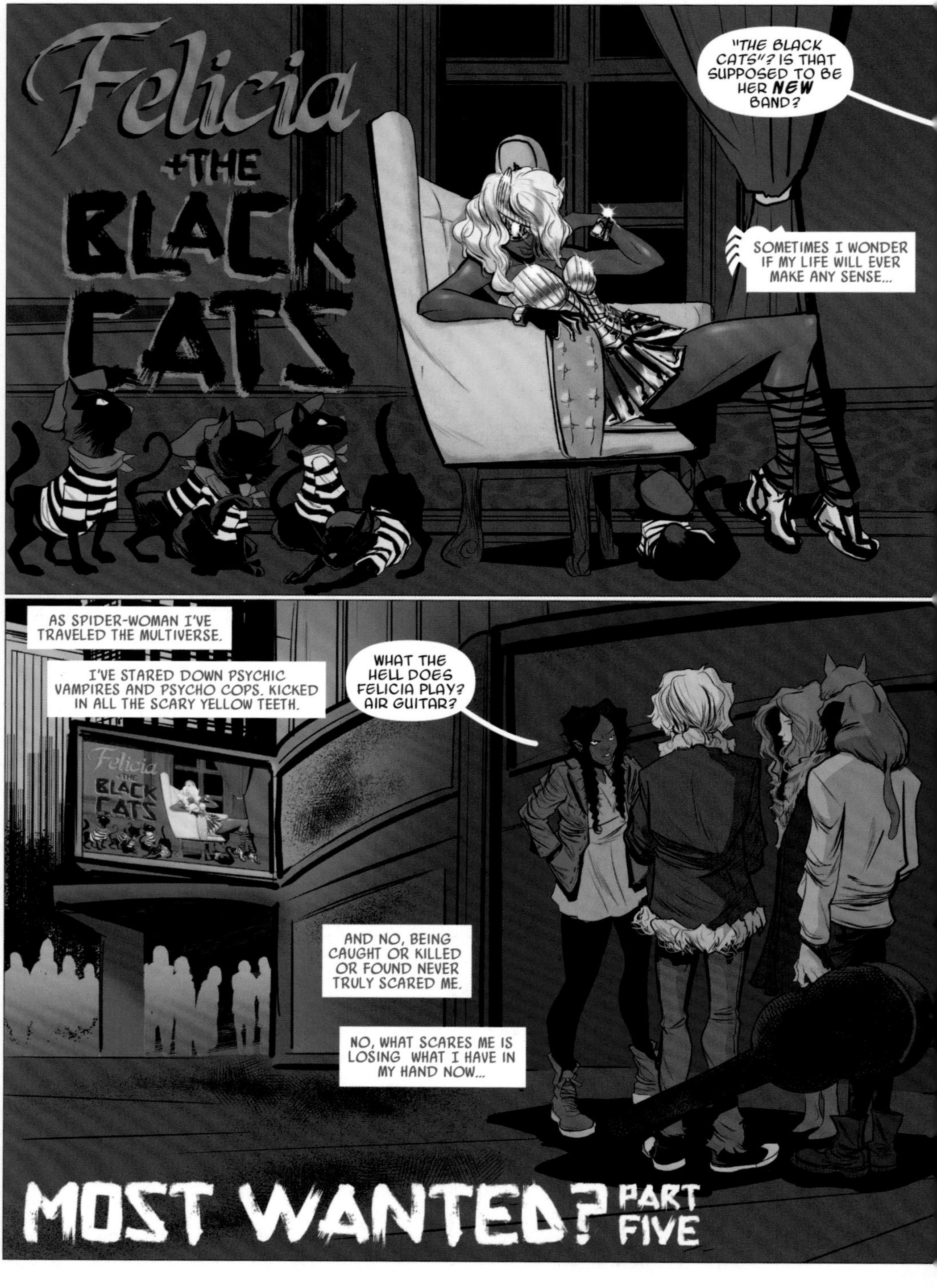
Felicia
+THE
BLACK
CATS
"THE BLACK CATS"? IS THAT SUPPOSED TO BE HER NEW BAND?
SOMETIMES I WONDER IF MY LIFE WILL EVER MAKE ANY SENSE...
AS SPIDER-WOMAN I'VE TRAVELED THE MULTIVERSE.
I'VE STARED DOWN PSYCHIC VAMPIRES AND PSYCHO COPS. KICKED IN ALL THE SCARY YELLOW TEETH.
WHAT THE HELL DOES FELICIA PLAY? AIR GUITAR?
Felicia +THE BLACK CATS
AND NO, BEING CAUGHT OR KILLED OR FOUND NEVER TRULY SCARED ME.
NO, WHAT SCARES ME IS LOSING WHAT I HAVE IN MY HAND NOW...
MOST WANTED? PART FIVE

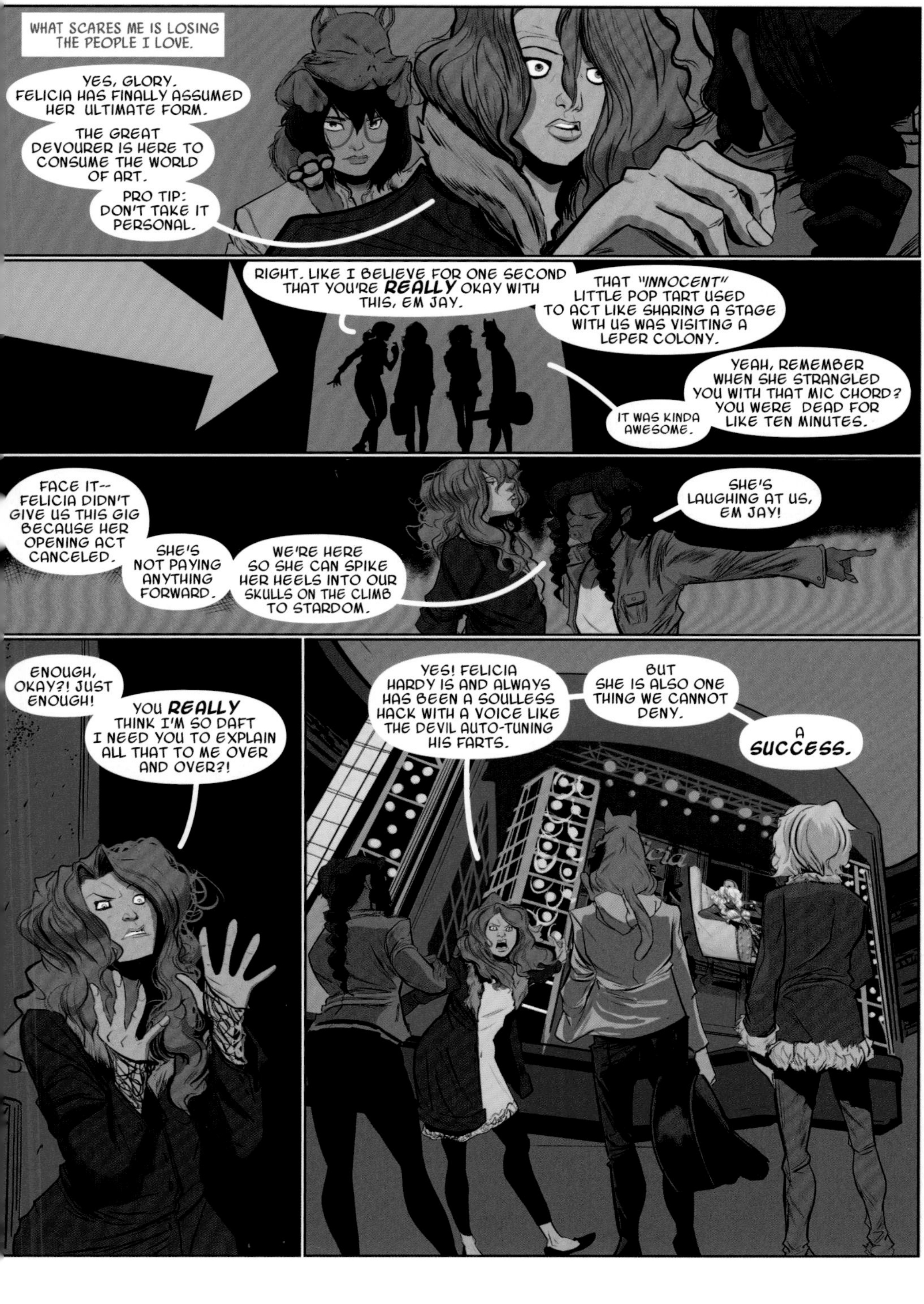
WHAT SCARES ME IS LOSING THE PEOPLE I LOVE.
YES, GLORY. FELICIA HAS FINALLY ASSUMED HER ULTIMATE FORM.
THE GREAT DEVOURER IS HERE TO CONSUME THE WORLD OF ART.
PRO TIP: DON'T TAKE IT PERSONAL.
RIGHT. LIKE I BELIEVE FOR ONE SECOND THAT YOU'RE **REALLY** OKAY WITH THIS, EM JAY.
THAT "INNOCENT" LITTLE POP TART USED TO ACT LIKE SHARING A STAGE WITH US WAS VISITING A LEPER COLONY.
YEAH, REMEMBER WHEN SHE STRANGLED YOU WITH THAT MIC CHORD? YOU WERE DEAD FOR LIKE TEN MINUTES.
IT WAS KINDA AWESOME.
FACE IT-- FELICIA DIDN'T GIVE US THIS GIG BECAUSE HER OPENING ACT CANCELED.
SHE'S NOT PAYING ANYTHING FORWARD.
WE'RE HERE SO SHE CAN SPIKE HER HEELS INTO OUR SKULLS ON THE CLIMB TO STARDOM.
SHE'S LAUGHING AT US, EM JAY!
ENOUGH, OKAY?! JUST ENOUGH!
YOU **REALLY** THINK I'M SO DAFT I NEED YOU TO EXPLAIN ALL THAT TO ME OVER AND OVER?!
YES! FELICIA HARDY IS AND ALWAYS HAS BEEN A SOULLESS HACK WITH A VOICE LIKE THE DEVIL AUTO-TUNING HIS FARTS.
BUT SHE IS ALSO ONE THING WE CANNOT DENY.
A **SUCCESS.**

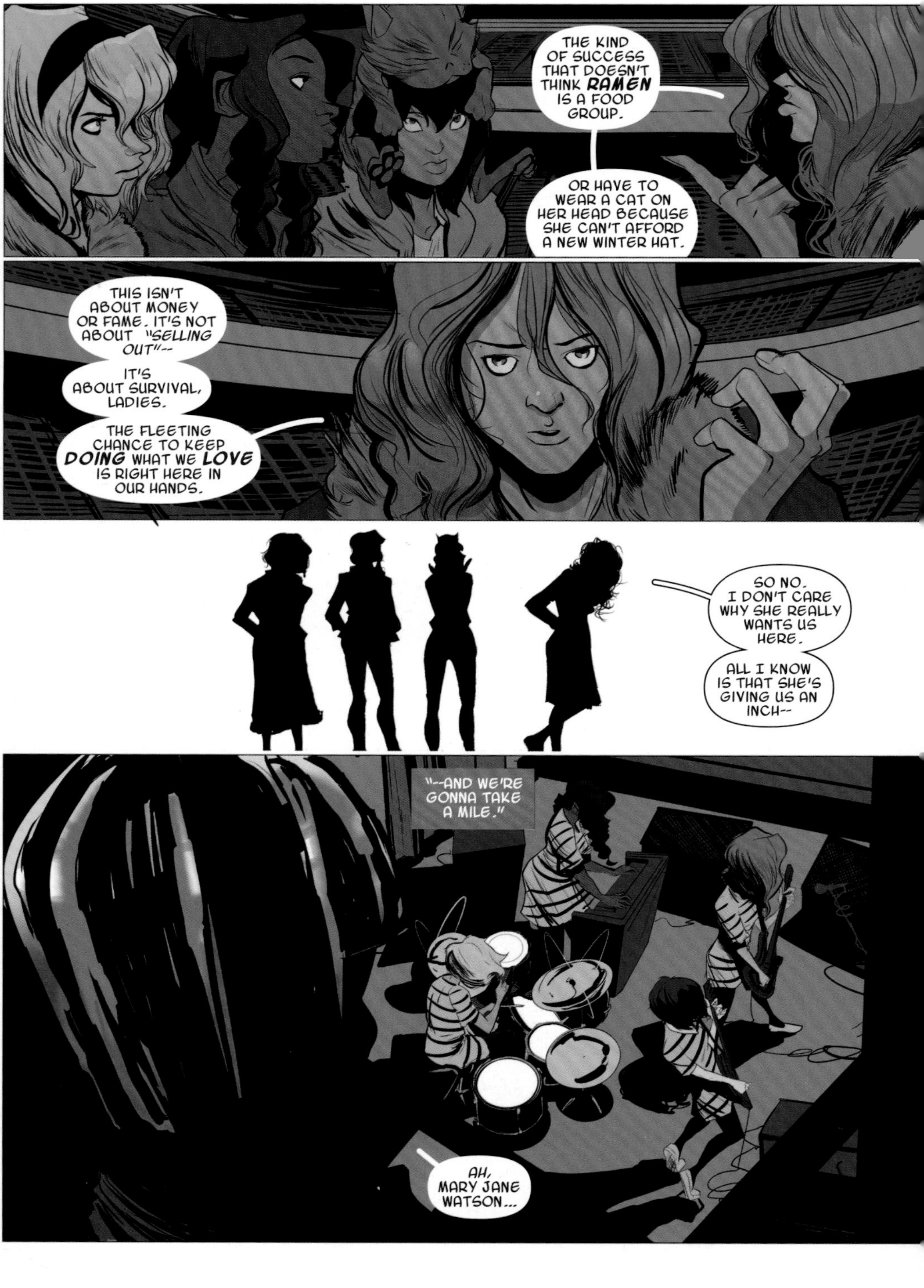
THE KIND OF SUCCESS THAT DOESN'T THINK RAMEN IS A FOOD GROUP.
OR HAVE TO WEAR A CAT ON HER HEAD BECAUSE SHE CAN'T AFFORD A NEW WINTER HAT.
THIS ISN'T ABOUT MONEY OR FAME. IT'S NOT ABOUT "SELLING OUT"--
IT'S ABOUT SURVIVAL, LADIES.
THE FLEETING CHANCE TO KEEP DOING WHAT WE LOVE IS RIGHT HERE IN OUR HANDS.
SO NO. I DON'T CARE WHY SHE REALLY WANTS US HERE.
ALL I KNOW IS THAT SHE'S GIVING US AN INCH--
"--AND WE'RE GONNA TAKE A MILE."
AH, MARY JANE WATSON...

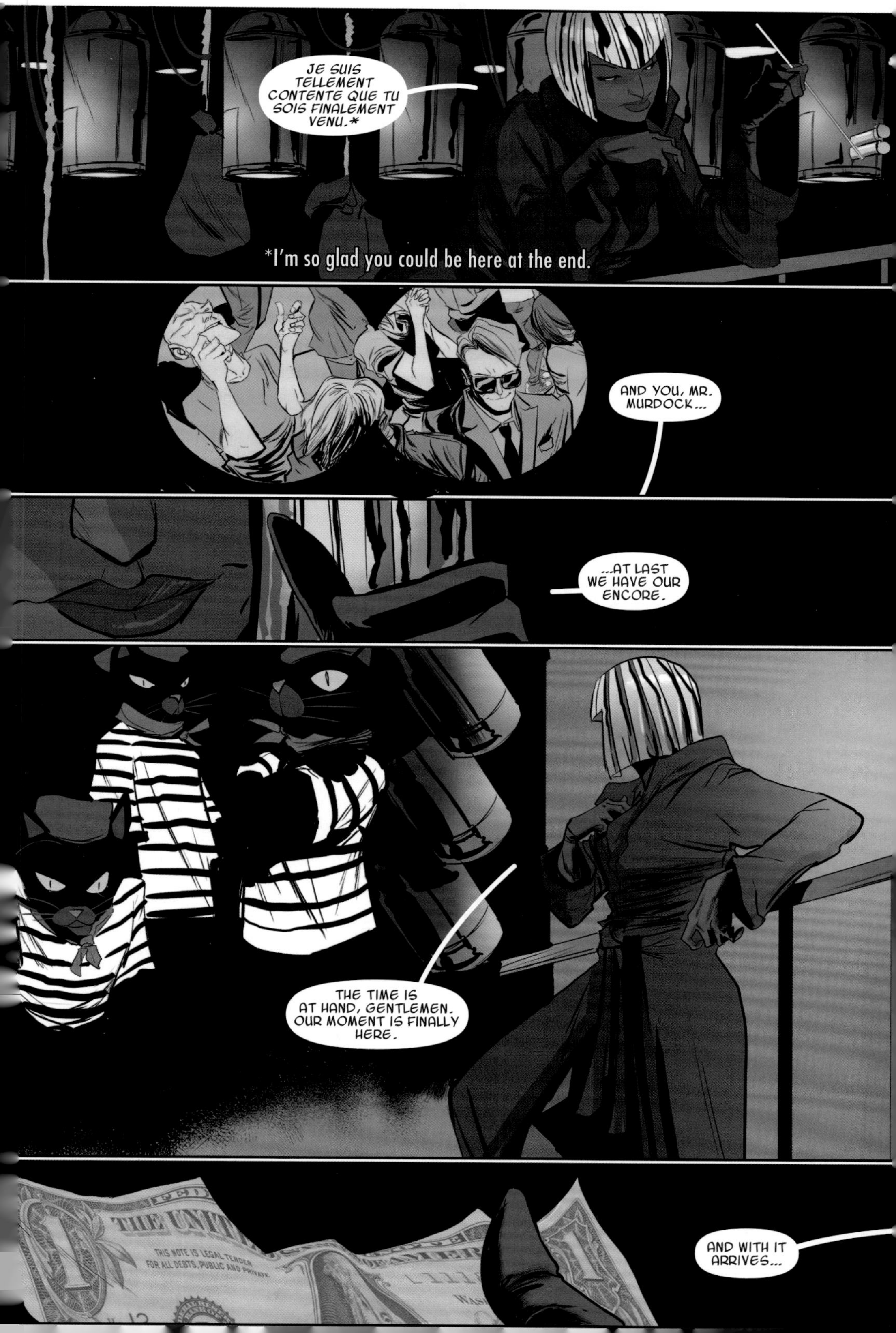
JE SUIS TELLEMENT CONTENTE QUE TU SOIS FINALEMENT VENU.*
*I'm so glad you could be here at the end.
AND YOU, MR. MURDOCK...
...AT LAST WE HAVE OUR ENCORE.
THE TIME IS AT HAND, GENTLEMEN. OUR MOMENT IS FINALLY HERE.
AND WITH IT ARRIVES...

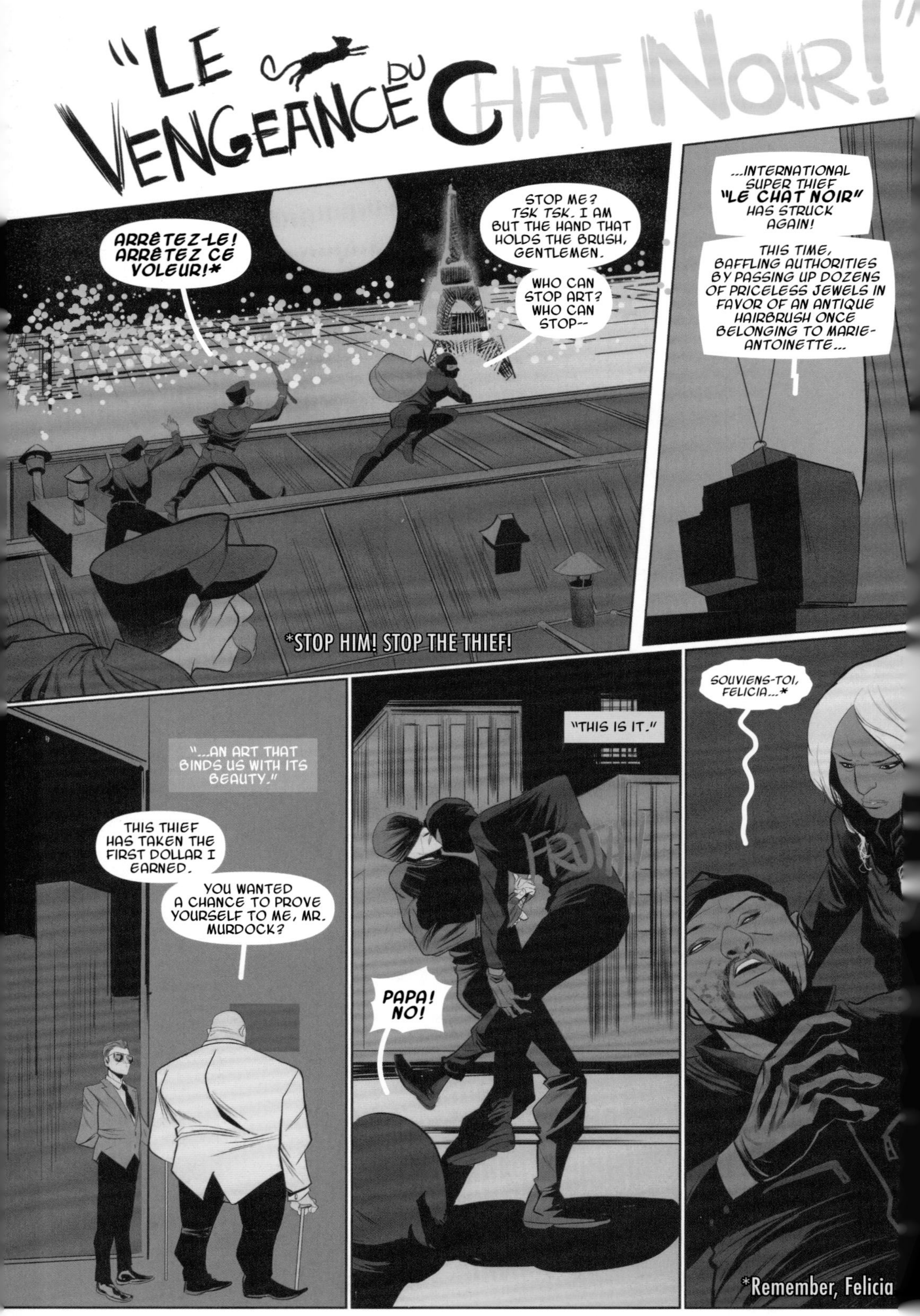
"LE VENGEANCE DU CHAT NOIR!"
ARRÊTEZ-LE! ARRÊTEZ CE VOLEUR!*
STOP ME? TSK TSK. I AM BUT THE HAND THAT HOLDS THE BRUSH, GENTLEMEN.
WHO CAN STOP ART? WHO CAN STOP--
*STOP HIM! STOP THE THIEF!
...INTERNATIONAL SUPER THIEF "LE CHAT NOIR" HAS STRUCK AGAIN!
THIS TIME, BAFFLING AUTHORITIES BY PASSING UP DOZENS OF PRICELESS JEWELS IN FAVOR OF AN ANTIQUE HAIRBRUSH ONCE BELONGING TO MARIE-ANTOINETTE...
"...AN ART THAT BINDS US WITH ITS BEAUTY."
THIS THIEF HAS TAKEN THE FIRST DOLLAR I EARNED.
YOU WANTED A CHANCE TO PROVE YOURSELF TO ME, MR. MURDOCK?
"THIS IS IT."
FRUTT!
PAPA! NO!
SOUVIENS-TOI, FELICIA...*
*Remember, Felicia

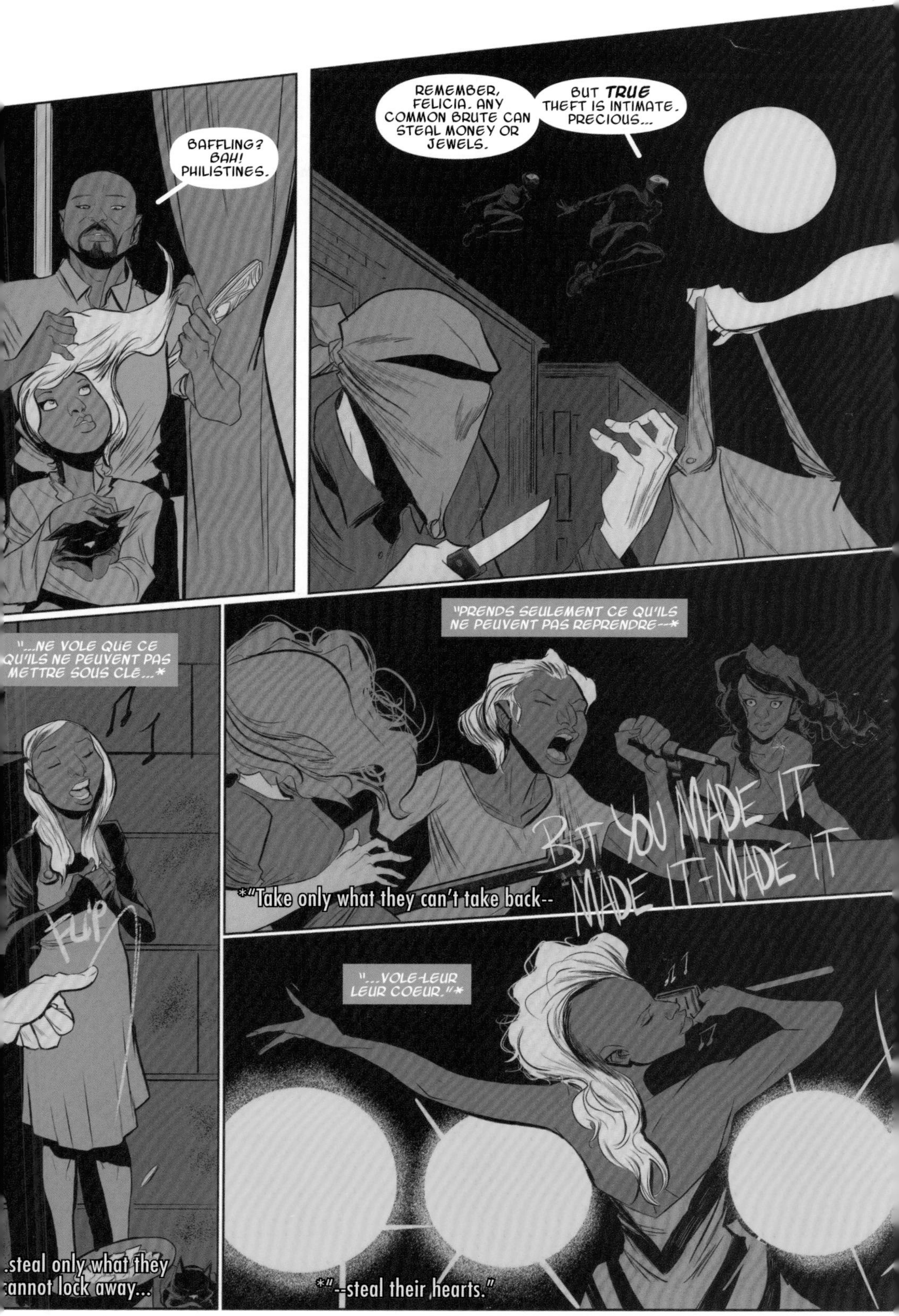

BAFFLING? BAH! PHILISTINES.
REMEMBER, FELICIA. ANY COMMON BRUTE CAN STEAL MONEY OR JEWELS.
BUT TRUE THEFT IS INTIMATE. PRECIOUS...
"...NE VOLE QUE CE QU'ILS NE PEUVENT PAS METTRE SOUS CLE...*
FUP
*...steal only what they cannot lock away...
"PRENDS SEULEMENT CE QU'ILS NE PEUVENT PAS REPRENDRE--*
BUT YOU MADE IT MADE IT-MADE IT
*"Take only what they can't take back--
"...VOLE-LEUR LEUR COEUR."*
*"--steal their hearts."

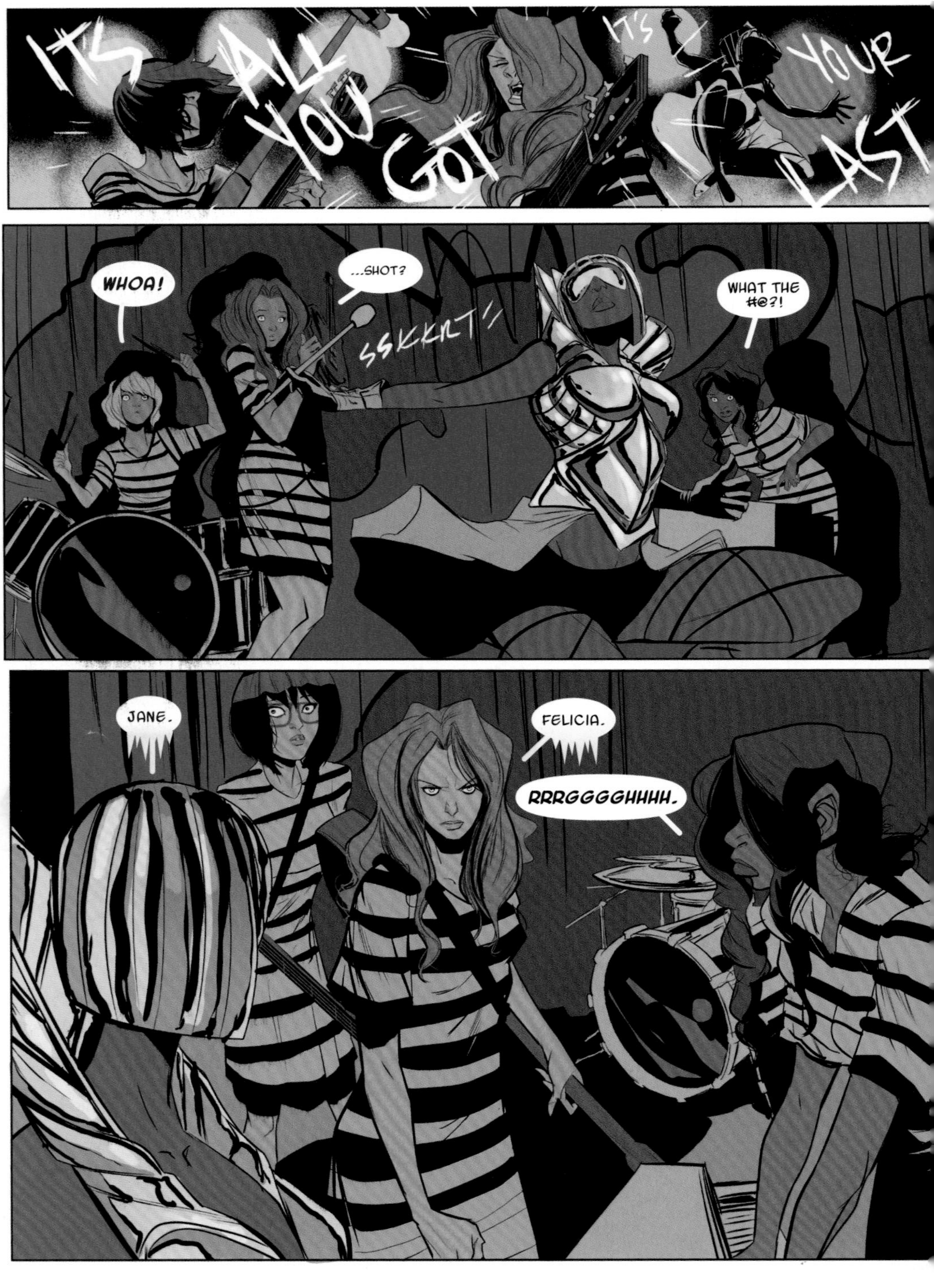
IT'S ALL YOU GOT
IT'S YOUR LAST
WHOA!
...SHOT?
SSKKRT
WHAT THE #@?!
JANE.
FELICIA.
RRRGGGGHHHH.

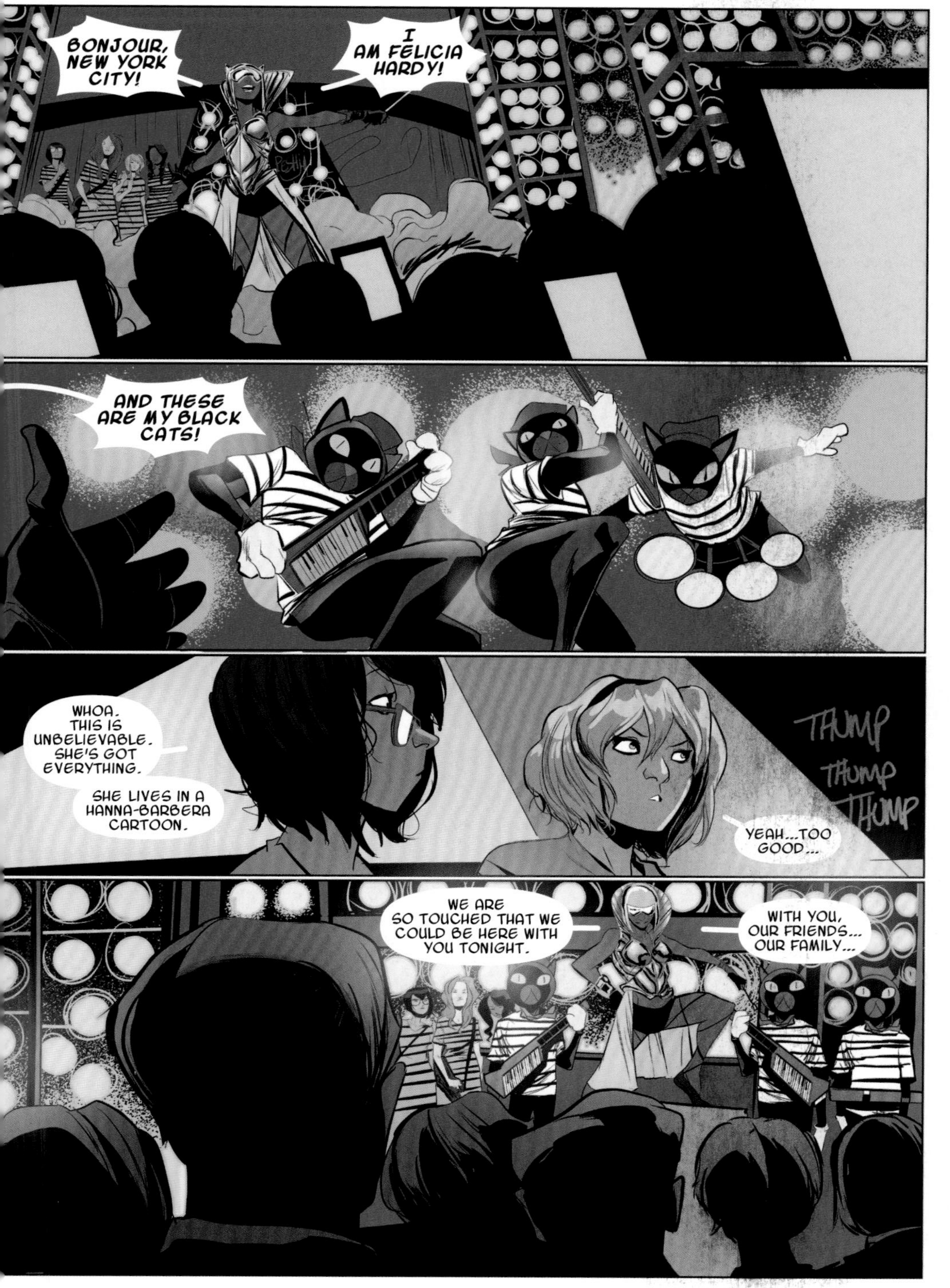
BONJOUR, NEW YORK CITY!
I AM FELICIA HARDY!
AND THESE ARE MY BLACK CATS!
WHOA. THIS IS UNBELIEVABLE. SHE'S GOT EVERYTHING.
SHE LIVES IN A HANNA-BARBERA CARTOON.
THUMP
THUMP
THUMP
YEAH...TOO GOOD...
WE ARE SO TOUCHED THAT WE COULD BE HERE WITH YOU TONIGHT.
WITH YOU, OUR FRIENDS... OUR FAMILY...

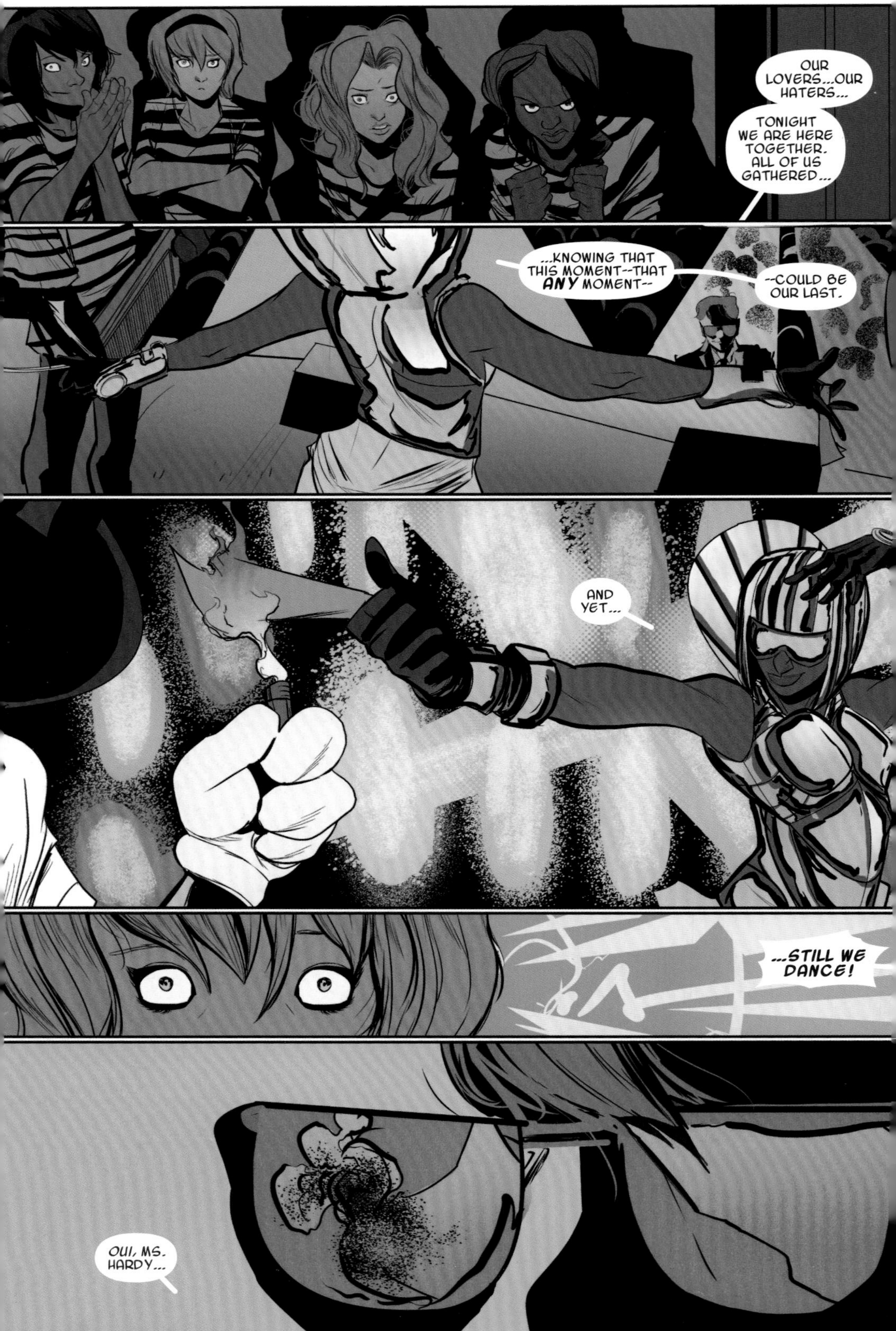
OUR LOVERS...OUR HATERS...
TONIGHT WE ARE HERE TOGETHER. ALL OF US GATHERED...
...KNOWING THAT THIS MOMENT--THAT ANY MOMENT--
--COULD BE OUR LAST.
AND YET...
...STILL WE DANCE!
OUI, MS. HARDY...

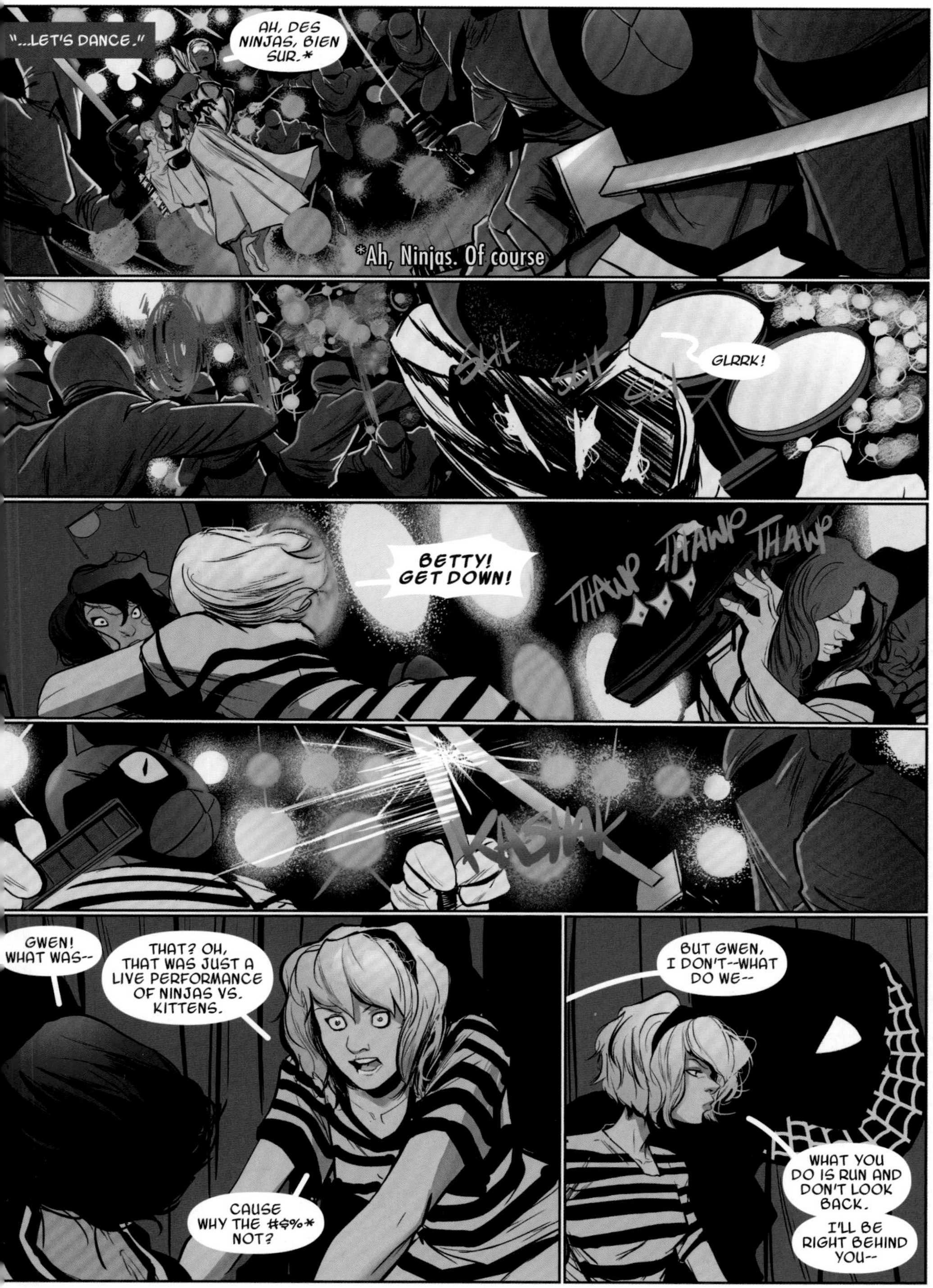
"...LET'S DANCE."
AH, DES NINJAS, BIEN SUR.*
*Ah, Ninjas. Of course
GLRRK!
BETTY! GET DOWN!
THAWP THAWP THAWP
KASHAK
GWEN! WHAT WAS--
THAT? OH, THAT WAS JUST A LIVE PERFORMANCE OF NINJAS VS. KITTENS.
CAUSE WHY THE #$%* NOT?
BUT GWEN, I DON'T--WHAT DO WE--
WHAT YOU DO IS RUN AND DON'T LOOK BACK.
I'LL BE RIGHT BEHIND YOU--

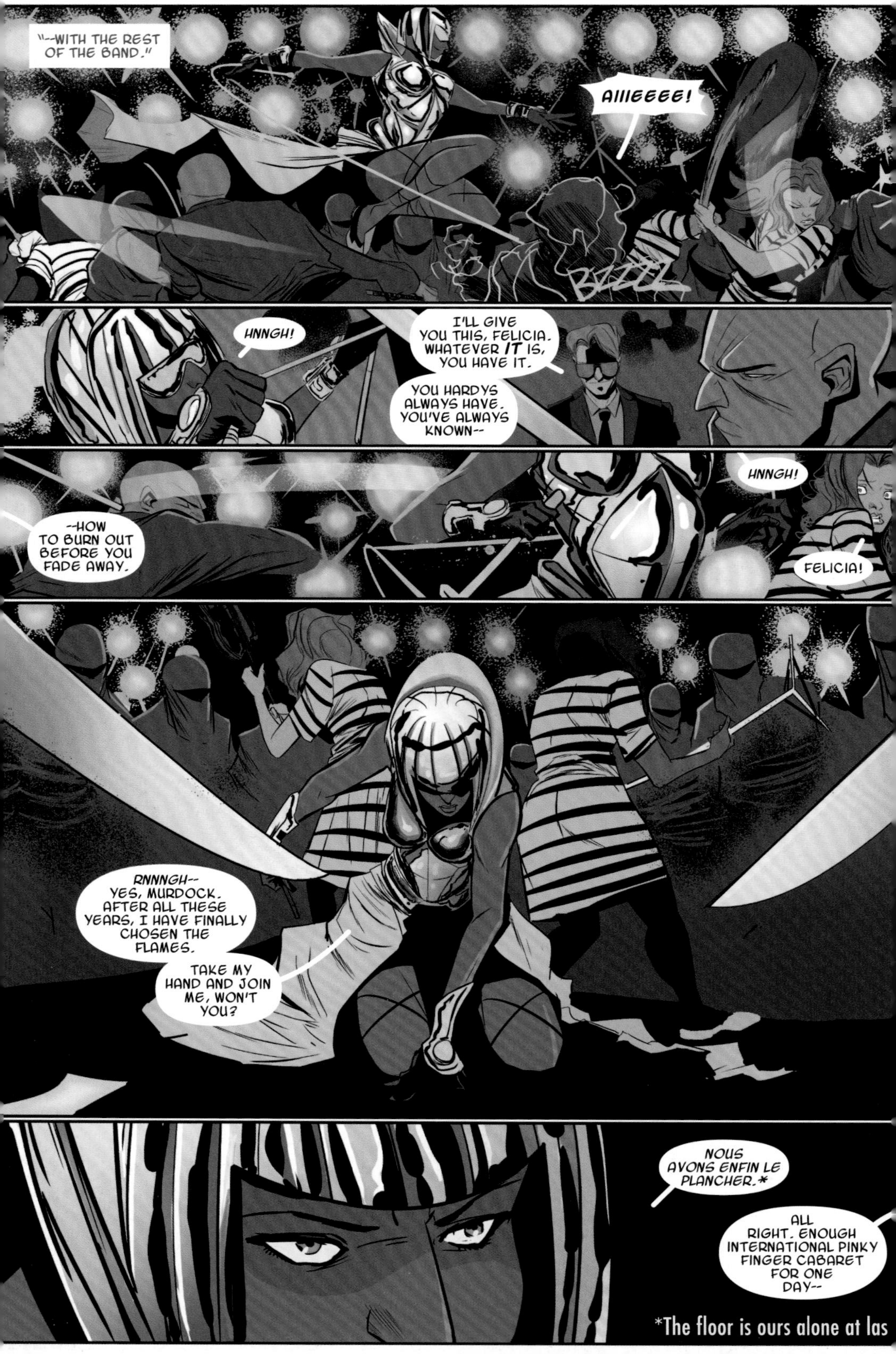
"--WITH THE REST OF THE BAND."
AIIIEEEE!
BZZZL
HNNGH!
I'LL GIVE YOU THIS, FELICIA. WHATEVER IT IS, YOU HAVE IT.
YOU HARDYS ALWAYS HAVE. YOU'VE ALWAYS KNOWN--
--HOW TO BURN OUT BEFORE YOU FADE AWAY.
HNNGH!
FELICIA!
RNNNGH-- YES, MURDOCK. AFTER ALL THESE YEARS, I HAVE FINALLY CHOSEN THE FLAMES.
TAKE MY HAND AND JOIN ME, WON'T YOU?
NOUS AVONS ENFIN LE PLANCHER.*
ALL RIGHT. ENOUGH INTERNATIONAL PINKY FINGER CABARET FOR ONE DAY--
*The floor is ours alone at las

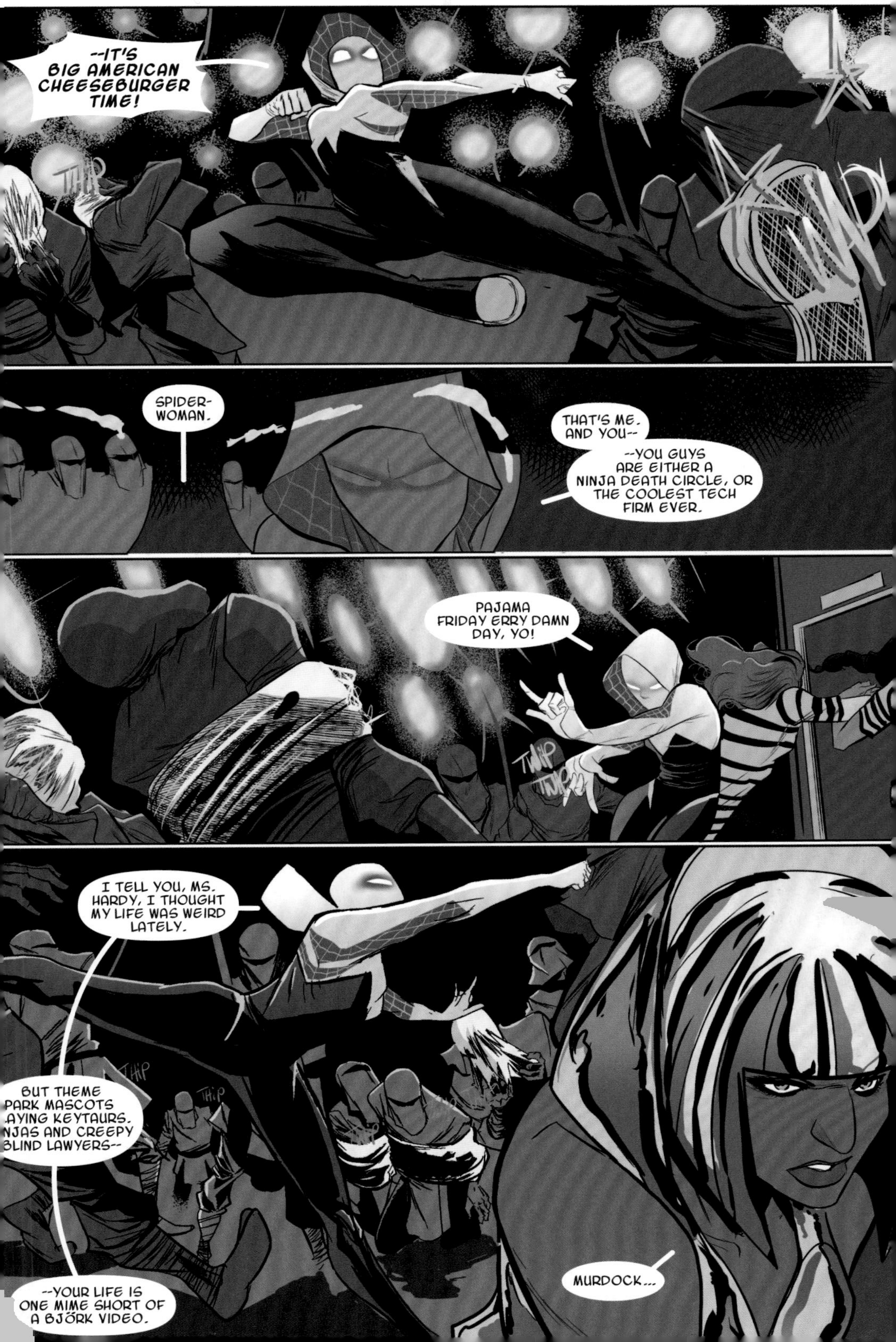
--IT'S BIG AMERICAN CHEESEBURGER TIME!
THIP
SPIDER-WOMAN.
THAT'S ME. AND YOU--
--YOU GUYS ARE EITHER A NINJA DEATH CIRCLE, OR THE COOLEST TECH FIRM EVER.
PAJAMA FRIDAY ERRY DAMN DAY, YO!
THIP THIP
I TELL YOU, MS. HARDY, I THOUGHT MY LIFE WAS WEIRD LATELY.
BUT THEME PARK MASCOTS LAYING KEYTAURS. NJAS AND CREEPY BLIND LAWYERS--
THIP
THIP
--YOUR LIFE IS ONE MIME SHORT OF A BJÖRK VIDEO.
MURDOCK...

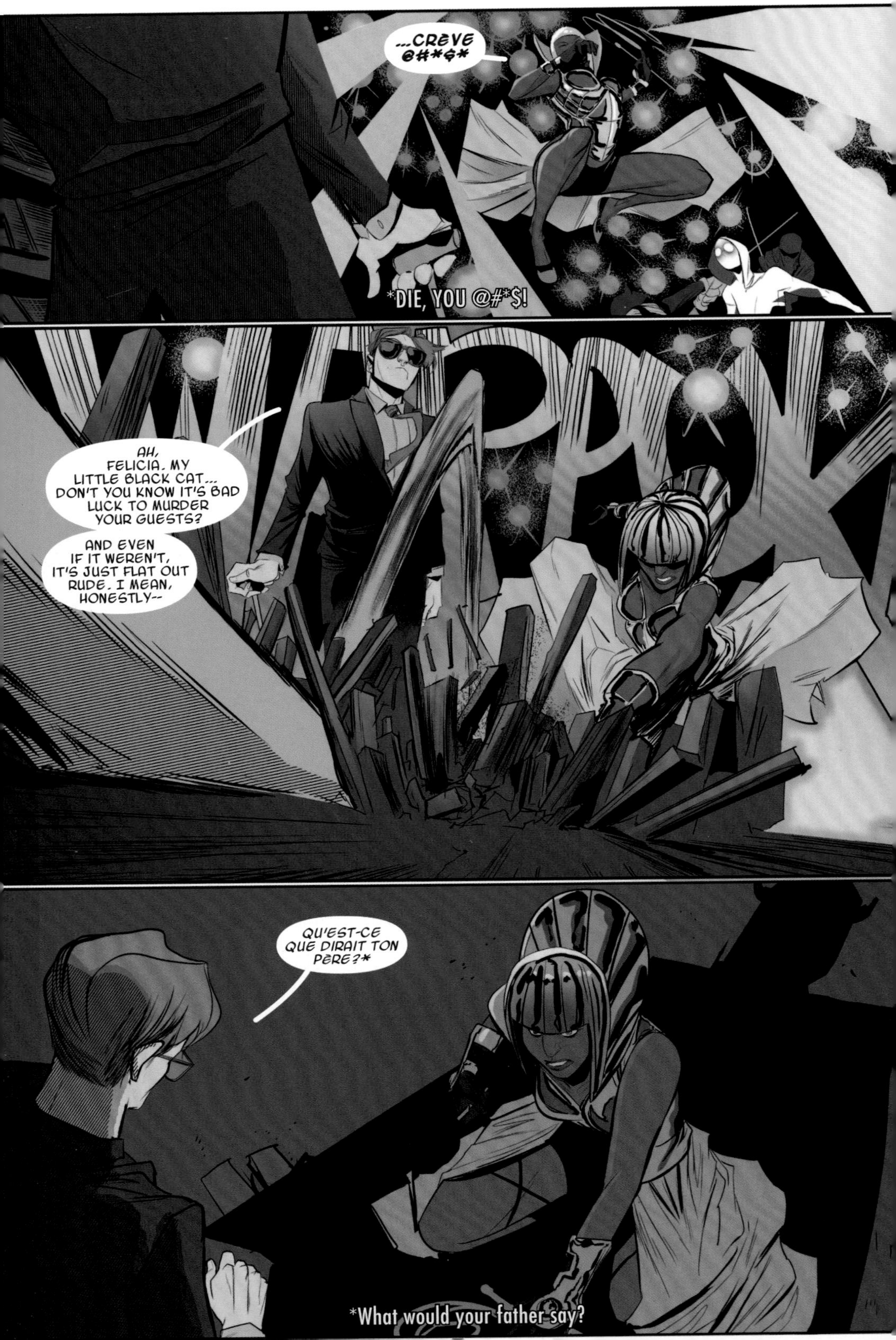
...CRÈVE @#*$*
DIE, YOU @#$!
AH, FELICIA. MY LITTLE BLACK CAT... DON'T YOU KNOW IT'S BAD LUCK TO MURDER YOUR GUESTS?
AND EVEN IF IT WEREN'T, IT'S JUST FLAT OUT RUDE. I MEAN, HONESTLY--
QU'EST-CE QUE DIRAIT TON PÈRE?*
*What would your father say?

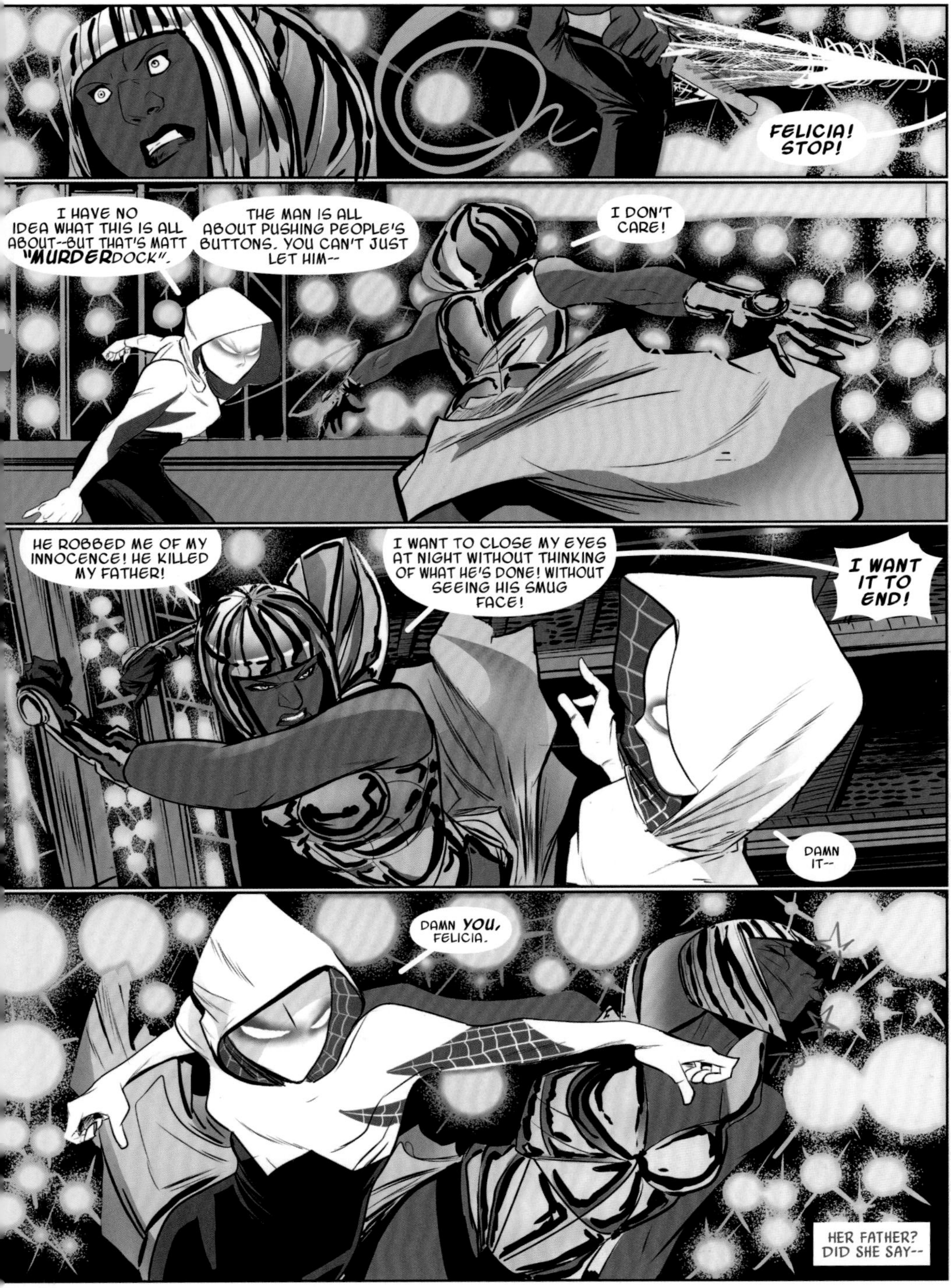
FELICIA! STOP!
I HAVE NO IDEA WHAT THIS IS ALL ABOUT--BUT THAT'S MATT "MURDERDOCK".
THE MAN IS ALL ABOUT PUSHING PEOPLE'S BUTTONS. YOU CAN'T JUST LET HIM--
I DON'T CARE!
HE ROBBED ME OF MY INNOCENCE! HE KILLED MY FATHER!
I WANT TO CLOSE MY EYES AT NIGHT WITHOUT THINKING OF WHAT HE'S DONE! WITHOUT SEEING HIS SMUG FACE!
I WANT IT TO END!
DAMN IT--
DAMN YOU, FELICIA.
HER FATHER? DID SHE SAY--

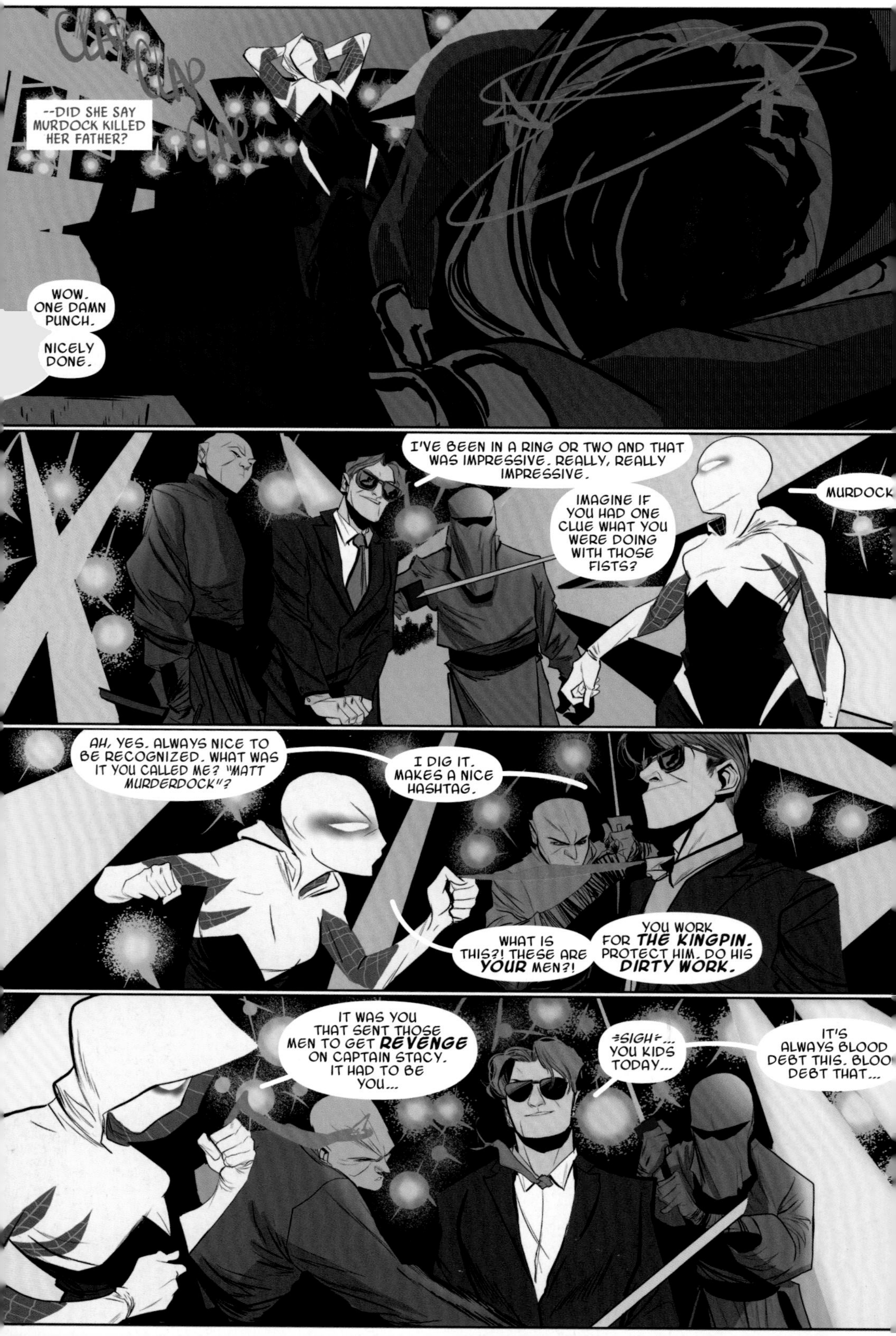
CLAP CLAP CLAP
--DID SHE SAY MURDOCK KILLED HER FATHER?
WOW. ONE DAMN PUNCH.
NICELY DONE.
I'VE BEEN IN A RING OR TWO AND THAT WAS IMPRESSIVE. REALLY, REALLY IMPRESSIVE.
IMAGINE IF YOU HAD ONE CLUE WHAT YOU WERE DOING WITH THOSE FISTS?
MURDOCK
AH, YES. ALWAYS NICE TO BE RECOGNIZED. WHAT WAS IT YOU CALLED ME? "MATT MURDERDOCK"?
I DIG IT. MAKES A NICE HASHTAG.
WHAT IS THIS?! THESE ARE YOUR MEN?!
YOU WORK FOR THE KINGPIN. PROTECT HIM. DO HIS DIRTY WORK.
IT WAS YOU THAT SENT THOSE MEN TO GET REVENGE ON CAPTAIN STACY. IT HAD TO BE YOU...
=SIGH=... YOU KIDS TODAY...
IT'S ALWAYS BLOOD DEBT THIS. BLOO DEBT THAT...

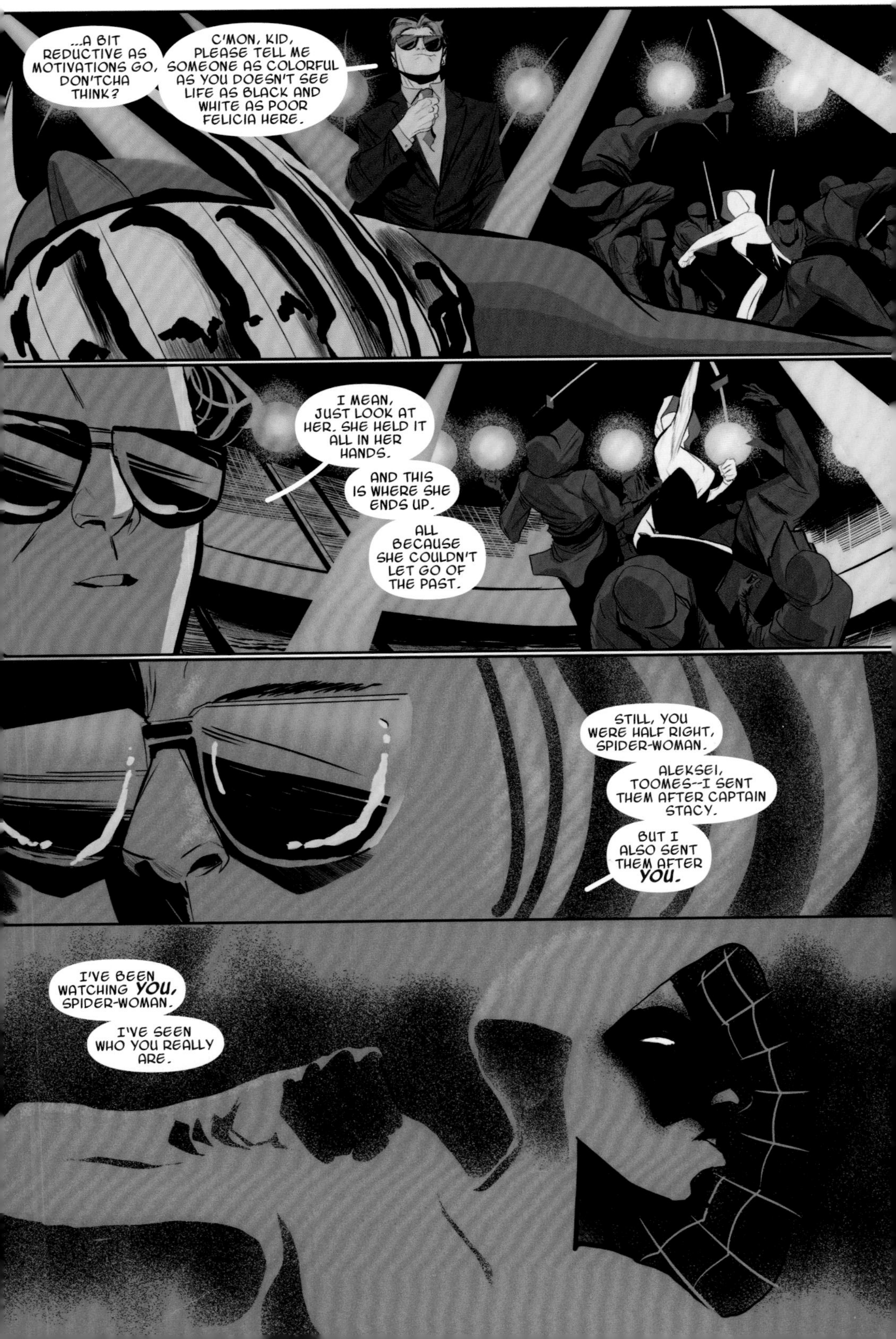
...A BIT REDUCTIVE AS MOTIVATIONS GO, DON'TCHA THINK?
C'MON, KID, PLEASE TELL ME SOMEONE AS COLORFUL AS YOU DOESN'T SEE LIFE AS BLACK AND WHITE AS POOR FELICIA HERE.
I MEAN, JUST LOOK AT HER. SHE HELD IT ALL IN HER HANDS.
AND THIS IS WHERE SHE ENDS UP.
ALL BECAUSE SHE COULDN'T LET GO OF THE PAST.
STILL, YOU WERE HALF RIGHT, SPIDER-WOMAN.
ALEKSEI, TOOMES--I SENT THEM AFTER CAPTAIN STACY.
BUT I ALSO SENT THEM AFTER YOU.
I'VE BEEN WATCHING YOU, SPIDER-WOMAN.
I'VE SEEN WHO YOU REALLY ARE.

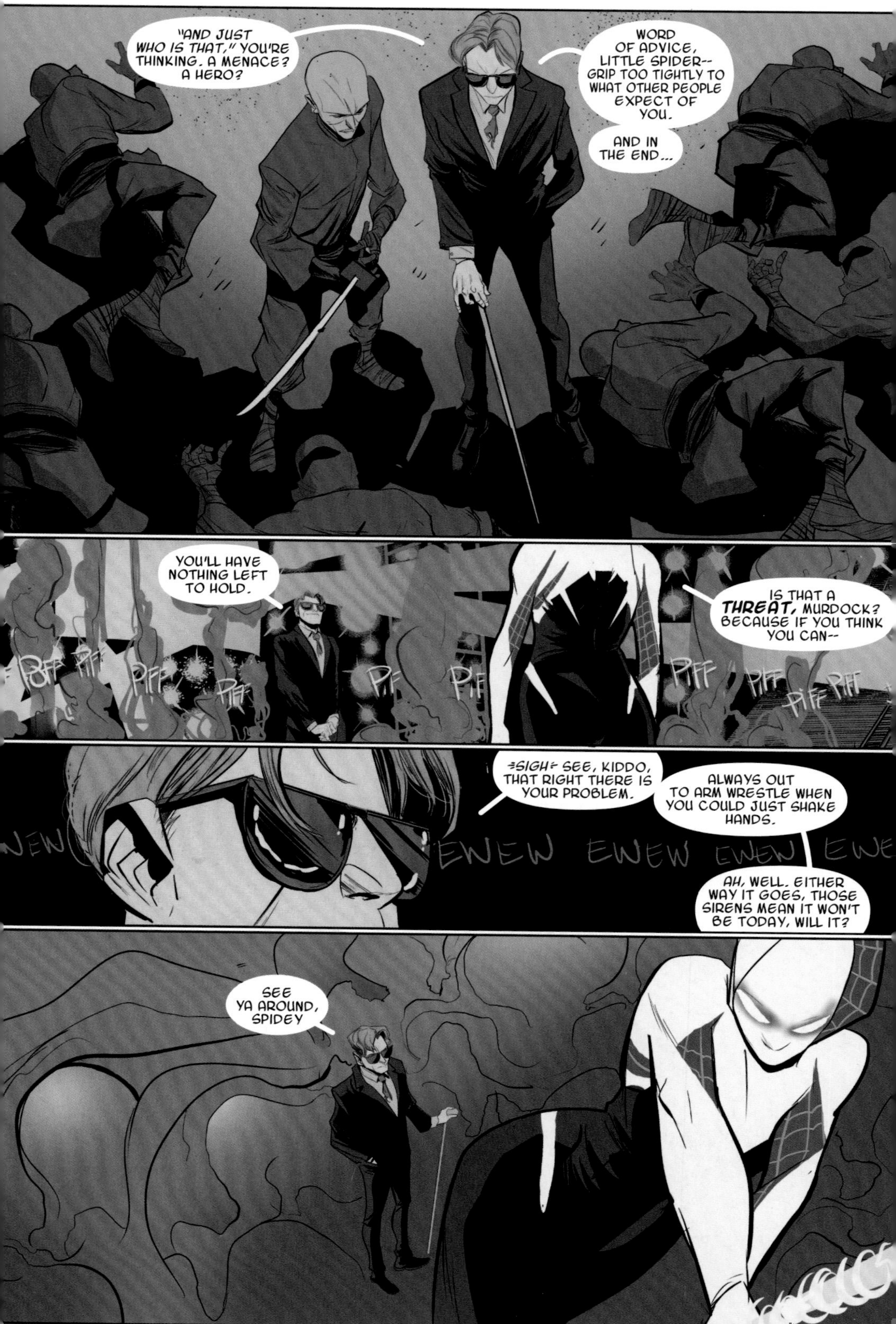
"AND JUST WHO IS THAT," YOU'RE THINKING. A MENACE? A HERO?
WORD OF ADVICE, LITTLE SPIDER-- GRIP TOO TIGHTLY TO WHAT OTHER PEOPLE EXPECT OF YOU.
AND IN THE END...
YOU'LL HAVE NOTHING LEFT TO HOLD.
IS THAT A THREAT, MURDOCK? BECAUSE IF YOU THINK YOU CAN--
PIFF PIFF PIFF PIFF PIFF PIFF PIFF PIFF PIFF PIFF PIFF
=SIGH= SEE, KIDDO, THAT RIGHT THERE IS YOUR PROBLEM.
ALWAYS OUT TO ARM WRESTLE WHEN YOU COULD JUST SHAKE HANDS.
EWEW EWEW EWEW EWEW EWE
AH, WELL. EITHER WAY IT GOES, THOSE SIRENS MEAN IT WON'T BE TODAY, WILL IT?
SEE YA AROUND, SPIDEY

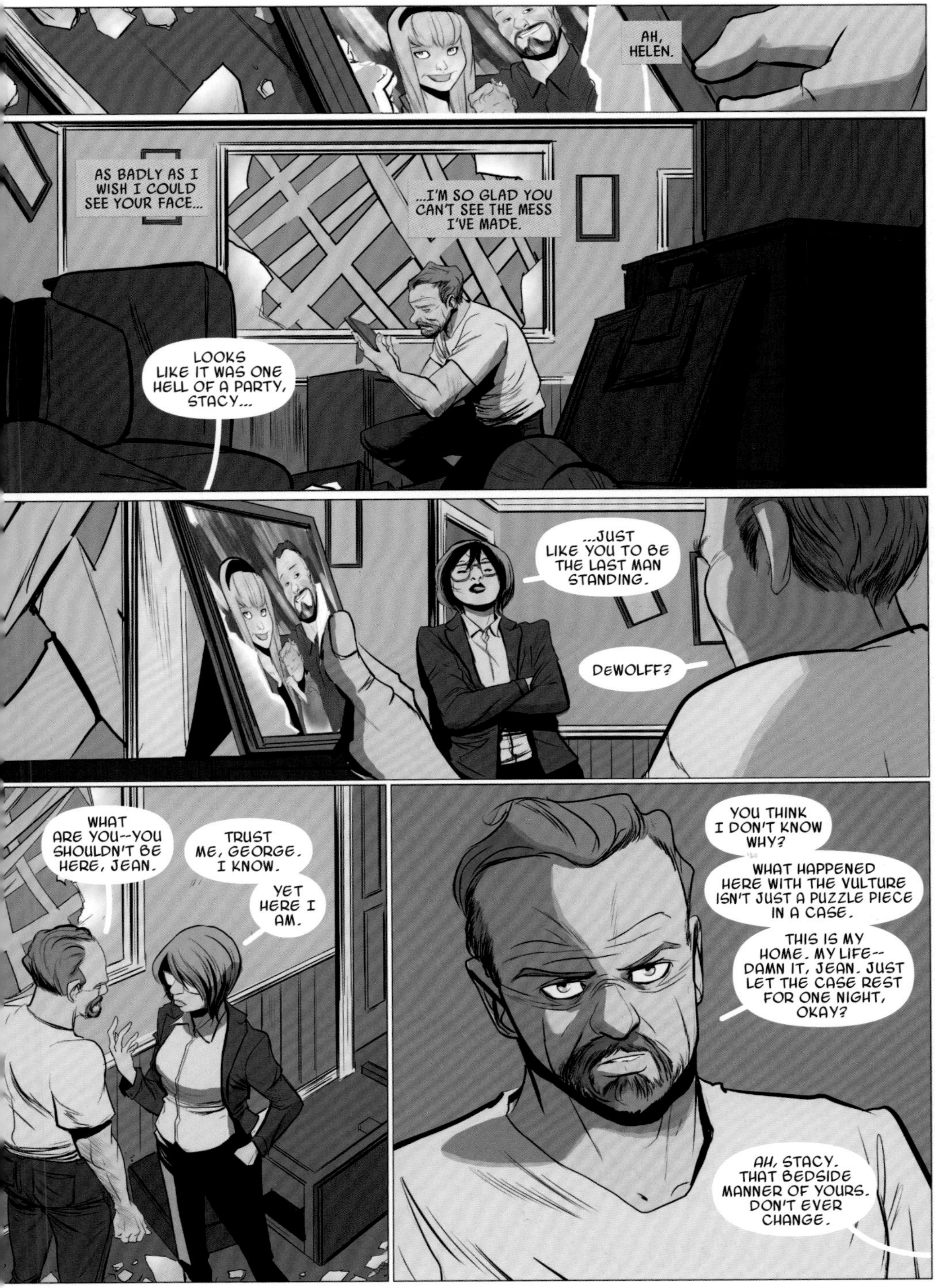
AH, HELEN.
AS BADLY AS I WISH I COULD SEE YOUR FACE...
...I'M SO GLAD YOU CAN'T SEE THE MESS I'VE MADE.
LOOKS LIKE IT WAS ONE HELL OF A PARTY, STACY...
...JUST LIKE YOU TO BE THE LAST MAN STANDING.
DeWOLFF?
WHAT ARE YOU--YOU SHOULDN'T BE HERE, JEAN.
TRUST ME, GEORGE. I KNOW.
YET HERE I AM.
YOU THINK I DON'T KNOW WHY?
WHAT HAPPENED HERE WITH THE VULTURE ISN'T JUST A PUZZLE PIECE IN A CASE.
THIS IS MY HOME. MY LIFE--DAMN IT, JEAN. JUST LET THE CASE REST FOR ONE NIGHT, OKAY?
AH, STACY. THAT BEDSIDE MANNER OF YOURS. DON'T EVER CHANGE.

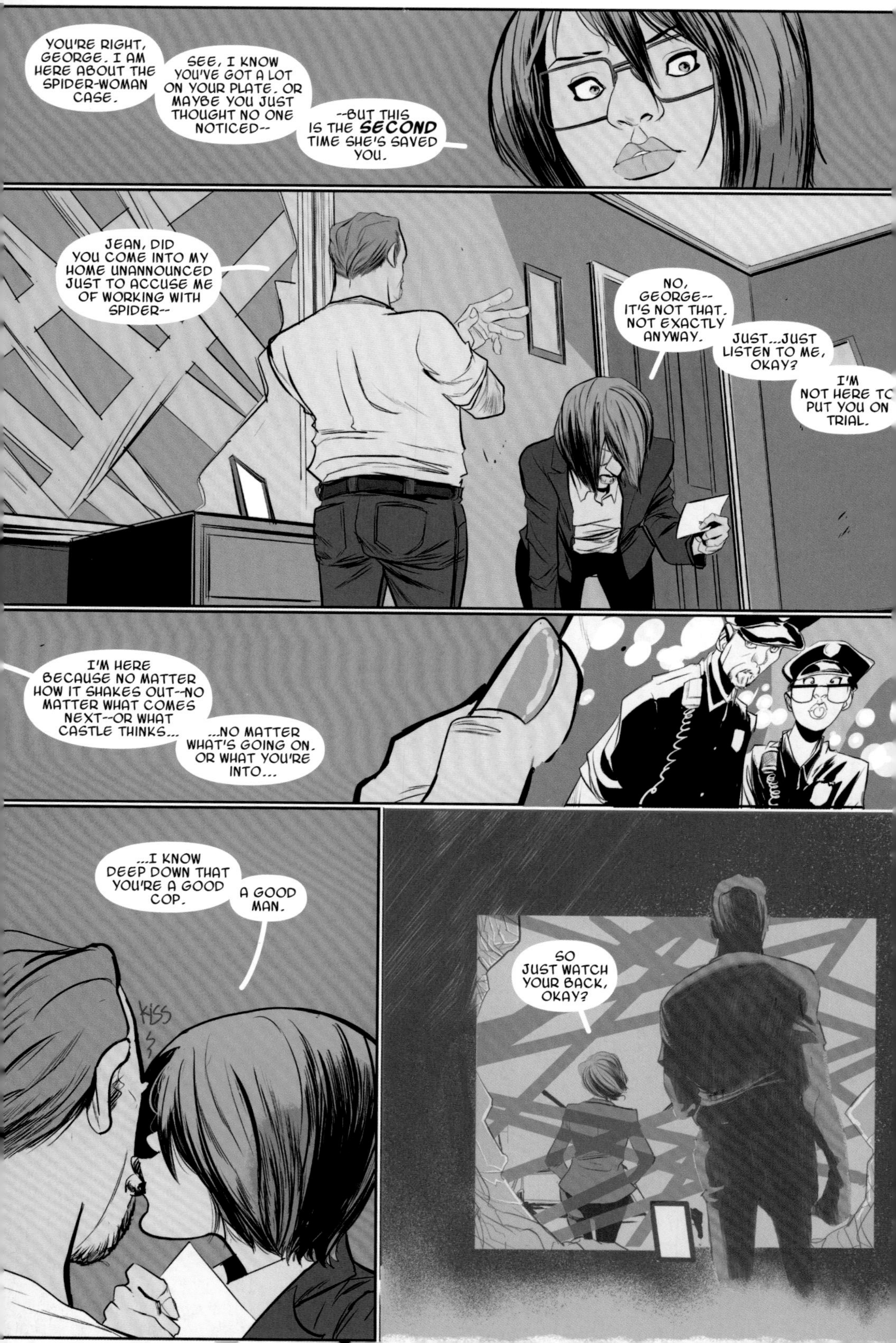
YOU'RE RIGHT, GEORGE. I AM HERE ABOUT THE SPIDER-WOMAN CASE.
SEE, I KNOW YOU'VE GOT A LOT ON YOUR PLATE. OR MAYBE YOU JUST THOUGHT NO ONE NOTICED--
--BUT THIS IS THE SECOND TIME SHE'S SAVED YOU.
JEAN, DID YOU COME INTO MY HOME UNANNOUNCED JUST TO ACCUSE ME OF WORKING WITH SPIDER--
NO, GEORGE-- IT'S NOT THAT. NOT EXACTLY ANYWAY.
JUST...JUST LISTEN TO ME, OKAY?
I'M NOT HERE TO PUT YOU ON TRIAL.
I'M HERE BECAUSE NO MATTER HOW IT SHAKES OUT--NO MATTER WHAT COMES NEXT--OR WHAT CASTLE THINKS...
...NO MATTER WHAT'S GOING ON. OR WHAT YOU'RE INTO...
...I KNOW DEEP DOWN THAT YOU'RE A GOOD COP.
A GOOD MAN.
KISS
SO JUST WATCH YOUR BACK, OKAY?

1B

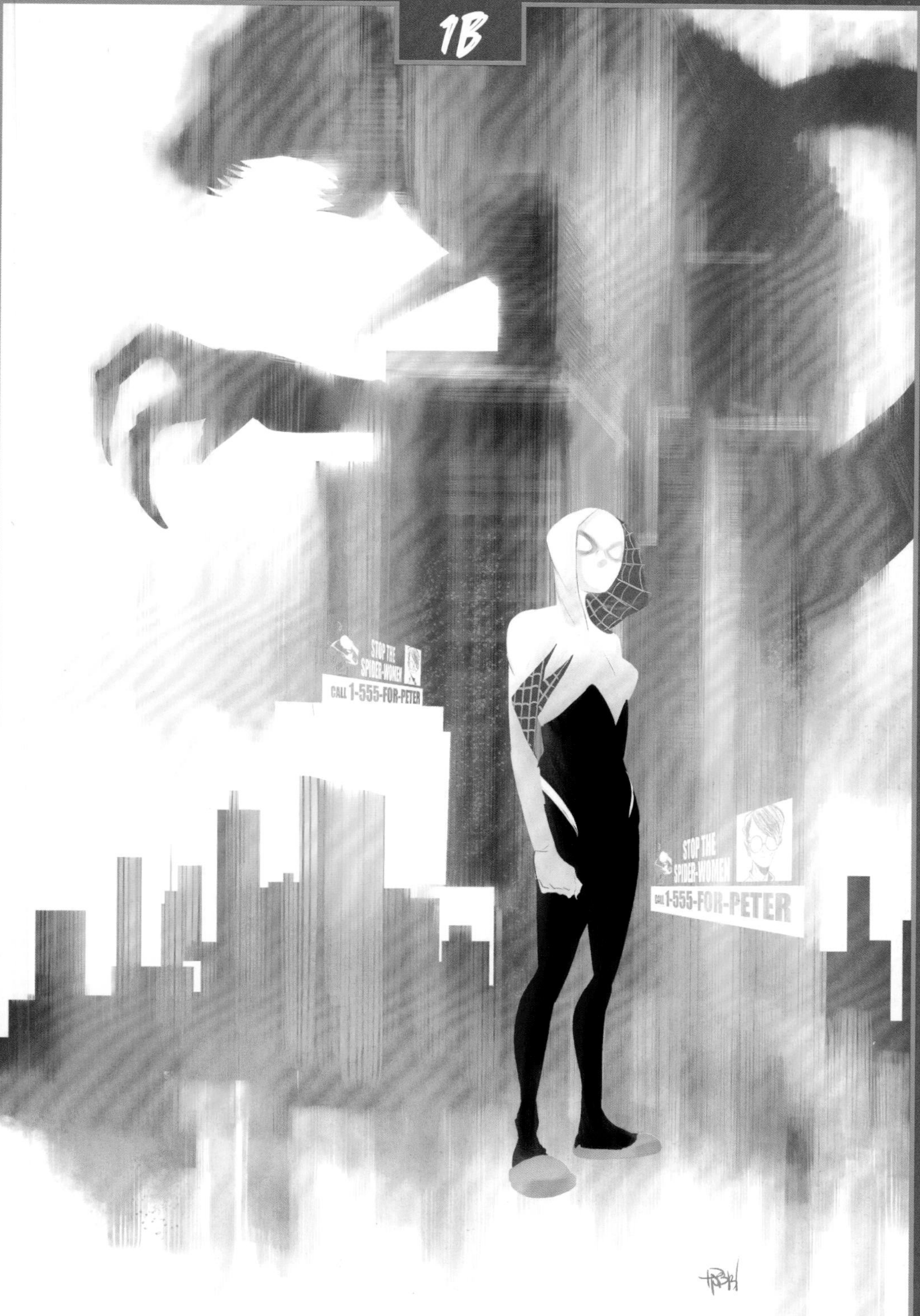
STOP THE
SPIDER-WOMEN
CALL 1-555-FOR-PETER
STOP THE
SPIDER-WOMEN
CALL 1-555-FOR-PETER

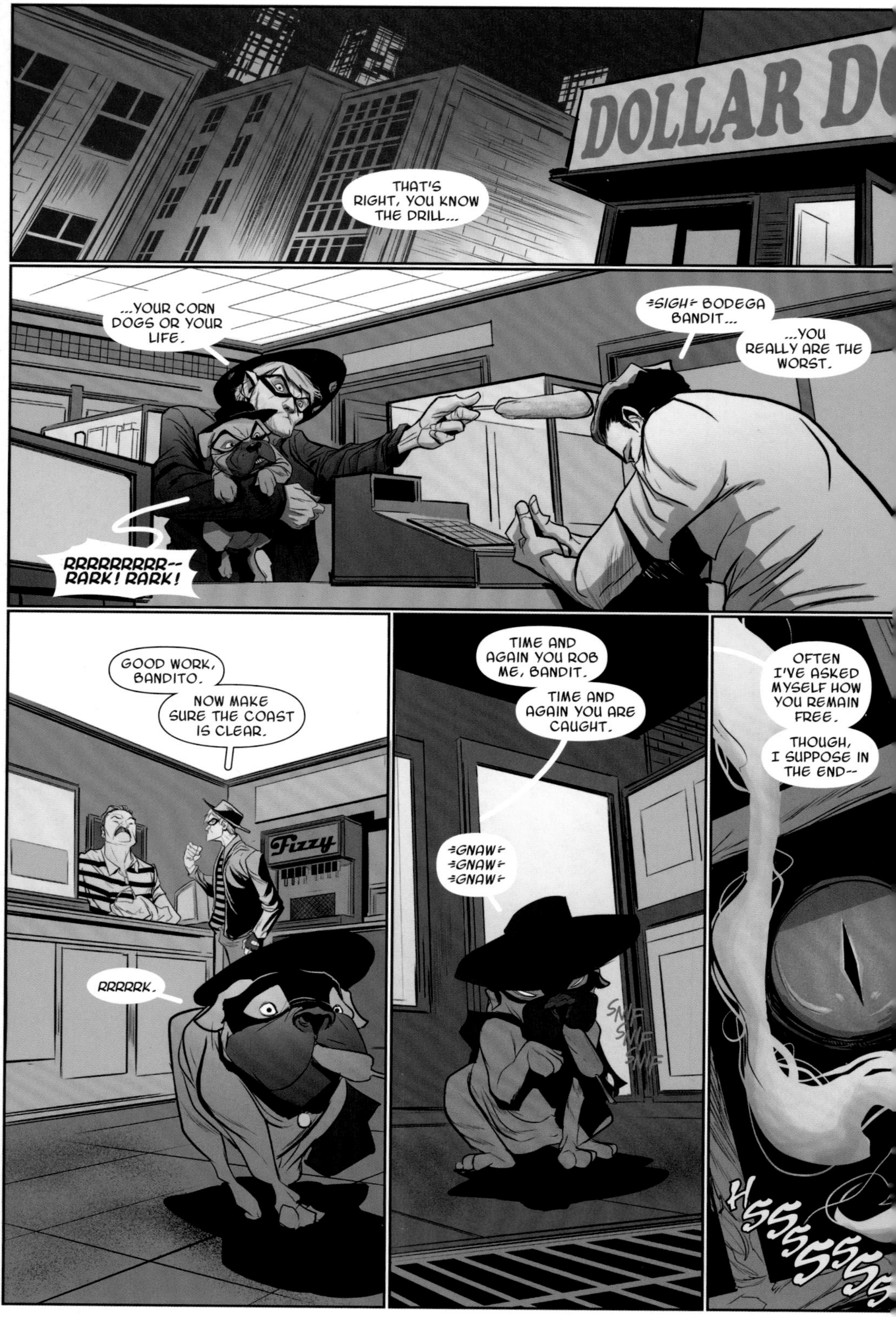
DOLLAR D
THAT'S RIGHT, YOU KNOW THE DRILL...
...YOUR CORN DOGS OR YOUR LIFE.
=SIGH= BODEGA BANDIT...
...YOU REALLY ARE THE WORST.
RRRRRRRRR--RARK! RARK!
GOOD WORK, BANDITO.
NOW MAKE SURE THE COAST IS CLEAR.
Fizzy
RRRRRK.
TIME AND AGAIN YOU ROB ME, BANDIT.
TIME AND AGAIN YOU ARE CAUGHT.
=GNAW= =GNAW= =GNAW=
SNIF SNIF SNIF
OFTEN I'VE ASKED MYSELF HOW YOU REMAIN FREE.
THOUGH, I SUPPOSE IN THE END--
HSSSSSSS

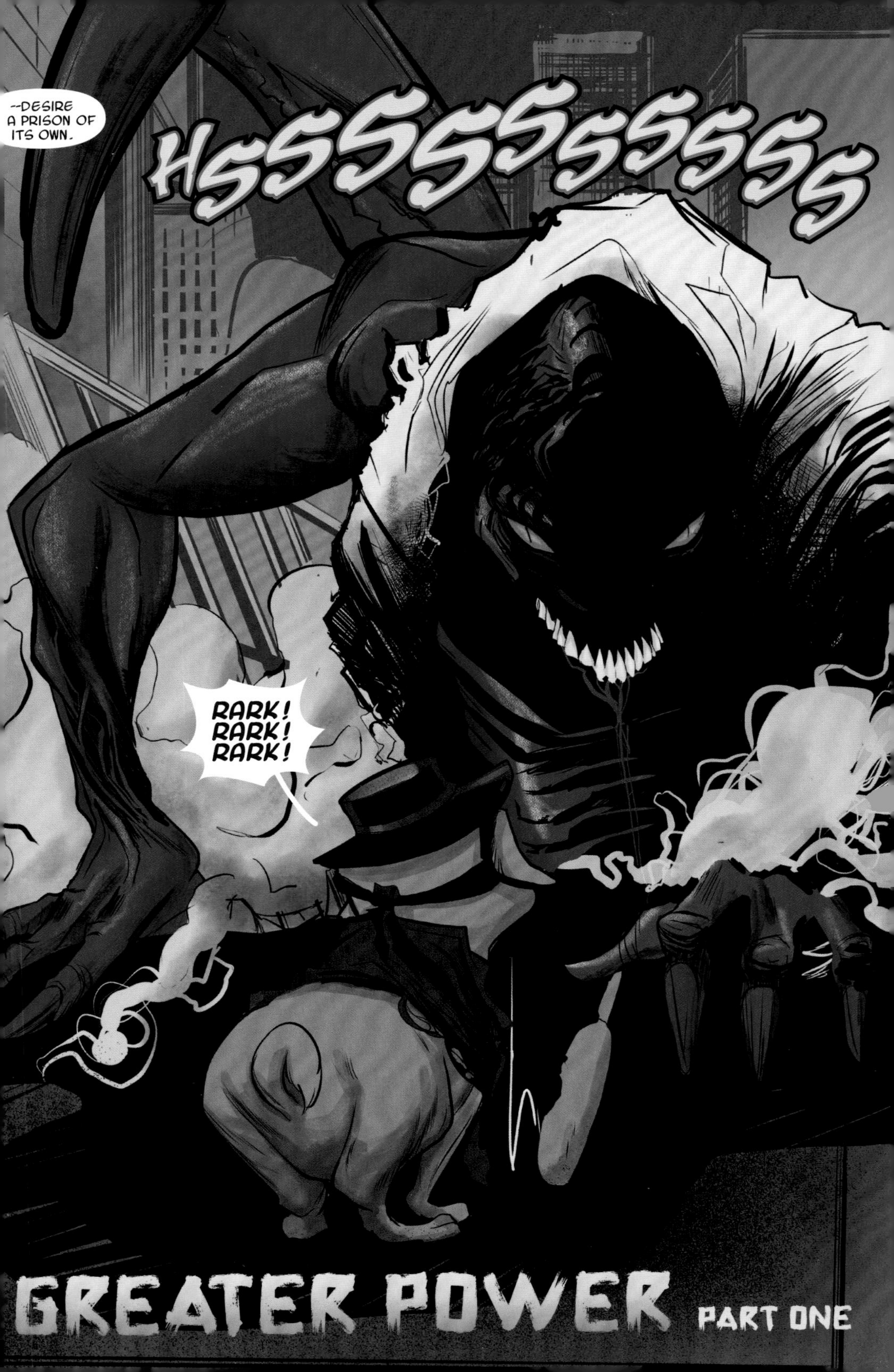
--DESIRE A PRISON OF ITS OWN.
HSSSSSSSSSS
RARK! RARK! RARK!
GREATER POWER PART ONE

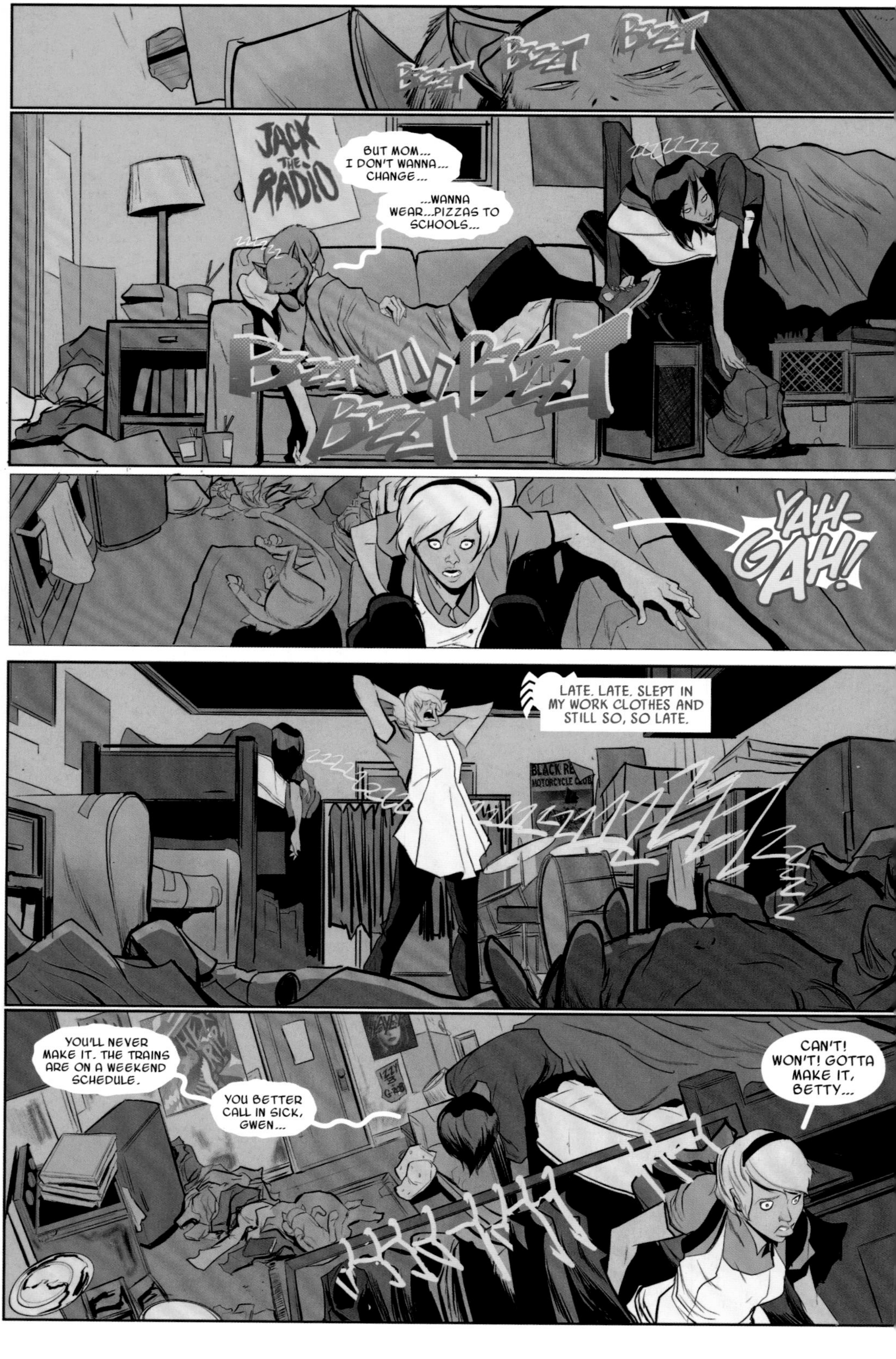
BEET BEET BEET
JACK THE RADIO
BUT MOM... I DON'T WANNA... CHANGE...
...WANNA WEAR...PIZZAS TO SCHOOLS...
ZZZZZZZZ
BEET BEET BEET BEET
YAH-GAH!
LATE. LATE. SLEPT IN MY WORK CLOTHES AND STILL SO, SO LATE.
BLACK RE MOTORCYCLE CLUB
YOU'LL NEVER MAKE IT. THE TRAINS ARE ON A WEEKEND SCHEDULE.
YOU BETTER CALL IN SICK, GWEN...
CAN'T! WON'T! GOTTA MAKE IT, BETTY...

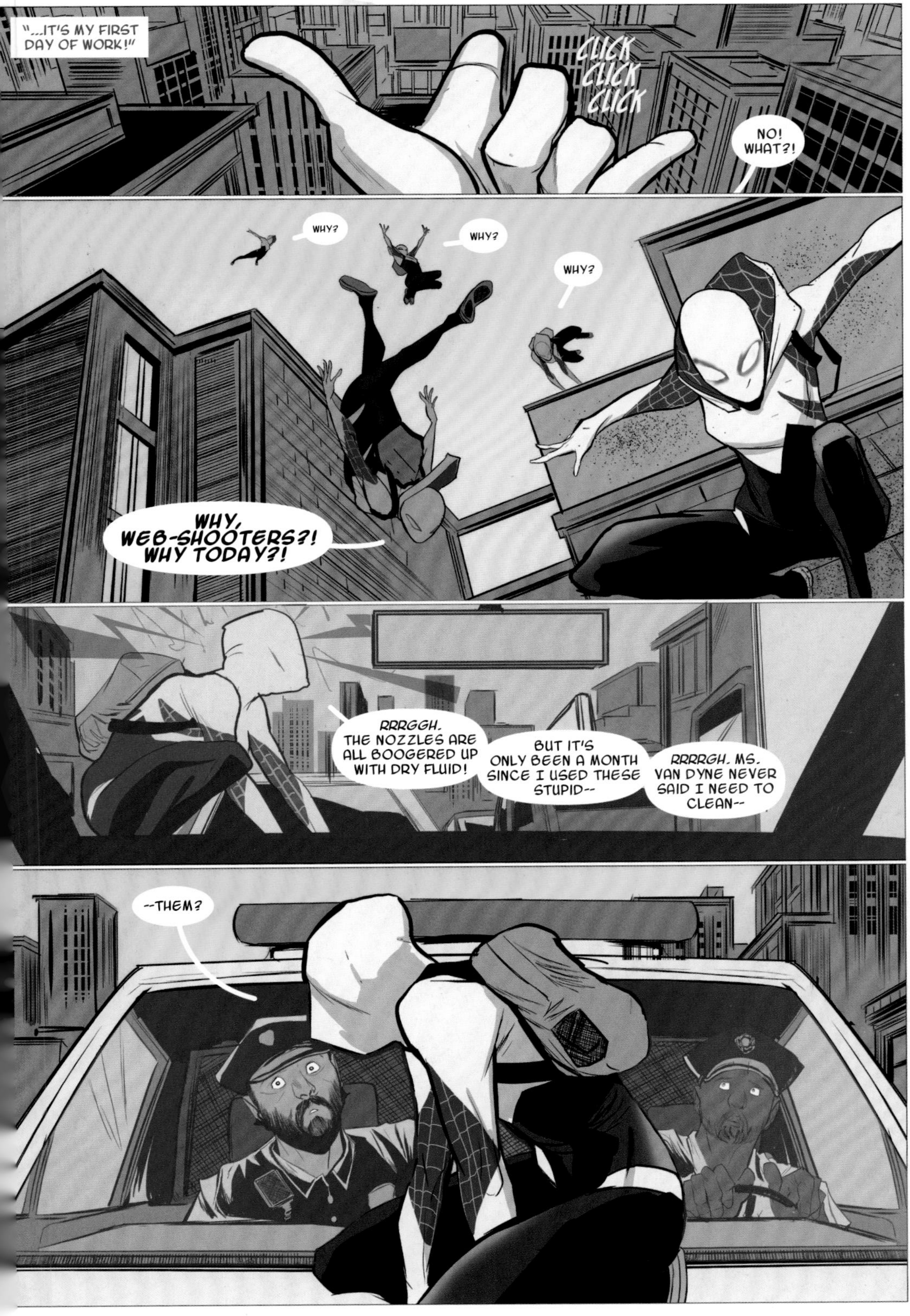
"...IT'S MY FIRST DAY OF WORK!"
CLICK CLICK CLICK
NO! WHAT?!
WHY?
WHY?
WHY?
WHY, WEB-SHOOTERS?! WHY TODAY?!
RRRGGH. THE NOZZLES ARE ALL BOOGERED UP WITH DRY FLUID!
BUT IT'S ONLY BEEN A MONTH SINCE I USED THESE STUPID--
RRRRGH. MS. VAN DYNE NEVER SAID I NEED TO CLEAN--
--THEM?

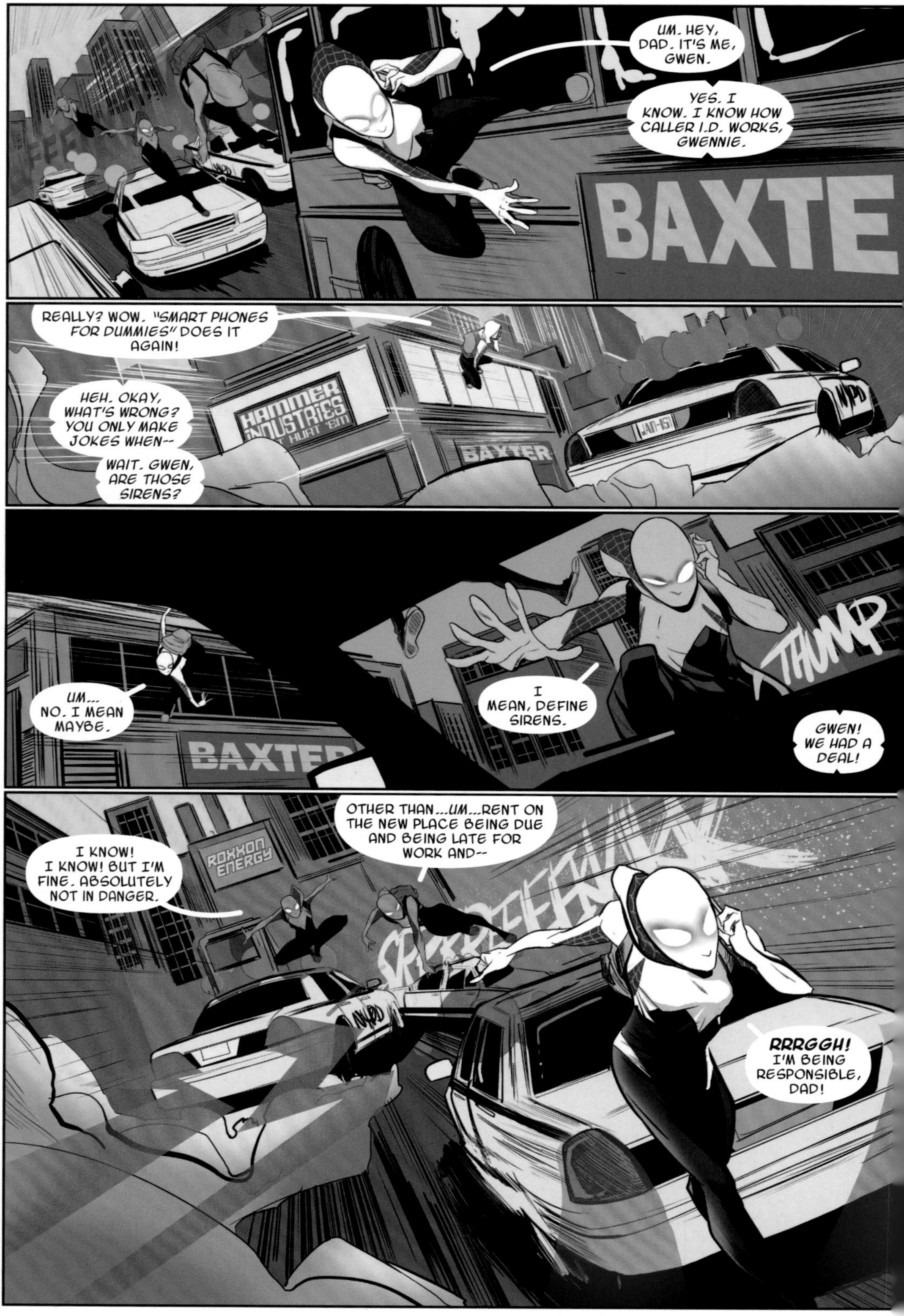
UM. HEY, DAD. IT'S ME, GWEN.
YES. I KNOW. I KNOW HOW CALLER I.D. WORKS, GWENNIE.
BAXTE
REALLY? WOW. "SMART PHONES FOR DUMMIES" DOES IT AGAIN!
HEH. OKAY, WHAT'S WRONG? YOU ONLY MAKE JOKES WHEN--
WAIT. GWEN, ARE THOSE SIRENS?
HAMMER INDUSTRIES
BAXTER
UM... NO. I MEAN MAYBE.
I MEAN, DEFINE SIRENS.
THUMP
GWEN! WE HAD A DEAL!
BAXTER
I KNOW! I KNOW! BUT I'M FINE. ABSOLUTELY NOT IN DANGER.
OTHER THAN...UM...RENT ON THE NEW PLACE BEING DUE AND BEING LATE FOR WORK AND--
ROXXON ENERGY
RRRGGH! I'M BEING RESPONSIBLE, DAD!

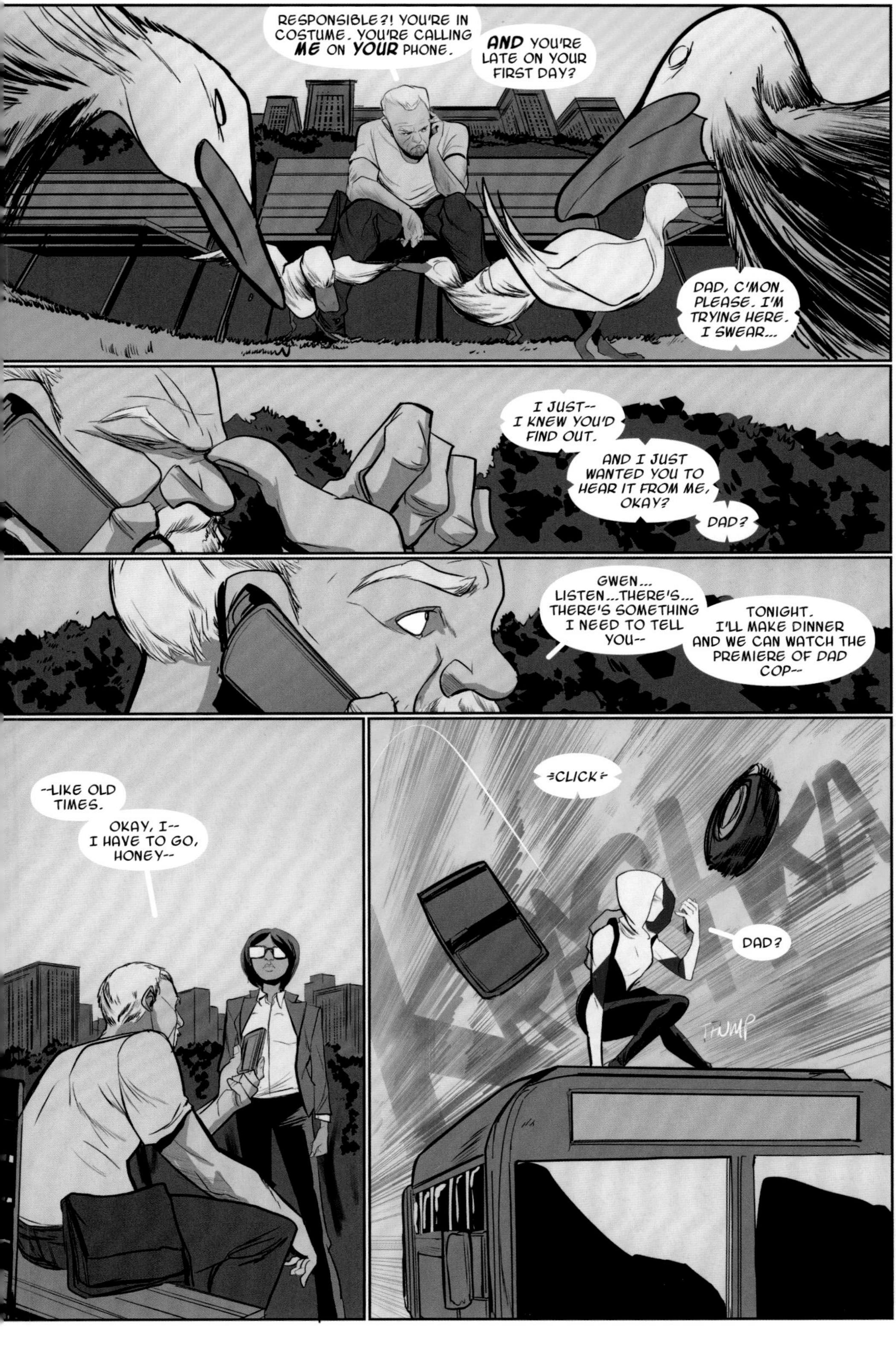
RESPONSIBLE?! YOU'RE IN COSTUME. YOU'RE CALLING ME ON YOUR PHONE.
AND YOU'RE LATE ON YOUR FIRST DAY?
DAD, C'MON. PLEASE. I'M TRYING HERE. I SWEAR...
I JUST-- I KNEW YOU'D FIND OUT.
AND I JUST WANTED YOU TO HEAR IT FROM ME, OKAY?
DAD?
GWEN... LISTEN...THERE'S... THERE'S SOMETHING I NEED TO TELL YOU--
TONIGHT. I'LL MAKE DINNER AND WE CAN WATCH THE PREMIERE OF DAD COP--
--LIKE OLD TIMES.
OKAY, I-- I HAVE TO GO, HONEY--
=CLICK=
DAD?
THUMP

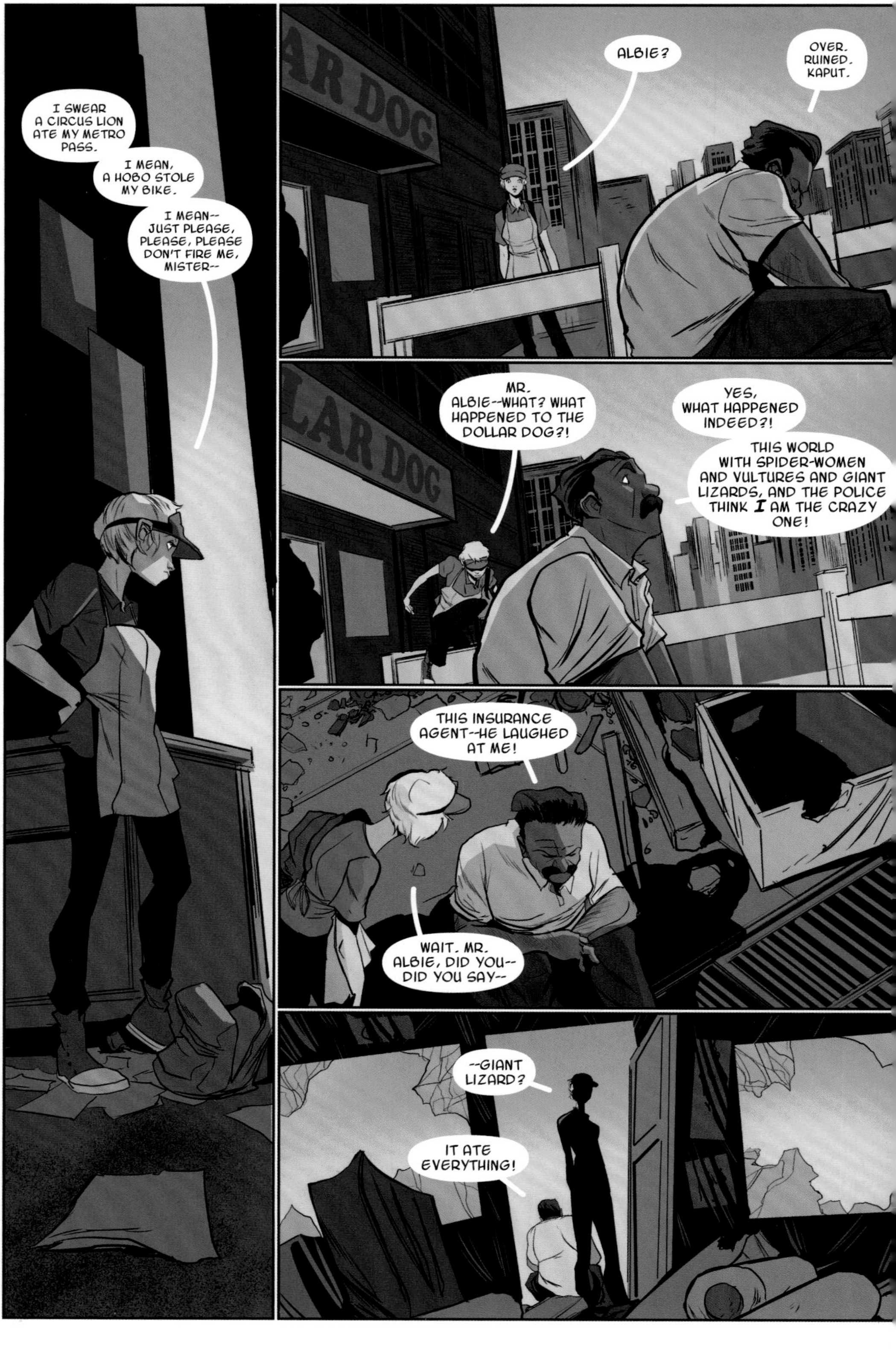
I SWEAR A CIRCUS LION ATE MY METRO PASS.
I MEAN, A HOBO STOLE MY BIKE.
I MEAN-- JUST PLEASE, PLEASE, PLEASE DON'T FIRE ME, MISTER--
AR DOG
ALBIE?
OVER. RUINED. KAPUT.
LAR DOG
MR. ALBIE--WHAT? WHAT HAPPENED TO THE DOLLAR DOG?!
YES, WHAT HAPPENED INDEED?!
THIS WORLD WITH SPIDER-WOMEN AND VULTURES AND GIANT LIZARDS, AND THE POLICE THINK *I* AM THE CRAZY ONE!
THIS INSURANCE AGENT--HE LAUGHED AT ME!
WAIT. MR. ALBIE, DID YOU-- DID YOU SAY--
--GIANT LIZARD?
IT ATE EVERYTHING!

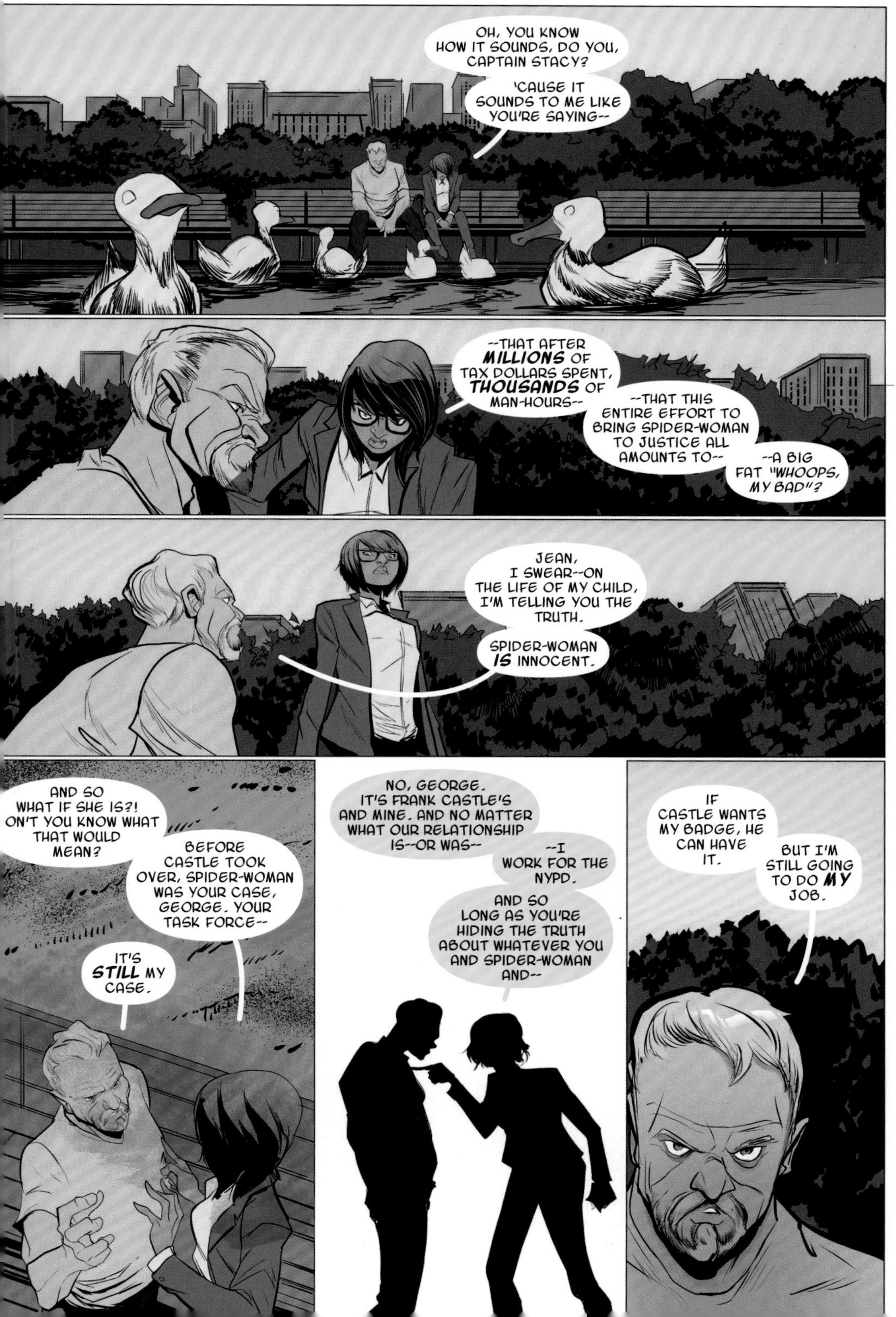

OH, YOU KNOW HOW IT SOUNDS, DO YOU, CAPTAIN STACY?
'CAUSE IT SOUNDS TO ME LIKE YOU'RE SAYING--
--THAT AFTER MILLIONS OF TAX DOLLARS SPENT, THOUSANDS OF MAN-HOURS--
--THAT THIS ENTIRE EFFORT TO BRING SPIDER-WOMAN TO JUSTICE ALL AMOUNTS TO--
--A BIG FAT "WHOOPS, MY BAD"?
JEAN, I SWEAR--ON THE LIFE OF MY CHILD, I'M TELLING YOU THE TRUTH.
SPIDER-WOMAN IS INNOCENT.
AND SO WHAT IF SHE IS?! ON'T YOU KNOW WHAT THAT WOULD MEAN?
BEFORE CASTLE TOOK OVER, SPIDER-WOMAN WAS YOUR CASE, GEORGE. YOUR TASK FORCE--
IT'S STILL MY CASE.
NO, GEORGE. IT'S FRANK CASTLE'S AND MINE. AND NO MATTER WHAT OUR RELATIONSHIP IS--OR WAS--
--I WORK FOR THE NYPD.
AND SO LONG AS YOU'RE HIDING THE TRUTH ABOUT WHATEVER YOU AND SPIDER-WOMAN AND--
IF CASTLE WANTS MY BADGE, HE CAN HAVE IT.
BUT I'M STILL GOING TO DO MY JOB.

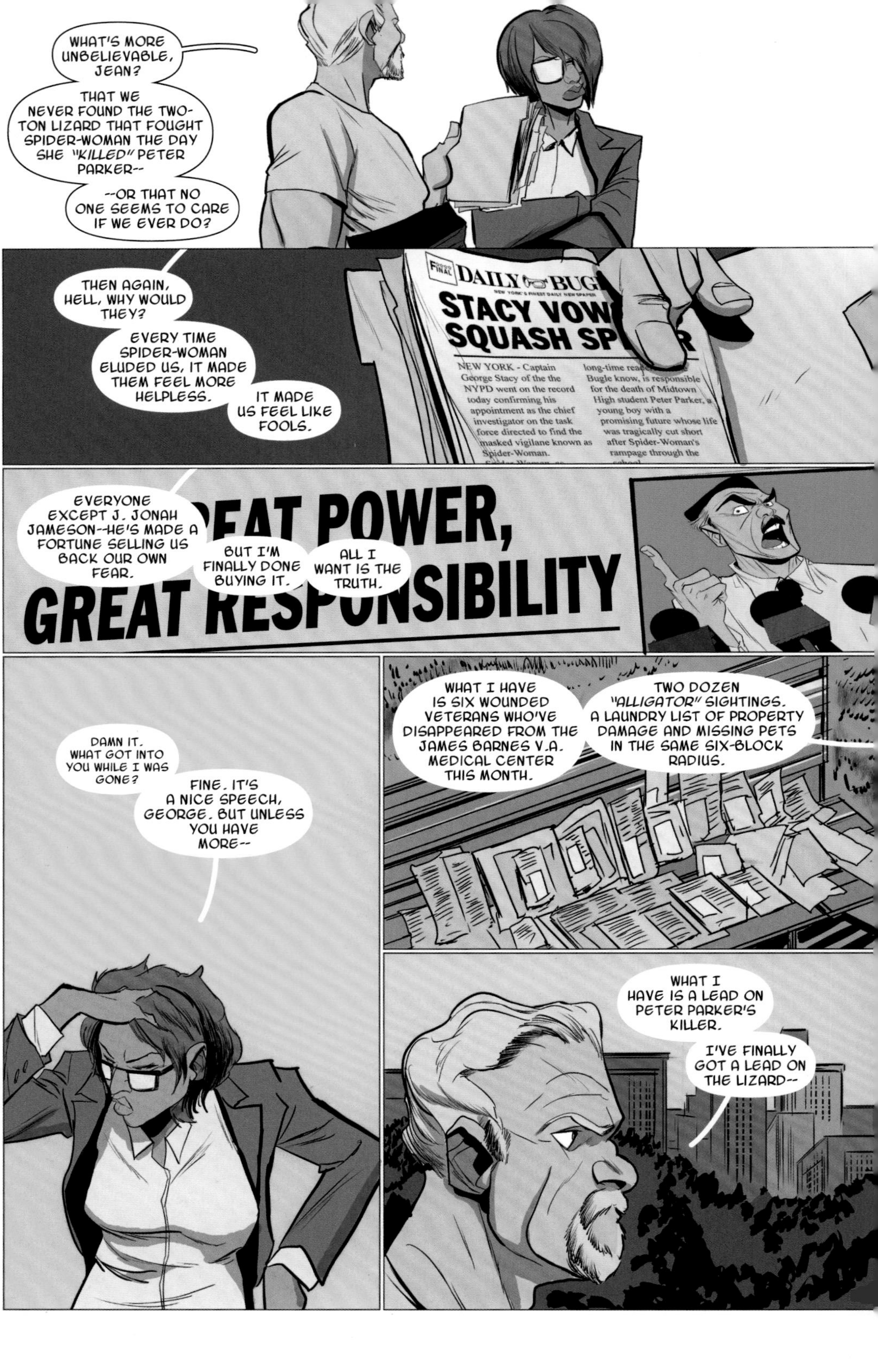

WHAT'S MORE UNBELIEVABLE, JEAN?
THAT WE NEVER FOUND THE TWO-TON LIZARD THAT FOUGHT SPIDER-WOMAN THE DAY SHE "KILLED" PETER PARKER--
--OR THAT NO ONE SEEMS TO CARE IF WE EVER DO?
THEN AGAIN, HELL, WHY WOULD THEY?
EVERY TIME SPIDER-WOMAN ELUDED US, IT MADE THEM FEEL MORE HELPLESS.
IT MADE US FEEL LIKE FOOLS.
DAILY BUGLE
STACY VOW
SQUASH SP
NEW YORK - Captain George Stacy of the the NYPD went on the record today confirming his appointment as the chief investigator on the task force directed to find the masked vigilane known as Spider-Woman.
long-time reade Bugle know, is responsible for the death of Midtown High student Peter Parker, a young boy with a promising future whose life was tragically cut short after Spider-Woman's rampage through the
EVERYONE EXCEPT J. JONAH JAMESON--HE'S MADE A FORTUNE SELLING US BACK OUR OWN FEAR.
BUT I'M FINALLY DONE BUYING IT.
ALL I WANT IS THE TRUTH.
EAT POWER,
GREAT RESPONSIBILITY
DAMN IT. WHAT GOT INTO YOU WHILE I WAS GONE?
FINE. IT'S A NICE SPEECH, GEORGE. BUT UNLESS YOU HAVE MORE--
WHAT I HAVE IS SIX WOUNDED VETERANS WHO'VE DISAPPEARED FROM THE JAMES BARNES V.A. MEDICAL CENTER THIS MONTH.
TWO DOZEN "ALLIGATOR" SIGHTINGS. A LAUNDRY LIST OF PROPERTY DAMAGE AND MISSING PETS IN THE SAME SIX-BLOCK RADIUS.
WHAT I HAVE IS A LEAD ON PETER PARKER'S KILLER.
I'VE FINALLY GOT A LEAD ON THE LIZARD--

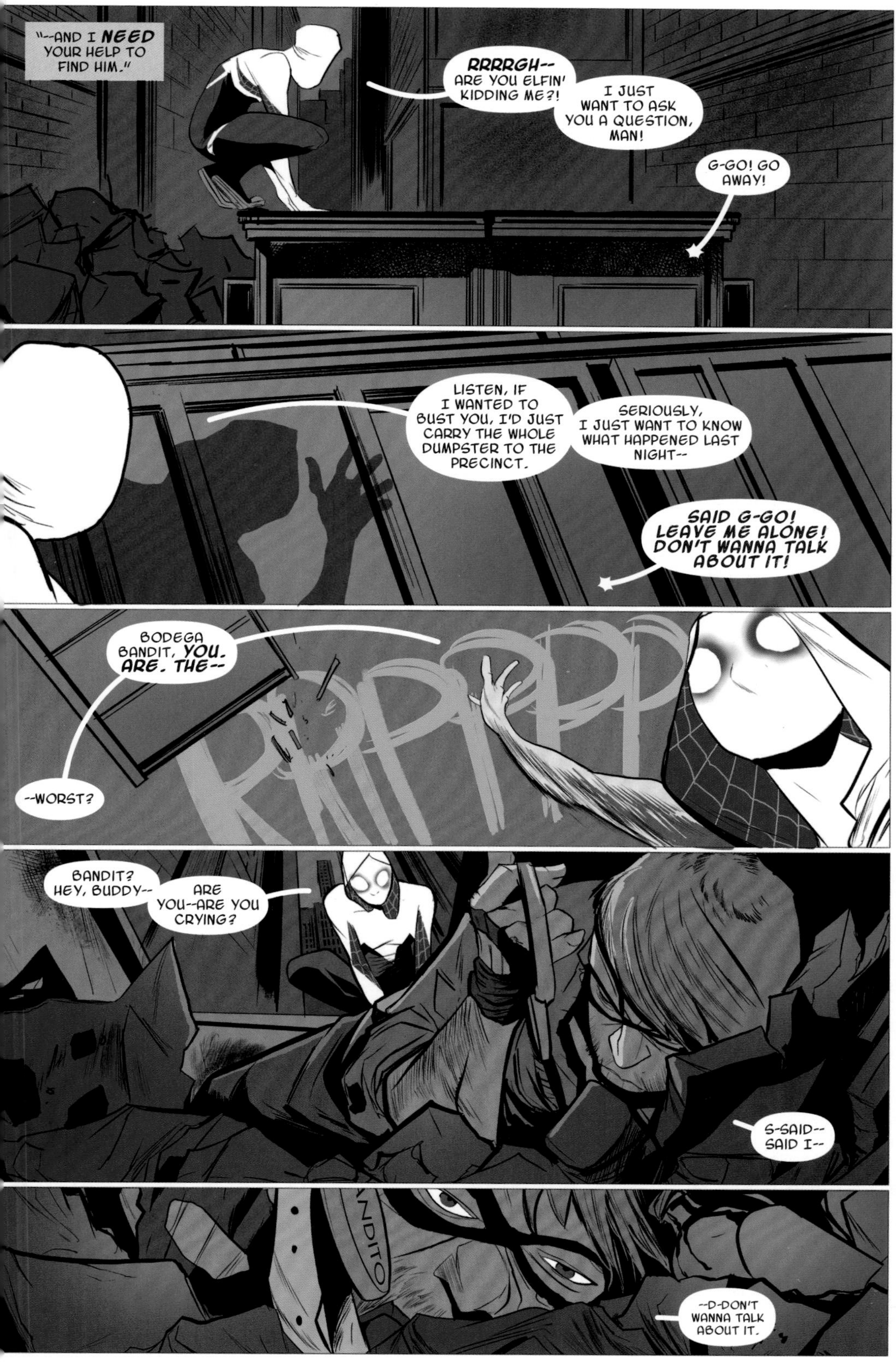
"--AND I NEED YOUR HELP TO FIND HIM."
RRRRGH-- ARE YOU ELFIN' KIDDING ME?!
I JUST WANT TO ASK YOU A QUESTION, MAN!
G-GO! GO AWAY!
LISTEN, IF I WANTED TO BUST YOU, I'D JUST CARRY THE WHOLE DUMPSTER TO THE PRECINCT.
SERIOUSLY, I JUST WANT TO KNOW WHAT HAPPENED LAST NIGHT--
SAID G-GO! LEAVE ME ALONE! DON'T WANNA TALK ABOUT IT!
BODEGA BANDIT, YOU. ARE. THE--
RRIPPPP
--WORST?
BANDIT? HEY, BUDDY--
ARE YOU--ARE YOU CRYING?
S-SAID-- SAID I--
--D-DON'T WANNA TALK ABOUT IT.

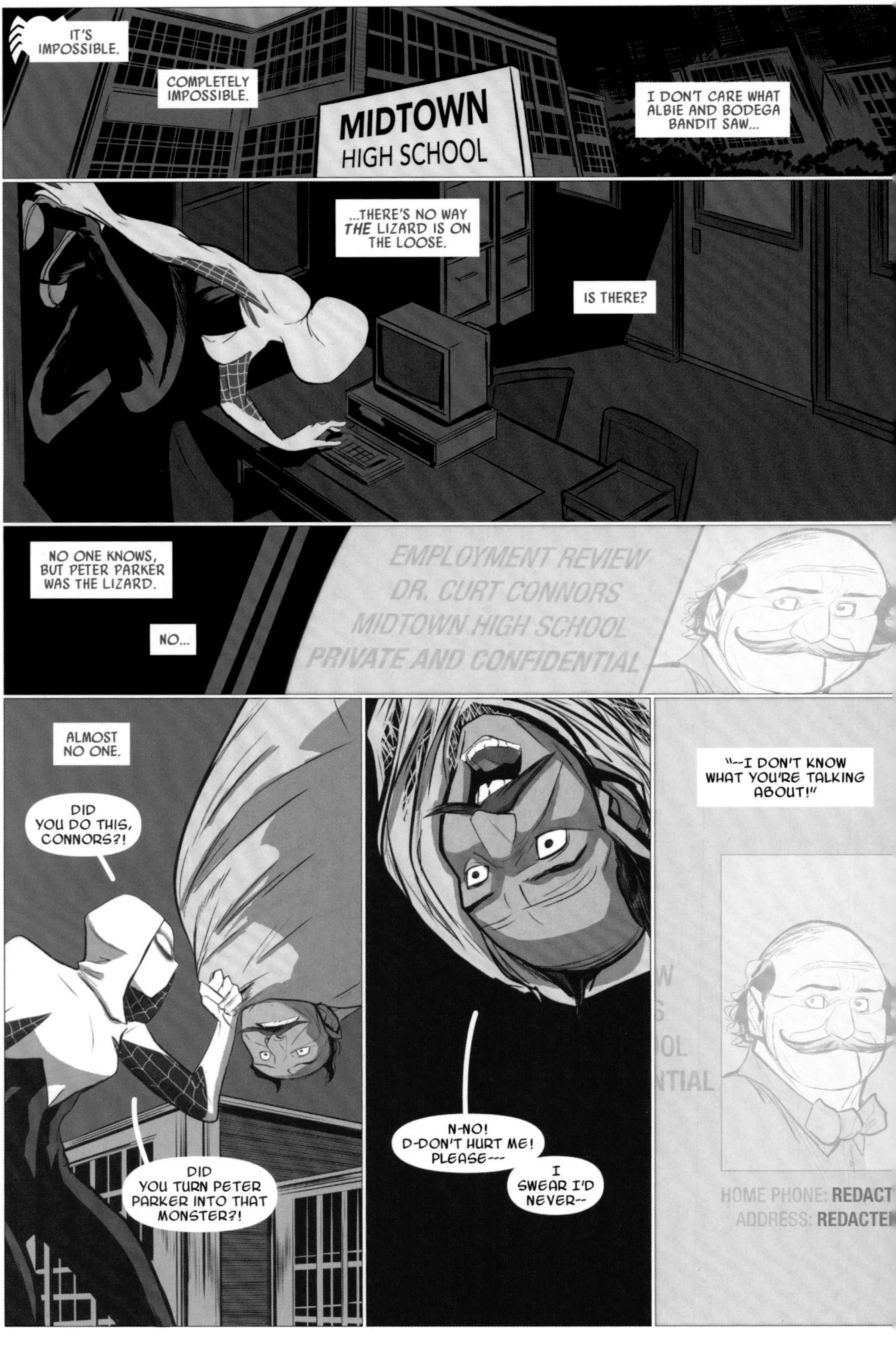
IT'S IMPOSSIBLE.
COMPLETELY IMPOSSIBLE.
MIDTOWN
HIGH SCHOOL
I DON'T CARE WHAT ALBIE AND BODEGA BANDIT SAW...
...THERE'S NO WAY THE LIZARD IS ON THE LOOSE.
IS THERE?
NO ONE KNOWS, BUT PETER PARKER WAS THE LIZARD.
NO...
EMPLOYMENT REVIEW
DR. CURT CONNORS
MIDTOWN HIGH SCHOOL
PRIVATE AND CONFIDENTIAL
ALMOST NO ONE.
DID YOU DO THIS, CONNORS?!
DID YOU TURN PETER PARKER INTO THAT MONSTER?!
N-NO! D-DON'T HURT ME! PLEASE---
I SWEAR I'D NEVER--
"--I DON'T KNOW WHAT YOU'RE TALKING ABOUT!"
HOME PHONE: REDACT
ADDRESS: REDACTE

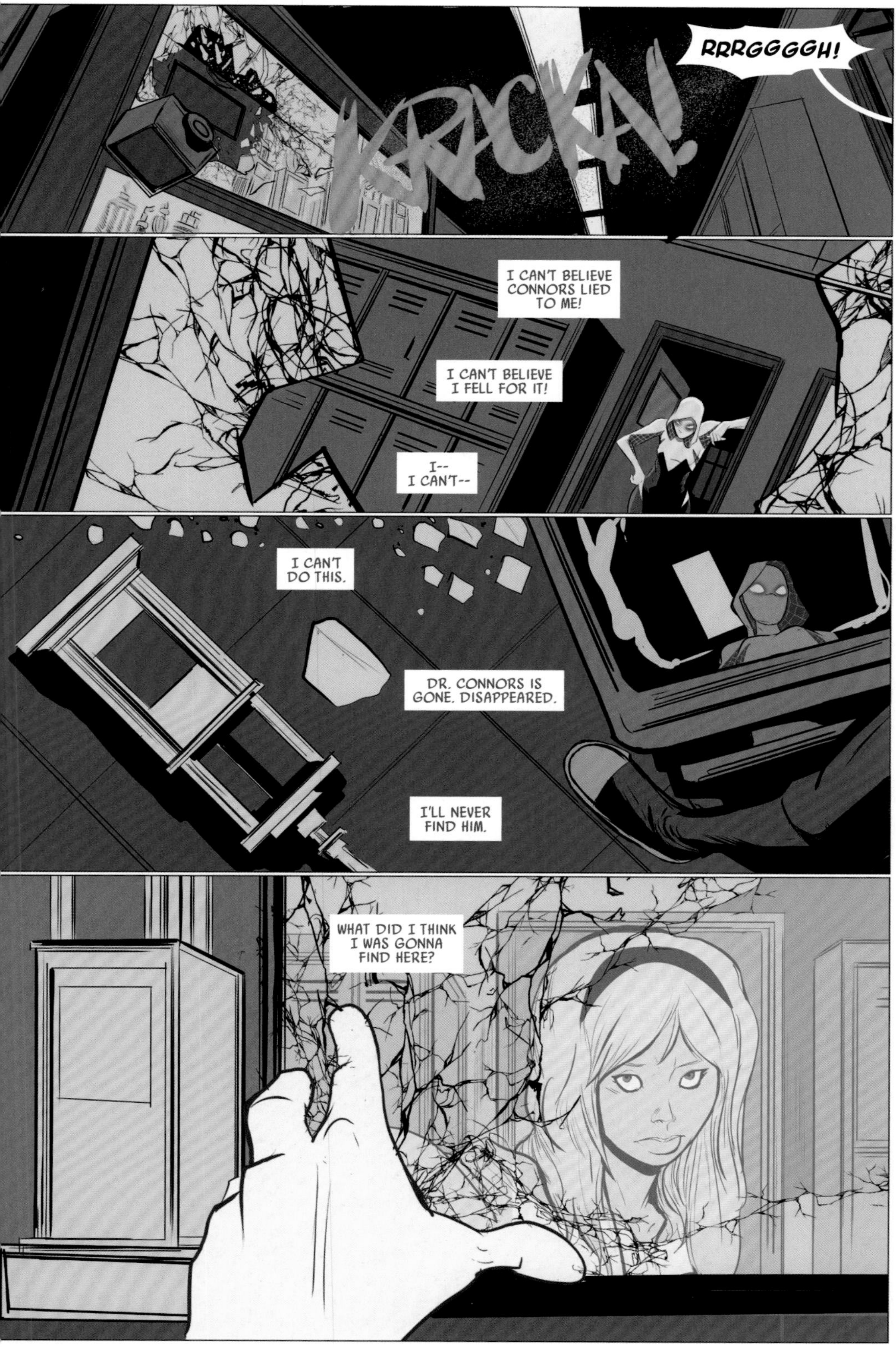
RRRGGGGH!
KRACKA!
I CAN'T BELIEVE CONNORS LIED TO ME!
I CAN'T BELIEVE I FELL FOR IT!
I-- I CAN'T--
I CAN'T DO THIS.
DR. CONNORS IS GONE. DISAPPEARED.
I'LL NEVER FIND HIM.
WHAT DID I THINK I WAS GONNA FIND HERE?

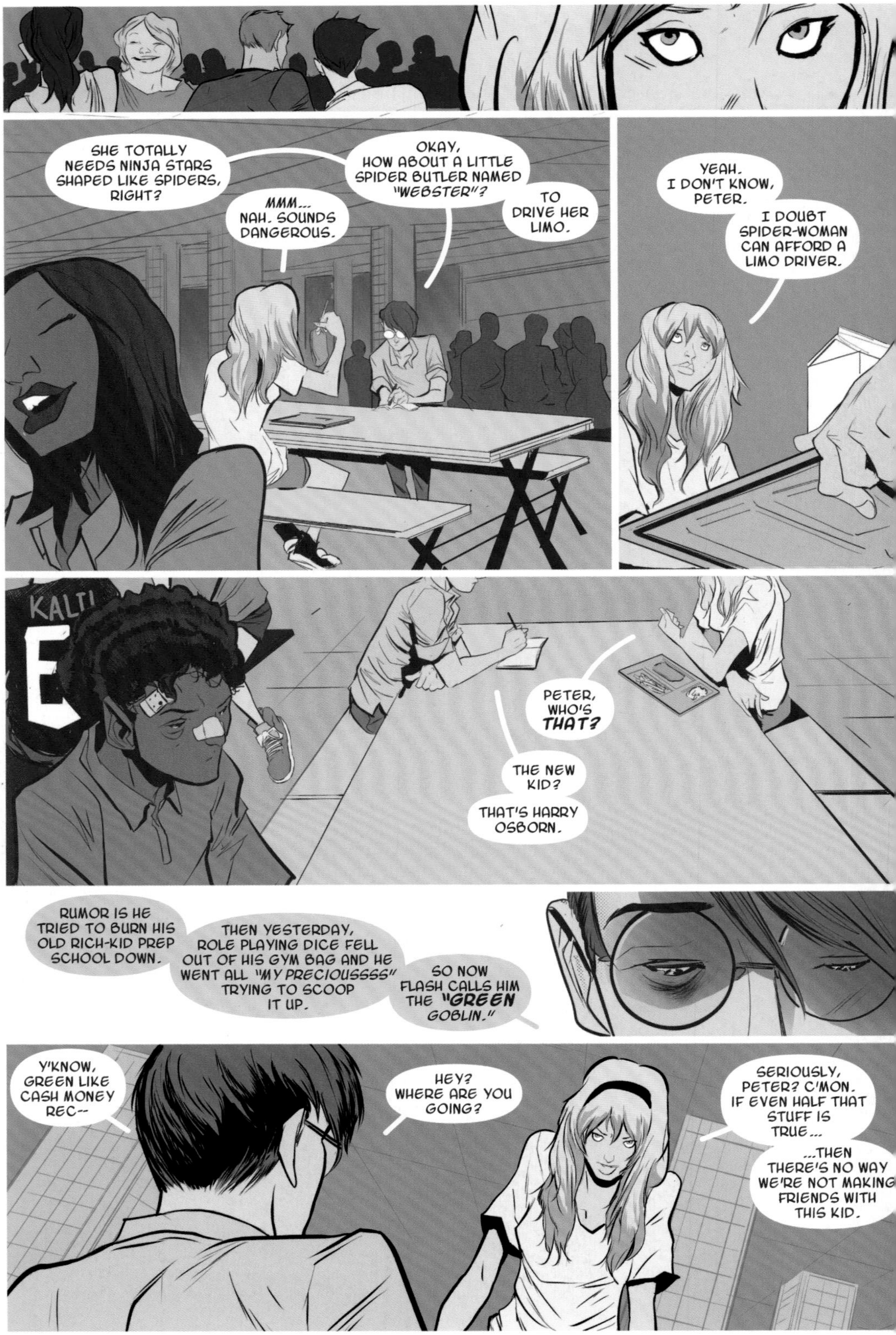
SHE TOTALLY NEEDS NINJA STARS SHAPED LIKE SPIDERS, RIGHT?
MMM... NAH. SOUNDS DANGEROUS.
OKAY, HOW ABOUT A LITTLE SPIDER BUTLER NAMED "WEBSTER"?
TO DRIVE HER LIMO.
YEAH. I DON'T KNOW, PETER.
I DOUBT SPIDER-WOMAN CAN AFFORD A LIMO DRIVER.
KALTI
PETER, WHO'S THAT?
THE NEW KID?
THAT'S HARRY OSBORN.
RUMOR IS HE TRIED TO BURN HIS OLD RICH-KID PREP SCHOOL DOWN.
THEN YESTERDAY, ROLE PLAYING DICE FELL OUT OF HIS GYM BAG AND HE WENT ALL "MY PRECIOUSSSS" TRYING TO SCOOP IT UP.
SO NOW FLASH CALLS HIM THE "GREEN GOBLIN."
Y'KNOW, GREEN LIKE CASH MONEY REC--
HEY? WHERE ARE YOU GOING?
SERIOUSLY, PETER? C'MON. IF EVEN HALF THAT STUFF IS TRUE...
...THEN THERE'S NO WAY WE'RE NOT MAKING FRIENDS WITH THIS KID.

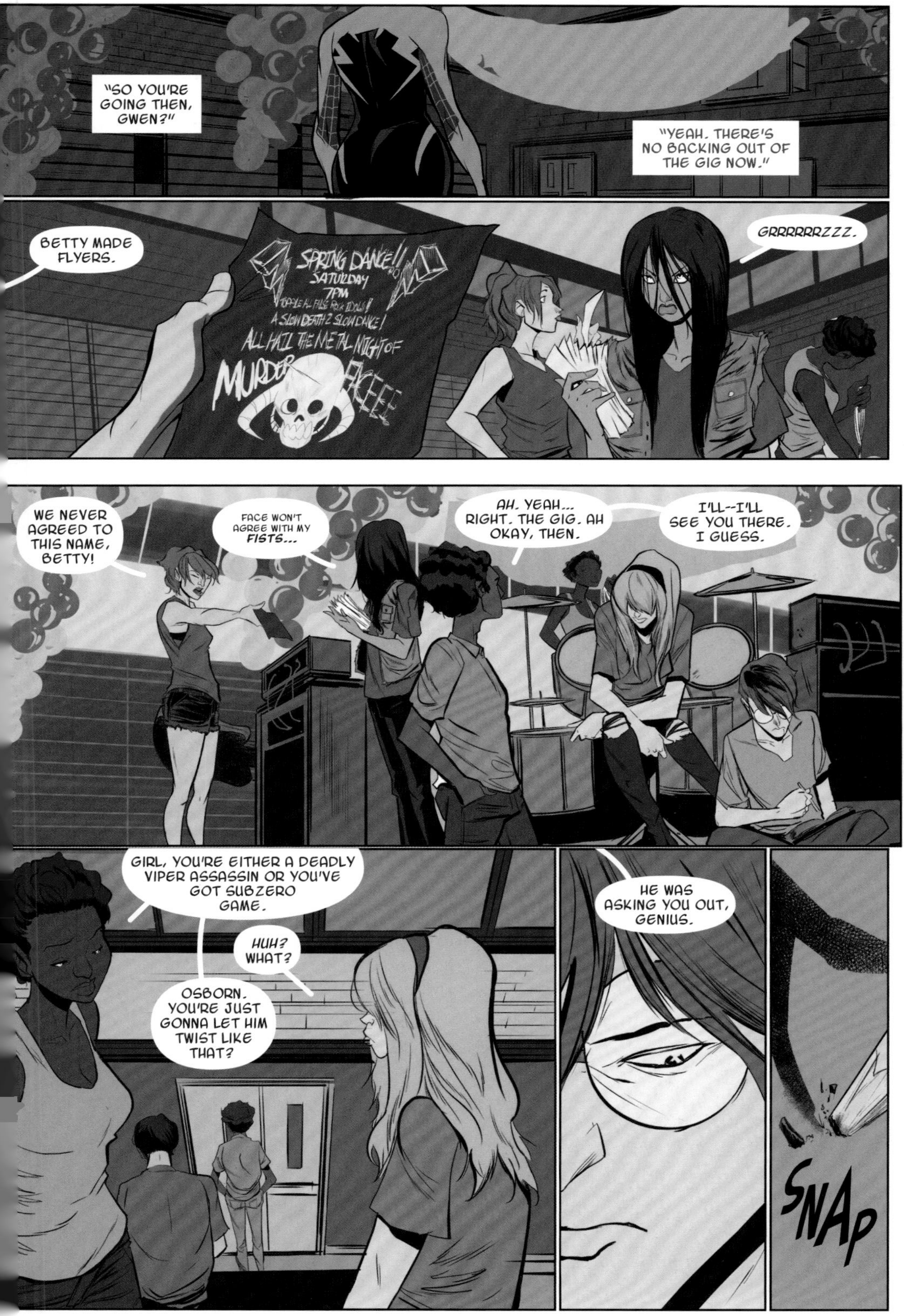
"SO YOU'RE GOING THEN, GWEN?"
"YEAH. THERE'S NO BACKING OUT OF THE GIG NOW."
BETTY MADE FLYERS.
SPRING DANCE!! SATURDAY 7PM
TOPPLE ALL FALSE ROCK IDOLS!
A SLOW DEATH 2 SLOW DANCE!
ALL HAIL THE METAL NIGHT OF MURDER FACEEE
GRRRRRRZZZ.
WE NEVER AGREED TO THIS NAME, BETTY!
FACE WON'T AGREE WITH MY *FISTS...*
AH. YEAH... RIGHT. THE GIG. AH OKAY, THEN.
I'LL--I'LL SEE YOU THERE. I GUESS.
GIRL, YOU'RE EITHER A DEADLY VIPER ASSASSIN OR YOU'VE GOT SUBZERO GAME.
HUH? WHAT?
OSBORN. YOU'RE JUST GONNA LET HIM TWIST LIKE THAT?
HE WAS ASKING YOU OUT, GENIUS.
SNAP

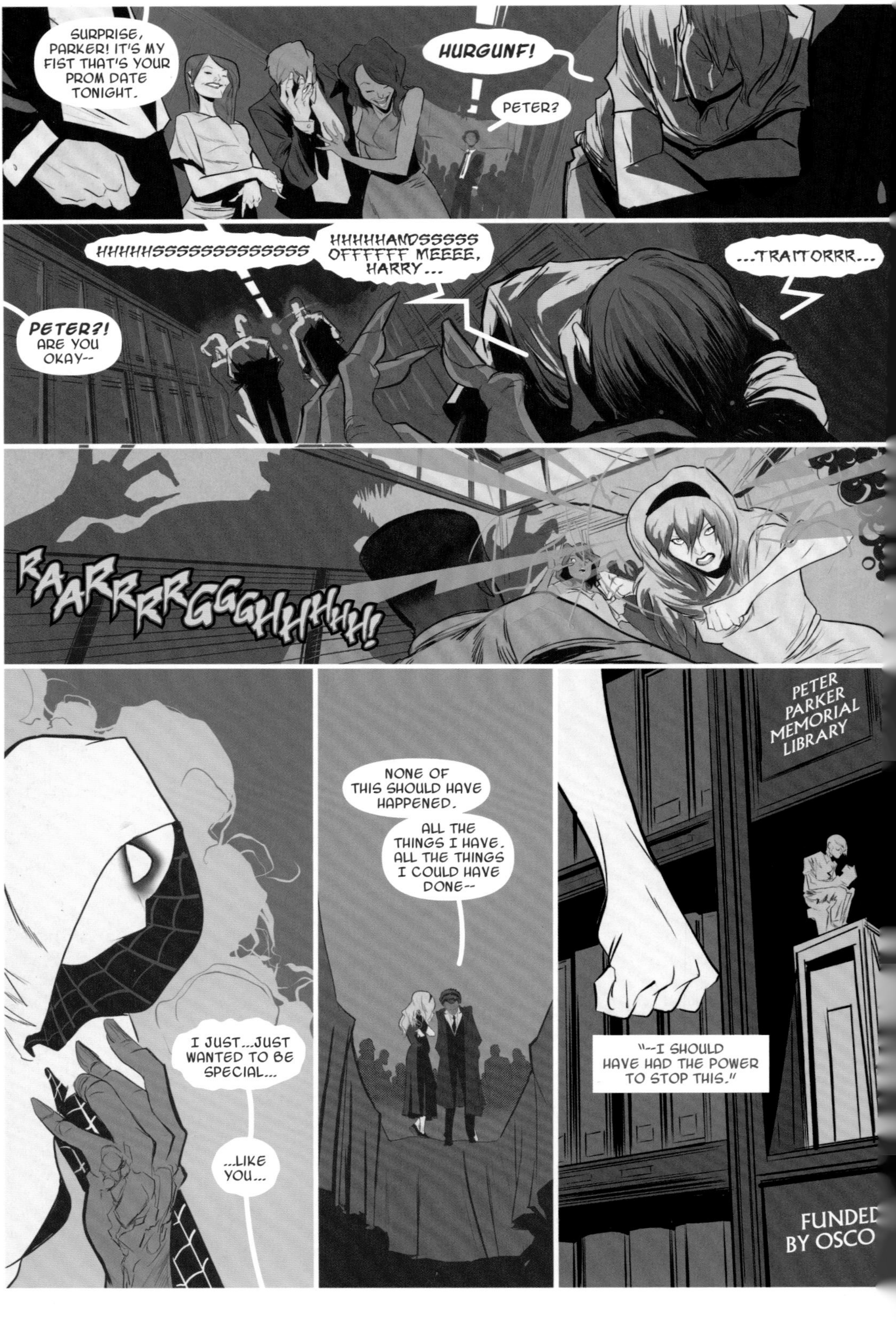
SURPRISE, PARKER! IT'S MY FIST THAT'S YOUR PROM DATE TONIGHT.
HURGUNF!
PETER?
HHHHHSSSSSSSSSSSSSS
HHHHHANDSSSSS OFFFFFF MEEEE, HARRY...
...TRAITORRR...
PETER?! ARE YOU OKAY--
RAARRRRGGGHHHHH!
I JUST...JUST WANTED TO BE SPECIAL...
...LIKE YOU...
NONE OF THIS SHOULD HAVE HAPPENED.
ALL THE THINGS I HAVE. ALL THE THINGS I COULD HAVE DONE--
PETER PARKER MEMORIAL LIBRARY
"--I SHOULD HAVE HAD THE POWER TO STOP THIS."
FUNDED BY OSCO

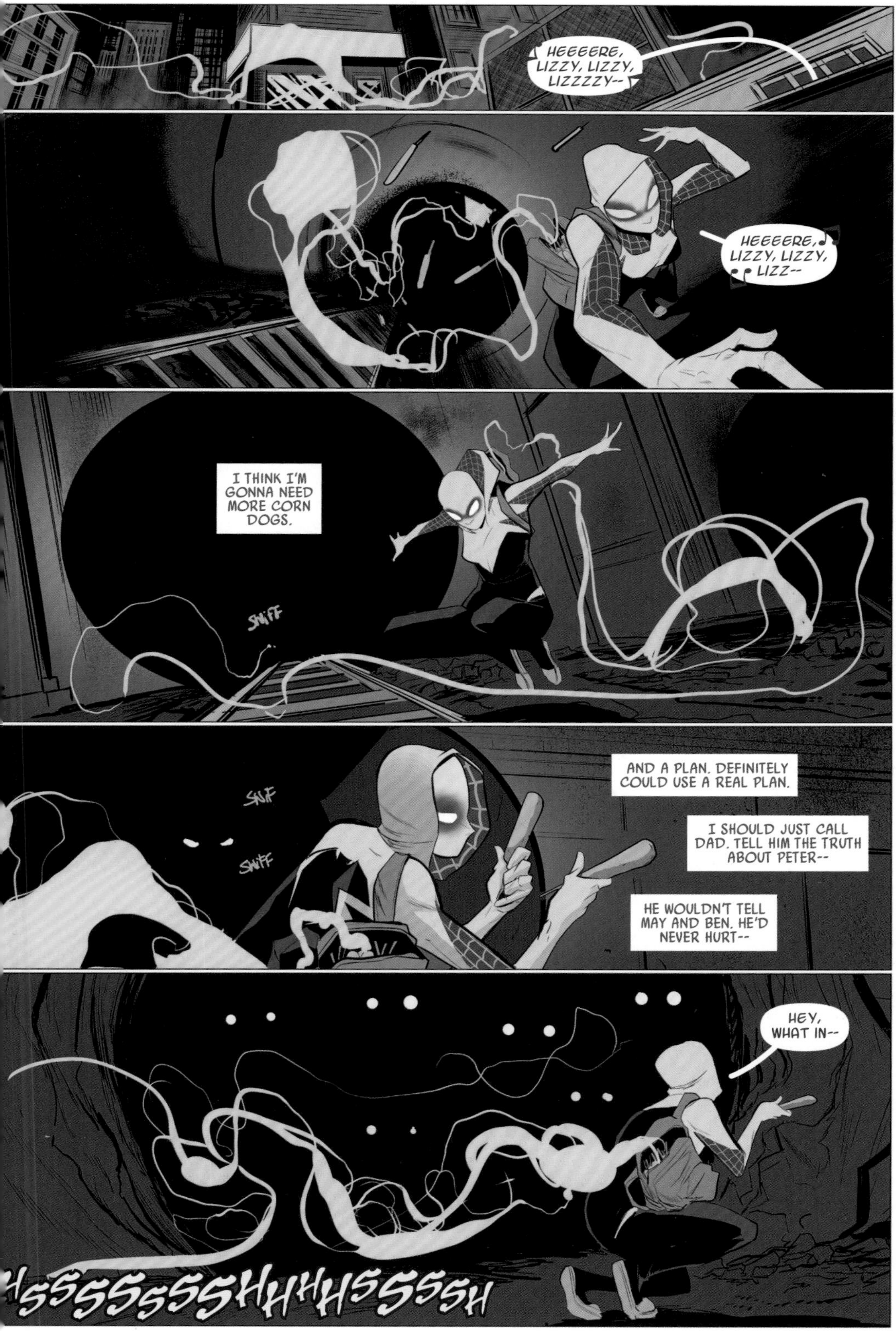
HEEEERE, LIZZY, LIZZY, LIZZZZY--
HEEEERE, LIZZY, LIZZY, LIZZ--
I THINK I'M GONNA NEED MORE CORN DOGS.
SNIFF
AND A PLAN. DEFINITELY COULD USE A REAL PLAN.
SNIFF
SNIFF
I SHOULD JUST CALL DAD. TELL HIM THE TRUTH ABOUT PETER--
HE WOULDN'T TELL MAY AND BEN. HE'D NEVER HURT--
HEY, WHAT IN--
HSSSSSSSHHHHSSSSH

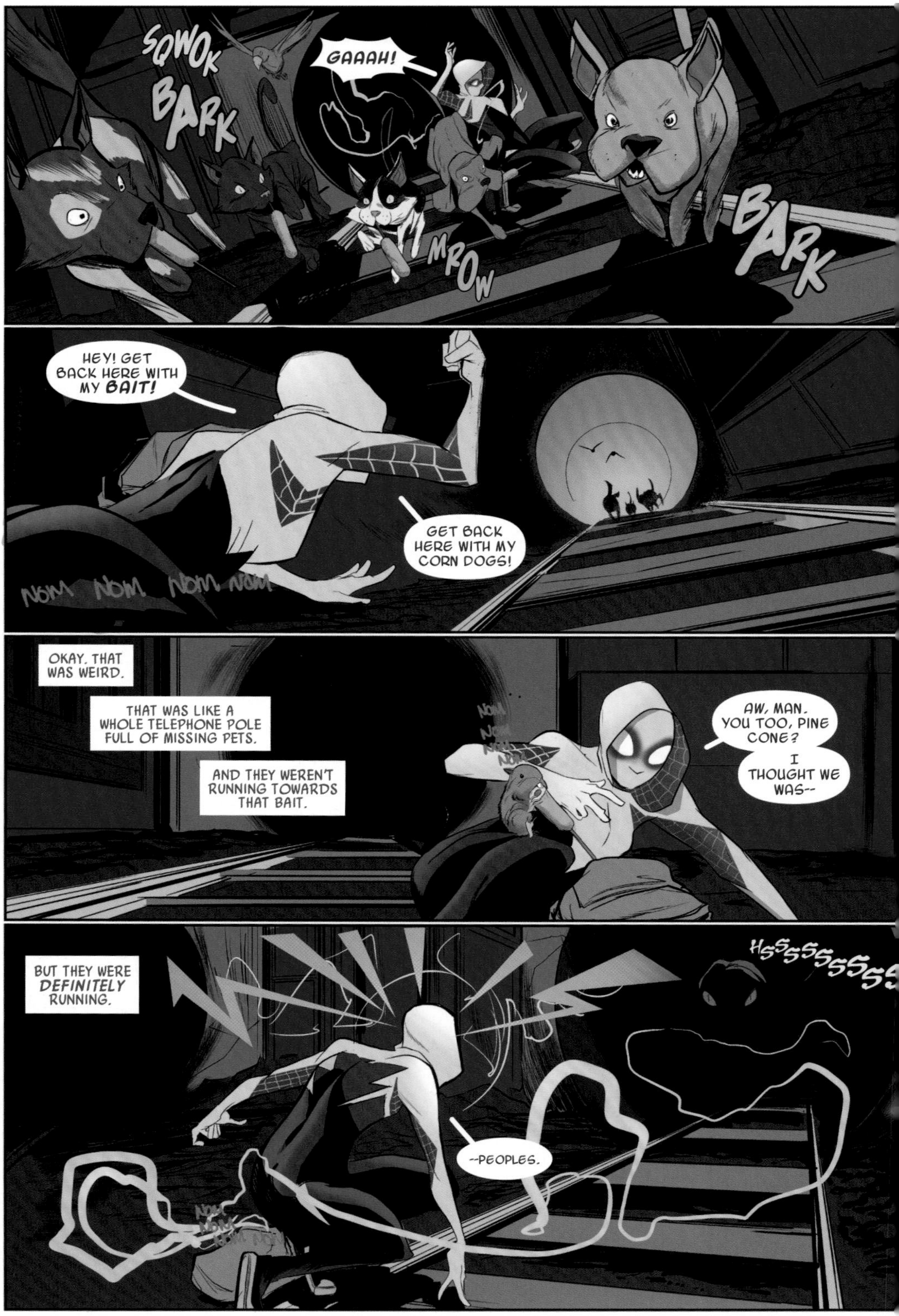
SQWOK
BARK
GAAAH!
MROW
BARK
HEY! GET BACK HERE WITH MY BAIT!
GET BACK HERE WITH MY CORN DOGS!
NOM NOM NOM NOM
OKAY. THAT WAS WEIRD.
THAT WAS LIKE A WHOLE TELEPHONE POLE FULL OF MISSING PETS.
AND THEY WEREN'T RUNNING TOWARDS THAT BAIT.
AW, MAN. YOU TOO, PINE CONE?
I THOUGHT WE WAS--
BUT THEY WERE DEFINITELY RUNNING.
HSSSSSSSS
--PEOPLES.

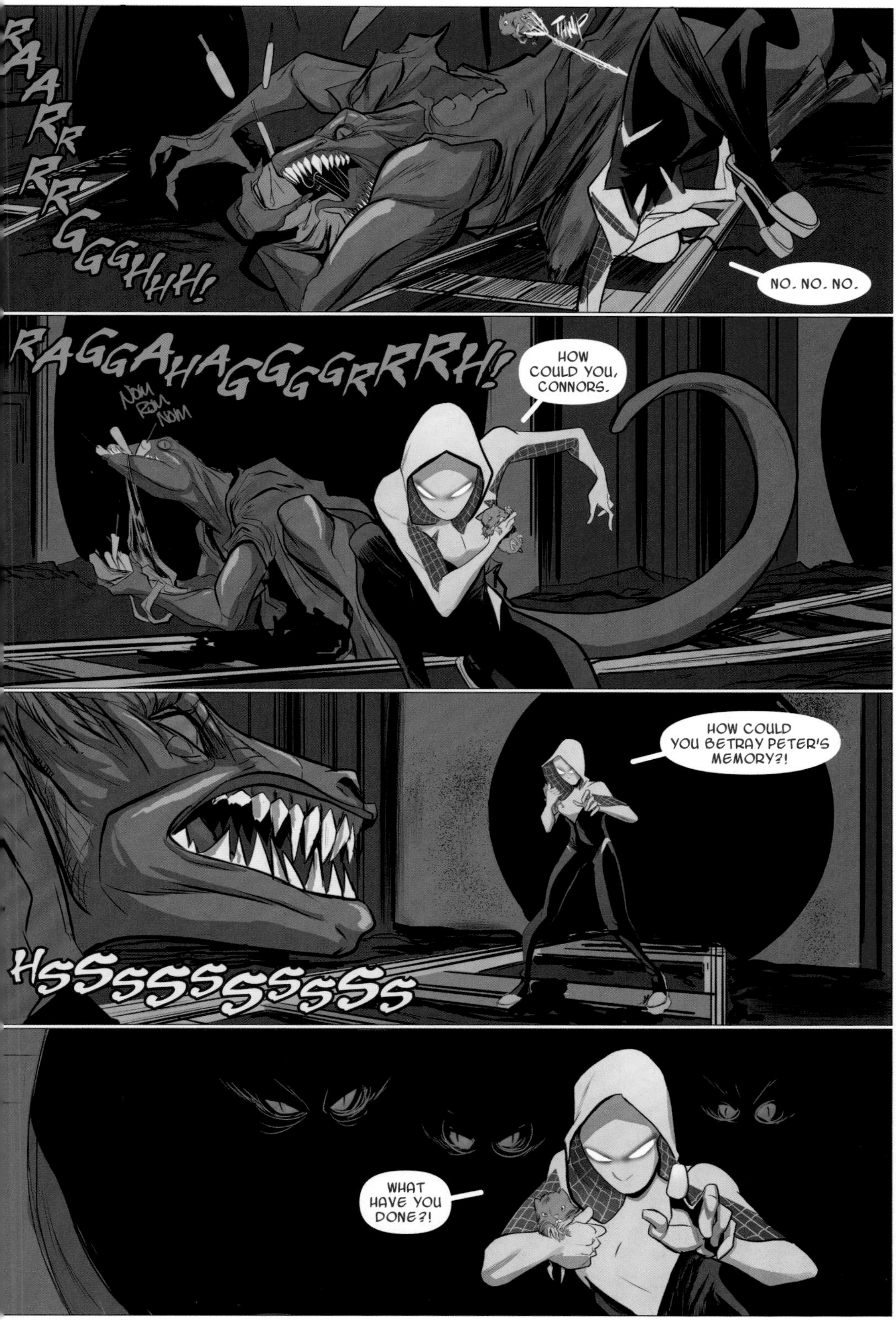
RAARRRRRGGGHHH!
THWIP
NO. NO. NO.
RAGGAHAGGGGRRRH!
NOM NOM NOM
HOW COULD YOU, CONNORS.
HOW COULD YOU BETRAY PETER'S MEMORY?!
HSSSSSSSSSSS
WHAT HAVE YOU DONE?!

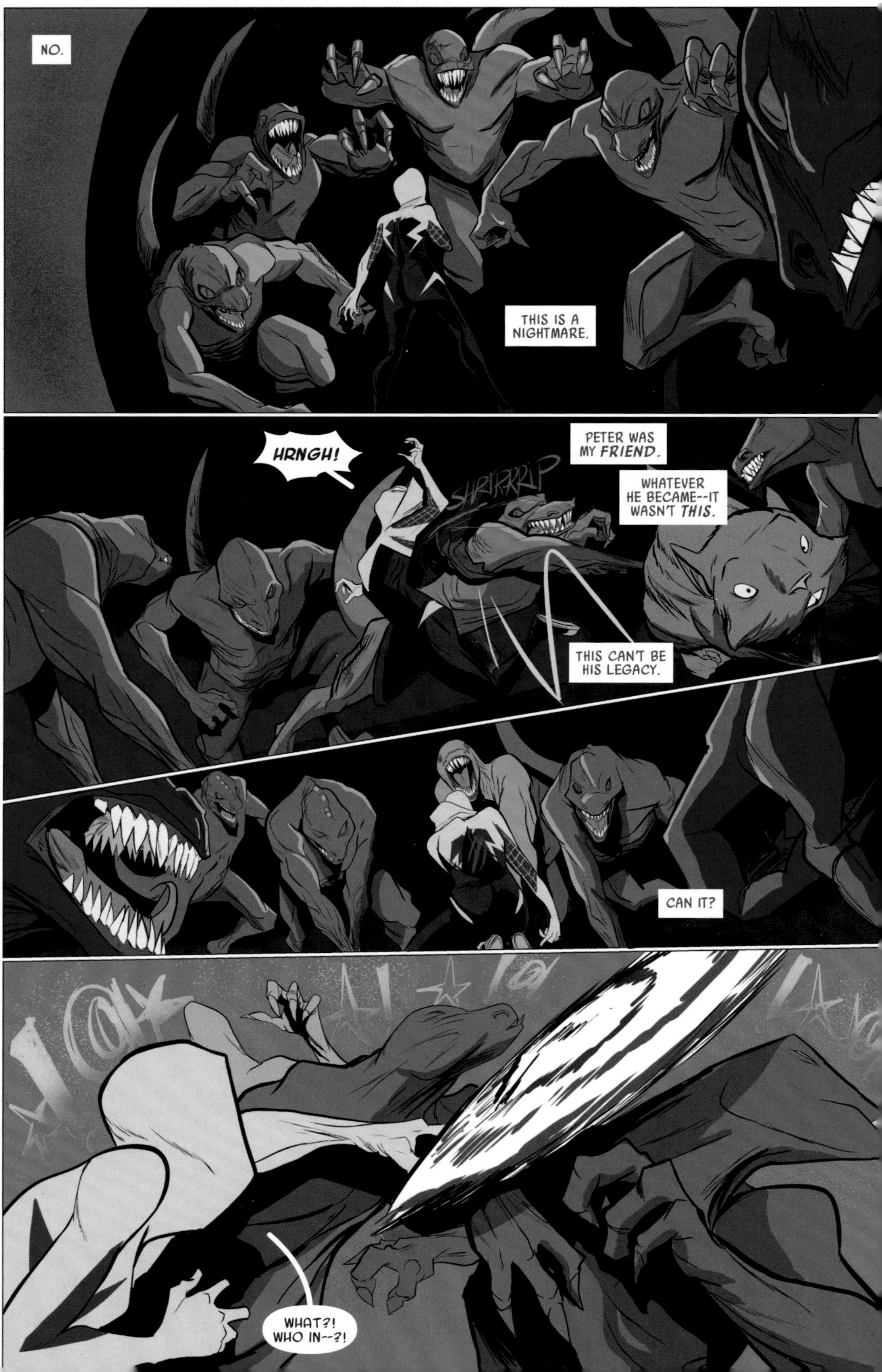

NO.
THIS IS A NIGHTMARE.
HRNGH!
SHRRRRRIP
PETER WAS MY FRIEND.
WHATEVER HE BECAME--IT WASN'T THIS.
THIS CAN'T BE HIS LEGACY.
CAN IT?
WHAT?! WHO IN--?!

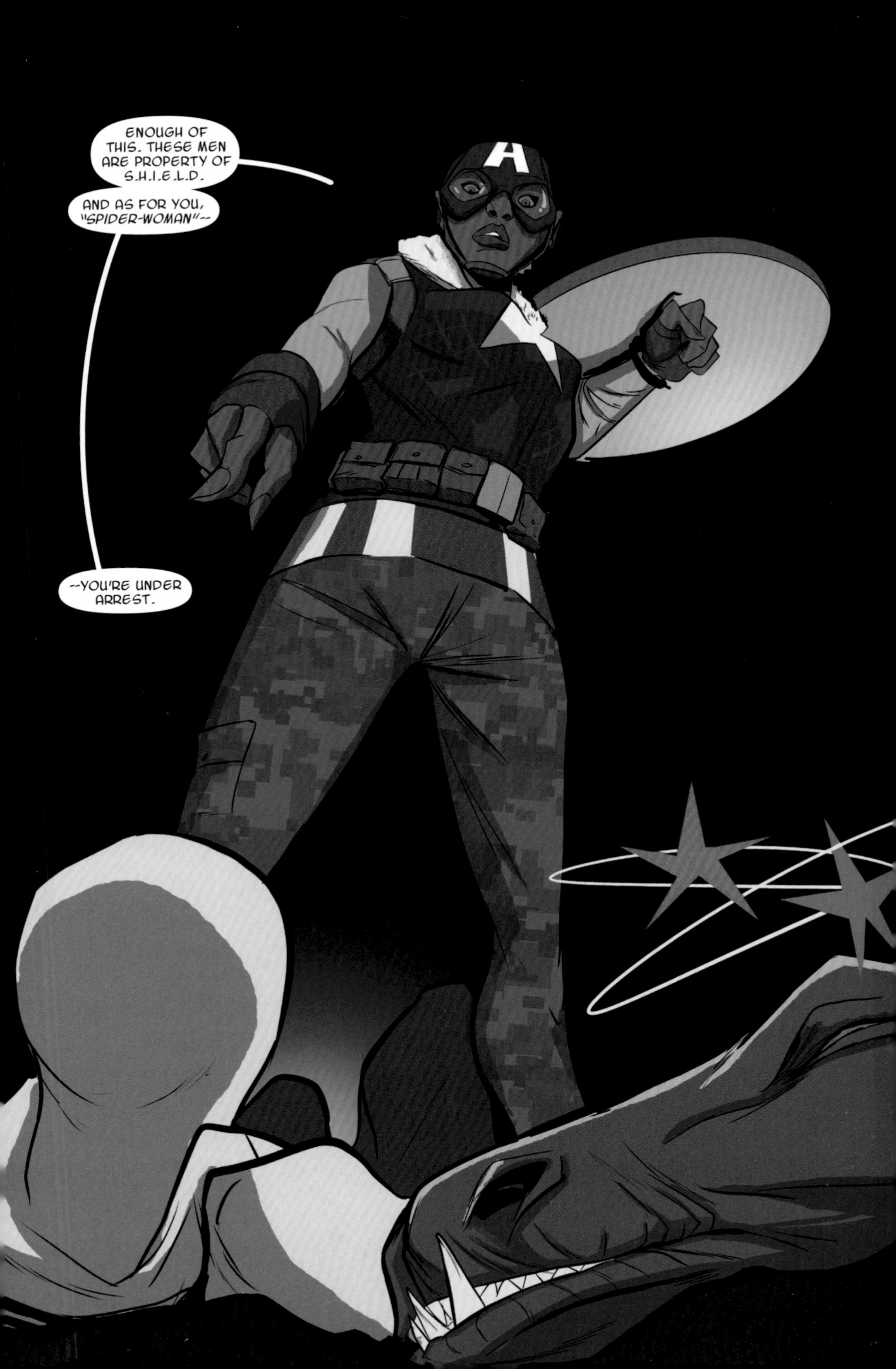
ENOUGH OF THIS. THESE MEN ARE PROPERTY OF S.H.I.E.L.D.
AND AS FOR YOU, "SPIDER-WOMAN"--
--YOU'RE UNDER ARREST.

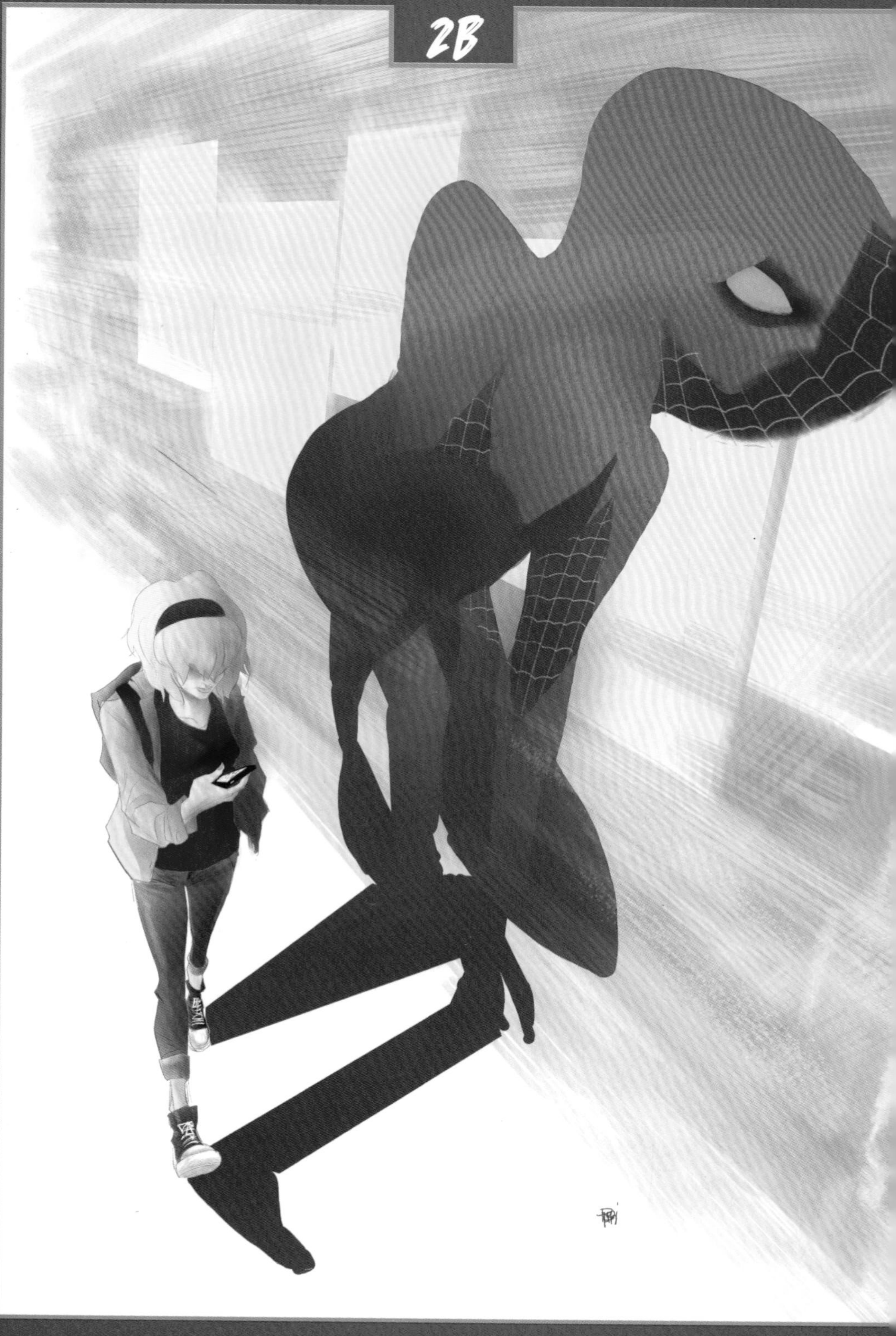
2B

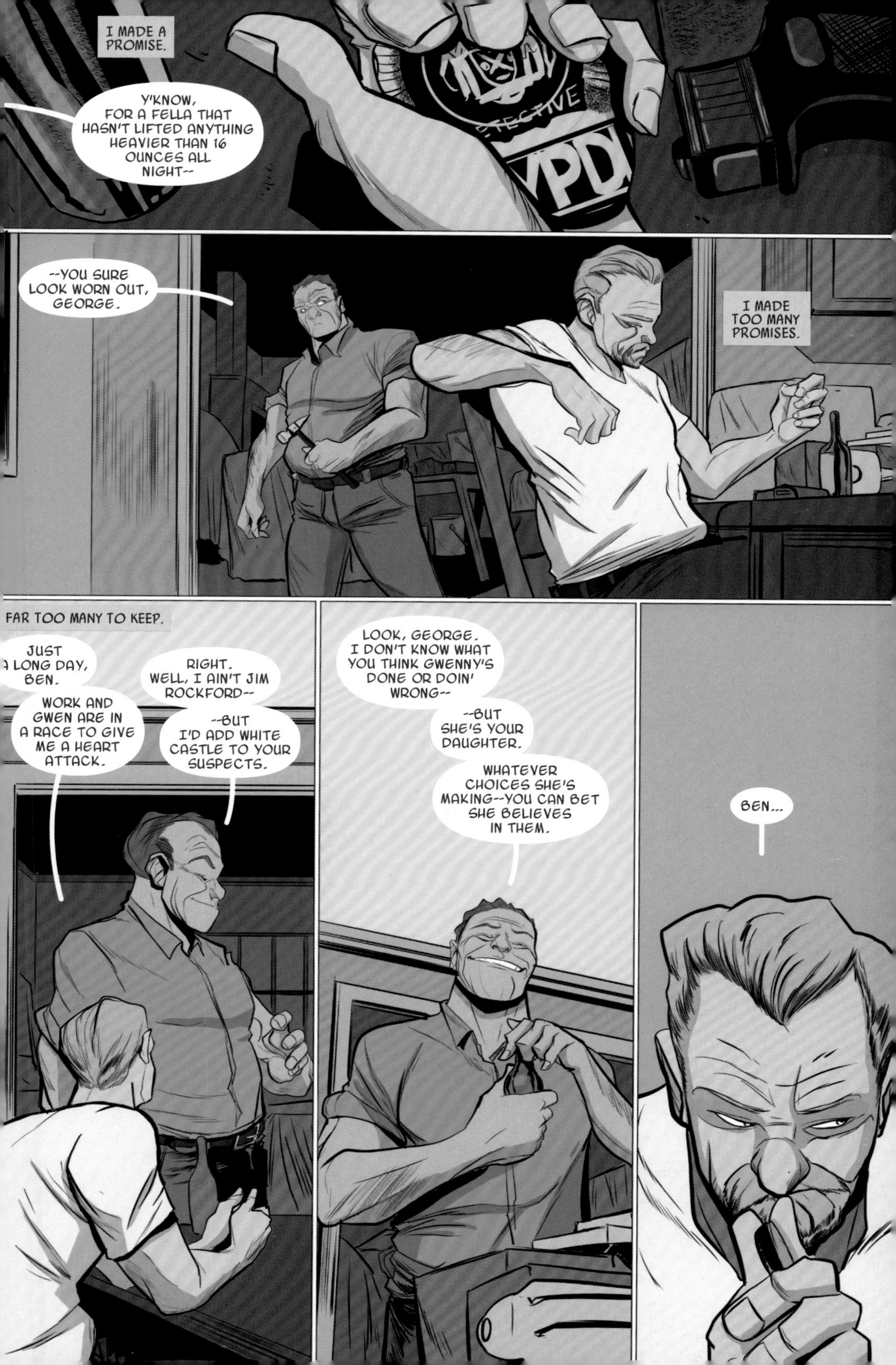
I MADE A PROMISE.
Y'KNOW, FOR A FELLA THAT HASN'T LIFTED ANYTHING HEAVIER THAN 16 OUNCES ALL NIGHT--
DETECTIVE
NYPD
--YOU SURE LOOK WORN OUT, GEORGE.
I MADE TOO MANY PROMISES.
FAR TOO MANY TO KEEP.
JUST A LONG DAY, BEN.
WORK AND GWEN ARE IN A RACE TO GIVE ME A HEART ATTACK.
RIGHT. WELL, I AIN'T JIM ROCKFORD--
--BUT I'D ADD WHITE CASTLE TO YOUR SUSPECTS.
LOOK, GEORGE. I DON'T KNOW WHAT YOU THINK GWENNY'S DONE OR DOIN' WRONG--
--BUT SHE'S YOUR DAUGHTER.
WHATEVER CHOICES SHE'S MAKING--YOU CAN BET SHE BELIEVES IN THEM.
BEN...

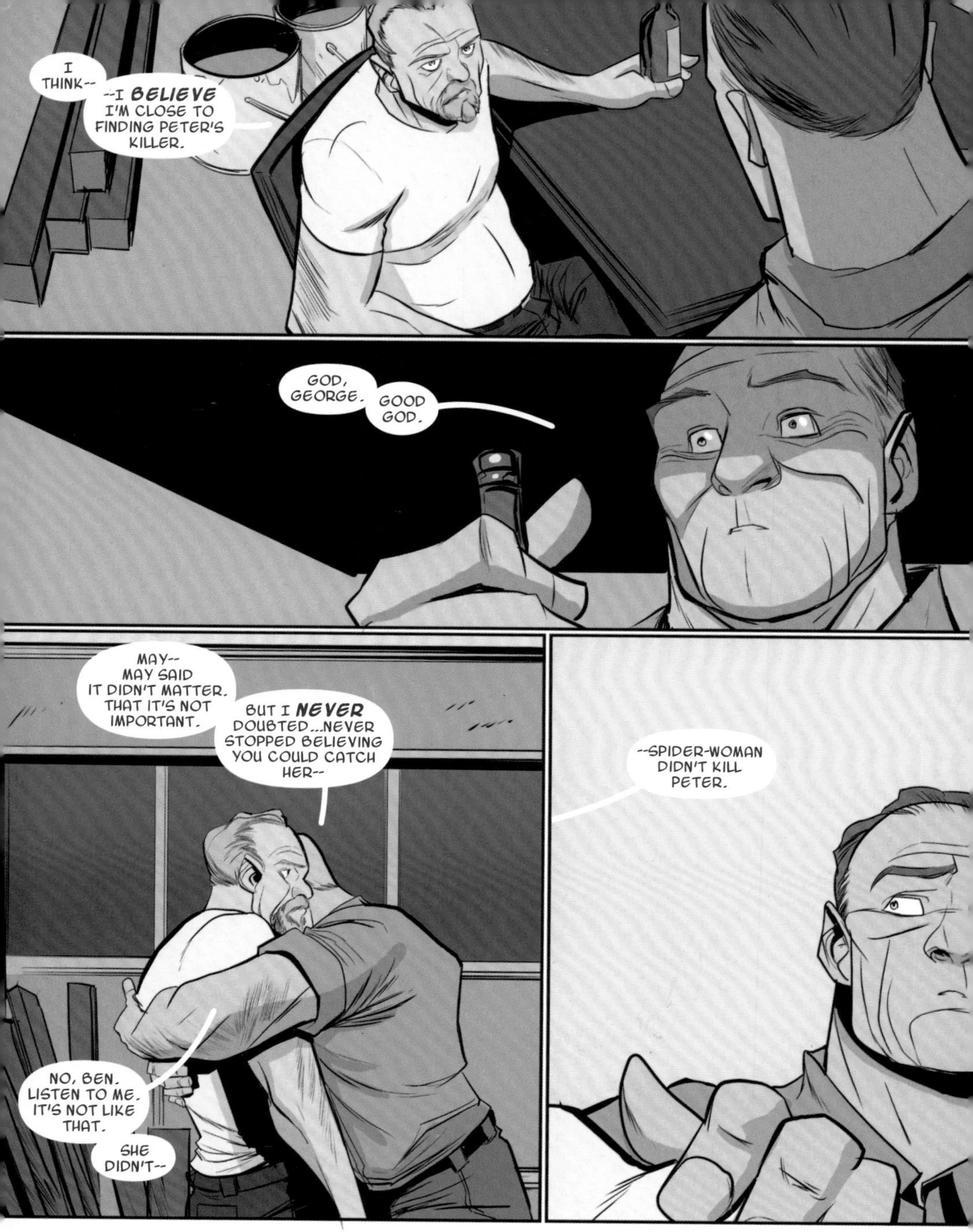
I THINK--
--I BELIEVE I'M CLOSE TO FINDING PETER'S KILLER.
GOD, GEORGE.
GOOD GOD.
MAY--MAY SAID IT DIDN'T MATTER. THAT IT'S NOT IMPORTANT.
BUT I NEVER DOUBTED...NEVER STOPPED BELIEVING YOU COULD CATCH HER--
NO, BEN. LISTEN TO ME. IT'S NOT LIKE THAT.
SHE DIDN'T--
--SPIDER-WOMAN DIDN'T KILL PETER.

GREATER POWER

PART TWO

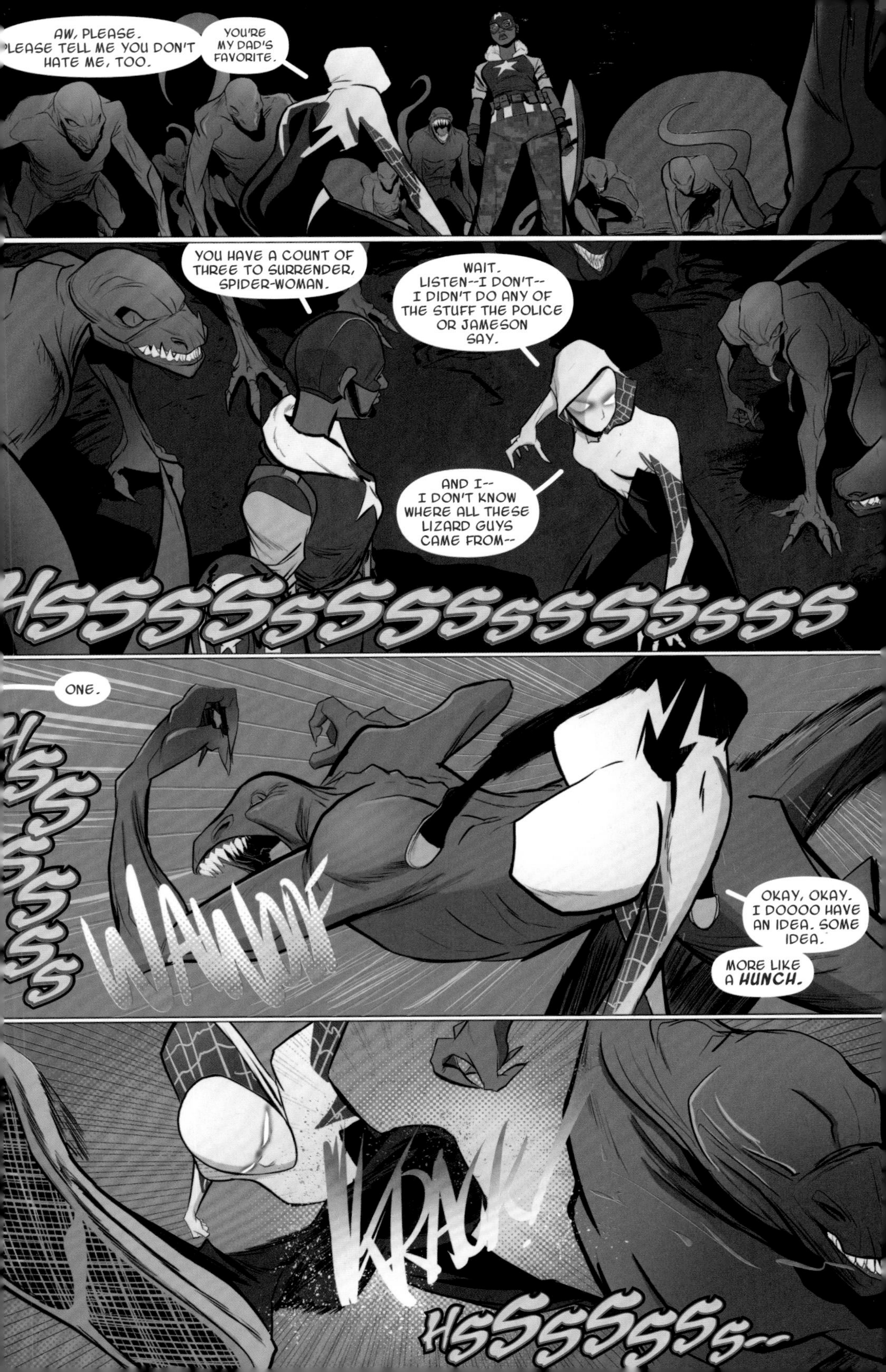
AW, PLEASE. PLEASE TELL ME YOU DON'T HATE ME, TOO.
YOU'RE MY DAD'S FAVORITE.
YOU HAVE A COUNT OF THREE TO SURRENDER, SPIDER-WOMAN.
WAIT. LISTEN--I DON'T-- I DIDN'T DO ANY OF THE STUFF THE POLICE OR JAMESON SAY.
AND I-- I DON'T KNOW WHERE ALL THESE LIZARD GUYS CAME FROM--
HSSSSSSSSSSSSSSSSS
ONE.
HSSSSSSSS
WAMF
OKAY, OKAY. I DOOOO HAVE AN IDEA. SOME IDEA.
MORE LIKE A HUNCH.
KRACK
HSSSSSSS--

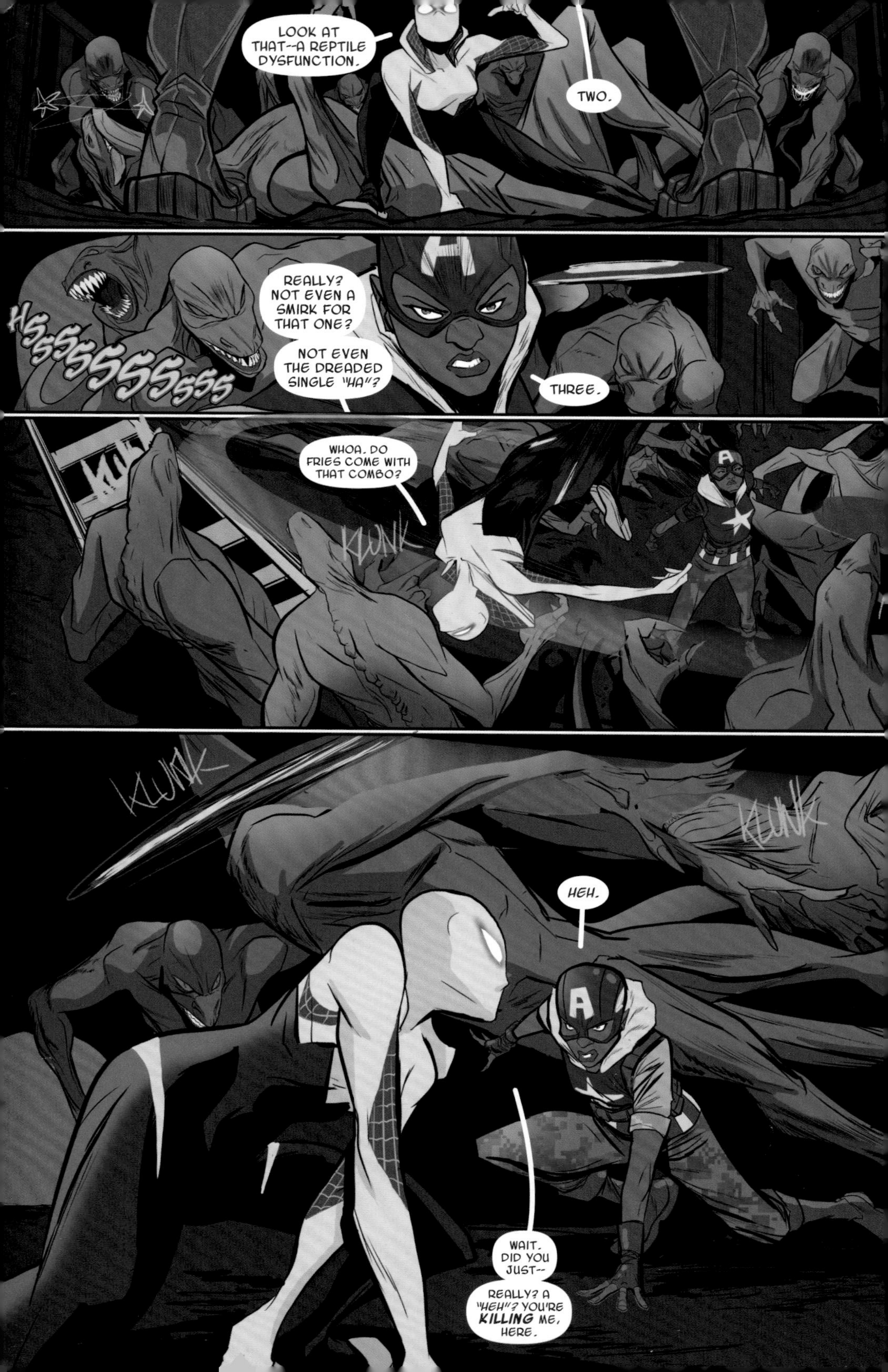
LOOK AT THAT--A REPTILE DYSFUNCTION.
TWO.
HSSSSSSSSsss
REALLY? NOT EVEN A SMIRK FOR THAT ONE?
NOT EVEN THE DREADED SINGLE "HA"?
THREE.
WHOA. DO FRIES COME WITH THAT COMBO?
KLUNK
KLUNK
KLUNK
HEH.
WAIT. DID YOU JUST--
REALLY? A "HEH"? YOU'RE **KILLING** ME, HERE.

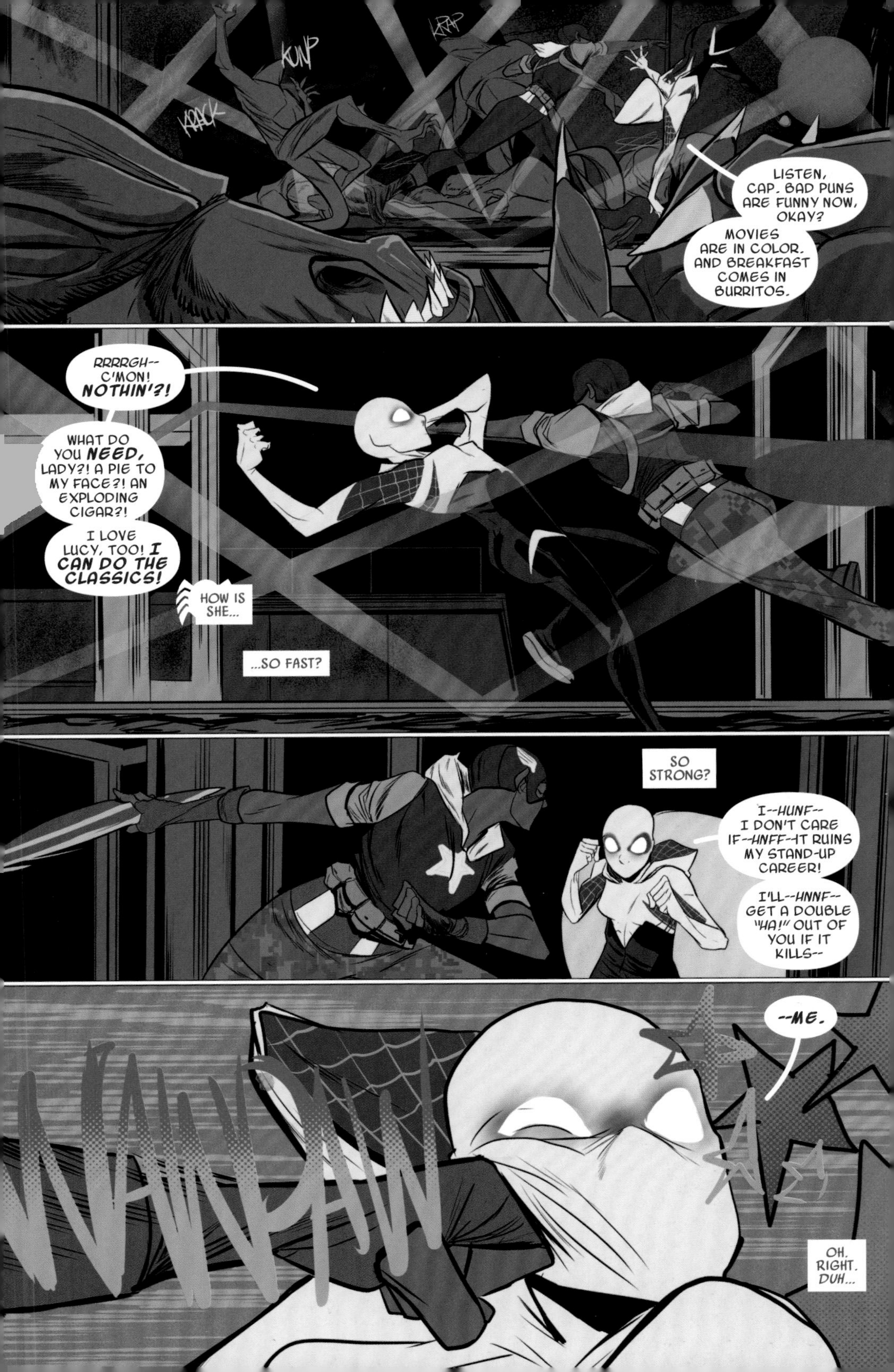
KUNP
KRAP
KRACK
LISTEN, CAP. BAD PUNS ARE FUNNY NOW, OKAY?
MOVIES ARE IN COLOR. AND BREAKFAST COMES IN BURRITOS.
RRRRGH-- C'MON! **NOTHIN'?!**
WHAT DO YOU **NEED,** LADY?! A PIE TO MY FACE?! AN EXPLODING CIGAR?!
I LOVE LUCY, TOO! **I CAN DO THE CLASSICS!**
HOW IS SHE...
...SO FAST?
SO STRONG?
I--*HUNF*-- I DON'T CARE IF--*HNFF*--IT RUINS MY STAND-UP CAREER!
I'LL--*HNNF*-- GET A DOUBLE "HA!" OUT OF YOU IF IT KILLS--
--ME.
OH. RIGHT. DUH...

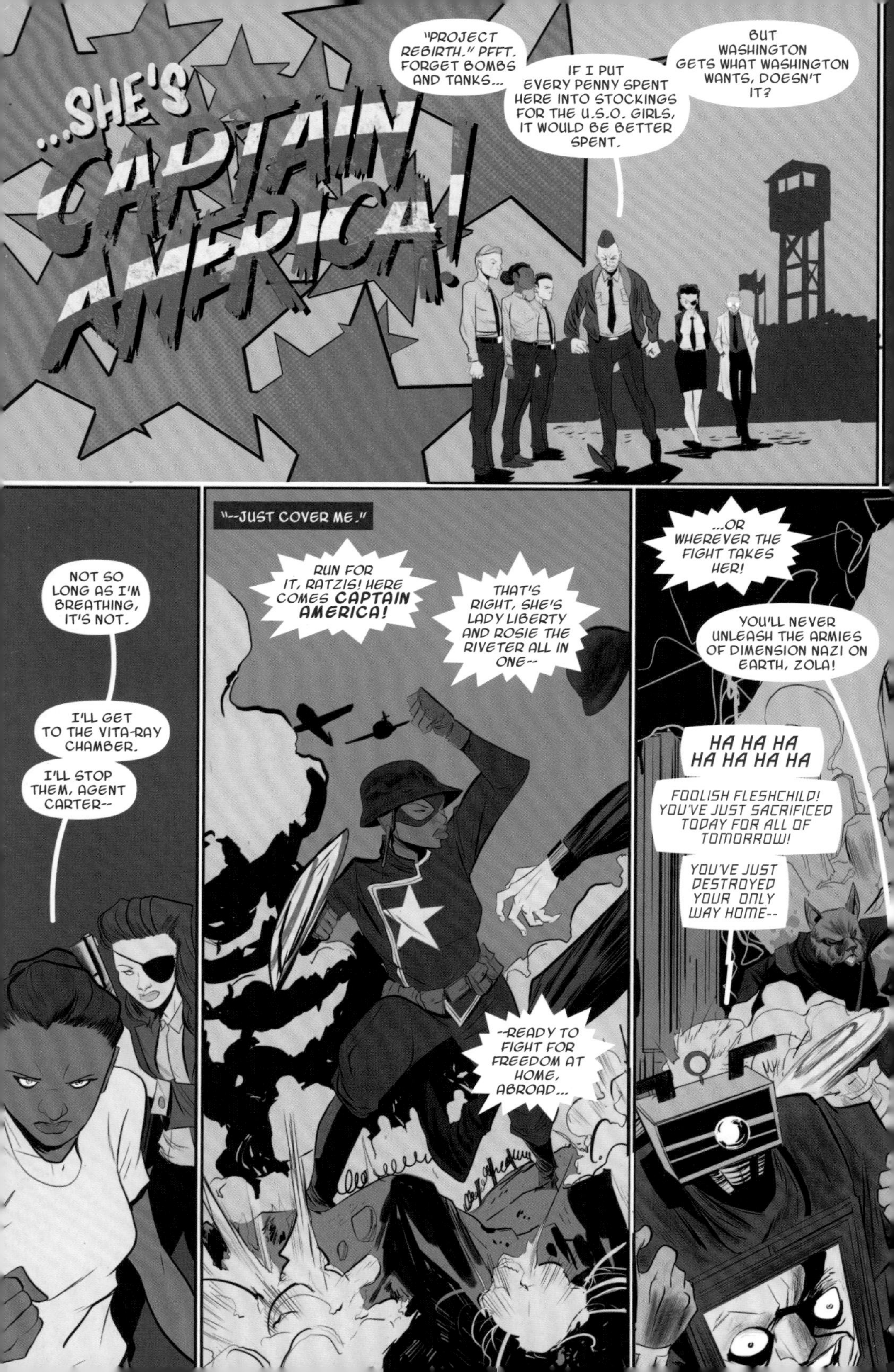
...SHE'S
CAPTAIN AMERICA!
"PROJECT REBIRTH." PFFT. FORGET BOMBS AND TANKS...
IF I PUT EVERY PENNY SPENT HERE INTO STOCKINGS FOR THE U.S.O. GIRLS, IT WOULD BE BETTER SPENT.
BUT WASHINGTON GETS WHAT WASHINGTON WANTS, DOESN'T IT?
NOT SO LONG AS I'M BREATHING, IT'S NOT.
I'LL GET TO THE VITA-RAY CHAMBER.
I'LL STOP THEM, AGENT CARTER--
"--JUST COVER ME."
RUN FOR IT, RATZIS! HERE COMES CAPTAIN AMERICA!
THAT'S RIGHT, SHE'S LADY LIBERTY AND ROSIE THE RIVETER ALL IN ONE--
--READY TO FIGHT FOR FREEDOM AT HOME, ABROAD...
...OR WHEREVER THE FIGHT TAKES HER!
YOU'LL NEVER UNLEASH THE ARMIES OF DIMENSION NAZI ON EARTH, ZOLA!
HA HA HA HA HA HA HA
FOOLISH FLESHCHILD! YOU'VE JUST SACRIFICED TODAY FOR ALL OF TOMORROW!
YOU'VE JUST DESTROYED YOUR ONLY WAY HOME--

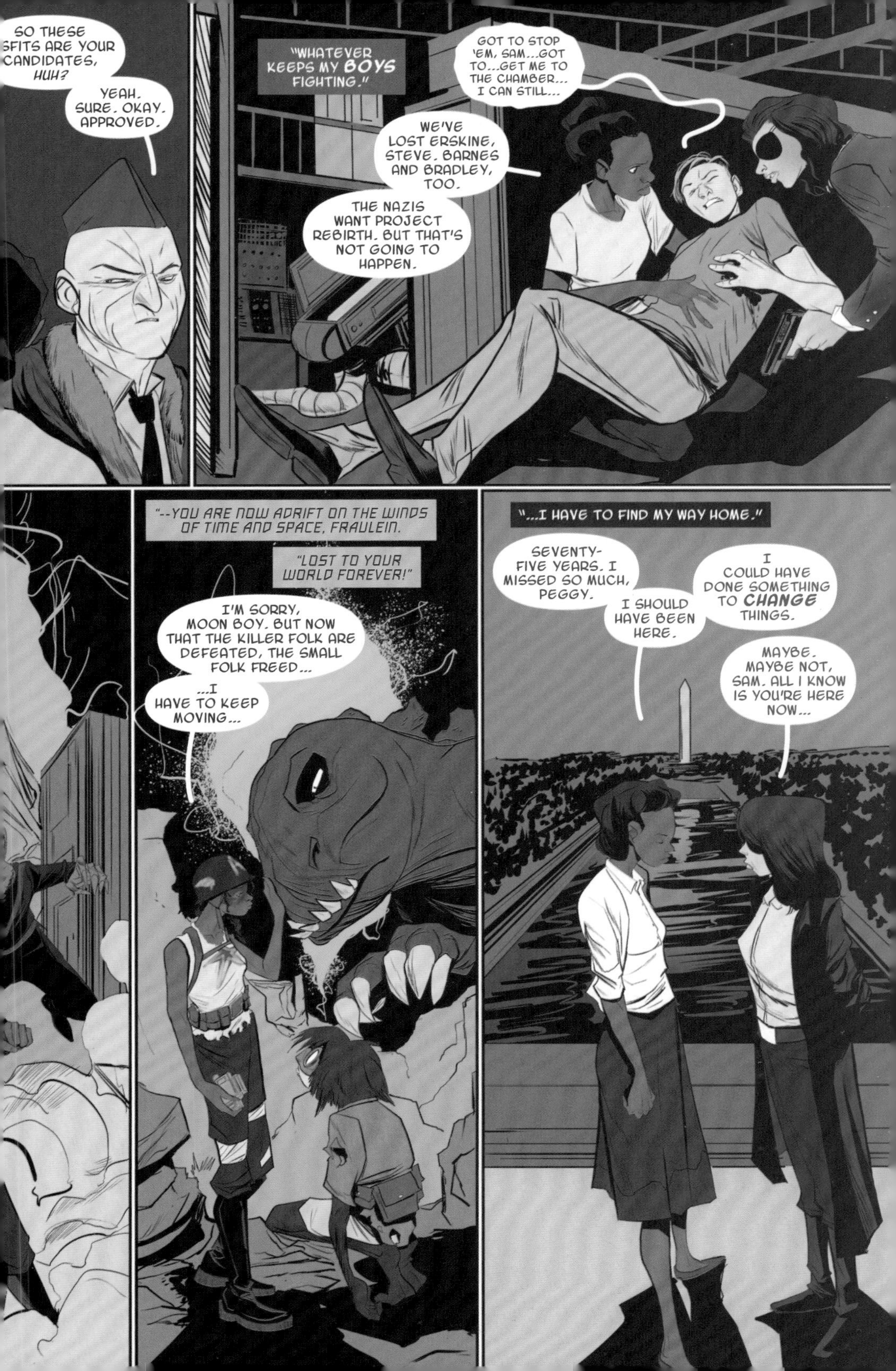
SO THESE
SFITS ARE YOUR CANDIDATES, HUH?
YEAH. SURE. OKAY. APPROVED.
"WHATEVER KEEPS MY BOYS FIGHTING."
GOT TO STOP 'EM, SAM...GOT TO...GET ME TO THE CHAMBER... I CAN STILL...
WE'VE LOST ERSKINE, STEVE. BARNES AND BRADLEY, TOO.
THE NAZIS WANT PROJECT REBIRTH. BUT THAT'S NOT GOING TO HAPPEN.
"--YOU ARE NOW ADRIFT ON THE WINDS OF TIME AND SPACE, FRAULEIN.
"LOST TO YOUR WORLD FOREVER!"
I'M SORRY, MOON BOY. BUT NOW THAT THE KILLER FOLK ARE DEFEATED, THE SMALL FOLK FREED...
...I HAVE TO KEEP MOVING...
"...I HAVE TO FIND MY WAY HOME."
SEVENTY-FIVE YEARS. I MISSED SO MUCH, PEGGY.
I SHOULD HAVE BEEN HERE.
I COULD HAVE DONE SOMETHING TO CHANGE THINGS.
MAYBE. MAYBE NOT, SAM. ALL I KNOW IS YOU'RE HERE NOW...

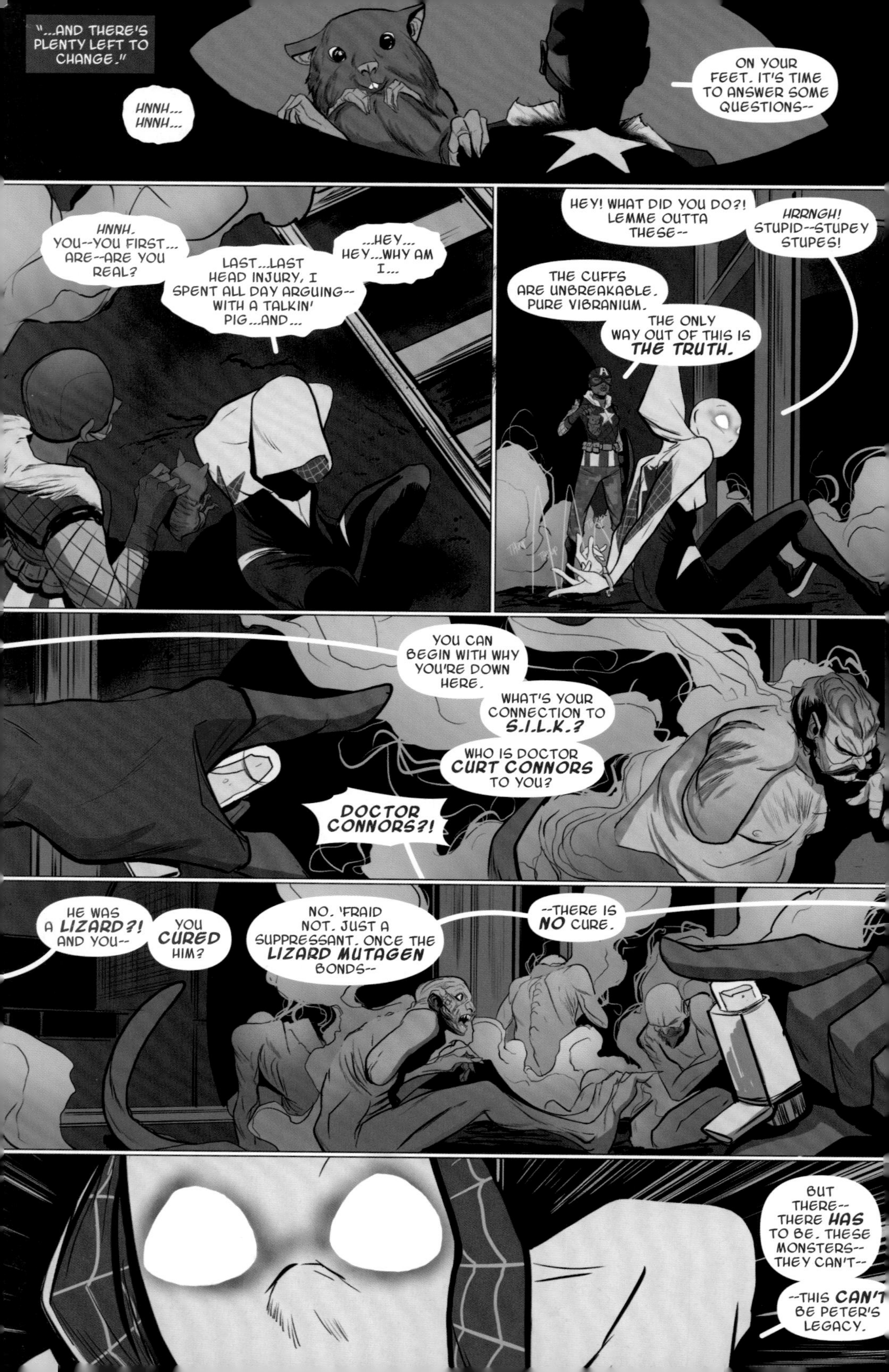

"...AND THERE'S PLENTY LEFT TO CHANGE."
HNNH... HNNH...
ON YOUR FEET. IT'S TIME TO ANSWER SOME QUESTIONS--
HNNH. YOU--YOU FIRST... ARE--ARE YOU REAL?
LAST...LAST HEAD INJURY, I SPENT ALL DAY ARGUING--WITH A TALKIN' PIG...AND...
...HEY... HEY...WHY AM I...
HEY! WHAT DID YOU DO?! LEMME OUTTA THESE--
HRRNGH! STUPID--STUPEY STUPES!
THE CUFFS ARE UNBREAKABLE. PURE VIBRANIUM.
THE ONLY WAY OUT OF THIS IS THE TRUTH.
YOU CAN BEGIN WITH WHY YOU'RE DOWN HERE.
WHAT'S YOUR CONNECTION TO S.I.L.K.?
WHO IS DOCTOR CURT CONNORS TO YOU?
DOCTOR CONNORS?!
HE WAS A LIZARD?! AND YOU--
YOU CURED HIM?
NO. 'FRAID NOT. JUST A SUPPRESSANT. ONCE THE LIZARD MUTAGEN BONDS--
--THERE IS NO CURE.
BUT THERE--THERE HAS TO BE. THESE MONSTERS--THEY CAN'T--
--THIS CAN'T BE PETER'S LEGACY.

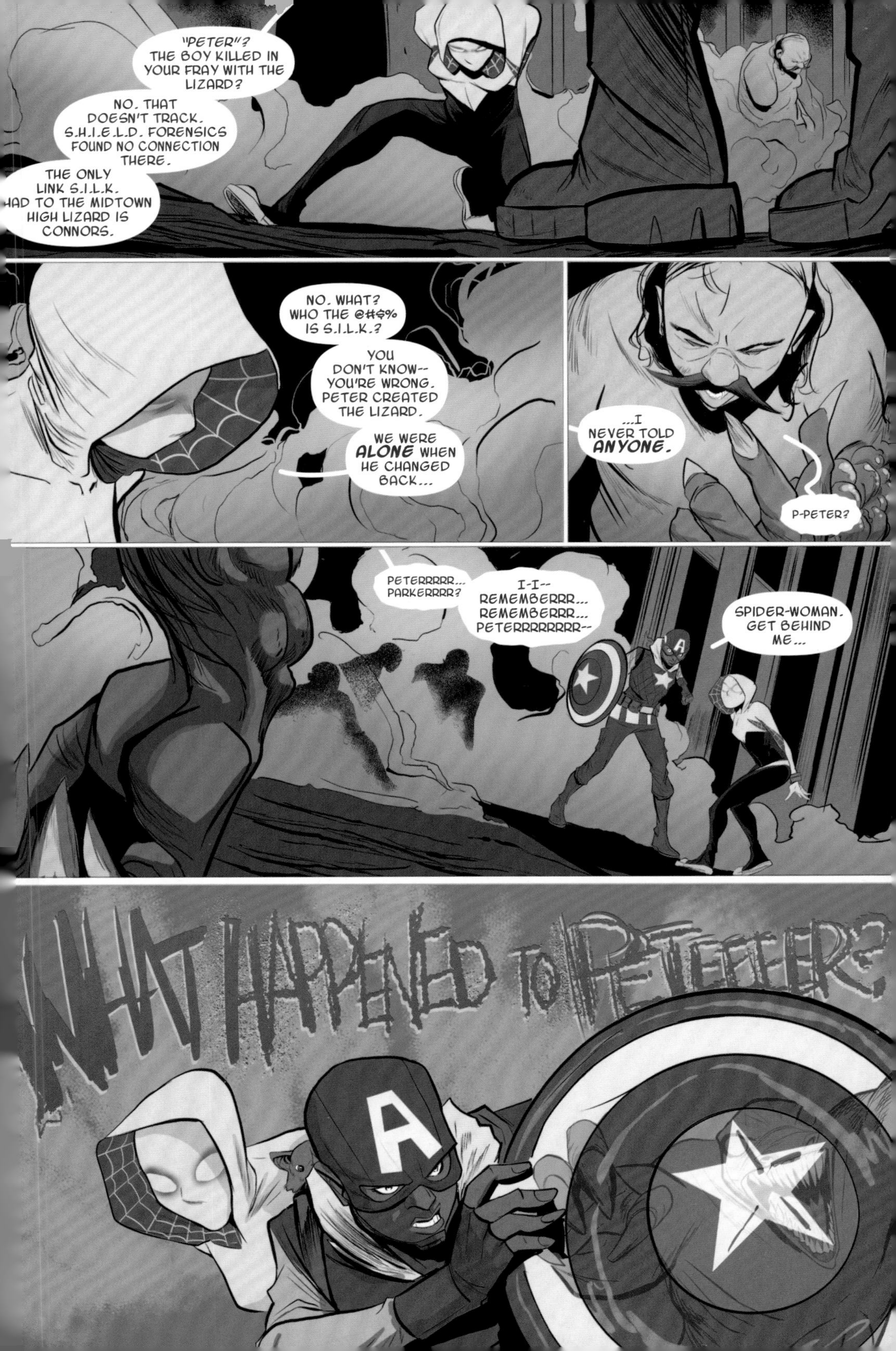
"PETER"? THE BOY KILLED IN YOUR FRAY WITH THE LIZARD?
NO. THAT DOESN'T TRACK. S.H.I.E.L.D. FORENSICS FOUND NO CONNECTION THERE.
THE ONLY LINK S.I.L.K. HAD TO THE MIDTOWN HIGH LIZARD IS CONNORS.
NO. WHAT? WHO THE @#$% IS S.I.L.K.?
YOU DON'T KNOW-- YOU'RE WRONG. PETER CREATED THE LIZARD.
WE WERE ALONE WHEN HE CHANGED BACK...
...I NEVER TOLD ANYONE.
P-PETER?
PETERRRRR... PARKERRRR?
I-I-- REMEMBERRR... REMEMBERRR... PETERRRRRRRR--
SPIDER-WOMAN. GET BEHIND ME...
WHAT HAPPENED TO PETEEEER?

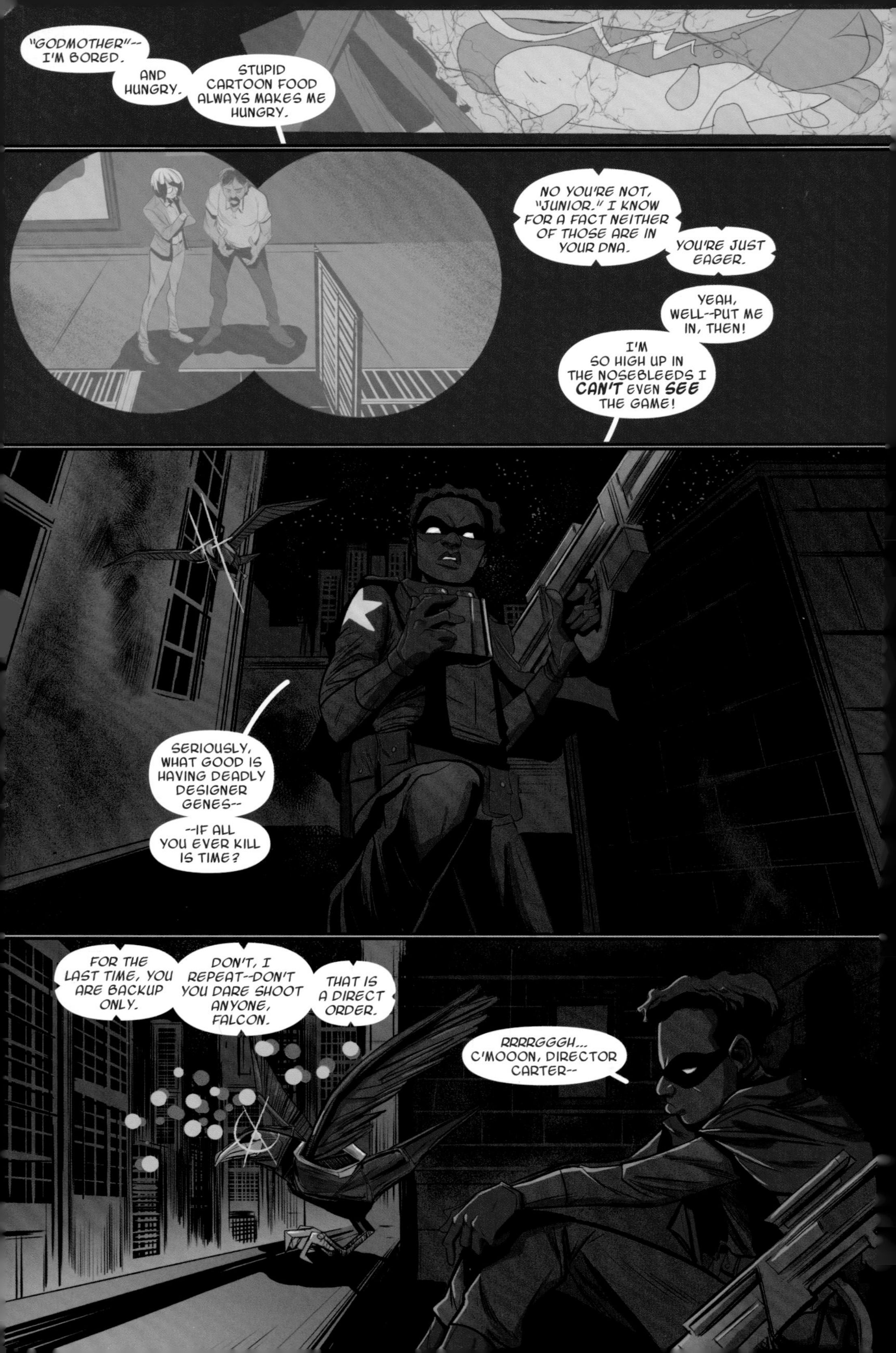
"GODMOTHER"-- I'M BORED.
AND HUNGRY.
STUPID CARTOON FOOD ALWAYS MAKES ME HUNGRY.
NO YOU'RE NOT, "JUNIOR." I KNOW FOR A FACT NEITHER OF THOSE ARE IN YOUR DNA.
YOU'RE JUST EAGER.
YEAH, WELL--PUT ME IN, THEN!
I'M SO HIGH UP IN THE NOSEBLEEDS I CAN'T EVEN SEE THE GAME!
SERIOUSLY, WHAT GOOD IS HAVING DEADLY DESIGNER GENES--
--IF ALL YOU EVER KILL IS TIME?
FOR THE LAST TIME, YOU ARE BACKUP ONLY.
DON'T, I REPEAT--DON'T YOU DARE SHOOT ANYONE, FALCON.
THAT IS A DIRECT ORDER.
RRRRGGGH... C'MOOON, DIRECTOR CARTER--

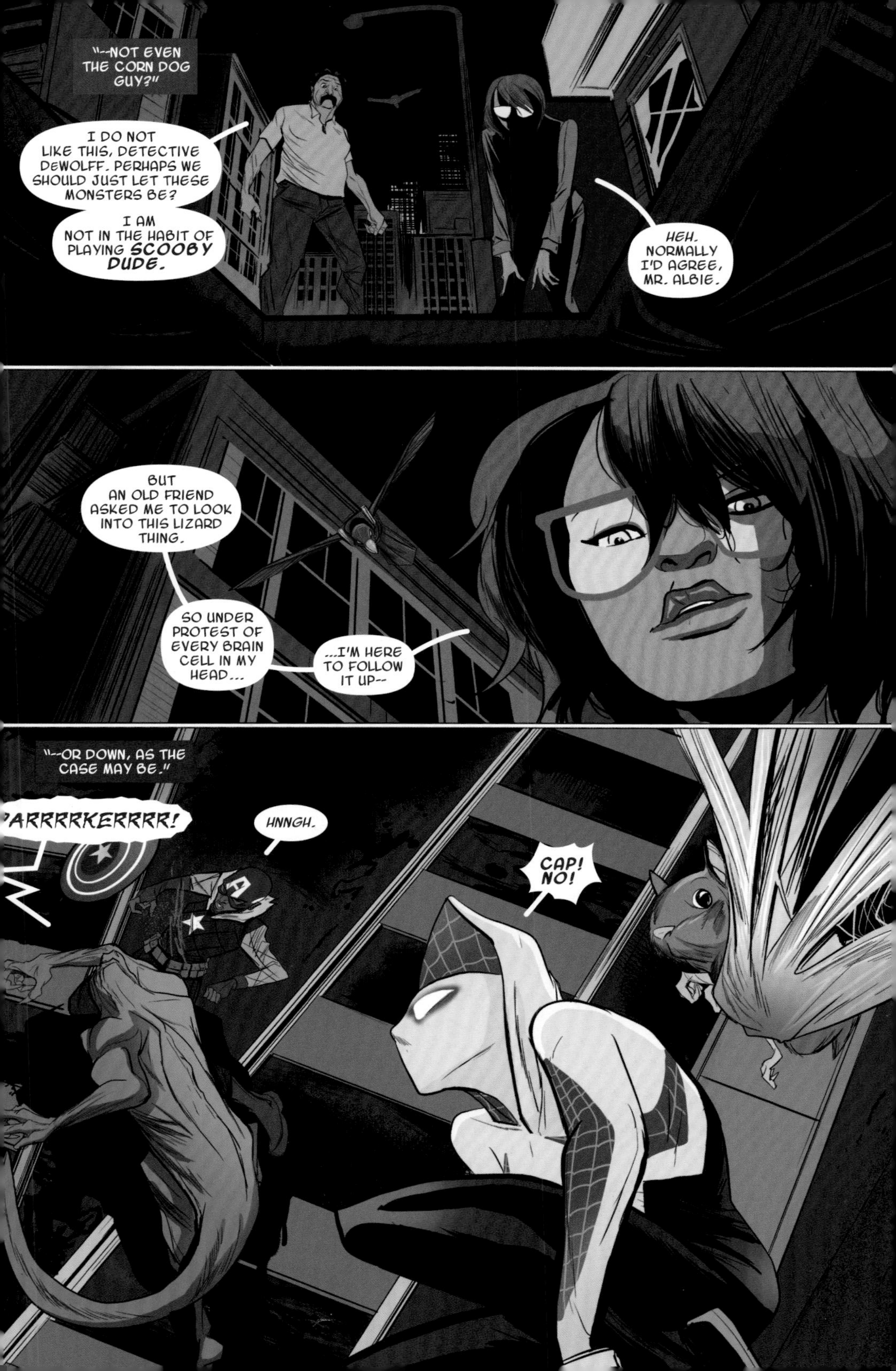
"--NOT EVEN THE CORN DOG GUY?"
I DO NOT LIKE THIS, DETECTIVE DEWOLFF. PERHAPS WE SHOULD JUST LET THESE MONSTERS BE?
I AM NOT IN THE HABIT OF PLAYING SCOOBY DUDE.
HEH. NORMALLY I'D AGREE, MR. ALBIE.
BUT AN OLD FRIEND ASKED ME TO LOOK INTO THIS LIZARD THING.
SO UNDER PROTEST OF EVERY BRAIN CELL IN MY HEAD...
...I'M HERE TO FOLLOW IT UP--
"--OR DOWN, AS THE CASE MAY BE."
PARRRRKERRRR!
HNNGH.
CAP! NO!

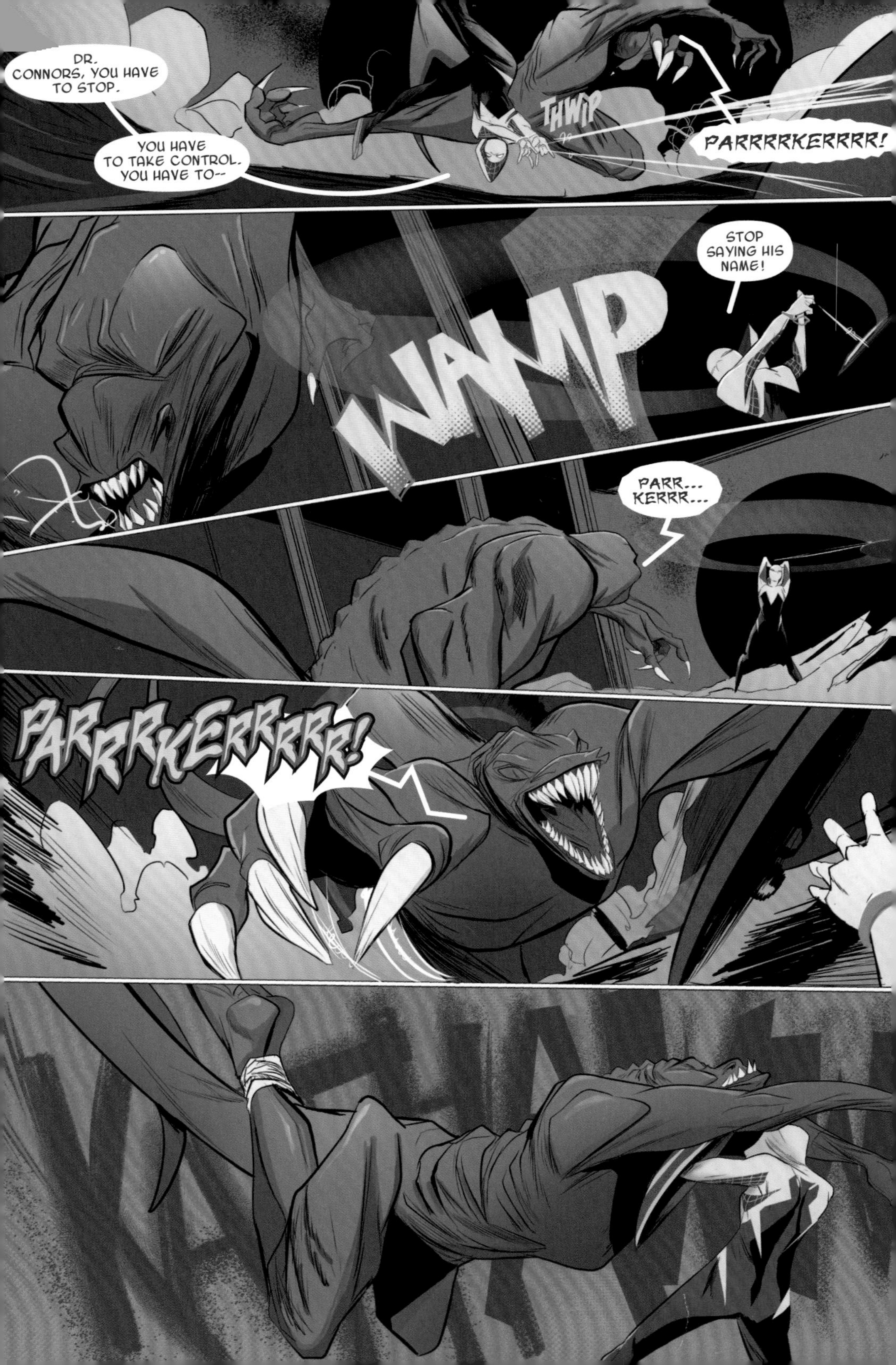
DR. CONNORS, YOU HAVE TO STOP.
THWIP
YOU HAVE TO TAKE CONTROL. YOU HAVE TO--
PARRRRKERRRR!
STOP SAYING HIS NAME!
WAMP
PARR... KERRR...
PARRRKERRRRR!

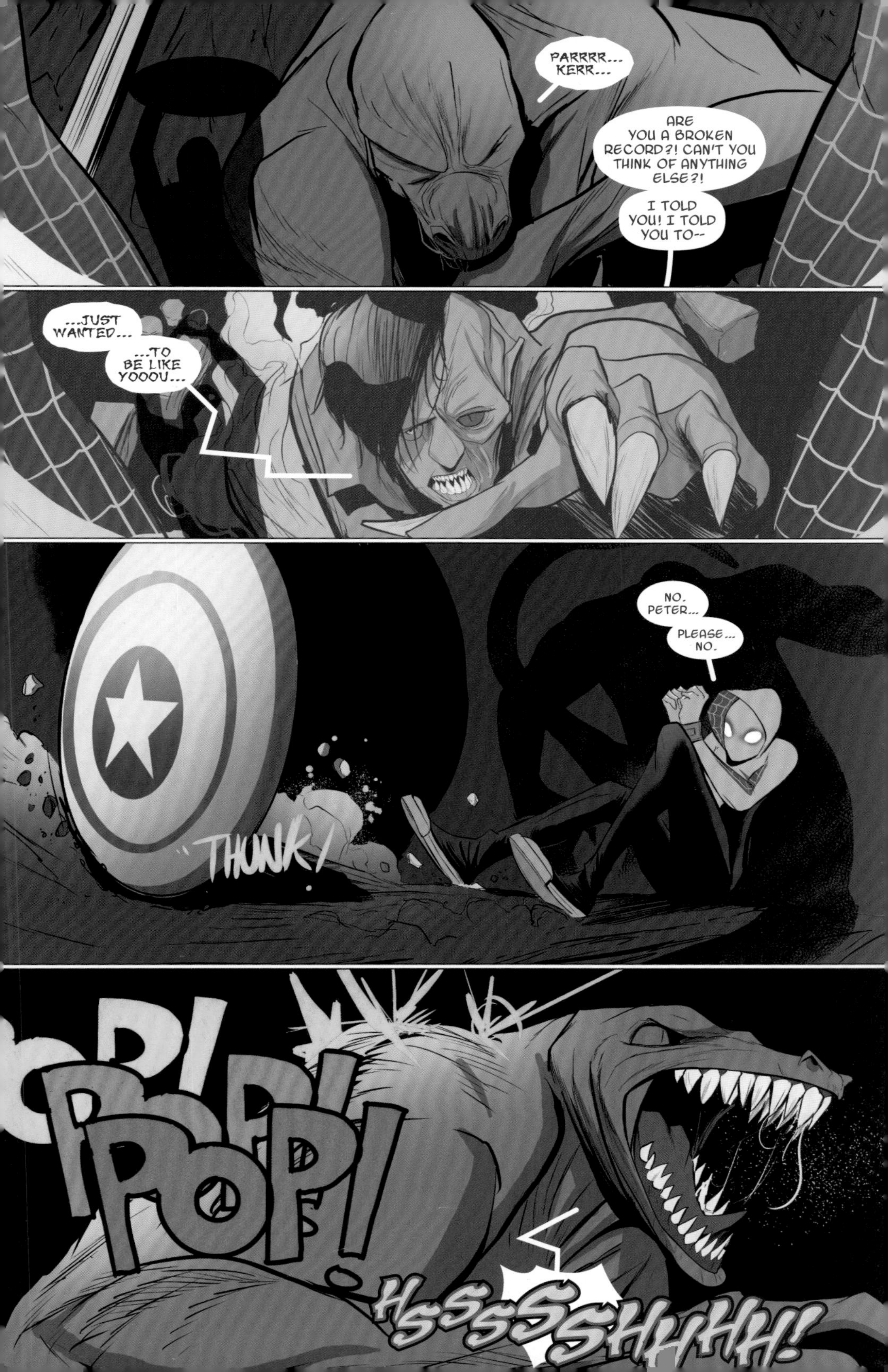
PARRRR... KERR...
ARE YOU A BROKEN RECORD?! CAN'T YOU THINK OF ANYTHING ELSE?!
I TOLD YOU! I TOLD YOU TO--
...JUST WANTED...
...TO BE LIKE YOOOU...
NO. PETER...
PLEASE... NO.
THUNK!
POP!
HSSSSSHHHH!

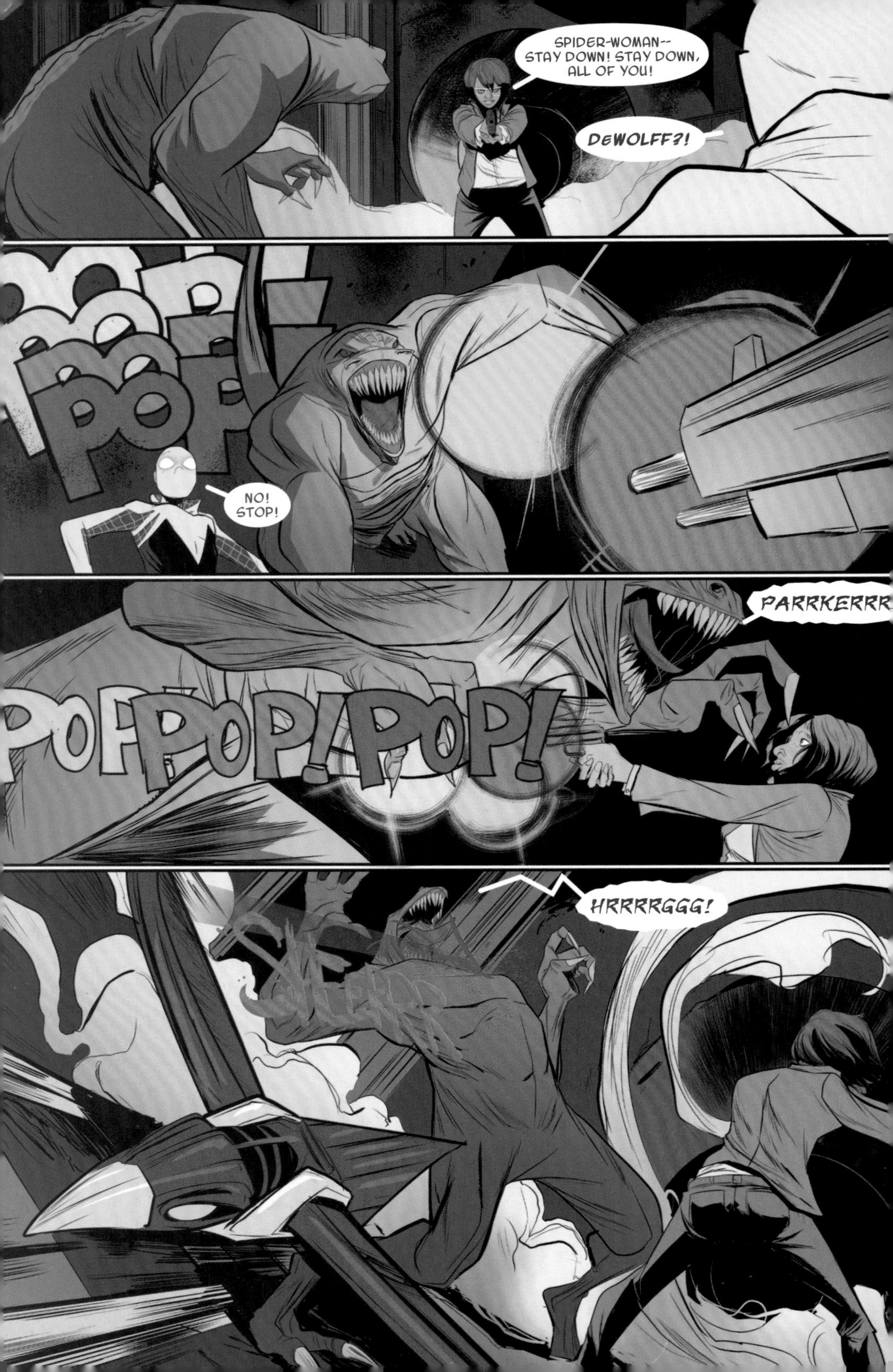
SPIDER-WOMAN-- STAY DOWN! STAY DOWN, ALL OF YOU!
DeWOLFF?!
POP POP POP POP!
NO! STOP!
PARRKERRR
POP POP! POP! POP!
HRRRRGGG!

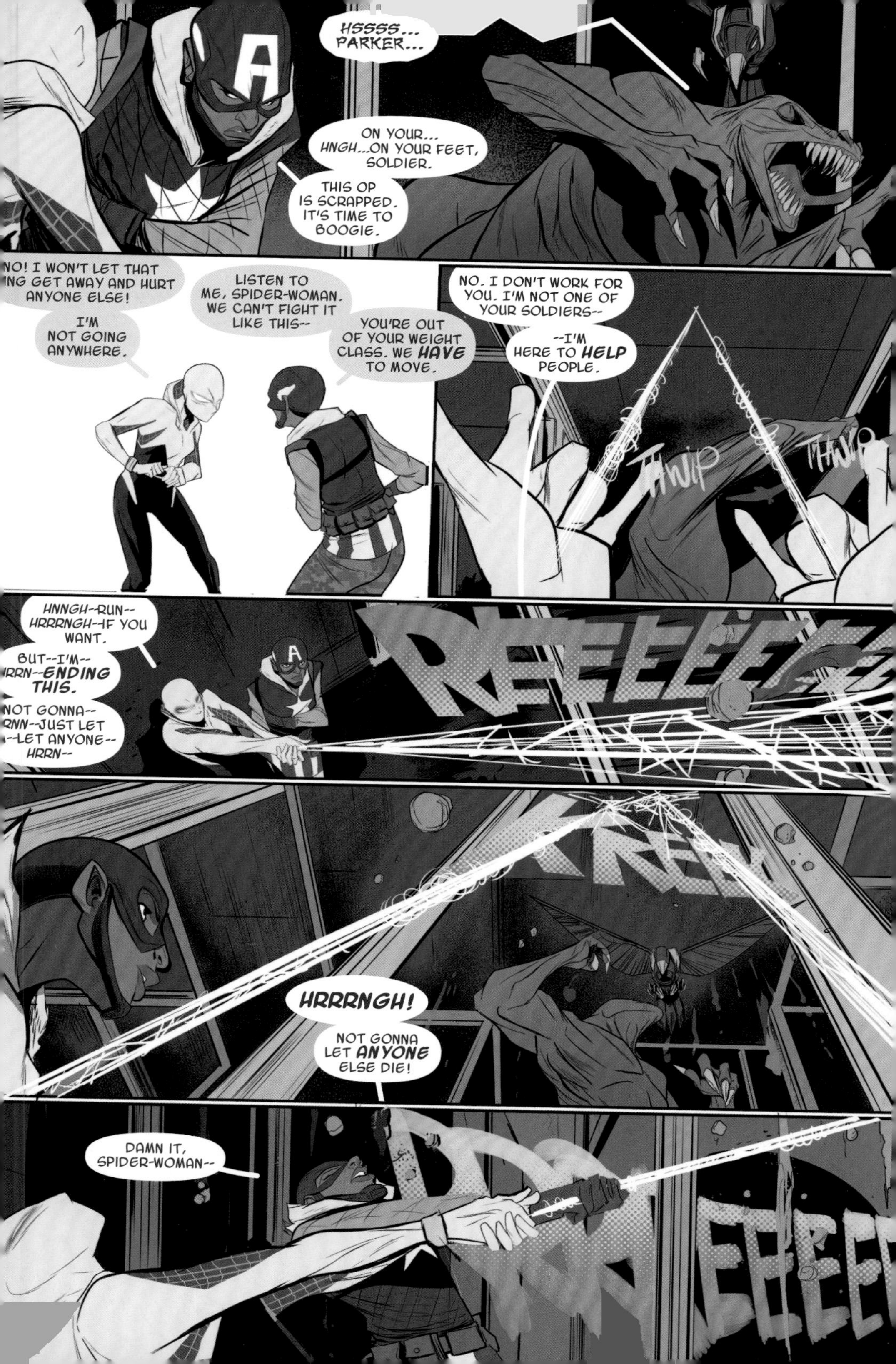
HSSSS... PARKER...
ON YOUR... HNGH...ON YOUR FEET, SOLDIER.
THIS OP IS SCRAPPED. IT'S TIME TO BOOGIE.
NO! I WON'T LET THAT
NG GET AWAY AND HURT ANYONE ELSE!
I'M NOT GOING ANYWHERE.
LISTEN TO ME, SPIDER-WOMAN. WE CAN'T FIGHT IT LIKE THIS--
YOU'RE OUT OF YOUR WEIGHT CLASS. WE HAVE TO MOVE.
NO. I DON'T WORK FOR YOU. I'M NOT ONE OF YOUR SOLDIERS--
--I'M HERE TO HELP PEOPLE.
THWIP
THWIP
HNNGH--RUN-- HRRRNGH--IF YOU WANT.
BUT--I'M-- RRN--ENDING THIS.
NOT GONNA-- RNN--JUST LET --LET ANYONE-- HRRN--
HRRRNGH!
NOT GONNA LET ANYONE ELSE DIE!
DAMN IT, SPIDER-WOMAN--

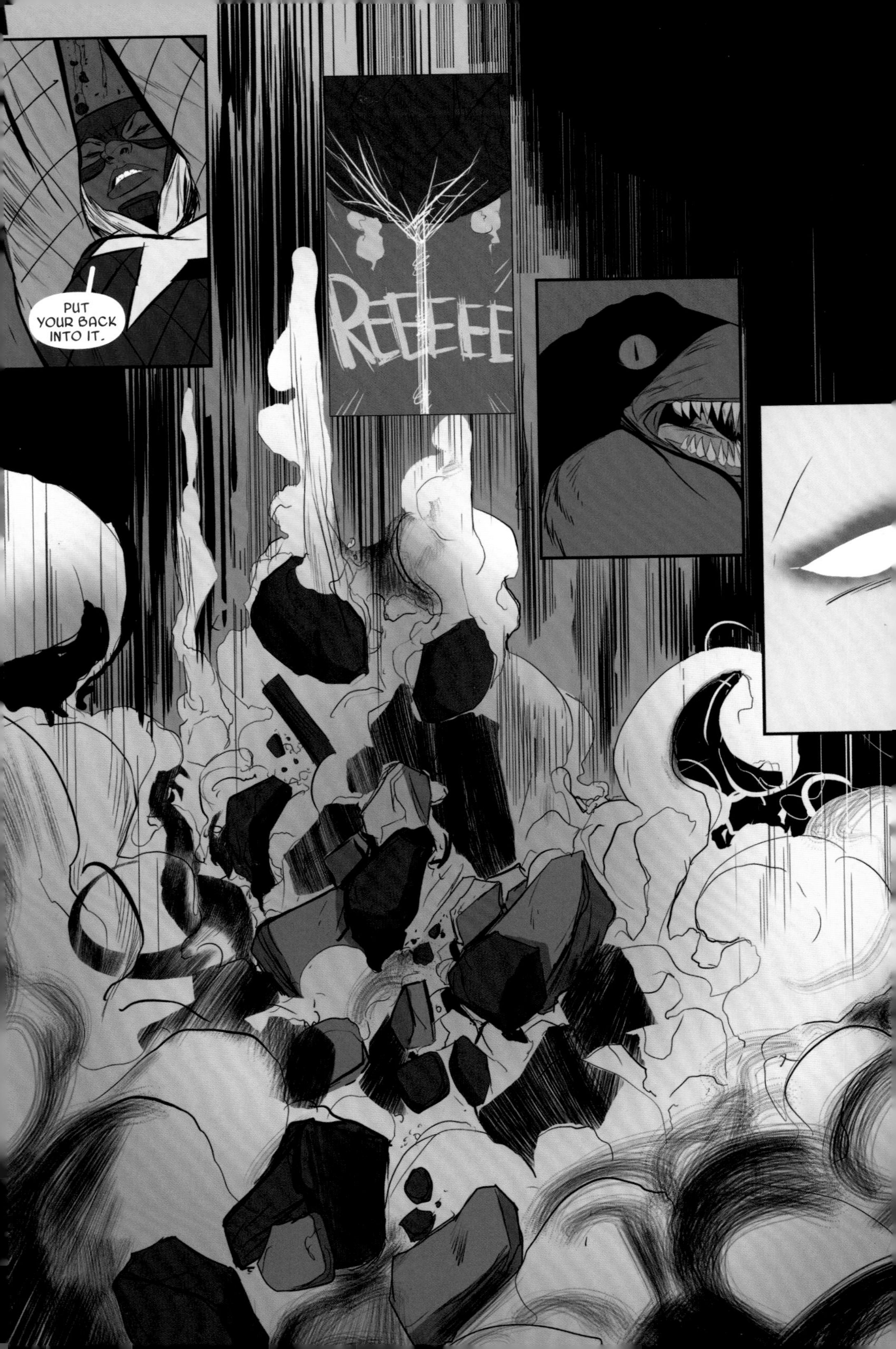
PUT YOUR BACK INTO IT.
REEEEE

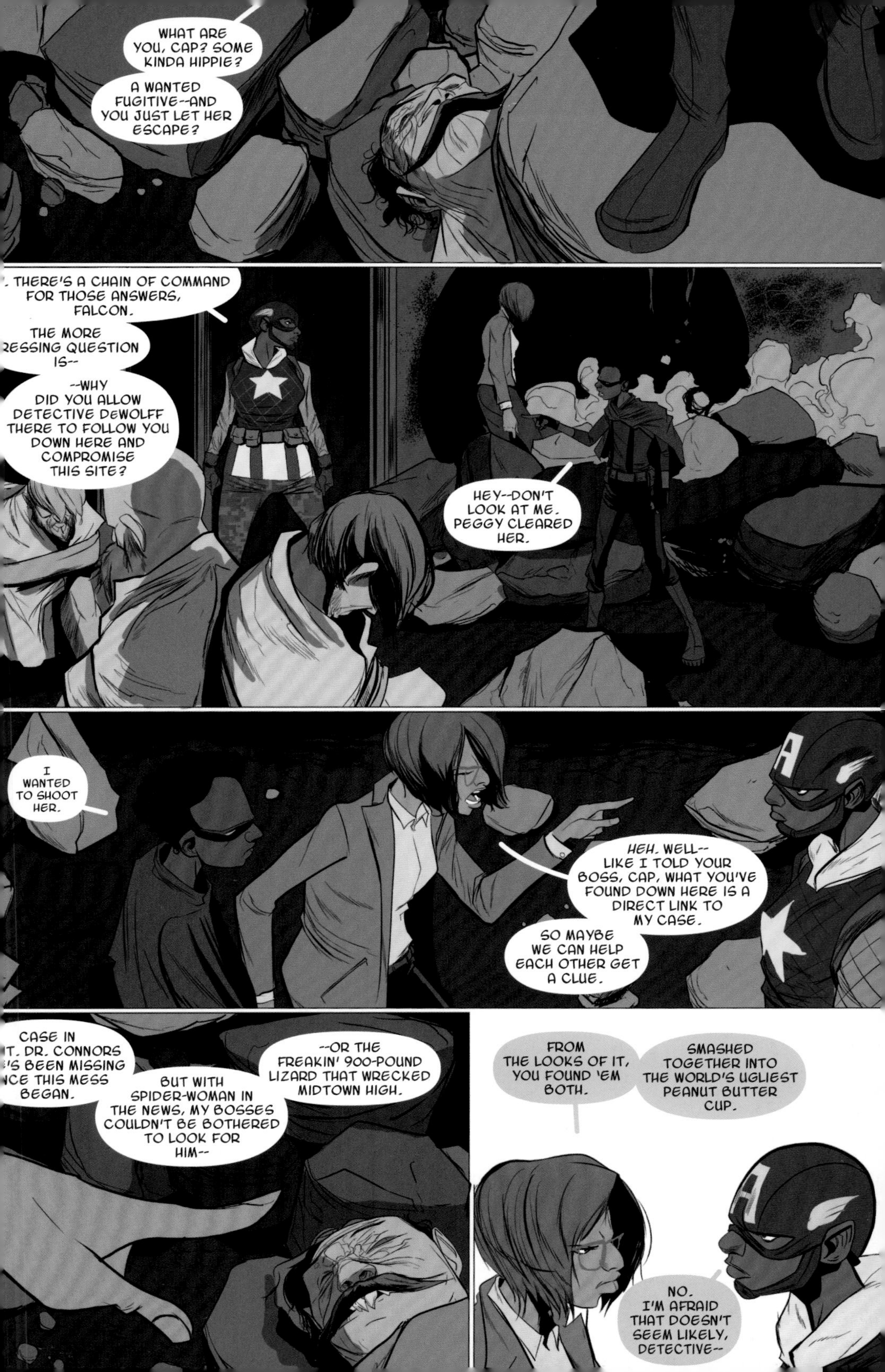
WHAT ARE YOU, CAP? SOME KINDA HIPPIE?
A WANTED FUGITIVE--AND YOU JUST LET HER ESCAPE?
THERE'S A CHAIN OF COMMAND FOR THOSE ANSWERS, FALCON.
THE MORE RESSING QUESTION IS--
--WHY DID YOU ALLOW DETECTIVE DEWOLFF THERE TO FOLLOW YOU DOWN HERE AND COMPROMISE THIS SITE?
HEY--DON'T LOOK AT ME. PEGGY CLEARED HER.
I WANTED TO SHOOT HER.
HEH. WELL-- LIKE I TOLD YOUR BOSS, CAP, WHAT YOU'VE FOUND DOWN HERE IS A DIRECT LINK TO MY CASE.
SO MAYBE WE CAN HELP EACH OTHER GET A CLUE.
CASE IN T. DR. CONNORS 'S BEEN MISSING NCE THIS MESS BEGAN.
BUT WITH SPIDER-WOMAN IN THE NEWS, MY BOSSES COULDN'T BE BOTHERED TO LOOK FOR HIM--
--OR THE FREAKIN' 900-POUND LIZARD THAT WRECKED MIDTOWN HIGH.
FROM THE LOOKS OF IT, YOU FOUND 'EM BOTH.
SMASHED TOGETHER INTO THE WORLD'S UGLIEST PEANUT BUTTER CUP.
NO. I'M AFRAID THAT DOESN'T SEEM LIKELY, DETECTIVE--

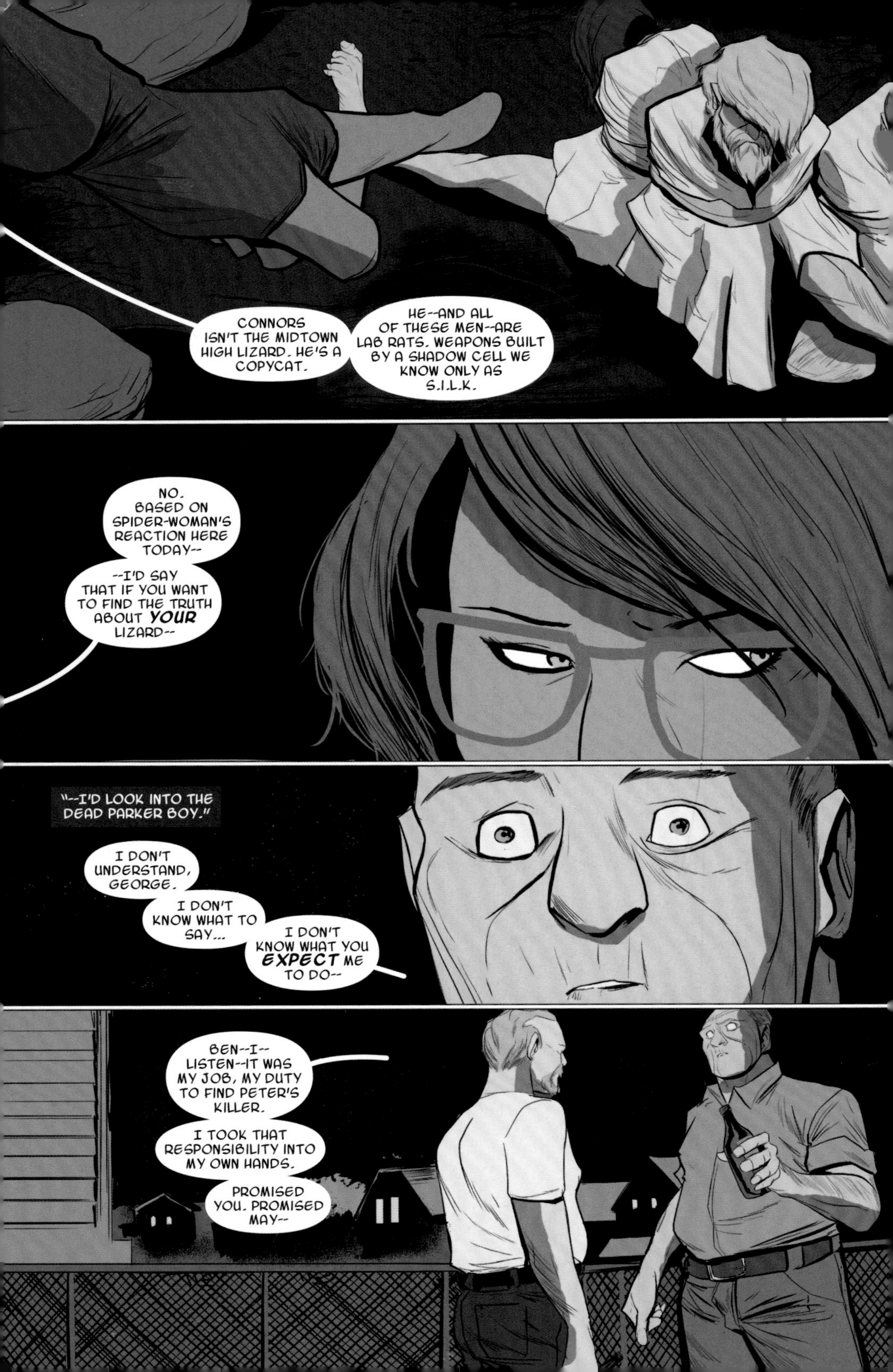
CONNORS ISN'T THE MIDTOWN HIGH LIZARD. HE'S A COPYCAT.
HE--AND ALL OF THESE MEN--ARE LAB RATS. WEAPONS BUILT BY A SHADOW CELL WE KNOW ONLY AS S.I.L.K.
NO. BASED ON SPIDER-WOMAN'S REACTION HERE TODAY--
--I'D SAY THAT IF YOU WANT TO FIND THE TRUTH ABOUT YOUR LIZARD--
"--I'D LOOK INTO THE DEAD PARKER BOY."
I DON'T UNDERSTAND, GEORGE.
I DON'T KNOW WHAT TO SAY...
I DON'T KNOW WHAT YOU EXPECT ME TO DO--
BEN--I--LISTEN--IT WAS MY JOB, MY DUTY TO FIND PETER'S KILLER.
I TOOK THAT RESPONSIBILITY INTO MY OWN HANDS.
PROMISED YOU. PROMISED MAY--

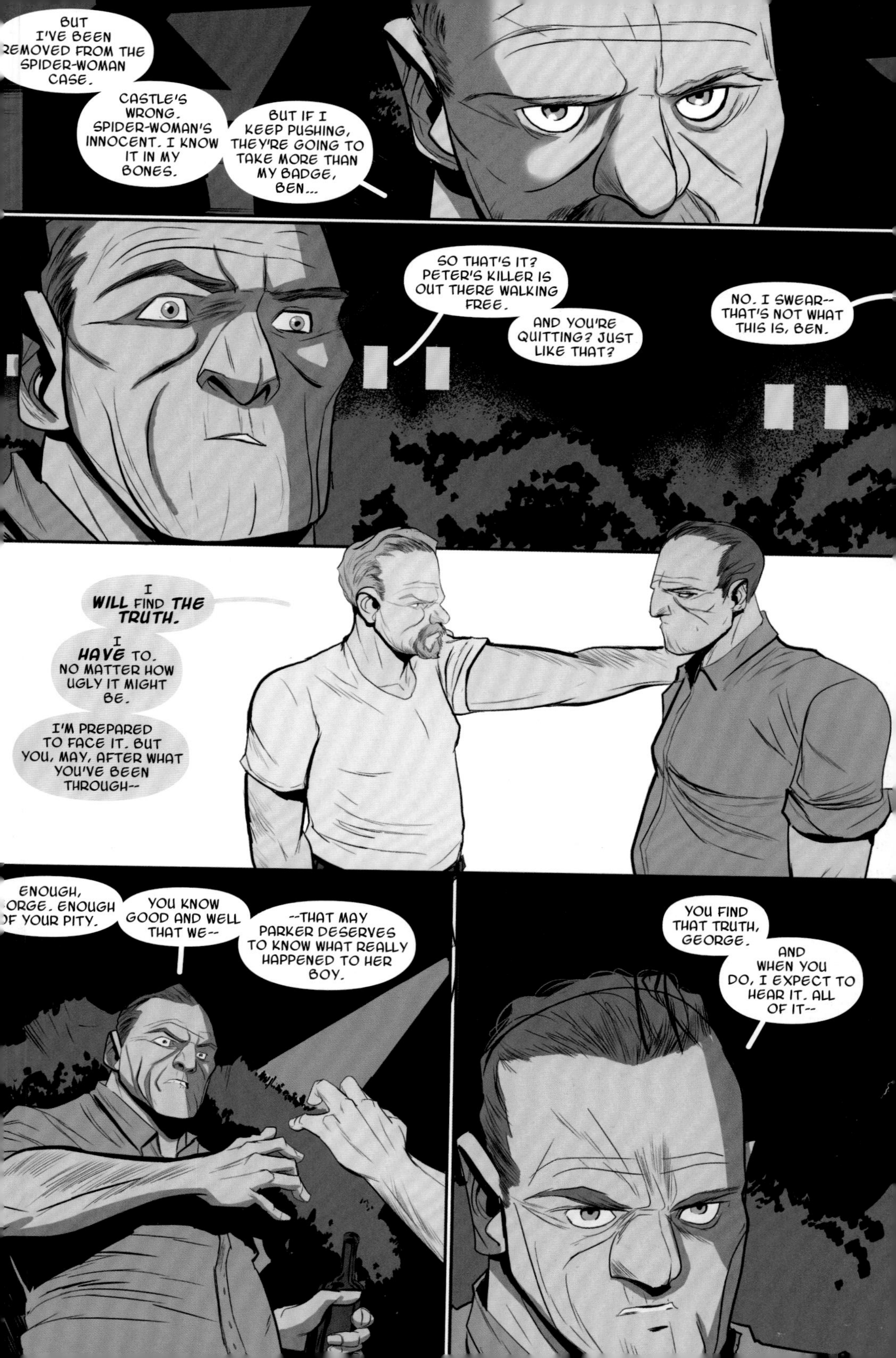
BUT I'VE BEEN REMOVED FROM THE SPIDER-WOMAN CASE.
CASTLE'S WRONG. SPIDER-WOMAN'S INNOCENT. I KNOW IT IN MY BONES.
BUT IF I KEEP PUSHING, THEY'RE GOING TO TAKE MORE THAN MY BADGE, BEN...
SO THAT'S IT? PETER'S KILLER IS OUT THERE WALKING FREE.
AND YOU'RE QUITTING? JUST LIKE THAT?
NO. I SWEAR-- THAT'S NOT WHAT THIS IS, BEN.
I WILL FIND THE TRUTH.
I HAVE TO. NO MATTER HOW UGLY IT MIGHT BE.
I'M PREPARED TO FACE IT. BUT YOU, MAY, AFTER WHAT YOU'VE BEEN THROUGH--
ENOUGH, ORGE. ENOUGH OF YOUR PITY.
YOU KNOW GOOD AND WELL THAT WE--
--THAT MAY PARKER DESERVES TO KNOW WHAT REALLY HAPPENED TO HER BOY.
YOU FIND THAT TRUTH, GEORGE.
AND WHEN YOU DO, I EXPECT TO HEAR IT. ALL OF IT--

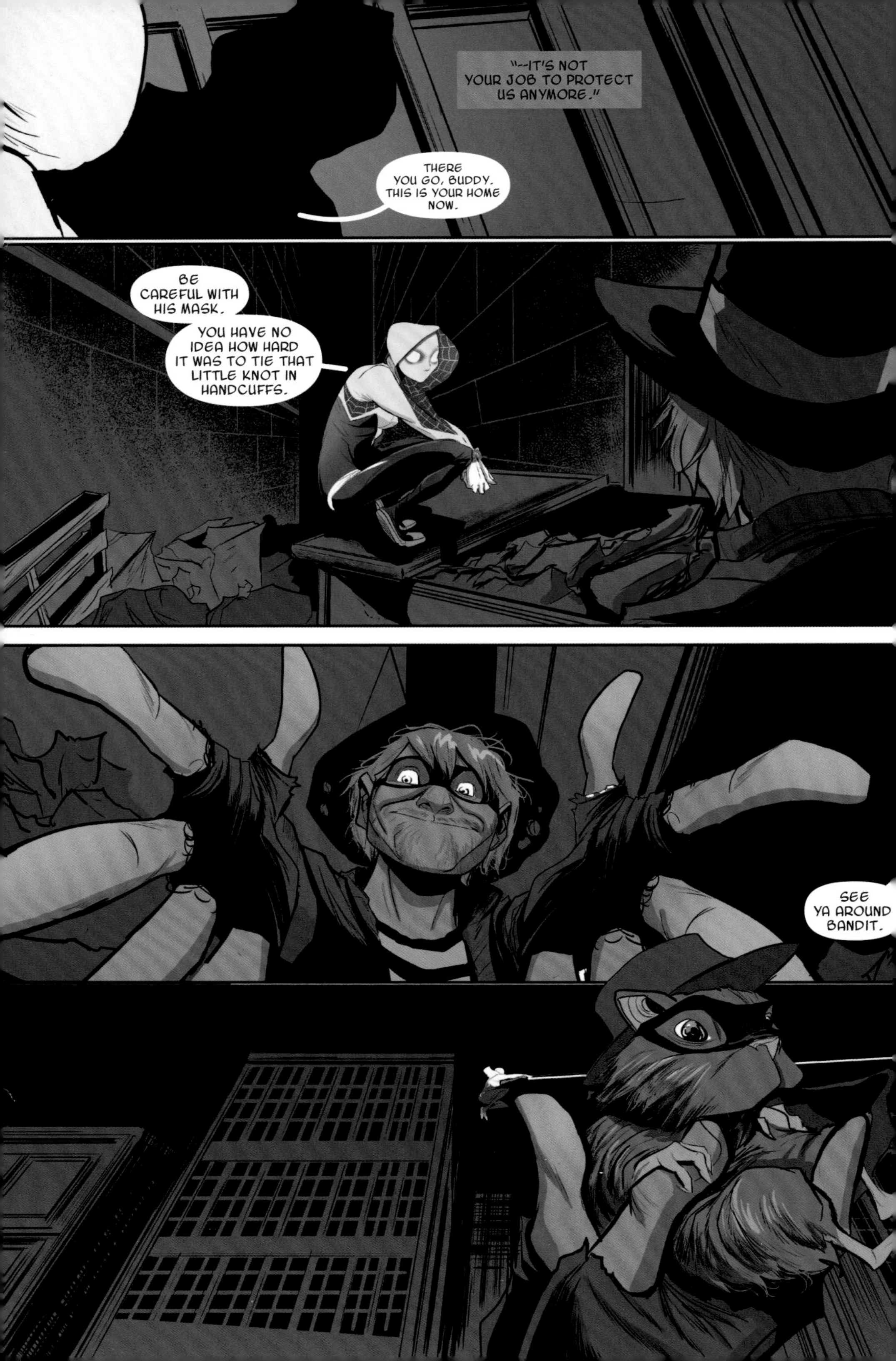
"--IT'S NOT YOUR JOB TO PROTECT US ANYMORE."
THERE YOU GO, BUDDY. THIS IS YOUR HOME NOW.
BE CAREFUL WITH HIS MASK.
YOU HAVE NO IDEA HOW HARD IT WAS TO TIE THAT LITTLE KNOT IN HANDCUFFS.
SEE YA AROUND BANDIT.

3B

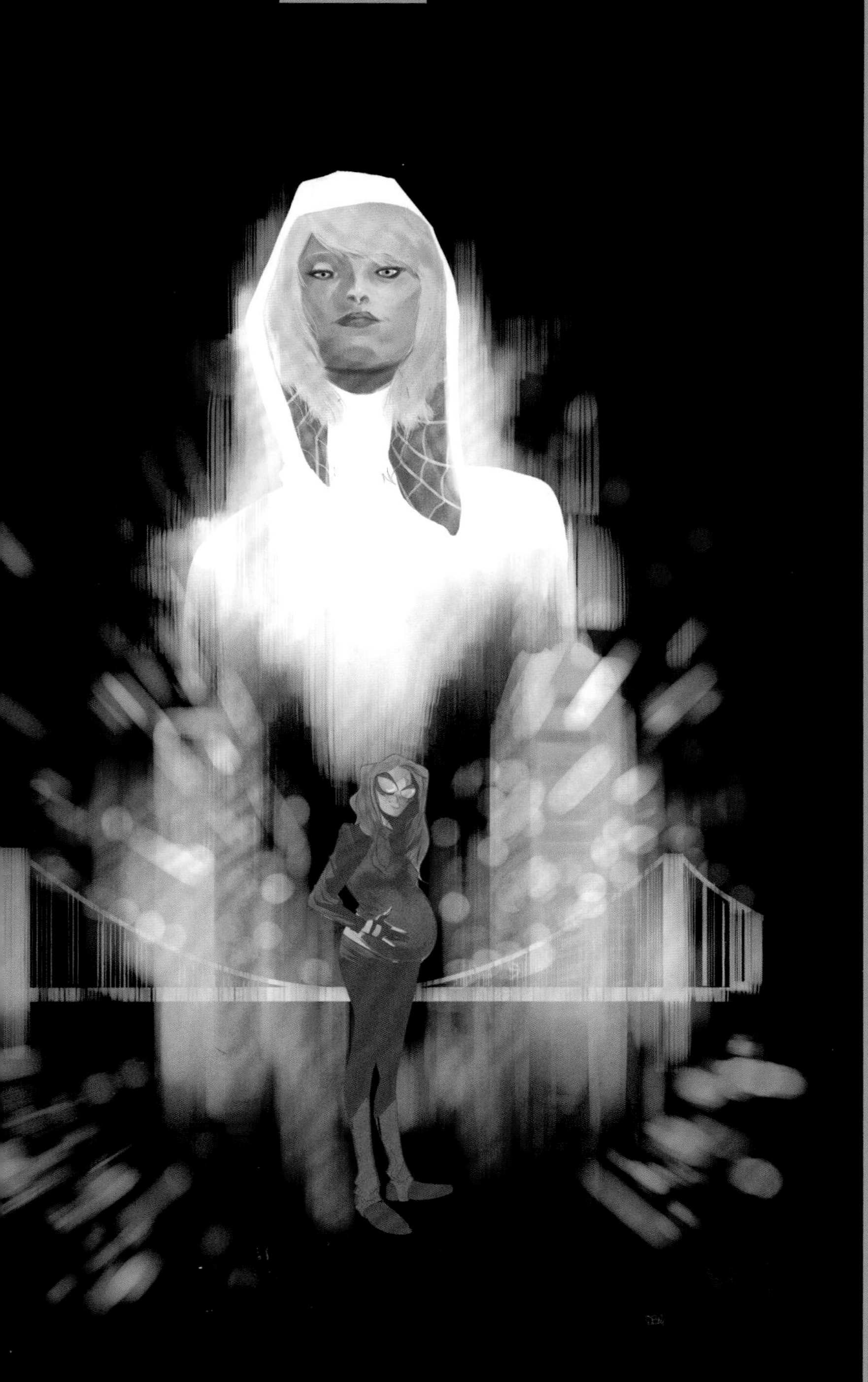

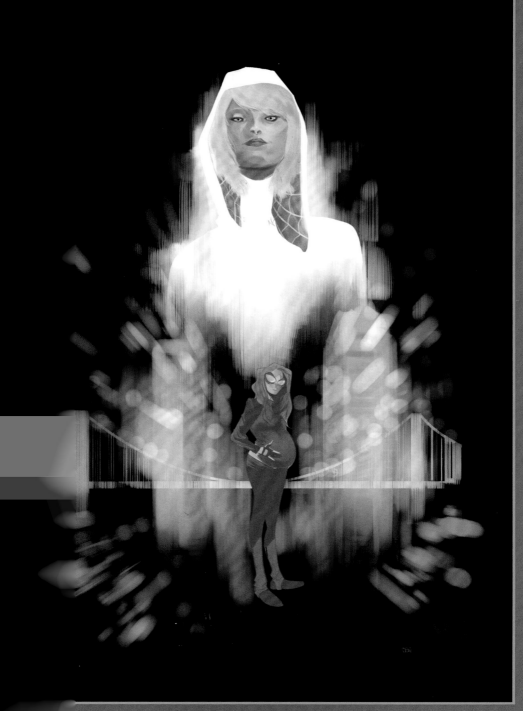

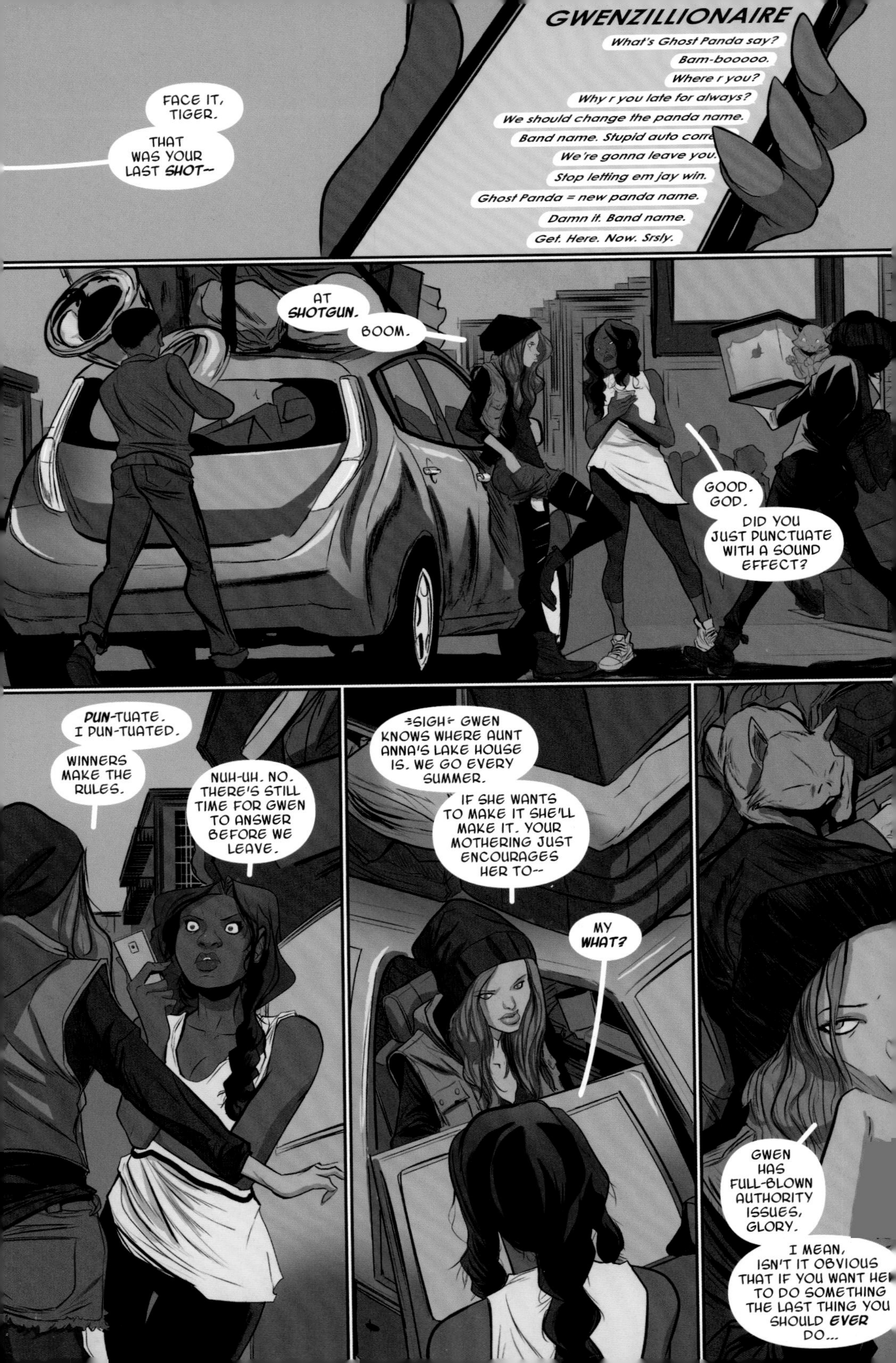
FACE IT, TIGER.
THAT WAS YOUR LAST SHOT--
GWENZILLIONAIRE
What's Ghost Panda say?
Bam-booooo.
Where r you?
Why r you late for always?
We should change the panda name.
Band name. Stupid auto corre
We're gonna leave you.
Stop letting em jay win.
Ghost Panda = new panda name.
Damn it. Band name.
Get. Here. Now. Srsly.
AT SHOTGUN.
BOOM.
GOOD. GOD.
DID YOU JUST PUNCTUATE WITH A SOUND EFFECT?
PUN-TUATE. I PUN-TUATED.
WINNERS MAKE THE RULES.
NUH-UH. NO. THERE'S STILL TIME FOR GWEN TO ANSWER BEFORE WE LEAVE.
=SIGH= GWEN KNOWS WHERE AUNT ANNA'S LAKE HOUSE IS. WE GO EVERY SUMMER.
IF SHE WANTS TO MAKE IT SHE'LL MAKE IT. YOUR MOTHERING JUST ENCOURAGES HER TO--
MY WHAT?
GWEN HAS FULL-BLOWN AUTHORITY ISSUES, GLORY.
I MEAN, ISN'T IT OBVIOUS THAT IF YOU WANT HE TO DO SOMETHING THE LAST THING YOU SHOULD EVER DO...

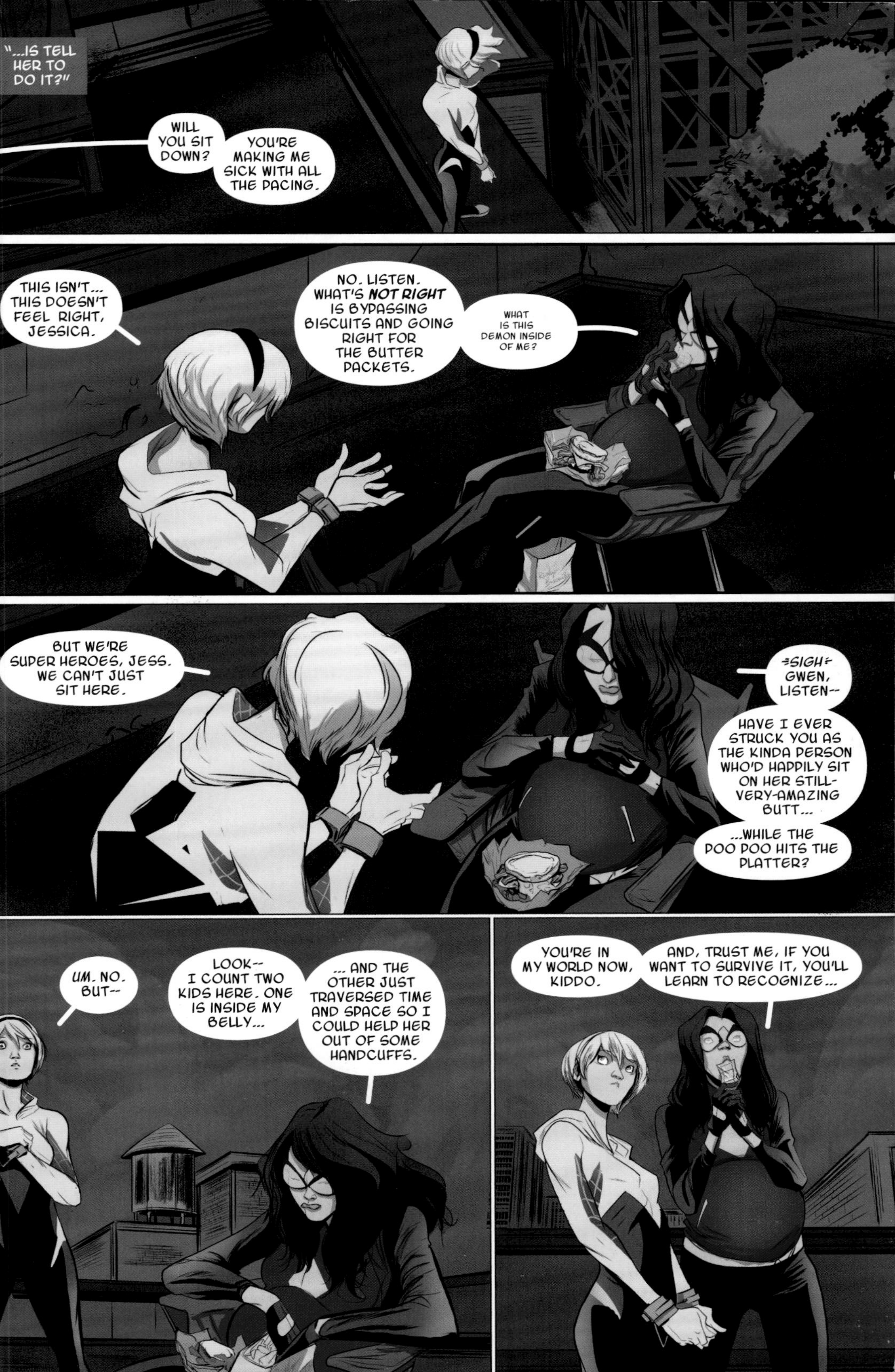
"...IS TELL HER TO DO IT?"
WILL YOU SIT DOWN?
YOU'RE MAKING ME SICK WITH ALL THE PACING.
THIS ISN'T... THIS DOESN'T FEEL RIGHT, JESSICA.
NO. LISTEN. WHAT'S **NOT RIGHT** IS BYPASSING BISCUITS AND GOING RIGHT FOR THE BUTTER PACKETS.
WHAT IS THIS DEMON INSIDE OF ME?
BUT WE'RE SUPER HEROES, JESS. WE CAN'T JUST SIT HERE.
=SIGH= GWEN, LISTEN--
HAVE I EVER STRUCK YOU AS THE KINDA PERSON WHO'D HAPPILY SIT ON HER STILL-VERY-AMAZING BUTT...
...WHILE THE POO POO HITS THE PLATTER?
UM. NO. BUT--
LOOK-- I COUNT TWO KIDS HERE. ONE IS INSIDE MY BELLY...
... AND THE OTHER JUST TRAVERSED TIME AND SPACE SO I COULD HELP HER OUT OF SOME HANDCUFFS.
YOU'RE IN MY WORLD NOW, KIDDO.
AND, TRUST ME, IF YOU WANT TO SURVIVE IT, YOU'LL LEARN TO RECOGNIZE...

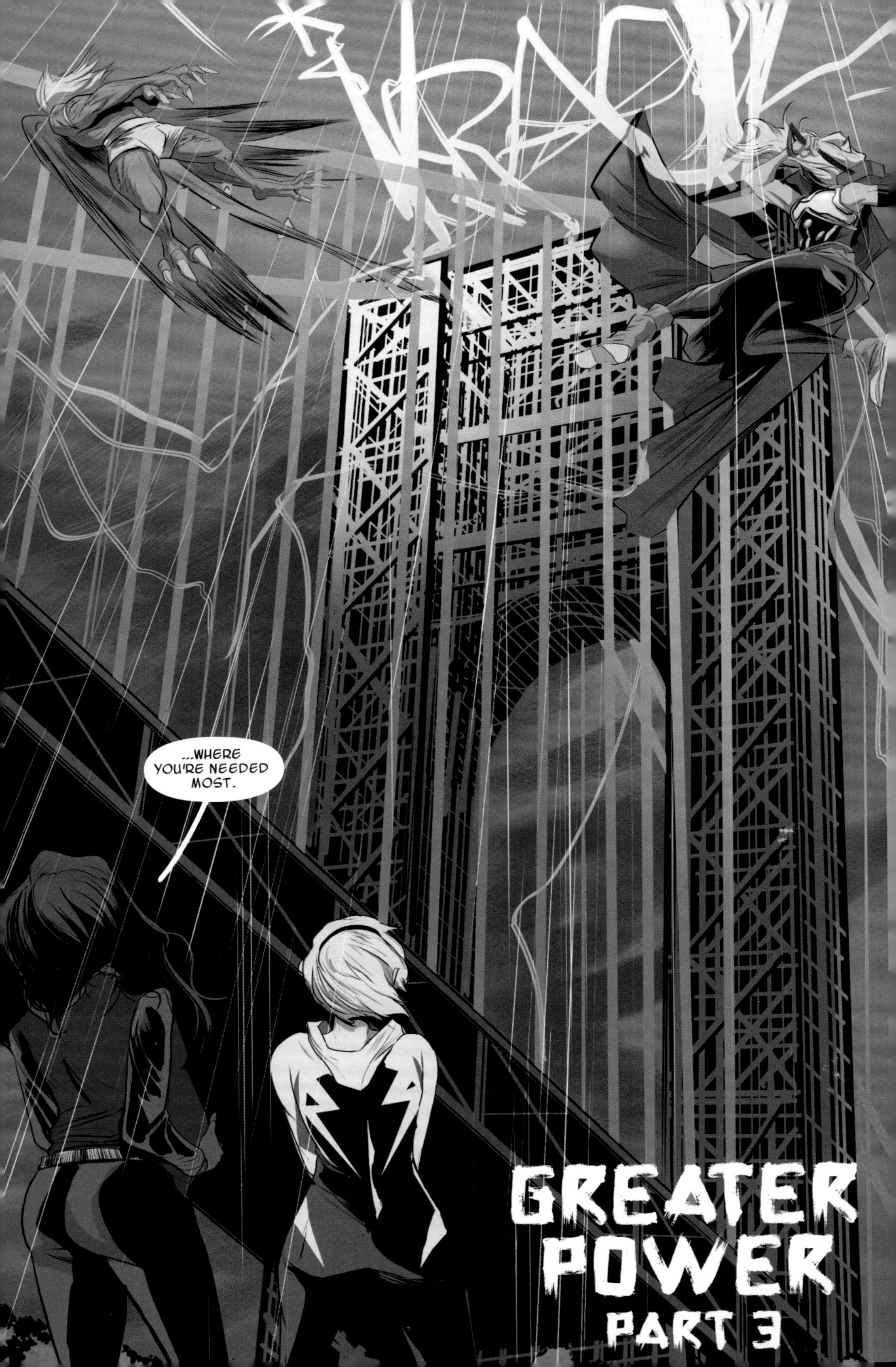
...WHERE YOU'RE NEEDED MOST.
GREATER POWER
PART 3

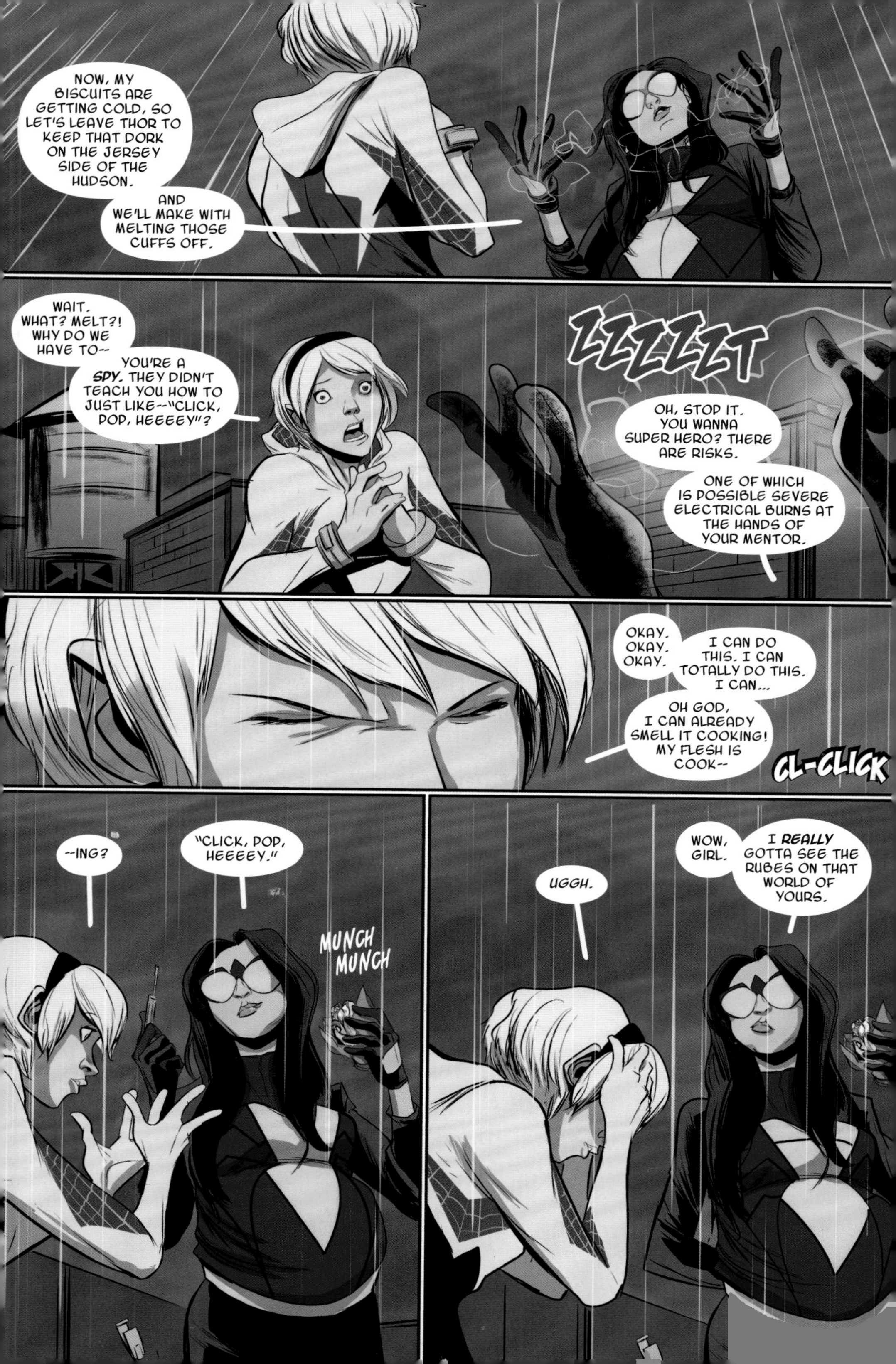
NOW, MY BISCUITS ARE GETTING COLD, SO LET'S LEAVE THOR TO KEEP THAT DORK ON THE JERSEY SIDE OF THE HUDSON.
AND WE'LL MAKE WITH MELTING THOSE CUFFS OFF.
WAIT. WHAT? MELT?! WHY DO WE HAVE TO--
YOU'RE A SPY. THEY DIDN'T TEACH YOU HOW TO JUST LIKE--"CLICK, POP, HEEEEY"?
ZZZZZT
OH, STOP IT. YOU WANNA SUPER HERO? THERE ARE RISKS.
ONE OF WHICH IS POSSIBLE SEVERE ELECTRICAL BURNS AT THE HANDS OF YOUR MENTOR.
OKAY. OKAY. OKAY.
I CAN DO THIS. I CAN TOTALLY DO THIS. I CAN...
OH GOD, I CAN ALREADY SMELL IT COOKING! MY FLESH IS COOK--
CL-CLICK
--ING?
"CLICK, POP, HEEEEY."
MUNCH MUNCH
UGGH.
WOW, GIRL.
I REALLY GOTTA SEE THE RUBES ON THAT WORLD OF YOURS.

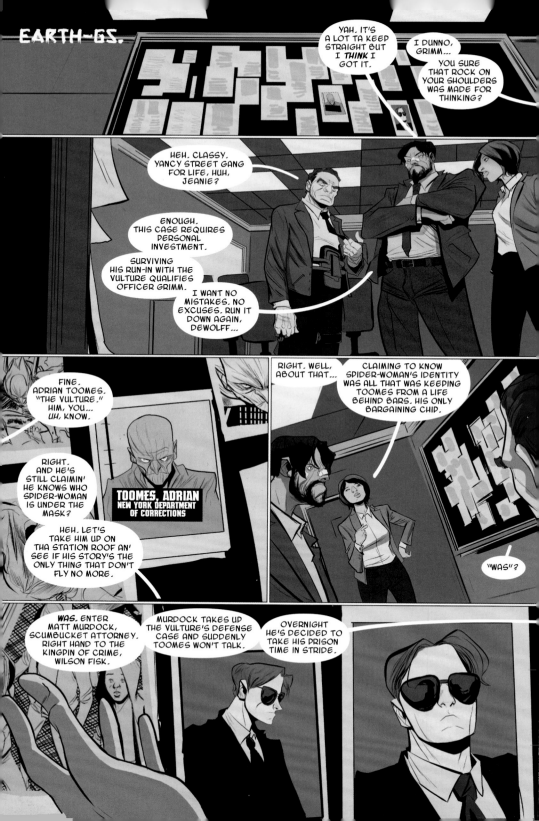

EARTH-65.

YAH. IT'S A LOT TA KEEP STRAIGHT BUT I *THINK* I GOT IT.

I DUNNO, GRIMM... YOU SURE THAT ROCK ON YOUR SHOULDERS WAS MADE FOR THINKING?

HEH. CLASSY. YANCY STREET GANG FOR LIFE, HUH, JEANIE?

ENOUGH. THIS CASE REQUIRES PERSONAL INVESTMENT.

SURVIVING HIS RUN-IN WITH THE VULTURE QUALIFIES OFFICER GRIMM. I WANT NO MISTAKES. NO EXCUSES. RUN IT DOWN AGAIN, DEWOLFF...

FINE. ADRIAN TOOMES. "THE VULTURE." HIM, YOU... UH, KNOW.

RIGHT. AND HE'S STILL CLAIMIN' HE KNOWS WHO SPIDER-WOMAN IS UNDER THE MASK?

HEH. LET'S TAKE HIM UP ON THA STATION ROOF AN' SEE IF HIS STORY'S THE ONLY THING THAT DON'T FLY NO MORE.

TOOMES, ADRIAN
NEW YORK DEPARTMENT OF CORRECTIONS

RIGHT. WELL, ABOUT THAT...

CLAIMING TO KNOW SPIDER-WOMAN'S IDENTITY WAS ALL THAT WAS KEEPING TOOMES FROM A LIFE BEHIND BARS. HIS ONLY BARGAINING CHIP.

"WAS"?

WAS. ENTER MATT MURDOCK, SCUMBUCKET ATTORNEY. RIGHT HAND TO THE KINGPIN OF CRIME, WILSON FISK.

MURDOCK TAKES UP THE VULTURE'S DEFENSE CASE AND SUDDENLY TOOMES WON'T TALK.

OVERNIGHT HE'S DECIDED TO TAKE HIS PRISON TIME IN STRIDE.

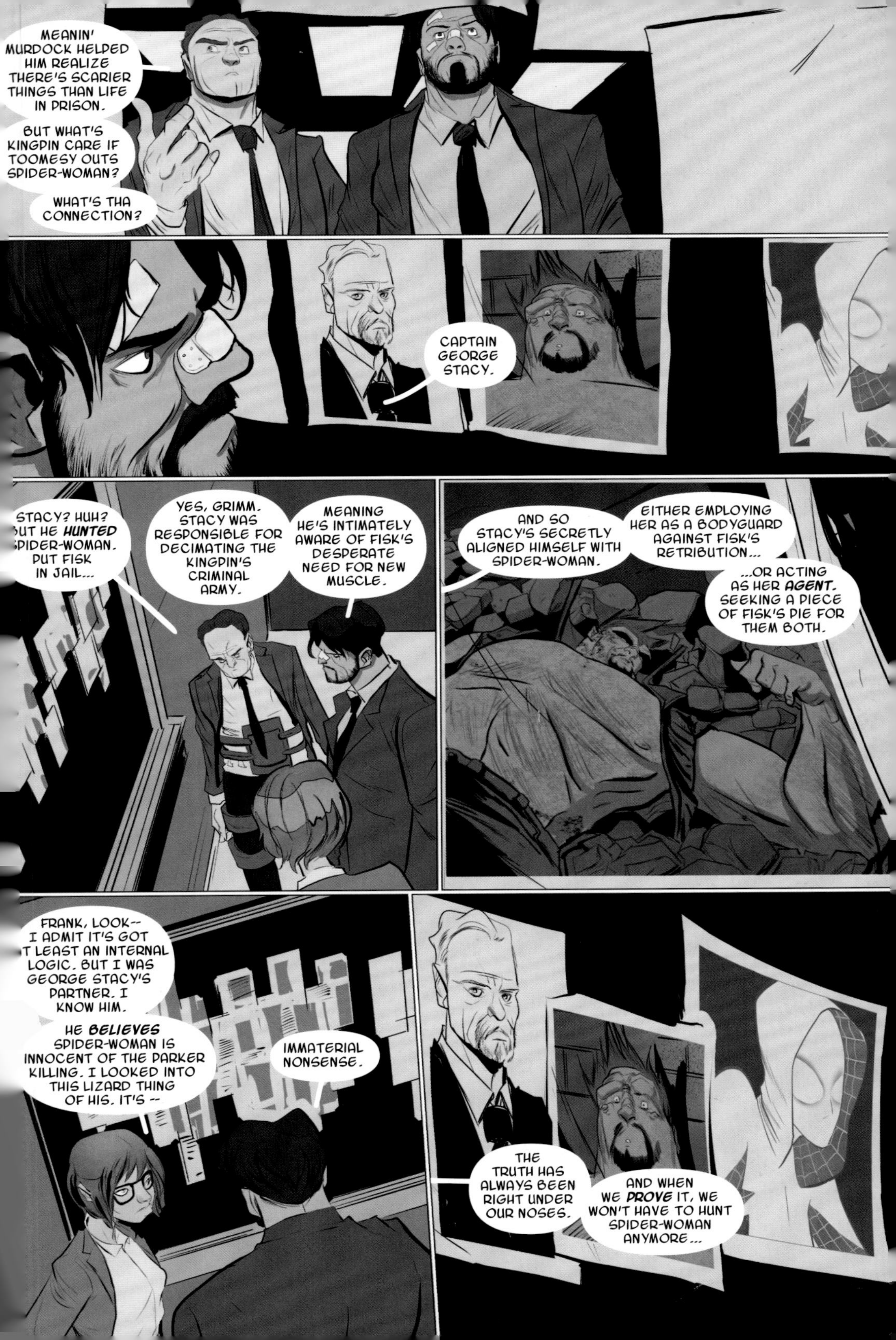
MEANIN' MURDOCK HELPED HIM REALIZE THERE'S SCARIER THINGS THAN LIFE IN PRISON.
BUT WHAT'S KINGPIN CARE IF TOOMESY OUTS SPIDER-WOMAN?
WHAT'S THA CONNECTION?
CAPTAIN GEORGE STACY.
STACY? HUH? BUT HE HUNTED SPIDER-WOMAN. PUT FISK IN JAIL...
YES, GRIMM. STACY WAS RESPONSIBLE FOR DECIMATING THE KINGPIN'S CRIMINAL ARMY.
MEANING HE'S INTIMATELY AWARE OF FISK'S DESPERATE NEED FOR NEW MUSCLE.
AND SO STACY'S SECRETLY ALIGNED HIMSELF WITH SPIDER-WOMAN.
EITHER EMPLOYING HER AS A BODYGUARD AGAINST FISK'S RETRIBUTION...
...OR ACTING AS HER AGENT. SEEKING A PIECE OF FISK'S PIE FOR THEM BOTH.
FRANK, LOOK-- I ADMIT IT'S GOT AT LEAST AN INTERNAL LOGIC. BUT I WAS GEORGE STACY'S PARTNER. I KNOW HIM.
HE BELIEVES SPIDER-WOMAN IS INNOCENT OF THE PARKER KILLING. I LOOKED INTO THIS LIZARD THING OF HIS. IT'S --
IMMATERIAL NONSENSE.
THE TRUTH HAS ALWAYS BEEN RIGHT UNDER OUR NOSES.
AND WHEN WE PROVE IT, WE WON'T HAVE TO HUNT SPIDER-WOMAN ANYMORE...

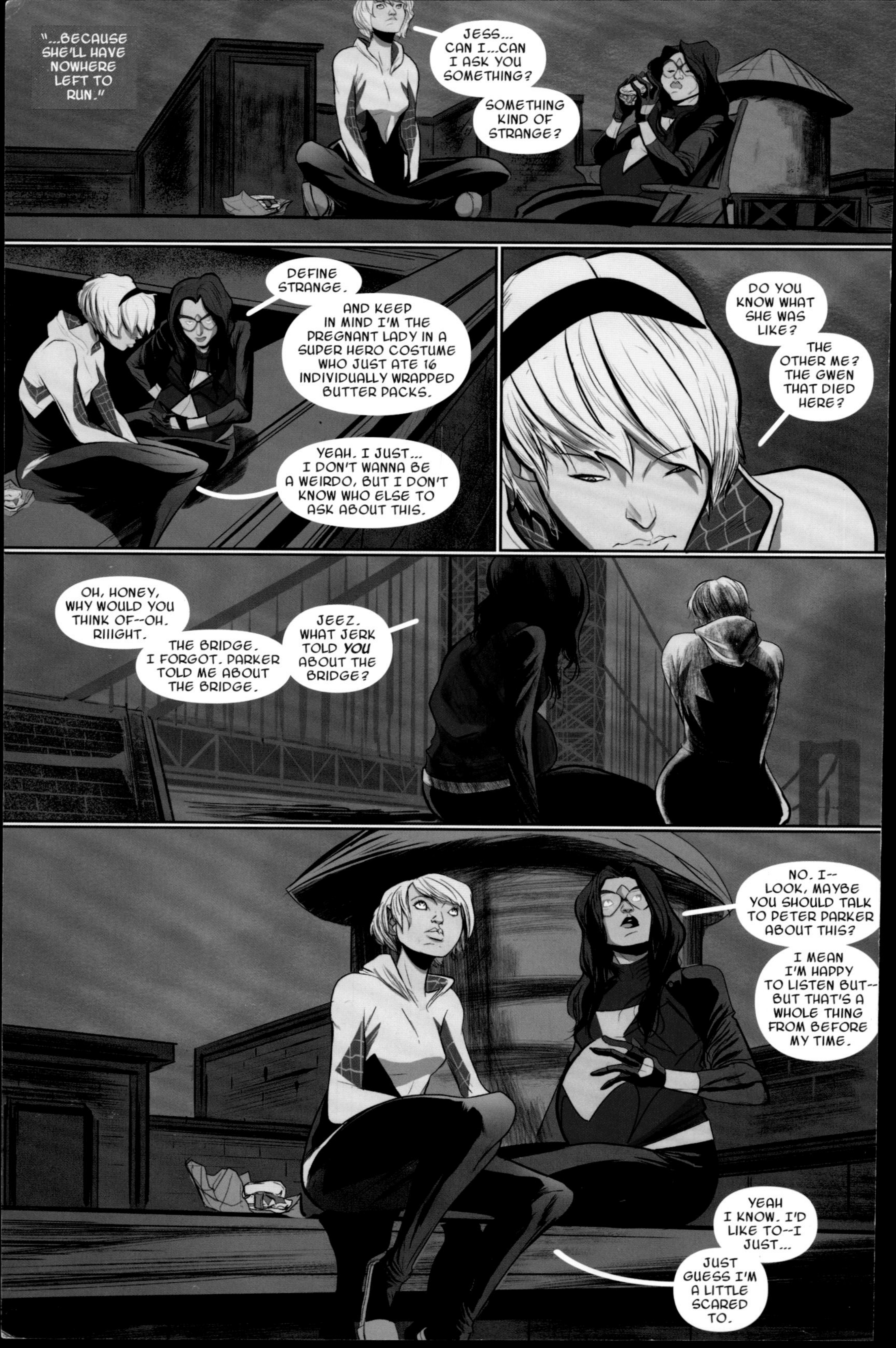
"...BECAUSE SHE'LL HAVE NOWHERE LEFT TO RUN."
JESS... CAN I...CAN I ASK YOU SOMETHING?
SOMETHING KIND OF STRANGE?
DEFINE STRANGE.
AND KEEP IN MIND I'M THE PREGNANT LADY IN A SUPER HERO COSTUME WHO JUST ATE 16 INDIVIDUALLY WRAPPED BUTTER PACKS.
YEAH. I JUST... I DON'T WANNA BE A WEIRDO, BUT I DON'T KNOW WHO ELSE TO ASK ABOUT THIS.
DO YOU KNOW WHAT SHE WAS LIKE?
THE OTHER ME? THE GWEN THAT DIED HERE?
OH, HONEY, WHY WOULD YOU THINK OF--OH. RIIIGHT.
THE BRIDGE. I FORGOT. PARKER TOLD ME ABOUT THE BRIDGE.
JEEZ. WHAT JERK TOLD *YOU* ABOUT THE BRIDGE?
NO. I-- LOOK, MAYBE YOU SHOULD TALK TO PETER PARKER ABOUT THIS?
I MEAN I'M HAPPY TO LISTEN BUT-- BUT THAT'S A WHOLE THING FROM BEFORE MY TIME.
YEAH I KNOW. I'D LIKE TO--I JUST...
JUST GUESS I'M A LITTLE SCARED TO.

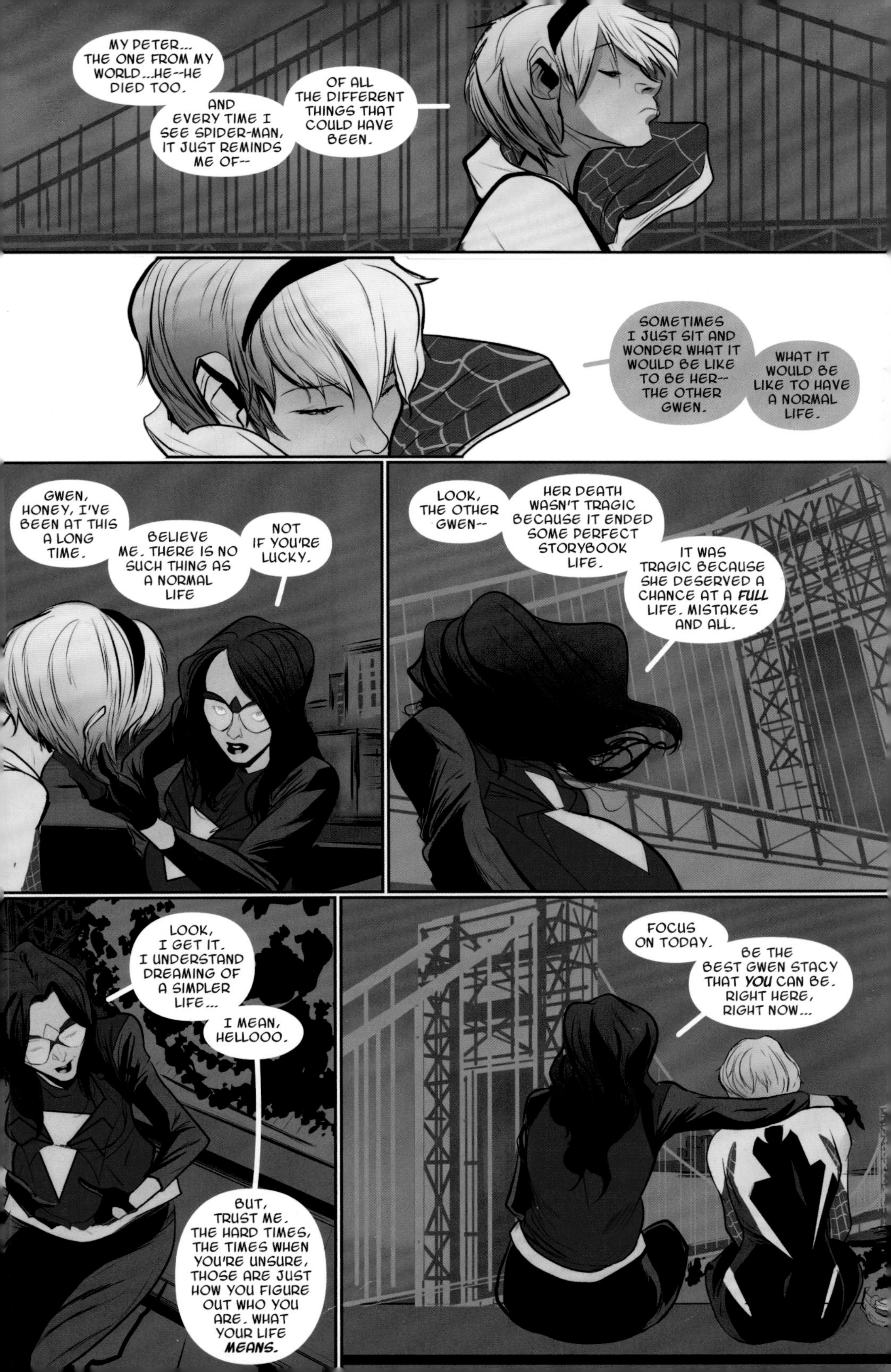

MY PETER... THE ONE FROM MY WORLD...HE--HE DIED TOO.
AND EVERY TIME I SEE SPIDER-MAN, IT JUST REMINDS ME OF--
OF ALL THE DIFFERENT THINGS THAT COULD HAVE BEEN.
SOMETIMES I JUST SIT AND WONDER WHAT IT WOULD BE LIKE TO BE HER-- THE OTHER GWEN.
WHAT IT WOULD BE LIKE TO HAVE A NORMAL LIFE.
GWEN, HONEY, I'VE BEEN AT THIS A LONG TIME.
BELIEVE ME. THERE IS NO SUCH THING AS A NORMAL LIFE
NOT IF YOU'RE LUCKY.
LOOK, THE OTHER GWEN--
HER DEATH WASN'T TRAGIC BECAUSE IT ENDED SOME PERFECT STORYBOOK LIFE.
IT WAS TRAGIC BECAUSE SHE DESERVED A CHANCE AT A FULL LIFE. MISTAKES AND ALL.
LOOK, I GET IT. I UNDERSTAND DREAMING OF A SIMPLER LIFE...
I MEAN, HELLOOO.
BUT, TRUST ME. THE HARD TIMES, THE TIMES WHEN YOU'RE UNSURE, THOSE ARE JUST HOW YOU FIGURE OUT WHO YOU ARE. WHAT YOUR LIFE MEANS.
FOCUS ON TODAY.
BE THE BEST GWEN STACY THAT YOU CAN BE. RIGHT HERE, RIGHT NOW...

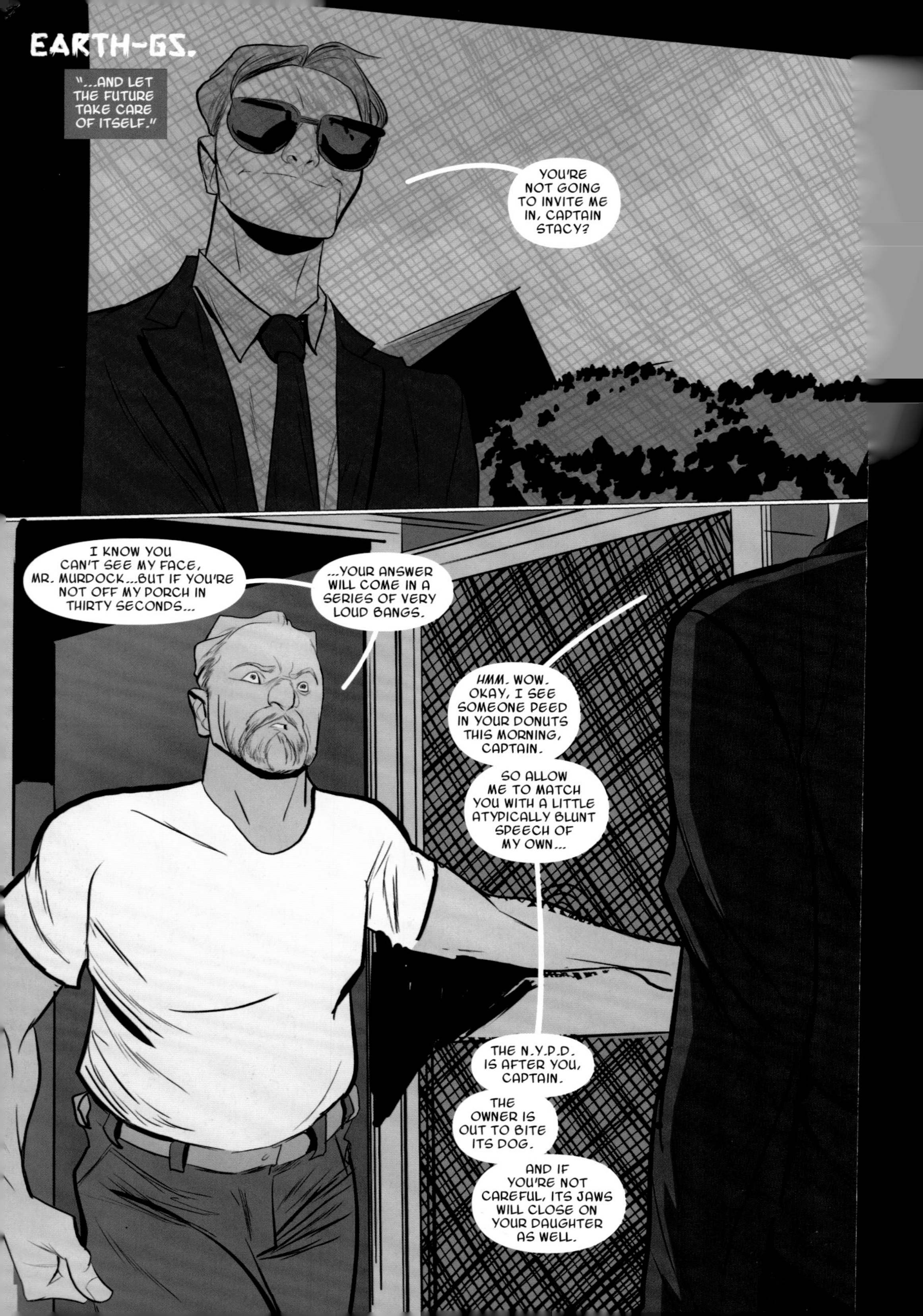
EARTH-65.
"...AND LET THE FUTURE TAKE CARE OF ITSELF."
YOU'RE NOT GOING TO INVITE ME IN, CAPTAIN STACY?
I KNOW YOU CAN'T SEE MY FACE, MR. MURDOCK...BUT IF YOU'RE NOT OFF MY PORCH IN THIRTY SECONDS...
...YOUR ANSWER WILL COME IN A SERIES OF VERY LOUD BANGS.
HMM. WOW. OKAY, I SEE SOMEONE PEED IN YOUR DONUTS THIS MORNING, CAPTAIN.
SO ALLOW ME TO MATCH YOU WITH A LITTLE ATYPICALLY BLUNT SPEECH OF MY OWN...
THE N.Y.P.D. IS AFTER YOU, CAPTAIN.
THE OWNER IS OUT TO BITE ITS DOG.
AND IF YOU'RE NOT CAREFUL, ITS JAWS WILL CLOSE ON YOUR DAUGHTER AS WELL.

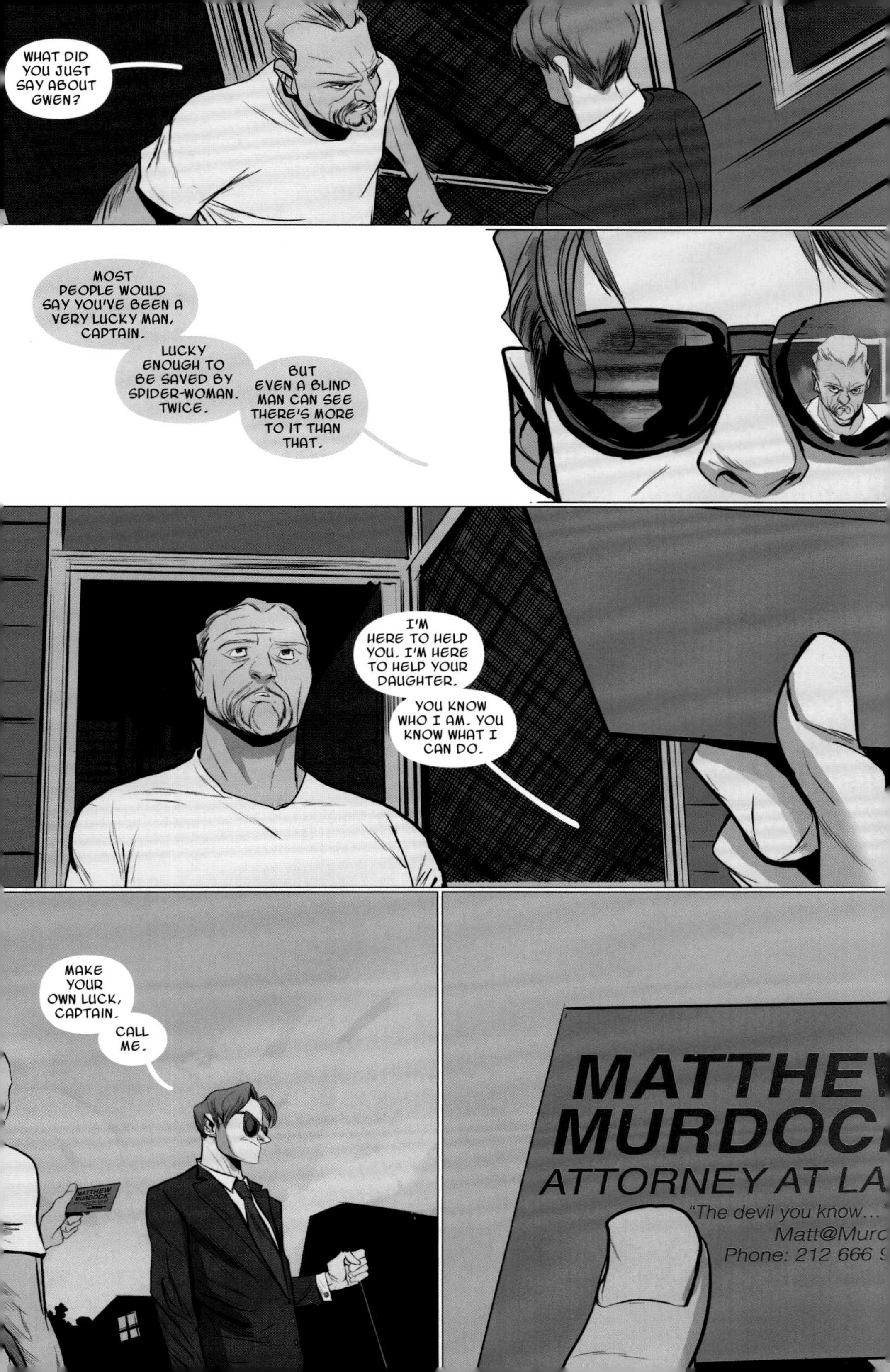
WHAT DID YOU JUST SAY ABOUT GWEN?
MOST PEOPLE WOULD SAY YOU'VE BEEN A VERY LUCKY MAN, CAPTAIN.
LUCKY ENOUGH TO BE SAVED BY SPIDER-WOMAN. TWICE.
BUT EVEN A BLIND MAN CAN SEE THERE'S MORE TO IT THAN THAT.
I'M HERE TO HELP YOU. I'M HERE TO HELP YOUR DAUGHTER.
YOU KNOW WHO I AM. YOU KNOW WHAT I CAN DO.
MAKE YOUR OWN LUCK, CAPTAIN.
CALL ME.
MATTHEW MURDOCK
ATTORNEY AT LA
"The devil you know..."
Matt@Murd
Phone: 212 666

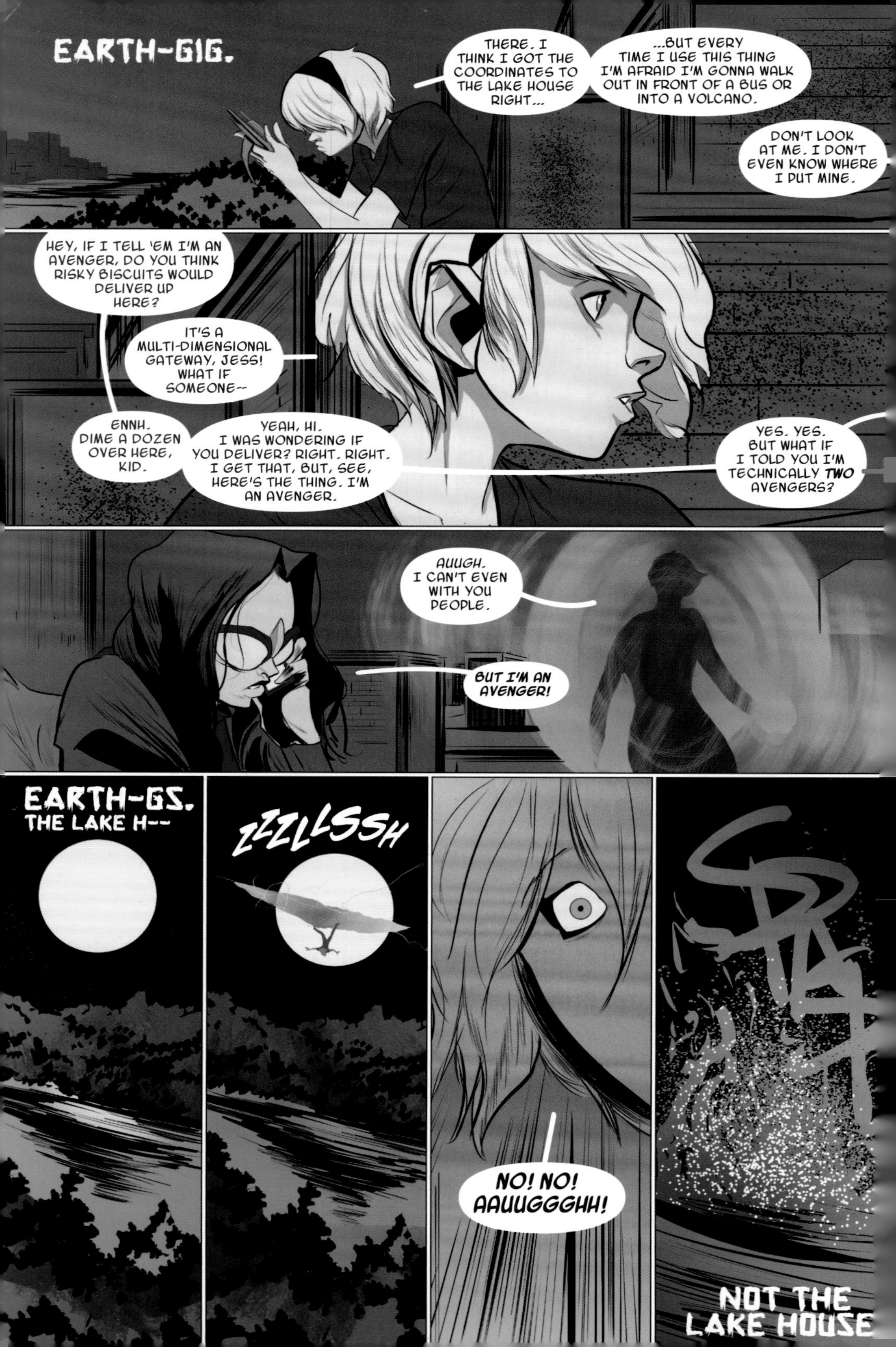
EARTH-616.
THERE. I THINK I GOT THE COORDINATES TO THE LAKE HOUSE RIGHT...
...BUT EVERY TIME I USE THIS THING I'M AFRAID I'M GONNA WALK OUT IN FRONT OF A BUS OR INTO A VOLCANO.
DON'T LOOK AT ME. I DON'T EVEN KNOW WHERE I PUT MINE.
HEY, IF I TELL 'EM I'M AN AVENGER, DO YOU THINK RISKY BISCUITS WOULD DELIVER UP HERE?
IT'S A MULTI-DIMENSIONAL GATEWAY, JESS! WHAT IF SOMEONE--
ENNH. DIME A DOZEN OVER HERE, KID.
YEAH, HI. I WAS WONDERING IF YOU DELIVER? RIGHT. RIGHT. I GET THAT, BUT, SEE, HERE'S THE THING. I'M AN AVENGER.
YES. YES. BUT WHAT IF I TOLD YOU I'M TECHNICALLY TWO AVENGERS?
AUUGH. I CAN'T EVEN WITH YOU PEOPLE.
BUT I'M AN AVENGER!
EARTH-65. THE LAKE H--
ZZZLLSSSH
NO! NO! AAUUGGGHH!
NOT THE LAKE HOUSE

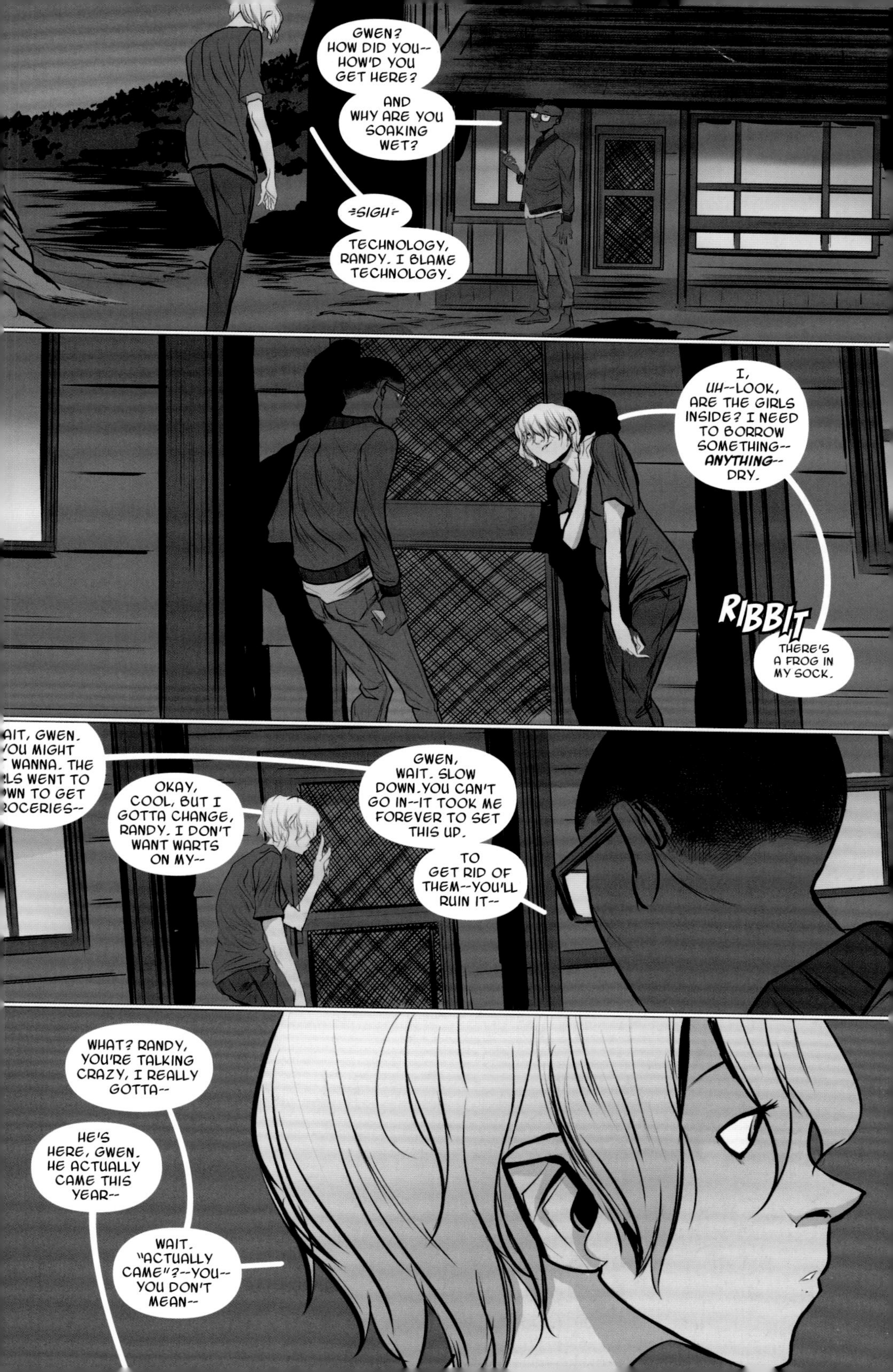
GWEN? HOW DID YOU-- HOW'D YOU GET HERE?
AND WHY ARE YOU SOAKING WET?
=SIGH=
TECHNOLOGY, RANDY. I BLAME TECHNOLOGY.
I, UH--LOOK, ARE THE GIRLS INSIDE? I NEED TO BORROW SOMETHING--ANYTHING--DRY.
RIBBIT
THERE'S A FROG IN MY SOCK.
AIT, GWEN. OU MIGHT WANNA. THE LS WENT TO WN TO GET ROCERIES--
OKAY, COOL, BUT I GOTTA CHANGE, RANDY. I DON'T WANT WARTS ON MY--
GWEN, WAIT. SLOW DOWN. YOU CAN'T GO IN--IT TOOK ME FOREVER TO SET THIS UP.
TO GET RID OF THEM--YOU'LL RUIN IT--
WHAT? RANDY, YOU'RE TALKING CRAZY, I REALLY GOTTA--
HE'S HERE, GWEN. HE ACTUALLY CAME THIS YEAR--
WAIT. "ACTUALLY CAME"?--YOU--YOU DON'T MEAN--

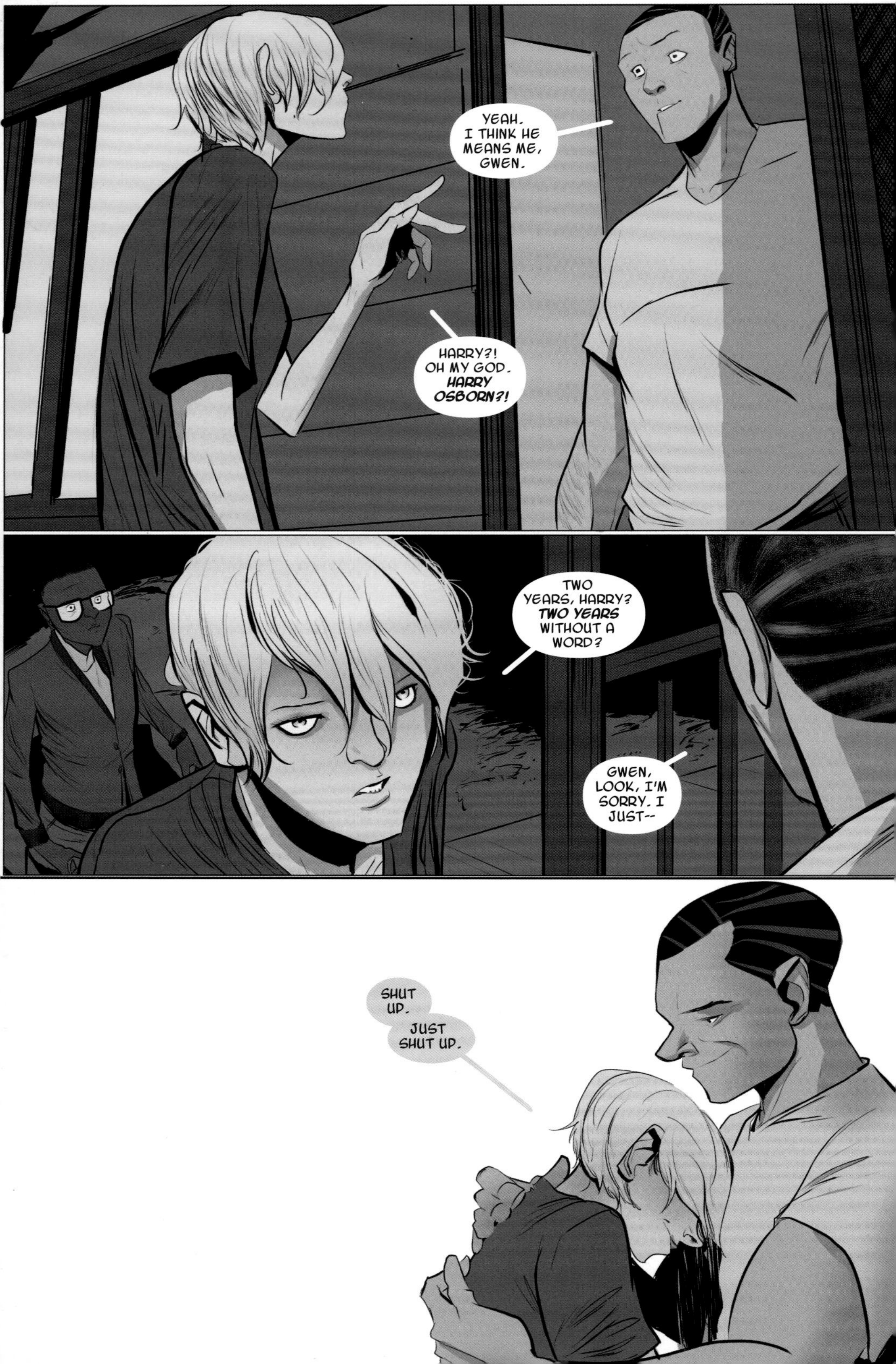
YEAH. I THINK HE MEANS ME, GWEN.
HARRY?! OH MY GOD. HARRY OSBORN?!
TWO YEARS, HARRY? TWO YEARS WITHOUT A WORD?
GWEN, LOOK, I'M SORRY. I JUST--
SHUT UP.
JUST SHUT UP.

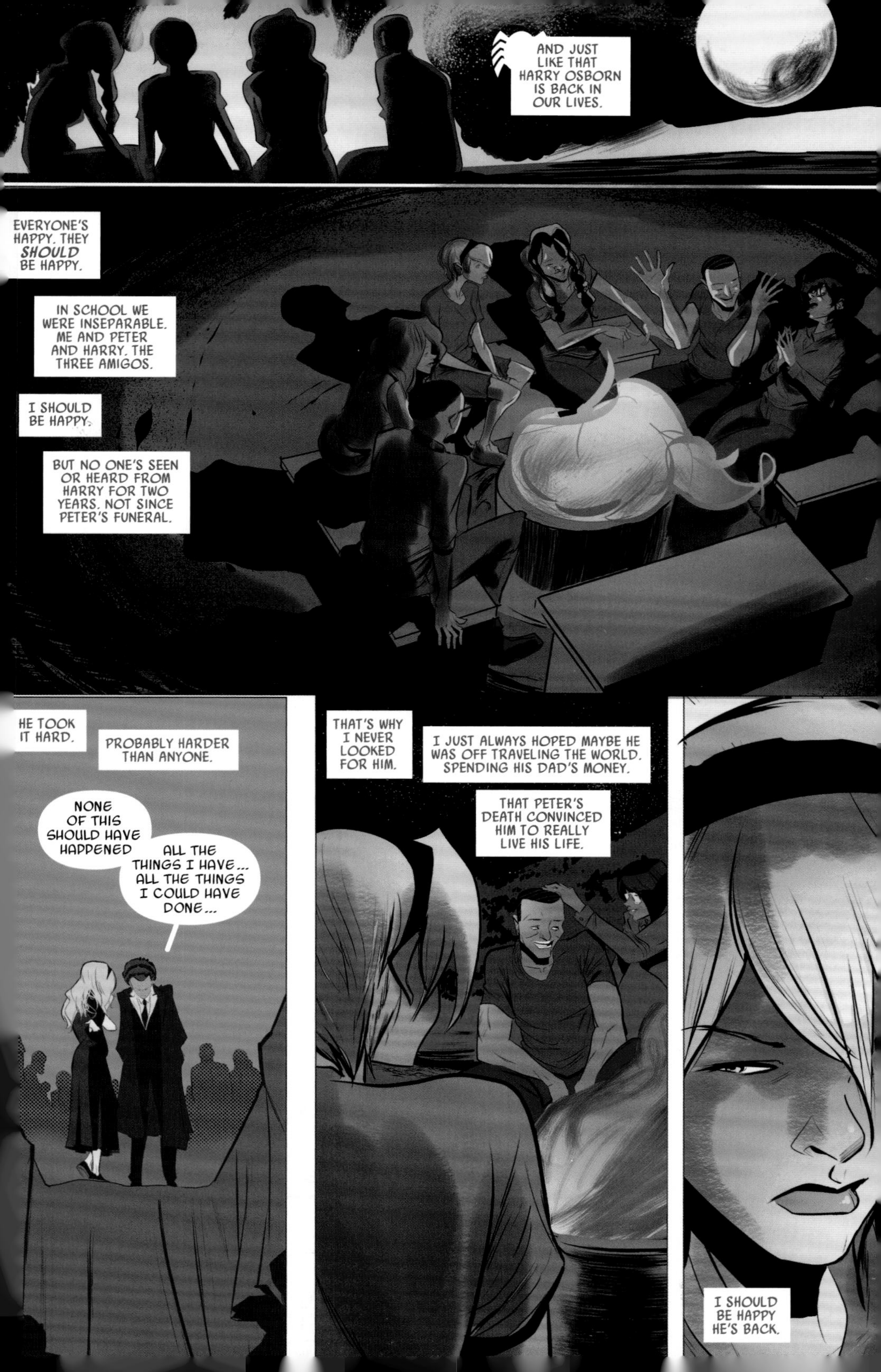
AND JUST LIKE THAT HARRY OSBORN IS BACK IN OUR LIVES.
EVERYONE'S HAPPY. THEY SHOULD BE HAPPY.
IN SCHOOL WE WERE INSEPARABLE. ME AND PETER AND HARRY. THE THREE AMIGOS.
I SHOULD BE HAPPY.
BUT NO ONE'S SEEN OR HEARD FROM HARRY FOR TWO YEARS. NOT SINCE PETER'S FUNERAL.
HE TOOK IT HARD.
PROBABLY HARDER THAN ANYONE.
NONE OF THIS SHOULD HAVE HAPPENED
ALL THE THINGS I HAVE... ALL THE THINGS I COULD HAVE DONE...
THAT'S WHY I NEVER LOOKED FOR HIM.
I JUST ALWAYS HOPED MAYBE HE WAS OFF TRAVELING THE WORLD. SPENDING HIS DAD'S MONEY.
THAT PETER'S DEATH CONVINCED HIM TO REALLY LIVE HIS LIFE.
I SHOULD BE HAPPY HE'S BACK.

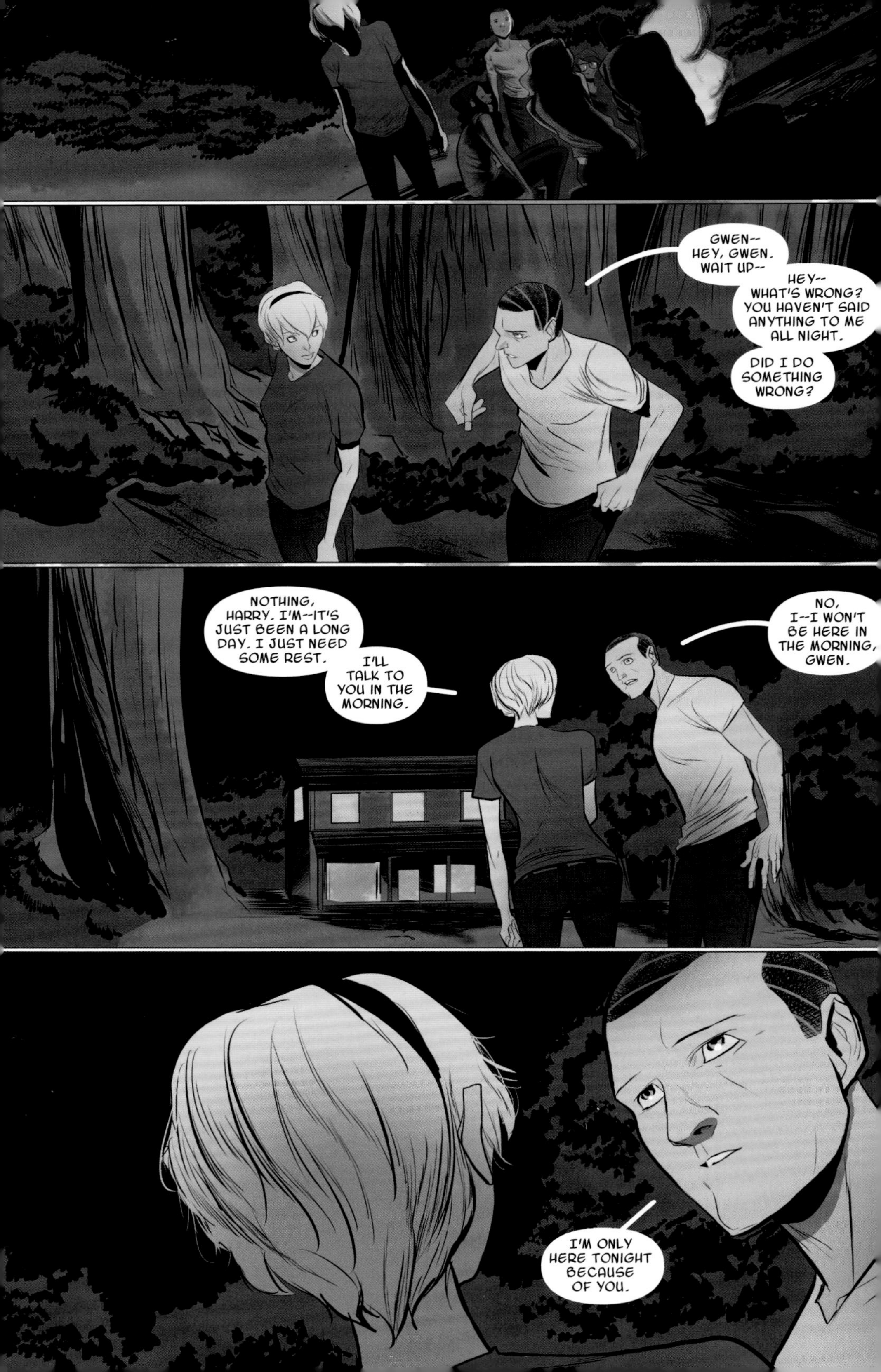
GWEN--
HEY, GWEN. WAIT UP--
HEY-- WHAT'S WRONG? YOU HAVEN'T SAID ANYTHING TO ME ALL NIGHT.
DID I DO SOMETHING WRONG?
NOTHING, HARRY. I'M--IT'S JUST BEEN A LONG DAY. I JUST NEED SOME REST.
I'LL TALK TO YOU IN THE MORNING.
NO, I--I WON'T BE HERE IN THE MORNING, GWEN.
I'M ONLY HERE TONIGHT BECAUSE OF YOU.

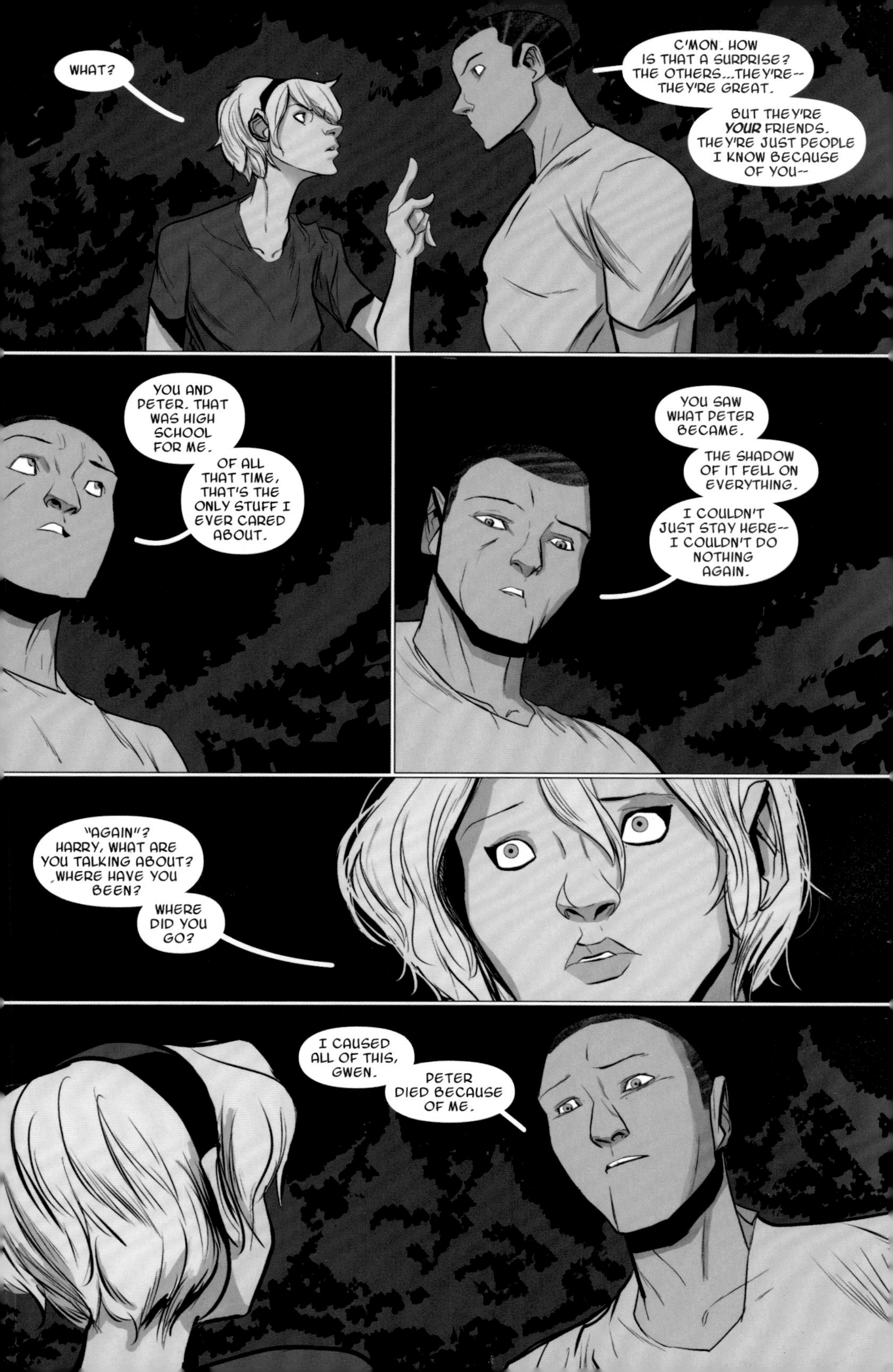
WHAT?
C'MON. HOW IS THAT A SURPRISE? THE OTHERS...THEY'RE-- THEY'RE GREAT.
BUT THEY'RE *YOUR* FRIENDS. THEY'RE JUST PEOPLE I KNOW BECAUSE OF YOU--
YOU AND PETER. THAT WAS HIGH SCHOOL FOR ME.
OF ALL THAT TIME, THAT'S THE ONLY STUFF I EVER CARED ABOUT.
YOU SAW WHAT PETER BECAME.
THE SHADOW OF IT FELL ON EVERYTHING.
I COULDN'T JUST STAY HERE-- I COULDN'T DO NOTHING AGAIN.
"AGAIN"? HARRY, WHAT ARE YOU TALKING ABOUT? WHERE HAVE YOU BEEN?
WHERE DID YOU GO?
I CAUSED ALL OF THIS, GWEN.
PETER DIED BECAUSE OF ME.

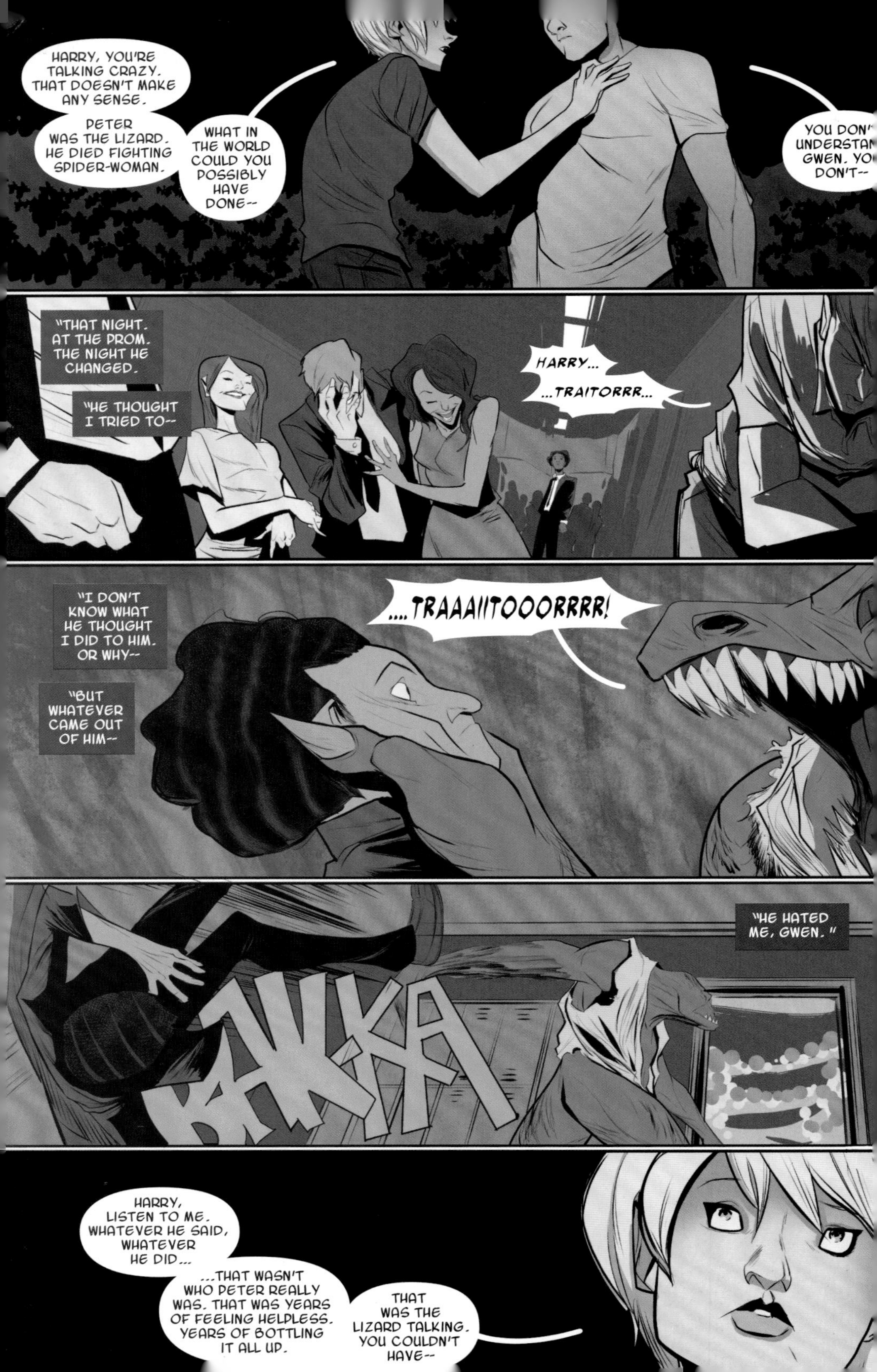
HARRY, YOU'RE TALKING CRAZY. THAT DOESN'T MAKE ANY SENSE.
PETER WAS THE LIZARD. HE DIED FIGHTING SPIDER-WOMAN.
WHAT IN THE WORLD COULD YOU POSSIBLY HAVE DONE--
YOU DON'T UNDERSTAN GWEN. YO DON'T--
"THAT NIGHT. AT THE PROM. THE NIGHT HE CHANGED.
"HE THOUGHT I TRIED TO--
HARRY... ...TRAITORRR...
"I DON'T KNOW WHAT HE THOUGHT I DID TO HIM. OR WHY--
"BUT WHATEVER CAME OUT OF HIM--
....TRAAAIITOOORRRR!
"HE HATED ME, GWEN."
BAK-KA
HARRY, LISTEN TO ME. WHATEVER HE SAID, WHATEVER HE DID...
...THAT WASN'T WHO PETER REALLY WAS. THAT WAS YEARS OF FEELING HELPLESS. YEARS OF BOTTLING IT ALL UP.
THAT WAS THE LIZARD TALKING. YOU COULDN'T HAVE--

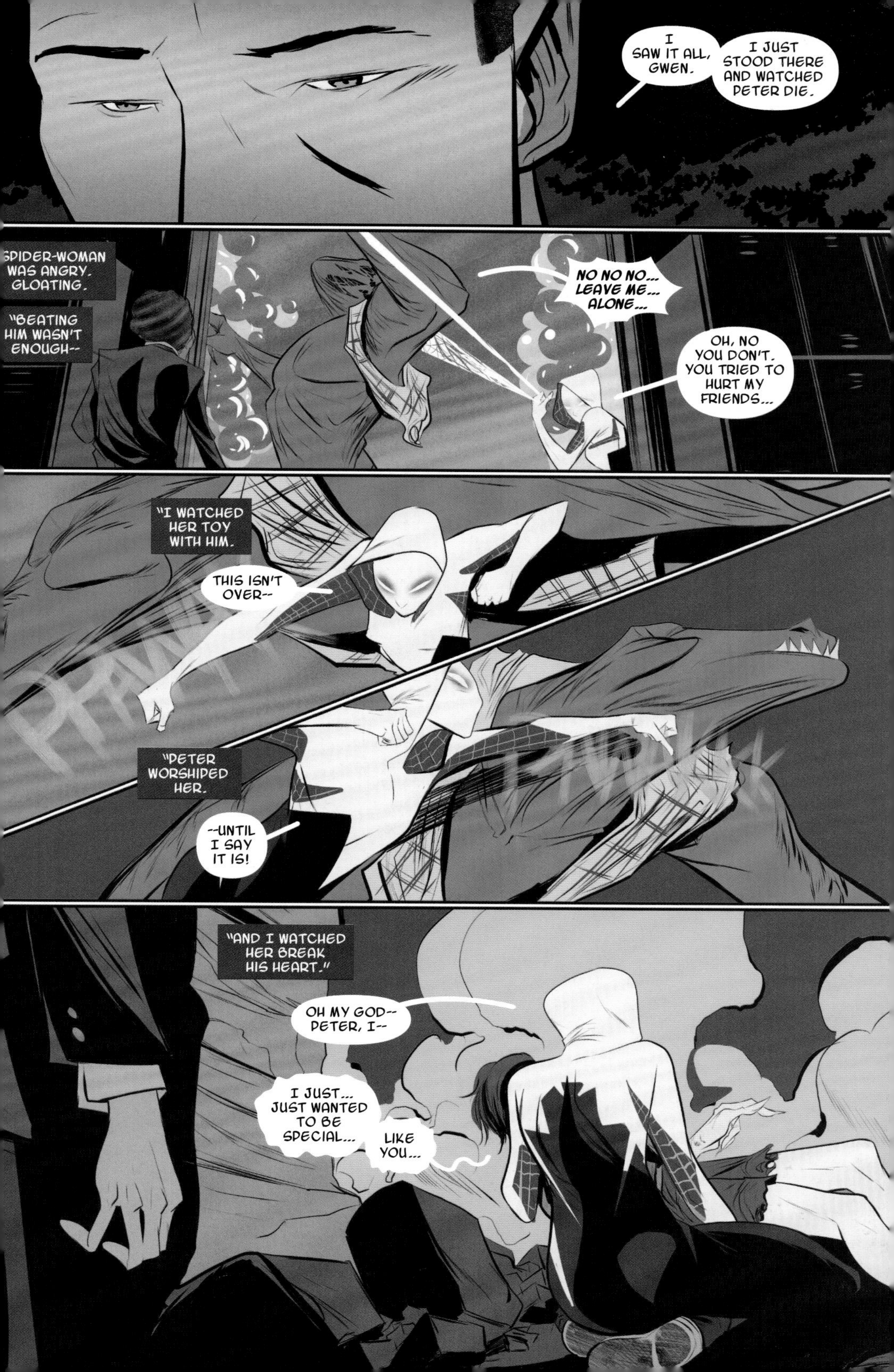
I SAW IT ALL, GWEN.
I JUST STOOD THERE AND WATCHED PETER DIE.
SPIDER-WOMAN WAS ANGRY. GLOATING.
"BEATING HIM WASN'T ENOUGH--
NO NO NO... LEAVE ME... ALONE...
OH, NO YOU DON'T. YOU TRIED TO HURT MY FRIENDS...
"I WATCHED HER TOY WITH HIM.
THIS ISN'T OVER--
"PETER WORSHIPED HER.
--UNTIL I SAY IT IS!
"AND I WATCHED HER BREAK HIS HEART."
OH MY GOD-- PETER, I--
I JUST... JUST WANTED TO BE SPECIAL...
LIKE YOU...

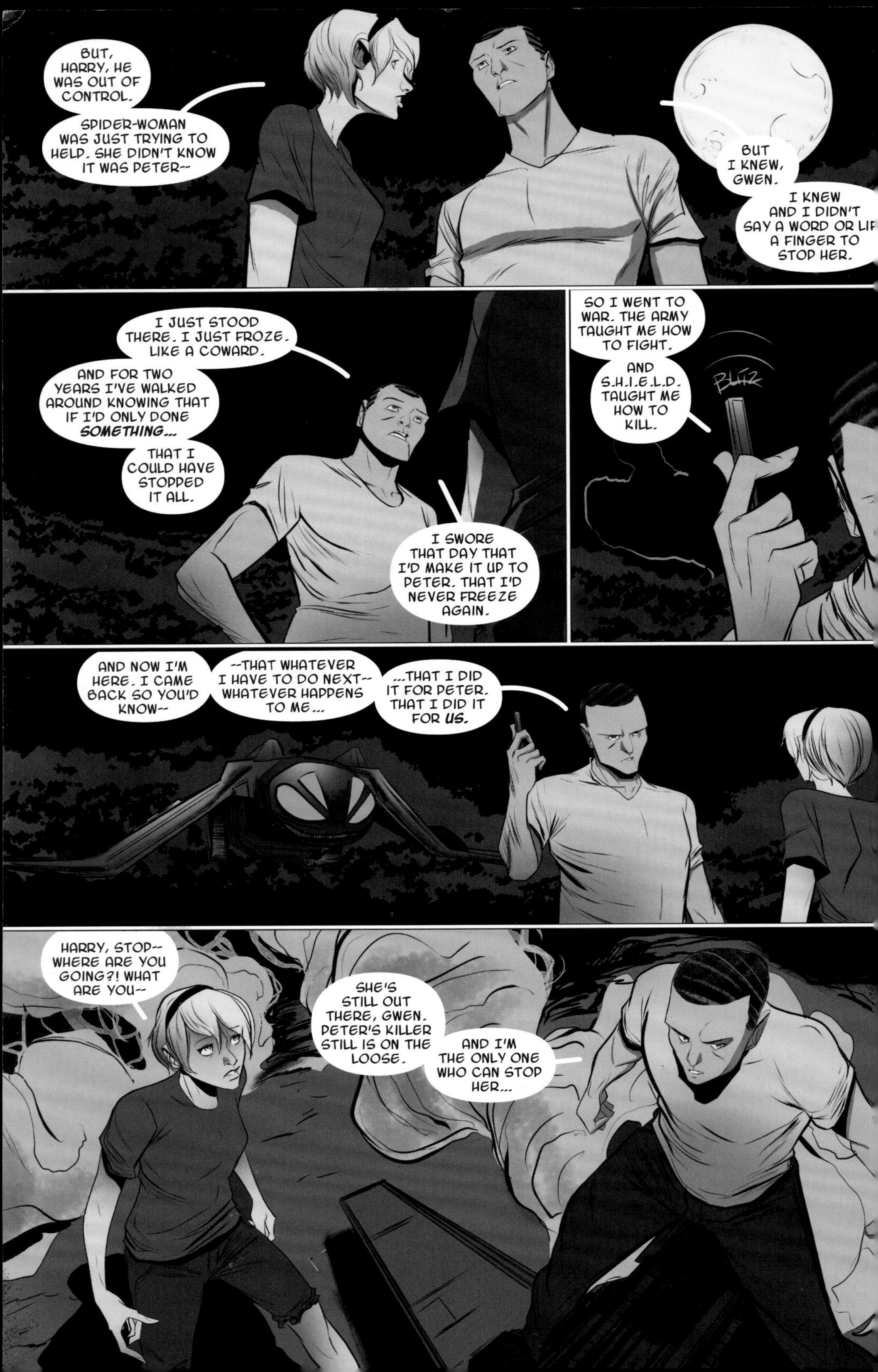
BUT, HARRY, HE WAS OUT OF CONTROL.
SPIDER-WOMAN WAS JUST TRYING TO HELP. SHE DIDN'T KNOW IT WAS PETER--
BUT I KNEW, GWEN.
I KNEW AND I DIDN'T SAY A WORD OR LIF A FINGER TO STOP HER.
I JUST STOOD THERE. I JUST FROZE. LIKE A COWARD.
AND FOR TWO YEARS I'VE WALKED AROUND KNOWING THAT IF I'D ONLY DONE SOMETHING...
THAT I COULD HAVE STOPPED IT ALL.
I SWORE THAT DAY THAT I'D MAKE IT UP TO PETER. THAT I'D NEVER FREEZE AGAIN.
SO I WENT TO WAR. THE ARMY TAUGHT ME HOW TO FIGHT.
AND S.H.I.E.L.D. TAUGHT ME HOW TO KILL.
BLITZ
AND NOW I'M HERE. I CAME BACK SO YOU'D KNOW--
--THAT WHATEVER I HAVE TO DO NEXT-- WHATEVER HAPPENS TO ME...
...THAT I DID IT FOR PETER. THAT I DID IT FOR US.
HARRY, STOP-- WHERE ARE YOU GOING?! WHAT ARE YOU--
SHE'S STILL OUT THERE, GWEN. PETER'S KILLER STILL IS ON THE LOOSE.
AND I'M THE ONLY ONE WHO CAN STOP HER...

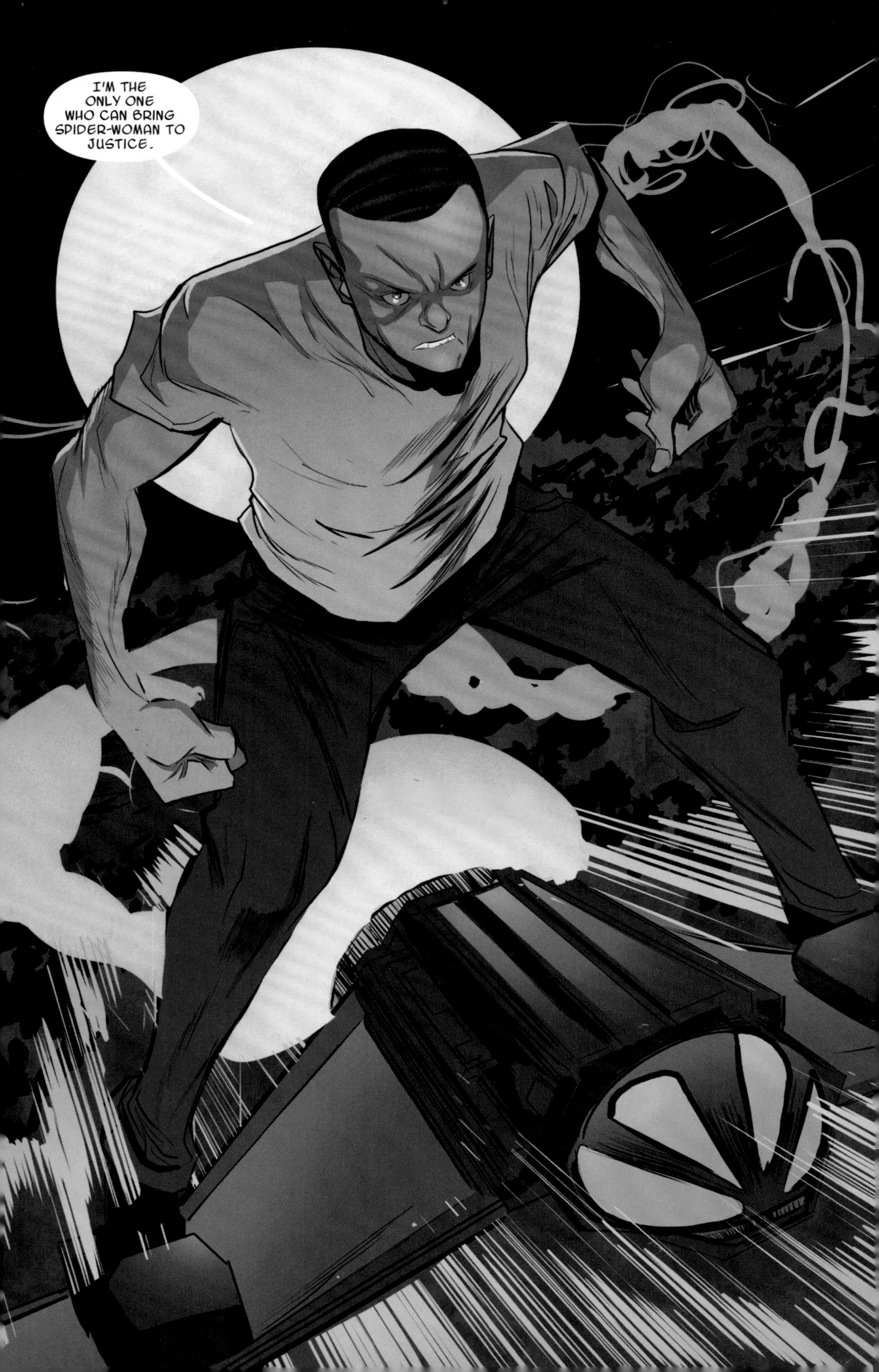
I'M THE ONLY ONE WHO CAN BRING SPIDER-WOMAN TO JUSTICE.

4B

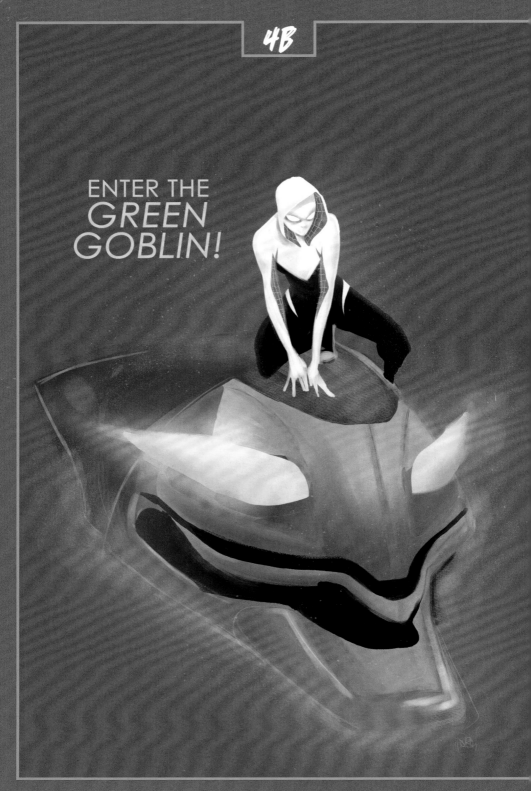

ENTER THE *GREEN GOBLIN!*

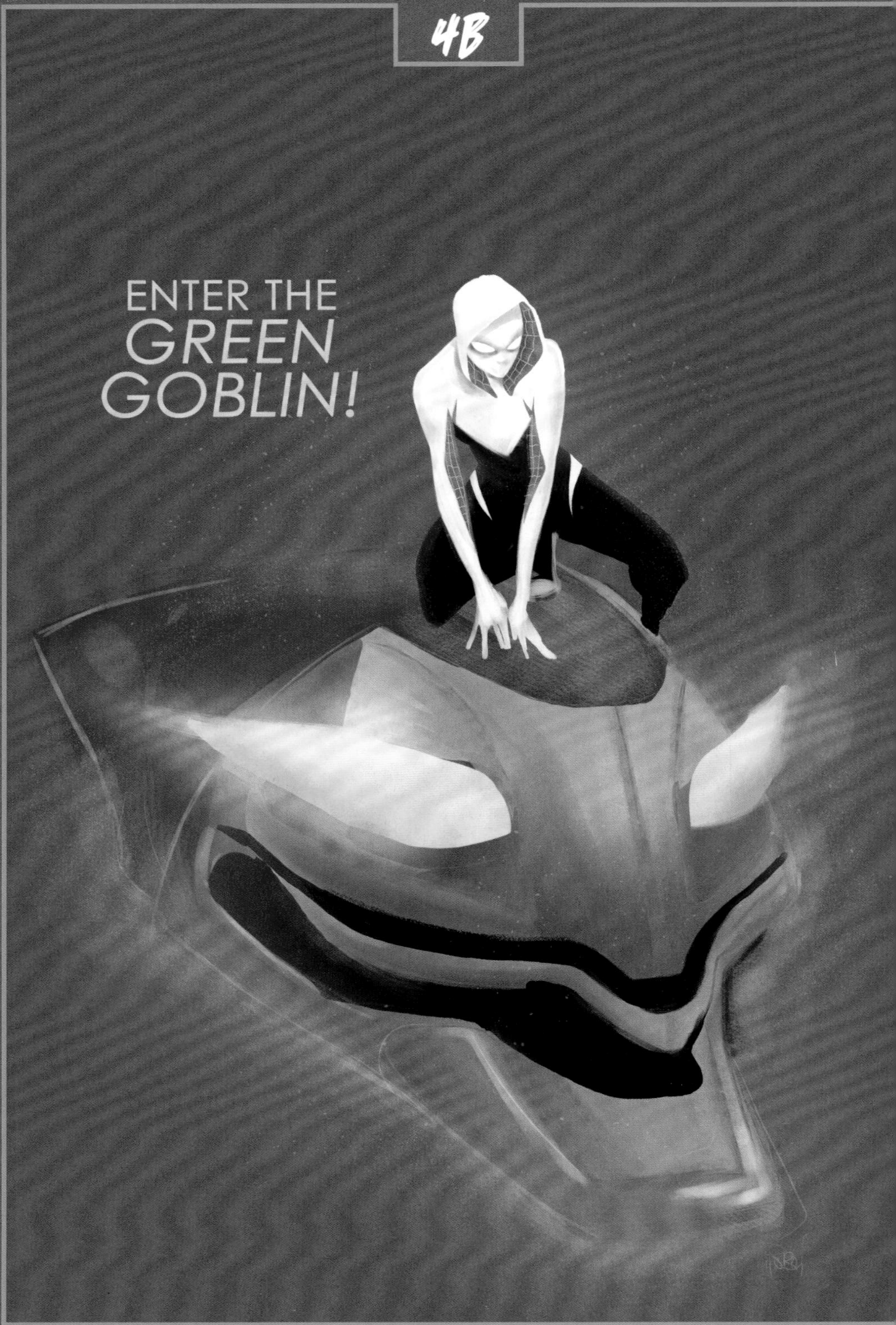

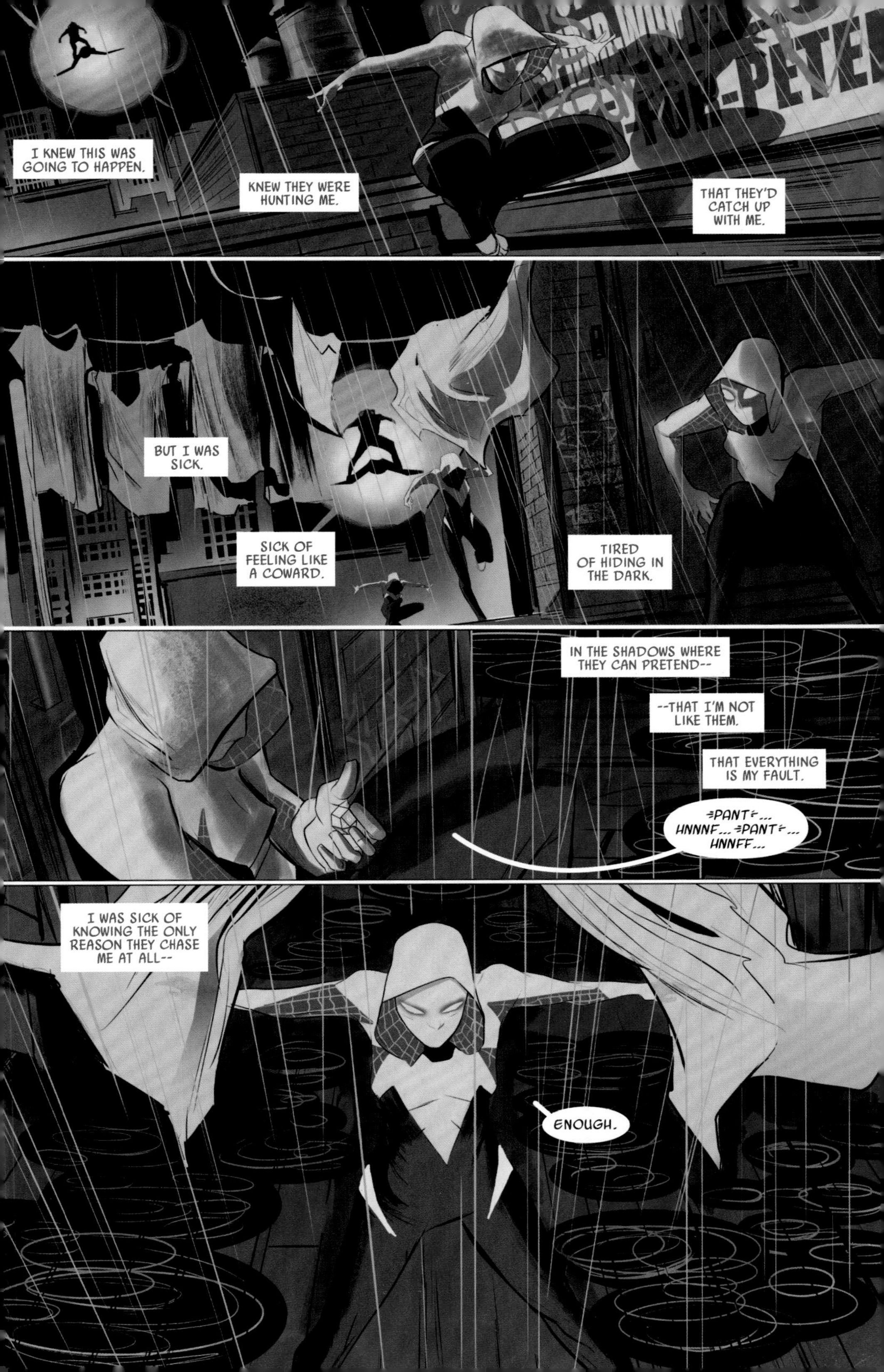

FOR-PETER
I KNEW THIS WAS GOING TO HAPPEN.
KNEW THEY WERE HUNTING ME.
THAT THEY'D CATCH UP WITH ME.
BUT I WAS SICK.
SICK OF FEELING LIKE A COWARD.
TIRED OF HIDING IN THE DARK.
IN THE SHADOWS WHERE THEY CAN PRETEND--
--THAT I'M NOT LIKE THEM.
THAT EVERYTHING IS MY FAULT.
=PANT=... HNNNF... =PANT=... HNNFF...
I WAS SICK OF KNOWING THE ONLY REASON THEY CHASE ME AT ALL--
ENOUGH.

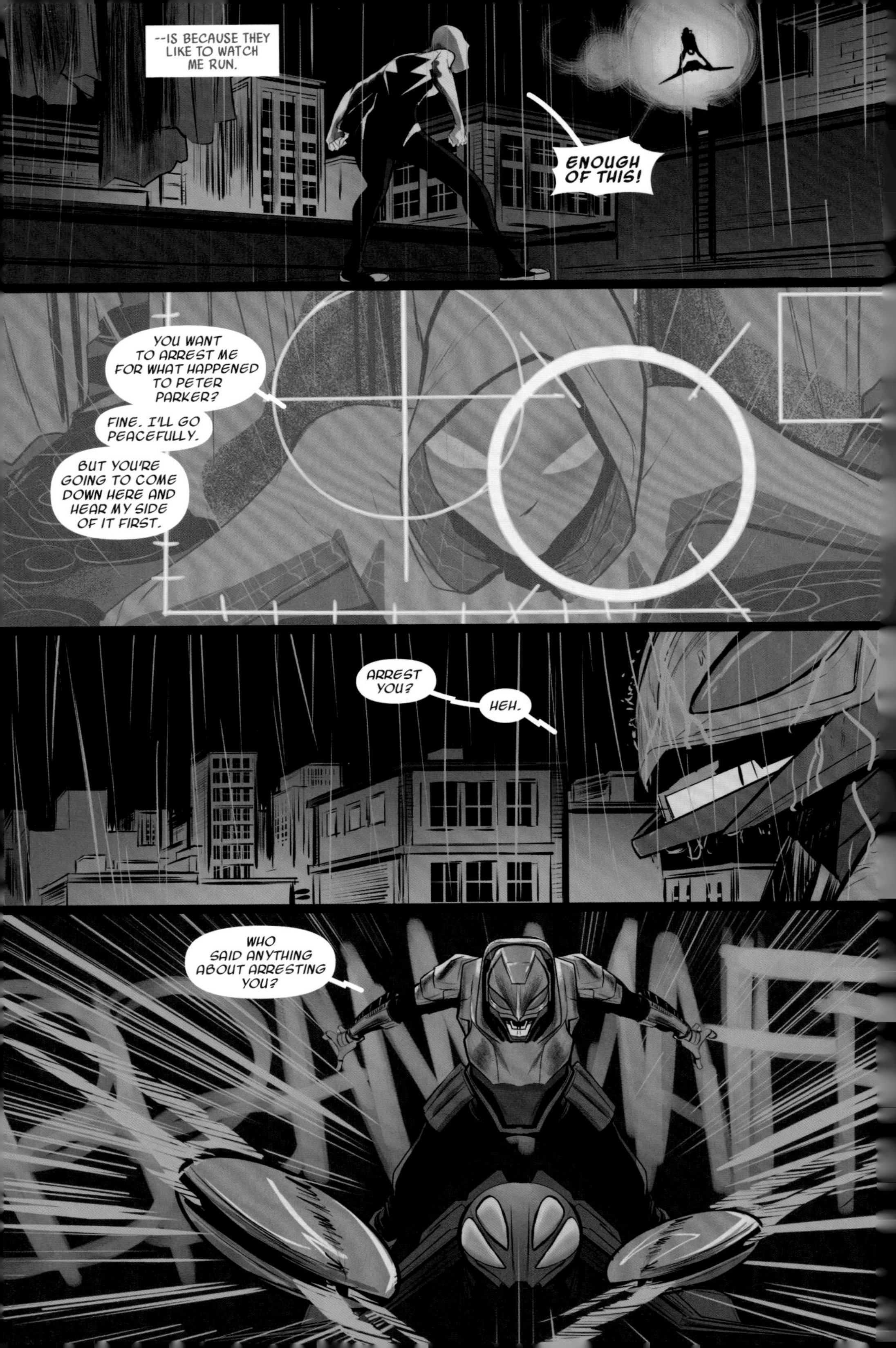
--IS BECAUSE THEY LIKE TO WATCH ME RUN.
ENOUGH OF THIS!
YOU WANT TO ARREST ME FOR WHAT HAPPENED TO PETER PARKER?
FINE. I'LL GO PEACEFULLY.
BUT YOU'RE GOING TO COME DOWN HERE AND HEAR MY SIDE OF IT FIRST.
ARREST YOU?
HEH.
WHO SAID ANYTHING ABOUT ARRESTING YOU?

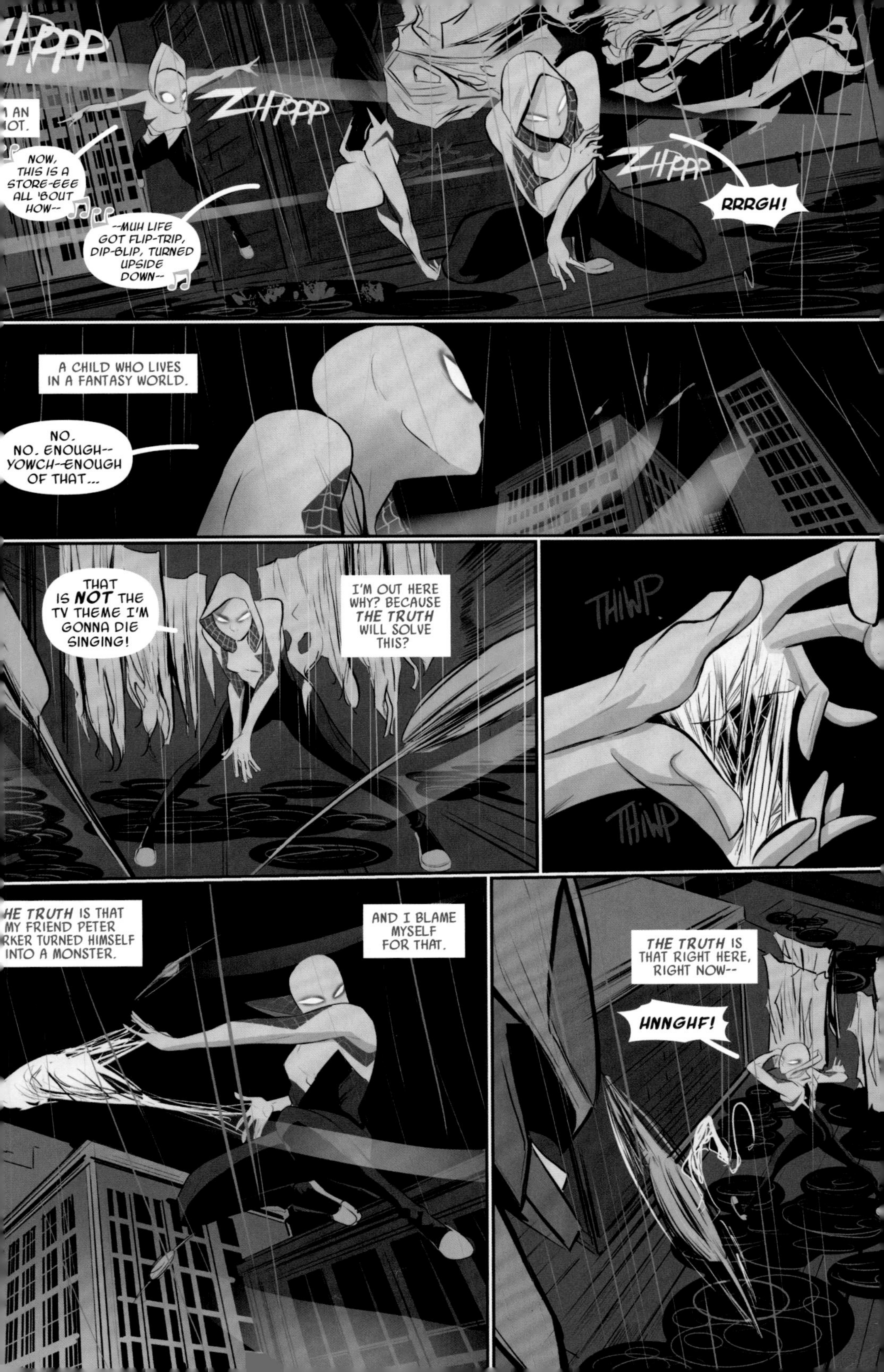
ZIPPPP
I AN
IOT.
NOW, THIS IS A STORE-EEE ALL 'BOUT HOW--
ZIPPPP
--MUH LIFE GOT FLIP-TRIP, DIP-BLIP, TURNED UPSIDE DOWN--
ZIPPPP
RRRGH!
A CHILD WHO LIVES IN A FANTASY WORLD.
NO. NO. ENOUGH-- YOWCH--ENOUGH OF THAT...
THAT IS NOT THE TV THEME I'M GONNA DIE SINGING!
I'M OUT HERE WHY? BECAUSE THE TRUTH WILL SOLVE THIS?
THIWP
THIWP
HE TRUTH IS THAT MY FRIEND PETER RKER TURNED HIMSELF INTO A MONSTER.
AND I BLAME MYSELF FOR THAT.
THE TRUTH IS THAT RIGHT HERE, RIGHT NOW--
HNNGHF!

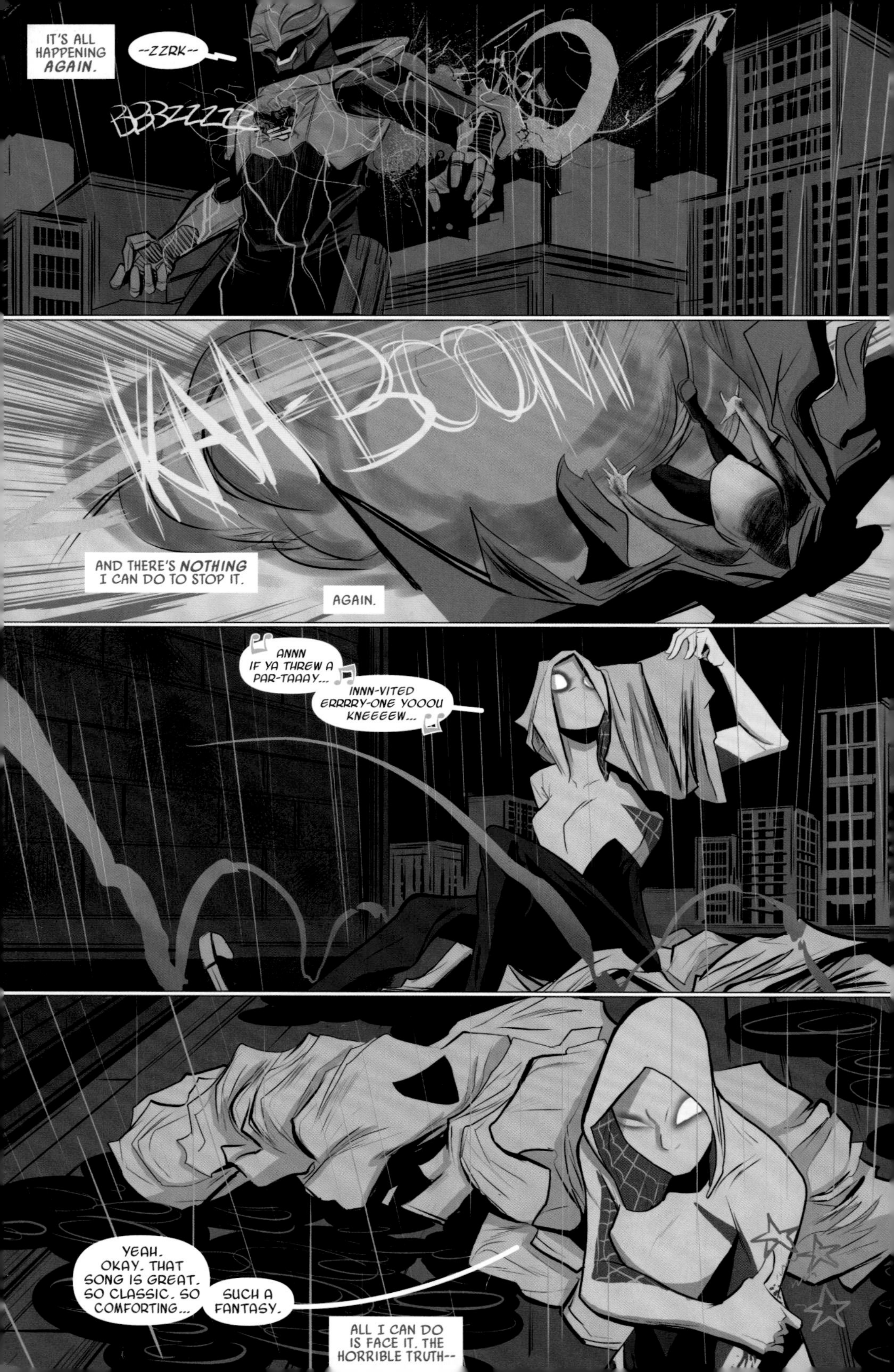
IT'S ALL HAPPENING AGAIN.
--ZZRK--
BBBZZZZZZ
KAA-BOOM!
AND THERE'S NOTHING I CAN DO TO STOP IT.
AGAIN.
ANNN IF YA THREW A PAR-TAAAY...
INNN-VITED ERRRRY-ONE YOOOU KNEEEEW...
YEAH. OKAY. THAT SONG IS GREAT. SO CLASSIC. SO COMFORTING...
SUCH A FANTASY.
ALL I CAN DO IS FACE IT. THE HORRIBLE TRUTH--

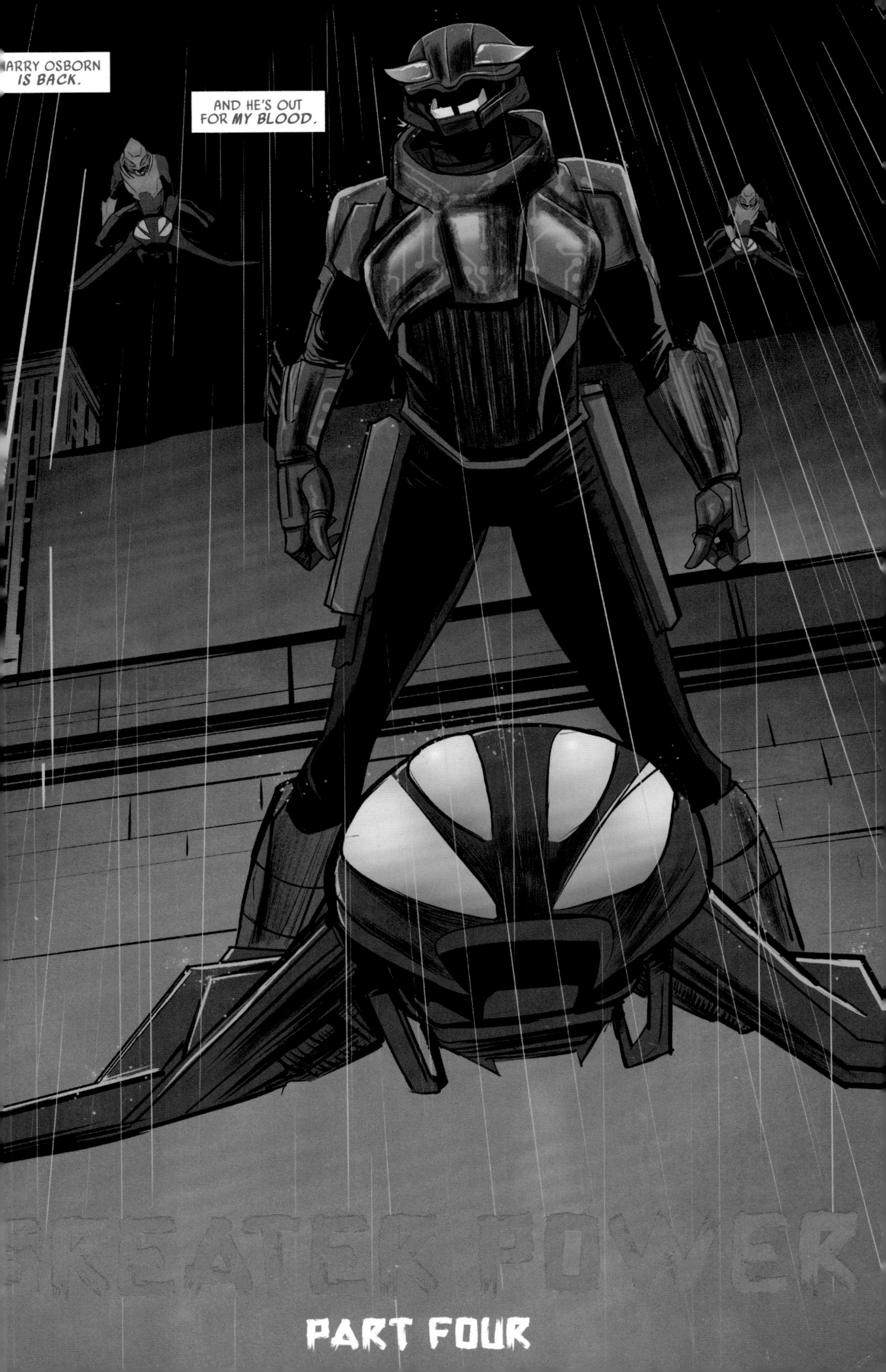
ARRY OSBORN IS BACK.
AND HE'S OUT FOR MY BLOOD.
REATER POWER
PART FOUR

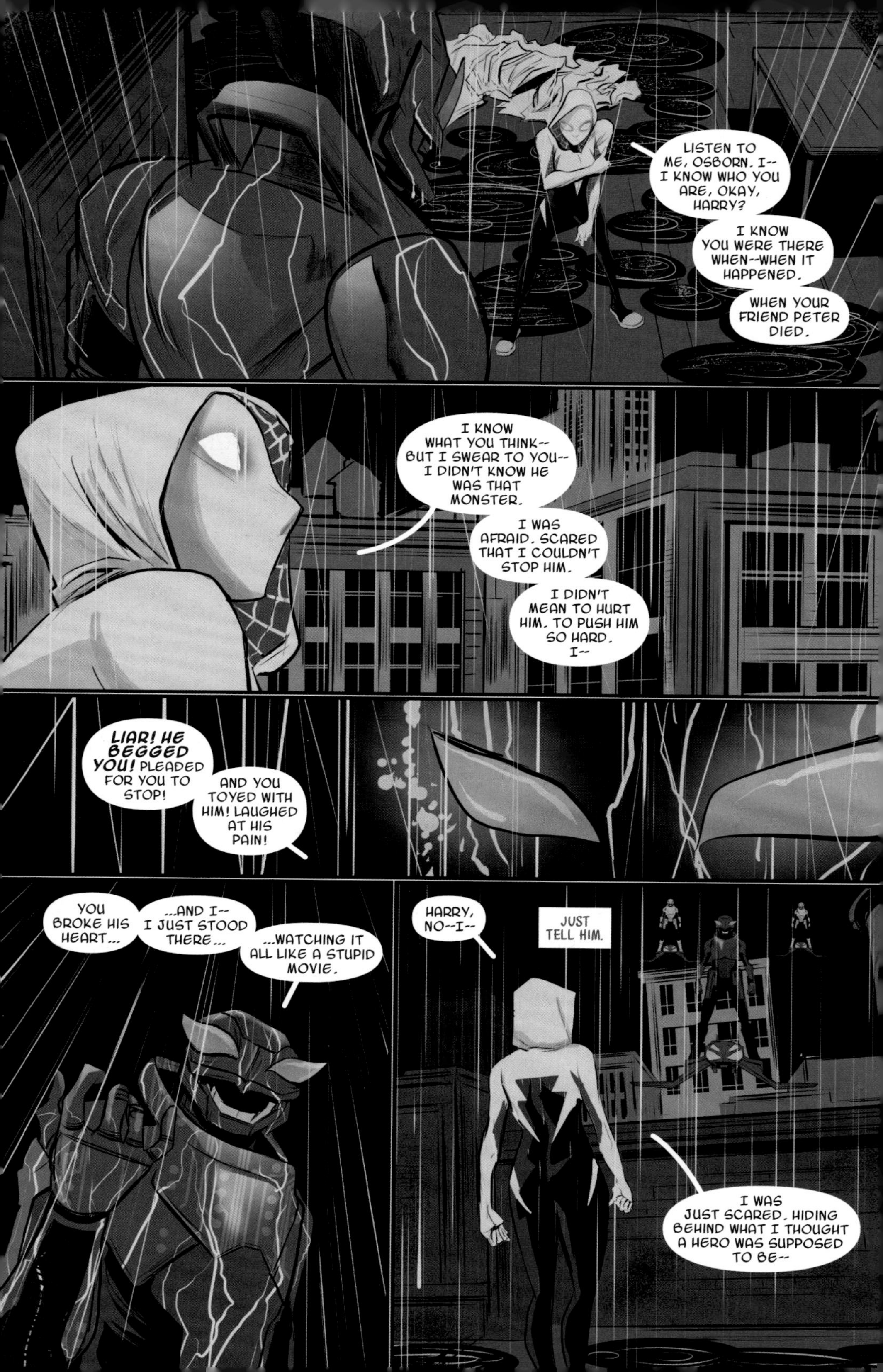
LISTEN TO ME, OSBORN. I-- I KNOW WHO YOU ARE, OKAY, HARRY?
I KNOW YOU WERE THERE WHEN--WHEN IT HAPPENED.
WHEN YOUR FRIEND PETER DIED.
I KNOW WHAT YOU THINK-- BUT I SWEAR TO YOU-- I DIDN'T KNOW HE WAS THAT MONSTER.
I WAS AFRAID. SCARED THAT I COULDN'T STOP HIM.
I DIDN'T MEAN TO HURT HIM. TO PUSH HIM SO HARD. I--
LIAR! HE BEGGED YOU! PLEADED FOR YOU TO STOP!
AND YOU TOYED WITH HIM! LAUGHED AT HIS PAIN!
YOU BROKE HIS HEART...
...AND I-- I JUST STOOD THERE...
...WATCHING IT ALL LIKE A STUPID MOVIE.
HARRY, NO--I--
JUST TELL HIM.
I WAS JUST SCARED. HIDING BEHIND WHAT I THOUGHT A HERO WAS SUPPOSED TO BE--

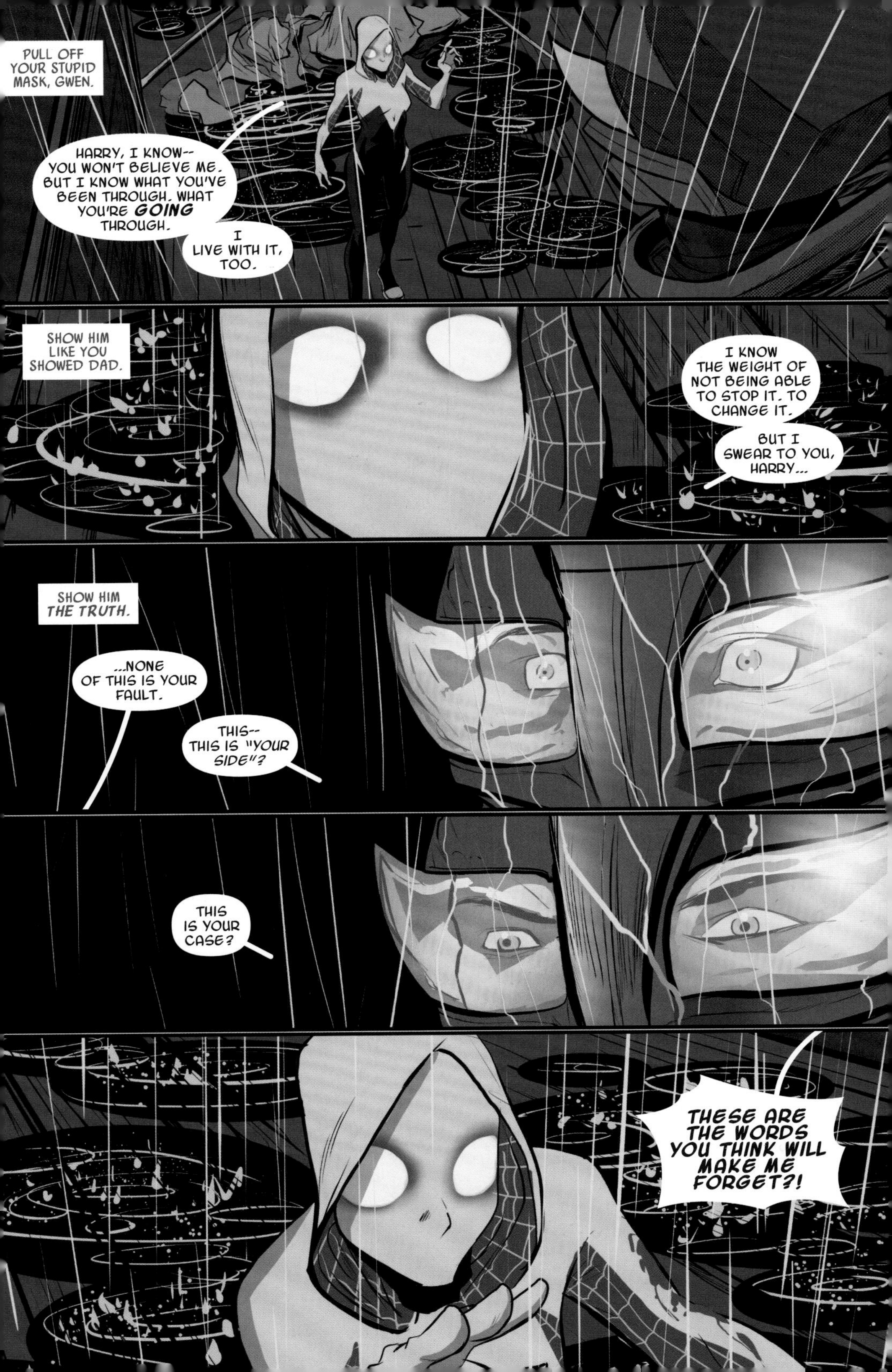

PULL OFF YOUR STUPID MASK, GWEN.
HARRY, I KNOW-- YOU WON'T BELIEVE ME. BUT I KNOW WHAT YOU'VE BEEN THROUGH. WHAT YOU'RE GOING THROUGH.
I LIVE WITH IT, TOO.
SHOW HIM LIKE YOU SHOWED DAD.
I KNOW THE WEIGHT OF NOT BEING ABLE TO STOP IT. TO CHANGE IT.
BUT I SWEAR TO YOU, HARRY...
SHOW HIM THE TRUTH.
...NONE OF THIS IS YOUR FAULT.
THIS-- THIS IS "YOUR SIDE"?
THIS IS YOUR CASE?
THESE ARE THE WORDS YOU THINK WILL MAKE ME FORGET?!

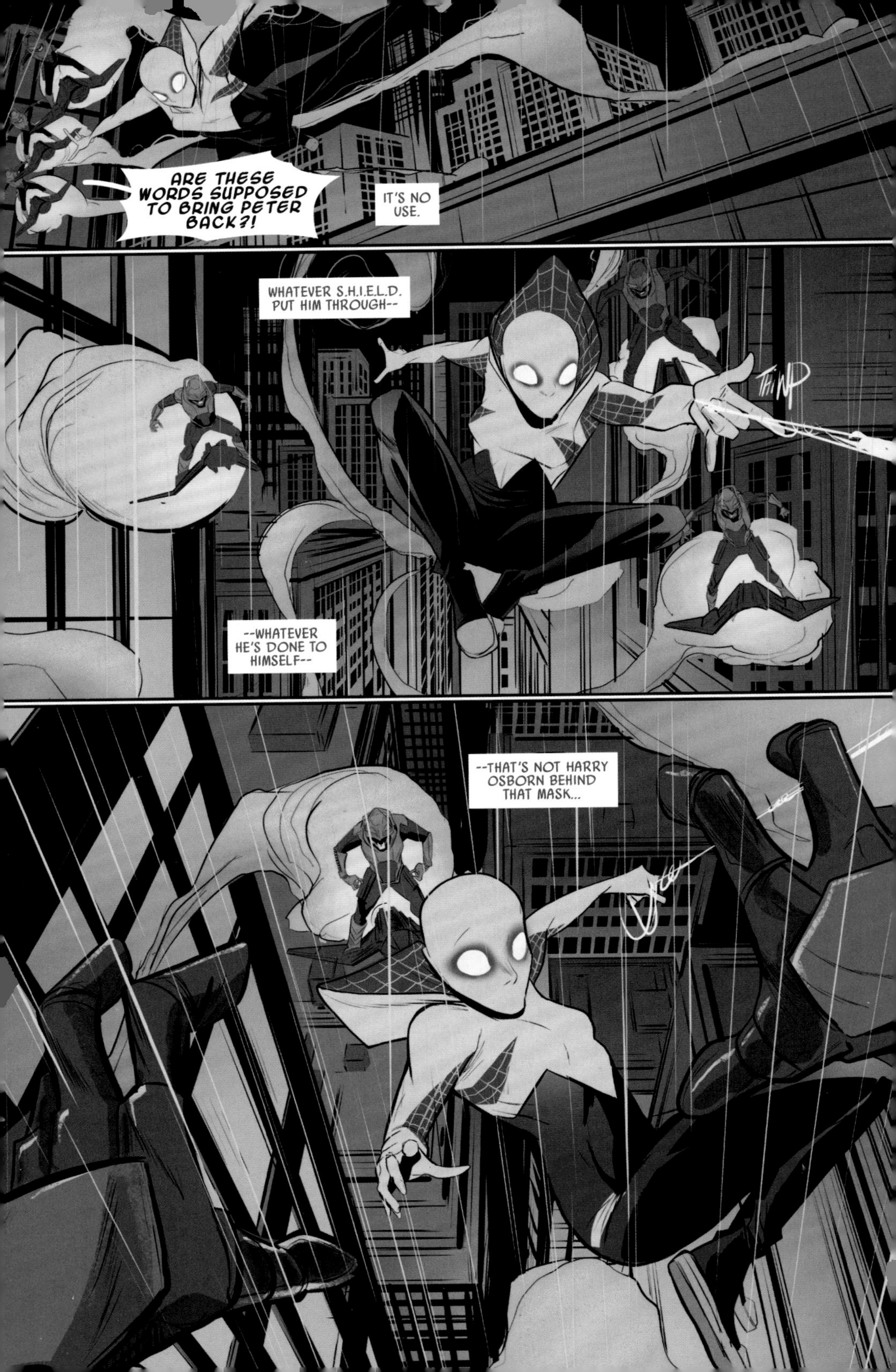

ARE THESE WORDS SUPPOSED TO BRING PETER BACK?!
IT'S NO USE.
WHATEVER S.H.I.E.L.D. PUT HIM THROUGH--
THWP
--WHATEVER HE'S DONE TO HIMSELF--
--THAT'S NOT HARRY OSBORN BEHIND THAT MASK...

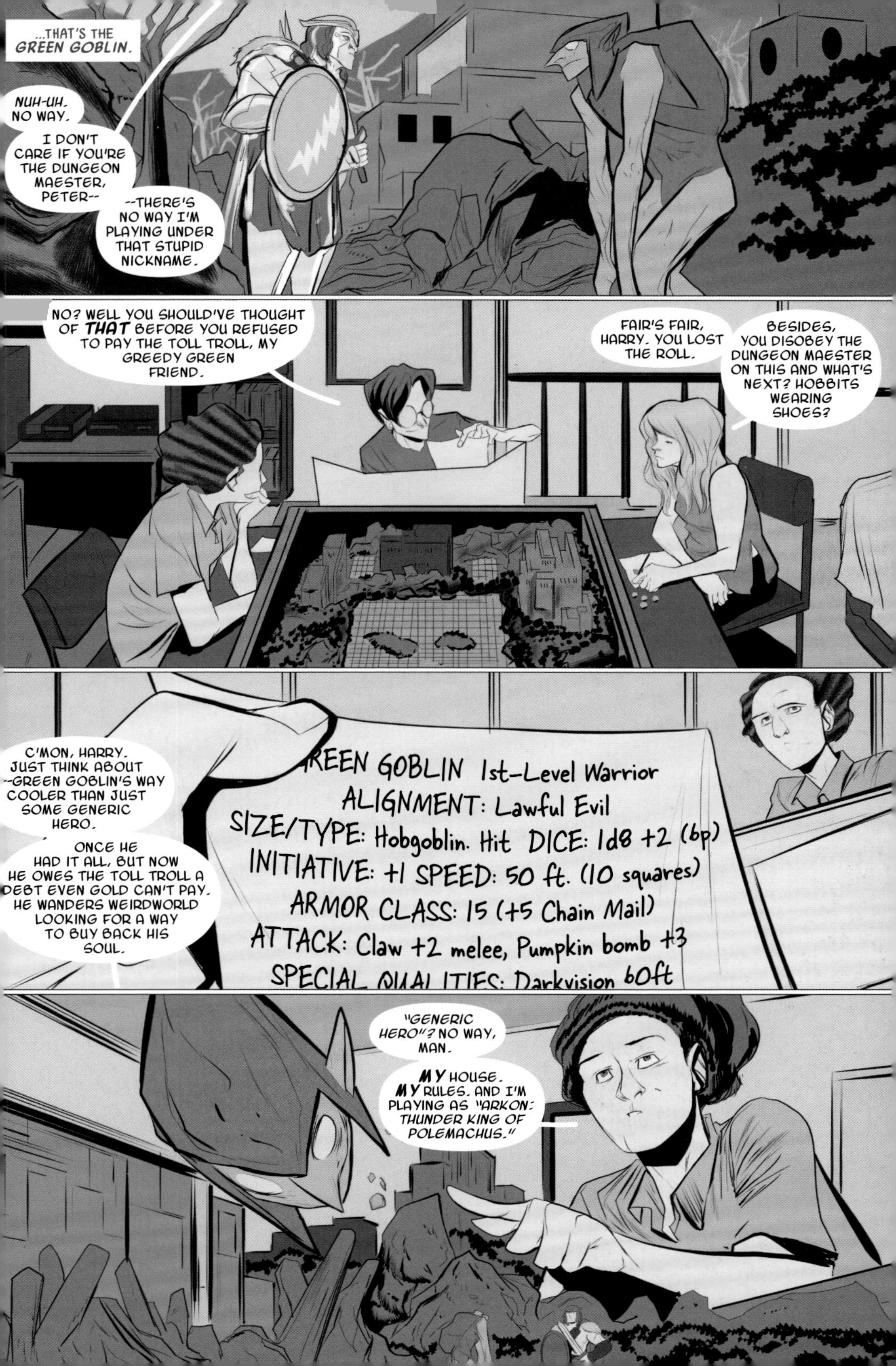
...THAT'S THE GREEN GOBLIN.
NUH-UH. NO WAY.
I DON'T CARE IF YOU'RE THE DUNGEON MAESTER, PETER--
--THERE'S NO WAY I'M PLAYING UNDER THAT STUPID NICKNAME.
NO? WELL YOU SHOULD'VE THOUGHT OF THAT BEFORE YOU REFUSED TO PAY THE TOLL TROLL, MY GREEDY GREEN FRIEND.
FAIR'S FAIR, HARRY. YOU LOST THE ROLL.
BESIDES, YOU DISOBEY THE DUNGEON MAESTER ON THIS AND WHAT'S NEXT? HOBBITS WEARING SHOES?
C'MON, HARRY. JUST THINK ABOUT --GREEN GOBLIN'S WAY COOLER THAN JUST SOME GENERIC HERO.
ONCE HE HAD IT ALL, BUT NOW HE OWES THE TOLL TROLL A DEBT EVEN GOLD CAN'T PAY. HE WANDERS WEIRDWORLD LOOKING FOR A WAY TO BUY BACK HIS SOUL.
REEN GOBLIN 1st-Level Warrior
ALIGNMENT: Lawful Evil
SIZE/TYPE: Hobgoblin. Hit DICE: 1d8 +2 (6p)
INITIATIVE: +1 SPEED: 50 ft. (10 squares)
ARMOR CLASS: 15 (+5 Chain Mail)
ATTACK: Claw +2 melee, Pumpkin bomb +3
"GENERIC HERO"? NO WAY, MAN.
MY HOUSE. MY RULES. AND I'M PLAYING AS "ARKON: THUNDER KING OF POLEMACHUS."

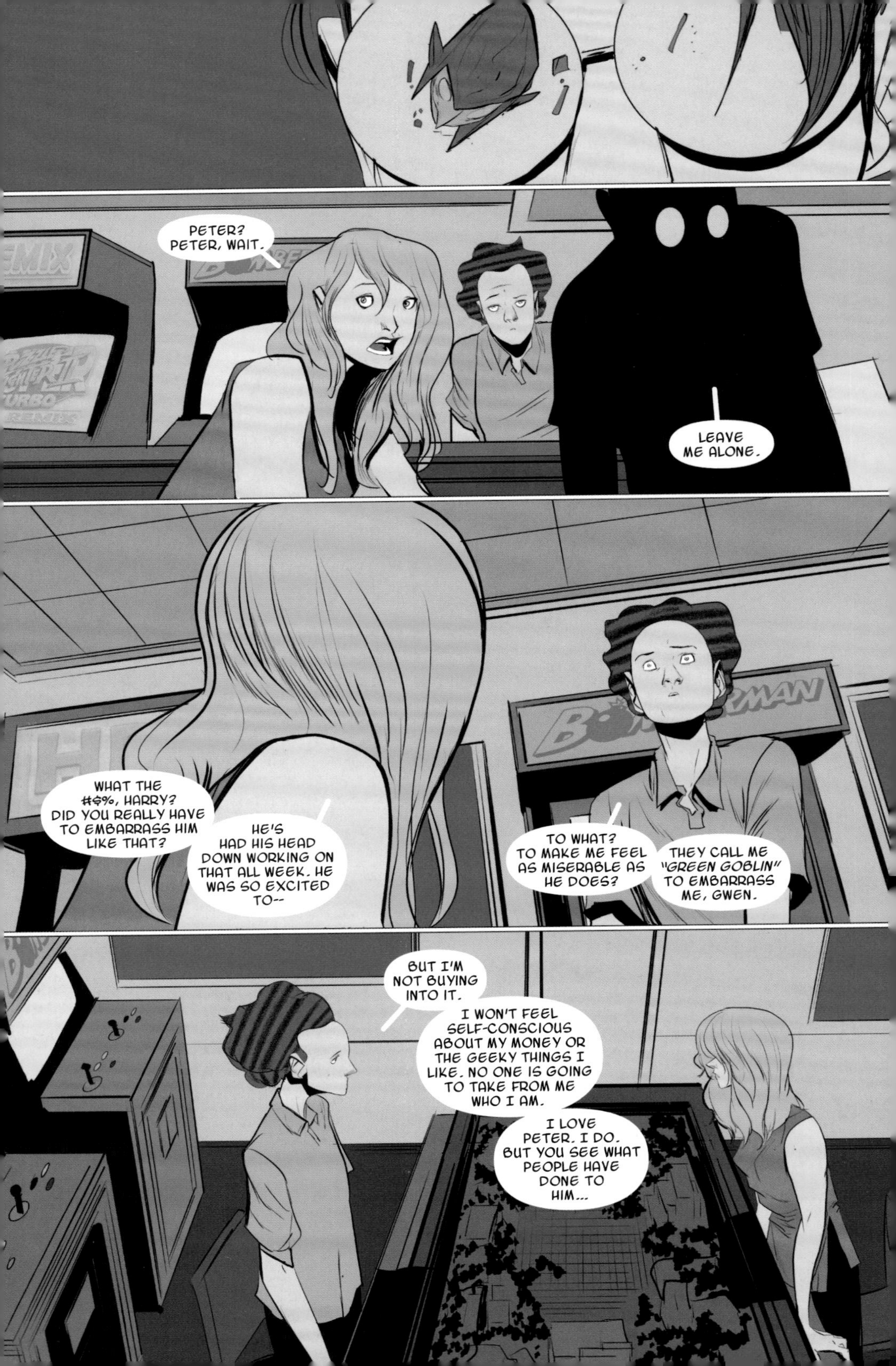
PETER? PETER, WAIT.
LEAVE ME ALONE.
WHAT THE #$%, HARRY? DID YOU REALLY HAVE TO EMBARRASS HIM LIKE THAT?
HE'S HAD HIS HEAD DOWN WORKING ON THAT ALL WEEK. HE WAS SO EXCITED TO--
TO WHAT? TO MAKE ME FEEL AS MISERABLE AS HE DOES?
THEY CALL ME "GREEN GOBLIN" TO EMBARRASS ME, GWEN.
BUT I'M NOT BUYING INTO IT.
I WON'T FEEL SELF-CONSCIOUS ABOUT MY MONEY OR THE GEEKY THINGS I LIKE. NO ONE IS GOING TO TAKE FROM ME WHO I AM.
I LOVE PETER. I DO. BUT YOU SEE WHAT PEOPLE HAVE DONE TO HIM...

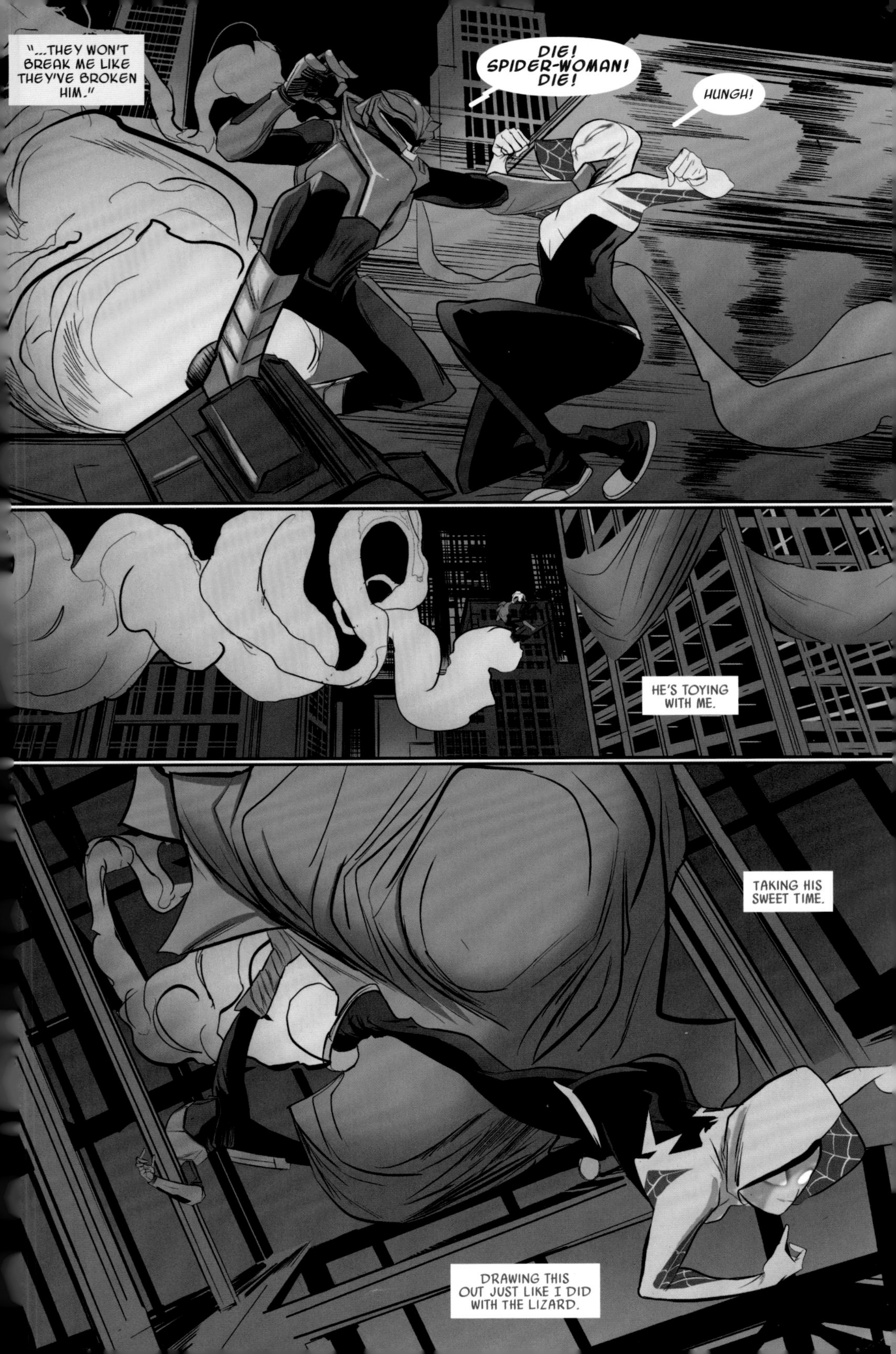
"...THEY WON'T BREAK ME LIKE THEY'VE BROKEN HIM."
DIE! SPIDER-WOMAN! DIE!
HUNGH!
HE'S TOYING WITH ME.
TAKING HIS SWEET TIME.
DRAWING THIS OUT JUST LIKE I DID WITH THE LIZARD.

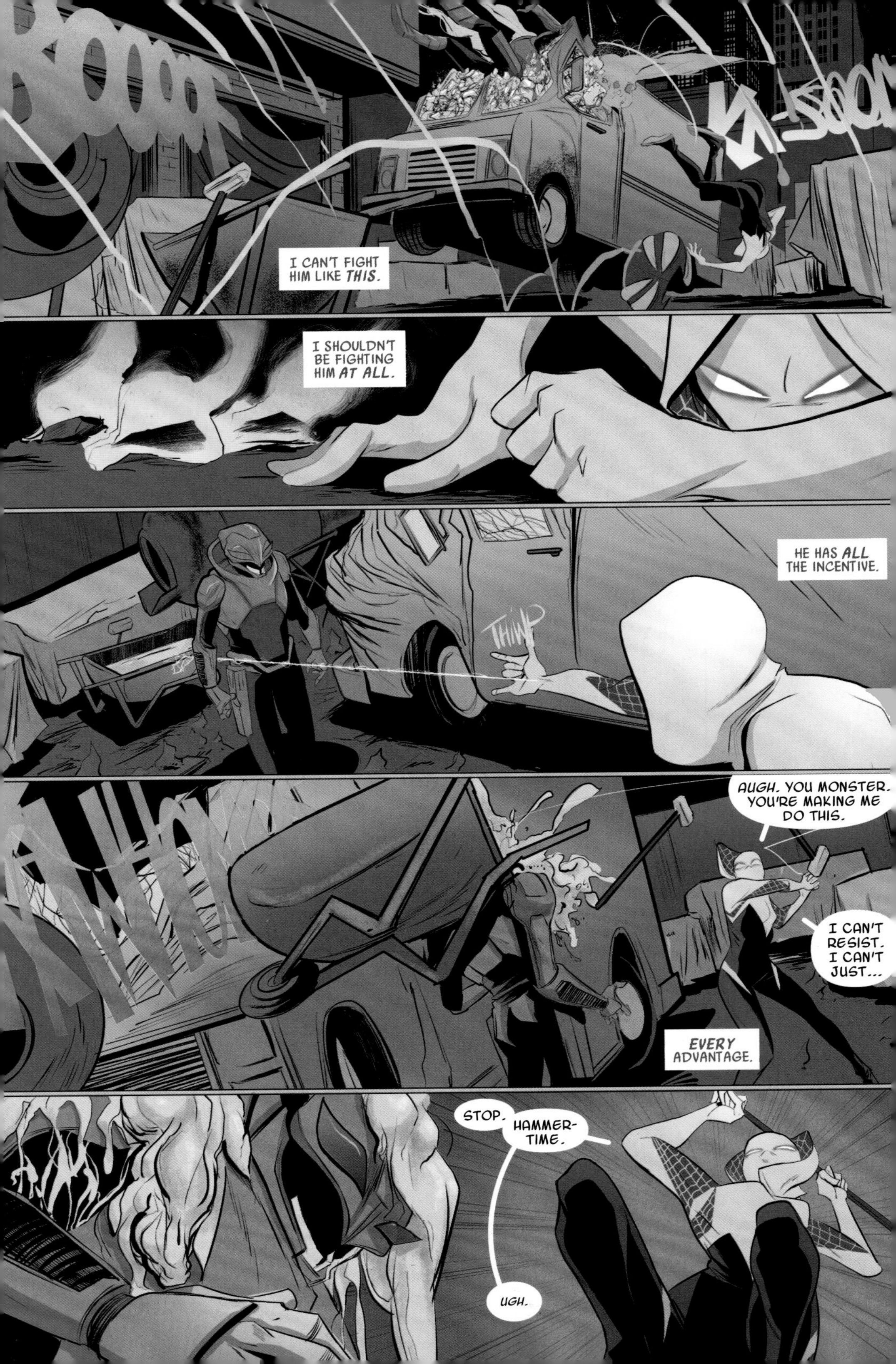
BOOOOM
KA-BOOM
I CAN'T FIGHT HIM LIKE THIS.
I SHOULDN'T BE FIGHTING HIM AT ALL.
HE HAS ALL THE INCENTIVE.
THWP
AUGH. YOU MONSTER. YOU'RE MAKING ME DO THIS.
I CAN'T RESIST. I CAN'T JUST...
EVERY ADVANTAGE.
STOP.
HAMMER-TIME.
UGH.

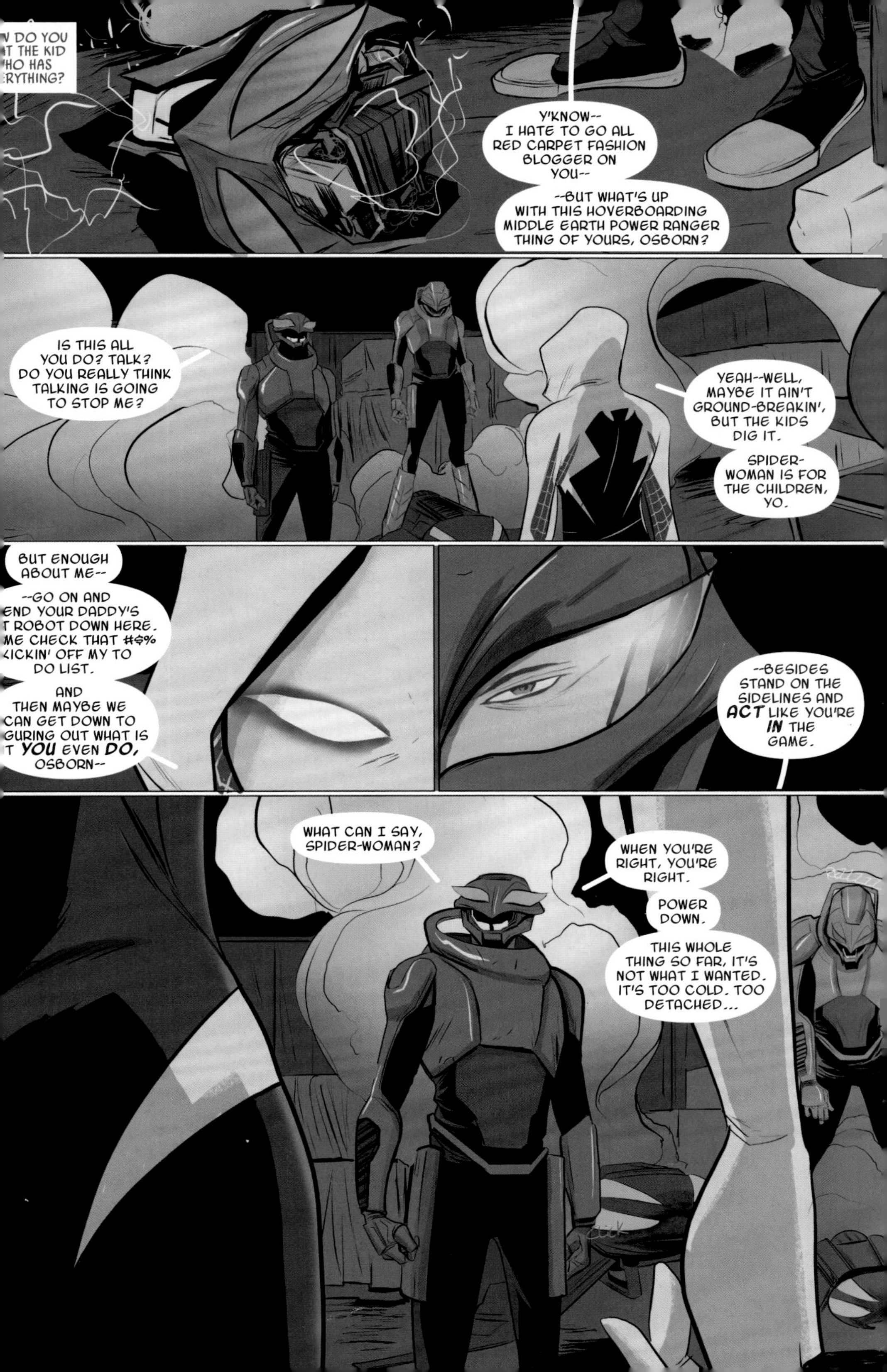
Y'KNOW-- I HATE TO GO ALL RED CARPET FASHION BLOGGER ON YOU--
--BUT WHAT'S UP WITH THIS HOVERBOARDING MIDDLE EARTH POWER RANGER THING OF YOURS, OSBORN?
IS THIS ALL YOU DO? TALK? DO YOU REALLY THINK TALKING IS GOING TO STOP ME?
YEAH--WELL, MAYBE IT AIN'T GROUND-BREAKIN', BUT THE KIDS DIG IT.
SPIDER-WOMAN IS FOR THE CHILDREN, YO.
BUT ENOUGH ABOUT ME--
--BESIDES STAND ON THE SIDELINES AND ACT LIKE YOU'RE IN THE GAME.
WHAT CAN I SAY, SPIDER-WOMAN?
WHEN YOU'RE RIGHT, YOU'RE RIGHT.
POWER DOWN.
THIS WHOLE THING SO FAR, IT'S NOT WHAT I WANTED. IT'S TOO COLD. TOO DETACHED...

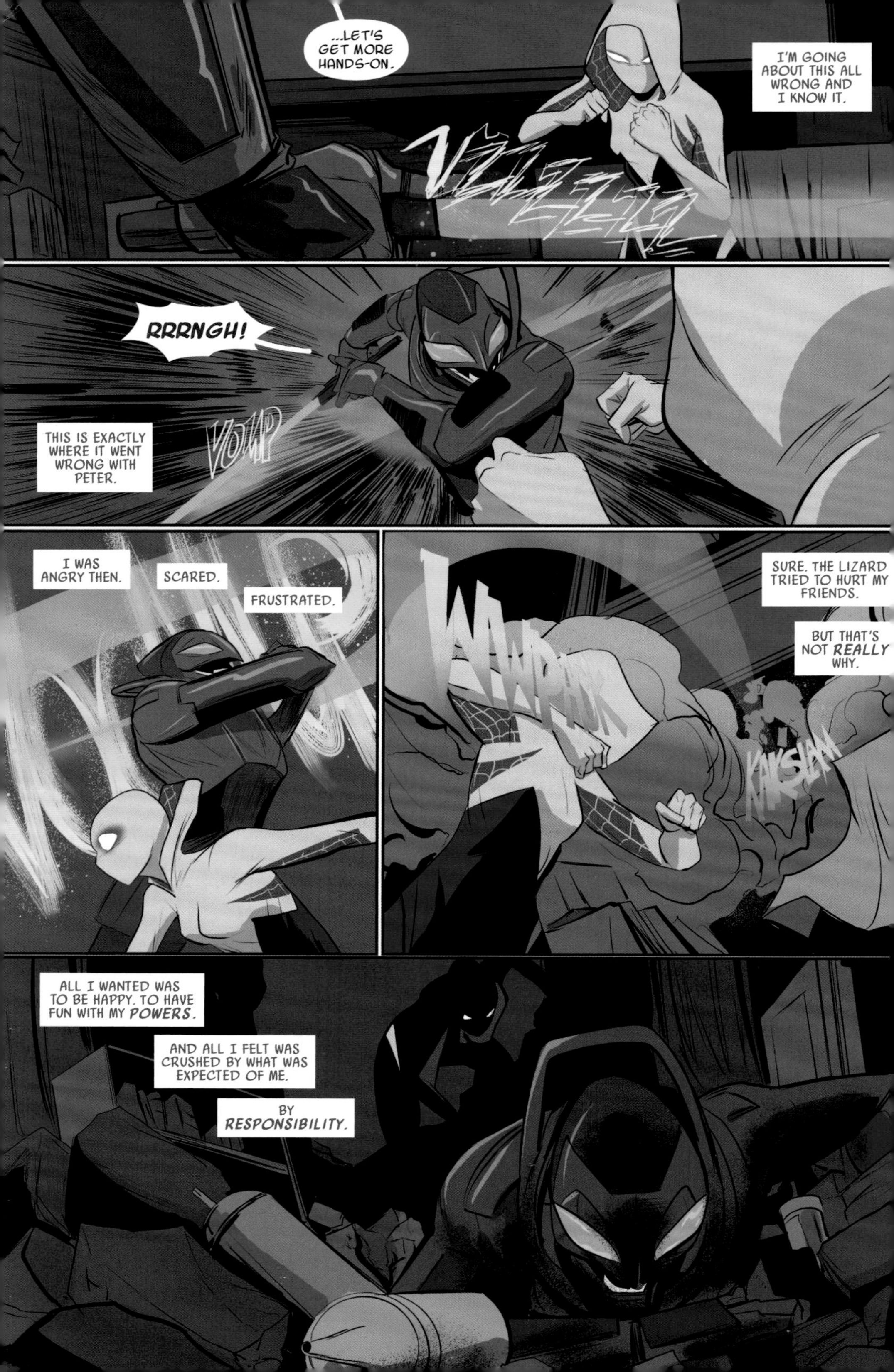
...LET'S GET MORE HANDS-ON.
I'M GOING ABOUT THIS ALL WRONG AND I KNOW IT.
RRRNGH!
THIS IS EXACTLY WHERE IT WENT WRONG WITH PETER.
VOMP
I WAS ANGRY THEN.
SCARED.
FRUSTRATED.
SURE, THE LIZARD TRIED TO HURT MY FRIENDS.
BUT THAT'S NOT REALLY WHY.
KRASLAM
ALL I WANTED WAS TO BE HAPPY. TO HAVE FUN WITH MY POWERS.
AND ALL I FELT WAS CRUSHED BY WHAT WAS EXPECTED OF ME.
BY RESPONSIBILITY.

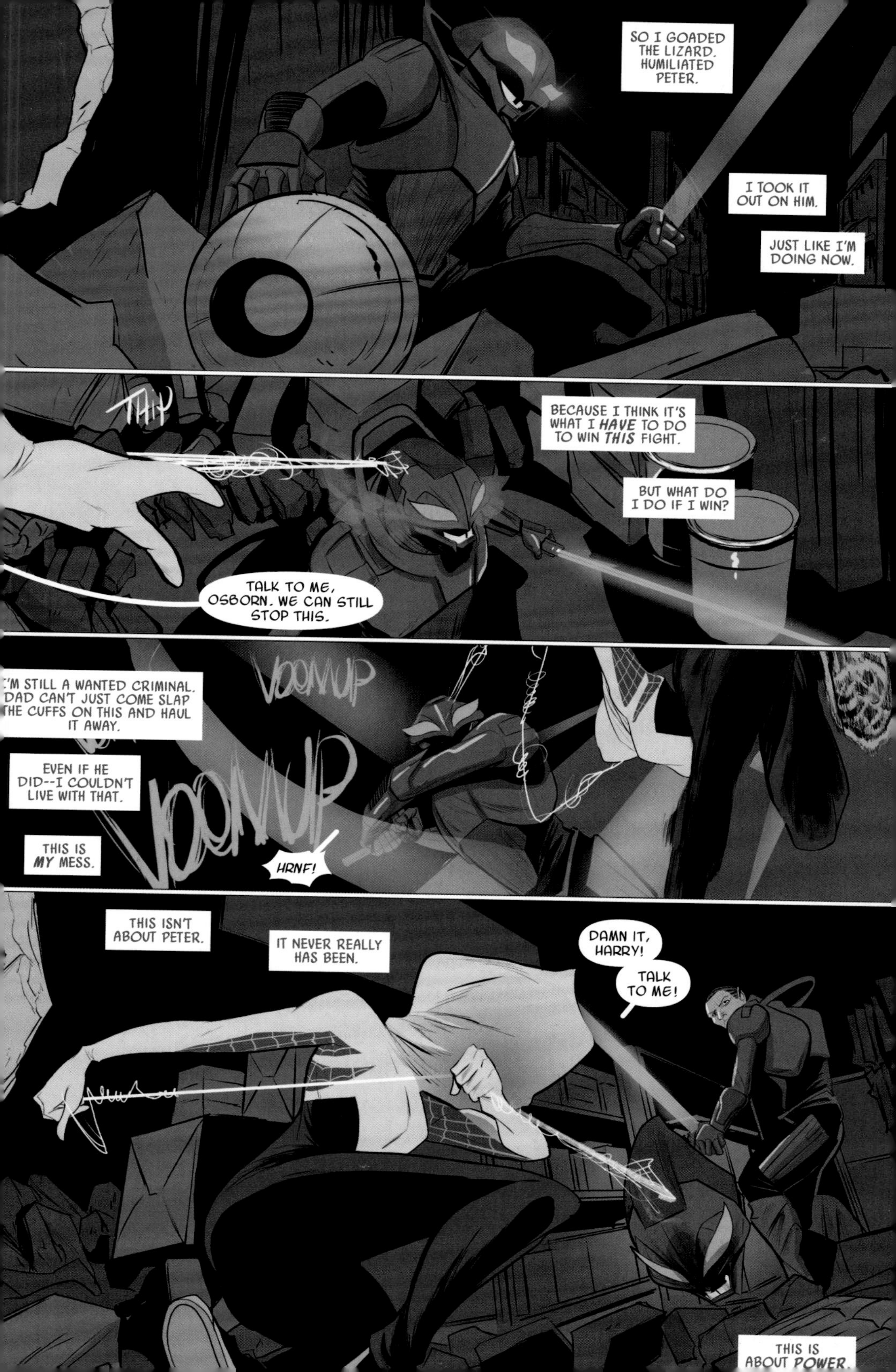

SO I GOADED THE LIZARD. HUMILIATED PETER.
I TOOK IT OUT ON HIM.
JUST LIKE I'M DOING NOW.
THIP
BECAUSE I THINK IT'S WHAT I HAVE TO DO TO WIN THIS FIGHT.
BUT WHAT DO I DO IF I WIN?
TALK TO ME, OSBORN. WE CAN STILL STOP THIS.
VOOMUP
I'M STILL A WANTED CRIMINAL. DAD CAN'T JUST COME SLAP THE CUFFS ON THIS AND HAUL IT AWAY.
EVEN IF HE DID--I COULDN'T LIVE WITH THAT.
VOOMUP
THIS IS MY MESS.
HRNF!
THIS ISN'T ABOUT PETER.
IT NEVER REALLY HAS BEEN.
DAMN IT, HARRY!
TALK TO ME!
THIS IS ABOUT POWER.

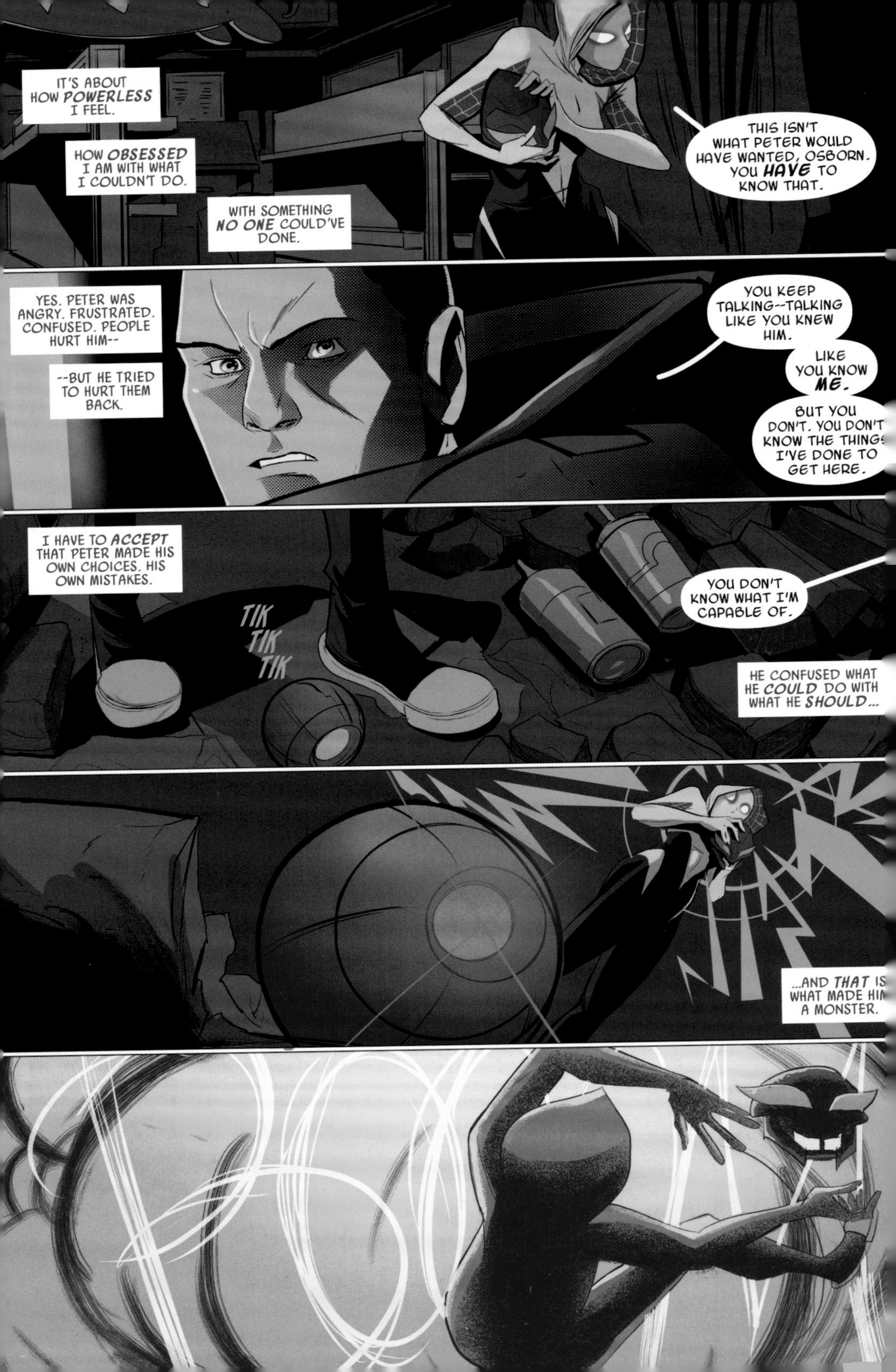
IT'S ABOUT HOW POWERLESS I FEEL.
HOW OBSESSED I AM WITH WHAT I COULDN'T DO.
WITH SOMETHING NO ONE COULD'VE DONE.
THIS ISN'T WHAT PETER WOULD HAVE WANTED, OSBORN. YOU HAVE TO KNOW THAT.
YES. PETER WAS ANGRY. FRUSTRATED. CONFUSED. PEOPLE HURT HIM--
--BUT HE TRIED TO HURT THEM BACK.
YOU KEEP TALKING--TALKING LIKE YOU KNEW HIM.
LIKE YOU KNOW ME.
BUT YOU DON'T. YOU DON'T KNOW THE THINGS I'VE DONE TO GET HERE.
I HAVE TO ACCEPT THAT PETER MADE HIS OWN CHOICES. HIS OWN MISTAKES.
TIK TIK TIK
YOU DON'T KNOW WHAT I'M CAPABLE OF.
HE CONFUSED WHAT HE COULD DO WITH WHAT HE SHOULD...
...AND THAT IS WHAT MADE HIM A MONSTER.

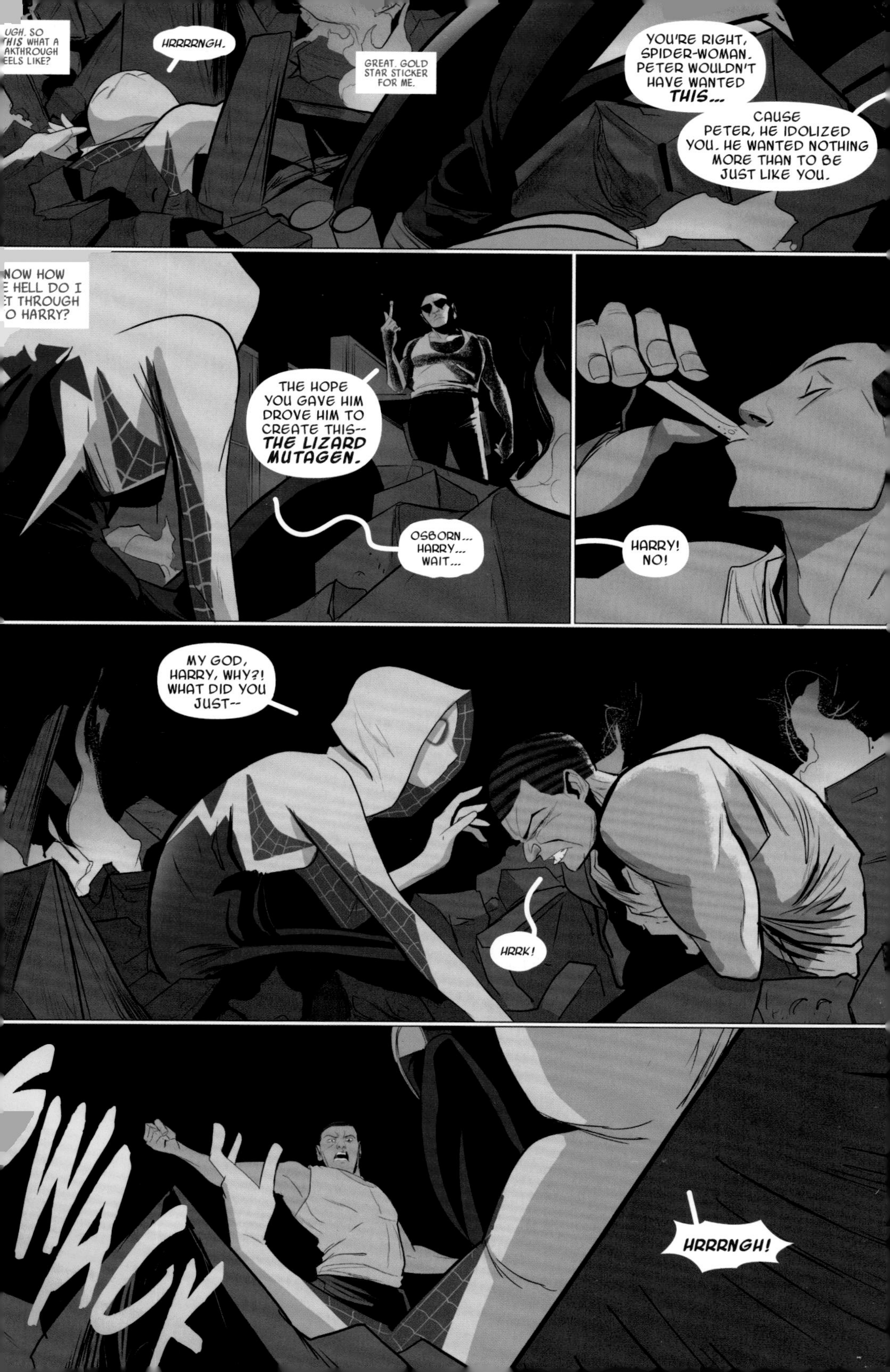
UGH. SO THIS WHAT A AKTHROUGH EELS LIKE?
HRRRRNGH.
GREAT. GOLD STAR STICKER FOR ME.
YOU'RE RIGHT, SPIDER-WOMAN. PETER WOULDN'T HAVE WANTED THIS...
CAUSE PETER, HE IDOLIZED YOU. HE WANTED NOTHING MORE THAN TO BE JUST LIKE YOU.
NOW HOW E HELL DO I ET THROUGH O HARRY?
THE HOPE YOU GAVE HIM DROVE HIM TO CREATE THIS-- THE LIZARD MUTAGEN.
OSBORN... HARRY... WAIT...
HARRY! NO!
MY GOD, HARRY, WHY?! WHAT DID YOU JUST--
HRRK!
SWACK
HRRRNGH!

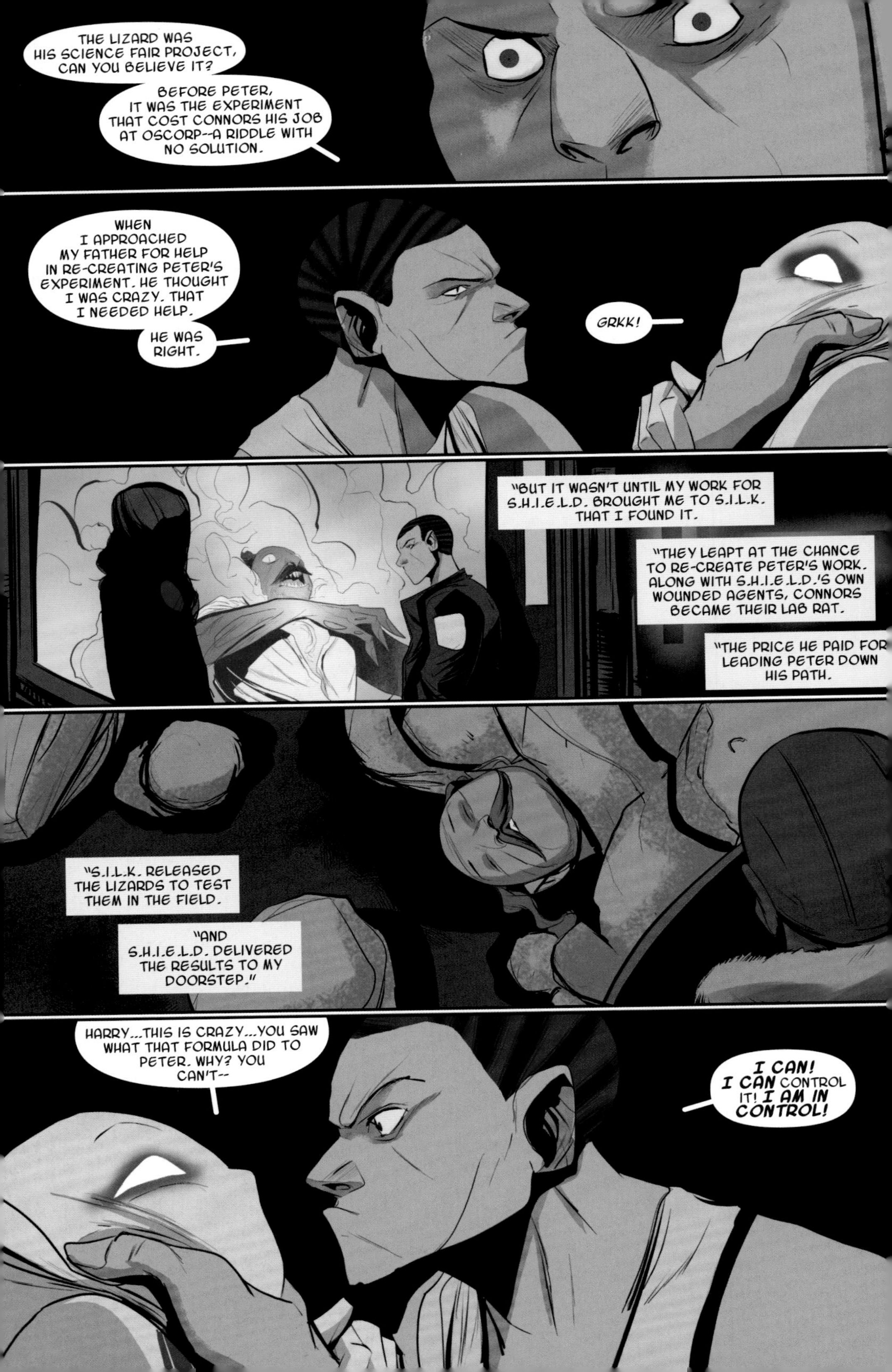
THE LIZARD WAS HIS SCIENCE FAIR PROJECT, CAN YOU BELIEVE IT?
BEFORE PETER, IT WAS THE EXPERIMENT THAT COST CONNORS HIS JOB AT OSCORP--A RIDDLE WITH NO SOLUTION.
WHEN I APPROACHED MY FATHER FOR HELP IN RE-CREATING PETER'S EXPERIMENT. HE THOUGHT I WAS CRAZY. THAT I NEEDED HELP.
HE WAS RIGHT.
GRKK!
"BUT IT WASN'T UNTIL MY WORK FOR S.H.I.E.L.D. BROUGHT ME TO S.I.L.K. THAT I FOUND IT.
"THEY LEAPT AT THE CHANCE TO RE-CREATE PETER'S WORK. ALONG WITH S.H.I.E.L.D.'S OWN WOUNDED AGENTS, CONNORS BECAME THEIR LAB RAT.
"THE PRICE HE PAID FOR LEADING PETER DOWN HIS PATH.
"S.I.L.K. RELEASED THE LIZARDS TO TEST THEM IN THE FIELD.
"AND S.H.I.E.L.D. DELIVERED THE RESULTS TO MY DOORSTEP."
HARRY...THIS IS CRAZY...YOU SAW WHAT THAT FORMULA DID TO PETER. WHY? YOU CAN'T--
I CAN! I CAN CONTROL IT! I AM IN CONTROL!

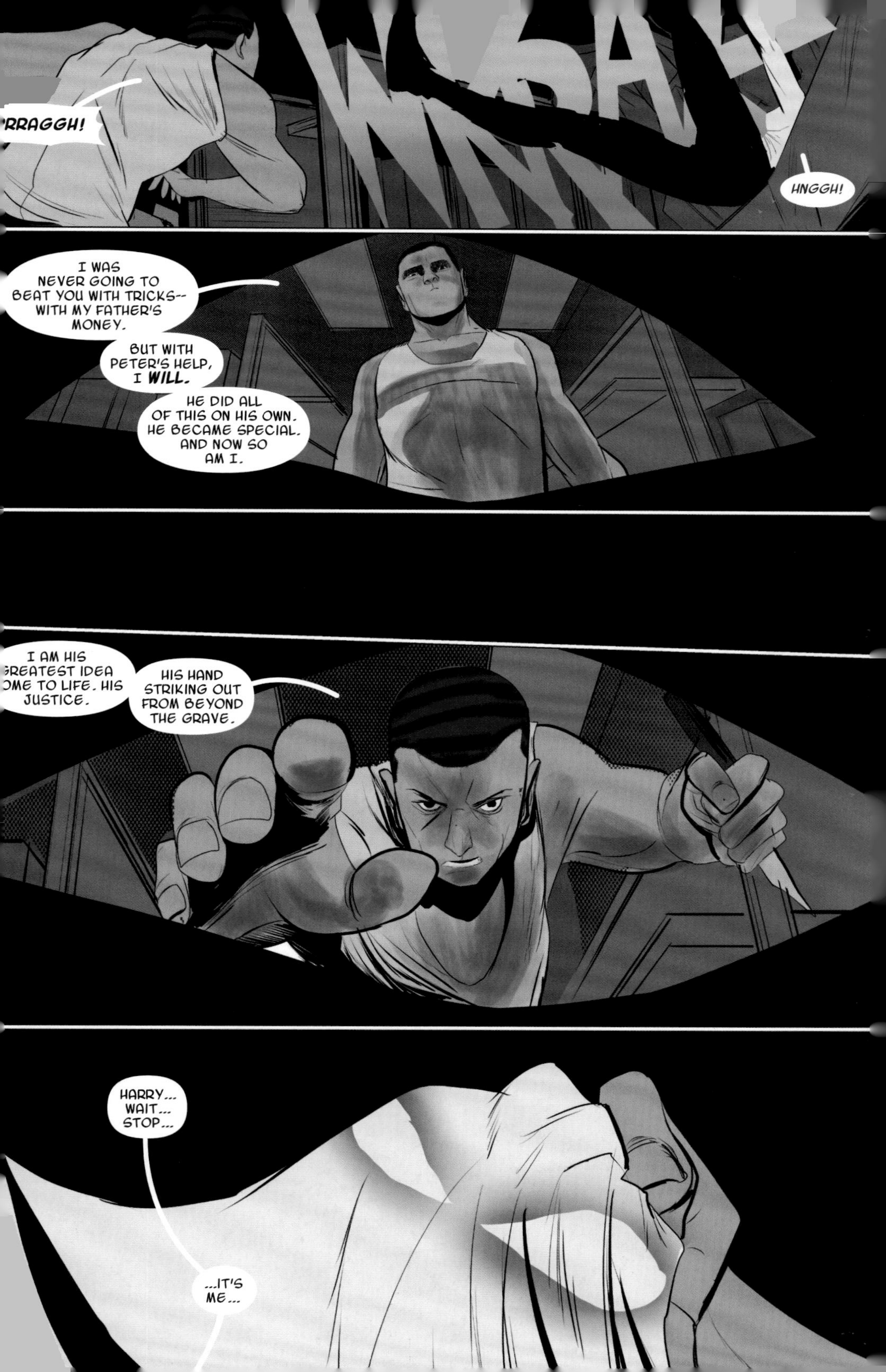
RRAGGH!
HNGGH!
I WAS NEVER GOING TO BEAT YOU WITH TRICKS-- WITH MY FATHER'S MONEY.
BUT WITH PETER'S HELP, I **WILL.**
HE DID ALL OF THIS ON HIS OWN. HE BECAME SPECIAL. AND NOW SO AM I.
I AM HIS GREATEST IDEA OME TO LIFE. HIS JUSTICE.
HIS HAND STRIKING OUT FROM BEYOND THE GRAVE.
HARRY... WAIT... STOP...
...IT'S ME...

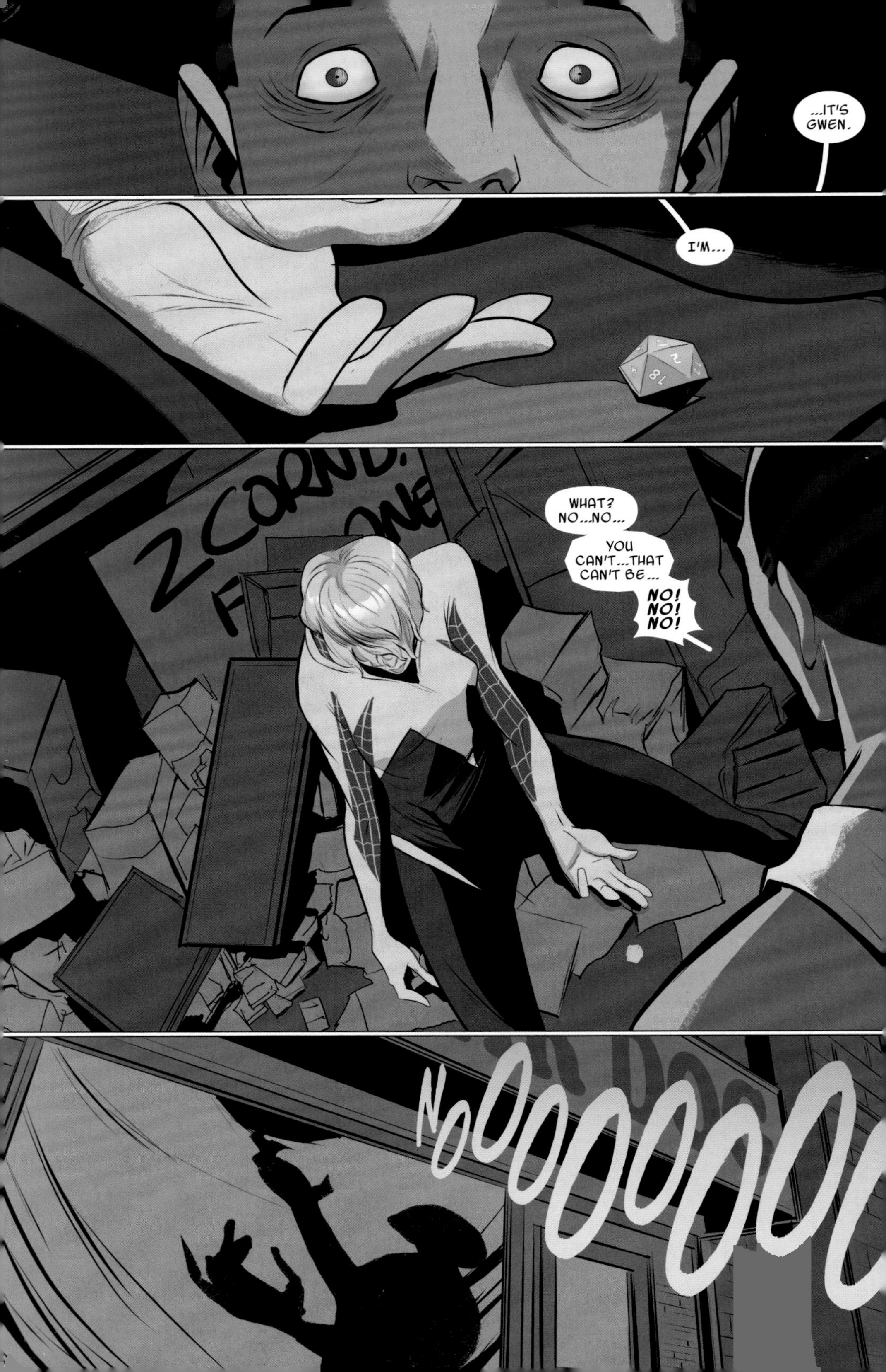
...IT'S GWEN.
I'M...
WHAT? NO...NO...
YOU CAN'T...THAT CAN'T BE...
NO! NO! NO!
NOOOOOOOOO

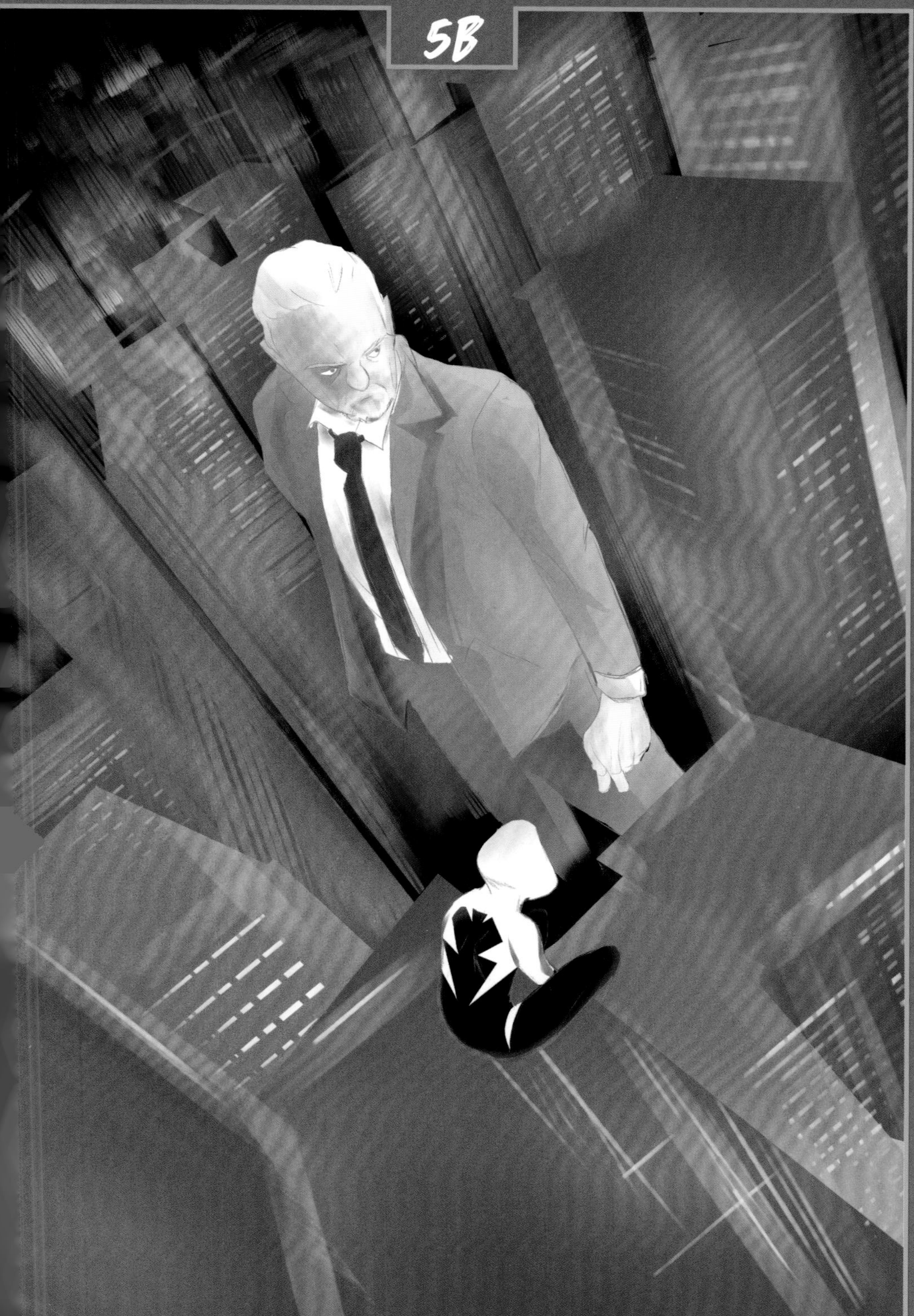
5B

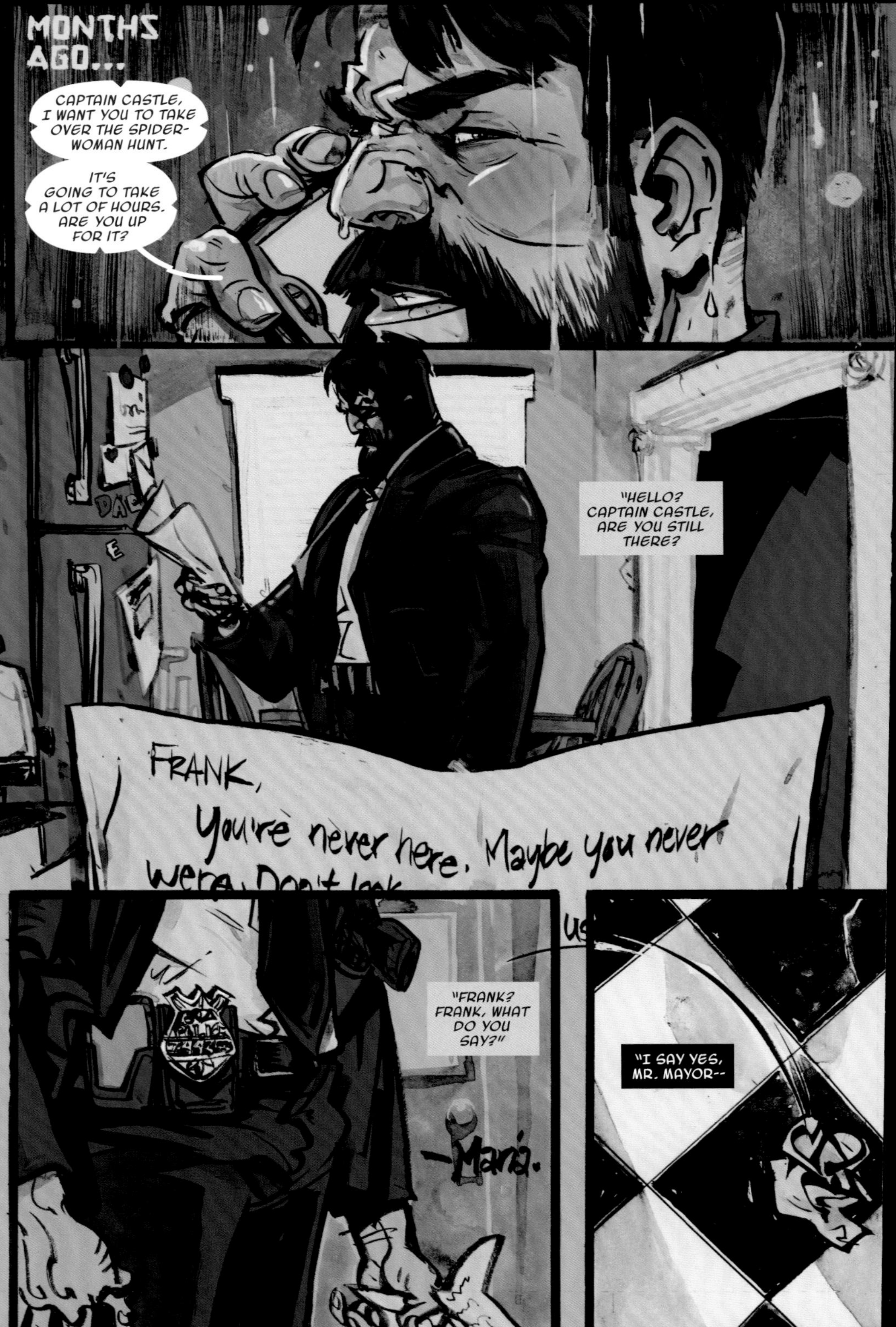

MONTHS AGO...
CAPTAIN CASTLE, I WANT YOU TO TAKE OVER THE SPIDER-WOMAN HUNT.
IT'S GOING TO TAKE A LOT OF HOURS. ARE YOU UP FOR IT?
"HELLO? CAPTAIN CASTLE, ARE YOU STILL THERE?
FRANK,
You're never here. Maybe you never
"FRANK? FRANK, WHAT DO YOU SAY?"
—María.
"I SAY YES, MR. MAYOR--

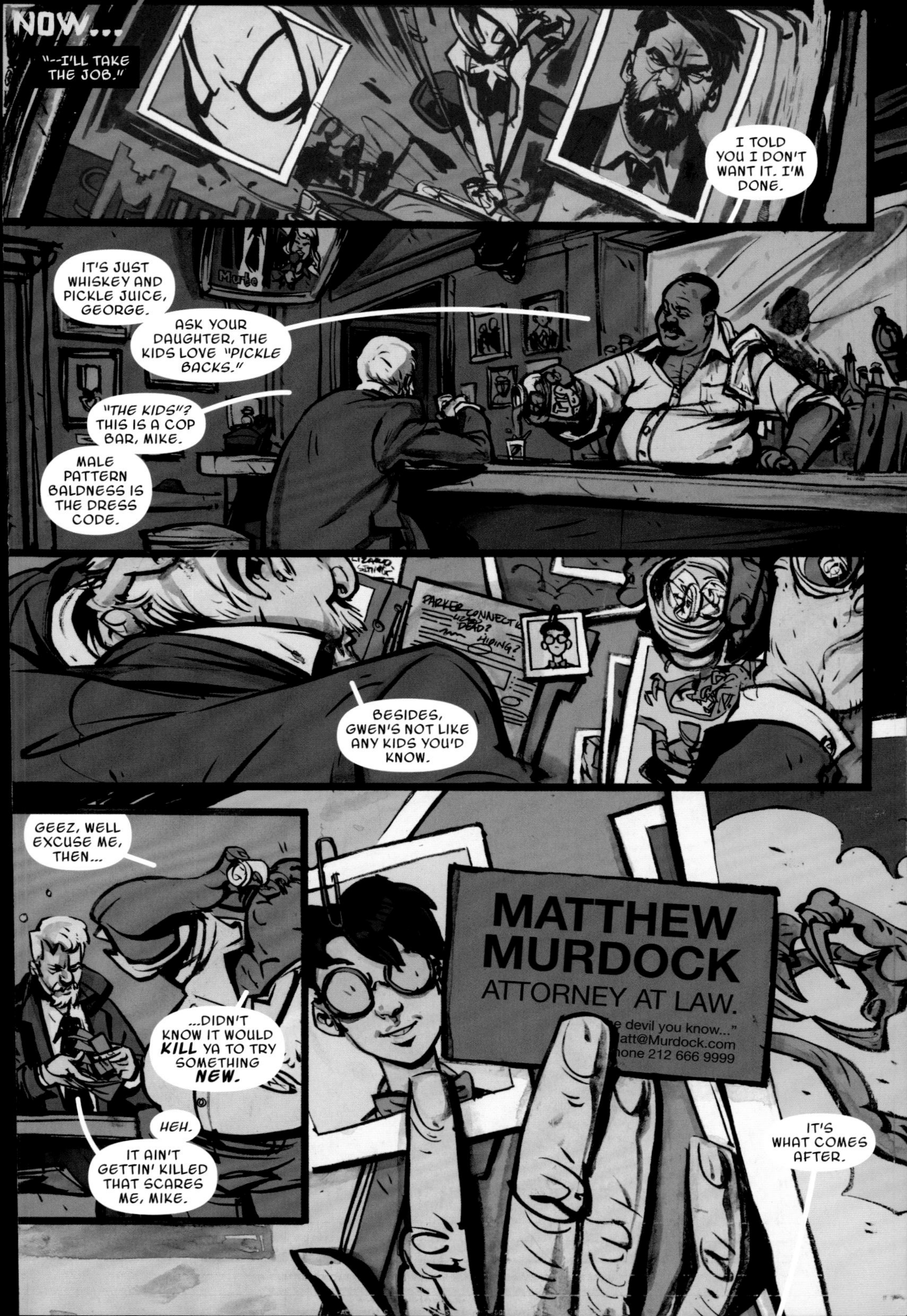
NOW...
"--I'LL TAKE THE JOB."
I TOLD YOU I DON'T WANT IT. I'M DONE.
IT'S JUST WHISKEY AND PICKLE JUICE, GEORGE.
ASK YOUR DAUGHTER, THE KIDS LOVE "PICKLE BACKS."
"THE KIDS"? THIS IS A COP BAR, MIKE.
MALE PATTERN BALDNESS IS THE DRESS CODE.
BESIDES, GWEN'S NOT LIKE ANY KIDS YOU'D KNOW.
GEEZ, WELL EXCUSE ME, THEN...
...DIDN'T KNOW IT WOULD KILL YA TO TRY SOMETHING NEW.
HEH.
IT AIN'T GETTIN' KILLED THAT SCARES ME, MIKE.
MATTHEW MURDOCK
ATTORNEY AT LAW.
e devil you know..."
att@Murdock.com
hone 212 666 9999
IT'S WHAT COMES AFTER.

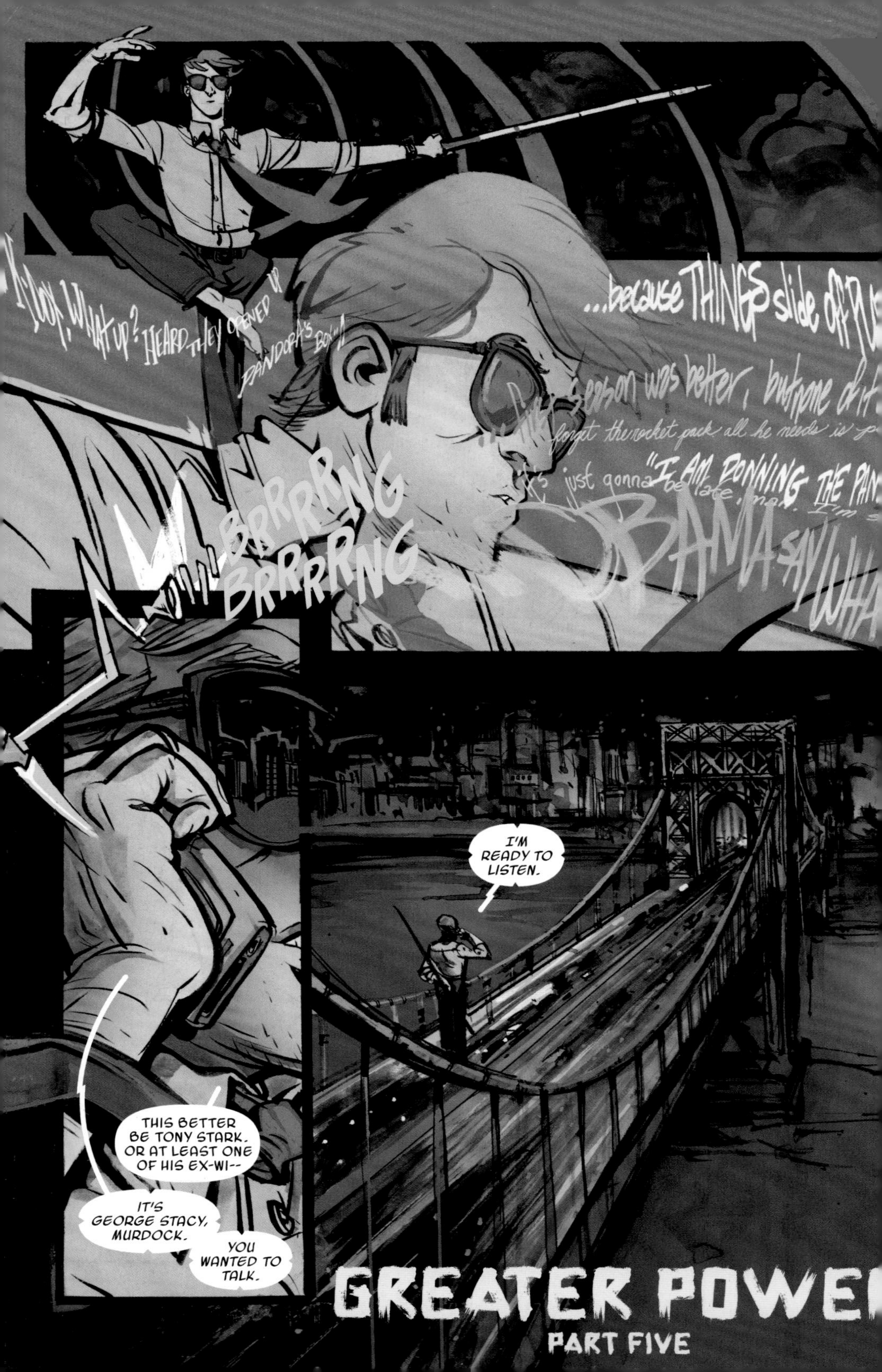
BRRRRNG
BRRRRNG
I'M READY TO LISTEN.
THIS BETTER BE TONY STARK. OR AT LEAST ONE OF HIS EX-WI--
IT'S GEORGE STACY, MURDOCK.
YOU WANTED TO TALK.
GREATER POWE
PART FIVE

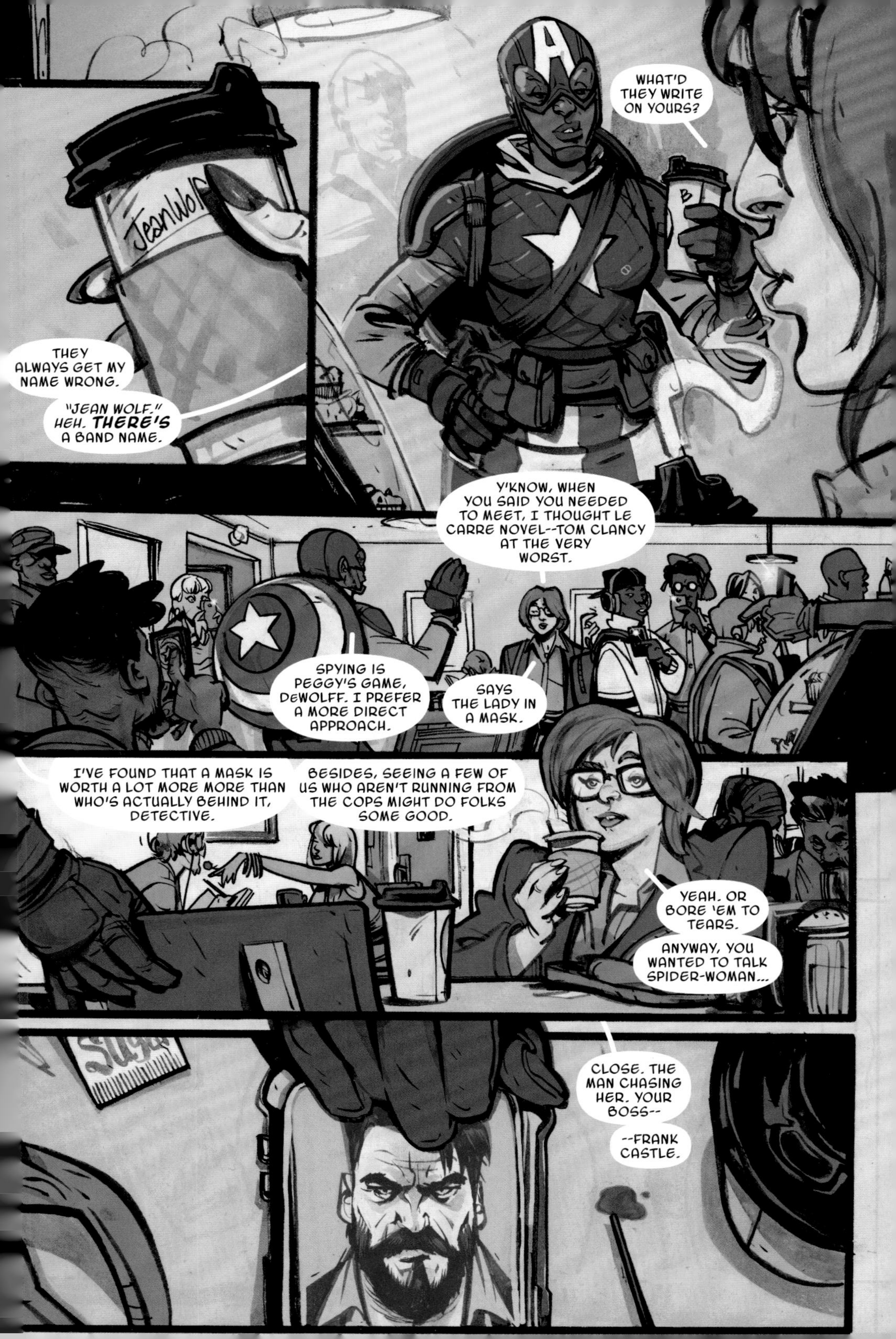
Jean Wolf
WHAT'D THEY WRITE ON YOURS?
B
THEY ALWAYS GET MY NAME WRONG.
"JEAN WOLF." HEH. **THERE'S** A BAND NAME.
Y'KNOW, WHEN YOU SAID YOU NEEDED TO MEET, I THOUGHT LE CARRE NOVEL--TOM CLANCY AT THE VERY WORST.
SPYING IS PEGGY'S GAME, DEWOLFF. I PREFER A MORE DIRECT APPROACH.
SAYS THE LADY IN A MASK.
I'VE FOUND THAT A MASK IS WORTH A LOT MORE MORE THAN WHO'S ACTUALLY BEHIND IT, DETECTIVE.
BESIDES, SEEING A FEW OF US WHO AREN'T RUNNING FROM THE COPS MIGHT DO FOLKS SOME GOOD.
YEAH. OR BORE 'EM TO TEARS.
ANYWAY, YOU WANTED TO TALK SPIDER-WOMAN...
CLOSE. THE MAN CHASING HER. YOUR BOSS--
--FRANK CASTLE.

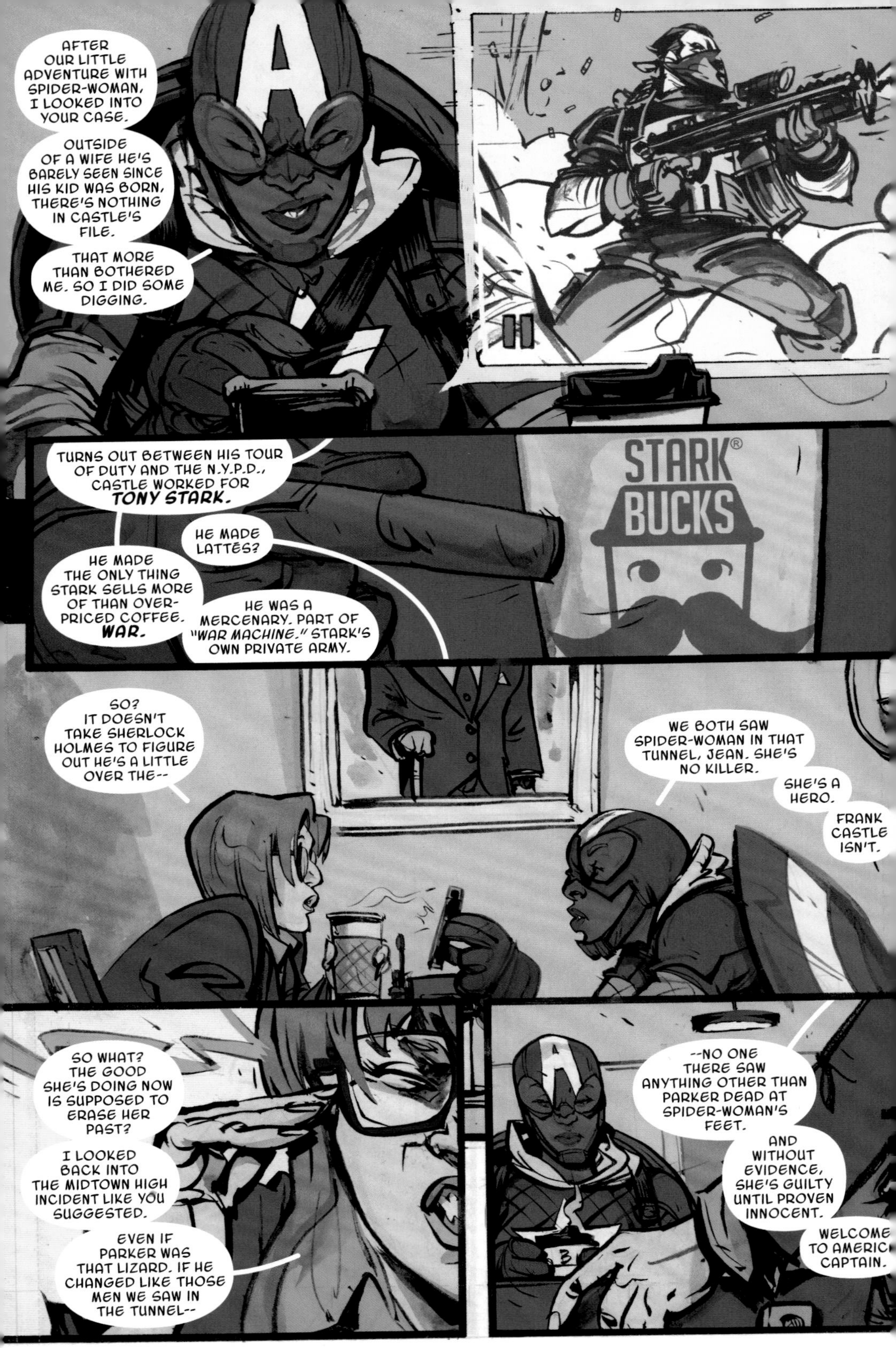
AFTER OUR LITTLE ADVENTURE WITH SPIDER-WOMAN, I LOOKED INTO YOUR CASE.
OUTSIDE OF A WIFE HE'S BARELY SEEN SINCE HIS KID WAS BORN, THERE'S NOTHING IN CASTLE'S FILE.
THAT MORE THAN BOTHERED ME. SO I DID SOME DIGGING.
TURNS OUT BETWEEN HIS TOUR OF DUTY AND THE N.Y.P.D., CASTLE WORKED FOR TONY STARK.
STARK® BUCKS
HE MADE LATTES?
HE MADE THE ONLY THING STARK SELLS MORE OF THAN OVER-PRICED COFFEE. WAR.
HE WAS A MERCENARY. PART OF "WAR MACHINE." STARK'S OWN PRIVATE ARMY.
SO? IT DOESN'T TAKE SHERLOCK HOLMES TO FIGURE OUT HE'S A LITTLE OVER THE--
WE BOTH SAW SPIDER-WOMAN IN THAT TUNNEL, JEAN. SHE'S NO KILLER.
SHE'S A HERO.
FRANK CASTLE ISN'T.
SO WHAT? THE GOOD SHE'S DOING NOW IS SUPPOSED TO ERASE HER PAST?
I LOOKED BACK INTO THE MIDTOWN HIGH INCIDENT LIKE YOU SUGGESTED.
EVEN IF PARKER WAS THAT LIZARD. IF HE CHANGED LIKE THOSE MEN WE SAW IN THE TUNNEL--
--NO ONE THERE SAW ANYTHING OTHER THAN PARKER DEAD AT SPIDER-WOMAN'S FEET.
AND WITHOUT EVIDENCE, SHE'S GUILTY UNTIL PROVEN INNOCENT.
WELCOME TO AMERIC CAPTAIN.

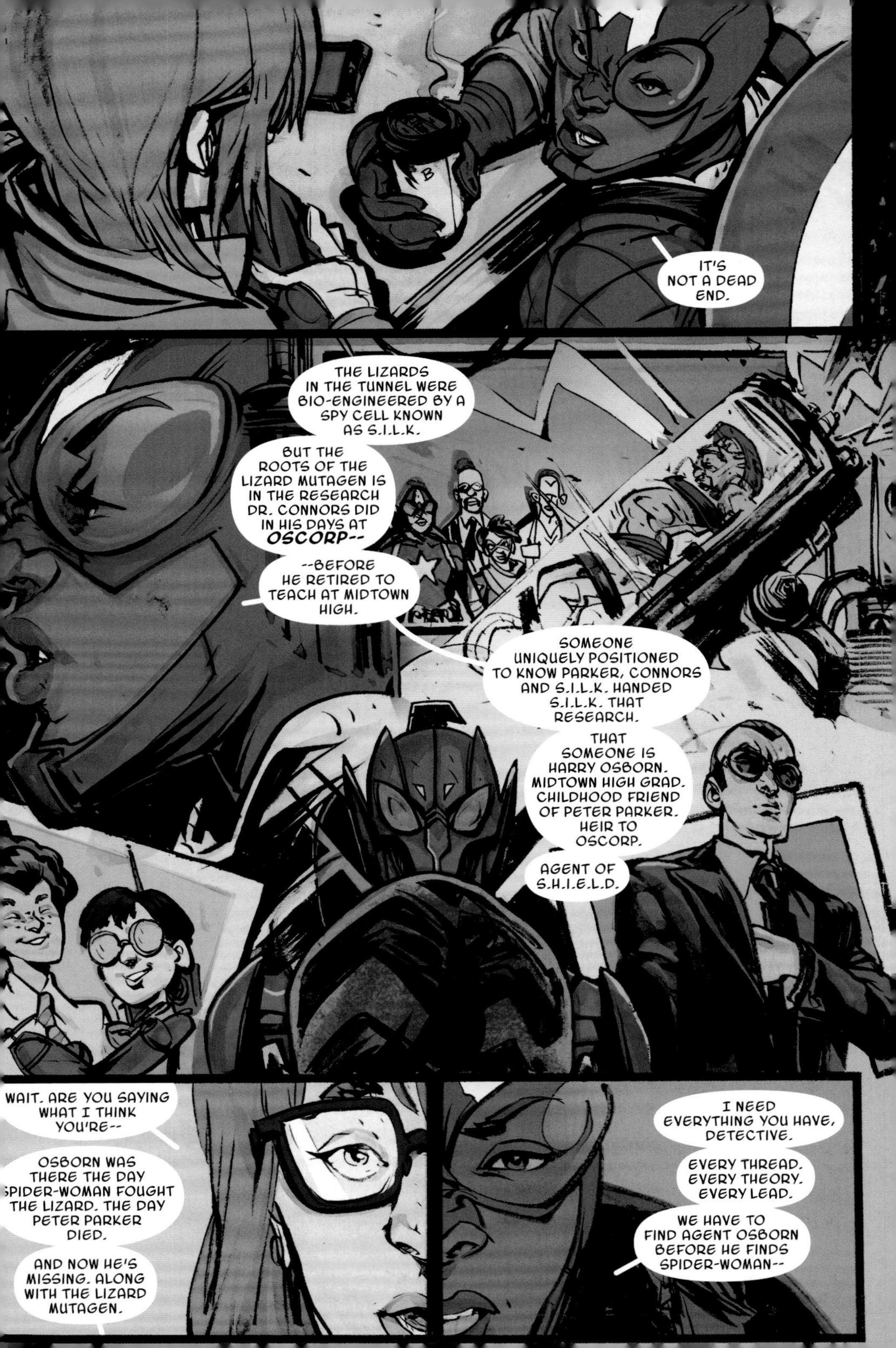
IT'S NOT A DEAD END.
THE LIZARDS IN THE TUNNEL WERE BIO-ENGINEERED BY A SPY CELL KNOWN AS S.I.L.K.
BUT THE ROOTS OF THE LIZARD MUTAGEN IS IN THE RESEARCH DR. CONNORS DID IN HIS DAYS AT OSCORP--
--BEFORE HE RETIRED TO TEACH AT MIDTOWN HIGH.
SOMEONE UNIQUELY POSITIONED TO KNOW PARKER, CONNORS AND S.I.L.K. HANDED S.I.L.K. THAT RESEARCH.
THAT SOMEONE IS HARRY OSBORN. MIDTOWN HIGH GRAD. CHILDHOOD FRIEND OF PETER PARKER. HEIR TO OSCORP.
AGENT OF S.H.I.E.L.D.
WAIT. ARE YOU SAYING WHAT I THINK YOU'RE--
OSBORN WAS THERE THE DAY SPIDER-WOMAN FOUGHT THE LIZARD. THE DAY PETER PARKER DIED.
AND NOW HE'S MISSING. ALONG WITH THE LIZARD MUTAGEN.
I NEED EVERYTHING YOU HAVE, DETECTIVE.
EVERY THREAD. EVERY THEORY. EVERY LEAD.
WE HAVE TO FIND AGENT OSBORN BEFORE HE FINDS SPIDER-WOMAN--

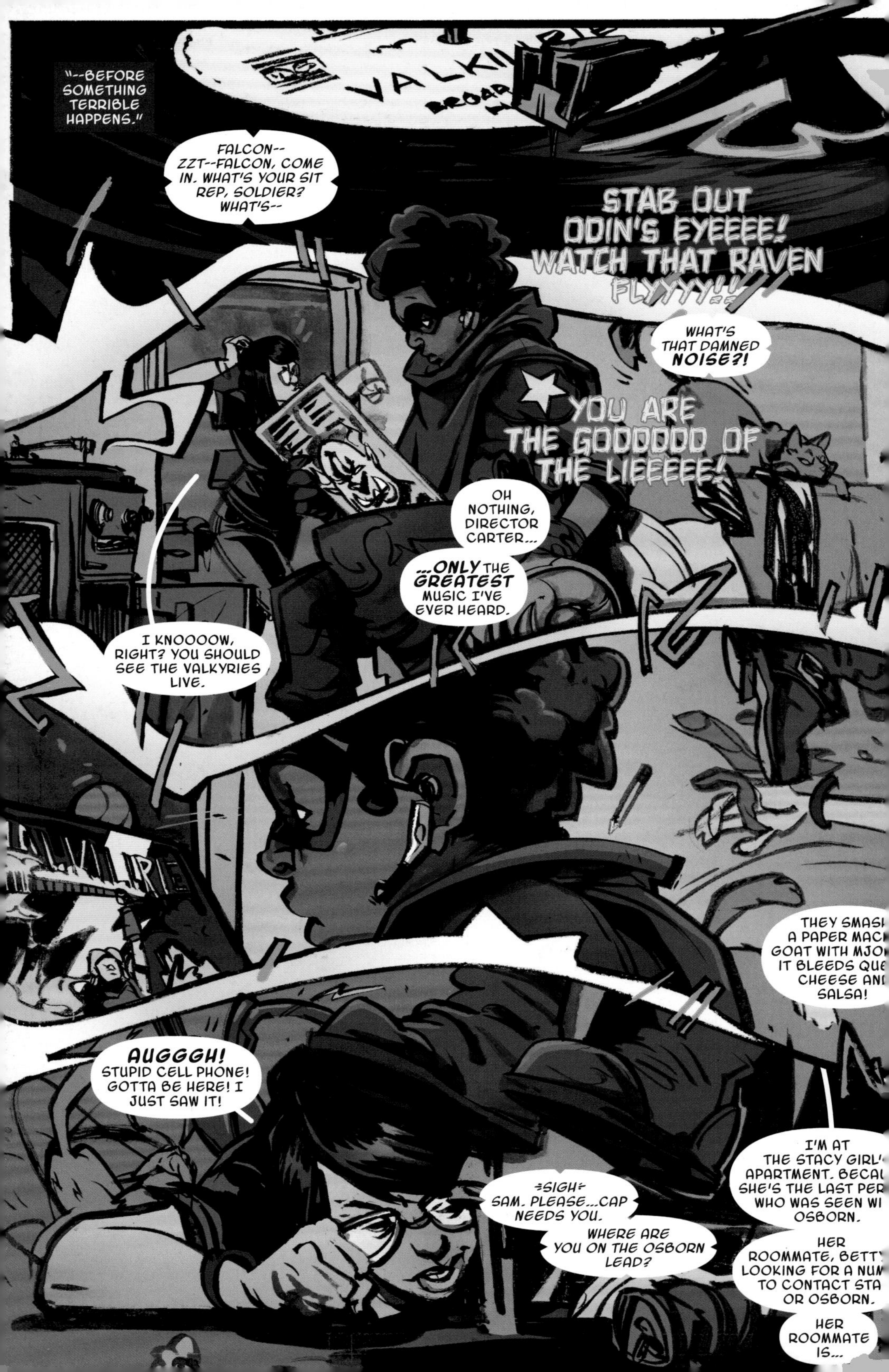
"--BEFORE SOMETHING TERRIBLE HAPPENS."
FALCON-- ZZT--FALCON, COME IN. WHAT'S YOUR SIT REP, SOLDIER? WHAT'S--
STAB OUT ODIN'S EYEEEE! WATCH THAT RAVEN FLYYYY!!
WHAT'S THAT DAMNED NOISE?!
YOU ARE THE GODDDDD OF THE LIEEEEE!
OH NOTHING, DIRECTOR CARTER...
...ONLY THE GREATEST MUSIC I'VE EVER HEARD.
I KNOOOOW, RIGHT? YOU SHOULD SEE THE VALKYRIES LIVE.
THEY SMASH A PAPER MACH GOAT WITH MJO IT BLEEDS QUE CHEESE AND SALSA!
AUGGGH! STUPID CELL PHONE! GOTTA BE HERE! I JUST SAW IT!
=SIGH= SAM. PLEASE...CAP NEEDS YOU.
WHERE ARE YOU ON THE OSBORN LEAD?
I'M AT THE STACY GIRL' APARTMENT. BECAU SHE'S THE LAST PER WHO WAS SEEN WI OSBORN.
HER ROOMMATE, BETTY LOOKING FOR A NUM TO CONTACT STA OR OSBORN.
HER ROOMMATE IS...

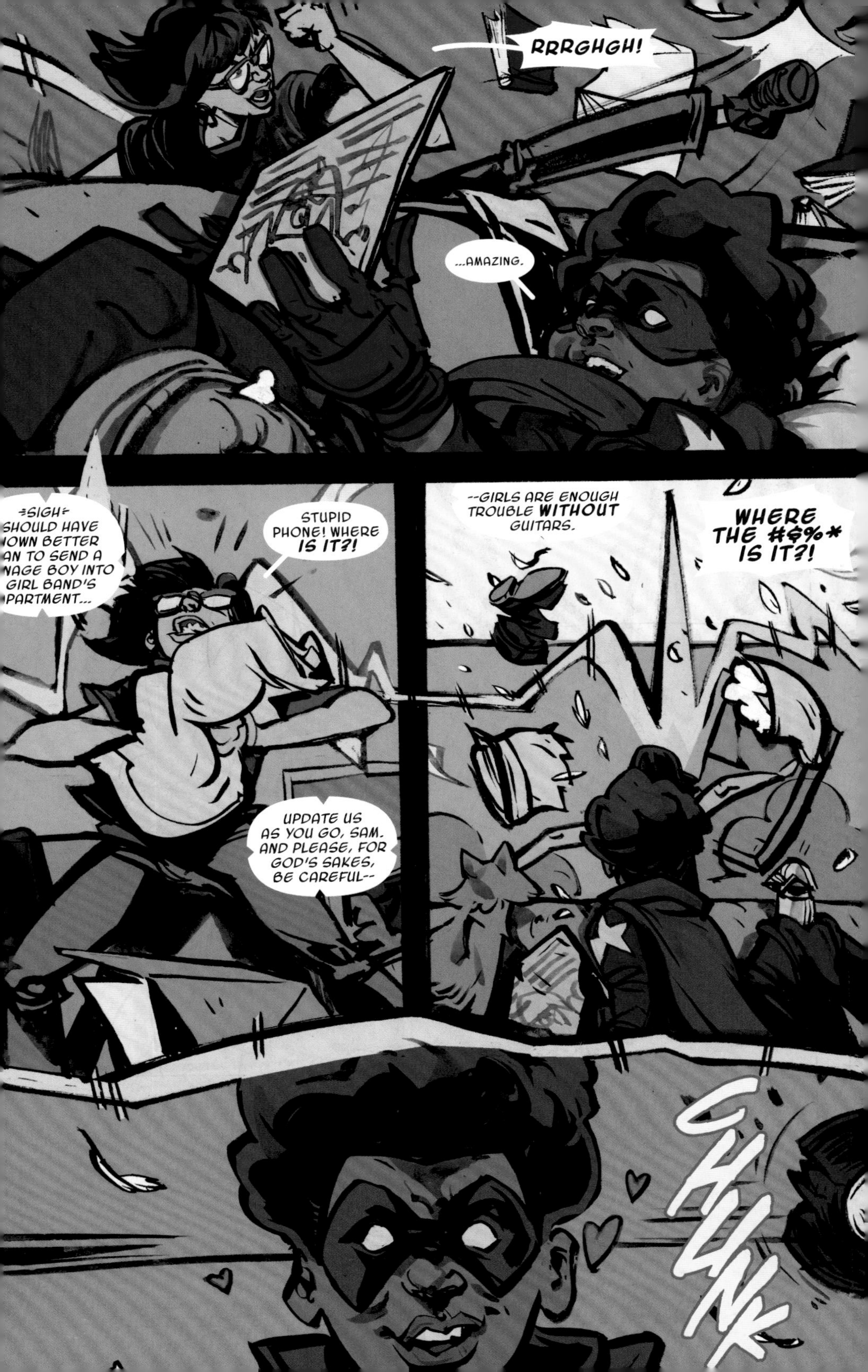
RRRGHGH!
...AMAZING.
=SIGH=
SHOULD HAVE
NOWN BETTER
AN TO SEND A
NAGE BOY INTO
GIRL BAND'S
PARTMENT...
STUPID PHONE! WHERE IS IT?!
UPDATE US AS YOU GO, SAM. AND PLEASE, FOR GOD'S SAKES, BE CAREFUL--
--GIRLS ARE ENOUGH TROUBLE WITHOUT GUITARS.
WHERE THE #$%* IS IT?!
CHUNK

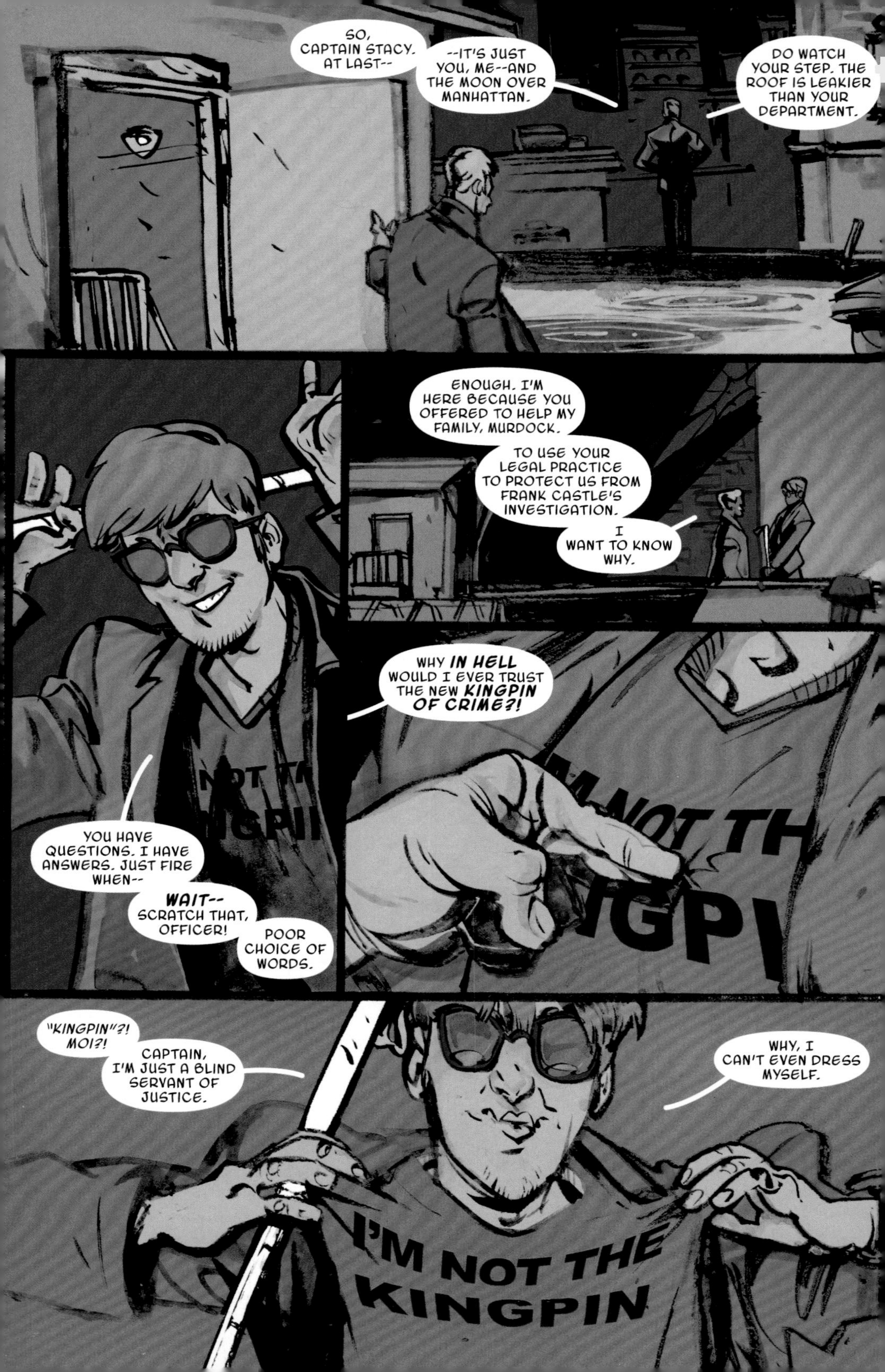
SO, CAPTAIN STACY. AT LAST--
--IT'S JUST YOU, ME--AND THE MOON OVER MANHATTAN.
DO WATCH YOUR STEP. THE ROOF IS LEAKIER THAN YOUR DEPARTMENT.
ENOUGH. I'M HERE BECAUSE YOU OFFERED TO HELP MY FAMILY, MURDOCK.
TO USE YOUR LEGAL PRACTICE TO PROTECT US FROM FRANK CASTLE'S INVESTIGATION.
I WANT TO KNOW WHY.
YOU HAVE QUESTIONS. I HAVE ANSWERS. JUST FIRE WHEN--
WAIT-- SCRATCH THAT, OFFICER!
POOR CHOICE OF WORDS.
WHY IN HELL WOULD I EVER TRUST THE NEW KINGPIN OF CRIME?!
"KINGPIN"?! MOI?!
CAPTAIN, I'M JUST A BLIND SERVANT OF JUSTICE.
WHY, I CAN'T EVEN DRESS MYSELF.
I'M NOT THE KINGPIN

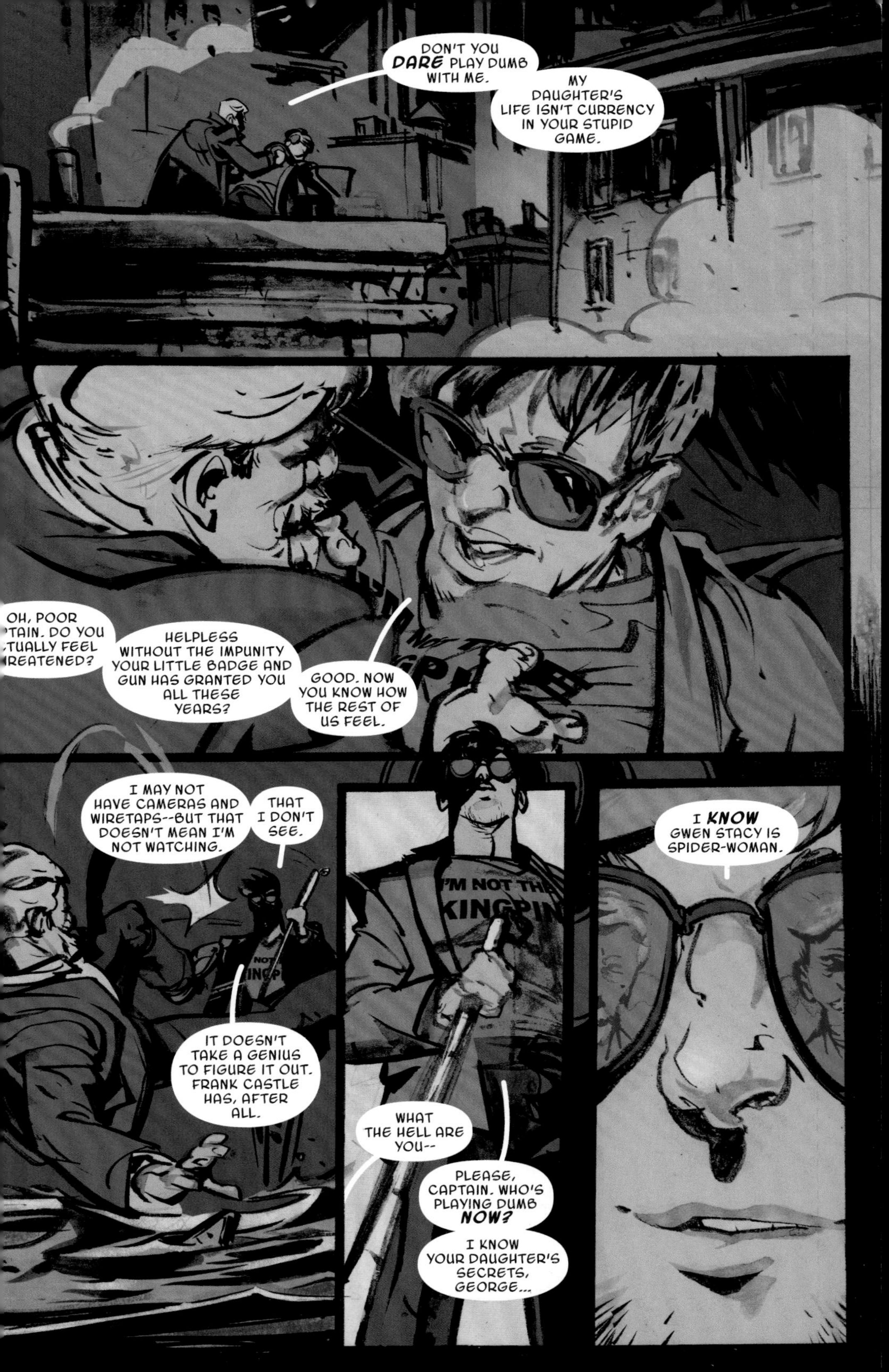
DON'T YOU DARE PLAY DUMB WITH ME.
MY DAUGHTER'S LIFE ISN'T CURRENCY IN YOUR STUPID GAME.
OH, POOR PTAIN. DO YOU TUALLY FEEL REATENED?
HELPLESS WITHOUT THE IMPUNITY YOUR LITTLE BADGE AND GUN HAS GRANTED YOU ALL THESE YEARS?
GOOD. NOW YOU KNOW HOW THE REST OF US FEEL.
I MAY NOT HAVE CAMERAS AND WIRETAPS--BUT THAT DOESN'T MEAN I'M NOT WATCHING.
THAT I DON'T SEE.
IT DOESN'T TAKE A GENIUS TO FIGURE IT OUT. FRANK CASTLE HAS, AFTER ALL.
I'M NOT THE KINGPIN
WHAT THE HELL ARE YOU--
PLEASE, CAPTAIN. WHO'S PLAYING DUMB NOW?
I KNOW YOUR DAUGHTER'S SECRETS, GEORGE...
I KNOW GWEN STACY IS SPIDER-WOMAN.

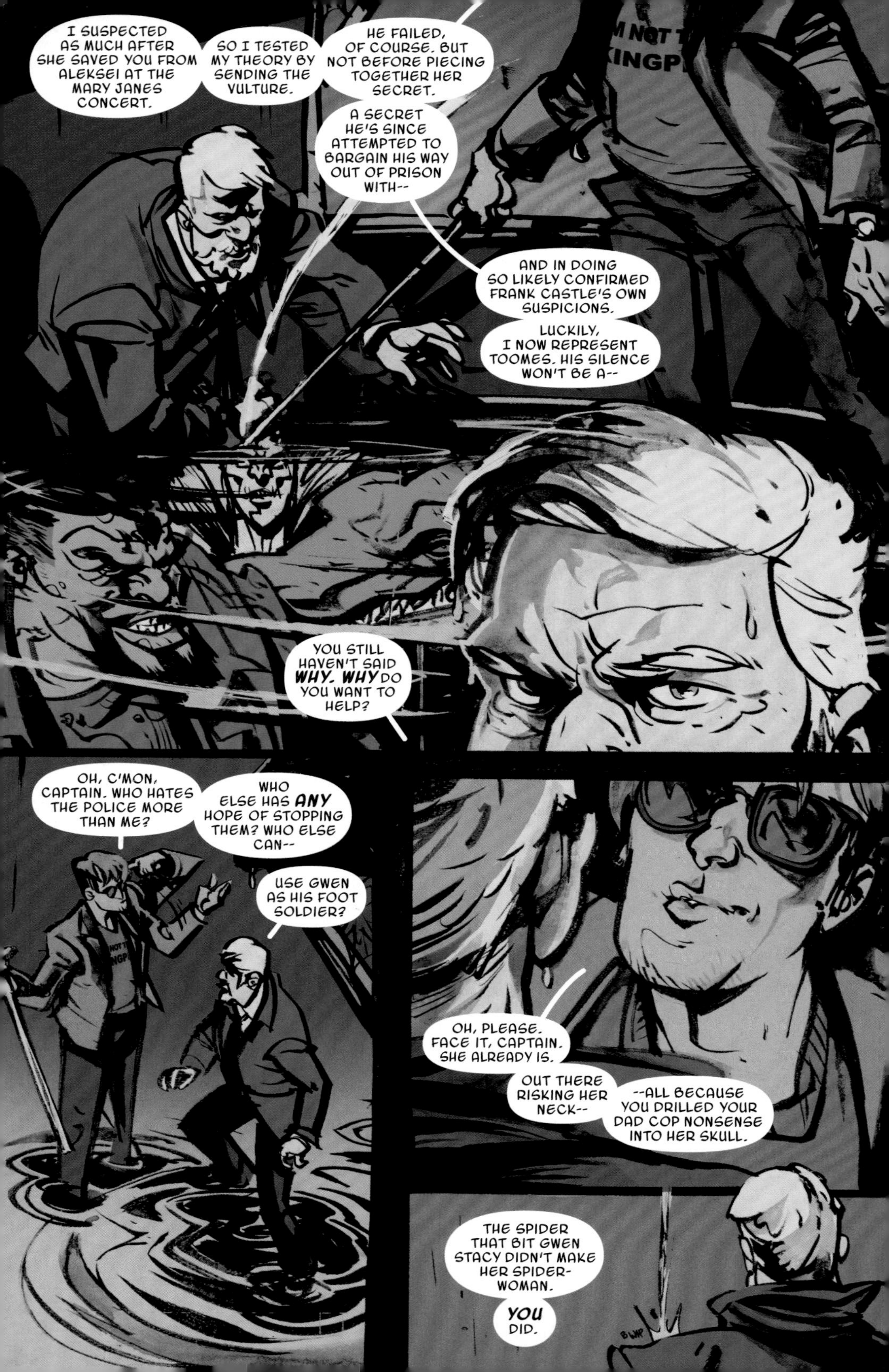
I SUSPECTED AS MUCH AFTER SHE SAVED YOU FROM ALEKSEI AT THE MARY JANES CONCERT.
SO I TESTED MY THEORY BY SENDING THE VULTURE.
HE FAILED, OF COURSE. BUT NOT BEFORE PIECING TOGETHER HER SECRET.
A SECRET HE'S SINCE ATTEMPTED TO BARGAIN HIS WAY OUT OF PRISON WITH--
AND IN DOING SO LIKELY CONFIRMED FRANK CASTLE'S OWN SUSPICIONS.
LUCKILY, I NOW REPRESENT TOOMES. HIS SILENCE WON'T BE A--
YOU STILL HAVEN'T SAID **WHY. WHY** DO YOU WANT TO HELP?
OH, C'MON, CAPTAIN. WHO HATES THE POLICE MORE THAN ME?
WHO ELSE HAS **ANY** HOPE OF STOPPING THEM? WHO ELSE CAN--
USE GWEN AS HIS FOOT SOLDIER?
OH, PLEASE. FACE IT, CAPTAIN. SHE ALREADY IS.
OUT THERE RISKING HER NECK--
--ALL BECAUSE YOU DRILLED YOUR DAD COP NONSENSE INTO HER SKULL.
THE SPIDER THAT BIT GWEN STACY DIDN'T MAKE HER SPIDER-WOMAN.
YOU DID.

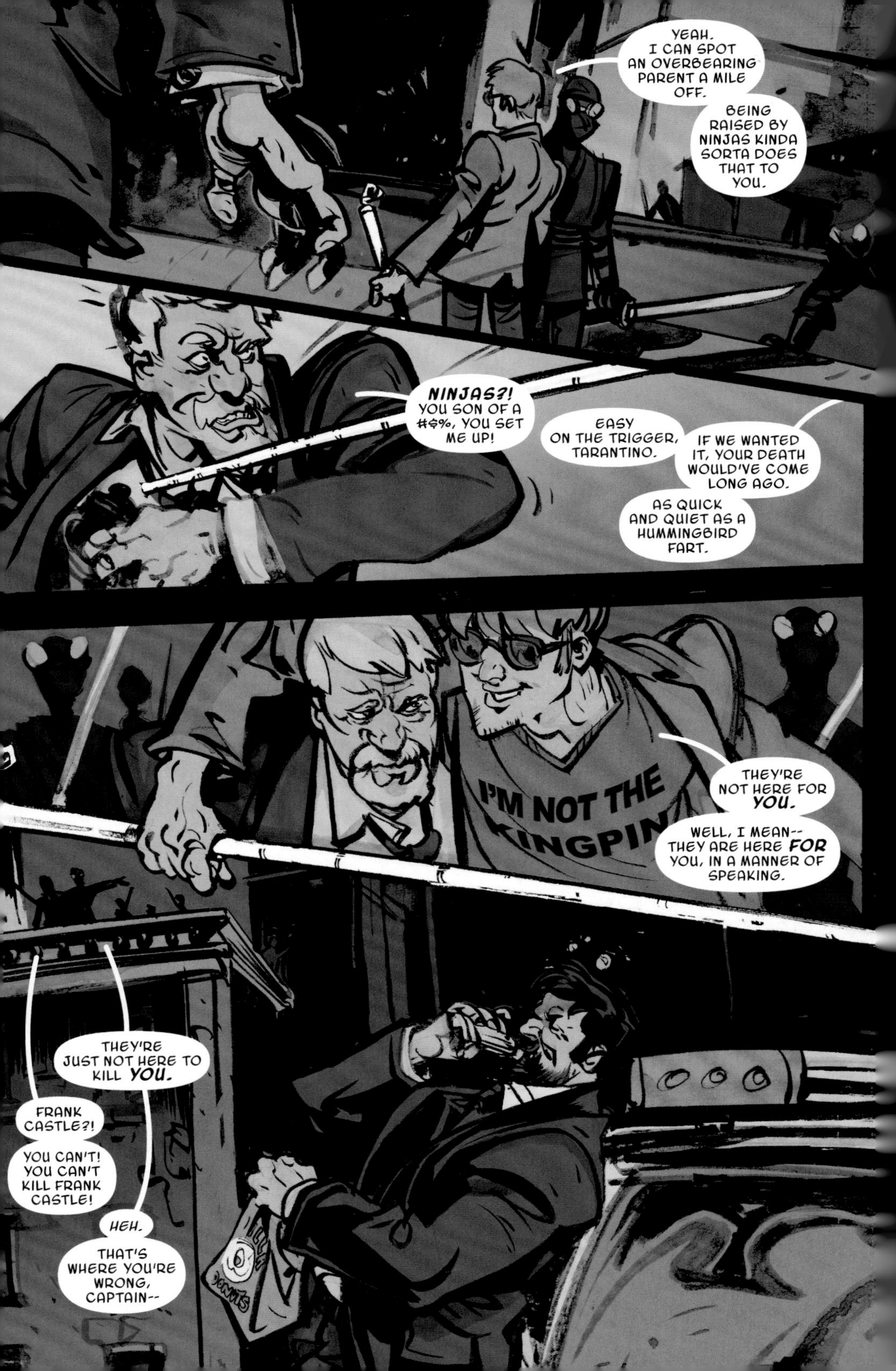
YEAH. I CAN SPOT AN OVERBEARING PARENT A MILE OFF.
BEING RAISED BY NINJAS KINDA SORTA DOES THAT TO YOU.
NINJAS?! YOU SON OF A #$%, YOU SET ME UP!
EASY ON THE TRIGGER, TARANTINO.
IF WE WANTED IT, YOUR DEATH WOULD'VE COME LONG AGO.
AS QUICK AND QUIET AS A HUMMINGBIRD FART.
I'M NOT THE KINGPIN
THEY'RE NOT HERE FOR YOU.
WELL, I MEAN-- THEY ARE HERE FOR YOU, IN A MANNER OF SPEAKING.
THEY'RE JUST NOT HERE TO KILL YOU.
FRANK CASTLE?!
YOU CAN'T! YOU CAN'T KILL FRANK CASTLE!
HEH.
THAT'S WHERE YOU'RE WRONG, CAPTAIN--

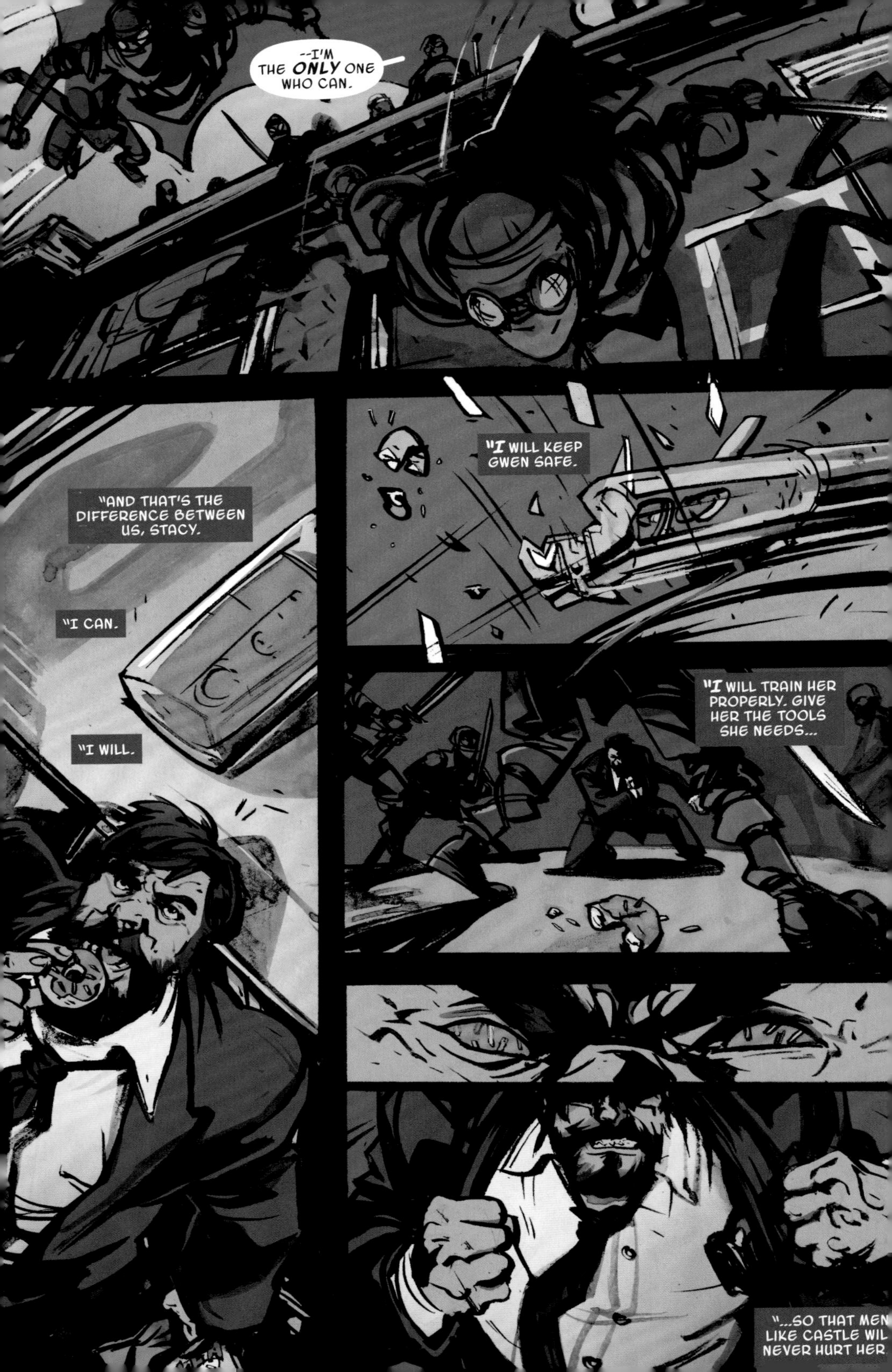
--I'M THE ONLY ONE WHO CAN.
"AND THAT'S THE DIFFERENCE BETWEEN US, STACY.
"I CAN.
"I WILL.
"I WILL KEEP GWEN SAFE.
"I WILL TRAIN HER PROPERLY. GIVE HER THE TOOLS SHE NEEDS...
"...SO THAT MEN LIKE CASTLE WIL NEVER HURT HER

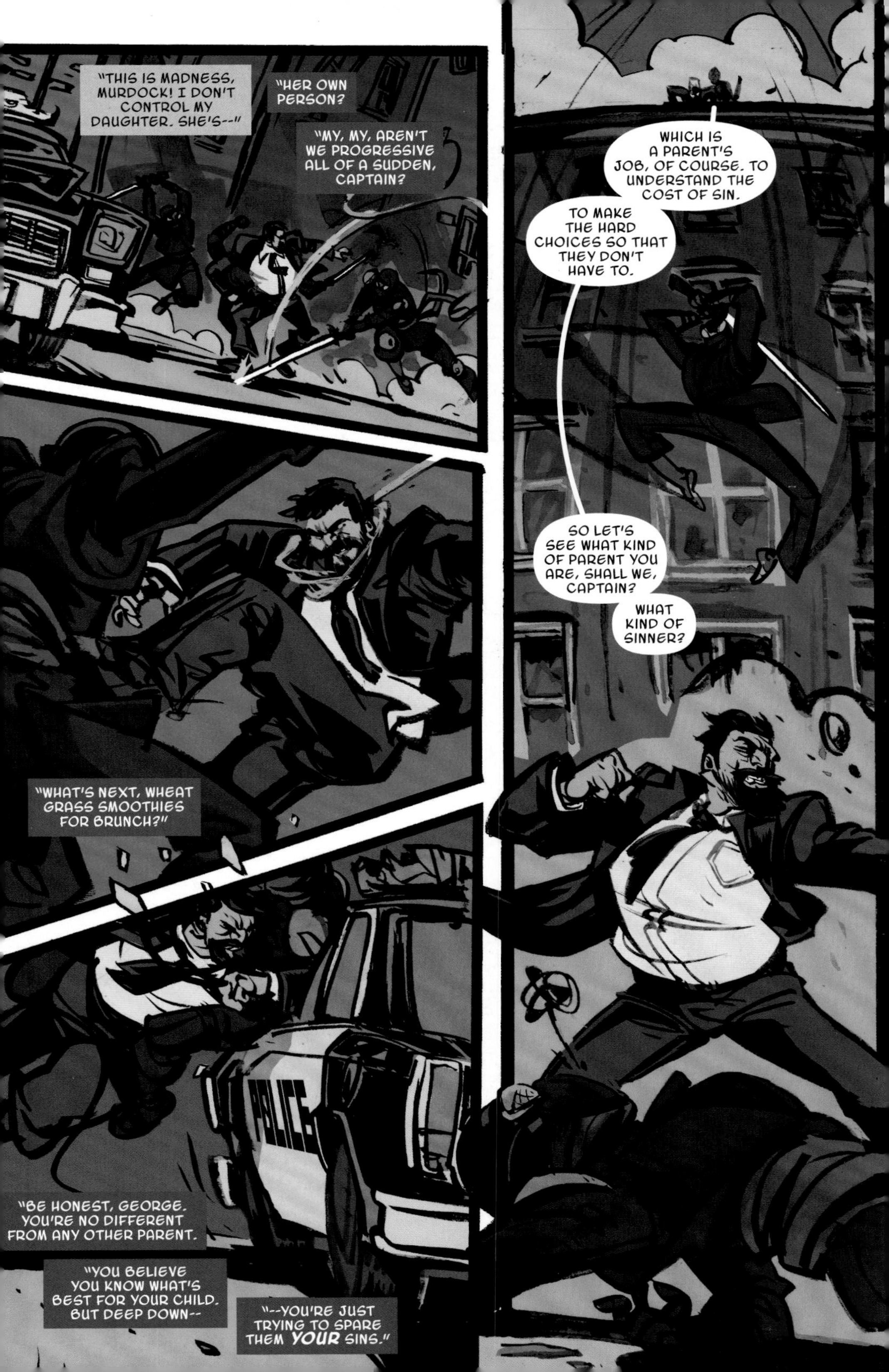
"THIS IS MADNESS, MURDOCK! I DON'T CONTROL MY DAUGHTER. SHE'S--"
"HER OWN PERSON?
"MY, MY, AREN'T WE PROGRESSIVE ALL OF A SUDDEN, CAPTAIN?
"WHAT'S NEXT, WHEAT GRASS SMOOTHIES FOR BRUNCH?"
"BE HONEST, GEORGE. YOU'RE NO DIFFERENT FROM ANY OTHER PARENT.
"YOU BELIEVE YOU KNOW WHAT'S BEST FOR YOUR CHILD. BUT DEEP DOWN--
"--YOU'RE JUST TRYING TO SPARE THEM *YOUR* SINS."
POLICE
WHICH IS A PARENT'S JOB, OF COURSE. TO UNDERSTAND THE COST OF SIN.
TO MAKE THE HARD CHOICES SO THAT THEY DON'T HAVE TO.
SO LET'S SEE WHAT KIND OF PARENT YOU ARE, SHALL WE, CAPTAIN?
WHAT KIND OF SINNER?

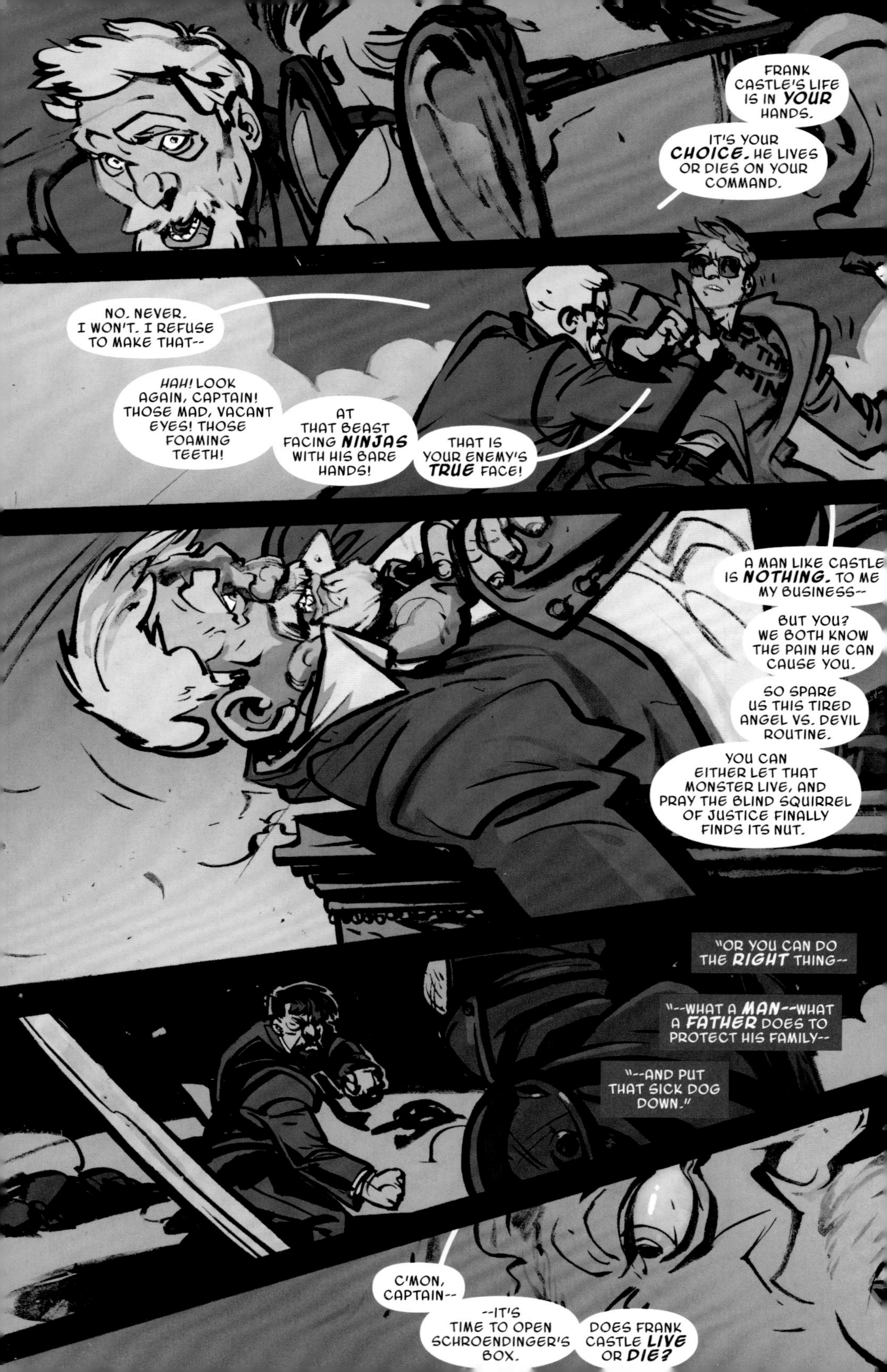

FRANK CASTLE'S LIFE IS IN YOUR HANDS.
IT'S YOUR CHOICE. HE LIVES OR DIES ON YOUR COMMAND.
NO. NEVER. I WON'T. I REFUSE TO MAKE THAT--
HAH! LOOK AGAIN, CAPTAIN! THOSE MAD, VACANT EYES! THOSE FOAMING TEETH!
AT THAT BEAST FACING NINJAS WITH HIS BARE HANDS!
THAT IS YOUR ENEMY'S TRUE FACE!
A MAN LIKE CASTLE IS NOTHING. TO ME MY BUSINESS--
BUT YOU? WE BOTH KNOW THE PAIN HE CAN CAUSE YOU.
SO SPARE US THIS TIRED ANGEL VS. DEVIL ROUTINE.
YOU CAN EITHER LET THAT MONSTER LIVE, AND PRAY THE BLIND SQUIRREL OF JUSTICE FINALLY FINDS ITS NUT.
"OR YOU CAN DO THE RIGHT THING--
"--WHAT A MAN--WHAT A FATHER DOES TO PROTECT HIS FAMILY--
"--AND PUT THAT SICK DOG DOWN."
C'MON, CAPTAIN--
--IT'S TIME TO OPEN SCHROENDINGER'S BOX.
DOES FRANK CASTLE LIVE OR DIE?

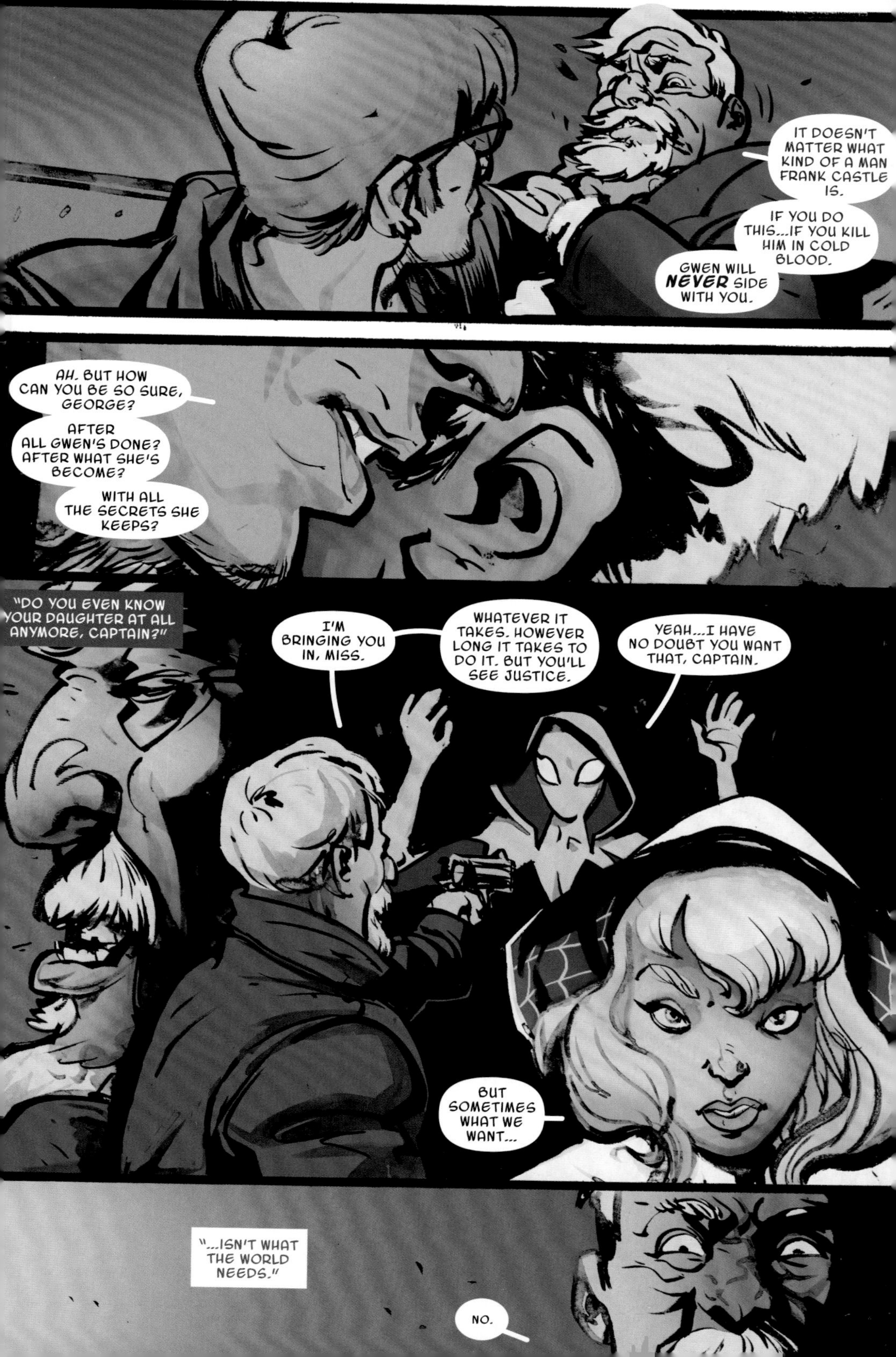
IT DOESN'T MATTER WHAT KIND OF A MAN FRANK CASTLE IS.
IF YOU DO THIS...IF YOU KILL HIM IN COLD BLOOD.
GWEN WILL **NEVER** SIDE WITH YOU.
AH. BUT HOW CAN YOU BE SO SURE, GEORGE?
AFTER ALL GWEN'S DONE? AFTER WHAT SHE'S BECOME?
WITH ALL THE SECRETS SHE KEEPS?
"DO YOU EVEN KNOW YOUR DAUGHTER AT ALL ANYMORE, CAPTAIN?"
I'M BRINGING YOU IN, MISS.
WHATEVER IT TAKES. HOWEVER LONG IT TAKES TO DO IT. BUT YOU'LL SEE JUSTICE.
YEAH...I HAVE NO DOUBT YOU WANT THAT, CAPTAIN.
BUT SOMETIMES WHAT WE WANT...
"...ISN'T WHAT THE WORLD NEEDS."
NO.

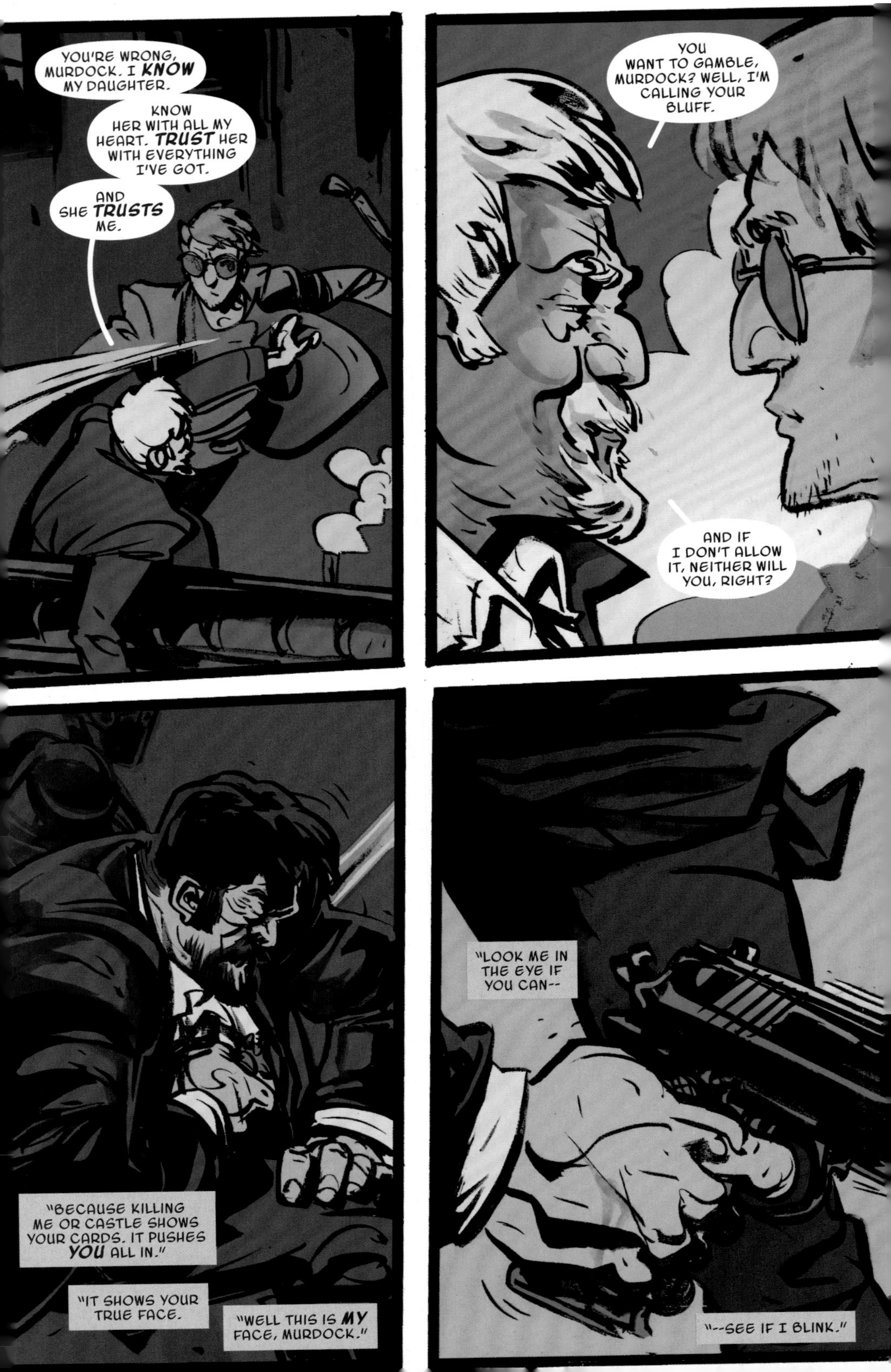
YOU'RE WRONG, MURDOCK. I KNOW MY DAUGHTER.
KNOW HER WITH ALL MY HEART. TRUST HER WITH EVERYTHING I'VE GOT.
AND SHE TRUSTS ME.
YOU WANT TO GAMBLE, MURDOCK? WELL, I'M CALLING YOUR BLUFF.
AND IF I DON'T ALLOW IT, NEITHER WILL YOU, RIGHT?
"BECAUSE KILLING ME OR CASTLE SHOWS YOUR CARDS. IT PUSHES YOU ALL IN."
"IT SHOWS YOUR TRUE FACE.
"WELL THIS IS MY FACE, MURDOCK."
"LOOK ME IN THE EYE IF YOU CAN--
"--SEE IF I BLINK."

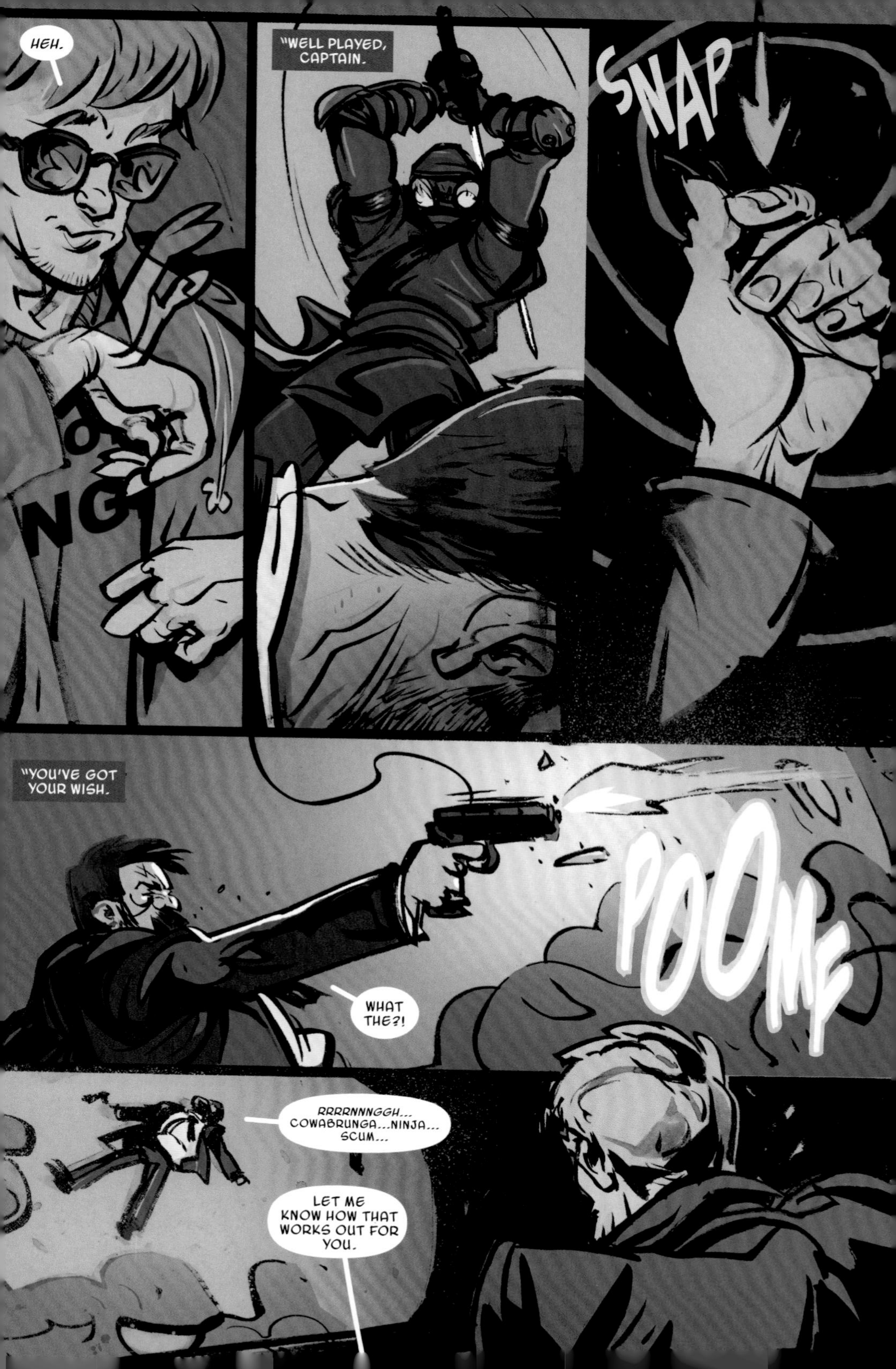
HEH.
"WELL PLAYED, CAPTAIN.
SNAP
"YOU'VE GOT YOUR WISH.
POOMF
WHAT THE?!
RRRRNNNGGH... COWABRUNGA...NINJA... SCUM...
LET ME KNOW HOW THAT WORKS OUT FOR YOU.

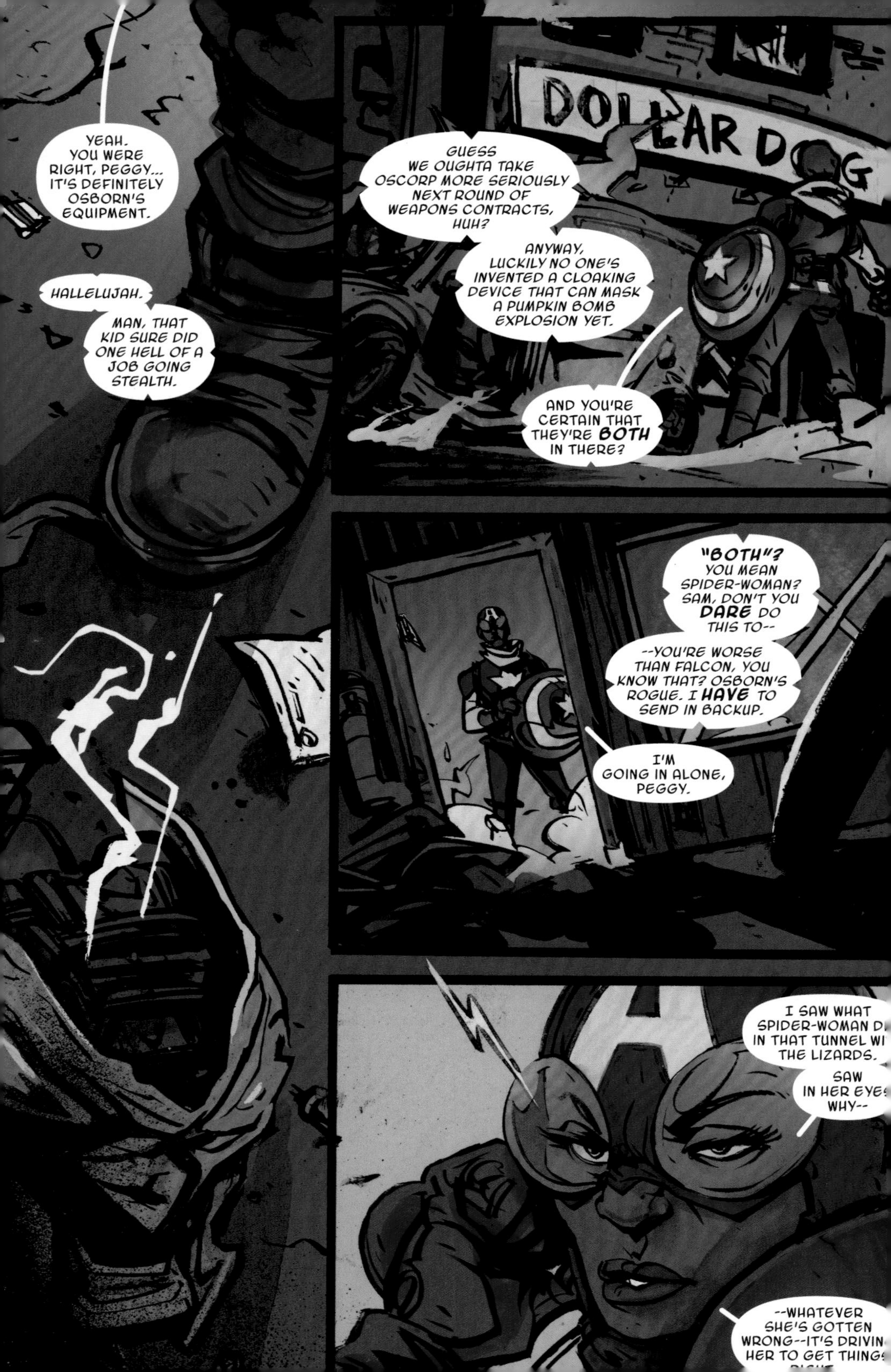
YEAH. YOU WERE RIGHT, PEGGY... IT'S DEFINITELY OSBORN'S EQUIPMENT.
HALLELUJAH.
MAN, THAT KID SURE DID ONE HELL OF A JOB GOING STEALTH.
DOLLAR DOG
GUESS WE OUGHTA TAKE OSCORP MORE SERIOUSLY NEXT ROUND OF WEAPONS CONTRACTS, HUH?
ANYWAY, LUCKILY NO ONE'S INVENTED A CLOAKING DEVICE THAT CAN MASK A PUMPKIN BOMB EXPLOSION YET.
AND YOU'RE CERTAIN THAT THEY'RE BOTH IN THERE?
"BOTH"? YOU MEAN SPIDER-WOMAN? SAM, DON'T YOU DARE DO THIS TO--
--YOU'RE WORSE THAN FALCON, YOU KNOW THAT? OSBORN'S ROGUE. I HAVE TO SEND IN BACKUP.
I'M GOING IN ALONE, PEGGY.
I SAW WHAT SPIDER-WOMAN D
IN THAT TUNNEL W
THE LIZARDS.
SAW IN HER EYE
WHY--
--WHATEVER SHE'S GOTTEN WRONG--IT'S DRIVIN
HER TO GET THING

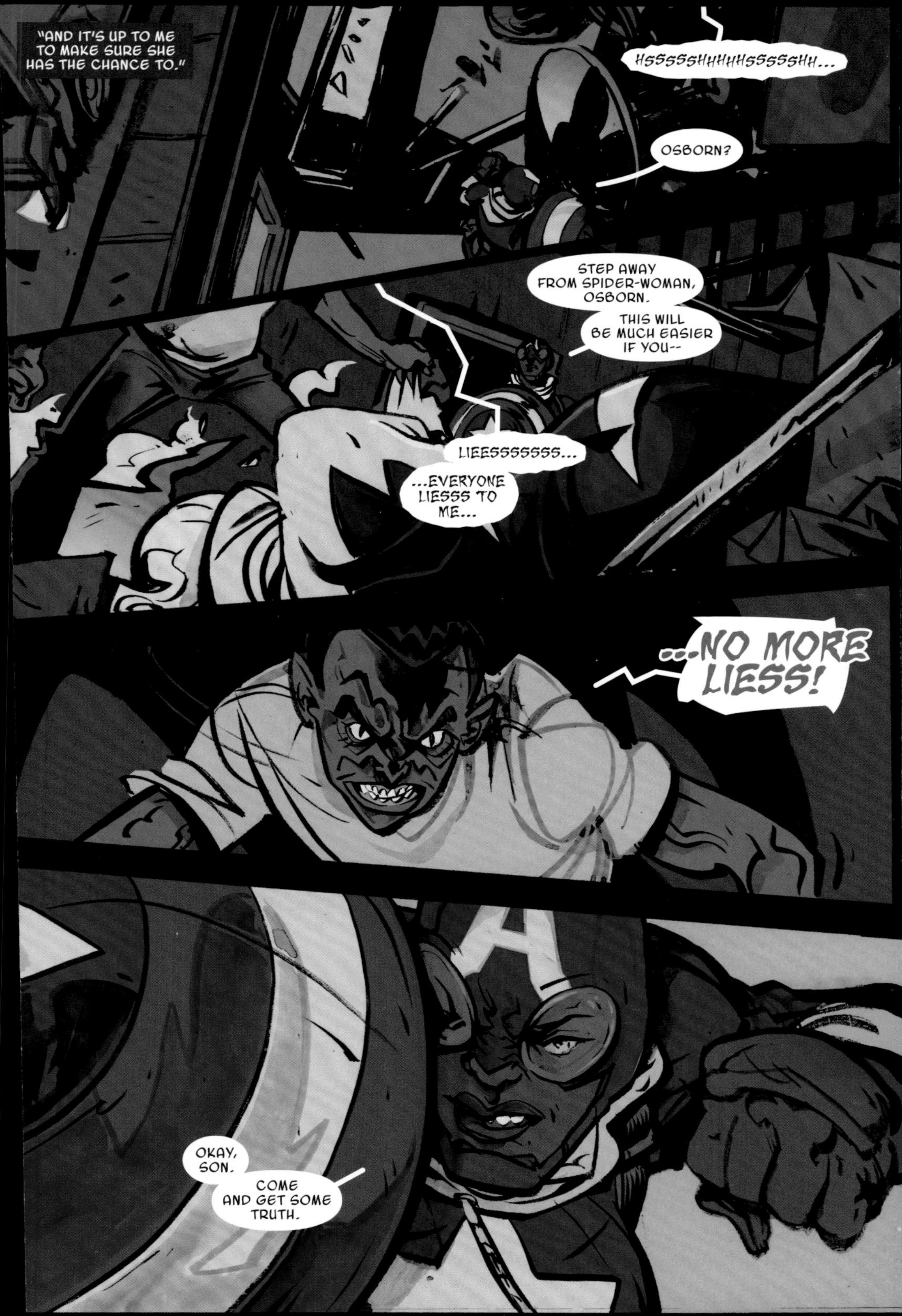
"AND IT'S UP TO ME TO MAKE SURE SHE HAS THE CHANCE TO."
HSSSSSHHHHHSSSSSHH...
OSBORN?
STEP AWAY FROM SPIDER-WOMAN, OSBORN.
THIS WILL BE MUCH EASIER IF YOU--
LIEESSSSSSSS...
...EVERYONE LIESSS TO ME...
...NO MORE LIESS!
OKAY, SON.
COME AND GET SOME TRUTH.

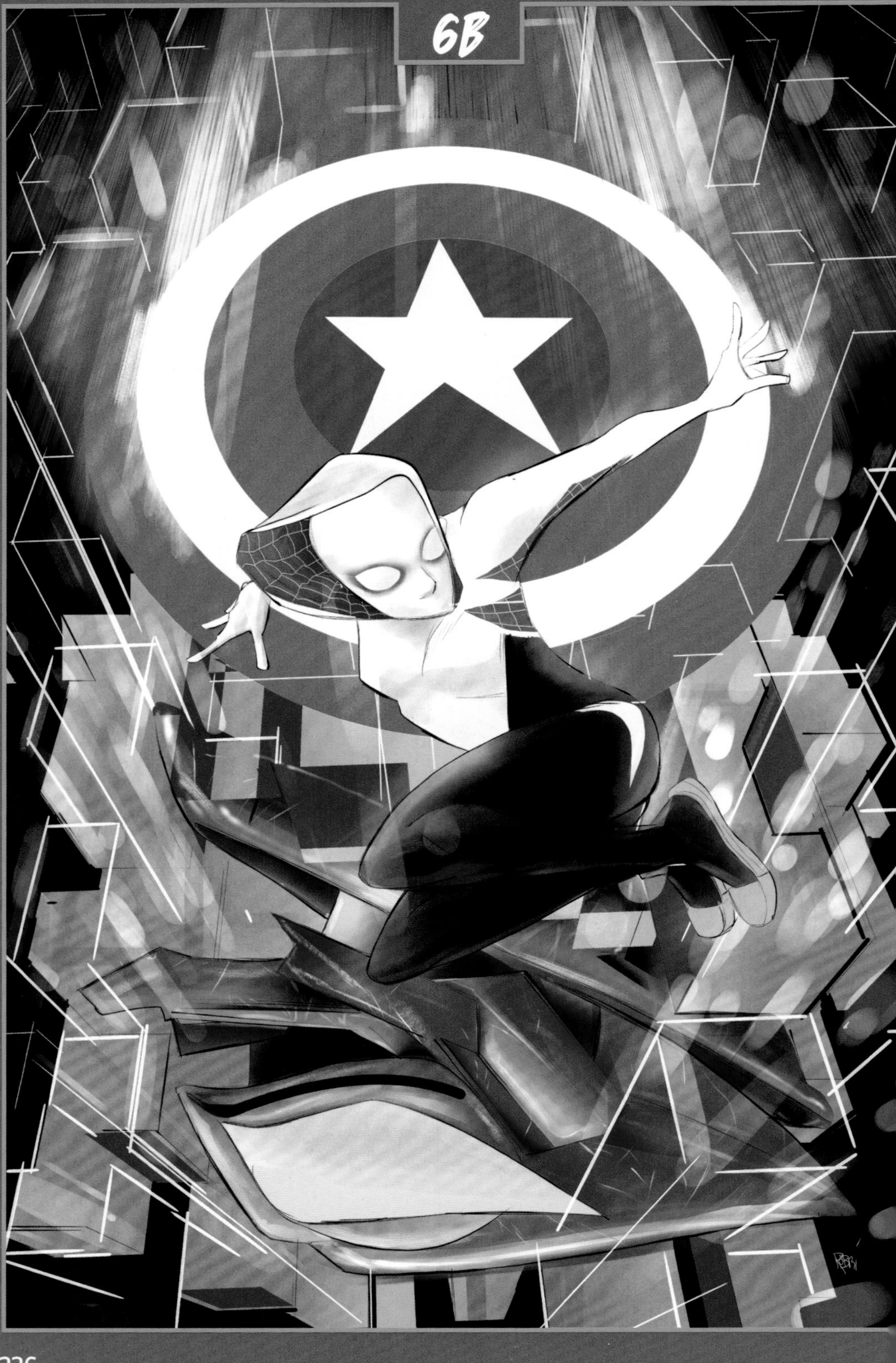
6B

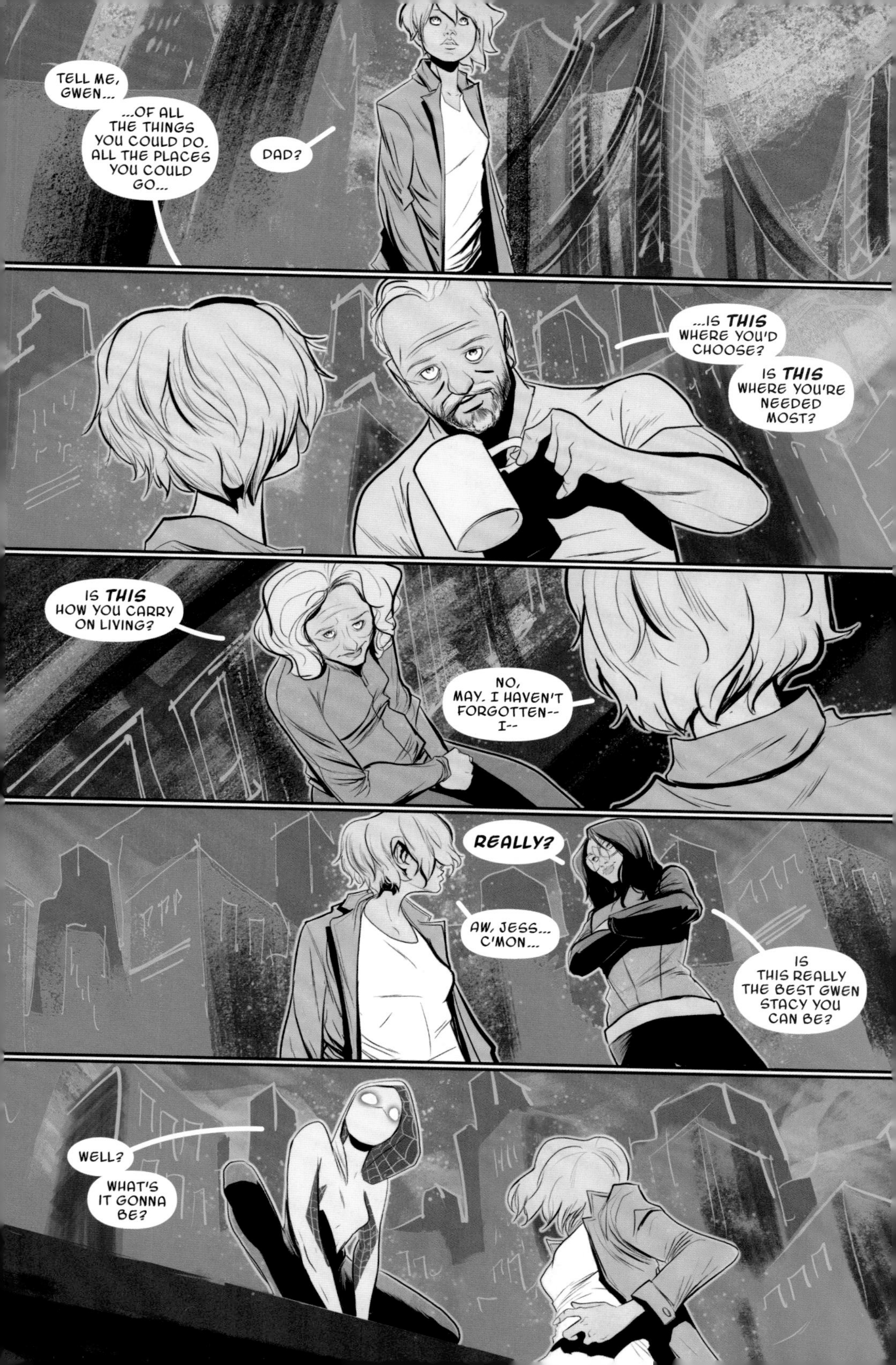
TELL ME, GWEN...
...OF ALL THE THINGS YOU COULD DO. ALL THE PLACES YOU COULD GO...
DAD?
...IS **THIS** WHERE YOU'D CHOOSE?
IS **THIS** WHERE YOU'RE NEEDED MOST?
IS **THIS** HOW YOU CARRY ON LIVING?
NO, MAY. I HAVEN'T FORGOTTEN-- I--
REALLY?
AW, JESS... C'MON...
IS THIS REALLY THE BEST GWEN STACY YOU CAN BE?
WELL?
WHAT'S IT GONNA BE?

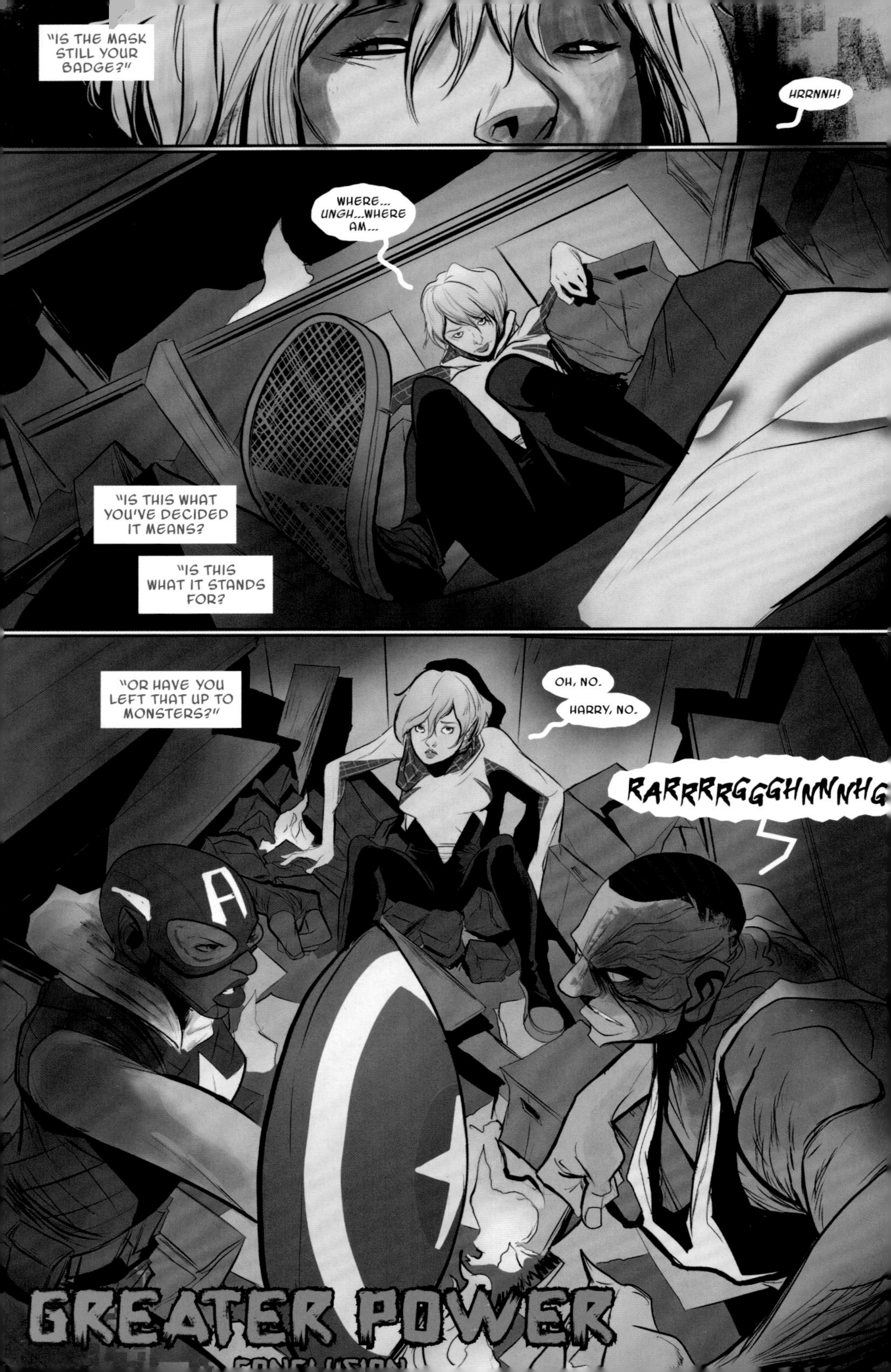
"IS THE MASK STILL YOUR BADGE?"
HRRNNH!
WHERE... UNGH...WHERE AM...
"IS THIS WHAT YOU'VE DECIDED IT MEANS?
"IS THIS WHAT IT STANDS FOR?
"OR HAVE YOU LEFT THAT UP TO MONSTERS?"
OH, NO.
HARRY, NO.
RARRRRGGGHNNNHG
GREATER POWER

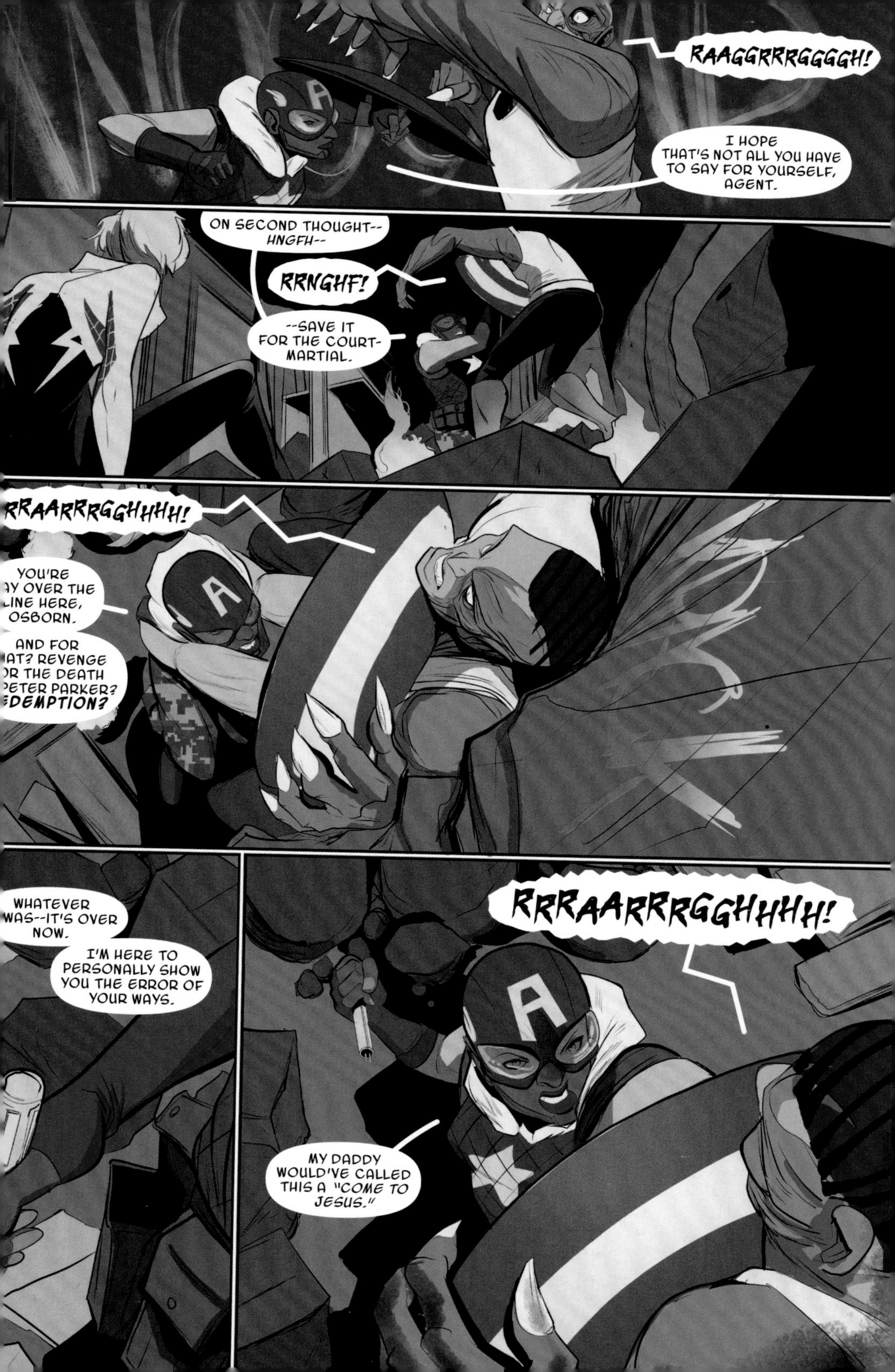
RAAGGRRRGGGGH!
I HOPE THAT'S NOT ALL YOU HAVE TO SAY FOR YOURSELF, AGENT.
ON SECOND THOUGHT-- HNGFH--
RRNGHF!
--SAVE IT FOR THE COURT-MARTIAL.
RRAARRRGGHHHH!
YOU'RE AY OVER THE LINE HERE, OSBORN.
AND FOR AT? REVENGE OR THE DEATH PETER PARKER? EDEMPTION?
WHATEVER WAS--IT'S OVER NOW.
I'M HERE TO PERSONALLY SHOW YOU THE ERROR OF YOUR WAYS.
RRRAARRRGGHHHH!
MY DADDY WOULD'VE CALLED THIS A "COME TO JESUS."

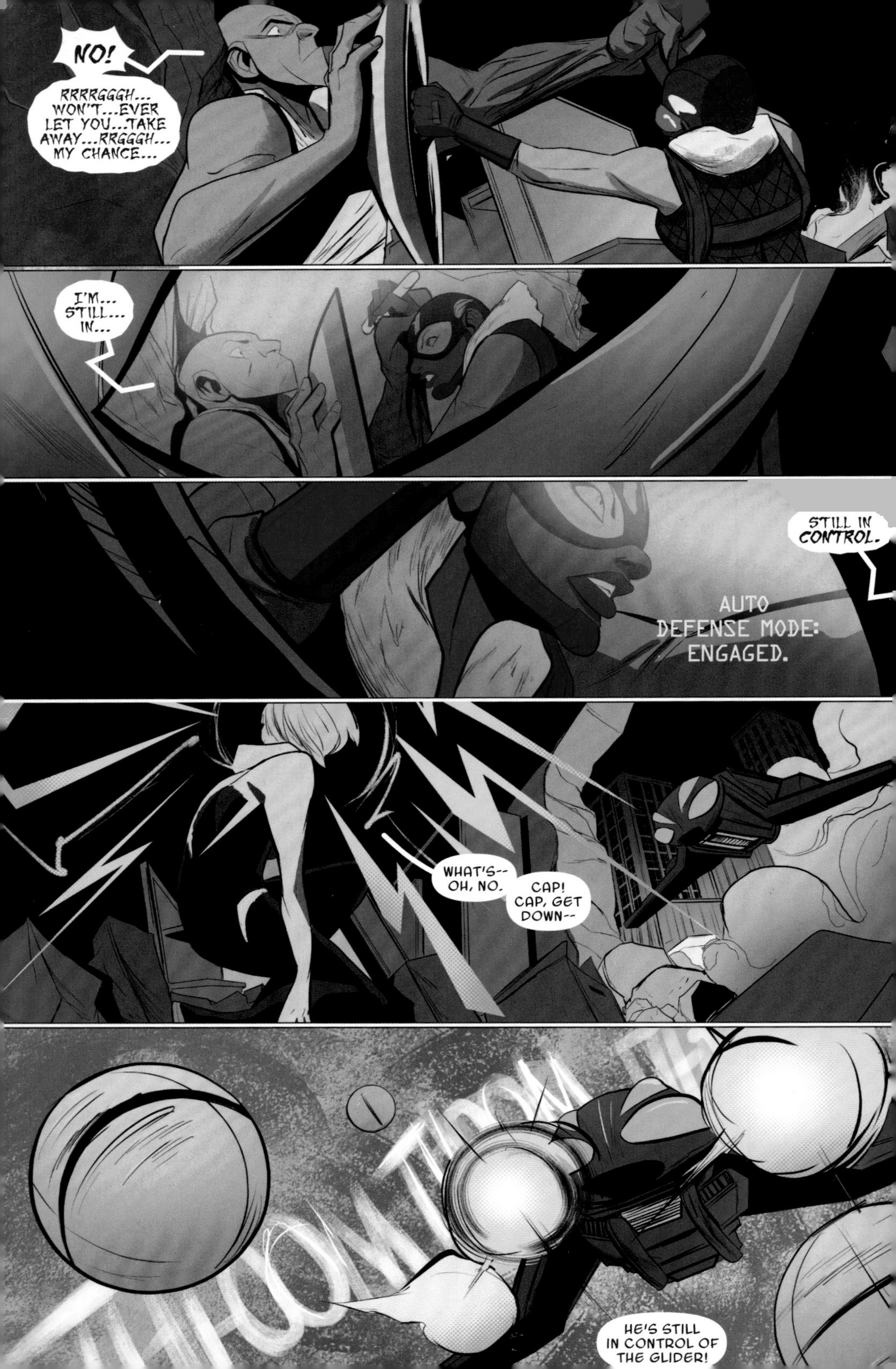
NO!
RRRRGGGH... WON'T...EVER LET YOU...TAKE AWAY...RRGGGH... MY CHANCE...
I'M... STILL... IN...
STILL IN CONTROL.
AUTO DEFENSE MODE: ENGAGED.
WHAT'S-- OH, NO.
CAP! CAP, GET DOWN--
THOOM THOOM THOOM
HE'S STILL IN CONTROL OF THE GLIDER!

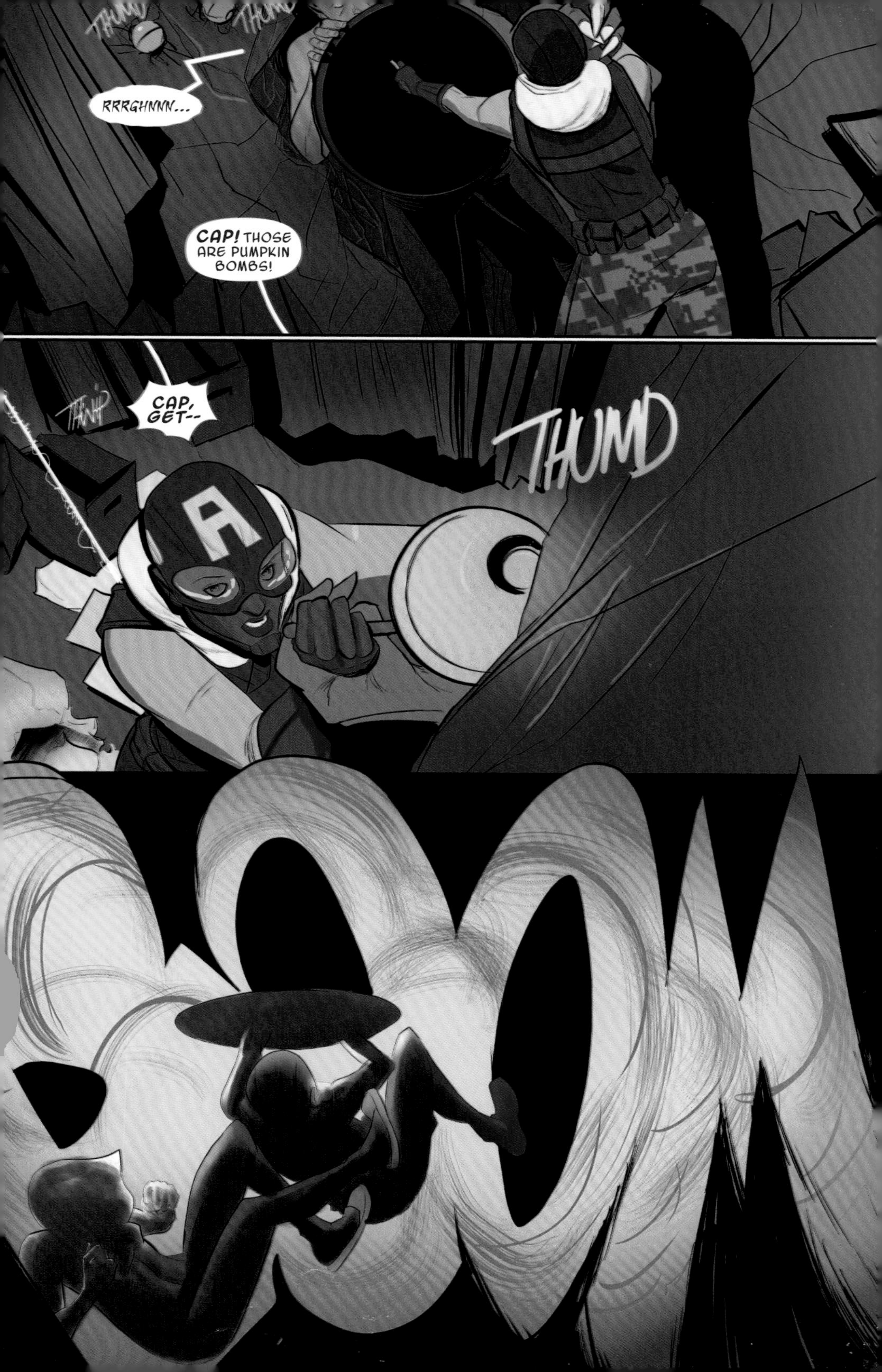
THUMD
THUMD
RRRGHNNN...
CAP! THOSE ARE PUMPKIN BOMBS!
THWIP
CAP, GET--
THUMD

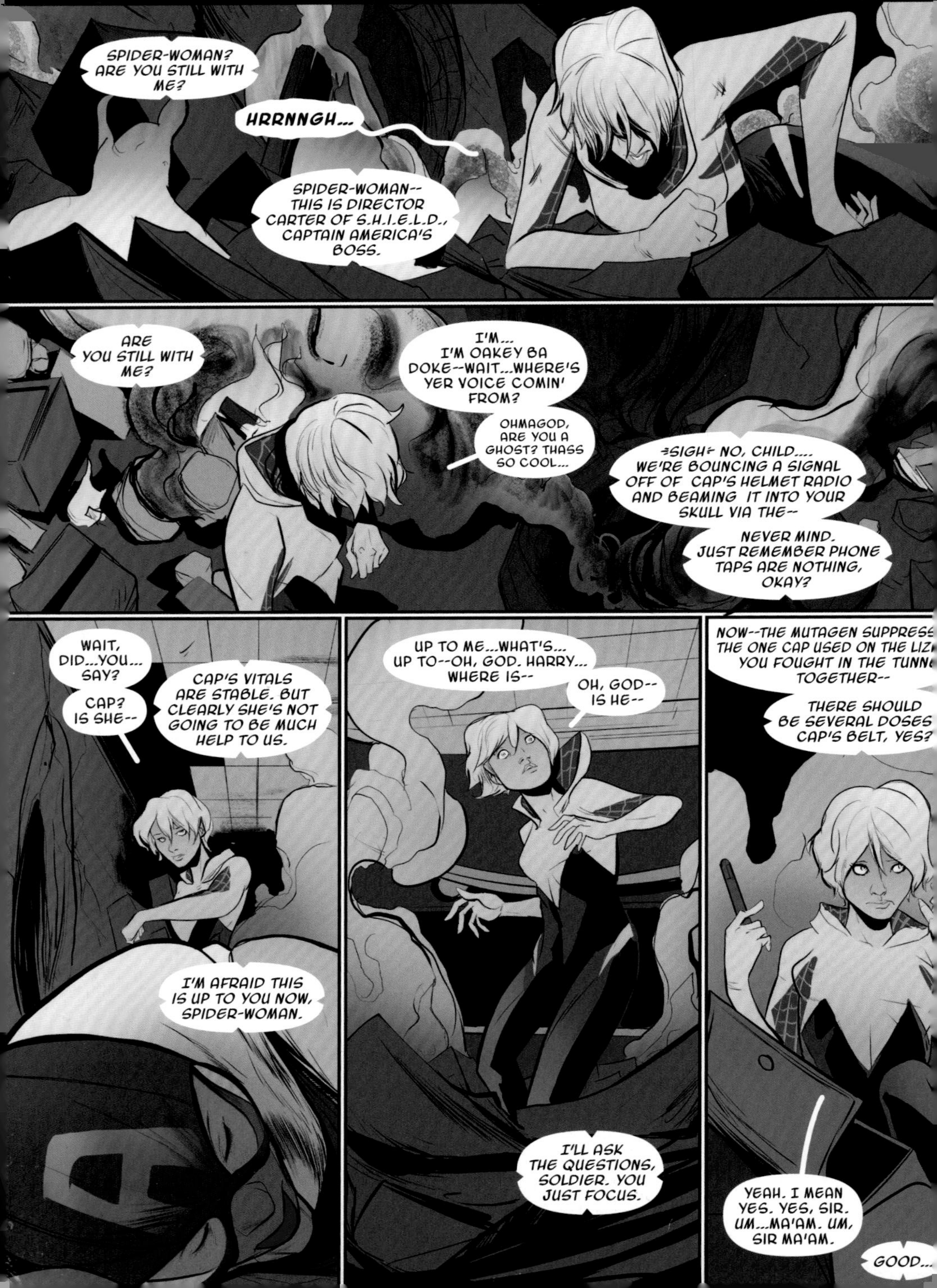
SPIDER-WOMAN? ARE YOU STILL WITH ME?
HRRNNGH...
SPIDER-WOMAN-- THIS IS DIRECTOR CARTER OF S.H.I.E.L.D., CAPTAIN AMERICA'S BOSS.
ARE YOU STILL WITH ME?
I'M... I'M OAKEY BA DOKE--WAIT...WHERE'S YER VOICE COMIN' FROM?
OHMAGOD, ARE YOU A GHOST? THASS SO COOL...
=SIGH= NO, CHILD.... WE'RE BOUNCING A SIGNAL OFF OF CAP'S HELMET RADIO AND BEAMING IT INTO YOUR SKULL VIA THE--
NEVER MIND. JUST REMEMBER PHONE TAPS ARE NOTHING, OKAY?
WAIT, DID...YOU... SAY?
CAP? IS SHE--
CAP'S VITALS ARE STABLE. BUT CLEARLY SHE'S NOT GOING TO BE MUCH HELP TO US.
I'M AFRAID THIS IS UP TO YOU NOW, SPIDER-WOMAN.
UP TO ME...WHAT'S... UP TO--OH, GOD. HARRY... WHERE IS--
OH, GOD-- IS HE--
I'LL ASK THE QUESTIONS, SOLDIER. YOU JUST FOCUS.
NOW--THE MUTAGEN SUPPRESS THE ONE CAP USED ON THE LIZ YOU FOUGHT IN THE TUNN TOGETHER--
THERE SHOULD BE SEVERAL DOSES CAP'S BELT, YES?
YEAH. I MEAN YES. YES, SIR. UM...MA'AM. UM, SIR MA'AM.
GOOD...

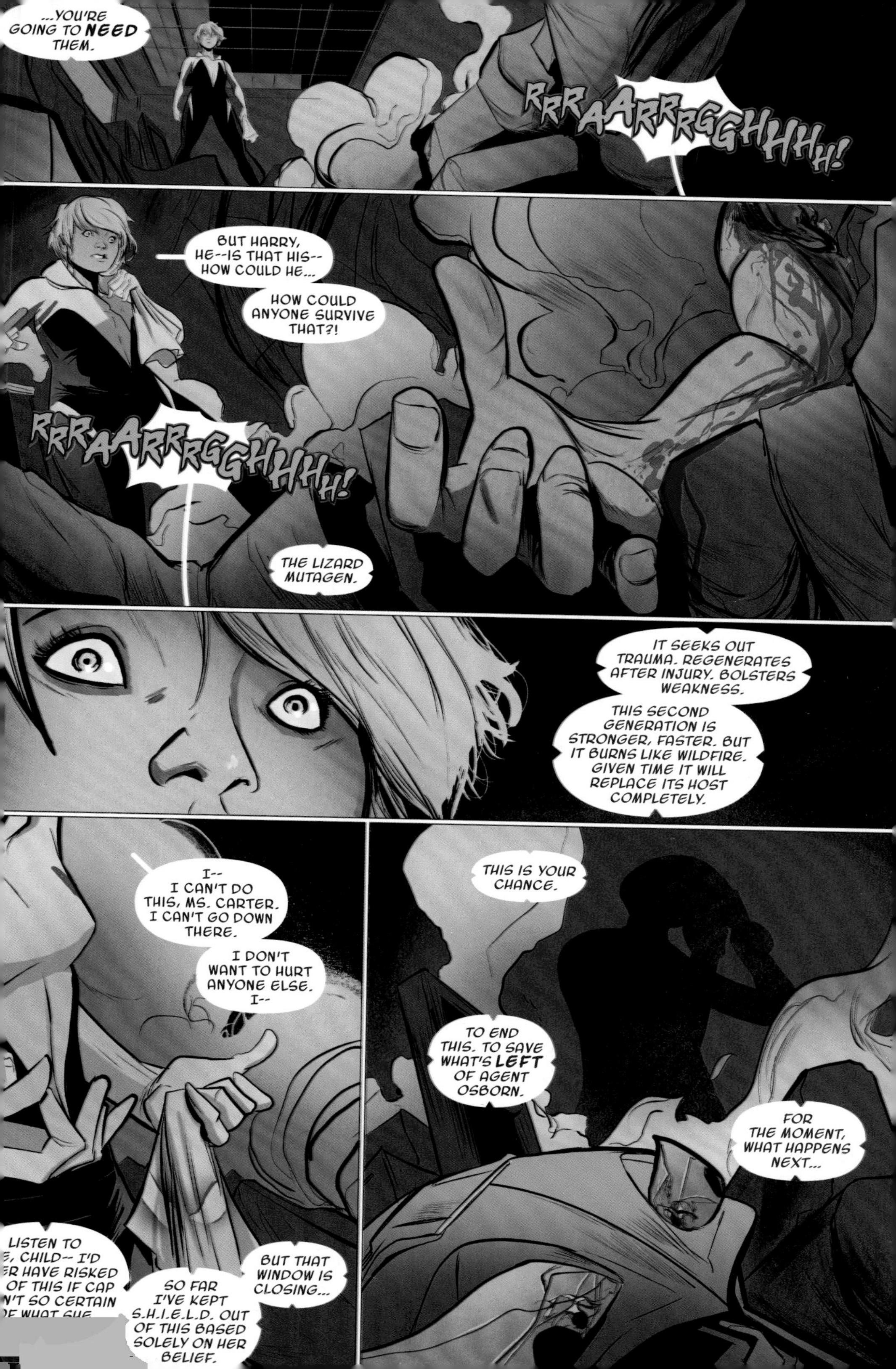

...YOU'RE GOING TO NEED THEM.
RRRAARRRGGHHHH!
BUT HARRY, HE--IS THAT HIS-- HOW COULD HE...
HOW COULD ANYONE SURVIVE THAT?!
RRRAARRRGGHHHH!
THE LIZARD MUTAGEN.
IT SEEKS OUT TRAUMA. REGENERATES AFTER INJURY. BOLSTERS WEAKNESS.
THIS SECOND GENERATION IS STRONGER, FASTER. BUT IT BURNS LIKE WILDFIRE. GIVEN TIME IT WILL REPLACE ITS HOST COMPLETELY.
I-- I CAN'T DO THIS, MS. CARTER. I CAN'T GO DOWN THERE.
I DON'T WANT TO HURT ANYONE ELSE. I--
LISTEN TO E, CHILD-- I'D ER HAVE RISKED OF THIS IF CAP N'T SO CERTAIN
SO FAR I'VE KEPT S.H.I.E.L.D. OUT OF THIS BASED SOLELY ON HER BELIEF.
BUT THAT WINDOW IS CLOSING...
THIS IS YOUR CHANCE.
TO END THIS. TO SAVE WHAT'S LEFT OF AGENT OSBORN.
FOR THE MOMENT, WHAT HAPPENS NEXT...

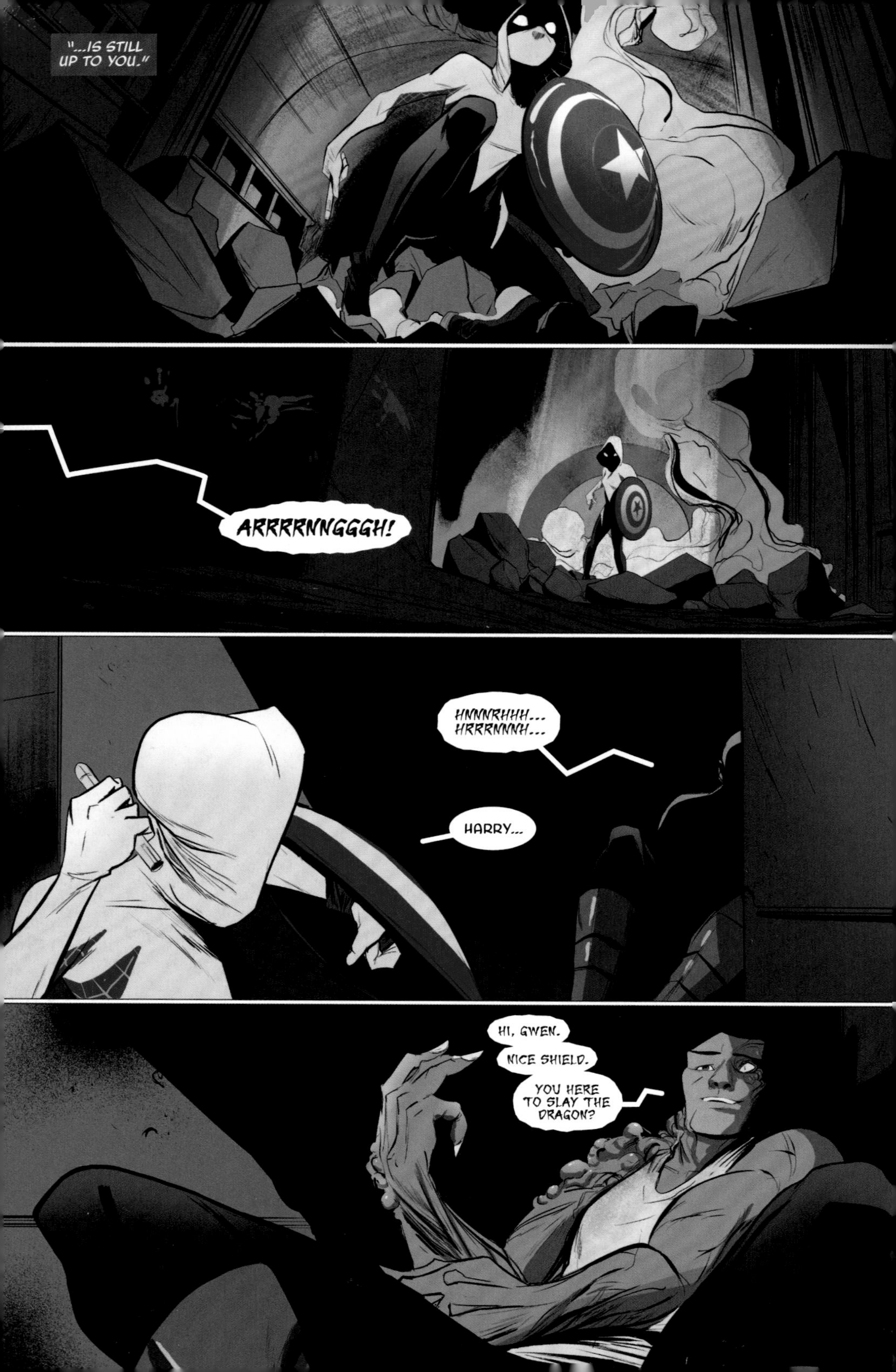
"...IS STILL UP TO YOU."
ARRRRNNGGGH!
HNNNRHHH... HRRRNNNH...
HARRY...
HI, GWEN.
NICE SHIELD.
YOU HERE TO SLAY THE DRAGON?

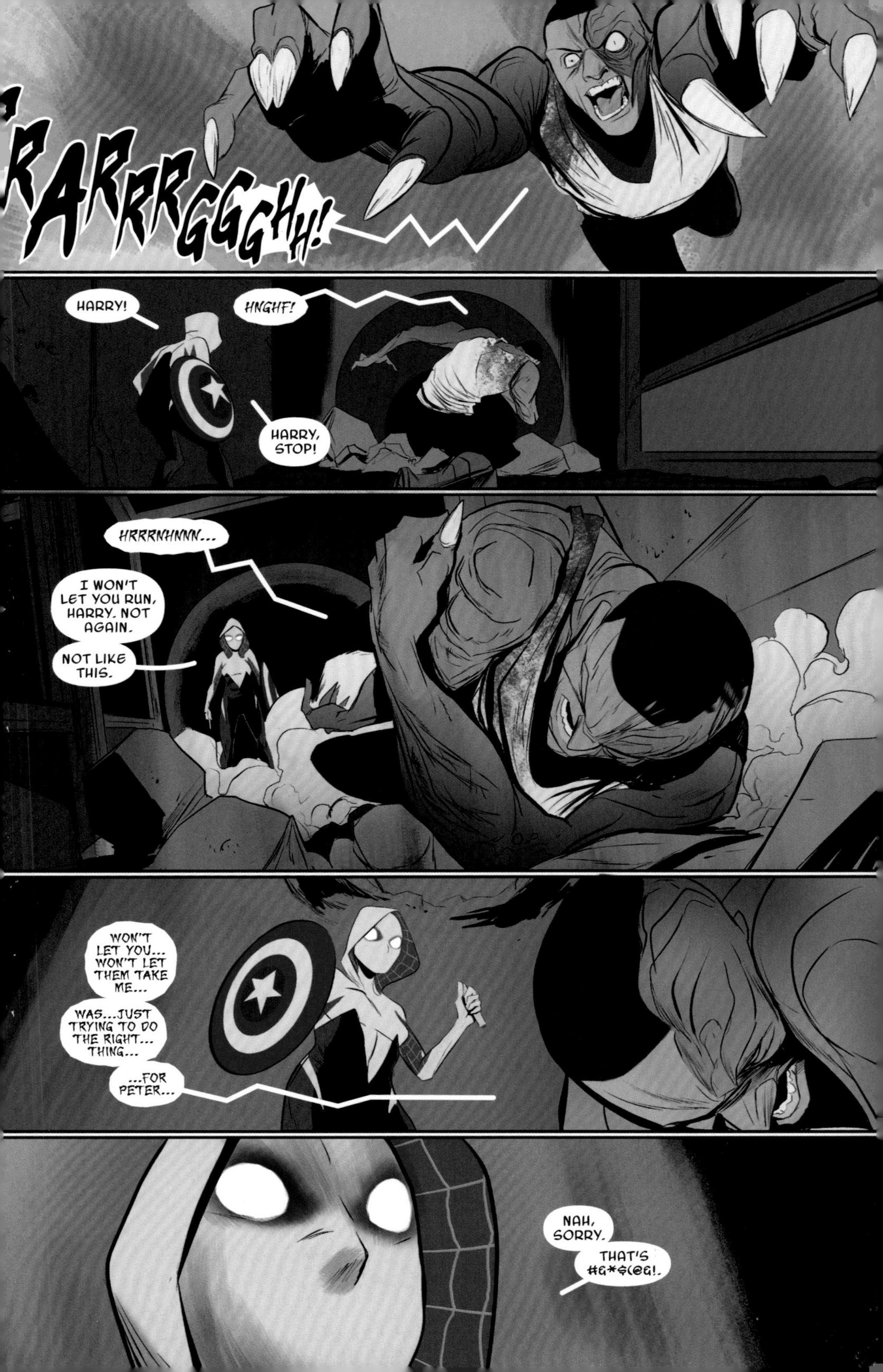
'RARRRGGGHH!
HARRY!
HNGHF!
HARRY, STOP!
HRRRNHNNN...
I WON'T LET YOU RUN, HARRY. NOT AGAIN.
NOT LIKE THIS.
WON'T LET YOU... WON'T LET THEM TAKE ME...
WAS...JUST TRYING TO DO THE RIGHT... THING...
...FOR PETER...
NAH, SORRY.
THAT'S #&*$(@&!.

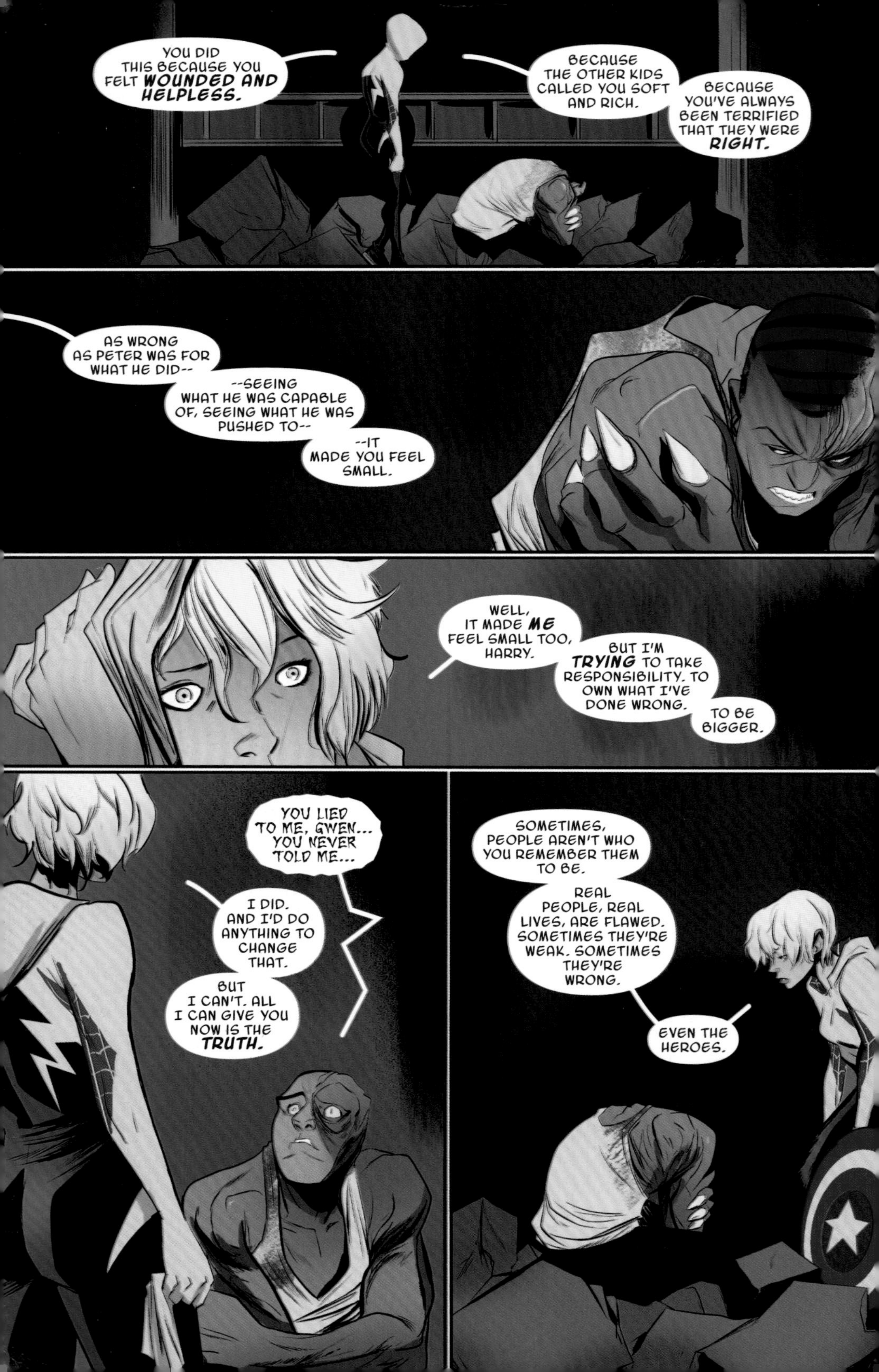
YOU DID THIS BECAUSE YOU FELT WOUNDED AND HELPLESS.
BECAUSE THE OTHER KIDS CALLED YOU SOFT AND RICH.
BECAUSE YOU'VE ALWAYS BEEN TERRIFIED THAT THEY WERE RIGHT.
AS WRONG AS PETER WAS FOR WHAT HE DID--
--SEEING WHAT HE WAS CAPABLE OF, SEEING WHAT HE WAS PUSHED TO--
--IT MADE YOU FEEL SMALL.
WELL, IT MADE ME FEEL SMALL TOO, HARRY.
BUT I'M TRYING TO TAKE RESPONSIBILITY. TO OWN WHAT I'VE DONE WRONG.
TO BE BIGGER.
YOU LIED TO ME, GWEN... YOU NEVER TOLD ME...
I DID. AND I'D DO ANYTHING TO CHANGE THAT.
BUT I CAN'T. ALL I CAN GIVE YOU NOW IS THE TRUTH.
SOMETIMES, PEOPLE AREN'T WHO YOU REMEMBER THEM TO BE.
REAL PEOPLE, REAL LIVES, ARE FLAWED. SOMETIMES THEY'RE WEAK. SOMETIMES THEY'RE WRONG.
EVEN THE HEROES.

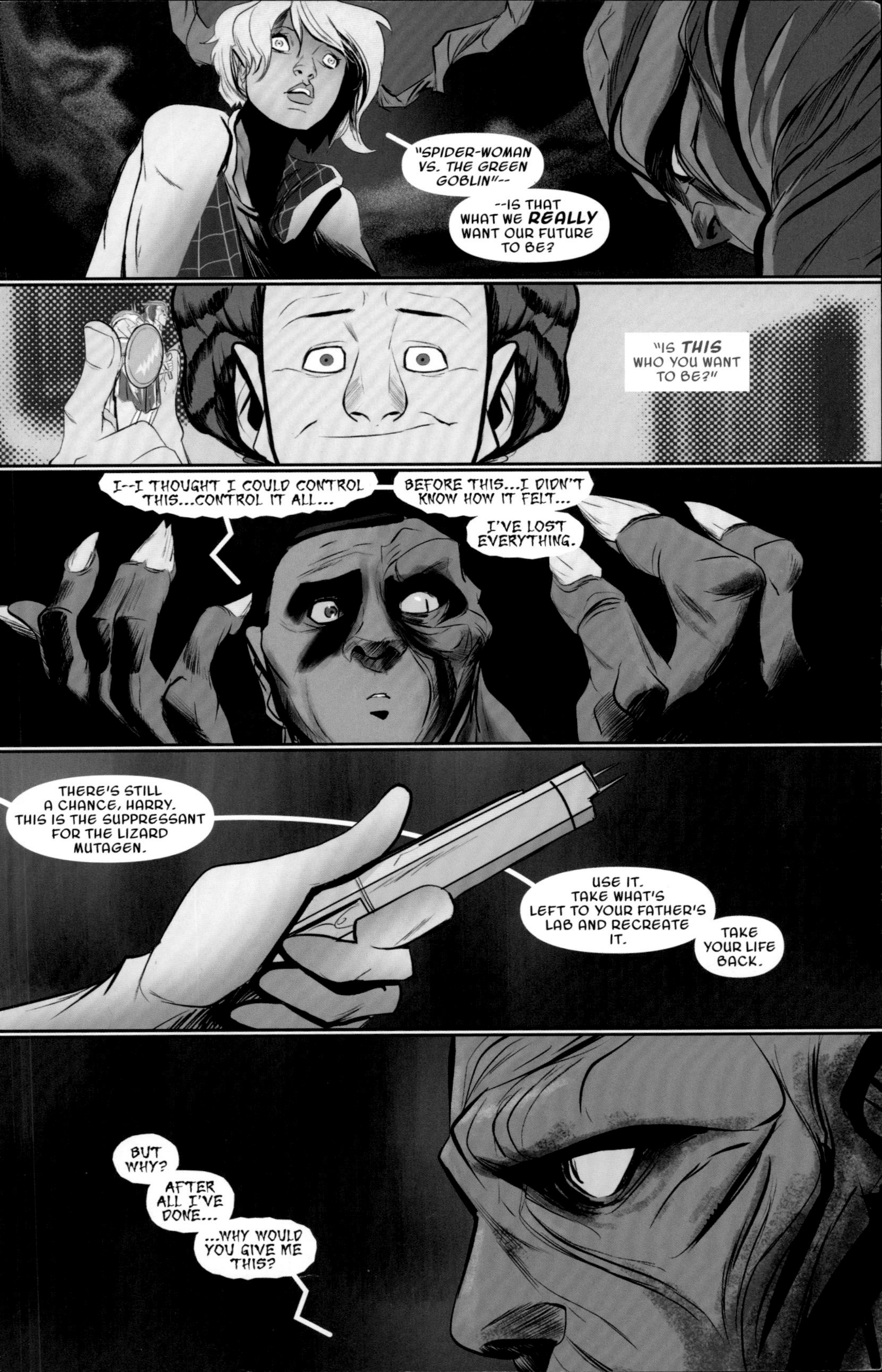
"SPIDER-WOMAN VS. THE GREEN GOBLIN"--
--IS THAT WHAT WE REALLY WANT OUR FUTURE TO BE?
"IS THIS WHO YOU WANT TO BE?"
I--I THOUGHT I COULD CONTROL THIS...CONTROL IT ALL...
BEFORE THIS...I DIDN'T KNOW HOW IT FELT...
I'VE LOST EVERYTHING.
THERE'S STILL A CHANCE, HARRY. THIS IS THE SUPPRESSANT FOR THE LIZARD MUTAGEN.
USE IT. TAKE WHAT'S LEFT TO YOUR FATHER'S LAB AND RECREATE IT.
TAKE YOUR LIFE BACK.
BUT WHY?
AFTER ALL I'VE DONE...
...WHY WOULD YOU GIVE ME THIS?

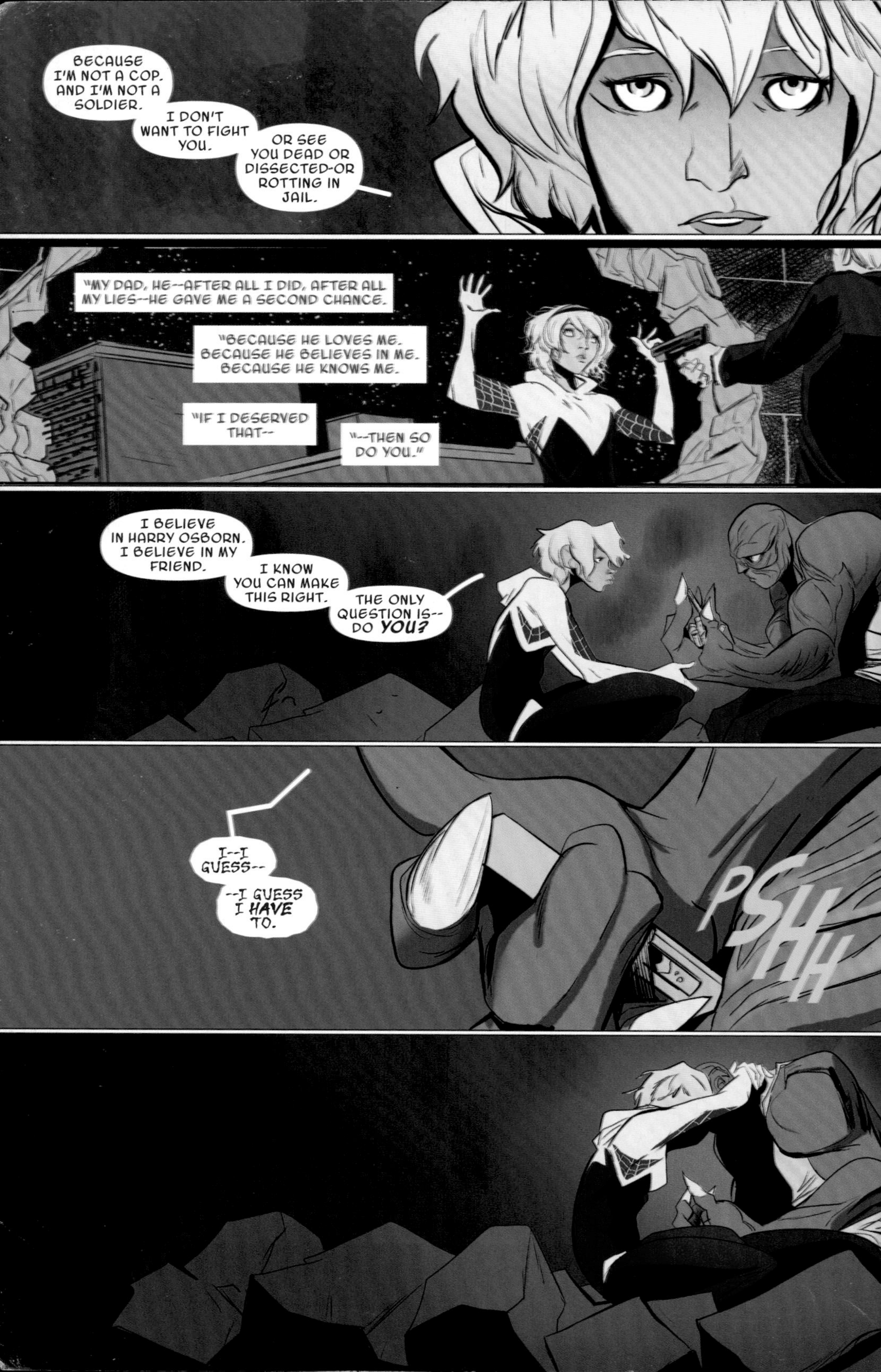
BECAUSE I'M NOT A COP. AND I'M NOT A SOLDIER.
I DON'T WANT TO FIGHT YOU.
OR SEE YOU DEAD OR DISSECTED-OR ROTTING IN JAIL.
"MY DAD, HE--AFTER ALL I DID, AFTER ALL MY LIES--HE GAVE ME A SECOND CHANCE.
"BECAUSE HE LOVES ME. BECAUSE HE BELIEVES IN ME. BECAUSE HE KNOWS ME.
"IF I DESERVED THAT--
"--THEN SO DO YOU."
I BELIEVE IN HARRY OSBORN. I BELIEVE IN MY FRIEND.
I KNOW YOU CAN MAKE THIS RIGHT.
THE ONLY QUESTION IS--DO YOU?
I--I GUESS--
--I GUESS I HAVE TO.
PSHH

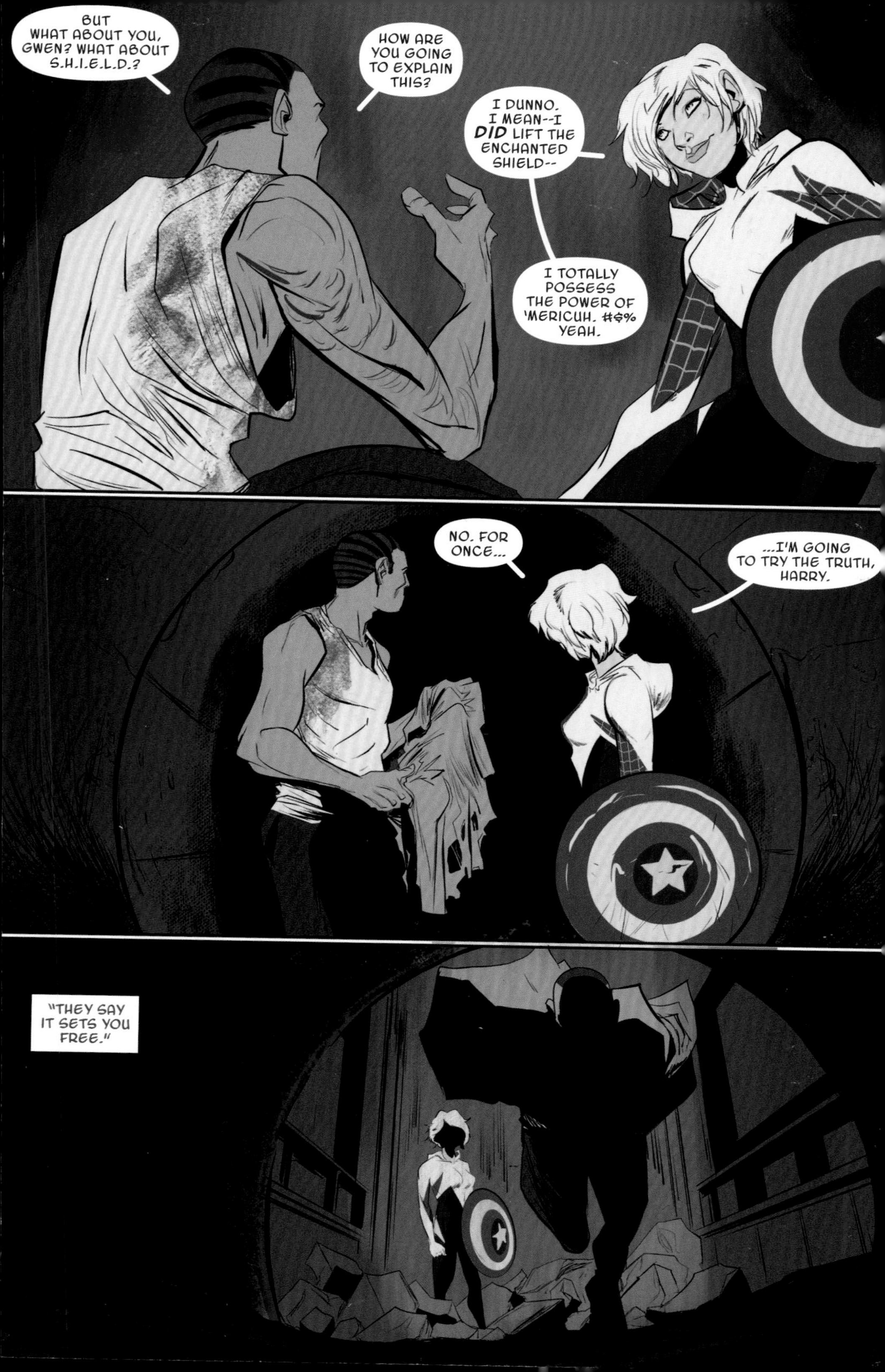

BUT WHAT ABOUT YOU, GWEN? WHAT ABOUT S.H.I.E.L.D.?
HOW ARE YOU GOING TO EXPLAIN THIS?
I DUNNO. I MEAN--I *DID* LIFT THE ENCHANTED SHIELD--
I TOTALLY POSSESS THE POWER OF 'MERICUH. #$% YEAH.
NO. FOR ONCE...
...I'M GOING TO TRY THE TRUTH, HARRY.
"THEY SAY IT SETS YOU FREE."

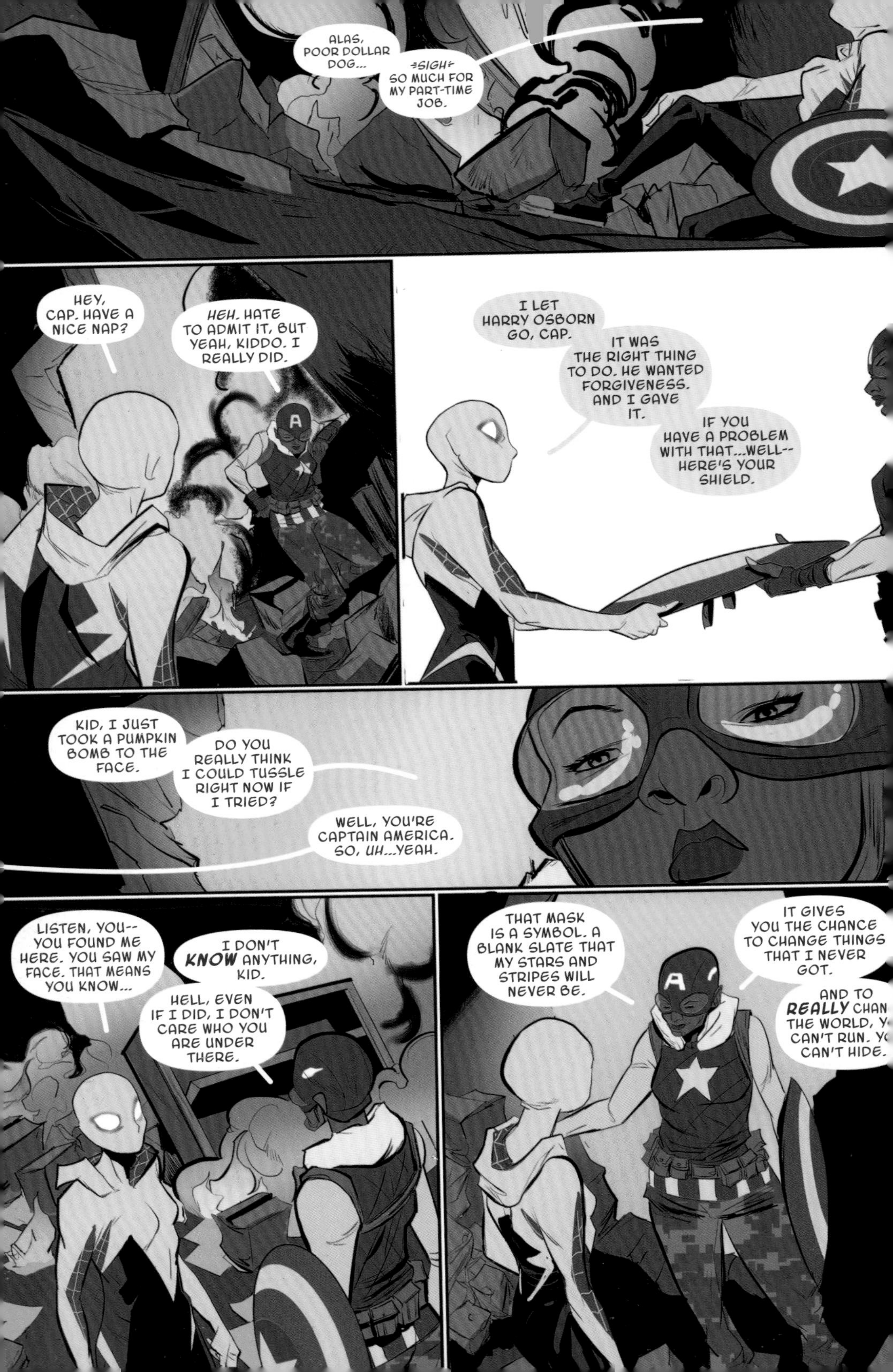
ALAS, POOR DOLLAR DOG...
=SIGH= SO MUCH FOR MY PART-TIME JOB.
HEY, CAP. HAVE A NICE NAP?
HEH. HATE TO ADMIT IT, BUT YEAH, KIDDO. I REALLY DID.
I LET HARRY OSBORN GO, CAP.
IT WAS THE RIGHT THING TO DO. HE WANTED FORGIVENESS. AND I GAVE IT.
IF YOU HAVE A PROBLEM WITH THAT...WELL--HERE'S YOUR SHIELD.
KID, I JUST TOOK A PUMPKIN BOMB TO THE FACE.
DO YOU REALLY THINK I COULD TUSSLE RIGHT NOW IF I TRIED?
WELL, YOU'RE CAPTAIN AMERICA. SO, UH...YEAH.
LISTEN, YOU--YOU FOUND ME HERE. YOU SAW MY FACE. THAT MEANS YOU KNOW...
I DON'T KNOW ANYTHING, KID.
HELL, EVEN IF I DID, I DON'T CARE WHO YOU ARE UNDER THERE.
THAT MASK IS A SYMBOL. A BLANK SLATE THAT MY STARS AND STRIPES WILL NEVER BE.
IT GIVES YOU THE CHANCE TO CHANGE THINGS THAT I NEVER GOT.
AND TO REALLY CHAN THE WORLD, Y CAN'T RUN. Y CAN'T HIDE.

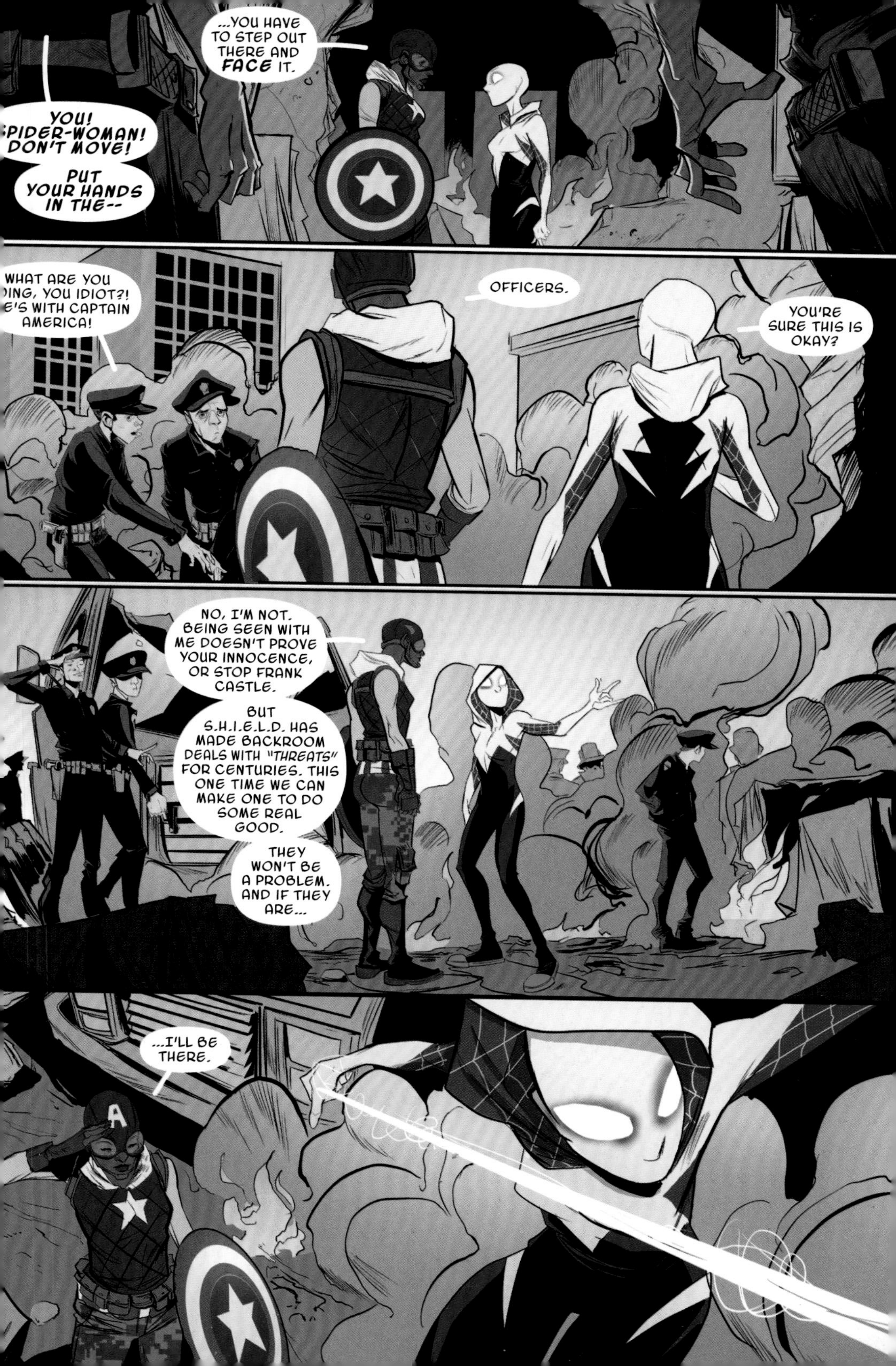
...YOU HAVE TO STEP OUT THERE AND FACE IT.
YOU! SPIDER-WOMAN! DON'T MOVE!
PUT YOUR HANDS IN THE--
WHAT ARE YOU DOING, YOU IDIOT?! SHE'S WITH CAPTAIN AMERICA!
OFFICERS.
YOU'RE SURE THIS IS OKAY?
NO, I'M NOT. BEING SEEN WITH ME DOESN'T PROVE YOUR INNOCENCE, OR STOP FRANK CASTLE.
BUT S.H.I.E.L.D. HAS MADE BACKROOM DEALS WITH "THREATS" FOR CENTURIES. THIS ONE TIME WE CAN MAKE ONE TO DO SOME REAL GOOD.
THEY WON'T BE A PROBLEM. AND IF THEY ARE...
...I'LL BE THERE.

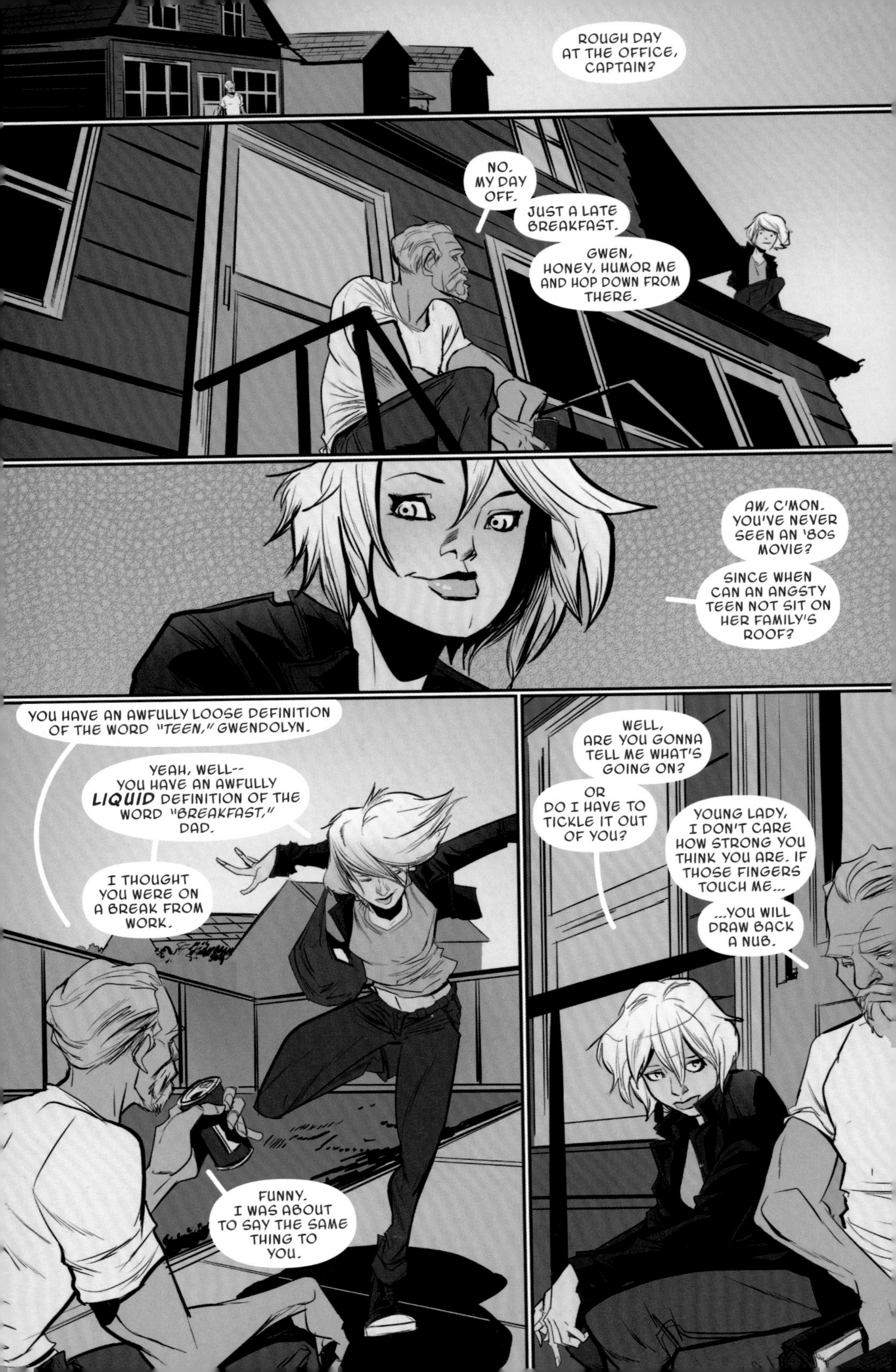
ROUGH DAY AT THE OFFICE, CAPTAIN?
NO. MY DAY OFF.
JUST A LATE BREAKFAST.
GWEN, HONEY, HUMOR ME AND HOP DOWN FROM THERE.
AW, C'MON. YOU'VE NEVER SEEN AN '80s MOVIE?
SINCE WHEN CAN AN ANGSTY TEEN NOT SIT ON HER FAMILY'S ROOF?
YOU HAVE AN AWFULLY LOOSE DEFINITION OF THE WORD "TEEN," GWENDOLYN.
YEAH, WELL-- YOU HAVE AN AWFULLY LIQUID DEFINITION OF THE WORD "BREAKFAST," DAD.
I THOUGHT YOU WERE ON A BREAK FROM WORK.
FUNNY. I WAS ABOUT TO SAY THE SAME THING TO YOU.
WELL, ARE YOU GONNA TELL ME WHAT'S GOING ON?
OR DO I HAVE TO TICKLE IT OUT OF YOU?
YOUNG LADY, I DON'T CARE HOW STRONG YOU THINK YOU ARE. IF THOSE FINGERS TOUCH ME...
...YOU WILL DRAW BACK A NUB.

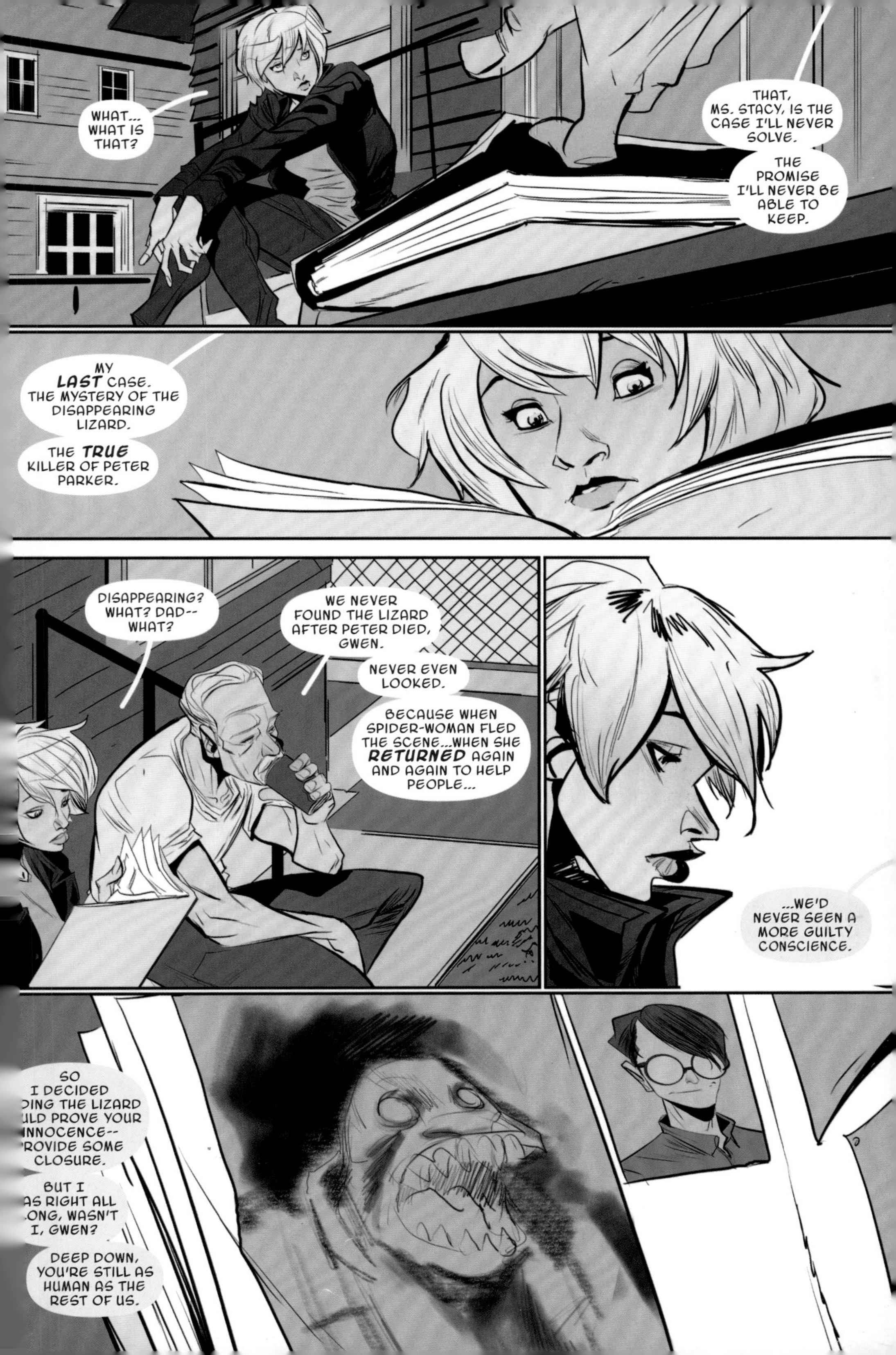

WHAT... WHAT IS THAT?
THAT, MS. STACY, IS THE CASE I'LL NEVER SOLVE.
THE PROMISE I'LL NEVER BE ABLE TO KEEP.
MY LAST CASE. THE MYSTERY OF THE DISAPPEARING LIZARD.
THE TRUE KILLER OF PETER PARKER.
DISAPPEARING? WHAT? DAD-- WHAT?
WE NEVER FOUND THE LIZARD AFTER PETER DIED, GWEN.
NEVER EVEN LOOKED.
BECAUSE WHEN SPIDER-WOMAN FLED THE SCENE...WHEN SHE RETURNED AGAIN AND AGAIN TO HELP PEOPLE...
...WE'D NEVER SEEN A MORE GUILTY CONSCIENCE.
SO I DECIDED DING THE LIZARD ULD PROVE YOUR INNOCENCE-- PROVIDE SOME CLOSURE.
BUT I AS RIGHT ALL ONG, WASN'T I, GWEN?
DEEP DOWN, YOU'RE STILL AS HUMAN AS THE REST OF US.

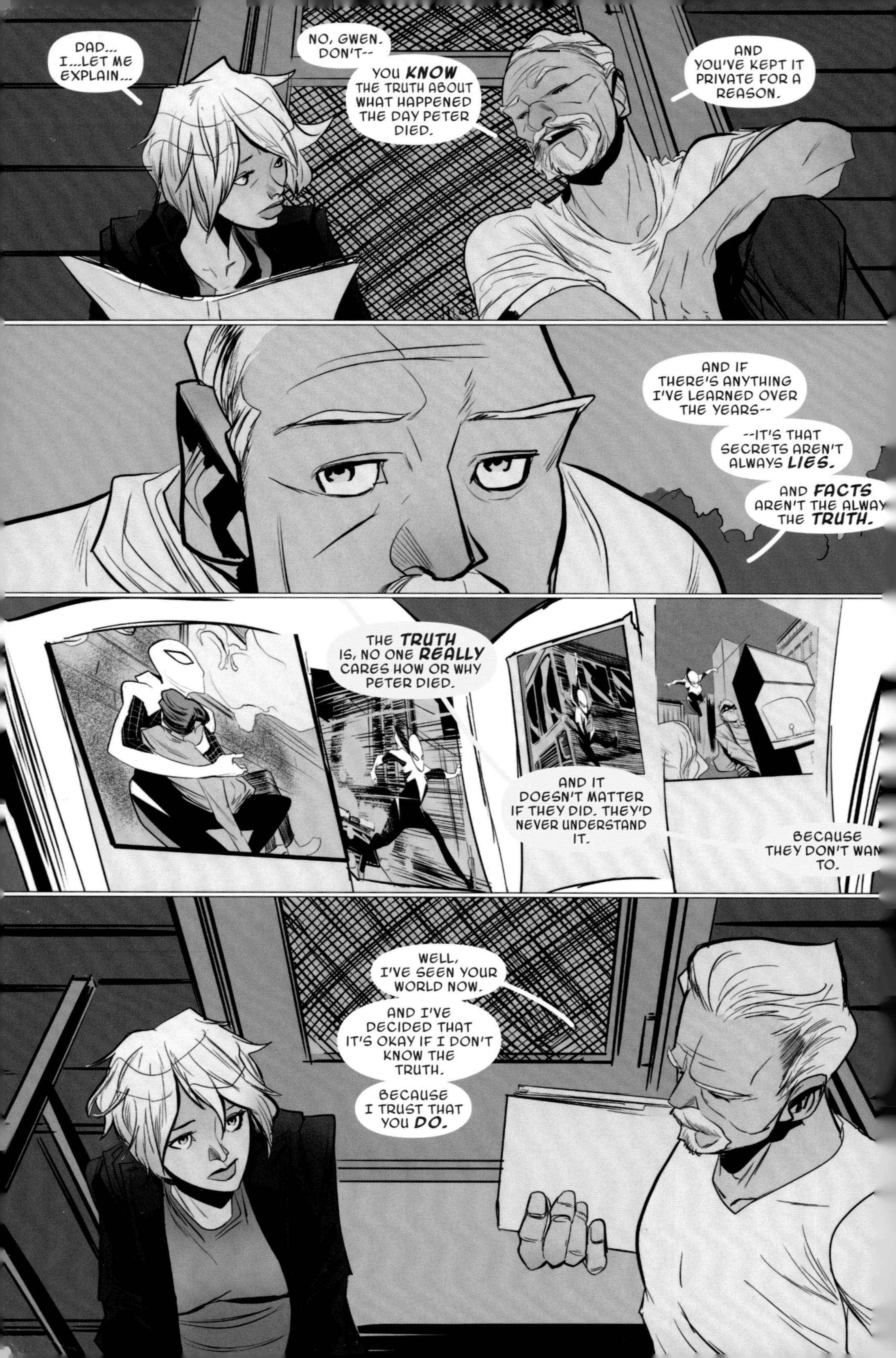
DAD... I...LET ME EXPLAIN...
NO, GWEN. DON'T--
YOU **KNOW** THE TRUTH ABOUT WHAT HAPPENED THE DAY PETER DIED.
AND YOU'VE KEPT IT PRIVATE FOR A REASON.
AND IF THERE'S ANYTHING I'VE LEARNED OVER THE YEARS--
--IT'S THAT SECRETS AREN'T ALWAYS **LIES.**
AND **FACTS** AREN'T THE ALWAY THE **TRUTH.**
THE **TRUTH** IS, NO ONE **REALLY** CARES HOW OR WHY PETER DIED.
AND IT DOESN'T MATTER IF THEY DID. THEY'D NEVER UNDERSTAND IT.
BECAUSE THEY DON'T WAN TO.
WELL, I'VE SEEN YOUR WORLD NOW.
AND I'VE DECIDED THAT IT'S OKAY IF I DON'T KNOW THE TRUTH.
BECAUSE I TRUST THAT YOU **DO.**

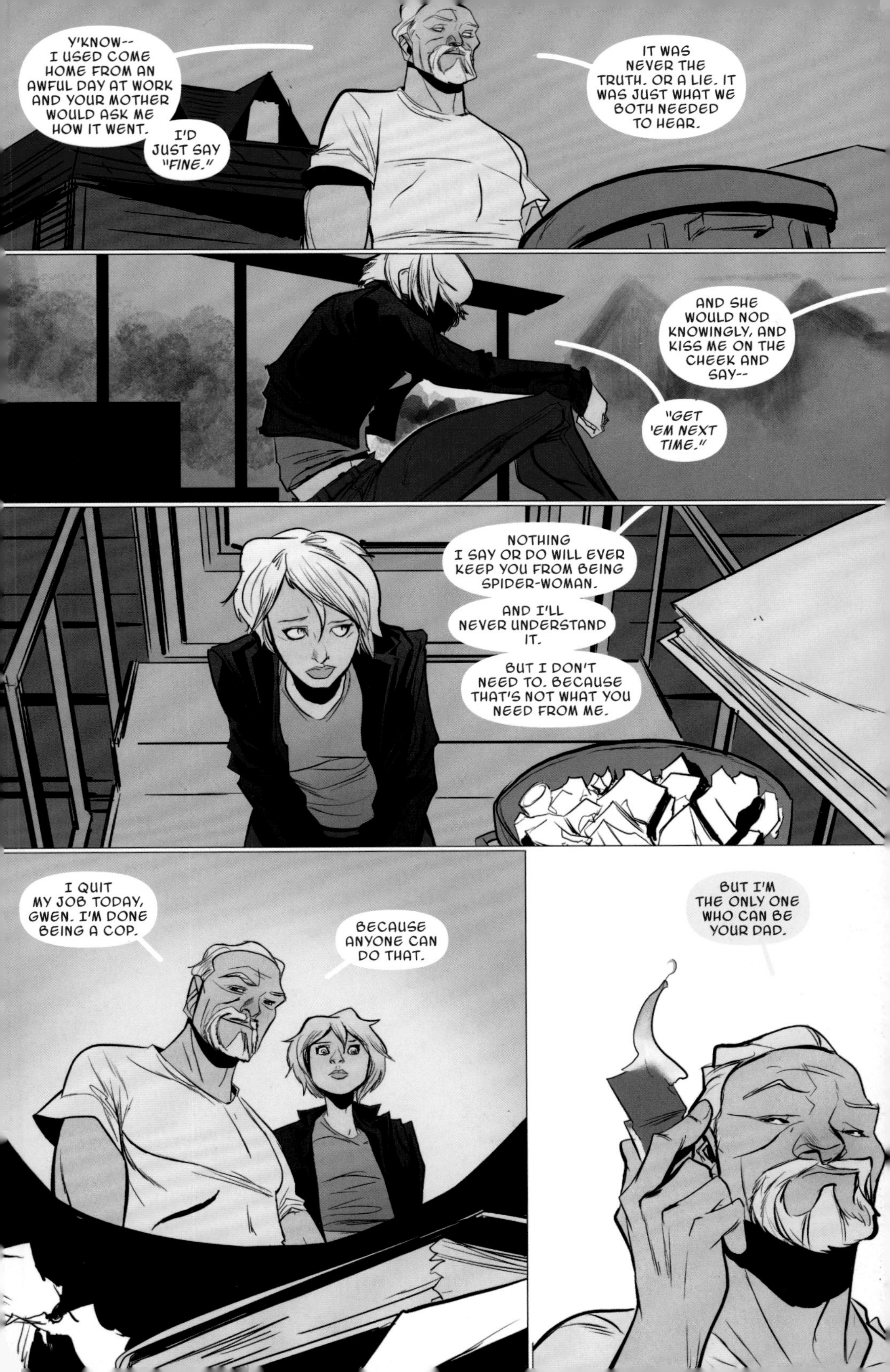

Y'KNOW-- I USED COME HOME FROM AN AWFUL DAY AT WORK AND YOUR MOTHER WOULD ASK ME HOW IT WENT.
I'D JUST SAY "FINE."
IT WAS NEVER THE TRUTH. OR A LIE. IT WAS JUST WHAT WE BOTH NEEDED TO HEAR.
AND SHE WOULD NOD KNOWINGLY, AND KISS ME ON THE CHEEK AND SAY--
"GET 'EM NEXT TIME."
NOTHING I SAY OR DO WILL EVER KEEP YOU FROM BEING SPIDER-WOMAN.
AND I'LL NEVER UNDERSTAND IT.
BUT I DON'T NEED TO. BECAUSE THAT'S NOT WHAT YOU NEED FROM ME.
I QUIT MY JOB TODAY, GWEN. I'M DONE BEING A COP.
BECAUSE ANYONE CAN DO THAT.
BUT I'M THE ONLY ONE WHO CAN BE YOUR DAD.

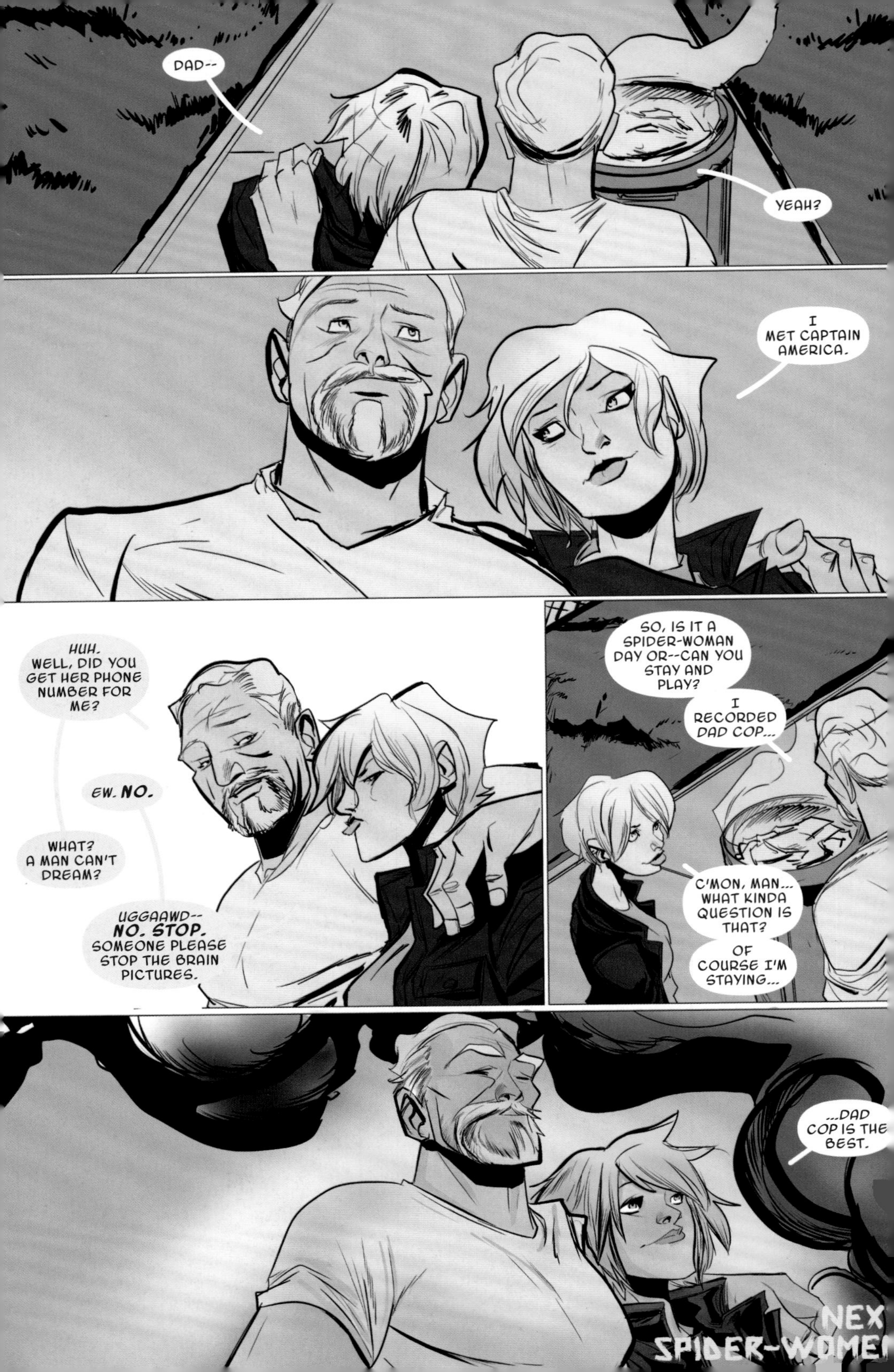
DAD--
YEAH?
I MET CAPTAIN AMERICA.
HUH. WELL, DID YOU GET HER PHONE NUMBER FOR ME?
EW. NO.
WHAT? A MAN CAN'T DREAM?
UGGAAWD-- NO. STOP. SOMEONE PLEASE STOP THE BRAIN PICTURES.
SO, IS IT A SPIDER-WOMAN DAY OR--CAN YOU STAY AND PLAY?
I RECORDED DAD COP...
C'MON, MAN... WHAT KINDA QUESTION IS THAT?
OF COURSE I'M STAYING...
...DAD COP IS THE BEST.
NEX
SPIDER-WOME

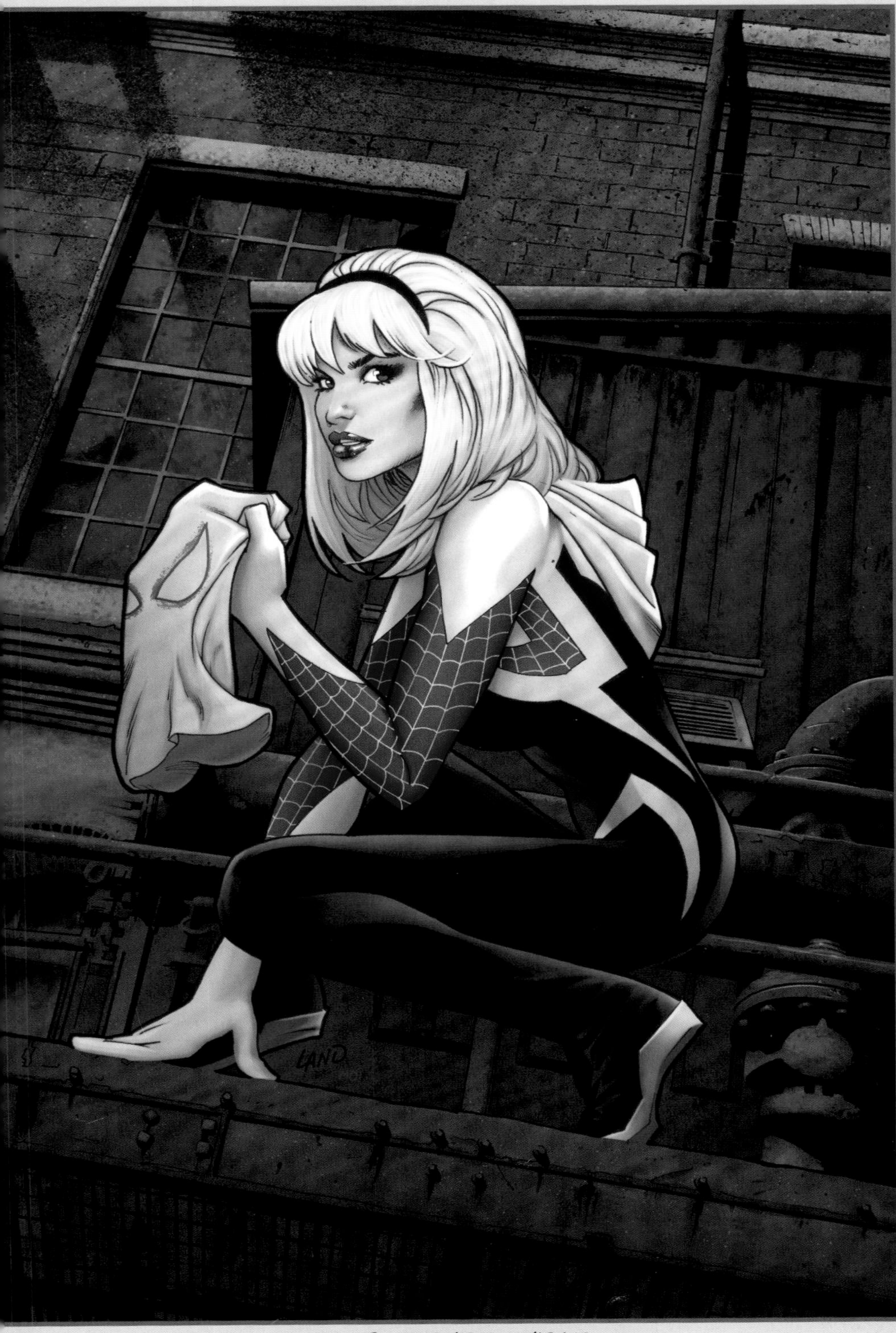

EDGE OF SPIDER-VERSE #2 VARIANT
BY GREG LAND & MORRY HOLLOWELL

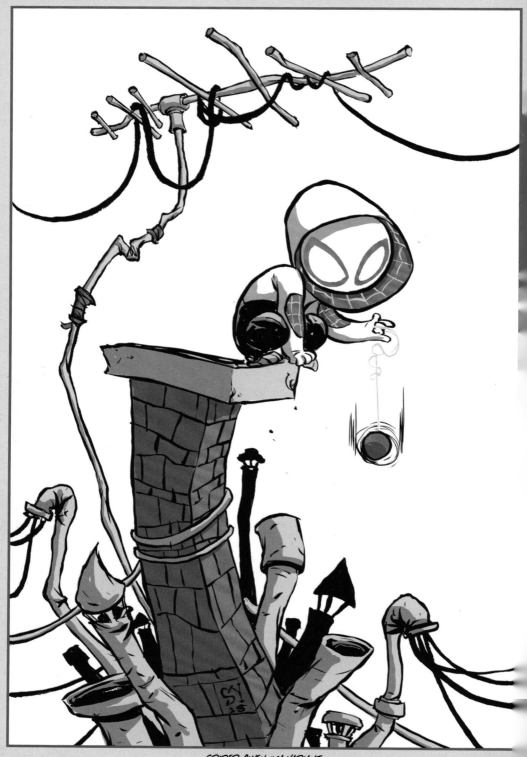

SPIDER-GWEN #1A VARIANT
BY SKOTTIE YOUNG

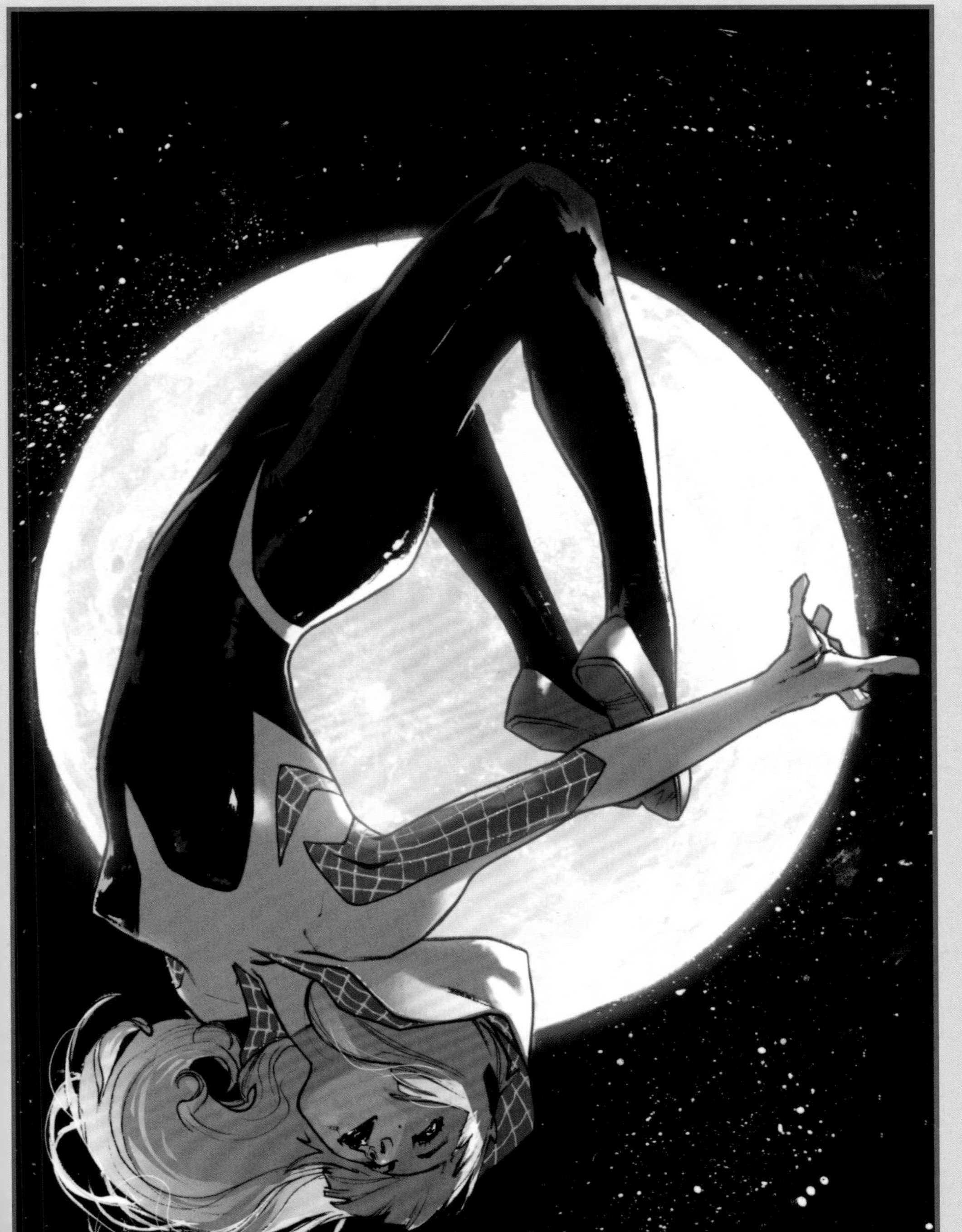

SPIDER-GWEN #2A VARIANT
BY SARA PICHELLI

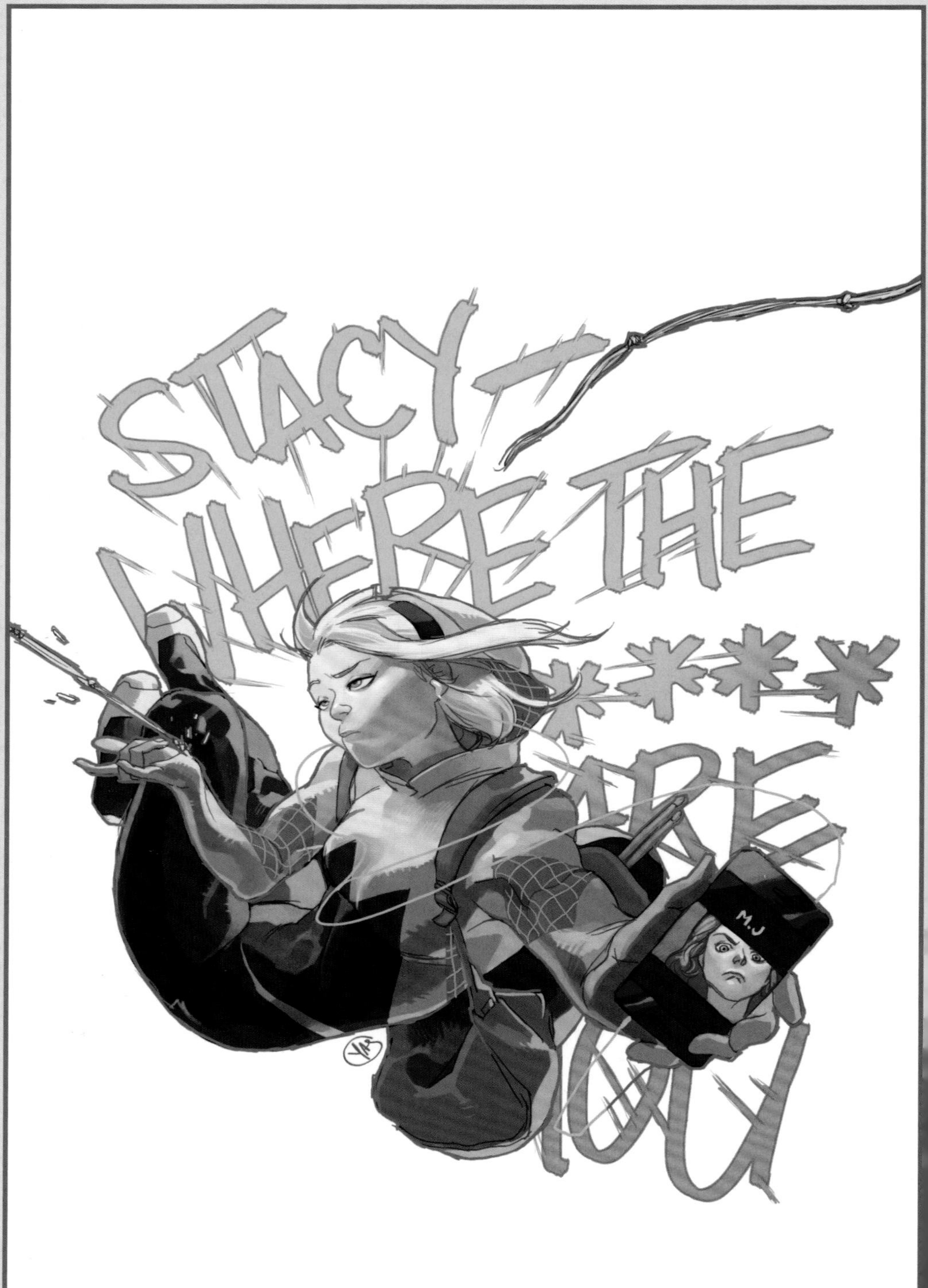
STACY—
WHERE THE
****
ARE
YOU
M.J

SPIDER-GWEN #3A VARIANT
BY YASMINE PUTRI

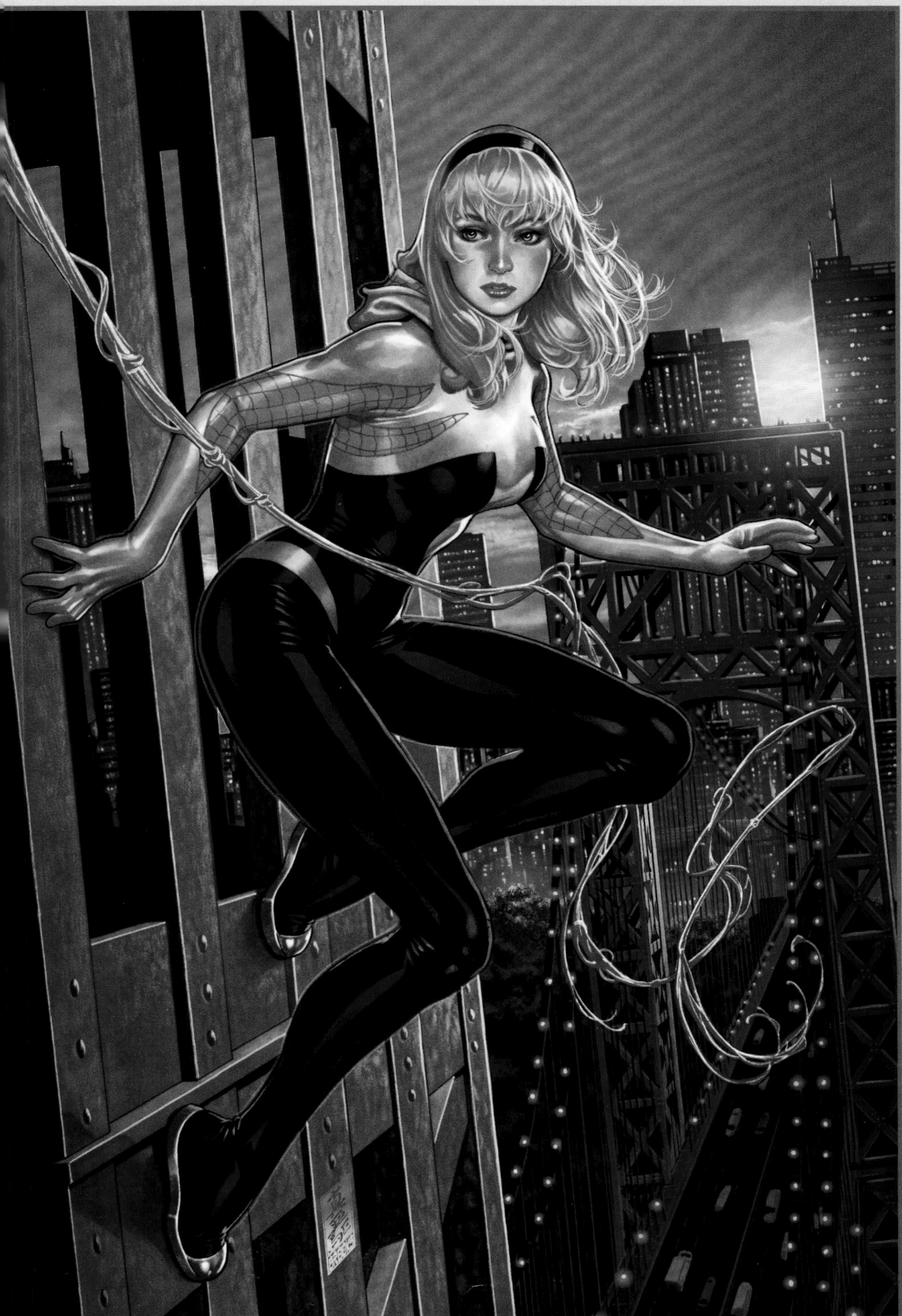

SPIDER-GWEN #4A VARIANT
BY MARK BROOKS

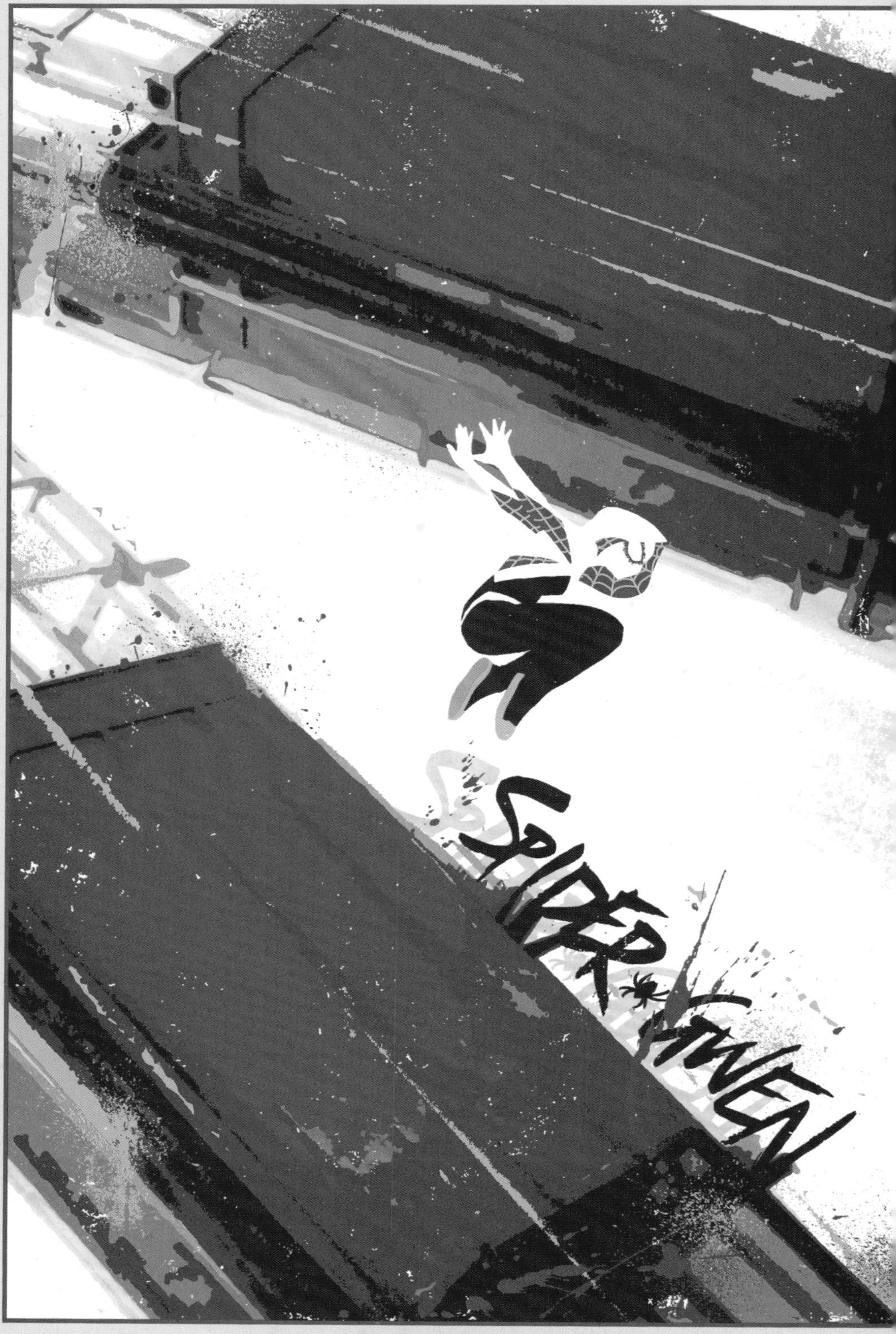
SPIDER-GWEN

SPIDER-GWEN #5A VARIANT
BY DAVID AJA

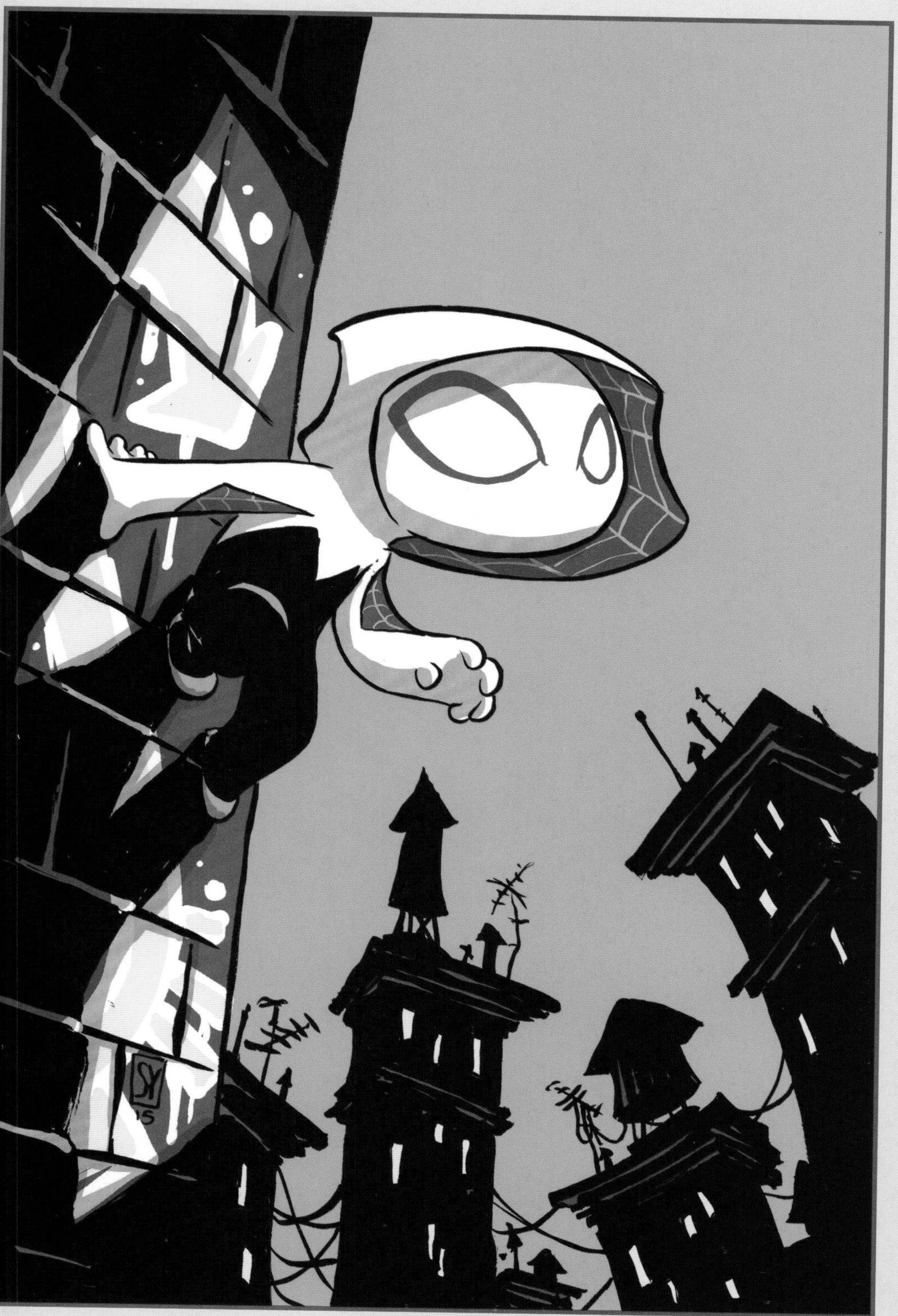

SPIDER-GWEN #1B VARIANT
BY SKOTTIE YOUNG

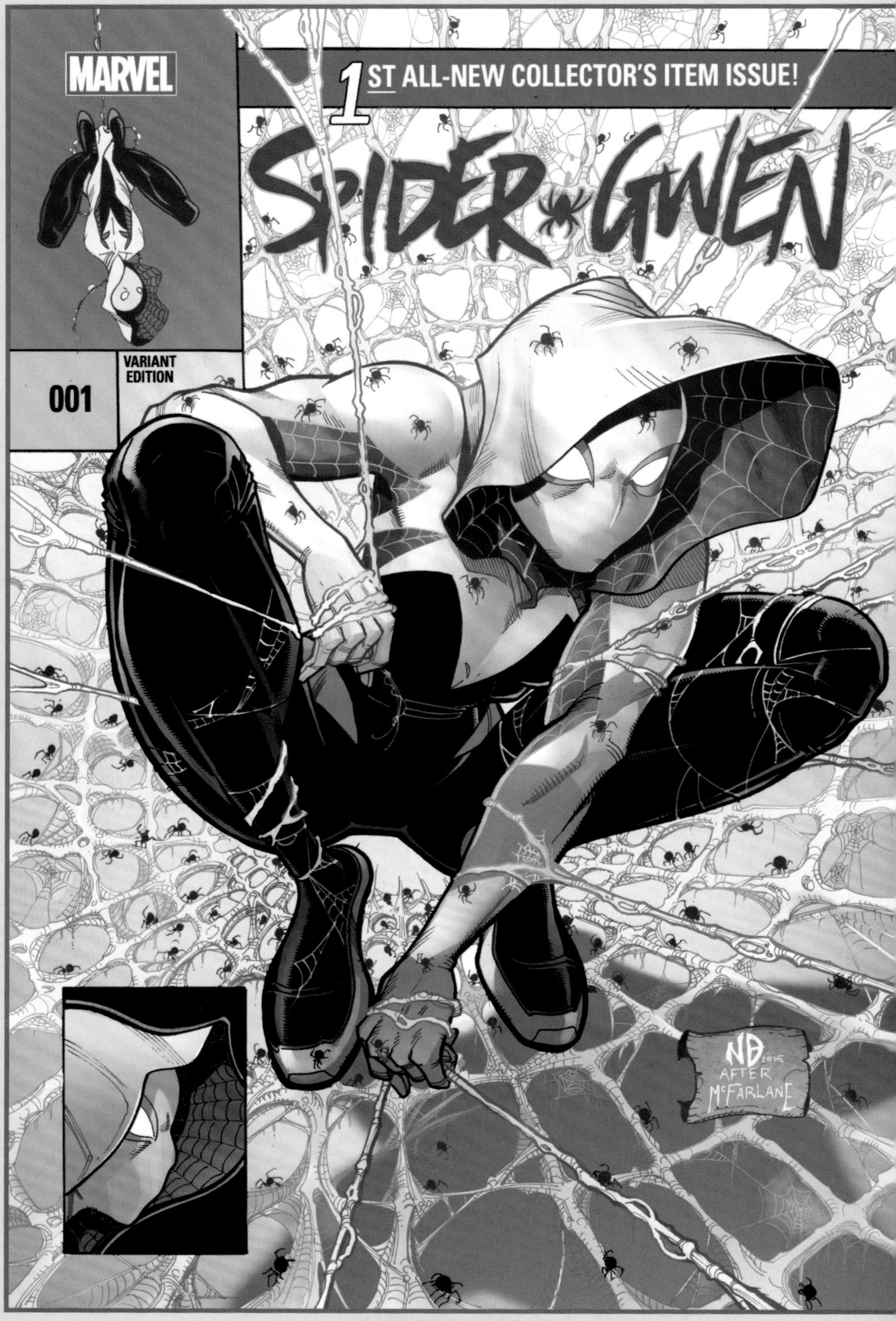
MARVEL
1 ST ALL-NEW COLLECTOR'S ITEM ISSUE!
SPIDER-GWEN
001
VARIANT EDITION
NB 2015 AFTER McFARLANE

SPIDER-GWEN #1A VARIANT
BY NICK BRADSHAW & SONIA OBACK

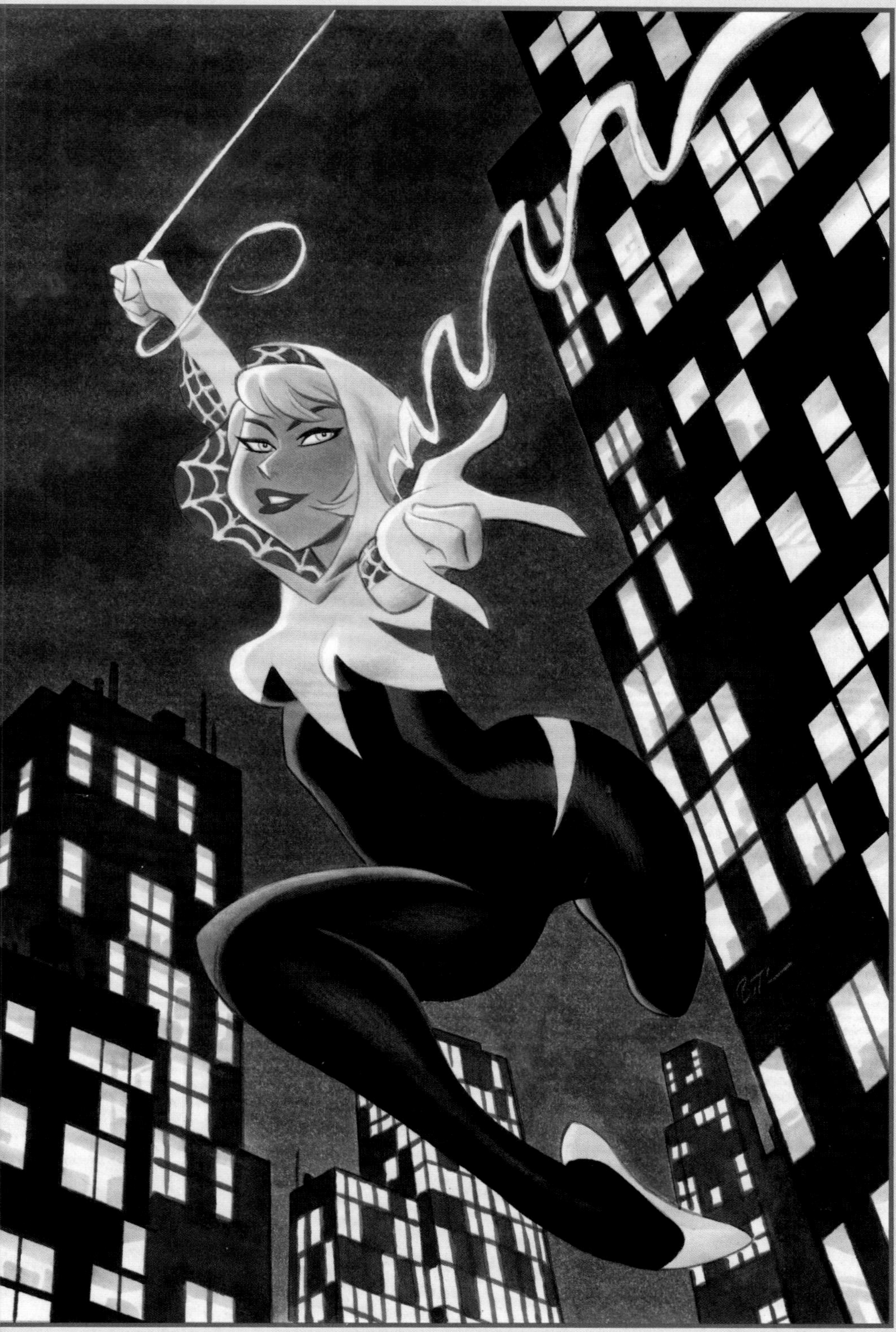

SPIDER-GWEN #1B VARIANT
BY BRUCE TIMM

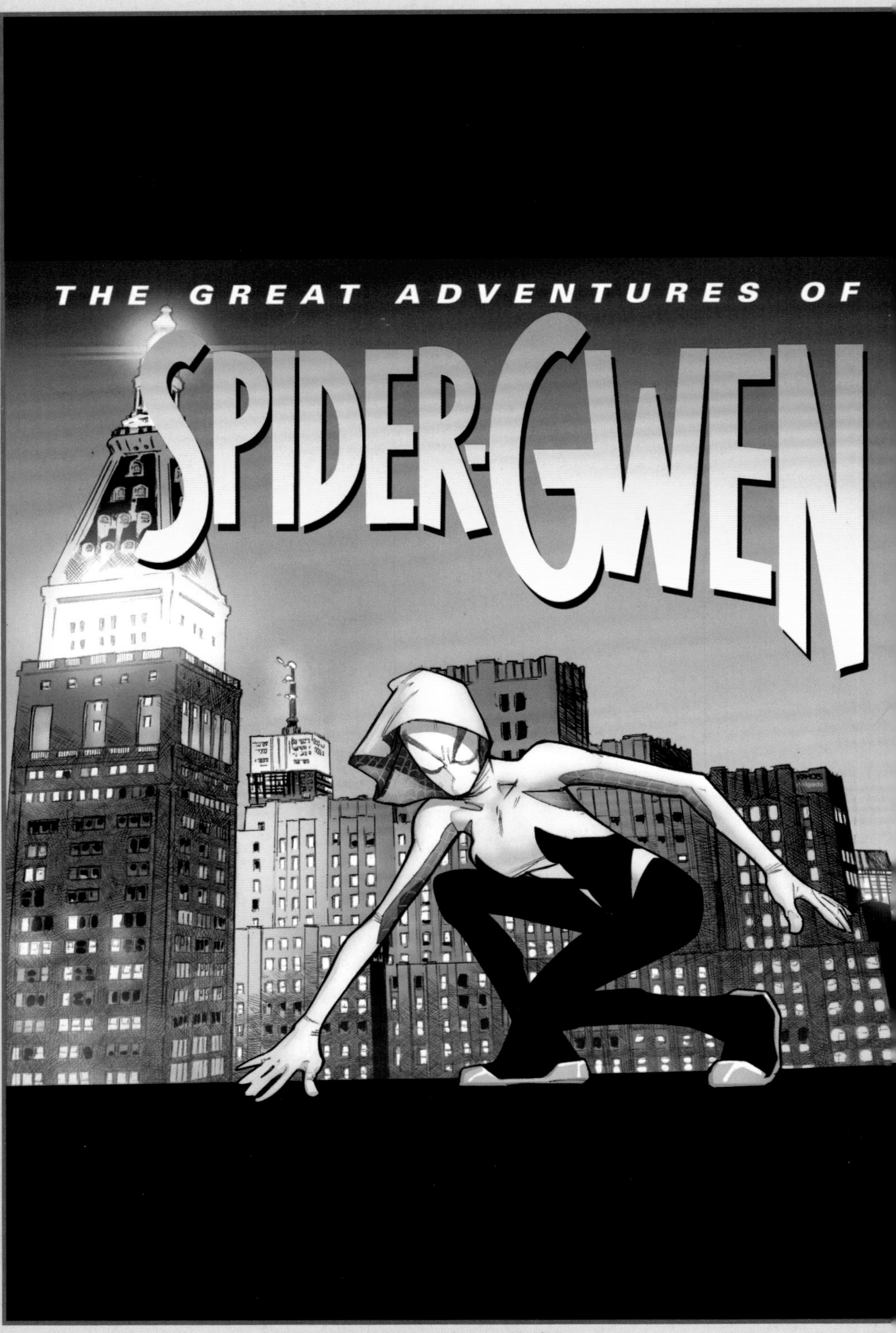
THE GREAT ADVENTURES OF
SPIDER-GWEN

SPIDER-GWEN #1B HIP-HOP VARIANT
BY HUMBERTO RAMOS & EDGAR DELGADO

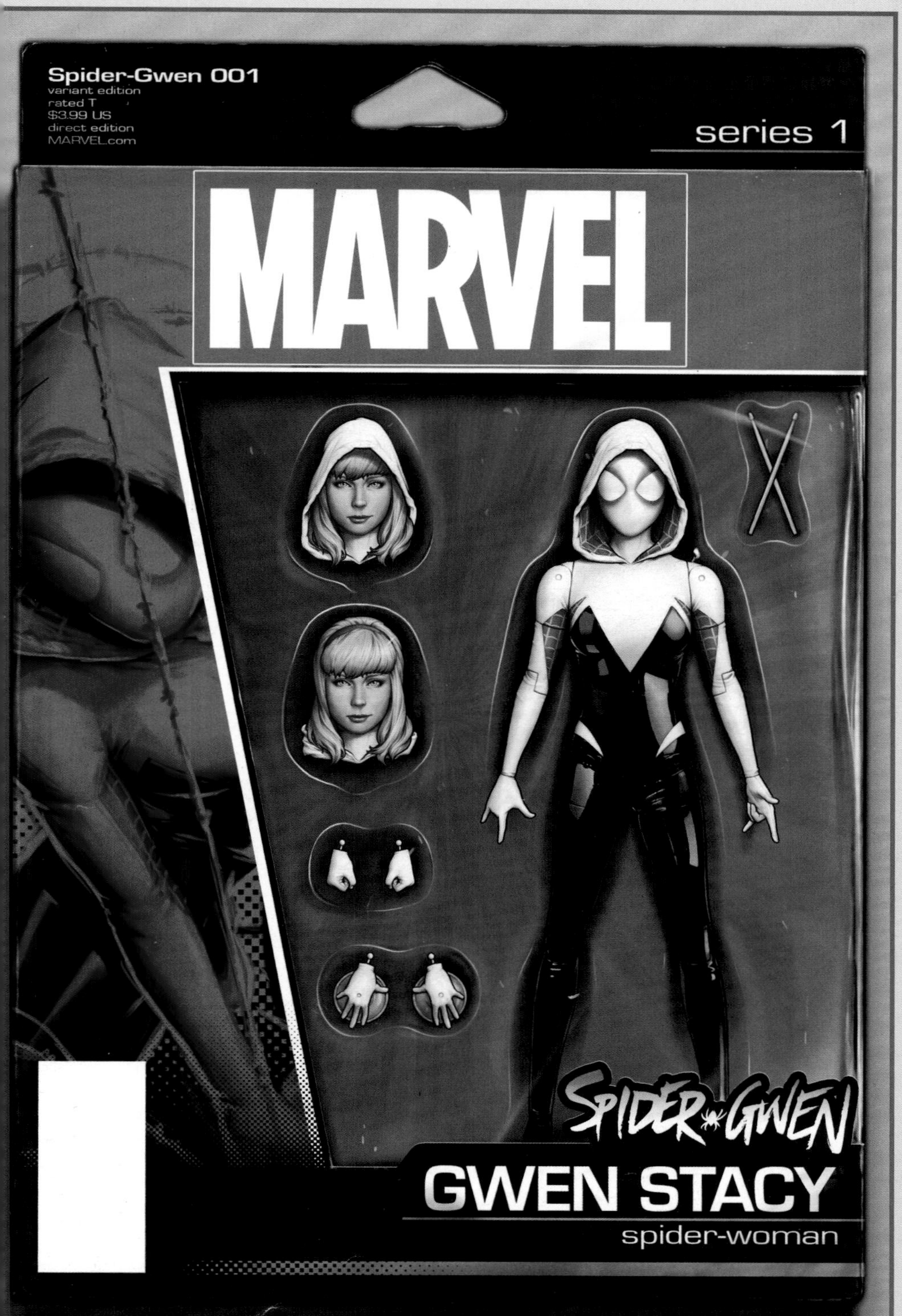
Spider-Gwen 001
variant edition
rated T
$3.99 US
direct edition
MARVEL.com
series 1
MARVEL
SPIDER-GWEN
GWEN STACY
spider-woman

SPIDER-GWEN #1B ACTION FIGURE VARIANT
BY JOHN TYLER CHRISTOPHER

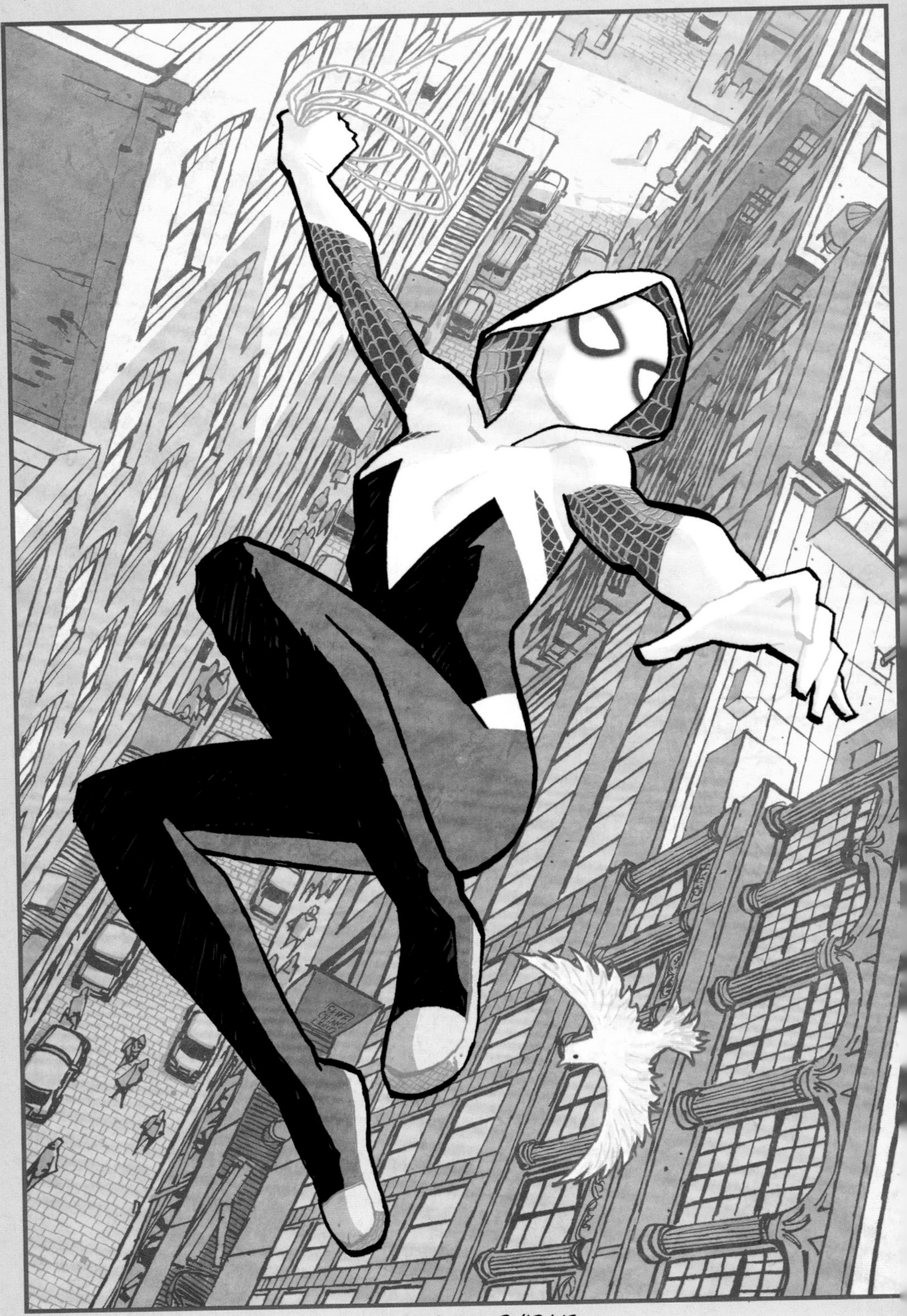

SPIDER-GWEN #2B VARIANT
BY CLIFF CHIANG

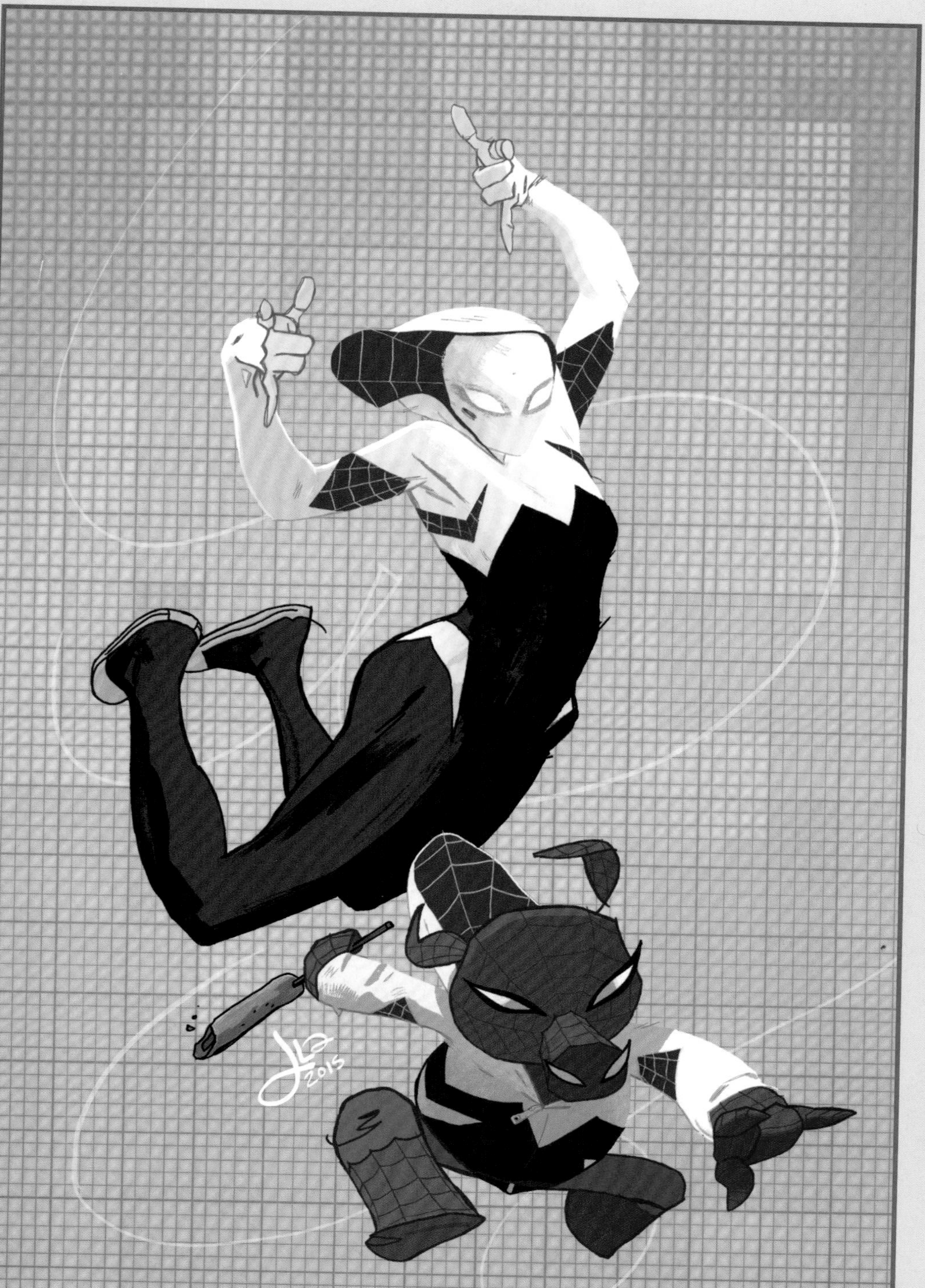

JL
2015

SPIDER-GWEN #3B VARIANT
BY JASON LATOUR

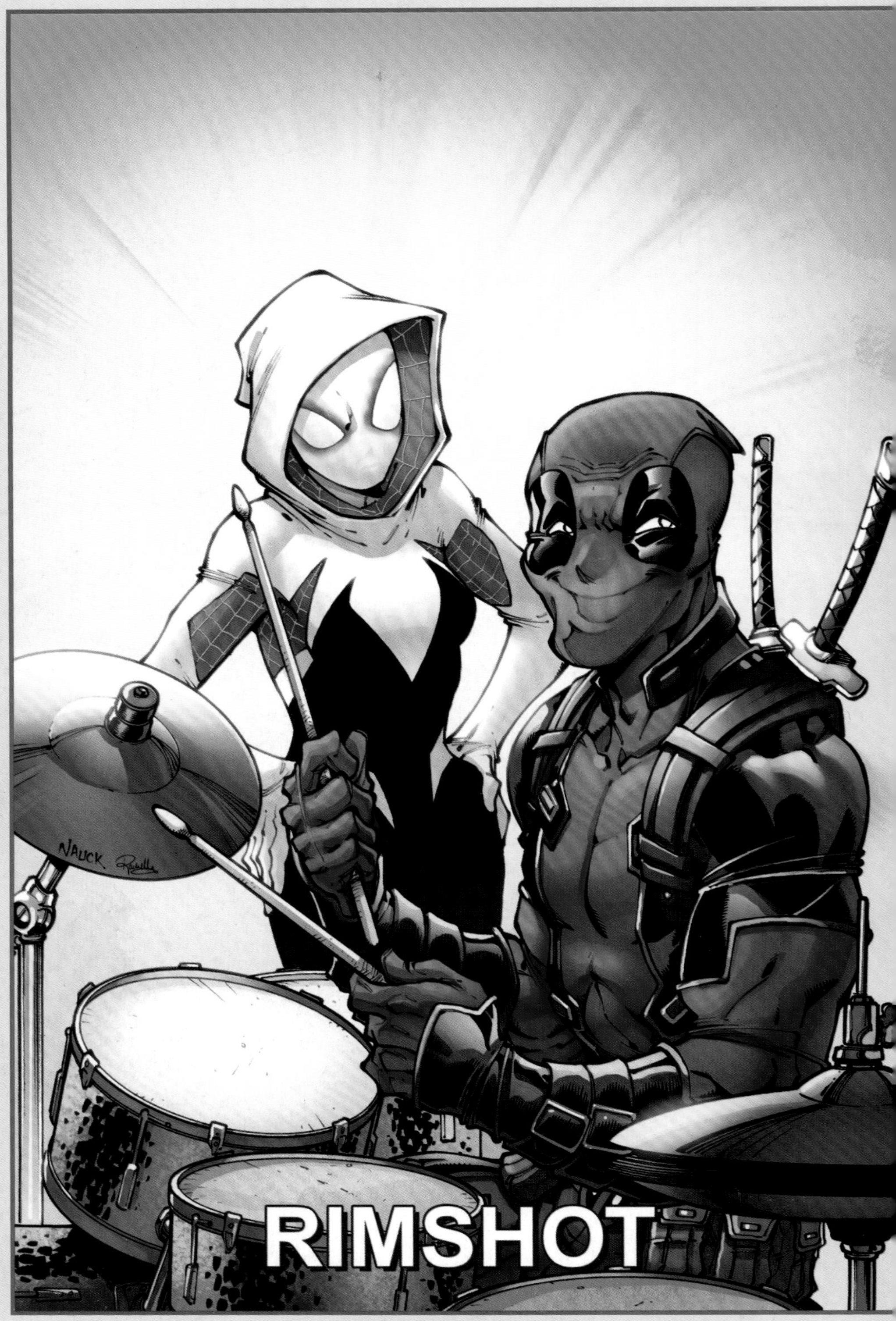
NAUCK
RIMSHOT

SPIDER-GWEN #4A DEADPOOL VARIANT
BY TODD NAUCK & RACHELLE ROSENBERG

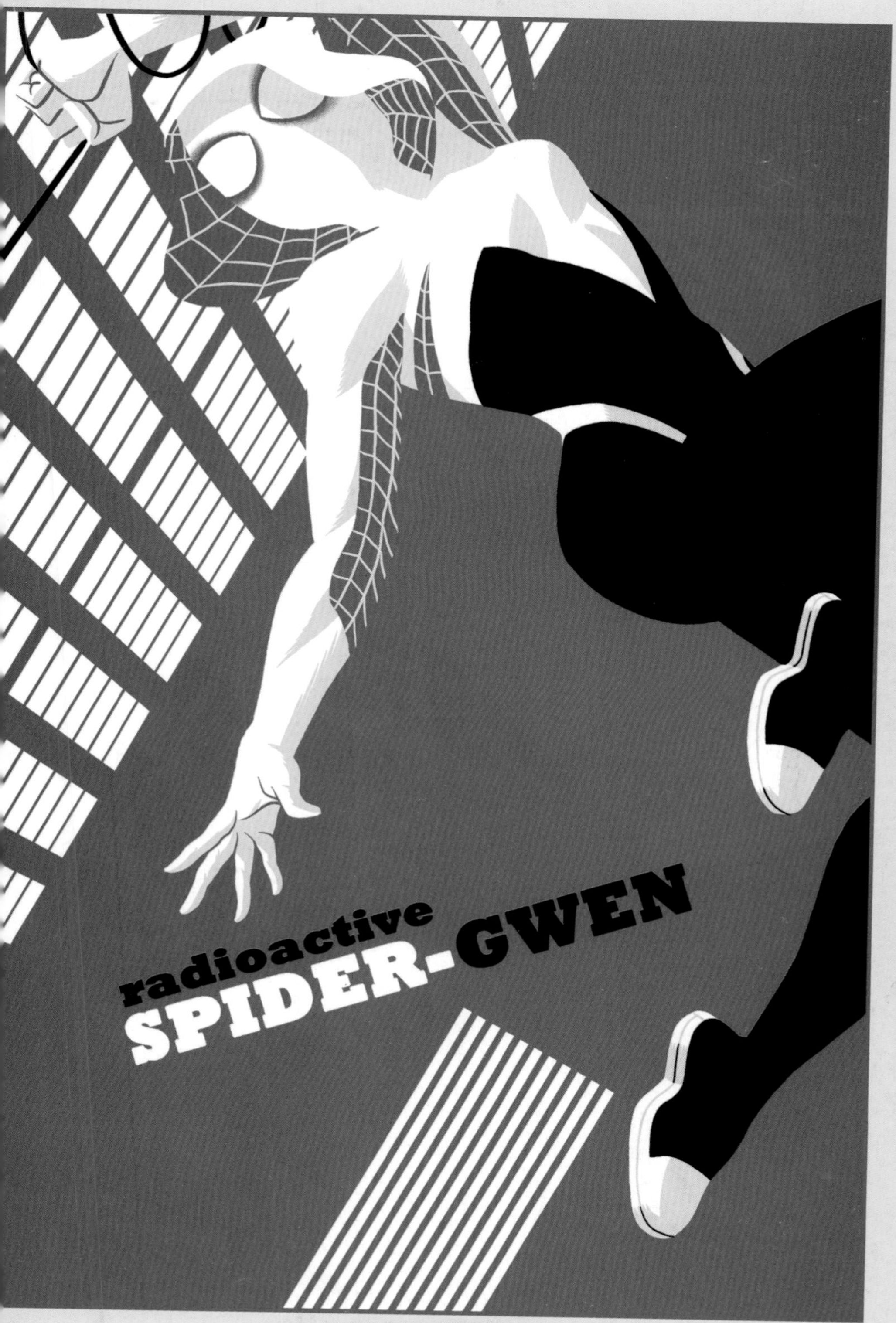
radioactive
SPIDER-GWEN

SPIDER-GWEN #5A VARIANT
BY MICHAEL CHO

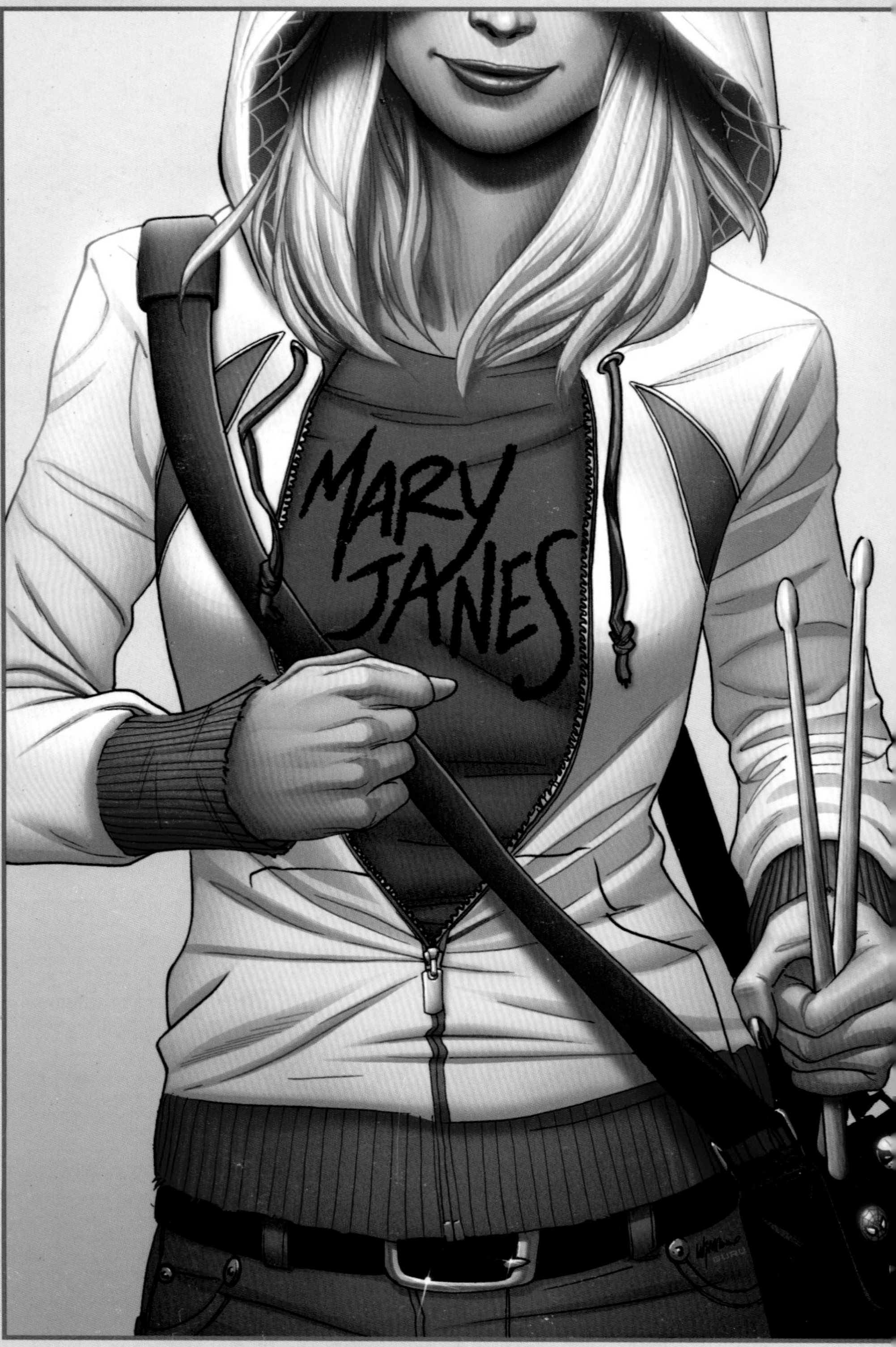
MARY JANES

SPIDER-GWEN #6B WOMEN OF POWER VARIANT
BY EMA LUPACCHINO & GURU-eFX